LOS GEMELOS TAPPER

ARRASAN LA CIUDAD

Lo siento mucho

Y más que lo sentirás

☠☠☠☠☠☠

LOS GEMELOS TAPPER

ARRASAN LA CIUDAD

SOCORRO, MAMÁ. ATRAPADO EN CAMIÓN

Es broma?

algarada: f. Alboroto o vocerío formado por un grupo de personas.

NO, D VIRDAD

GEOFF RODKEY

RBA

Este libro es una obra de ficción. Salvo en lo que se indica más abajo, los nombres, personajes, lugares, nombres de productos y servicios, organizaciones y acontecimientos que aparecen en el libro son producto de la imaginación del autor o se utilizan de forma ficticia. Cualquier parecido con personas, lugares, productos, servicios o hechos reales es pura coincidencia.

Con vistas a dar realismo a la historia, en el libro se han utilizado algunos nombres de lugares reales, pero los acontecimientos descritos en el mismo son imaginarios y los lugares reales se utilizan de forma ficticia. crónut® es una marca registrada de Dominique Ansel Bakery.

Título original inglés: *Tapper Twins Tear Up New York.*

Publicado de acuerdo con Little, Brown and Company, Nueva York, Nueva York, USA.
Las páginas 267-269 constituyen una ampliación de esta página de copyright.

Avda. Diagonal, 189 - 08018 Barcelona.
rbalibros.com

Primera edición: mayo de 2016.

RBA MOLINO
Ref.: MONL336
ISBN: 978-84-272-0979-4
Depósito legal: B.8073-2016.

Impreso en España - *Printed in Spain*

CRÓNICA DE LA PRIMERA
CAZA DEL TESORO BENÉFICA
DEL COLEGIO CULVERT
que tuvo lugar en
la ciudad de Nueva York
el
sábado, 25 de octubre
(y que NUNCA provocó disturbios)

entrevistas realizadas por
CLAUDIA TAPPER
a

Reese Tapper
Akash Gupta
Parvati Gupta
Carmen Gutierrez
Sophie Koh
Kalisha Hendricks
Jens Kuypers
Xander Billington
Wyatt Templeman
James Mantolini
Dimitri Sharansky
Toby Zimmerman
la subdirectora Joanna Bevan
el letrado Eric S. Tapper
y a quien haya podido olvidar.

Para consultas de prensa, sírvanse dirigirse a:
Claudia Tapper (claudaroo@gmail.com)

Para pleitos/citaciones/etc.:
Eric Tapper (eric.steven.tapper@gmail.com)

ÍNDICE

PRÓLOGO

CLAUDIA

Esta es la historia oficial de la Primera Caza del Tesoro Benéfica del Colegio Culvert.

La escribo porque ha corrido MUCHA información falsa sobre lo que pasó. Sobre todo por culpa de aquel estúpido artículo del *New York Star*.

FALSO

UNA CAZA DEL TESORO ESCOLAR ACABA EN DISTURBIOS

Niños y padres de un colegio privado montan una algarada durante una recaudación benéfica

(un poquito cierto)

O sea, totalmente falso. NADIE en NINGÚN momento causó «disturbios».

Vale, quizás un par de minutos hacia el final. Pero eso lo puedo explicar.

Confieso que lo que ocurrió fue técnicamente una «algarada». Pero, teniendo en cuenta que casi nadie sabe lo que significa, es bastante ridículo ponerlo en un titular.

DICCIONARIO

algarada

algarada: f.
Alboroto o vocerío formado por un grupo de personas.

Además, algunas de las cosas que pasaron con el equipo de mi hermano Reese no fueron nada buenas. Ni legales.

Pero, en general, fue TODO UN ÉXITO. Recaudamos 8.748,75 dólares para el Banco de Alimentos de Manhattan, y eso es SIMPLEMENTE ALUCINANTE. Gracias a nuestra caza del tesoro MUCHA gente que pasa hambre va a poder comer algo decente.

Claro que esto no te lo contarán en el estúpido *New York Star*.

Por eso, insisto, he decidido escribir esta crónica, elaborada a partir de entrevistas a todos los implicados. Porque, para mí, que no solo tuve la idea de la caza del tesoro, sino que además la organicé, toda esta información falsa es muy frustrante y me hace mucho daño.

excepto los que no han querido hablar conmigo

También resulta muy frustrante saber que nunca habrá una Segunda Caza del Tesoro, porque la subdirectora Bevan la ha prohibido para siempre.

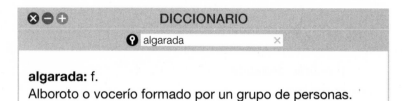

Y, sinceramente, creo que su reacción ha sido desproporcionada. Nadie nos ha puesto una demanda. Al final no han pasado de amenazas.

(hasta ahora)

REESE

Todo lo que puedo decir es que nada de lo que pasó con nuestro equipo fue culpa mía. Por lo visto violamos un montón de leyes que yo ni siquiera sabía que eran leyes. O sea, que no deberían contar.

Y en el fondo no habría pasado nada si mi padre hubiera cumplido mejor su papel de acompañante del equipo.

No es que quiera echarle toda la culpa a él, pero es verdad que casi todo el problema empezó por ahí.

Mi madre aún sigue enfadadísima con él.

NUESTROS PADRES (Mensajes copiados del móvil de mamá)

Q sepas q Claudia dice q está escribiendo otra crónica ← MAMÁ

PAPÁ → Sobre qué?

Adivina

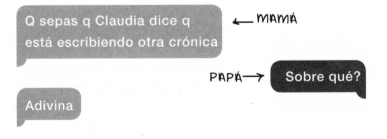

La caza del tesoro no, por favor!

Sí

Arghh! Esta vez no le dejarás usar nuestros mensajes, verdad?

Por qué no?

PQ PARECERÉ EL PEOR PADRE D LA HISTORIA

Y el peor marido. No olvides esa parte

Lo sé! Y pido perdón por enésima vez. No le dejes, te lo suplico!

No le dejaré

Gracias!!!!

A no ser q esté mintiendo... Pq todos SABEMOS mentir en los mensajes, VERDAD, ERIC?

Lo sieeeentooo muuchooo!!!

Lo sé. Y t perdono

Y no le dejarás usar los mensajes, verdad?

Verdad?

Cariño?

Sin comentarios

¡Gracias, mamá!

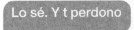

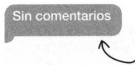

CAPÍTULO 1
TENGO UNA IDEA BUENÍSIMA (CON ALGO DE AYUDA DE MI HERMANO)

CLAUDIA

La idea de la caza del tesoro se me ocurrió mientras atravesaba el Central Park en el autobús M79 de camino al colegio.

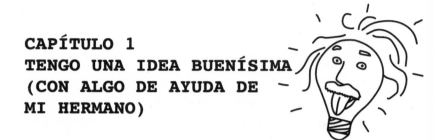

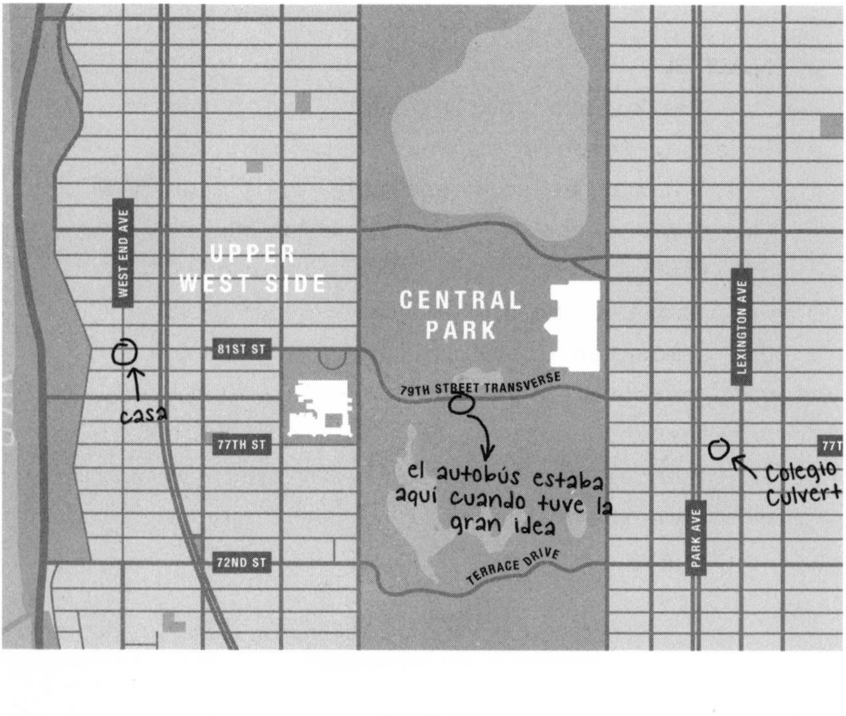

REESE

¡Tú no tuviste ninguna idea!¡La idea fue MÍA!

Me la copiaste enterita, ¡y nunca lo has querido reconocer!

CLAUDIA

¿En serio quieres que diga que fue idea tuya? ¿Con todo lo que pasó?

REESE

Ah, claro… Es verdad. Olvídalo.

CLAUDIA

Por cierto, por si hay alguien que no lo sabe, Reese y yo somos gemelos.

Lo cual es sorprendente, porque no nos parecemos mucho. De hecho, somos MUY distintos.

Ahora no me voy a poner a explicar en QUÉ somos tan distintos, porque creo que cada persona es única y especial, y que si ponemos etiquetas a una persona es como si la encerráramos en una cajita sin espacio para moverse y sin poder ser ella misma.

Y eso, obviamente, no mola.

Sin embargo, si no tuviera más REMEDIO que etiquetarnos, yo sería La Lista.

Y Reese sería El Deportista.

O también podría ser El Maloliente.

O incluso El que Desperdicia su Vida Jugando a Videojuegos mientras su Hermana Trabaja para Hacer un Mundo Mejor.

si fuéramos mascotas, yo sería...

y Reese sería...

¿Ves lo que quiero decir con lo de las etiquetas? Son muy injustas.

Aunque sean acertadas.

Volvamos al autobús M79.

autobús M79 = megalento
(pero más rápido que ir andando) (aunque no mucho más)

Estaba sentada al lado de Reese escribiendo mi discurso para el Consejo de Alumnos sobre mi propuesta de montar un acto benéfico a favor del Banco de Alimentos de Manhattan.

Eso de que haya gente en Nueva York que no tenga suficiente para comer me preocupa DE VERDAD. Sobre todo cuando piensas lo forradas que están muchas de las familias de Culvert. Me parece muy mal y totalmente injusto que en una parte de la ciudad haya niños que pasan hambre mientras otros como Athena Cohen tienen tanto dinero que pueden ir cada semana en avión privado a las Bermudas.

Por eso, como presidenta, decidí que debía hacer algo al respecto.

REESE

Pero tú ya sabes que solo eres presidenta del curso de primero, ¿verdad?

O sea, que no eres presidenta de toda la ciudad…

CLAUDIA

Vale: A) No me digas.

B) Nueva York tiene ALCALDE, no presidente.

el alcalde de Nueva York vive aquí
(casi tan bonita como la Casa Blanca)
(pero difícil de fotografiar por culpa de árboles/mur

Y C) ¿No has oído nunca aquello de «Piensa globalmente, actúa localmente»?

REESE

Creo que sí. ¿Salía en un anuncio de Burger King?

CLAUDIA

Estoy casi completamente segura de que no.

REESE

Ah, pues entonces no.

CLAUDIA

Es penoso, Reese. En serio.

Volvamos al autobús. Yo estaba preparando mi discurso y Reese iba farfullando algo sobre MetaWorld.

REESE

MetaWorld es el mejor videojuego de la historia universal. No es solo un juego, es como cincuenta juegos distintos estrupujados en uno.

esta palabra no existe

Y uno de esos juegos es MetaTesoro, que va de una caza del tesoro a lo bestia, pero MUCHO mejor que una caza del tesoro normal, porque aquí puedes cargarte a otros jugadores para quedarte con sus cosas. Así, si matas a muchos, ni siquiera hace falta que te pongas a buscar más cosas.

MetaTesoro tiene esta pinta:

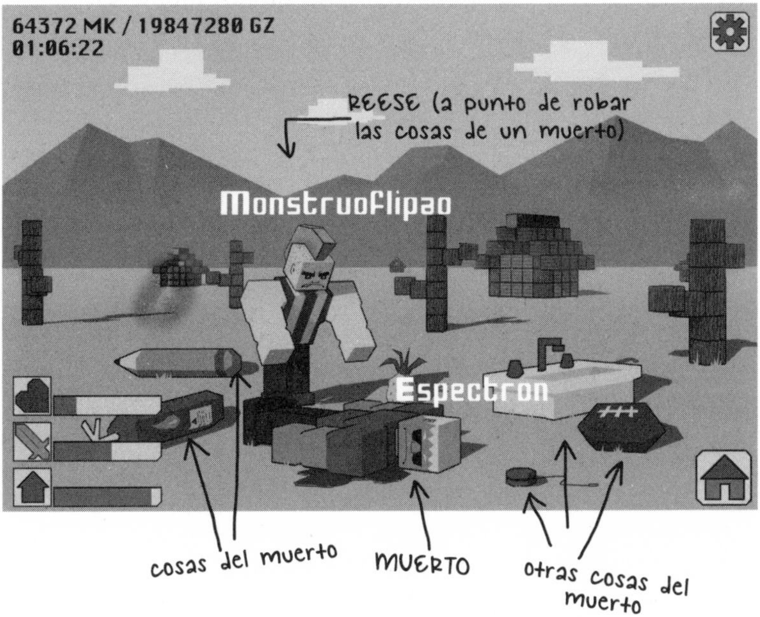

He pasado horas y horas jugando al MetaTesoro, y un día se me ocurrió que sería alucinante montar una caza del tesoro de verdad por toda Nueva York.

Claro que no podríamos ir matándonos y tal. Pero igualmente molaría.

Por eso, cuando Claudia me dijo «Calla, Reese, que estoy escribiendo mi discurso para el Consejo de Alumnos», yo le contesté: «¡A esos deberías decirles que monten una caza del tesoro! ¡Para todo el colegio!».

Y Claudia me dijo: «Es la idea más ESTÚPIDA que he… ¡Un momento!».

CLAUDIA

Y así es básicamente como empezó todo.

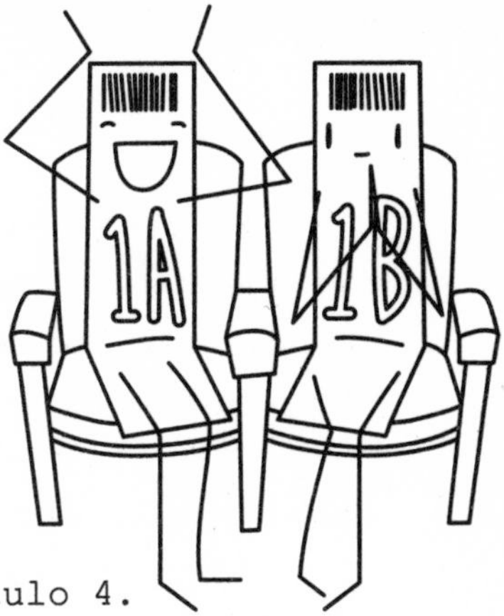

CAPÍTULO 4
LA FIEBRE DE LA CAZA DEL TESORO INVADE CULVERT

CLAUDIA

Ya ves, esto es el Capítulo 4.

Y te preguntarás por qué no hay capítulos 2 y 3.

Antes los había. Y a mí, la verdad, me parecían fascinantes.

Pero todos los que leyeron el primer borrador dijeron que eran muy aburridos.

Sophie
Parvati
Carmen
Mamá

Así que los suprimí. Pero, por si te interesa, el Capítulo 2 iba sobre el discurso que pronuncié y que convenció al Consejo de Alumnos para aprobar un acuerdo de creación de la Primera Caza del Tesoro Benéfica del Colegio Culvert.

No es por presumir, pero fue un discurso muy eficaz. Cité a Miranda Fleet Y a Gandhi.

Miranda Fleet: la mejor cantautora del mundo

Gandhi: el mejor manifestante pacífico del mundo

El Capítulo 3 iba sobre cómo planeamos la caza del tesoro. Cuando digo "planea*mos*" me refiero sobre todo a mí y a Akash Gupta, mi copresidente del Comité de la Caza del Tesoro. Y también a la subdirectora Bevan, porque ella tenía que aprobarlo todo.

Akash va a dos cursos por encima del mío. Es el hermano mayor de una de mis (Parvati) mejores amigas, y es básicamente un genio, aunque por eso mismo a veces es difícil trabajar con él.

AKASH GUPTA, copresidente del Comité de la Caza del Tesoro

¡No puedo creer que hayas suprimido el Capítulo 3! ¡Era el mejor!

CLAUDIA

¿Verdad que sí? Pues todo el mundo decía que era mortal.

AKASH

La gente es idiota. Con la programación informática pasa igual. Todo el mundo quiere jugar a Vacas Explosivas, pero a nadie le importa cómo se ha hecho.

Vacas Explosivas: aplicación la mar de tonta (pero que engancha mucho)

Y planear la caza del tesoro fue realmente complicado. Sobre todo cuando tú te rajaste y yo tuve que hacerlo todo solo.

CLAUDIA

¡NO me rajé! Pero cuando decidí que no solo quería PLANEAR la caza del tesoro, sino también PARTICIPAR en ella, la señora Bevan me hizo dimitir de copresidenta para evitar sospechas de corrupción.

AKASH

Sí, claro. Tú sigue con ese cuento. Lo que sea por dormir tranquila, rajada.

CLAUDIA

¿Ves a qué me refería cuando decía que a veces es difícil trabajar con Akash?

La cosa fue así: en principio yo no pensaba participar. Pero una de las funciones que teníamos asignadas Akash y yo era idear premios para los que ganaran.

Y, como lo que nos permitía gastar la señora Bevan no daba para nada, el segundo y tercer premios eran penosillos.

AKASH

¿Perdón? ¿Un vale de 20 dólares para el Starbucks? ¿Con cuatro jugadores por equipo? ¡Es ridículo! Eso no da ni para un *frappuccino* grande por persona.

Y el tercer premio ni te cuento. Esos estuches para lápices de Culvert son pura basura. Por un dólar te podrían dar diez.

~~La señora Bevan es una rata que te c...~~ ~~No, esto no lo pongas.~~

¡Glups! ¡Perdón, Akash, olvidé quitarlo!

CLAUDIA

~~No lo pondré.~~

Pero el primer premio era otra cosa. El padre de Allegra Bell tiene no sé qué cargo importante en el pabellón Madison Square Garden. Y Akash convenció a Allegra para que su padre donara, como primer premio, cuatro asientos de primera fila para CUALQUIER EVENTO.

Y, claro, eso era lo más, una locura, increíble, asombroso, pasmoso y COMPLETAMENTE ALUCINANTE.

Porque en el Madison no solo estaban programados los partidos de baloncesto de los Knicks, los partidos de hockey de los Rangers y los combates de lucha libre que tanto les gusta a unos del último curso de primaria. No, también había conciertos de Fiddy K, Deondra Y Miranda Fleet.

Y eso era demasiado para mí. Miranda Fleet no solo es la mejor cantautora del mundo y mi ídolo; es todo lo que quiero ser de mayor, además de presidenta del país. Poder verla desde la PRIMERA FILA… era una oportunidad que no podía dejar escapar.

Casi todo el colegio pensó lo mismo. En cuanto corrió la voz sobre los asientos de primera fila, el interés por la caza del tesoro básicamente se desbordó.

SOPHIE KOH, mejor amiga de Claudia

La gente se volvió LOCA con lo de las entradas del Madison. No se habló de otra cosa durante días.

PARVATI GUPTA, segunda mejor amiga de Claudia (empatada con Carmen)

Solo una cosa: cuando supe que podía conseguir entradas de primera fila para Deondra casi me hago pis encima. ¡Deondra ES LO MÁS!

CARMEN GUTIERREZ, segunda mejor amiga de Claudia (empatada con Parvati)

Yo tenía un verdadero dilema ético. Porque no sabía a quién prefería ver, si a Miranda Fleet o a Deondra. Pero, en cualquier caso, grité: «¡YUJUUUU!».

REESE

Al principio, muchos de mis amigos decían: «¿Es una caza del tesoro y no podemos matar a nadie para llevarnos sus cosas? ¡No tiene sentido!».

Pero cuando se enteraron de que podían conseguir entradas gratis para ver a los Knicks o a Fiddy K, ¡FLIPANDEARON!

↖ esta palabra no existe

WYATT TEMPLEMAN, amigo de Reese (y tirando a burro)

Yo me quedé a cuadros. Dicen que, si te sientas en la primera fila de un partido de los Knicks, los jugadores ¡te sudan encima! ¿Te imaginas QUÉ gozada?

(PUES NO, ¡puaaj!)

XANDER BILLINGTON, amigo de Reese (y MUCHO más que burro)

Yo dije: «¿VER A FIDDY K A UN PALMO DE LA NAPIA? ¡APARTA QUE ALLÁ VOY!».

Y todo por la *FACE*. Bro, ¡yo me apunto!

CLAUDIA

Una pequeña advertencia sobre Xander Billington: no solo es mucho más que burro, también es miembro de una de las familias más antiguas de Estados Unidos. Se ve que los Billington vinieron de Inglaterra con los primeros peregrinos en el *Mayflower*.

Siempre que pienso en esto me dan mucha pena los peregrinos.

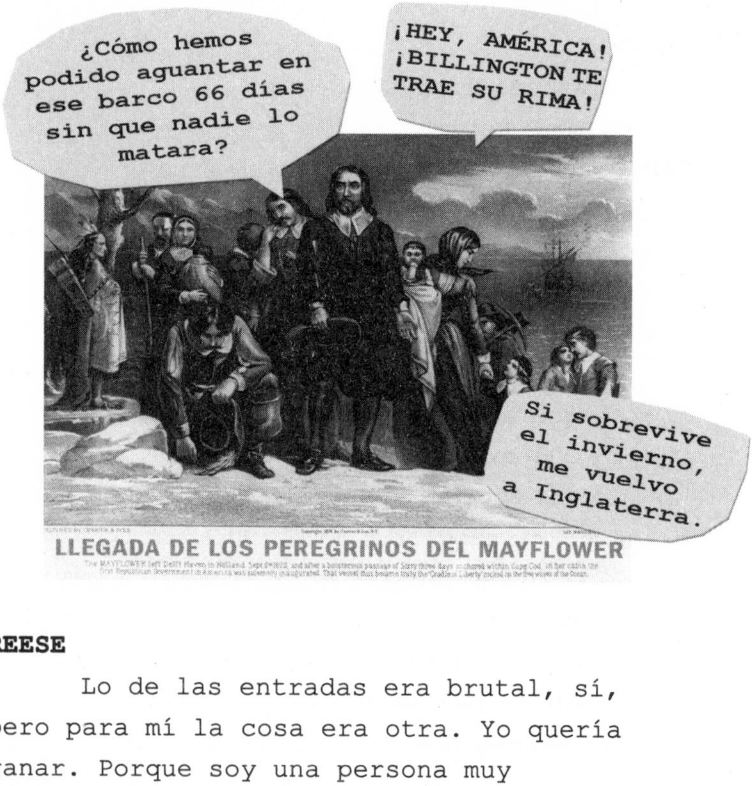

¿Cómo hemos podido aguantar en ese barco 66 días sin que nadie lo matara?
¡HEY, AMÉRICA! ¡BILLINGTON TE TRAE SU RIMA!
Si sobrevive el invierno, me vuelvo a Inglaterra.
LLEGADA DE LOS PEREGRINOS DEL MAYFLOWER

REESE

Lo de las entradas era brutal, sí, pero para mí la cosa era otra. Yo quería ganar. Porque soy una persona muy competitiva. Pregúntale a quien quieras de mi equipo de fútbol: ¡no hay quien me pare ni en los entrenamientos!

no existe

Y una oportunidad como esa de panzarse a todo un colegio no se da todos los días.

Bueno, vale, la Batalla de los Libros. Pero es muy injusto. Porque la única forma de ganar esa batalla es… ya sabes…

CLAUDIA

¿Leyendo libros?

REESE

Sí. Y ese no es mi fuerte. Pero ¿una caza del tesoro? ¡Eso es lo mío!

CLAUDIA

La fiebre de la caza del tesoro era tan fuerte que hasta contagió a las fembots. Tendré que explicar algo de las fembots.

O no. Porque, como presidenta de primero, mi labor es representar a todo mi curso de forma justa e igualitaria. Incluidas las fembots.

Sería MUY poco presidencial por mi parte hablar mal de nadie.

De manera que dejaré que lo haga Sophie.

SOPHIE

A ver, básicamente es como… si Satán y la más mala de las *Mujeres Descerebradas* tuvieran una hija, sería una fembot. Son un grupito de Culvert formado por chicas desesperadamente ricas y que se lo tienen muy creído, como Athena Cohen y Ling Chen, y otras quiero y no puedo, como Meredith y Clarissa.

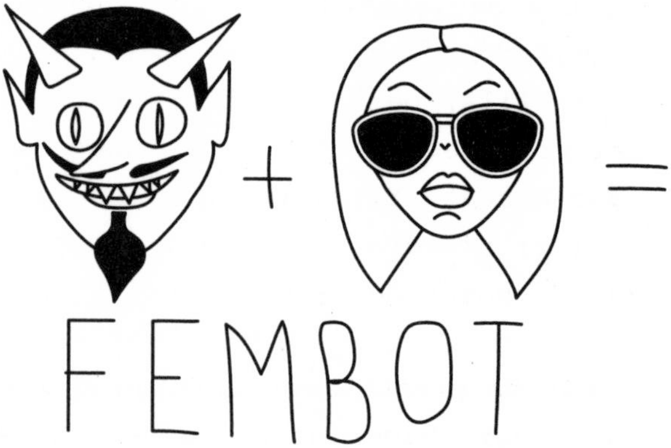

CARMEN

No creo que a las fembots les importaran lo más mínimo las entradas. El padre de Athena, sin ir más lejos, prácticamente puede COMPRAR el Madison Square Garden. Imagino que no les gustó la idea de que ocurriera algo en Culvert que no tuviera que ver con ellas.

O quizá se apuntaron porque todos los guapos del curso siguiente al nuestro lo hacían.

CLAUDIA

Fuera por lo que fuese, el día después de anunciar lo de las entradas, Parvati y yo comentamos en clase de lengua si yo debía o no participar en la caza del tesoro.

Era una decisión difícil, porque hubiera matado por ver a Miranda Fleet desde la primera fila, pero estaba a punto de preparar con Akash la lista de cosas que había que buscar. Y, claro, que una misma persona (yo) hiciera la lista Y luego buscara las cosas de la lista no era muy justo.

Le estaba preguntando a Parvati qué creía que debía hacer cuando Athena Cohen oyó nuestra conversación. Se dio la vuelta y dijo con esa voz tan repelente que tiene: «¿DE VERDAD CREÉIS que tenéis la más mínima oportunidad de ganar esas entradas? ¿Qué pensáis hacer? ¿Recorrer Manhattan con vuestros patinetes rosas?».

PARVATI

¡Menuda TONTERÍA! No hemos usado los patinetes desde, no sé, ¿los ocho años?

patinete rosa (lo he tenido que sacar del trastero para hacer la foto porque hace AÑOS que no lo uso)

CLAUDIA

Pero eso es muy típico de Athena. En el fondo nos estaba diciendo: «Sois unas pueblerinas que circuláis en patinete y yo soy increíblemente rica y tengo un avión particular».

PARVATI

Yo le dije: «¿Y tú qué vas a hacer, Athena? ¿Pedirle a tu mayordomo que te lleve a caballito de un sitio a otro?».

Y ella puso morros y dijo: «Haré lo que haga falta, Pobreti».

Te juro que lo dijo así, tal cual: «Pobreti» en lugar de «Parvati».

CLAUDIA

Lo sé, estaba delante. Se pasó tres pueblos.

PARVATI

Y yo me di la vuelta y empecé: «¡Porfa, porfa, Claude! TIENES que estar en nuestro equipo porque AHORA ES PERSONAL».

CLAUDIA

No podía estar más de acuerdo.

Así que fui a ver a la señora Bevan y me dijo que, si dimitía del Comité de la Caza del Tesoro antes de empezar a hacer la lista, tenía permiso para participar.

Así que dimití oficialmente de la copresidencia y dediqué toda mi energía a reunir un equipo irresistible para vencer a las fembots y ganar la prueba.

Aunque la misión se reveló peliaguda.

CAPÍTULO 5
MONTAMOS UN EQUIPO IRRESISTIBLE (TRAS UNA LIGERA DISCUSIÓN)

CLAUDIA

Akash propuso que los equipos de la caza del tesoro fueran de cuatro personas. Para nosotras era ideal porque así Sophie, Parvati, Carmen y yo podíamos formar equipo, al que llamamos Equipo Revoltijo por nuestra diversidad étnica.

asiático-americana
indio-americana
cubano-americana
diverso-americana (yo)

Por desgracia, la caza del tesoro era en sábado. Y los sábados Sophie tiene la agenda a tope.

SOPHIE

Tengo ballet de 9 a 11 y clases de conversación de coreano de 2 a 4. Pero es que además aquel día tenía un recital de violín y no podía ni plantearme lo de saltármelo. Llevo una ETERNIDAD practicando el Concierto para violín n.º 3.

CLAUDIA

Lo entendía y lo respetaba, aunque me daba mucha pena. No solo porque perdíamos una pieza muy valiosa del equipo, sino porque es mi mejor amiga del mundo mundial.

Total, que necesitábamos una cuarta persona para el Revoltijo. Y Carmen, Parvati y yo teníamos un importante desacuerdo al respecto.

Yo decía que había que buscar a alguien con aptitudes que nosotras no tuviéramos. Por ejemplo, me parecía una buena idea reclutar a un chico por si teníamos que buscar cosas propias de chicos.

cómics, cartas de Pokemon, cosas que dan asco, etc.

Y también pensaba que nos convenía un chico atlético y deportista, porque a Parvati, Carmen y a mí no nos mata lo de la actividad física.

Además, como las tres hemos nacido aquí, me pareció interesante contar con alguien de fuera, por si necesitábamos un «punto de vista foráneo».

Sumando todo lo anterior, el candidato evidente era Jens Kuypers, porque es: A) chico, B) muy atlético, y C) llegó el verano pasado procedente de los Países Bajos.

PARVATI

Perdón, pero ¿y si intentas ser sincera? La ÚNICA razón por la que querías que Jens estuviera en el equipo es porque: D) ES TU NOVIO.

CARMEN

En serio, Claudia, metiste a tu holandesito en el equipo con calzador.

CLAUDIA

Voy a responder sobre este asunto sin rodeos y con la verdad por delante.

En primer lugar, Jens NO es técnicamente mi novio. Básicamente, porque no creo que a nuestra edad se pueda hablar de «novio» o «novia». Eso, si acaso, a partir del curso que viene.

Aunque es cierto que Jens y yo estamos saliendo. No voy a entrar en detalles sobre nuestra relación porque no es asunto de nadie más. Solo diré que llevamos juntos casi dos semanas y media y que nos va estupendamente bien.

Sin embargo, eso no tiene NADA QUE VER con el hecho de que quisiera a Jens en nuestro equipo. Creía sinceramente que sería mucho más útil para ganar a las fembots que la candidata de Parvati y Carmen, Kalisha Hendricks.

PARVATI

Y yo le solté: «Pero ¡qué dices! ESO ES RIDÍCULO».

Vale que Jens es mono y simpático y tal pero, sin ánimo de ofender, a mí siempre me ha parecido bastante vago.

Y lo siento, pero Kalisha es brillante.

CARMEN

¡Sí, es un COCO! ¡Es la más inteligente de la clase!

CLAUDIA

ESO habría que verlo. Vale, sí, Kalisha es muy lista, no lo niego.

Pero en nuestra clase hay MUCHA gente inteligente. Mirad, si no, el examen de mates de la semana pasada. Kalisha sacó solo un 9,4. Y sé de buena fuente que AL MENOS otra persona sacó un 9,6.

PARVATI

¿Quién? ¿Tú?

CLAUDIA

Lo importante no es quién. Era por poner un ejemplo.

Insisto en que Jens nos podía aportar un conocimiento masculino específico que no teníamos y…

PARVATI

¡Kalisha también! ¡Porque vive en Queens! NO sabes nada de ese barrio si no vives allí.

De verdad lo digo. Yo, por ejemplo, ni siquiera sé muy bien dónde está Queens.

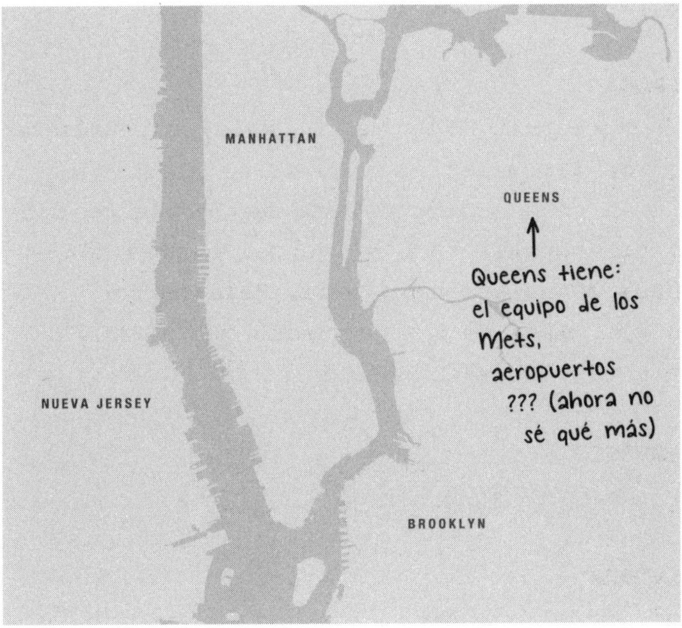

CARMEN

¡Kalisha nos habría ayudado TANTO! ADEMÁS, le hacía mucha ilusión estar en nuestro equipo.

CLAUDIA

Quiero dejar constancia de que a Kalisha no le molestó NO estar finalmente en nuestro equipo.

KALISHA HENDRICKS, una de las más listas de nuestra clase (pero no necesariament LA más lista)

No pasa nada. Me pasé al equipo de Yun y Charlotte, y luego fichamos a Max.

CLAUDIA

Y otro dato: Jens NO es vago, solo es un poco relajado. Y estaba muy motivado para ir a por todas.

JENS KUYPERS, amigo NO técnicamente novio (véanse págs. 28-29)

Sí, es verdad. La caza del tesoro sonaba muy divertida. Recorrer Nueva York buscando cosas, como vivo aquí poco tiempo, yo pienso: «¡Qué guay!».

CLAUDIA

Por otra parte, no quiero ser mala, pero creo que Jens agradeció que lo rescataran de un equipo en el que no tenía absolutamente ninguna oportunidad de ganar.

Claro que mi hermano no pensó lo mismo.

REESE

¡NO podía creer que mi propia hermana nos hubiera robado a Jens, tío! Me había llevado días enteros montar el Escuadrón Bestial. ¡Xander, Wyatt, Jens y yo hubiéramos formado un equipo alucinante, un dream team!

De hecho, pensamos en llamarnos así, Dream Team, en vez de Escuadrón Bestial.

CLAUDIA

Otra vez sin ánimos de ser cruel, pero lo de Dream Team hubiera sido un nombre mucho mejor, porque ni soñando hubieran ganado. Tenían las mismas posibilidades de ganar que una bola de nieve de salir con una cerilla.

¿lo pillas?
(es una bola de nieve)
(sin ningún futuro)
(como el equipo
de Reese)

Básicamente, todo aquello en lo que Reese y sus amigos son buenos —dar cabezazos a un balón, eructar el alfabeto completo o disputar combates de lucha en nuestro salón rompiendo muebles— no sirve de nada en una caza del tesoro. (ha pasado DOS veces)

Pero eso no impidió que se quedaran a cuadros cuando Jens decidió unirse al Equipo Revoltijo. Mira la conversación que encontré en el muro de ClickChat de Jens:

POSTS EN EL MURO PÚBLICO DE CLICKCHAT DE JENS KUYPERS

Xander XLoRemata JK, BRO, KE DISE K NOS PLANTAS POR TIAS?
Jens kuypersjens ¿qué significa eso?
XLoRemata REESE DISE K TE LAS PIRAS. ME LO FIRMAS?
kuypersjens Lo siento, Xander, pero no entiendo qué me dices.
Reese MONSTRUOFLIPAO En serio te vas al equipo de mi hermana para caza tesoro?
kuypersjens ah sí, lo siento, chicos
XLoRemata ¡¡¡¡¡JUDAS!!!!!!
MONSTRUOFLIPAO Dijiste que venías con nosotros!
Wyatt KillKill Y ahora de dónde sacamos el cuarto?
XLoRemata TAS PASAO CHAVAL!
kuypersjens lo siento chicos Claudia es mi novia y tengo que ir con ella

técnicamente solo estamos SALIENDO (Jens aún no domina el idioma)

REESE

Me mosquée bastante cuando se fue Jens. Pero pensé: «No pasa nada, seremos un trío. ¡Igualmente arrasaremos!».

CLAUDIA

Pero, por desgracia para el Escuadrón Bestial, dos días antes de la prueba, la subdirectora Bevan dijo que, como había un hueco, iba a incorporar a James Mantolini al equipo.

Debería hablaros de James Mantolini.

Aunque, bien mirado, mejor que lo haga Reese.

REESE

No me gusta hablar mal de la gente, pero creo que a James Mantolini le pasa algo, en serio.

No es fácil explicarlo. Es como si la Tierra no fuera su planeta de origen.

Por ejemplo, tú le preguntas: «James, ¿dos y dos?» y seguro que él te contesta: «¡Salchichas!».

Y en el cole se mete en MUCHOS problemas. De toda la vida. Cuando estábamos en preescolar lo mandaron a ver al director por comerse el pelo de Molly Preston. Mientras aún estaba enganchado a su cabeza.

Fue un momento potente. Yo estaba sentado al lado de Molly cuando pasó y te aseguro que NUNCA me quitaré esa imagen de la cabeza.

James Mantolini comiéndose el pelo de Molly Preston (recreación de la artista) (nota: la artista soy yo)

Por eso no era de extrañar que nadie quisiera a James en su equipo. Y cuando la señora Bevan lo metió en el Escuadrón Bestial, Xander, Wyatt y yo nos quedamos bastante espucharrados.

EPNE ("Esta Palabra No Existe")

Ahora no voy a culpar a James de TODOS los líos en que nos metimos y las cosas ilegales que hicimos.

Aunque de la mitad de ellos sí.

La otra mitad fueron culpa de mi padre.

CAPÍTULO 6
EL TEMITA DEL ACOMPAÑANTE

CLAUDIA

Como presidenta de mi curso, soy muy consciente de la responsabilidad que conlleva el liderazgo. Cuando algo sale mal, un buen líder tiene que dar un paso al frente y aceptar su parte de culpa.

Pero yo no tengo la menor culpa del temita del acompañante.

Porque la repentina decisión de la señora Bevan de que todos los equipos tenían que ir acompañados se produjo solo tres días antes de la prueba. De forma que Akash y yo tuvimos que encontrar, con tan poca antelación, a 25 padres que se ofrecieran voluntarios. Y acabamos con algunos candidatos poco idóneos.

Como mi padre.

Mi padre es abogado, y a los abogados les pasa una cosa: suelen trabajar los sábados. Y los domingos. Y básicamente todos los días. Y noches. (y en vacaciones, cortas o largas, y en cumpleaños, etc.)

Confieso que, aunque siempre está trabajando, mi padre se preocupa mucho por nosotros. Por eso acabó aceptando ser acompañante en cuanto mi madre le metió una pizca de presión.

NUESTROS PADRES (Mensajes de móvil)

Tienes q hacer d acompañante d Reese en caza tesoro sábado 10 a 14

No puedes tú?
Estoy machacado esta semana

Yo ya soy acompañante del equipo de Claudia

Y no pueden ir en mismo equipo?

Conoces a nuestros hijos?

Vale. Pero puede q lleve portátil y trabaje desde allí

Sí, claro. Muy realista

Detecto sarcasmo?

Mucho.

PERO T QUIERO

Yo tb! Compro algo para cenar de camino a casa?

Son las 12 d la noche. Hace horas q he cenado. Me voy a dormir

Buf! Tengo q cambiar de trabajo

Pues sí

CLAUDIA

Por cierto, mi padre también tuvo problemas con la hoja de recaudaciones de Reese.

REESE

Tenía clarísimo que iba a conseguir un montón de recaudaciones. Pero el día que repartieron las hojas tenía entreno y la mía acabó en el fondo de la mochila, debajo de las botas de fútbol.

Y luego ya me olvidé de ella hasta diez minutos, creo, antes de la prueba.

Otras cosas que Reese ha olvidado/perdido en el fondo de la mochila:
- las notas
- la autorización de salida para excursión
- calcetines sucios (muy malolientes)
- sándwich de la semana pasada (muy MUY maloliente)

CLAUDIA

Para que quede constancia, la hoja de recaudaciones de Reese acabó así:

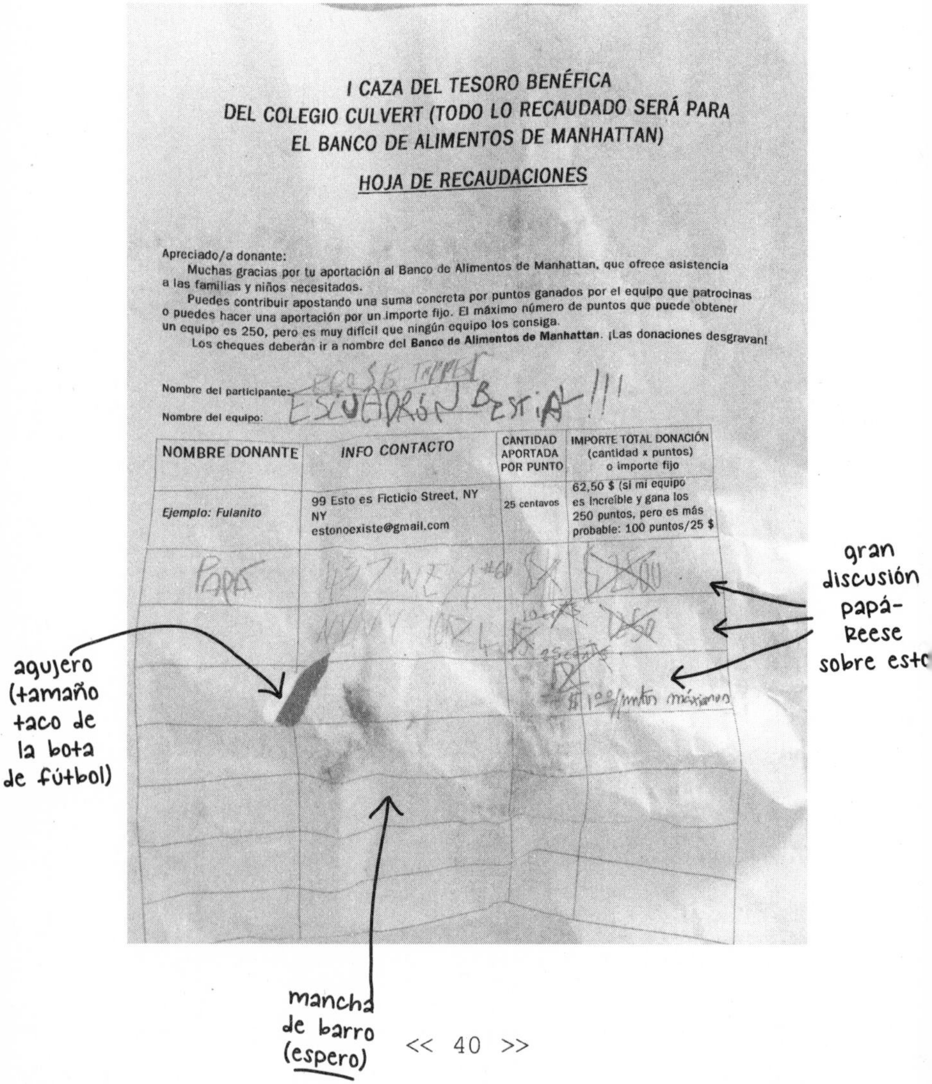

I CAZA DEL TESORO BENÉFICA
DEL COLEGIO CULVERT (TODO LO RECAUDADO SERÁ PARA
EL BANCO DE ALIMENTOS DE MANHATTAN)

HOJA DE RECAUDACIONES

Apreciado/a donante:

Muchas gracias por tu aportación al Banco de Alimentos de Manhattan, que ofrece asistencia a las familias y niños necesitados.

Puedes contribuir apostando una suma concreta por puntos ganados por el equipo que patrocinas o puedes hacer una aportación por un importe fijo. El máximo número de puntos que puede obtener un equipo es 250, pero es muy difícil que ningún equipo los consiga.

Los cheques deberán ir a nombre del **Banco de Alimentos de Manhattan**. ¡Las donaciones desgravan!

Nombre del participante: Reese Tapper

Nombre del equipo: ESCUADRÓN BESTIA!!!

NOMBRE DONANTE	INFO CONTACTO	CANTIDAD APORTADA POR PUNTO	IMPORTE TOTAL DONACIÓN (cantidad x puntos) o importe fijo
Ejemplo: Fulanito	99 Esto es Ficticio Street, NY NY estonoexiste@gmail.com	25 centavos	62,50 $ (si mi equipo es increíble y gana los 250 puntos, pero es más probable: 100 puntos/25 $
Papá	[illegible]	[illegible]	[illegible]
	[illegible]	[illegible]	[illegible]
			[illegible] puntos máximos

No es que quiera presumir ni nada por el estilo, pero MI hoja estaba así:

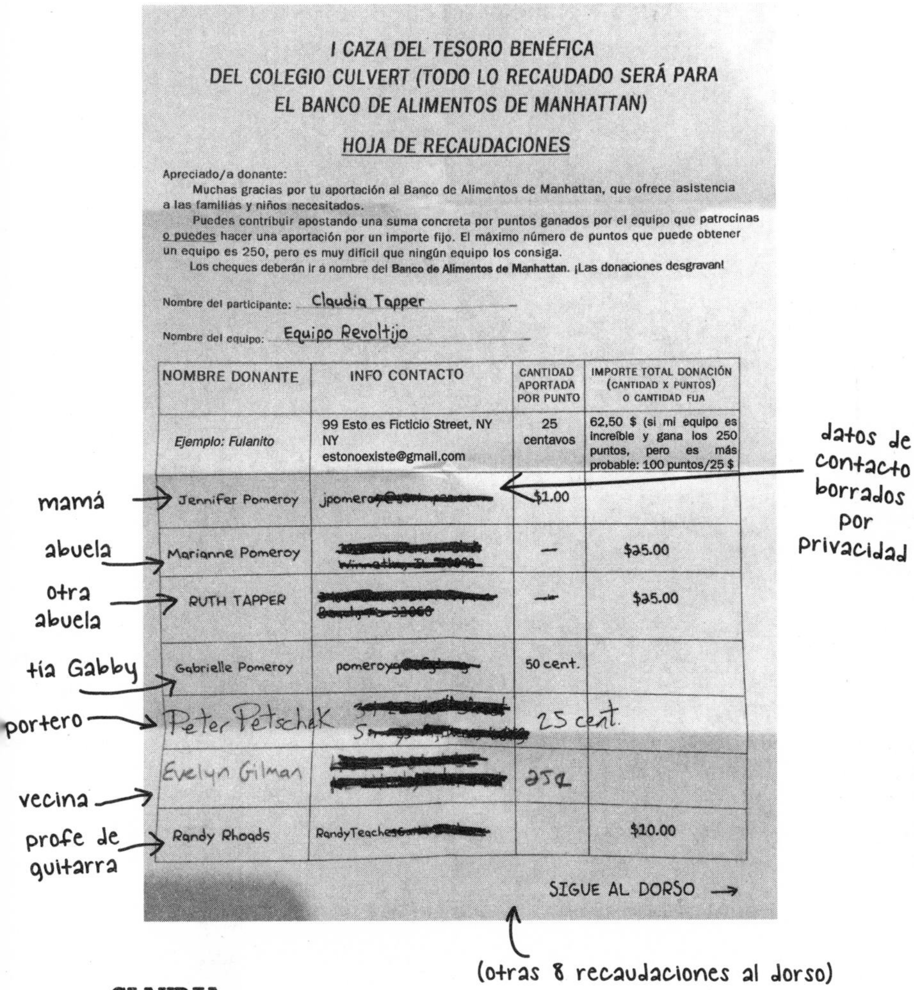

I CAZA DEL TESORO BENÉFICA
DEL COLEGIO CULVERT (TODO LO RECAUDADO SERÁ PARA
EL BANCO DE ALIMENTOS DE MANHATTAN)

HOJA DE RECAUDACIONES

Apreciado/a donante:

Muchas gracias por tu aportación al Banco de Alimentos de Manhattan, que ofrece asistencia a las familias y niños necesitados.

Puedes contribuir apostando una suma concreta por puntos ganados por el equipo que patrocinas o puedes hacer una aportación por un importe fijo. El máximo número de puntos que puede obtener un equipo es 250, pero es muy difícil que ningún equipo los consiga.

Los cheques deberán ir a nombre del **Banco de Alimentos de Manhattan.** ¡Las donaciones desgravan!

Nombre del participante: Claudia Tapper

Nombre del equipo: Equipo Revoltijo

NOMBRE DONANTE	INFO CONTACTO	CANTIDAD APORTADA POR PUNTO	IMPORTE TOTAL DONACIÓN (CANTIDAD X PUNTOS) O CANTIDAD FIJA
Ejemplo: Fulanito	99 Esto es Ficticio Street, NY NY estonoexiste@gmail.com	25 centavos	62,50 $ (si mi equipo es increíble y gana los 250 puntos, pero es más probable: 100 puntos/25 $
Jennifer Pomeroy	jpomero[redacted]	$1.00	
Marianne Pomeroy	[redacted]	—	$25.00
RUTH TAPPER	[redacted]	—	$25.00
Gabrielle Pomeroy	pomeroy[redacted]	50 cent.	
Peter Petschek	[redacted]	25 cent.	
Evelyn Gilman	[redacted]	25¢	
Randy Rhoads	RandyTeaches[redacted]		$10.00

SIGUE AL DORSO →

CLAUDIA

Al principio no era tan obvio que mi

padre acabaría siendo un problema. De hecho, la mañana de la prueba yo estaba mucho más preocupada por mi madre.

La noche anterior habíamos quedado en que, como yo tenía que estar en el cole antes de las 9:00 para ayudar a Akash y a la señora Bevan a prepararlo todo, saldríamos todos juntos de casa a las 8:45.

A las 8:41 yo ya estaba en la puerta de casa esperando para salir.

A las 8:50 SEGUÍA en la puerta de casa, cada vez más enfadada con mi familia.

Mi madre se estaba secando el pelo. Reese aún iba en calzoncillos. Y mi padre acababa de recibir una llamada de alguien del trabajo que se llamaba Larry.

Eso lo supe porque mi padre no paraba de gritar cosas como «Larry, es factible…». Y «¡Larry, lo solucionaremos…!». Y «¡LARRY! ¡PONERSE HISTÉRICO NO SIRVE DE NADA! ¡ESTO NO ES UNA CRISIS!».

Lo que era un poco raro, porque: A) el que parecía estar histérico ERA mi padre, y B) sonaba como una crisis.

A las 8:53, mi madre estaba por fin lista y decidimos salir hacia el cole sin esperarlos.

REESE

Lo de no esperarnos estuvo fatal. ¡Yo ya estaba listo!

CLAUDIA

Pero ¿qué dices? ¡Si ni siquiera llevabas pantalones!

REESE

Me los habría puesto en el ascensor.

CLAUDIA

No pienso ni molestarme en explicar por qué eso es una mala idea.

ascensor del
edificio —
entrar ahí
sin pantalones
COMO QUE NO

Total, que mi madre y yo cogimos un taxi en West End Avenue y, en cuanto se puso en marcha, mi madre dijo: «Creo que hoy vamos a pasarlo muy bien... ¡Ya tenía ganas de conocer a Jens!».

Fue entonces cuando me di cuenta de que tener a mi madre de acompañante en un equipo en el que estaba el chico con el que salía podía ser el error más gordo de mi vida.

Pasamos el resto del viaje estableciendo las reglas básicas para cualquier interacción entre mi madre y Jens. Cuando llegamos al colegio, mi madre ya había aceptado fingir que no sabía que Jens y yo salíamos, que ni siquiera había oído hablar de él y hacerle solo las preguntas típicas que se hacen por pura educación.

la mayoría,
reglas no escritas (p
falta de tiempo)
(y pq es muy difíc
escribir en un tax

También elegimos un código para que, en el caso de que ella dijera o hiciera algo embarazoso, yo pudiera pararla: «bálsamo labial».

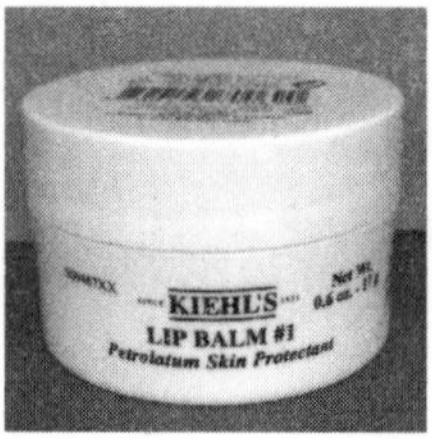

útil para labios cortados
y/o como código

Mientras bajábamos del taxi pensé que ese código podía ser un problema si realmente tenía que pedirle a mi madre el bálsamo labial.

Pero, en cuanto vi el Misterioso Coche Negro delante del cole, olvidé por completo el bálsamo y todo lo demás.

Si esto fuera una peli,
aquí empezaría a sonar
MÚSICA DE SUSPENSE DE COCHE
NEGRO

CAPÍTULO 7
EL MISTERIOSO COCHE NEGRO

CLAUDIA

Era uno de esos coches de alquiler con ventanillas tintadas y chófer. Y estaba allí plantado, junto a la acera, como esperando a alguno de los equipos para llevarlo todo el día de un lado a otro de la ciudad.

MISTERIOSO COCHE NEGRO (en verdad no era este) (pero se parecía mucho) (excepto por las ventanillas tintadas)

Y eso olía a hacer trampa GORDA.

Aunque técnicamente no lo sería… A MENOS que diera tiempo a añadir «PROHIBIDO

USAR COCHES» en el reglamento. Así que salí corriendo hacia el auditorio para proponer a Akash y a la señora Bevan un cambio de última hora.

Pero no me escucharon porque estaban enfrascados en una discusión monumental.

AKASH

¡Era ridículo! ¡Lo del puente de Brooklyn era una de las mejores pruebas de la lista! ¡Y me la hizo quitar! ¡Por una razón INCREÍBLEMENTE tonta!

CLAUDIA

Aquí yo estaba de acuerdo con la señora Bevan. Para coger aquel objeto del puente de Brooklyn había que arriesgar la vida.

AKASH

¡Pues claro! ¡POR ESO VALÍA VEINTE PUNTOS!

CLAUDIA

En teoría, en las cazas del tesoro no muere gente.

AKASH

¡EN LAS DIVERTIDAS, SÍ! Aquello era una pesadilla: ¡había creado una obra de arte y la señora Bevan me la arruinó con sus normas tontas! Me planteé dimitir como señal de protesta.

CLAUDIA

Cuando Akash aceptó por fin no dimitir ni marcharse a casa, les planteé lo de prohibir los coches. Pero la señora Bevan estaba demasiado estresada —tachando la línea sobre el puente de Brooklyn de todas las listas que iban a repartir— como para escucharme.

Para entonces ya había empezado a llegar todo el mundo, y a cada equipo se le daba un sobre en el que ponía **«NO ABRIR»**, una copia del reglamento y un gato Calvin.

GATOS CALVIN

Calvin es la mascota de Culvert, y los gatos que daban eran los mismos peluches que el colegio regala a los niños el primer día de preescolar. Al principio no entendí muy bien por qué los daban.

AKASH

La mitad de las pruebas eran fotos, y había que asegurarse de que se tomaban durante la caza. Así que decidimos dar a cada equipo un objeto que tendría que aparecer en todas las fotos.

Y yo tuve unas cuantas ideas GENIALES para eso. Pero todas costaban dinero, y la señora Bevan me obligó a recurrir a los estúpidos gatos Calvin, porque tenía un montón en un armario y no sabía qué hacer con ellos. Y ya sabéis que esa mujer es una...

~~(rata)~~
(perdón otra vez, Akash)

CLAUDIA

Los gatos Calvin confundieron bastante al personal. Cuando salí del auditorio en busca del resto de mi equipo, vi al imbécil de Xander, el amigo de mi hermano, tirando el del Escuadrón Bestial a la papelera.

XANDER

¡Hombre, claro!¡No era el primer día de párvulos, man!

CLAUDIA

Estaba a punto de avisar a Xander de que posiblemente Calvin tenía algo que ver con la caza del tesoro cuando aparecieron Parvati y Carmen.

Traían cara de alucine. Parvati me dijo, prácticamente gritando: «¿HAS VISTO TODOS ESOS COCHAZOS?».

El pánico me invadió. Porque yo solo había visto un coche.

PARVATI

Yo dije: «¡Dios mío, Claude! ¡¡¡HAY CUATRO!!!».

CLAUDIA

Lo primero que pensé fue: «Si CUATRO equipos diferentes se mueven en coche con chófer por la ciudad… ¡estamos perdidos!».

CARMEN

Yo intentaba tranquilizaros. Porque, si hay mucho tráfico —como cuando hay algún desfile, o ferias callejeras—, es más rápido ir en metro. O sea que lo del coche de alquiler tampoco era tanta ventaja.

CLAUDIA

Las tres nos sentamos a pensar qué equipos eran lo bastante ricos y repelentes como para pagar un servicio de coche con chófer durante las seis horas de la prueba.

Uno tenía que ser obviamente el de las fembots, que se habían puesto de nombre Diosas y Cía., aunque les pegaría mucho más Las Novias de Satán.

Pero, quitando un par de equipos que jamás en la vida harían algo así, como los Avada Kedavras, casi todos los demás podían ser sospechosos.

equipo de Kalisha

Posibles usuarios de coches con chófer:
- Las Fieras
- Las Guapis
- Gingivitis
- Los Caballeros de la Mesa Cuadrada
- Brigada Cuatro
- Killers
- Los Olakease

Estábamos repasando la lista cuando llegó Jens. Nos preguntó de qué hablábamos y, cuando se lo contamos, dijo: «¿No vamos a ir andando?».

Carmen y Parvati lo miraron bastante mal.

CARMEN

Yo le contesté: «¿Perdón? Manhattan tiene VEINTE KILÓMETROS DE LARGO».

en realidad, 21,5 km (ya iba bien)

JENS

Yo le dije a Carmen: «¡Pero hoy hace un día muy bonito! ¡Ideal para pasear!».

en esto tenía razón, hacía muy BUEN DÍA

PARVATI

No voy a mentir. A mí esa actitud de Jens me dejó megapreocupada, te lo juro. Va y dice: «Oh, vamos a dar una vuelta y a oler flores».

Y yo: «Perdona, pero aquí vamos a PELEARNOS A MUERTE. Y las fembots van en coche con chófer. Y otros tres equipos también. No sé si lo ves, pero estamos en plena crisis».

CLAUDIA

Iba a llevarme a Jens aparte para explicarle lo importante que era ganar para el resto del Equipo Revoltijo, pero justo entonces apareció mi madre. Me preparé para un encuentro incómodo mamá-Jens, pero ni siquiera lo miró.

Lo que hizo fue preguntar, con voz muy estresada: «¿Has visto a tu hermano?».

No lo había visto. Probablemente porque en ese mismo momento, él y mi padre estaban corriendo como locos por la calle 77.

CAPÍTULO 8
REESE Y MI PADRE CASI SE LO PIERDEN

REESE

Yo ya me había puesto los pantalones y mi padre aún seguía al teléfono, así que me senté a jugar un poco a MetaWorld y perdí la noción del tiempo hasta que me llegó un mensaje de Wyatt diciendo: «¿DÓNDE ESTÁS?».

Entonces vi que eran las diez menos cinco.

Y entré en modo pánico. Hice que mi padre colgara el teléfono —lo que le estresó MUCHÍSIMO— y nos marcamos un eskateo por las escaleras hasta pillar un taxi.

EPNE

En el taxi, mi padre leyó un mail del trabajo en el móvil y soltó un «arghhh» como si le hubieran dado un puñetazo en el estómago.

Luego me miró y me dijo: «Una cosa, hijo…» con esa voz, como susurrando, que utiliza, por ejemplo, cuando se te ha muerto el pez y lo va a tirar por el váter.

única foto conocida del pez de Reese Aletillas (vivió 3 días)

Por eso supe que lo que iba a decir no podía ser bueno.

Mi padre me dijo: «¿Hasta qué punto necesitáis un acompañante?».

Y yo le dije: «Papá… NI SE TE OCURRA dejarnos plantados».

Entonces el taxi se quedó parado en un atasco y tuvimos que bajar y empezar a correr.

NUESTROS PADRES (Mensajes de móvil)

Ya habéis salido? Empieza en 10 min

5 min

Por favor dime q estáis de camino y no hablando por tel otra vez

3 min

DÓNDE ESTÁIS???

ERIC????!!!!!!

YA EMPIEZA

comiendo

QUÉ?!

corriendo

DEPRISA!

CLAUDIA

La señora Bevan nos agradeció a todos la asistencia y nos recordó que la prueba tenía fines benéficos y que todos éramos ganadores por el solo hecho de participar para ayudar al Banco de Alimentos de Manhattan, y que no había que ser demasiado competitivos.

Consejo ampliamente ignorado por todos, que mientras tanto pensábamos: «¡ENTRADAS DE PRIMERA FILA EN EL MADISON! ¡PASARÉ POR ENCIMA DEL CADÁVER DE QUIEN SEA PARA GANARLAS!».

Luego empezó a repasar el reglamento. A efectos históricos —y porque algunas reglas acabaron siendo MUY importantes—, os reproduzco la hoja que repartió.

1.ª CAZA DEL TESORO BENÉFICA DEL COLEGIO CULVERT

REGLAMENTO

OBJETIVO: Reunir el máximo de puntos recogiendo cuantos más objetos de la lista sea posible. Atención: la puntuación varía para cada objeto.

EQUIPOS: Los equipos tendrán como máximo cuatro miembros. Los miembros del equipo deberían permanecer juntos durante la caza.

ACOMPAÑANTES: Todos los equipos deberán llevar un acompañante adulto en todo momento.

TRAMPAS: Todos los objetos y fotografías de la lista deberán conseguirse o hacerse DURANTE la caza, y solo por los miembros del equipo. El equipo que infrinja esta regla quedará descalificado.

FOTOS: Para ganar los puntos correspondientes, en todas las fotos TIENE QUE aparecer el Gato Calvin.

SEGUIMIENTO: Todos los equipos deberán presentarse en el muro oficial de la caza del tesoro de Clickchat (@ZarDeLaCaza) como mínimo cada hora.

HORA DE FINALIZACIÓN: La caza acaba a las 16:00 horas EN PUNTO. A esa hora tiene que estar presente en el auditorio del colegio TODO el equipo con los objetos que haya encontrado. Los que lleguen tarde quedarán descalificados.

PREMIOS:
PRIMER PREMIO: cuatro (4) entradas de primera fila para CUALQUIER EVENTO del Madison Square Garden que se celebre entre hoy y el último día de clase (14 de junio).
SEGUNDO PREMIO: Un (1) vale regalo de Starbucks por valor de 20 $ para repartir entre los cuatro miembros del equipo.
TERCER PREMIO: Cuatro (4) estuches de lápices de Culvert.
CUARTO PREMIO: No hay cuarto premio.

EN CASO DE URGENCIA: Para problemas graves, llamar/enviar mensaje de móvil a la señora Bevan: [redacted] Para problemas no graves, enviar un mensaje de ClickChat a Akash G. (@ZarDeLaCaza)

RECAUDACIONES: Deberán ser entregadas en el despacho de la señora Bevan como muy tarde el lunes 3 de noviembre al final del día. Los cheques deberán emitirse a favor del Banco de Alimentos de Manhattan.

CLAUDIA

Cuando acabó de leer el reglamento, la señora Bevan preguntó si había alguna duda.

Todo el mundo creía que ya podíamos

empezar, así que la mayoría se puso en pie… pero justo entonces la madre de Dimitri Sharansky levantó la mano y preguntó si algún objeto de la lista podía contener trazas de frutos secos.

potencialmente mortal para Dimitri Sharansky

La señora Bevan tardó una eternidad contestar, porque tuvo que googlear algunas cosas en su móvil. Y todo el mundo se enfadó con la madre de Dimitri, sobre todo Dimitri (aunque su alergia a los frutos secos es realmente grave).

En algún momento de todo ese lío, aparecieron Reese y mi padre.

REESE

Fue bastante sorprendente. Llegamos corriendo, sin aliento y sudados, y nos encontramos a todo el auditorio mirando cómo la señora Bevan miraba su móvil.

CLAUDIA

Al final, la señora Bevan dijo: «¡No! No hay trazas de frutos secos en nada. ¿Alguna pregunta más…? ¿No? Pues… ¡QUE EMPIECE LA CAZA!».

El auditorio entero pareció rasgarse cuando abrimos los sobres para leer la lista:

1.ª CAZA DEL TESORO BENÉFICA DEL COLEGIO CULVERT
LISTA DE OBJETOS POR BARRIOS
¡¡¡EN TODAS LAS FOTOS TIENE QUE SALIR UN GATO DE PELUCHE CALVIN!!!

punto de libro de la librería Strand (Greenwich Village) - 3 puntos
foto del Toro de Wall Street (Distrito Financiero) - 3 p.
chapa de Coca-Cola 5 centavos máquina Tekserve (Chelsea) - 3 p.
rascador de espalda de bambú de la tienda Ting's (Chinatown) - 3 p.
mosaico de Imagine en Strawberry Fields (Central Park) - 3 p.
horario de trenes de línea Metro-North Harlem (estación Grand Central) - 3 p.
servilleta con logo del hotel Waldorf Astoria (Upper East Side) - 3 p.
carta de pizzería con raciones a 99 centavos o menos - 4 p.
caca de gato de mentira de la tienda New York Costumes (Greenwich Village) - 4 p.
mapa del Museo de Historia Natural (Upper West Side) - 4 p.
tres caramelos de sabor palomitas con mantequilla de Dylan's Candy Bar (Upper Eas Side) - 4 p.
bolsa de la tienda Forbidden Planet (Greenwich Village) - 4 p.
estatuilla (máx. 7 cm) del Empire State (Midtown) - 5 p.
revista de Broadway (Times Square) - 5 p.
ticket del restaurante Katz's Delicatessen (Lower East Side) - 5 p.
recibo de taxi para un recorrido de más de 1,5 km - 5 p.
hoja de pedido del restaurante Nom Wah Tea Parlor (Chinatown) - 5 p.
foto de la bandera nacional de la India en la sede de la ONU (Midtown) - 6 p.
folleto de exposición individual de una galería de arte de Chelsea (Chelsea) - 6 p.
foto de cuadro en el que salga un perro del Museo Metropolitano de Arte (Upper East Side) - 6 p.
foto de la fuente de Bethesda tomada desde el centro del lago de las barcas (Central Park) - 7 p.
un dulce del Caffe Palermo (Little Italy) - 8 p.
folleto de los próximos espectáculos del teatro Apollo (Harlem) - 8 p.
foto de etiqueta de precio de un artículo de más de 100.000 $ del centro comercial Bloomingdale's (Upper East Side) - 8 p.
postal del Centro de Visitantes de la isla Roosevelt (Isla Roosevelt) - 8 p.
foto de tipo vestido de Flubby con el Gato Calvin en la mano (Times Square) - 8 p.
foto de la puerta 4 del estadio de los Yankees (Bronx) - 10 p.
vídeo de las 4 primeras notas de la Quinta Sinfonía de Beethoven tocadas en el piano de la juguetería FAO Schwarz (Midtown) - 10 p.
foto de la Estatua de la Libertad tomada desde la cubierta del ferry de Staten Island (Hudson) -10 p.
foto de paseante de perros llevando al menos 4 perros atados - 12 p. (+ 2 p. por cada perro adicional)
foto de la Unisphere de la exposición universal (Queens) - 12 p.
foto tomada desde el primer vagón del Cyclone de Coney Island (Brooklyn) - 15 p.
[redacted]
un crónut de la pastelería de Dominique Ansel (SoHo) - 30 p.
foto del Gato Calvin recibiendo un beso de Deondra - 500 p.

aquí iba lo
del puente de
Brooklyn

AKASH

Incluso sin lo del puente de Brooklyn, la lista era una obra de arte.

CLAUDIA

Si no fuera por un enorme error que acabó teniendo terribles consecuencias para todo el mundo.

AKASH

Yo no tengo la culpa de que la gente no sepa entender una broma.

CLAUDIA

Se produjo un silencio de algunos segundos mientras la gente repasaba la lista. Y luego, la estampida hacia la salida.

Lo primero que vimos al salir a la calle fue a Meredith Timms entrando en uno de los coches de alquiler mientras un chófer de uniforme le sostenía la puerta.

Luego a Ling Chen, entrando en el segundo coche…

Seguida de Clarissa Parker, desapareciendo en el tercero…

Y, por último, Athena Cohen y su madre, caminando hacia el cuarto.

Las cuatro fembots. En cuatro coches distintos.

CARMEN

A mí casi me dio un ataque al corazón.

PARVATI

No estoy segura, pero creo que grité. Y, si no, casi.

recreación de la
artista:
Parvati al ver a las
fembots irse en
cuatro coches distintos
(Parvati NO es así)
(si no lo pillas,
busca el cuadro El
grito
en Internet)

CLAUDIA

Fue más bien un aullido. Pero sí: gritaste.

Lo que era totalmente comprensible. Porque llevábamos solo dos minutos de caza y las fembots ya nos estaban machacando.

CAPÍTULO 9
EL EQUIPO DE MI HERMANO ES RARO Y ASQUEROSO

CLAUDIA

Voy a dejar que sea Reese quien explique lo que ocurrió con el Escuadrón Bestial, porque: A) yo no estaba, y B) aún no he entendido la mitad de la historia. Es demasiado penosa.

REESE

Cuando la señora Bevan nos soltó por fin, Xander y Wyatt corrieron hacia nosotros y Wyatt dijo: «¡Xander ha tirado nuestro Calvin!».

Mi padre y yo dijimos: «¿Einn?». Como acabábamos de llegar, ni siquiera sabíamos que habían repartido un Calvin a cada equipo para que saliera en las fotos.

Xander dijo: «Bro, ya lo pillo yo». Y se metió casi de cabeza en un cubo de basura.

Yo pregunté: «¿Tenemos que buscar cosas en los cubos de basura? Porque ¡menudo espuchurreo!».

↑
EPNE

WYATT

En ese momento llegó James Mantolini diciendo: «¿Preparados para montarla gorda?».

Pero lo dijo con una voz muy chunga, como si hablara con acento extranjero. Algo así como: «¿Prrreparrados parra montarrla gorrdaaa?». Ese chaval es muy raro.

REESE

Xander sacó la cabeza del cubo de basura diciendo: «BUF, BRO, ¡QUÉ ASCADA!».

XANDER

Algún desgraciado había vaciado un Starbucks entero en ese cubo. Total que cuando pillé el gato estaba un pelín mojado, era como un estropajo lleno de café…

WYATT

Daba bastante asco. El pobre Calvin chorreaba café. Todo caliente.

Todos soltamos: «¿Y ahora qué?».

Y James va y dice: «Hay que hacerle una foto, que a lo mejor está en garantía».

REESE

Yo le dije: «Pero, tío, ¿eso de qué nos va a servir? Lo tenemos que arreglar ¡y AHORA!».

Y va James y dice: «Pasa nada. Yo le saco el café de un chupetazo».

JAMES MANTOLINI, miembro del Escuadrón Bestial/persona muy rara

Lo hice para defender el planeta… por lo de reciclar el café.

REESE

Pues eso, que James cogió y se metió toda la cabeza del gato en la boca. Y básicamente le dio una arcada y empezó a ahogarse…

El Gato Calvin del Escuadrón Bestial después de bañarse en café (y en la boca de James) (puaaaj)

CLAUDIA

Perdón, siento interrumpir. ¿Podrías pasar a alguna parte que no dé asco?

REESE

Perdón. Total, que James decidió no morir ahogado y entre todos estrujamos a Calvin para sacar todo el café. Pero seguía mojado y marrón…

CLAUDIA

En serio. Sáltatelo.

REESE

¡Vaaale! Pesada.

Repasamos la lista y vimos que todo lo que valía muchos puntos estaba al final. Por eso pensamos que lo más inteligente era empezar por el final e ir hacia atrás.

Lo primero que había valía 500 puntos: una foto de Calvin recibiendo un beso de Deondra.

un crónut de la pastelería Dominique Ansel (SoHo) - 30 p.
foto del Gato Calvin recibiendo un beso de Deondra - 500 p.

Asomé la cabeza al interior del auditorio, donde aún estaba Akash y grité:

«¡EO, AKASH! ¿LO DE DEONDRA ES UNA BROMA?».

Y Akash: «¡¡CLARO QUE ES UNA BROMA!!».

WYATT

Luego dije: «Si lo conseguimos nos daréis 500 puntos, ¿no?».

Y Akash contestó: «¡Por supuesto! No tenéis más que localizar a la cantante más famosa del mundo antes de las cuatro de la tarde, convencerla para que le dé un besito a vuestro peluche y ¡hala, conseguido!».

Imagino que Akash estaba siendo sarcástico. Pero que conste que yo lo habría intentado si no fuera porque Calvin acababa de salir de la boca de James. Y de la basura. Supuse que, aunque encontráramos a Deondra, no estaría muy dispuesta a besarlo.

REESE

Lo siguiente con más puntos -30- era un «crónut».

Así que grité: «¡EO, AKASH! ¿QUÉ ES UN CRÓNUT?».

Y él me gritó todo alterado: «¡DEJAD DE HACERME PREGUNTAS!».

Y Xander soltó: «¡Un crónut, man, cómo rima!».

XANDER

¡El crónut es el REY! Como te digo. ¡Está bueno que lo flipas!

REESE

Te cuento lo que he aprendido sobre los crónuts: están riquísimos. Pero solo hay una pastelería en la ciudad que los venda. Y solo hacen unos pocos al día. Y la gente madruga y hace HORAS de cola para comprarlos.

XANDER

Lo firmo. Cuando me pilla la cronutitis mi vieja le paga al que nos pasea el perro cincuenta de los grandes para que vaya a la cola de madrugada y lo batalle para traerme uno directo a la panza.

REESE

¿Que tu madre le paga a un tipo cincuenta pavos para que te traiga un crónut? ¡Qué fuerte!

XANDER

Te lo juro. Mami quiere mucho a su X-Man.

esto explicaría por qué
Xander es tan desagradable
(malísima educación)

REESE

Cuando Xander nos contó lo difícil que era conseguir un crónut, empecé a pensar que a lo mejor no valía la pena. Pero mi padre —que había estado todo el tiempo, escribiendo mails en su móvil— soltó de pronto: «¿La pastelería de los crónuts del SoHo? ¡VAMOS!».

Antes de que nos diéramos cuenta, nos había metido a todos en un taxi hacia el SoHo.

Que daba la casualidad que estaba de camino a su oficina.

SoHo = "SOuth of HOuston Street"
(al sur de la calle Houston)
montones de tiendas
(y turistas)
(y cerca de la oficina de mi padre)

CAPÍTULO 10
MI EQUIPO EMPIEZA CON EL PIE IZQUIERDO (PERO SIGUE CON EL DERECHO)

CLAUDIA

Para el Equipo Revoltijo, los primeros minutos de la caza son recuerdos confusos. Nos pusimos a gritar y a correr, y es difícil hacer ambas cosas a la vez.

Gritábamos porque cada cual tenía su opinión sobre cómo había que responder a las fembots. Lo de los cuatro coches parecía completamente ilegal según la norma de «permanecer juntos durante la prueba».

EQUIPOS: Los equipos tendrán como máximo cuatro miembros. Los miembros del equipo deberían permanecer juntos durante la prueba.

Pero no nos poníamos de acuerdo sobre si intentábamos reventárselo nosotras o esperábamos a que lo hiciera otro equipo.

Y corríamos porque teníamos que movernos deprisa para tener alguna posibilidad de ganar si las fembots no eran descalificadas.

Íbamos hacia el Museo Metropolitano, porque era el único sitio cerca del colegio con un objeto de muchos puntos (6 puntos por una foto de algún cuadro en el que salga un perro).

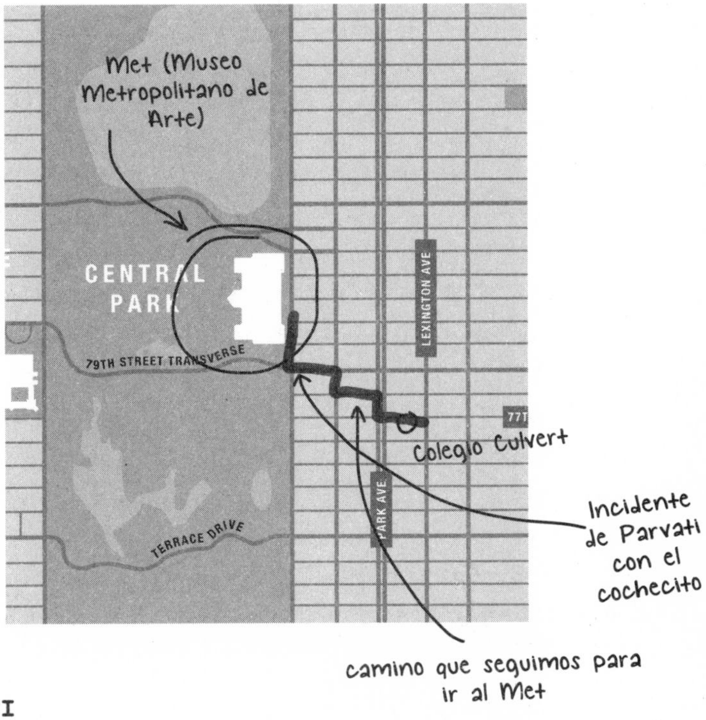

PARVATI

Y yo, en plan: «TENEMOS que hacer que descalifiquen a las fembots».

Y tu madre: «Lo que tenemos que hacer es concentrarnos en lo nuestro y no preocuparnos por otros equipos».

Y tú: «Mamá… ¡BÁLSAMO LABIAL!».

Que ya me dirás a cuento de qué venía.

el código no funcionó pq mi madre no se acordaba

CARMEN

Y yo dije: «¿CÓMO ES QUE TU NOVIO TAN DEPORTISTA CORRE TAN DESPACIO?».

JENS

No creía que había que correr. Si lo sabía, habría llevado otros zapatos.

CLAUDIA

Os explico: en comparación con los demás chicos de 12 años, Jens tiene un gusto para vestir ALUCINANTE. Esto casi siempre mola mucho. Pero para la caza del tesoro era más bien un problema porque iba con unos zapatos superguays de cuero azul y gris que le quedaban genial con lo que llevaba, pero que no parecían lo mejor para correr.

los zapatos de Jens = muy guays (pero NO lo mejor para correr)

Y eso nos estaba frenando un poco.

Aunque Parvati TAMBIÉN nos estaba frenando, porque intentaba marcar el número de la señora Bevan mientras corría como una loca por la acera y nos gritaba.

Y eso, por cierto, la convertía en una amenaza andante. Hubo un momento en que casi tropieza con un cochecito y se lleva por delante a un niño de dos años y a su canguro.

PARVATI

Mira, lo siento, pero esa canguro no hacía bien su trabajo. Tendría que haberme visto venir y haberse apartado a tiempo.

Lo importante es que conseguí hablar con la señora Bevan, que me dijo: «Gracias por la información, lo investigaré».

Una respuesta muy POCO satisfactoria, por cierto. Por eso, cuando llegamos al museo, decidí colgarlo en el muro de ClickChat para avergonzar públicamente a las fembots.

CLAUDIA

El museo estaba a tope de turistas, y la cola para sacar las entradas era una locura.

Museo Met: con unas colas HORRIBLES los sábados

Por suerte, Carmen es muy aficionada al arte y es socia del Met, y en la cola de socios solo había una persona. Al cabo de un minuto, Carmen se dirigía a una de las galerías con nuestro Gato Calvin para sacar una foto de algún cuadro en el que saliera un perro.

Las demás nos sentamos a esperarla en un banco del vestíbulo. Y fue cuando las cosas se pusieron incómodas entre mi madre y Jens. Mi madre empezó con lo de: «No nos han presentado oficialmente...». Y luego siguió con lo de: «¿Eres nuevo en Culvert? ¿Dónde estabas antes...?». Y: «¡HOLANDA! ¡Fantástico! ¿Qué te ha traído a Nueva York...?».

Como sabía que Jens es muy educado y se

le dan bien los adultos, intenté ignorarlos mientras comprobaba en el móvil el muro de la caza del tesoro en ClickChat. Parvati acababa de denunciar a las fembots por hacer trampas y el ambiente se estaba calentando:

POSTS EN EL MURO PÚBLICO DE CLICKCHAT «CAZA DEL TESORO DE CULVERT»

Parvati — Parversa: Q sepáis q Equipo Diosas (Athena, Ling, etc.) ha salido en 4 coches diferentes.

Parversa: eso es trampa y tienen q descalificarlas

Athena (fembot) — diosastupenda: hay celos?

Parversa: hay trampas?

Dimitri (Los ...balleros de la ...sa Cuadrada) — Sabad02: Yo tb lo he visto! Es ilegal!!

Brittany (...s Fieras) — BritSeavs: 4 COCHES ES TRAMPA DESCARADA!!

Akash — ZarDeLaCaza: estamos investigando estas alegaciones

Meredith (fembot) — mdith_timms: ya te vale irle a llorar a tu hermano, Parvati.

ZarDeLaCaza: El Zar es justo e imparcial y no permite favoritismos. Ni siquiera con los parientes sanguíneos

mdith_tims: Sí claro.

ZarDeLaCaza: la subdirectora Bevan ha decidido descalificar a las Diosas y Cía. con arreglo al párrafo 2 del reglamento.

diosastupenda: QUÉ????

mdith_tims: QUÉ DICES?!!

BritSeavs: LO QUE LEES!!!

CLAUDIA

Cuando vimos el mensaje de Akash diciendo que las fembots estaban descalificadas, Parvati y yo pegamos un grito tan fuerte que asustamos a mi madre, a Jens y a un grupo de turistas japoneses.

Justo en ese momento apareció Carmen con la foto que necesitábamos.

CARMEN

Fui directa a la sala de arte moderno europeo, la primera época, porque, entonces, a la gente le iban MUCHO los perros. Vaya, que si lanzas un hueso en esa sala, te salta un perro de cada cuadro.

CLAUDIA

Todos chocamos los cinco para celebrarlo mientras bajábamos las escaleras del Met. Luego fuimos hacia Central Park para buscar otros objetos. Recuerdo que mientras entrábamos en el parque pensé que lo de la descalificación de las fembots era demasiado bueno para ser verdad.

Por desgracia, tenía razón.

CAPÍTULO 11
MERCADO NEGRO DE CRÓNUTS

CLAUDIA

Mientras el Equipo Revoltijo estaba en el museo, el Escuadrón Bestial se dirigió hacia la pastelería de los crónuts.

REESE

Mi padre se pasó todo el camino en taxi hacia el SoHo escribiendo mails en el móvil. En un momento dado pasamos por delante de la juguetería FAO Schwarz, que tiene un piano gigante en el suelo que se puede tocar saltando sobre él.

Y todos dijimos: «¡Hay que parar aquí para hacer el vídeo tocando lo de Beethoven en el piano gigante! ¡Vale diez puntos!».

piano gigante de
FAO Schwarz

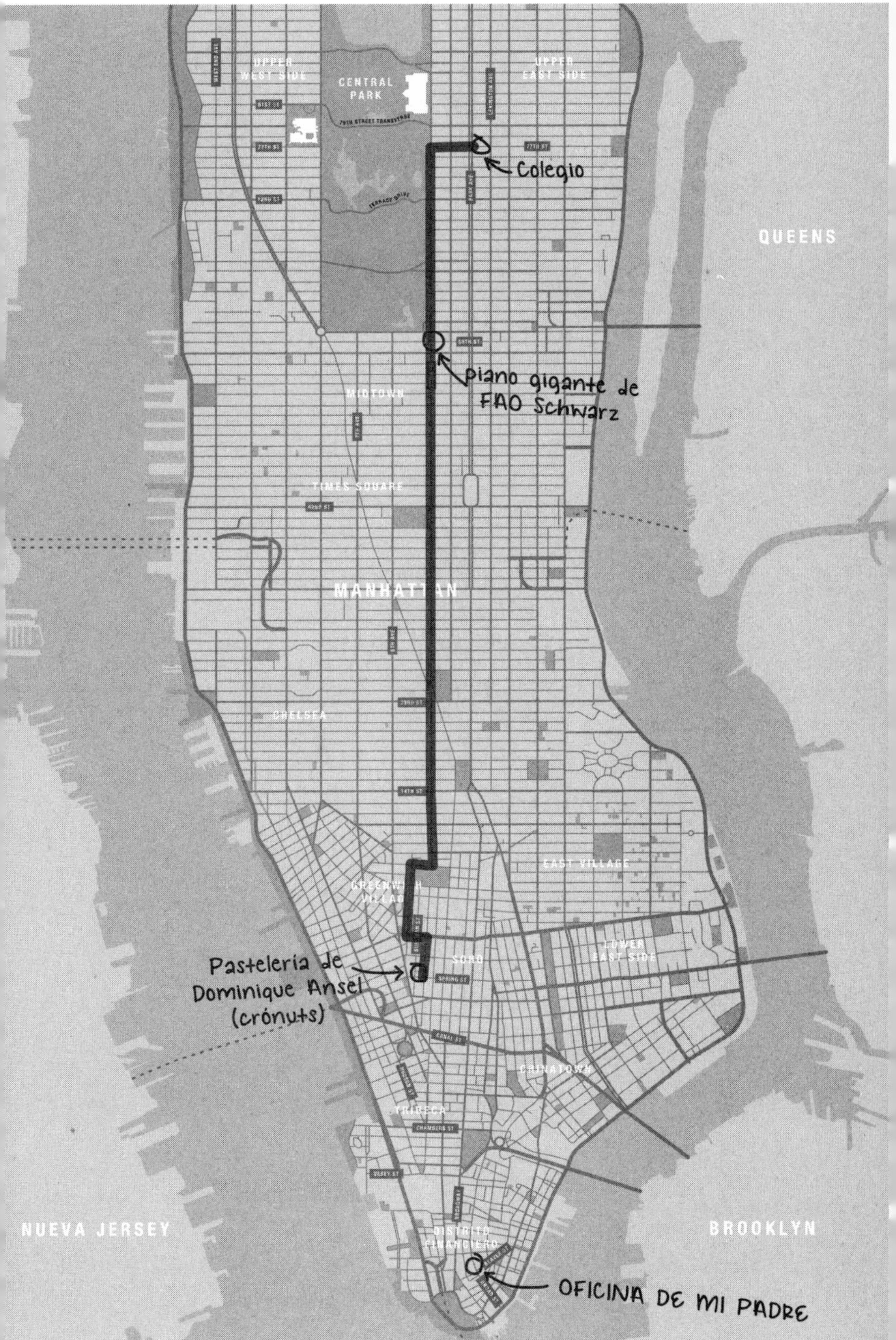

UPPER WEST SIDE
CENTRAL PARK
UPPER EAST SIDE
Colegio
QUEENS
piano gigante de FAO Schwarz
MIDTOWN
TIMES SQUARE
MANHATTAN
CHELSEA
EAST VILLAGE
GREENWICH VILLAGE
SOHO
LOWER EAST SIDE
Pastelería de Dominique Ansel (crónuts)
CHINATOWN
TRIBECA
NUEVA JERSEY
BROOKLYN
DISTRITO FINANCIERO
OFICINA DE MI PADRE

Y va mi padre y dice: «¡Ya lo haremos luego! ¡Ahora vamos al SoHo!».

Lo que tampoco era tan mala idea, porque en el equipo no nos poníamos de acuerdo sobre cómo sonaba la Quinta Sinfonía de Beethoven.

Primero, yo dije: «¡Lo sé! Es ¡tantanCHÁN, tantanCHÁN, tanTACHÁN!».

WYATT

Y los demás en plan: «Reese, tío, ¡eso es la Marcha Imperial de Darth Vader!».

Pero por su culpa a todos se nos pegó la Marcha Imperial. Y cada vez que alguien intentaba cantar la Quinta de Beethoven, le salía la Marcha Imperial.

REESE

Cuando Wyatt logró encontrar la canción en Internet con el móvil —era ¡tantataCHÁÁÁN!— ya hacía treinta calles que habíamos pasado la juguetería, o sea que ya era demasiado tarde.

Pero conseguimos los cinco puntos del «recibo de taxi para un recorrido de más de 1,5 km».

la de Dominique Ansel

Cuando llegamos a la pastelería de los crónuts, pensamos que habíamos tenido suerte porque contamos solo treinta y siete personas en la cola.

Cola para crónuts

WYATT

Pero resultó que es que casi se les habían acabado los crónuts. Cuando nos pusimos en la cola, los que teníamos delante nos dijeron: «¿Estáis locos? ¡Nosotros llevamos horas aquí y es muy probable que nos quedemos SIN crónuts!».

REESE

Y va mi padre y dice: «En fin, vamos a

tomar la foto de la estatua del Toro de Wall Street».

Que está justo a una calle de su oficina.

Pero yo no caí en ese detalle. Le dije: «¡Papá! ¡El Toro solo vale tres puntos! ¡Un crónut vale TREINTA!».

Y los cuatro nos pusimos a suplicarle que nos dejara quedarnos en la cola para intentarlo.

Mi padre dijo: «Voy a investigar un poco». Se fue hacia la entrada de la tienda para hacer un cálculo mientras los demás hacíamos cola, que daba la vuelta a la manzana.

Wyatt sacó el móvil para mirar el muro de ClickChat. Había un follón con el equipo de Athena Cohen y nos pusimos a leer los mensajes.

WYATT

Y ahí es cuando nuestro Calvin fue atropellado por un camión.

JAMES

La culpa fue de Xander.

XANDER

¿Qué dices, tío? TODA la culpa fue de

apodo que Xander le ha puesto a ...ames Mantolini (debería ser "Jota Eme", pero Xander es burro)

Jotaemo. Yo lo único que hice fue darle un par de veces en la cabeza con el Calvin de marras.

Pero fue Jotaemo quien me lo arrancó de las manos y lo tiró a mitad de la calle justo cuando pasaba el camión.

WYATT

Yo hasta oí cómo le petaba la cabeza. La rueda del camión la pilló de PLENO.

Pero por suerte el relleno aún estaba mojado por el café, y no salió volando. Se quedó enganchado, todo mojado.

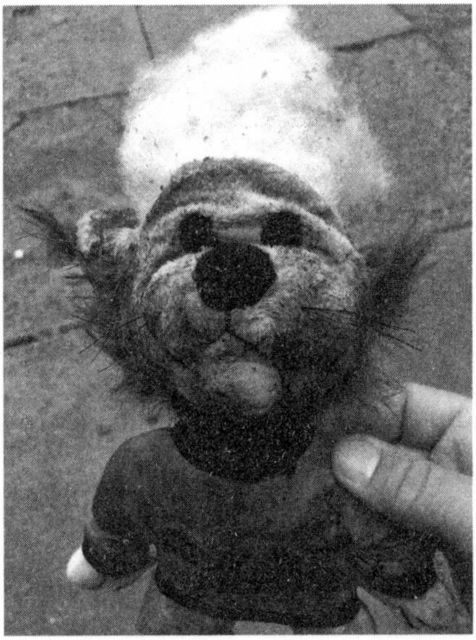

El Gato Calvin del Escuadrón Bestial (tras ser atropellado)

REESE

Y James, en plan: «¡Abran paso, soy médico!». Intentó volver a meter todo el relleno en la cabeza de Calvin. Pero no sabíamos cómo cerrarla.

Justo cuando Wyatt y yo íbamos a ir a comprar celo, volvió mi padre.

Y dijo: «Tengo una noticia mala… y otra buena».

La mala era que ya no quedaban crónuts.

La buena era que había conocido a un tipo que acababa de comprar un crónut y estaba dispuesto a vendérnoslo.

Pero pedía MUCHÍSIMO dinero por él. Mi padre no quería decirnos cuánto.

WYATT

Y yo: «¿Son más de cincuenta pavos?».

Y tu padre: «Sí».

Y yo: «¿Son más de cien?».

Y tu padre: «Sin comentarios».

REESE

Entonces mi padre bajó la voz y dijo: «Os ofrezco un trato, chicos: estoy dispuesto a compraros ese crónut. PERO… a cambio… os pediré que me hagáis un favor MUY grande».

Cuando aún no nos había dicho cuál era el favor, apareció un tipo con perilla que llevaba una cajita amarilla en la mano con el nombre de la pastelería.

cajita amarilla

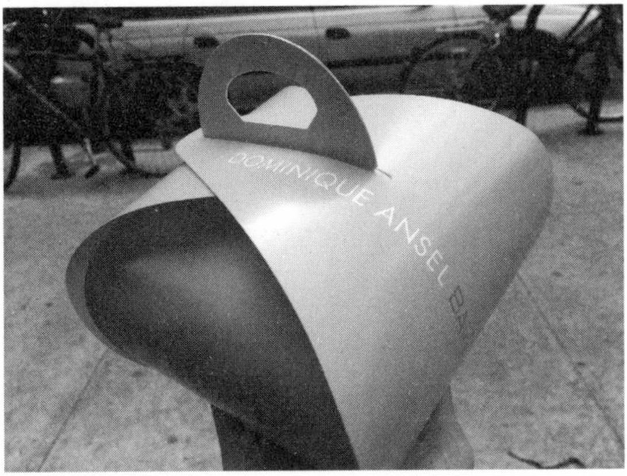

Y dijo: «Oye, tú, ¿lo hacemos o no? Porque, si no, me como el crónut».

Mi padre nos miró y repitió: «Chicos, ¿cerramos el trato? ¿Yo os compro el crónut y vosotros me hacéis un favor muy grande?».

XANDER

Y yo: «¡DISPARA, chavalote!».

WYATT

Yo estaba un poco preocupado. No por el dinero ni por lo del favor, sino porque el tipo que nos quería vender el crónut daba bastante mal rollo.

Y encima va James y le grita: «¿CUÁNTO COBRAS POR MATAR A ALGUIEN?».

JAMES

A ver, es fácil: alguien que vende crónuts en el mercado negro también debe de tener MUCHAS otras ocupaciones. Como asesinatos por encargo.

Y yo tengo algunos enemigos muy poderosos que me gustaría ver neutralizados.

CLAUDIA

¿Ah, sí? ¿Por ejemplo?

JAMES

Eso no lo diré nunca. Porque, cuando pase, no quiero que encuentres mi rastro.

James está como una CABRA

REESE

Total, que Xander tuvo que hacerle a James una llave de cuello para que estuviera callado el tiempo justo para que mi padre pudiera pagar al tipo de la perilla no sé cuánta pasta. El tipo soltó la caja y fuimos a sentarnos a un banco de un parque que había allí al lado para abrirla.

Yo tenía bastante curiosidad porque, hasta ese día, no había oído hablar nunca de los crónuts.

Era básicamente un dónut tirando a cuadrado con cobertura morada.

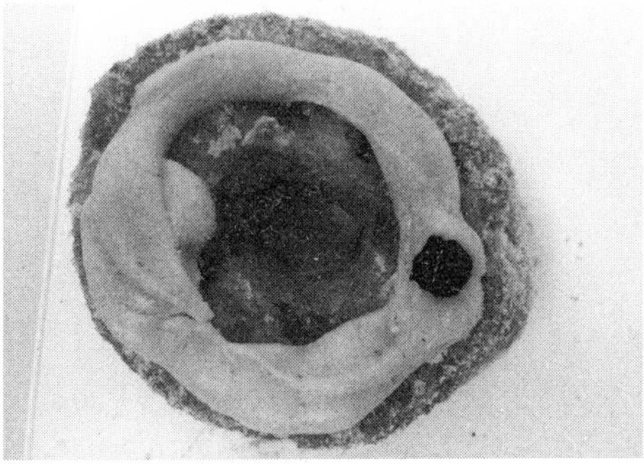

Xander saltó: «¡Eh, tíos, esto no es un crónut!».

XANDER

Yo solo sé que la última vez que comí un crónut el campeón era de chocolate. Y este llevaba encima una cosa como de fruta lila.

REESE

Mi padre dijo: «Por favor, por favor, no me digas que he comprado un crónut falso».

Y Wyatt dijo: «¡Anda, es verdad! ¡Podría ser una falsificación!».

WYATT

Tenía sentido. Vaya, es lo mismo que cuando compras un Rolex en Chinatown por veinte pavos, pero no es un Rolex, claro.

Una vez mi madre le compró a un tipo de la calle un bolso de Louis Vuitton por 40 dólares. Era más falso que los dientes de mi abuela y se rompió en tres días.

Mi madre no quiere que lo vaya contando. Pero es verdad.

REESE

Cuando Wyatt y Xander le dijeron que había pagado toda aquella pasta por un crónut falso, mi padre se puso blanco, como si le fuera a dar un ataque al corazón.

Luego le hizo una foto al crónut y se la envió a mi madre por el móvil.

NUESTROS PADRES (Mensajes de móvil)

Crees q este crónut es auténtico?

Ni siquiera sé qué es eso

Me temo q me han vendido uno falso

Ahora mismo tengo problemas MUCHO más graves. Has visto el muro d ClickChat?

REESE

Al final, mi padre decidió que, aun suponiendo que el crónut fuera falso, la caja parecía auténtica, de manera que la presentaríamos para ver si nos daban los treinta puntos.

Luego dijo: «En cuanto al favor que os quería pedir…».

Y ahí es donde empezó todo el lío.

¡CEREEEBROS!

CAPÍTULO 12
LAS FEMBOTS Y LA ZOMBI DE SU ABOGADA

CLAUDIA

Mientras tanto, la cabeza del Gato Calvin del Escuadrón Bestial no era la única que había reventado. La mía también.

No literalmente, pero casi.

Volvamos atrás en la historia. Al salir del museo, el Equipo Revoltijo nos dirigimos al lago de Central Park para alquilar una barca y poder ganar los 7 puntos de la «foto de la fuente de Bethesda tomada desde el centro del lago de las barcas».

Pero había una cola de MORIRSE.

COLA PARA ALQUILAR BARCAS
2. La cola da la vuelta aquí
3. La cola acaba allí al fondo, en la caseta de las barcas (no sale en la foto)
1. La cola empieza aquí

CARMEN

No sabía que esto de las barquitas gustaba tanto. Aquella cola era de, COMO MÍNIMO, una hora. Absolutamente imposible que nos quedáramos a hacerla.

Pero Parvati tuvo una idea genial.

PARVATI

La lista no decía: «Alquilad una barca». Solo decía: «Tomad una foto desde el lago de las barcas».

Por eso dije: «¡Oye! ¡Nos metemos un poco en el agua y hacemos la foto!».

CARMEN

A lo que yo contesté: «¡Qué AS-CO!». Porque el agua de ese estanque es de color verde, pero no precisamente verde sano natural, sino más bien verde enfermedad incurable. Yo desde luego no iba a entrar.

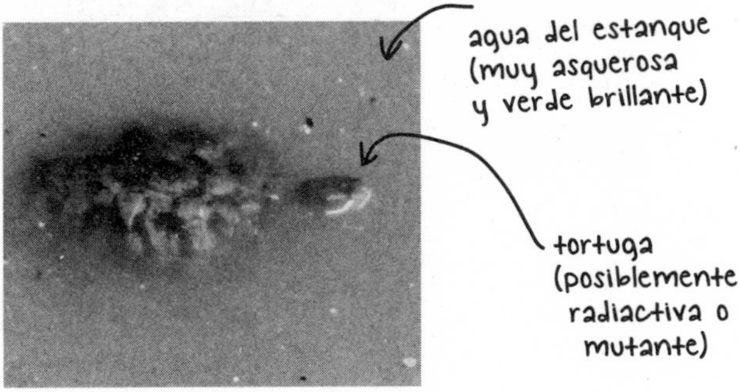

PARVATI

Y yo dije: «¡Oye! ¡Para eso tenemos a un chico en el equipo, ¿no?! ¡Para encargarse de la parte desagradable!».

JENS

Parvati me pidió que me meta en el agua. Pero yo dije no. Malo para mis zapatos.

PARVATI

Yo grité: «¿En serio? ¡PUES QUÍTATE LOS ZAPATOS Y ARREMÁNGATE LOS PANTALONES!».

JENS

Eso con mis pantalones no se puede. Son… ¿cómo se dice? ¿Pitillo? Muy difícil de enrollar.

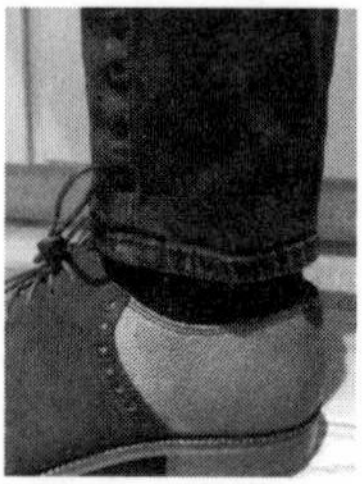

Pantalones de Jens (elegantísimos, pero imposible enrollarlos)

PARVATI

En serio, no me podía creer que Jens fuera tan inútil. Nada, le dije: «Vale. Como quieras. Ya entro yo».

CLAUDIA

Parvati corrió hasta el estanque, se quitó los zapatos, se arremangó los pantalones y entró en el agua con Calvin en una mano y el móvil en la otra.

PARVATI

Por cierto, ¿sabes lo que NO me esperaba? El barro. El fondo de ese lago está enfangado DEL TODO.

Y va tu madre y dice: «Parvati, creo que no es buena idea».

Y luego grita: «¡QUE VIENE LA POLICÍA!».

CLAUDIA

Solo era un guardia del parque, pero señaló a Parvati y le gritó: «¡EH, TÚ! ¡SAL DE AHÍ AHORA MISMO!».

Carmen y yo gritamos: «¡HAZ LA FOTO!». Y Parvati se asustó y casi se cae de culo.

PARVATI

¡Menudo susto! ¡Pensé que se me iba a ESTROPEAR el móvil! ¡Y la ropa! Pero no, los salvé. ¡Con foto y todo!

CLAUDIA

Parvati estuvo muy bien. Y, después de que ella y mi madre se disculparan, el guardia la dejó marchar con una advertencia.

Si te soy sincera, creo que eso es lo único que pueden hacer los guardias del parque.

PARVATI

Cuando les conté a mis padres que me había metido en el estanque, me hicieron poner la vacuna del tétanos.

Pero está claro que valió MUCHO la pena.

CLAUDIA

La foto que hizo Parvati fue lo mejor de la mañana. Porque, a partir de ahí, todo fue de mal en peor.

Primero, le costó una eternidad (y unas mil servilletas del puesto de perritos calientes) quitarse el barro de los pies. Luego fuimos a Strawberry Fields —que es una zona dedicada a John Lennon, de los Beatles, los segundos mejores compositores de la historia después de Miranda Fleet— y sacamos una foto de 3 puntos.

En Strawberry Fields empezamos a discutir a dónde iríamos después… lo bastante alto como para que el hippy de la guitarra acústica dejara de cantar *Yesterday* y nos dijera: «¡Chis! ¡Estamos en un lugar sagrado!».

Lo que era RIDÍCULO. *Yesterday* ni siquiera es una canción de Lennon. Todo el mundo sabe que la escribió Paul McCartney.

Al final decidimos ir a la parte este de la ciudad y visitar Dylan's Candy Bar y Bloomingdale's, pero no llegábamos nunca.

Primero tuvimos que deshacer todo el camino por el parque hasta volver a la Quinta Avenida. Luego no había forma de encontrar un taxi.

De manera que tuvimos que hacer todo el camino básicamente corriendo, y todos acabamos sudados y enfadados.

Y creo que a Jens le estaba saliendo una ampolla.

JENS

Mis zapatos eran muy malos para correr. Y los calcetines tampoco eran buenos.

(pero eran muy bonitos)

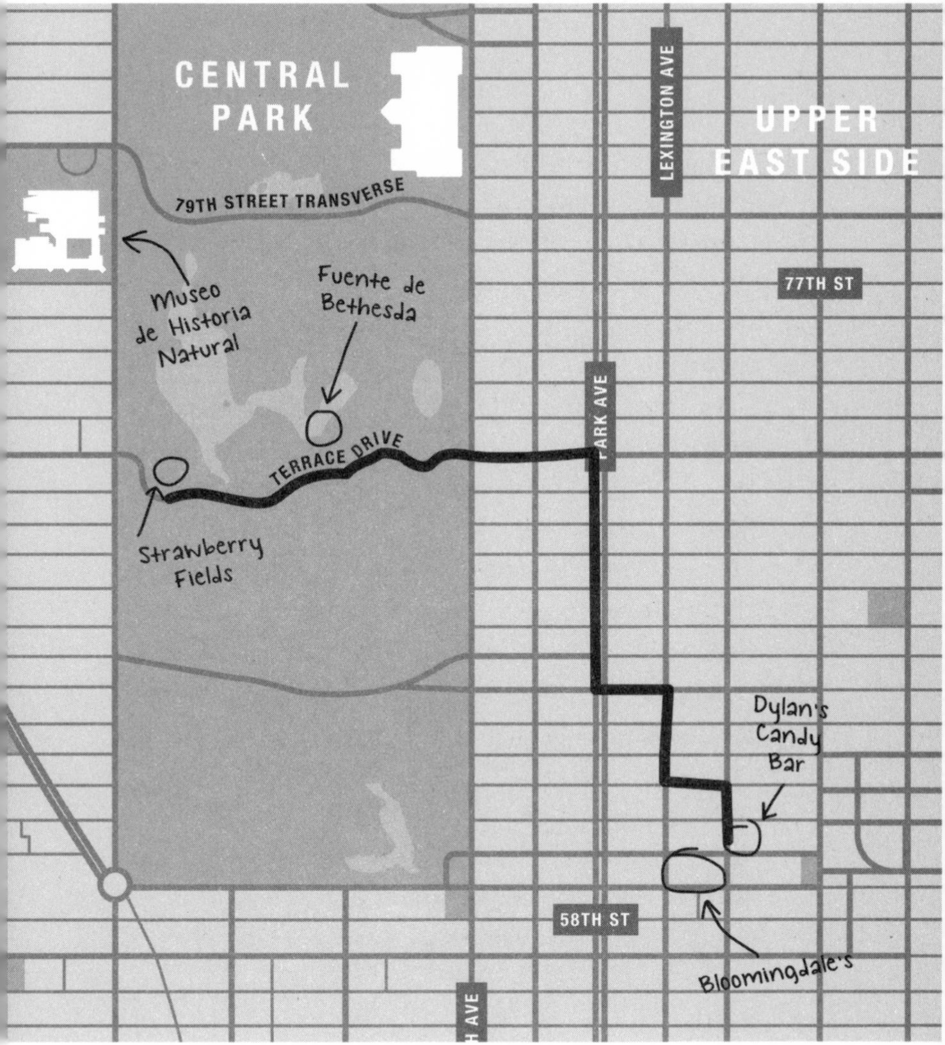

CLAUDIA

Como íbamos corriendo todo el rato, nadie se paró a comprobar el muro de ClickChat.

Por eso nos sorprendió tanto ver salir del Dylan's Candy Bar a una fembot, Ling, con una bolsa gigantesca que parecía que pesaba diez kilos como mínimo.

PARVATI

Y yo, en plan: «¡Eo, Ling, perdona, pero os han descalificado!».

CARMEN

Ling se rio con la nariz y dijo: «¡Qué más quisieras!».

Entonces hizo ese horrible gesto de echarse el pelo hacia atrás que un día de estos le va a dar un latigazo en el cuello. Ojalá.

Luego su chófer o lo que fuera le aguantó la puerta mientras entraba en el coche. Y cuando arrancaron, Ling gritó: «¡Suerte con los caramelos!».

CLAUDIA

Me acuerdo que pensé: «A) ¿A qué se referirá con lo de los caramelos?, y B) ¿Por qué sigue buscando cosas cuando la han descalificado?».

Entonces fue cuando todos sacamos los móviles y miramos el muro de ClickChat.

POSTS EN EL MURO PÚBLICO DE CLICKCHAT «CAZA DEL TESORO DE CULVERT»

madre Athena

diosastupenda Hola, soy la madre de Athena Cohen y la acompañante del Equipo Diosas y Cía. Su decisión de descalificar a nuestro equipo conforme al párrafo 2 no tiene fundamento y exijo su inmediata revocación.

Akash

ZarDeLaCaza Er... lo siento, pero no.

atasha (Los akease)

tasa_manda Es verdad lo de 500 puntos por foto Deondra?

ZarDeLaCaza LO DE FOTO DEONDRA ERA BROMA. Parad de preguntarlo.

diosastupenda El párrafo 2 del reglamento dice que «los miembros del equipo DEBERÍAN permanecer juntos durante la prueba». En condicional. No dice «DEBERÁN permanecer juntos». Tal como está redactado es evidente que no es obligatorio, y tienen que readmitirnos.

ZarDeLaCaza Pero ES obligatorio. Los equipos no se pueden separar.

diosastupenda No es lo que dice su reglamento.

ZarDeLaCaza Sí que lo dice.

diosastupenda No, no lo dice. Estoy licenciada en Derecho por Harvard y le puedo asegurar que mi interpretación es correcta. Haga el favor de readmitirnos de inmediato.

Hunter (Killers)

buhovigilante Esto es flipador!

ZarDeLaCaza El reglamento es claro. Los equipos no se pueden separar.

diosastupenda No. Su reglamento dice que DEBERÍAN permanecer juntos. Si se fijan, en el pár. 3 dice: «Todos los equipos DEBERÁN llevar un acompañante adulto en todo momento». Aquí se ve la diferencia material: el futuro tiene carácter obligatorio, el condicional es deseable pero no obligatorio. Por consiguiente, Diosas y Cía. no puede ser descalificado.

ZarDeLaCaza Eso es buscarle tres pies al gato.

diosastupenda Da igual, es correcto. Readmítanos ahora mismo.

ZarDeLaCaza No puedo. Las ha descalificado la señora Bevan.
diosastupenda SOY UNA LICENCIADA EN DERECHO POR HARVARD. Si no readmite a Diosas y Cía. apelaré esa decisión con todas las consecuencias jurídicas posibles, que serán graves tanto para Culvert como para los organizadores de la prueba, incluido usted.
ZarDeLaCaza ¿Me está diciendo que me va a demandar?
diosastupenda Sí. Y pediré daños y perjuicios.
buhovigilante TOMA YA! ESTO SE PONE BUENO
ZarDeLaCaza Soy la señora Bevan escribiendo desde la cuenta de Akash. Sra. Cohen, si me da su número de teléfono, la llamo.
diosastupenda 917 [redacted]
J_KOPP Bueno buenísimo.
buhovigilante A que sí? Me pasas las palomitas?
daniR ¿Alguien sabe dónde puede estar Deondra?
J_KOPP Que era broma. No hay Deondra
daniR Pues qué pena, yo quería conocerla
J_KOPP Sí claro. Pues hala suerte
ZarDeLaCaza AVISO A TODOS LOS EQUIPOS: SEGÚN EL REGLAMENTO *NO* ES ESTRICTAMENTE NECESARIO QUE TODOS LOS MIEMBROS ESTÉN JUNTOS. SIN EMBARGO, SE RECOMIENDA ENCARECIDAMENTE POR MOTIVOS DE SEGURIDAD QUE PERMANEZCÁIS JUNTOS TODO EL TIEMPO POSIBLE.
ZarDeLaCaza Otra cosa: el equipo Diosas y Cía. ha sido readmitido. Los organizadores lamentan sinceramente la confusión.

Josh, (Gingivitis)

Daniella R. (Las Fieras)

NOTA: aquí me reventó la cabeza

CLAUDIA

Fue entonces cuando me reventó la cabeza.

Y luego fue a peor. Porque cuando bajamos al sótano del Dylan's Candy Bar para comprar tres caramelos de sabor palomitas con mantequilla (cuatro puntos), encontramos esto:

De pronto, aquella gigantesca (y pesada) bolsa que Ling llevaba al salir de la tienda cobró todo el (perverso) sentido.

Había comprado TODOS los caramelos de palomitas con mantequilla.

O sea que no solo la madre «licenciada en Derecho por Harvard» de Athena había hecho que las fembots se levantaran de entre los muertos como zombis, sino que además ahora se dedicaban a sabotear a todos los demás.

Y además estaba a punto de tener una bronca monumental con mi madre en plena sección de muebles de Bloomingdale's.

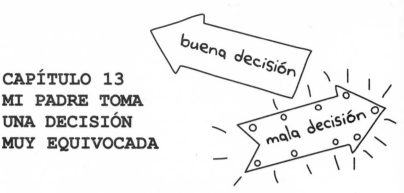

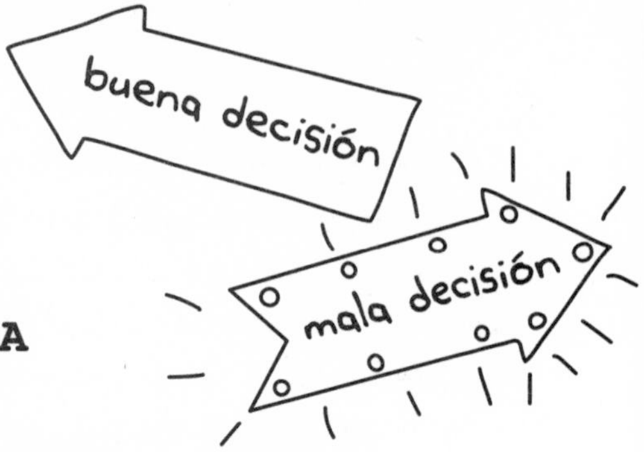

CAPÍTULO 13
MI PADRE TOMA UNA DECISIÓN MUY EQUIVOCADA

REESE

Al final resultó que el favor que mi padre nos quería pedir a cambio de lo del crónut era que lo acompañáramos a su oficina porque tenía que trabajar.

Nos dijo: «Solo necesito apagar un fuego. Diez minutos. ¡Os invitaré a algo para picar! ¿Qué me decís?».

Casi lo matamos. Porque, ahora que teníamos el crónut de 30 puntos, se suponía que estábamos ganando, y PARA NADA íbamos a dejar que se nos escapara la oportunidad perdiendo un montón de tiempo en su oficina.

Cuando vio que no picábamos, mi padre dijo: «Dejadme ver otra vez la lista».

La repasó deprisa y dijo: «Vale, ¿y si...?».

aquí empieza la decisió equivoca

Entonces se calló, se mordió el labio un segundo, como si estuviera muy estresado.

Y dijo: «Voy a sugerir algo... pero me tenéis que prometer que NUNCA SE LO DIRÉIS A NADIE...».

Y James gritó: «¡SOCORRO, NOS SECUESTRAN!».

Claro, Xander tuvo que hacerle otra llave de cuello para que se callara.

JAMES

Reconozco un intento de secuestro en cuanto lo veo.

REESE

Básicamente, mi padre proponía dejarnos en el ferry de Staten Island y marcharse corriendo a la oficina. Nosotros haríamos la foto de la Estatua de la Libertad —que valía diez puntos— desde el barco y luego nos encontraríamos en la estatua del Toro de Wall Street, que valía tres puntos y estaba

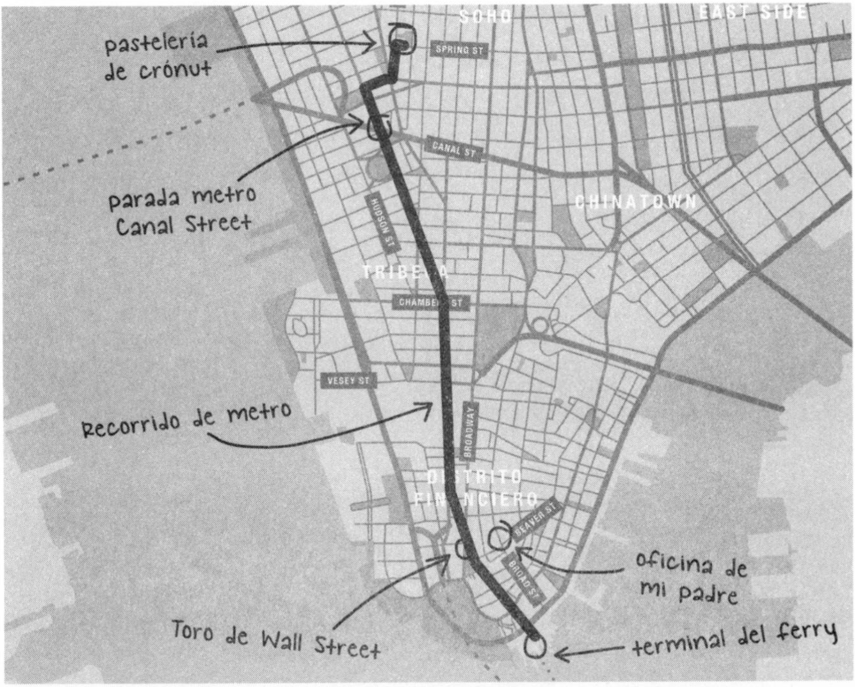

a medio camino entre la terminal del ferry y el despacho de mi padre.

Sabíamos que sin acompañante nos podían descalificar, pero tampoco nos iban a pillar si era solo durante el trayecto del ferry.

Y además mi padre nos dio veinte dólares a cada uno para que no nos chiváramos.

CLAUDIA

Si al leer esto piensas: «Hay algo aquí que empieza a ser poco ético, y el padre de Claudia ha tomado una decisión tremendamente equivocada», estoy de acuerdo contigo.

REESE

Como no encontramos ningún taxi grande que nos llevara al centro, tuvimos que coger el metro en Canal Street. El cartel del andén decía que el siguiente tren hacia el ferry llegaría en 4 minutos.

El tiempo JUSTO para que nuestro Gato Calvin cayera a la vía y fuera escuchimirrado por un tren. EPNE

Ahora no entraré a discutir de quién fue la culpa, pero está claro que no fue ni mía, ni de mi padre ni de Wyatt.

XANDER

Mis manos están limpias, man. Yo solo le metí el gato a Jotaemo por la camiseta. Y luego defendí mi espacio cuando él intentó metérmelo por la MÍA.

Si Jotaemo no me hubiera dado la brasa, yo no habría lanzado al bicho a la otra punta del andén.

JAMES

Tengo una teoría: ese gato tenía impulsos suicidas.

No me preguntes por qué. Yo no sé qué le andaba rondando por la cabeza. O por lo que quedaba de su cabeza, porque había perdido mucho relleno con lo del atropello del camión.

Pero creo que está bastante claro que ese gato quería morir.

Y que conste que NO tenía siete vidas. Como mucho, tres.

REESE

Cuando vimos que el metro pasaba por encima del gato, nos quedamos helados. ¡Sin el gato no podríamos hacer ni una sola foto!

Teníamos que recuperarlo. Pero cuando se te cae algo a la vía del metro NUNCA JAMÁS puedes ir a buscarlo. Eso es megapeligroso. Y, si lo intentas, es muy fácil que te mate un tren.

Al menos eso es lo que mi padre dijo después de gritar a Xander cuando vio que lo iba a intentar. Nunca en la vida le había oído gritar tan fuerte.

Pero resulta que muchas paradas de metro tienen jefe de estación. Y, si lo encuentras, él puede hacer una llamada para que paren todos los trenes de esa línea mientras viene otro tipo con una especie de pinzas gigantes de caucho muy raras y las usa para sacar a Calvin de la vía.

O, en este caso, los dos trozos de Calvin. Porque las ruedas del metro lo habían partido por la mitad.

También descubrimos que si llamas a un jefe de estación para que detenga todos los trenes porque se te ha caído algo superimportante a la vía y descubre que la cosa superimportante es un animal de peluche,

se enfadará mucho MUCHÍSIMO e insultará a tu padre. En tu idioma y en el suyo.

Pero habrás conseguido tus dos trozos de animal de peluche.

Resumiendo, veinte minutos después estábamos en la terminal del ferry de Staten Island.

Mi padre nos enseñó en qué calle estaba la estatua del Toro de Wall Street y nos dijo: «Enviadme un mensaje cuando estéis a medio trayecto del ferry y nos encontraremos delante del Toro».

Ferry de Staten Island

WYATT

Yo le dije: «Una cosa: ¿cada cuánto sale el ferry?».

Y tu padre me contestó: «Cada media hora».

Hicimos el cálculo y nos dimos cuenta de que íbamos a tardar AL MENOS una hora en hacer solo esa foto.

XANDER

Yo dije: «¡Eso es demasiado, man! ¡Hay que separarse!».

Ya vi que el Gran Papi Tapper iba a decirnos que NANAY, pero justo entonces algún tipejo del trabajo lo llamó al móvil.

REESE

Mi padre nos dijo: «JURADME que no os separaréis».

EPNE

Y eso era flipador, porque acabábamos de enterarnos en ClickChat de que el reglamento ya no prohibía que nos separásemos.

Cuando le íbamos a contestar, recibió una llamada de su jefe e hizo eso de «con-este-dedo-alzado-quiero-decir-que-esto-es-superimportante-y-no-me-habléis».

Y nosotros, en plan: «Vale… ¡ADIÓS!». Y nos metimos corriendo en la terminal sin darle tiempo a colgar el teléfono.

En ese momento creo que solo pensábamos separarnos un rato y no nos parecía tan mala idea, porque encontraríamos muchas más cosas y nos sobraría tiempo para reunirnos con mi padre. Por eso, en lugar de esperar a que colgara para discutir con él, nos pareció mejor salir corriendo.

Y ahí la cagamos.

CAPÍTULO 13½
MI PADRE QUIERE QUE SEPÁIS QUE NO ES MALO

CLAUDIA

No suelo entrevistar a mis padres cuando recopilo una crónica como esta, porque creo que sus mensajes de móvil hablan por ellos.

Pero en este caso haré una excepción. Sobre todo porque mi padre me ha rogado que le deje explicar su versión.

↖ y amenazado (con prohibiciones ordenador/iPad)

MI PADRE (también conocido como Eric Tapper, o progenitor de Claudia y Reese)

Hola, guapa.

CLAUDIA

Hola, papá.

MI PADRE

Antes que nada, quiero agradecer la oportunidad de…

CLAUDIA

Limítate a los hechos, papá. Rapidito.

MI PADRE

Vale, bueno.

Pues, er… Tú sabes que papá os quiere mucho a ti y a tu hermano, ¿verdad? Y que vuestra seguridad personal es muy importante para él y que nunca haría nada para poneros en peligro salvo en circunstancias realmente excepcionales, ¿verdad?

CLAUDIA

Por supuesto.

MI PADRE

Y también sabes que es MUY caro vivir aquí, ¿verdad? Y que aún es MÁS caro ir a un colegio como Culvert. Y que tanto vuestro padre como vuestra madre trabajan MUY DURO para ganar dinero y poder pagarlo todo. Eso lo sabes, ¿verdad?

CLAUDIA

¿Adónde quieres ir a parar, papá?

MI PADRE

Tu padre tiene un trabajo muy difícil, en un bufete de abogados muy grande, y está a las órdenes de un hombre que es, básicamente, el demonio.

Pues eso, papá tiene un jefe demonio. Y el jefe demonio de papá…

CLAUDIA

¿Podrías dejar de hablar de ti en tercera persona? Suena muy raro.

MI PADRE

Tienes razón, perdona. No sé porqué estaba hablando así.

CLAUDIA

Yo tampoco. Es muy paternalista.

DICCIONARIO

paternalismo

paternalismo: m. Tendencia a aplicar las formas de autoridad y protección propias del padre en la familia tradicional a relaciones sociales de otro tipo; políticas, laborales.

MI PADRE

Has utilizado muy bien la palabra.

CLAUDIA

Gracias, es que leo mucho.

MI PADRE

Lo sé. Eres un sol.

CLAUDIA

Nos estamos desviando del tema.

MI PADRE

Es verdad. ¿Por dónde iba?

CLAUDIA

Jefe demonio.

MI PADRE

Ah, sí. Pues eso, que trabajo para un hombre que no sabe mucho de compasión humana. Y mucho menos de conciliación familiar o de lo que supone ser padre…

CLAUDIA

Lo pillamos. Es el demonio. ¿Qué más?

MI PADRE

Vale, pues… el día de la caza del colegio coincidió con la fusión de dos empresas muy grandes. Y el bufete de papá… perdón, MI bufete representaba a una de ellas. Y había incertidumbres sobre las implicaciones fiscales de la fusión.

Total, que el jefe demonio de papá… perdón, mi jefe demonio me dijo: «Si no vienes al despacho y solucionas esto AHORA MISMO, te quedarás sin trabajo y no tendrás dinero para comer. Ni para pagar un colegio privado».

O sea que no tenía otra alternativa. TENÍA que ir a la oficina. O perdía el trabajo.

cuesta un OJO de la cara en NY (precio actual de un sándwich de queso en restaurante, 6,95 $)

DOS OJOS de la cara (mi padre no quiere decirme cuánto)

CLAUDIA

Eso lo entiendo muy bien. Yo, personalmente, preferiría que NO perdieras el trabajo.

Pero ¿por qué mentiste a mamá sobre lo que pasó?

MI PADRE

Bueno, eso, er…

Eso fue… er, yo…

Eso fue una decisión equivocada.

Sí, muy equivocada. Un gran error, claramente.

CLAUDIA

Mamá piensa igual.

MI PADRE

Lo sé. Lo hemos hablado. No paramos de hablarlo, de hecho.

muy cierto
(a mamá le está costando
mucho soltar la presa)

CAPÍTULO 14
MI MADRE Y YO TENEMOS UNA BRONCA EN LA SECCIÓN DE MUEBLES DEL CENTRO COMERCIAL

CLAUDIA

Técnicamente, la bronca con mi madre comenzó mientras cruzábamos la Tercera Avenida para pasar del Dylan's Candy Bar a Bloomingdale's, que son unos grandes almacenes alucinantes pero carísimos. Aunque, a decir verdad, hasta que vi en la lista lo de «foto de etiqueta de precio de un artículo de más de 100.000 $ de Bloomingdale's (8 puntos)», no tenía ni idea de lo caros que podían llegar a ser.

CENTRO COMERCIAL BLOOMINGDALE'S (Bloomie's)

La discusión fue sobre si el Equipo Revoltijo podía separarse o no. Con las fembots y su flota de coches de alquiler de vuelta a la competición, era obvio que no podríamos ganarlas a menos que nos moviéramos como MÍNIMO en dos direcciones distintas.

Y fue aún más obvio cuando encontramos a Kalisha Hendricks en la sección de perfumería femenina, saliendo del ascensor a toda pastilla.

CARMEN

Cuando Kalisha nos vio juntos nos dijo: «Ya sabéis que nos podemos separar, ¿verdad?».

Por la forma en que lo dijo se notaba que estaba pensando: «Y, si NO os separáis, estáis PERDIDOS».

Creo que se imaginó que ya no teníamos salvación, porque Kalisha es muy competitiva y, si hubiera creído que éramos una amenaza, no nos habría regalado los caramelos.

también muy inteligente (y competitiva)

KALISHA, miembro del equipo Avada Kedavras

Me sobraban caramelos de palomitas con mantequilla porque el expendedor se había vuelto loco y había dejado caer dos docenas en la bolsa. Y cuando me contasteis cómo Ling las había comprado todas, tuve clarísimo que tenía que compartir las mías. Porque sencillamente no es justo.

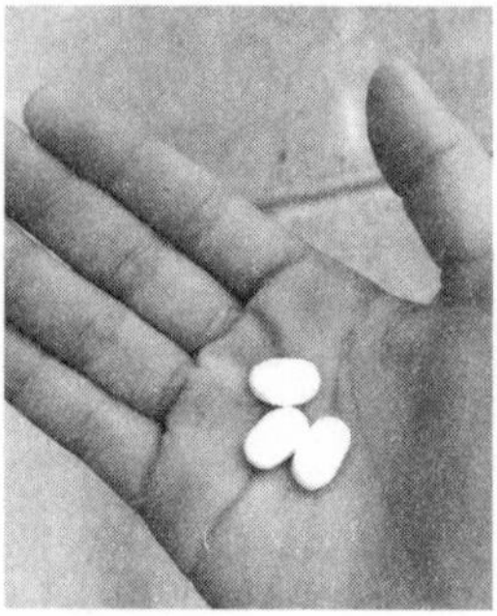

caramelos de palomitas con mantequilla (cortesía de Kalisha)

PARVATI

Solo una cosa: Kalisha se enrolló mucho y se portó megabien. Y ADEMÁS nos dijo dónde estaba lo que buscábamos en Bloomingdale's.

CLAUDIA

Cuando ya iba a salir corriendo, Kalisha se dio la vuelta y nos dijo: «Por cierto, lo de aquí buscadlo en la quinta planta».

Pero, como ha dicho Carmen, Kalisha es supercompetitiva. Por eso me mostré un poco escéptica.

PARVATI

¿«Un poco escéptica», dices? Te pusiste a gritar: «¡ES UNA TRAMPA! ¡LO DICE PARA DESPISTAR!».

CLAUDIA

Yo NO grité. Me limité a señalar una posibilidad lógica, con toda la calma.

CARMEN

Lo siento, pero de calma NADA. Ni siquiera querías subir al ascensor. Yo te dije: «Claro, Claudia, y los caramelos deben de estar ENVENENADOS». (sarcasmo)

PARVATI

¡Kalisha es la MEJOR! Con ella en el equipo, habríamos arrasado.

CLAUDIA

No empieces otra vez. Y, por cierto, la bromita sobre el calzado de Kalisha no venía a cuento. Y fue cruel con Jens.

PARVATI

Lo único que hice fue señalar que Kalisha llevaba unas deportivas que NO le producían ampollas. Y Jens ni siquiera pilló que me metía con él. Como no habla bien…

CLAUDIA

Sin comentarios.

Total, que fuimos a la quinta planta y

empezamos a mirar etiquetas de sofás y tocadores. La mayoría valían en torno a 10.000 dólares. O sea, carísimos... pero no lo suficiente.

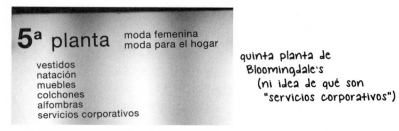

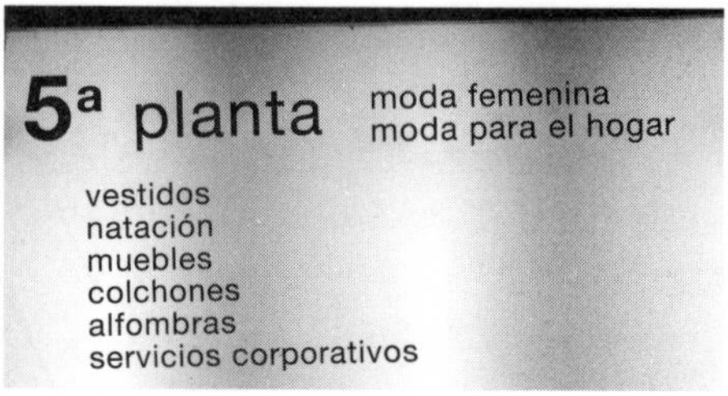

quinta planta de Bloomingdale's (ni idea de qué son "servicios corporativos")

Ahí es donde empezó mi pelea con mi madre. Porque, aunque era totalmente obvio que TENÍAMOS QUE SEPARARNOS, ella insistía en que no tenía permiso de los padres de Carmen, Parvati y Jens para «dejarlos deambular solos por la ciudad».

Eso me irritaba, porque: A) no iban a «deambular», sino CORRER (dependiendo del calzado), y B) nadie se quedaría solo, porque únicamente nos podíamos dividir en tantos equipos como gatos Calvin teníamos. Y solo podíamos contar con un Calvin más.

CARMEN

Yo todavía conservaba el mío de preescolar.

Lo iba a tirar el año pasado, pero mi

madre me dijo que si era un recuerdo importante y tal...

Me pareció muy ridi, pero, mira por dónde, nos fue bien.

CLAUDIA

La bronca fue principalmente entre mi madre y yo. Porque, aunque Parvati y Carmen estaban de mi parte, no puedes pelearte con la madre de otro. Es una especie de regla no escrita.

Y Jens se quedó un paso atrás, haciendo como que no iba con nosotras, porque los conflictos le resultan incómodos.

Mi madre interrumpía la discusión de vez en cuando para enviar mensajes a mi padre pidiéndole su opinión. No era muy buena idea, si tenemos en cuenta que mi padre acababa de dejar al equipo de Reese deambulando sin él por la ciudad.

Pero eso mi madre no lo sabía.

NUESTROS PADRES (Mensajes de móvil)

¿Has visto el muro d ClickChat?

No

Se ve q los equipos se pueden separar. Claudia quiere. Yo creo q es mala idea pq no es seguro que deambulen solos por la ciudad sin un adulto

Quizá no es para tanto

No estarás dejando q tu equipo se separe?

No, están juntos

Le digo a Claudia q no, ¿verdad?

Tú misma

Pero lo del acompañante era para garantizar la seguridad d los niños, no?

Supongo

Claudia está furiosa. Agotador. Dime q está bien no ceder y mantenerlos juntos aunque perjudique al equipo

En serio, ¿q hago? En los dos casos me siento mala madre

Eric?

Reunido

Cómo q estás reunido?

Perdona, prisa

T llamo

No puedo hablar

POR??

En metro

Sin señal

Pero si estás enviando mensajes!

Adiós

CLAUDIA

La discusión duró una eternidad, pero al final se me ocurrió un plan que mi madre no podía rebatir: ella se iría con Parvati y Carmen, y Jens y yo nos iríamos solos.

Tenía sentido porque: A) así mi madre seguiría siendo la acompañante de Parvati y Carmen, B) mi madre admitió que yo soy lo bastante responsable como para ir sin ella a condición de no ir sola, y C) Jens y yo la convencimos de que tiene unos padres muy flexibles y no les importaría en absoluto.

De hecho, los padres de Jens son tan flexibles que no estaba seguro de si sabían que estaba participando en una caza del tesoro.

JENS

Los padres holandeses no son tan… ¿cómo se dice?

CLAUDIA

¿Severos?

JENS

Sí, los holandeses son más inseveros.

no existe (pero suena muy BONITO)

CLAUDIA

Cuando mi madre se «inseveró» por fin, Carmen encontró las alfombras.

sección de alfombras

CARMEN

¡MADRE MÍA! ¡LO QUE VALÍAN ESAS ALFOMBRAS! ¡INCREÍBLE!

CLAUDIA

La sección de alfombras estaba junto a la de muebles y, en cuanto nos pusimos a mirar etiquetas de precios entre las alfombras persas tejidas a mano, supimos que lo habíamos encontrado.

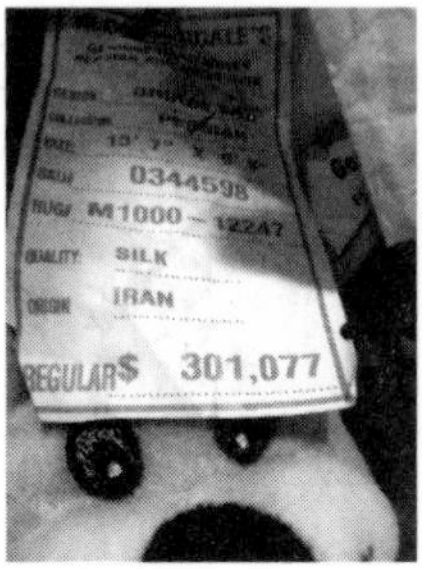

ALFOMBRA CON EL ESCANDALOSO PRECIO DE 300.000 $

PARVATI

Lo primero que pensé es qué pasa cuando tienes perro y compras esa alfombra y va el perro y se hace pis en la alfombra.

Lo digo en serio, ¿te lo imaginas? ¿Qué pasa? ¿Los ricos no tienen perro o qué?

CARMEN

Yo creo que debe de haber una sección secreta en el sótano de Bloomingdale's donde venden perros que no hacen ni pis ni caca. A juego con la alfombra de 300.000 dólares.

Perros que valen 400.000 dólares, por ejemplo.

CLAUDIA

Encontrar la alfombra (¡ocho puntos!) nos puso a todos de buen humor. Mi madre se fue con Parvati y Carmen a buscar más cosas por el East Side, mientras Jens y yo nos dirigimos hacia Times Square y el West Side.

Claro que primero tuve que encontrar a Jens, porque había desaparecido…

MENSAJES DE MÓVIL (Claudia y Jens)

DÓNDE ESTÁS??????

Sección calzado. Te gusta?
Mejor para correr

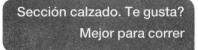

OMG! VUELVE A MUEBLES
AHORA MISMO

PERO ANTES COMPRA ZAPATILLAS

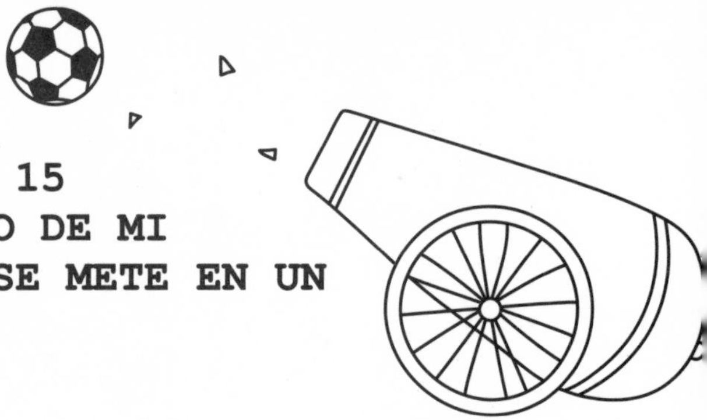

CAPÍTULO 15
EL EQUIPO DE MI HERMANO SE METE EN UN BUEN LÍO

CLAUDIA

Mientras que yo soy una persona muy responsable a la que definitivamente se puede dejar sola en mitad de Manhattan durante más de diez minutos sin que provoque ningún desastre, mi hermano no lo es.

Y menos los burros de sus amigos.

REESE

En la cola del ferry a Staten Island había MILES de personas. Muy sorprendente, porque las ligas menores de béisbol habían terminado. Y, si no vas a ver un partido de béisbol, ¿para qué narices vas a ir allí?

multitud esperando el ferry de Staten Island

CLAUDIA

Quizá porque, no sé, ¿vives allí? ¿Como hace MEDIO MILLÓN de personas?

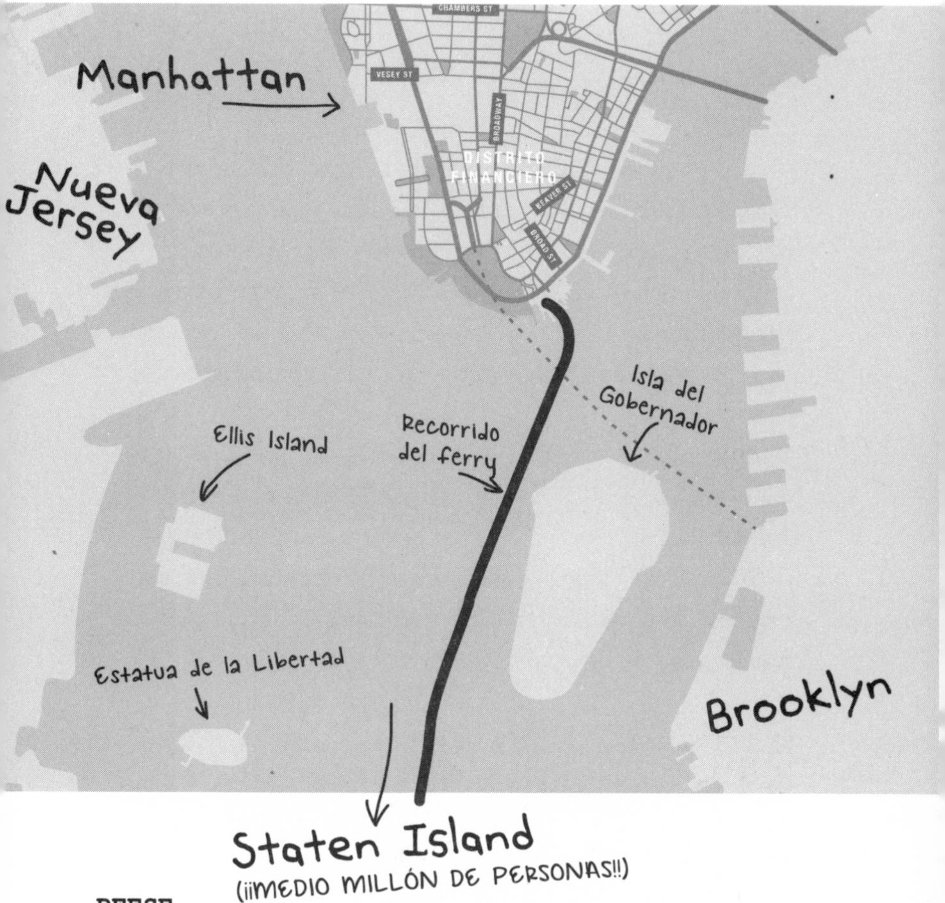

REESE

Ah, claro. Tiene sentido. Guau, debe de ser una isla bastante grande.

Bueno, el caso es que Xander le dijo a Wyatt que subiera al ferry para hacerle una foto a Calvin con la Estatua de la Libertad de fondo.

WYATT

Yo dije: «¿Y por qué yo?».

XANDER

Y yo contesté: «Porque yo paso».

REESE

Y yo, en plan: «Yo me mareo. Lo juro». Y es verdad. Soy de los que vomito.

lamentablemente cierto (también le pasa en el asiento trasero de los coches) (#DuroDeAguantar)

JAMES

Hay una orden de arresto contra mí en Staten Island. Para nada puedo poner los pies allí.

REESE

Me cuesta mucho creerlo, pero en fin.

WYATT

Entonces dije: «¡Yo no quiero ir a Staten Island solo!».

REESE

Y yo contesté: «Pues alguien tiene que hacerlo. ¿Por qué no votamos?».

Y votamos.

El resultado fue tres votos a favor de que fuera Wyatt y uno que decía «cualquiera menos Wyatt».

WYATT

Os portasteis fatal conmigo.

REESE

Así que Wyatt intentó escaquearse. Dijo: «¡No podemos separarnos! ¡Solo tenemos un Gato Calvin!».

JAMES

Yo dije: «De hecho, tenemos dos. ¿Qué quieres, la cabeza o las patas?».

WYATT

Elegí las patas. Porque se ve que en el metro la cabeza había caído sobre agua de alcantarillas o algo así, y olía muy asqueroso. NAUSEABUNDO. No entiendo cómo nadie pilló una enfermedad incurable

REESE

Dejamos a Wyatt esperando el ferry y

salimos de la terminal pensando: «¡Vamos a arrasar!».

Hasta que nos dimos cuenta de que no teníamos la lista de la caza del tesoro. La llevaba mi padre y a nadie se le ocurrió cogérsela antes de salir corriendo.

JAMES

Para alguien con memoria fotográfica esto no hubiera sido ningún problema.

Pero ninguno de nosotros tenía memoria fotográfica.

O sea que era un problema.

REESE

Pasamos un par de minutos diciendo: «¿Qué era lo de Times Square…? Había algo de Chinatown… ¿verdad?».

Lo único que recordábamos bien era lo el piano de la juguetería FAO Schwarz y lo del Cyclone de Coney Island, que es una montaña rusa brutal que está en la otra punta de Brooklyn.

Entonces Xander dijo: «¡El Toro, man!».

Así que nos fuimos caminando hasta la estatua del Toro de Wall Street y le hicimos la foto de tres puntos.

Luego decidimos ir a Coney Island.

Reese dice que Xander les obligó a hacer la foto por detrás, lo cual es COMPLETAMENTE INFANTIL

XANDER

Y yo, en plan: «¡Al Cyclone, man! ¡Ese campeón da muchos puntos!». Busqué Coney Island en el Google Maps y vi que teníamos que pillar la línea 4 y luego hacer transbordo.

Así que fuimos hacia el metro. Pero entonces vimos un bar donde daban el Chelsea-Liverpool.

REESE

El equipo favorito de Xander es el Chelsea. Aquel día jugaba contra el Liverpool y había un gran cartel en la acera que decía: «¡HOY PARTIDO CHELSEA-LIVERPOOL!».

Al pasar por delante del bar oímos un montón de gente gritando, como si acabaran de marcar un gol.

Y Xander dijo: «¡Hey! ¡Vamos a ver el gol, man!».

Y yo solté: «¡No hay tiempo para eso!». Pero Xander ya se había metido en el bar. Así que James y yo lo seguimos.

(al final, TODOS los locales de NY cierran y se convierten en farmacias)

Aquí estaba Hooligans (al cabo de una semana cerró y se convirtió en una farmacia)

CLAUDIA

Ya sabes que con 12 años está prohibido que entres a un bar sin un adulto, ¿verdad?

REESE

Bueno, lo sé AHORA. Entonces no lo sabía.

Tampoco me di cuenta de que el bar se llamaba Hooligans. Que NO es el mejor nombre para un bar en el que pasan partidos de la liga inglesa de fútbol.

Otra idea igual de MALA es entrar en un bar como ese con James Mantolini.

Para más info, busca en Internet "hooligans ingleses". Es una LOCURA

JAMES

A mí lo de los deportes no me va mucho. O sea que para mí solo eran una panda de tíos sudados y broncas gritándole a una tele.

Por eso pensé: «¡Pues yo también!».

REESE

Total, que entramos y veo que es claramente un bar del Liverpool, porque estaba a petar de hinchas suyos. Había un ejército entero de tíos calvos con camisetas rojas.

Y Xander había desaparecido. Del todo.

XANDER

Fui tal cual al meadero. X-Man tenía que regar las plantas.

REESE

El Liverpool acababa de marcar un gol y todo el bar estaba cantando. Había tanto ruido que costaba mucho entender qué decía la canción. Pero era algo guarro, seguro. Y se metía MUCHO con los aficionados del Chelsea. Y con los jugadores. Y con las madres de los jugadores.

Al acabar la canción hubo un momento de silencio en el que nadie gritaba nada.

Y justo entonces James aulló: «¡ABAJO LOS DEL LIVERPOOL!».

no es nada, nada pero que NADA inteligente hacer esto en un bar lleno de descomunales hinchas del Liverpool

JAMES

Solo quería meterme en el ambiente. Todo el mundo gritaba cosas. Pensé que apreciarían oír opiniones diversas sobre su querido equipo de fútbol.

Pero quedó claro que no lo apreciaron.

Prefirieron intentar matarnos.

REESE

Por suerte estábamos junto a la puerta. Si hubiéramos estado tres metros más lejos, creo sinceramente que ahora mismo estaríamos muertos.

Me cuesta recordar con claridad lo que pasó los dos minutos siguientes. Sé que corríamos y que yo estaba muy pero que muy asustado. Y que nos seguía un grupo de hinchas del Liverpool. Lo que no sé es cuántos.

XANDER

Yo solo sé que cuando salí descansado, la mitad del bar se había ido.

¡Una molada, porque había donde sentarse! Pillé un sitio y me puse a ver el partido.

Y me pedí unas alitas. Porque X-Man tenía hambre.

REESE

Te juro que nunca había pasado tanto miedo. Estaba corriendo a mil y no podía mirar hacia atrás. Pero oía a los tipos del Liverpool que no dejaban de gritarnos: «¡OS VAMOS A MATAR!». Y además con muchas palabrotas.

Como las calles de esa parte de la ciudad son muy cortas y estrechas, estuvimos hacheando por todas las esquinas en busca de algún sitio donde escondernos.

EPNE: esta palabra no existe

Y en esto que hacheamos una esquina y vemos un camión de reparto

EPSSE: esta palabra sigue sin existir

parado con las puertas de atrás abiertas de par en par. Y dentro no se veía nada.

camión de reparto (no el de verdad) (pero Reese dice que se parecía mucho a este)

De pronto, James subió de un salto al camión y desapareció.

Así que fui tras él.

JAMES

Ahora que lo pienso, Reese no me ha agradecido nunca que le salvara la vida subiendo a aquel camión. De hecho, más bien lo contrario, ha sido bastante desagradecido.

REESE

¡Tú eras la causa de que nuestras vidas corrieran peligro!

JAMES

Pero luego las SALVÉ. Lo uno por lo otro.

REESE

Sí, claro.

Total, que James y yo nos agachamos detrás de unas cajas. Y oímos pasar de largo a todos los hinchas rugiendo a la vez, «¡GROARRR!».

Después, silencio. Estábamos a punto de incorporarnos para bajar cuando oímos que venía alguien y volvimos a agacharnos. Al cabo de un segundo oímos un ruido estruendoso como de algo que vibraba.

Supongo que era la puerta de persiana del camión, que se estaba cerrando. Porque de repente nos quedamos completamente a oscuras, y no se veía nada.

Al cabo de otro segundo, oímos la puerta de la cabina que se abría y cerraba muy deprisa. Y el motor arrancó.

Así es como nos quedamos atrapados en la parte de atrás de un camión que iba hacia Nueva Jersey.

CAPÍTULO 16
SABOTAJE EN TIMES SQUARE

CLAUDIA

Aunque Jens ya llevaba más tres meses en Nueva York, nunca había bajado al metro, porque a su madre le da miedo. Por eso estaba tan emocionado cuando cogimos la línea 6 en dirección Grand Central y luego hicimos transbordo para ir a Times Square.

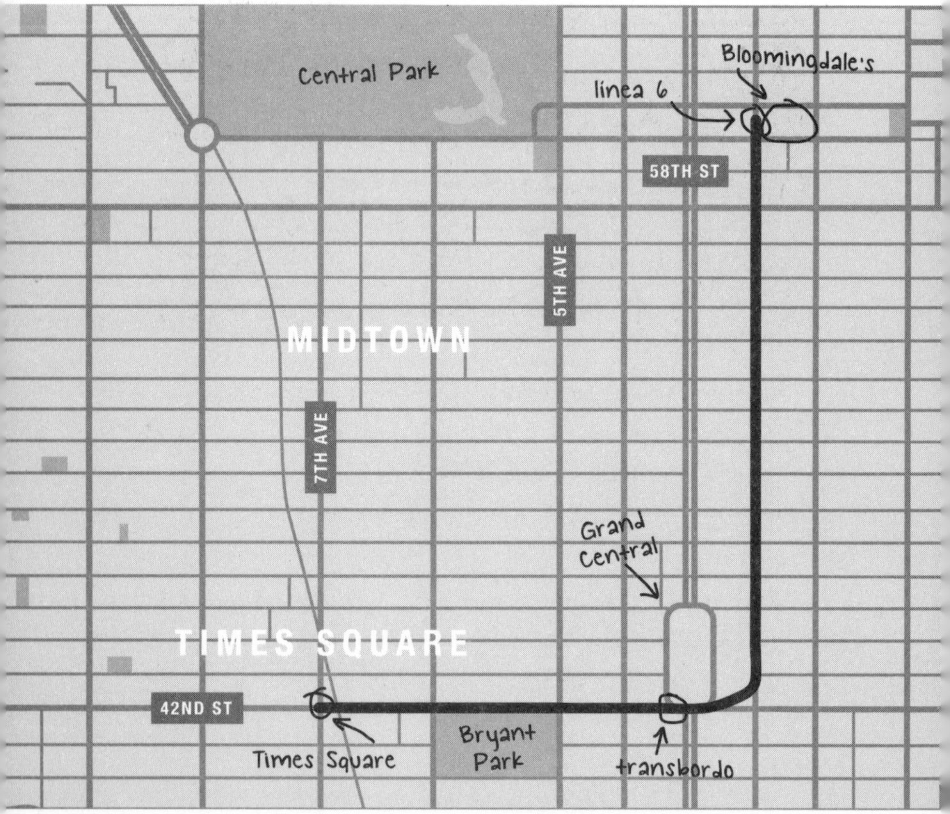

JENS

Me sorprendió. Creía que habría mal olor, pero bien.

CLAUDIA

Solo huele muy mal en verano.

estación de metro de Times Square
(el olor no sale en la foto)

Íbamos hacia Times Square a por dos cosas: un ejemplar de la revista de Broadway (5 puntos) y una foto de un tipo vestido de Flubby con el Gato Calvin en la mano (8 puntos).

Conseguir la revista era fácil. Bastaba con ir a algún teatro y pedirla.

obra MUY divertida
(convencí a mi madre para que me llevara a verla dos semanas después de la caza del tesoro)
(además: mi padre me dice que, a efectos legales, DEBO aclarar que la revista NO prestó apoyo a esta caza del tesoro")

Pero, volviendo a los puntos, lo más importante era lo de la foto con Flubby. Por si nunca has tenido tres años o por si has crecido sin televisión, te explico que Flubby es un personaje del programa *Barrio Perejil*. Es básicamente una estrella de rock para todos los niños de tres años del mundo.

JENS

En Holanda no lo llamamos Flubby, sino *Fluuber*.

¡Qué MONO!

CLAUDIA

Casi todos los días hay media docena de personas disfrazadas de Flubby deambulando por Times Square, cobrando a los turistas que se hacen fotos con ellos.

Es un poco extraño, la verdad, pero en Times Square casi todo lo es.

No tardamos nada en encontrar un Flubby, y parecía perfectamente dispuesto a que le hiciéramos una foto… hasta que saqué el Gato Calvin del bolso.

Cuando vio a Calvin, empezó a mover su gran cabeza de Flubby de un lado a otro, como diciendo «¡Nooooo!».

Imaginé que era porque aún no le había enseñado el dinero, así que saqué unos dólares y se los ofrecí. Y él empezó a agitar las manos como diciendo: «¡No, no, no!».

Y yo pregunté: «¿Por qué no?».

Y va el tipo y se da la vuelta y se va corriendo.

Flubby (yéndose corriendo)

Teniendo en cuenta lo mucho que veía *Barrio Perejil* cuando era pequeña, ver a un Flubby huyendo de mí de aquella manera fue bastante traumático.

Pero lo que pasó después aún lo fue más.

JENS

Al principio todo fue muy raro. Todos los *Fluubers* cuando veían a Calvin, cruzaban los brazos y no lo cogían.

CLAUDIA

Era como si fueran vampiros Flubby y nuestro Calvin estuviera hecho de ajo.

Siempre pasaba lo mismo: nos acercábamos a un Flubby, nos soltaba un «¡Hola!» muy amable y tal, pero en cuanto yo sacaba el Calvin, le entraba la paranoia y se negaba a cogerlo.

Al quinto Flubby que lo hizo, me sentí muy frustrada y le grité: «Pero ¿por qué no lo quieres tocar? ¡Solo es un gato!».

Y una voz cavernosa y amortiguada que salía de dentro de la cabeza del Flubby dijo con acento hispano: «¡He prometido a la chica nadie más!».

«¿Qué chica?», pregunté.

«La chica rica», contestó el Flubby hispano.

otros Flubby que se negaron: -Flubby enfadado, Flubby gandul (llevaba Crocs en los pies), Flubby con descosidos, Flubby rojo (este puede que fuera Elmo)

Enseguida supe qué había pasado: sabotaje fembot.

«¿Te ha pagado una chica para que no te hagas fotos con este gato?», le pregunté.

El Flubby hispano asintió con su gran cabeza.

«¿Cómo era?».

«Pelo largo. Coche negro. Ropa cara».

Athena Cohen.

Claro que también podía haber sido Meredith. O Ling. O Clarissa. Según lo mucho que le pagara o lo cara que fuera la ropa.

«¿Cuánto te ha pagado?».

«Cincuenta dólares».

Athena, estaba clarísimo. Solo ella era lo suficientemente rica y mala para sobornar a todos los Flubby de Times Square.

«Sería solo una foto, por favor», le supliqué, «y ella nunca lo sabrá!

«No», dijo el Flubby hispano. «Lo prometí».

«¡Se lo suplico!».

«No, lo siento. Flubby es un modelo para los niños. Flubby tiene que cumplir promesas».

muy admirable de su parte (pero ¡qué rabia!)

JENS

Cuando se lo pedías y *Fluuber* te decía que no y que no, estabas muy triste. Yo quería animarte.

CLAUDIA

Jens me abrazó y me dijo: «No te preocupes. No es más que un juego. Vamos a comer».

Y eso sí que me hizo ENFADAR. Porque pensé que, si no conseguíamos ni siquiera una foto de Flubby de 8 puntos, nos ganarían definitivamente las fembots. Y yo no quería que a Jens le diera igual. Quería que se enfadara y que se activara a tope conmigo.

Pero cuando se lo iba a decir oí otra voz desde dentro de una cabeza de Flubby que gritaba: «¡Oye, chica!».

Me giré y vi a otro de los Flubby de pie detrás de nosotros. No sé si era uno de los que nos había dicho que no u otro completamente nuevo. Cuesta mucho diferenciarlos. a lo mejor era el "Flubby enfadado" (véase más arriba)

Me dijo: «¿Quieres una foto con el gato?».

Este Flubby tenía un acento neoyorquino, tipo «olvídalo-tío», como el que tienen los taxistas en las películas malas (lo que, por cierto, es RIDÍCULO porque la mayoría de los taxistas de Nueva York son extranjeros y no tienen ese acento).

Contesté: «¡Sí! ¿Se la hará?».

El Flubby «olvídalo-tío», dijo: «Cincuenta pavos».

Una locura, porque yo no soy Athena Cohen. Además, era imposible, solo llevaba veintitrés dólares, así que iba a decirle: «¿Qué tal veinte?».

Pero justo entonces el Flubby hispano amenazó con su gran dedo azul al Flubby «olvídalo-tío» y le gritó: «¡No puedes hacerlo! ¡Promesa a la chica! ¡Te ha pagado!».

El Flubby «olvídalo-tío» mandó al Flubby hispano a paseo, pero utilizando un tipo de lenguaje que NO debería salir nunca de la boca de un Flubby.

si un niño de 3 años lo oyera, quedaría marcado para toda la vida

El Flubby hispano le dijo algo como: «¡Debería darte vergüenza! ¡Vergüenza! ¡Llevas el traje de Flubby! ¡No tienes honor!».

Entonces el Flubby «olvídalo-tío» pegó un puñetazo en la cabeza al Flubby hispano.

Creo que no le dolió, porque no le dio en su cabeza de verdad, sino en su enorme cabeza falsa.

Pero luego empezaron a darse patadas, y ESO sí que parecía doler.

Y después la cosa se puso *heavy*. Me entró la paranoia y empecé a gritar. No era lo mejor que podía hacer, pero, claro, no había dedicado mucho tiempo en mi vida a reflexionar sobre qué haría si algún día veía a dos Flubby pegándose en Times Square.

Mientras yo gritaba, Jens hacía fotos.

JENS

Al principio, pensé «¡Qué mal! ¡Tenemos que irnos!».

Pero luego pensé: «¡Dos *Fluubers* pegándose! No creo que vuelva a ver esto en la vida. Tengo que hacer fotos».

LAS FOTOS CON LOS
PERSONAJES DISFRAZADOS
SON GRATUITAS.
LA PROPINA ES OPCIONAL.

En caso de reclamación, hable con
algún policía o llame al 911

CLAUDIA

Por suerte, estábamos en Times Square, así que había dos polis muy cerca. Al oír mis gritos, vinieron corriendo y pararon la pelea.

Nos preguntaron quién había empezado; les dijimos que el Flubby «olvídalo-tío» había dado el primer puñetazo, y lo esposaron.

no hay foto de Flubby esposado
(pq le dije a Jens que no era muy enrollado hacerla)

Luego salimos de allí corriendo porque yo sabía que, si nos hacía ir a declarar a comisaría, nunca volveríamos a la caza.

Quisiera hacer constar, sin embargo, que la violencia de Flubby contra Flubby nunca se habría producido si Athena Cohen no los hubiera sobornado antes.

También me gustaría señalar que al final no conseguimos la foto del Flubby de 8 puntos. Y, sin ella, el Equipo Revoltijo ya lo podía dar todo básicamente por perdido.

A menos que se nos ocurriera alguna idea brillante y que diera la vuelta a la situación.

Pero eso ya da para otro capítulo.

(concretamente, el 18)

CAPÍTULO 17
MI HERMANO QUEDA ATRAPADO DENTRO DE UN CAMIÓN DE REPARTO EN DIRECCIÓN AL TÚNEL HOLLAND

CLAUDIA

A esas alturas, la situación de crisis de mi padre en el trabajo ya había terminado, pero la de la caza del tesoro no había hecho más que empezar.

REESE

Me estaba entrando muy mal rollo dentro del camión, porque había mucho ruido, todo rebotaba y la única luz que había era la de nuestros móviles.

vista del interior del camión (recreación de la artista) (la foto es del cuarto de baño)
luz de los móviles

James y yo empezamos en plan: «¡¡OIGA!! ¡Señor Conductor! ¡Ayúdenos!». Pero no nos oía. Debía de llevar la radio muy alta o yo qué sé.

Y va James y dice: «Creo que vamos a morir aquí dentro, DEFINITIVAMENTE».

Y yo le pregunté: «¿Cómo?».

Y James: «Probablemente de hambre».

Al oír eso, me entró el pánico.

Por eso me comí el crónut.

CLAUDIA

Sigo sin poder creer que te comieras el crónut. ¡VALÍA TREINTA PUNTOS!

REESE

¡Tú no sabes lo que es estar encerrado en la parte de atrás de un camión! ¡Es superagobiante!

A ver, ya sé que solo llevábamos encerrados un par de minutos, pero yo creía de verdad que nunca volvería a comer. Además, aquel día había desayunado poco.

JAMES

Yo le dije que no se comiera el crónut.

Pero, como no me hizo caso, le pedí la mitad.

REESE

En cuanto nos acabamos el crónut —que seguro que al final era auténtico, porque estaba buenísimo—, envié un mensaje a mi padre.

REESE Y NUESTRO PADRE (Mensajes copiados del móvil de Reese)

SOCORRO, PAPÁ. ATRAPADO EN CAMIÓN

REESE

Supongo que estaba aún en alguna reunión, porque no me contestó enseguida. Así que escribí a mi madre.

REESE Y NUESTRA MADRE (Mensajes copiados del móvil de mamá)

SOCORRO, MAMÁ. ATRAPADO EN CAMIÓN

Es broma?

NO, D VIRDAD

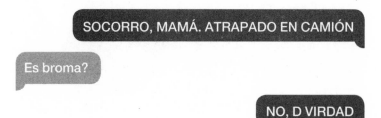

REESE

Mi madre me llamó al momento, y le conté todo lo que había pasado.

Nos dijo: «Poneos a gritar. Los dos. Con todas vuestras fuerzas».

Así que James y yo nos pusimos a gritar.

¡Y funcionó! Porque justo entonces el camión se paró. Y oímos al conductor bajar del camión y le gritamos: «¡ESTAMOS AQUÍ!».

El hombre subió la persiana y nos dejó salir.

Estaba bastante enfadado.

JAMES

El conductor del camión me pareció muy inestable, incluso más que los hinchas de fútbol, si quieres que te diga la verdad.

conductor del camión (recreación de la artista) (a partir de testimonios oculares)

REESE

El tipo se puso a decir: «¡HARÉ QUE OS DETENGAN POR ALLANAMIENTO! ¡LA POLI OS MANDARÁ AL REFORMATORIO!».

Entonces James lanzó al aire la apestosa cabeza de Calvin, muy alto.

Supongo que lo hizo para distraer, porque, mientras el conductor del camión y yo nos quedamos mirando cómo volvía a caer, James salió por patas.

El tío corría gritando por la calle, literalmente. Así: «¡AAAAAAAAHH!».

JAMES

Si hubieras visto al conductor del camión, sabrías que no estaba hecho para correr largas distancias. Por eso me pareció una buena estrategia.

REESE

Ver a James correr de aquella forma confundió mucho al conductor. No sabía qué hacer. Se notaba las vueltas que le estaba dando al coco, en plan: «¿Persigo al chico? Pero entonces el otro se escapará. Y, si NO pillo al primero, NADIE irá al reformatorio…».

Hasta que se rindió. Dijo: «¡Bah, paso!». Y arrancó el camión y se fue.

Entonces miré el móvil y vi que mi padre me había enviado algunos mensajes.

REESE Y NUESTRO PADRE (Mensajes copiados del móvil de Reese)

SOCORRO, PAPÁ. ATRAPADO EN CAMIÓN

Dónde?

Reese? Es broma?

Dónde estás?

He acabado trabajo. Voy hacia estatua toro. D verdad estás atrapado en un camión?

REESE, CONTESTA!!!

Todo bien. Ya fuera d camión

Dónde estás?

Ni idea. Quizá Nueva Jersey

NO estaba en Nueva Jersey (per camión debía de ir hacia allí pq estaba cerca del Túnel Holland)

Los demás están contigo?

No. Estoy solo

Dónde están los demás?

Chambers St

Están en Chambers St?

Ellos no, yo

T llamo

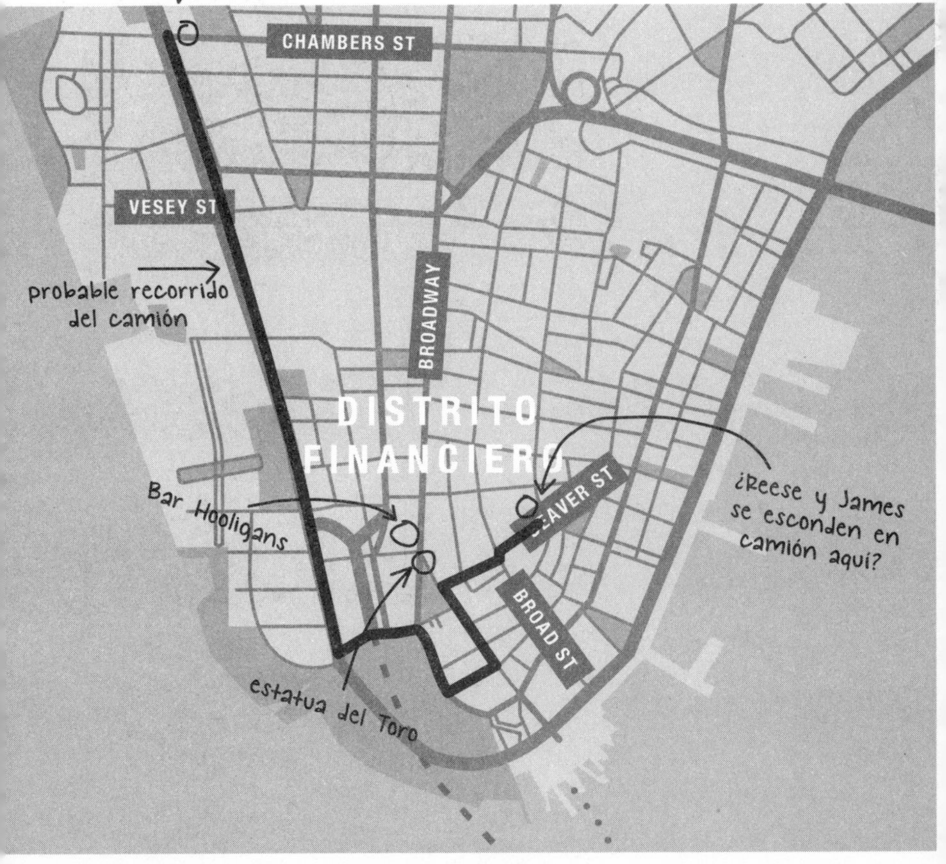

REESE

Estuve hablando por teléfono con mi padre y, cuando se imaginó dónde estaba, me dijo que siguiera por Chambers Street hasta Broadway y que luego girara a la derecha y bajara hacia el centro para reunirme con él en la estatua del Toro.

Y colgó enseguida para ponerse a buscar a los demás.

WYATT Y NUESTRO PADRE (Mensajes copiados del móvil de Wyatt)

Wyatt, soy el padre d Reese. Dónde estás?

Staten Island. Mire q foto

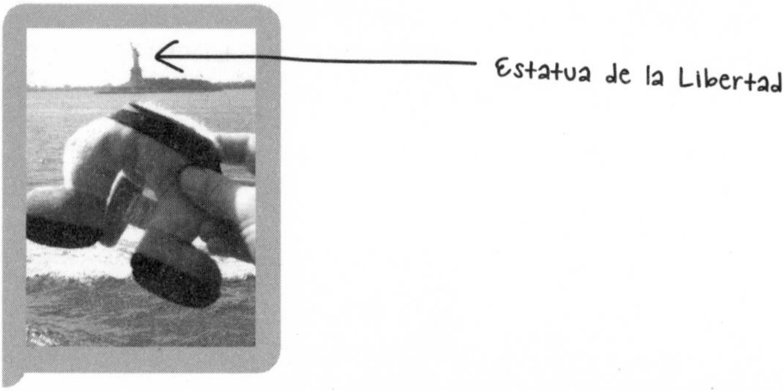

Quizá mejor foto con cabeza, no?

Se la han llevado los demás

Dónde están?

Sr. Tapper?

Adiós

Nos vemos en toro

XANDER Y NUESTRO PADRE (Mensajes copiados del móvil de Xander)

Xander, soy el padre d Reese. Dónde estás?

En un bar

No en un bar d verdad, espero

Sí, un bar

Sal inmediatamente d ahí y ve a estatua toro

No puedo

Xander, sal d ahí ya. Nos vemos en toro

Pero he pedido alitas d poyo

Xander es incapaz de escribir bien una palabra de 4 letras. Triste

Xander, es ILEGAL q estés solo en un bar

Ya estan aKi las alitas!

Xander, en serio, sal ahora mismo

Xander?

Ya has salido del bar?

No pued escbr, dedos prngosos

JAMES Y NUESTRO PADRE (Mensajes copiados del móvil de James)

James, soy el padre d Reese. Dónde estás?

Se equivoca de número

Disculpe

James, seguro q no eres tú?

Aquí no hay nadie
q se llame James

Este es el núm que sale en el
directorio de Culvert en Internet
para James Mantolini

SI ESTE ACOSO PROSIGUE
LLAMARÉ A LA POLICÍA

James, deja la broma. Dónde
estás? Como acompañante tengo
q saber dónde estás y si estás bien

SU CONDUCTA ES ILEGAL

ES UN DELITO GRAVE

HE ENVIADO SU NÚMERO
AL DPTO POLICÍA PARA
QUE INVESTIGUE

Si no es James, ruego acepte
mis más sinceras disculpas

REESE

Seguro que era James.

JAMES

Puede que sí, puede que no.

CLAUDIA

Era él. James me ha dejado copiar los mensajes desde su móvil.

REESE

De verdad que no entiendo nada de lo que hace James Mantolini.

Total, que yo fui por Chambers Street hasta Broadway como me había dicho mi padre. Y por el camino me di cuenta de que no le había dicho que había hablado con mi madre, y creo que eso le puso las cosas bastante más difíciles.

NUESTROS PADRES (Mensajes copiados del móvil de mamá)

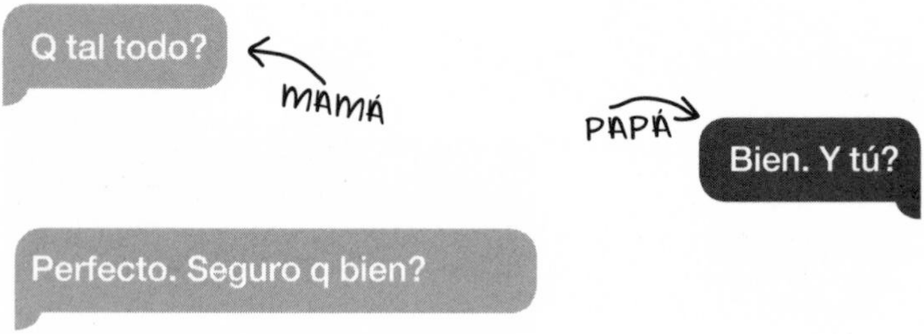

Sí, vamos genial

Los chavales bien?

P q preguntas?

Curiosidad. Nada q contar?

Muy frenético pero bien

Estupendo!

Sí! Divertido

O sea q cuando mi único hijo varón me manda «ATRAPADO EN CAMIÓN Y TEMO POR MI VIDA» yo tengo q contestarle «LOL»?

T llamo

Cariño?

Por favor coge el tel

Puedo explicarlo

Estoy buscando la mejor forma d expresar mi ira

hongos producidos por bombas atómicas (¿o simples árboles?) (no creo, más bien bombas)

Ya lo tengo

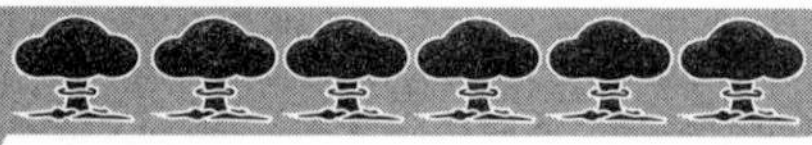

Lo siento mucho

Ni la mitad de lo q lo sentirás

CAPÍTULO 18
A JENS Y A MÍ SE NOS OCURRE UNA IDEA GENIAL PARA DARLE LA VUELTA A LA SITUACIÓN

CLAUDIA

Después de que nos fembotearan en Times Square, Jens y yo fuimos hacia el centro con la línea 1 del metro para conseguir la chapa de Coca-Cola de 5 centavos de la máquina de Tekserve (que no teníamos ni idea de lo que era).

Yo estaba bastante enfadada con nuestra situación general. Eran las 12:42, o sea, ya habíamos gastado casi la mitad del tiempo de la caza, y había tantas cosas en la lista que no habíamos conseguido —sobre todo cosas que estaban lejísimos, como el estadio de los Yankees y Coney Island— que parecía totalmente imposible ganar.

Y seguro que las fembots, con los cuatro coches circulando en distintas direcciones —y su enfermiza manía de sabotear a todo el mundo—, estaban arrasando.

Y, en esa situación, lo único en lo que pensaba Jens era en ir a comer.

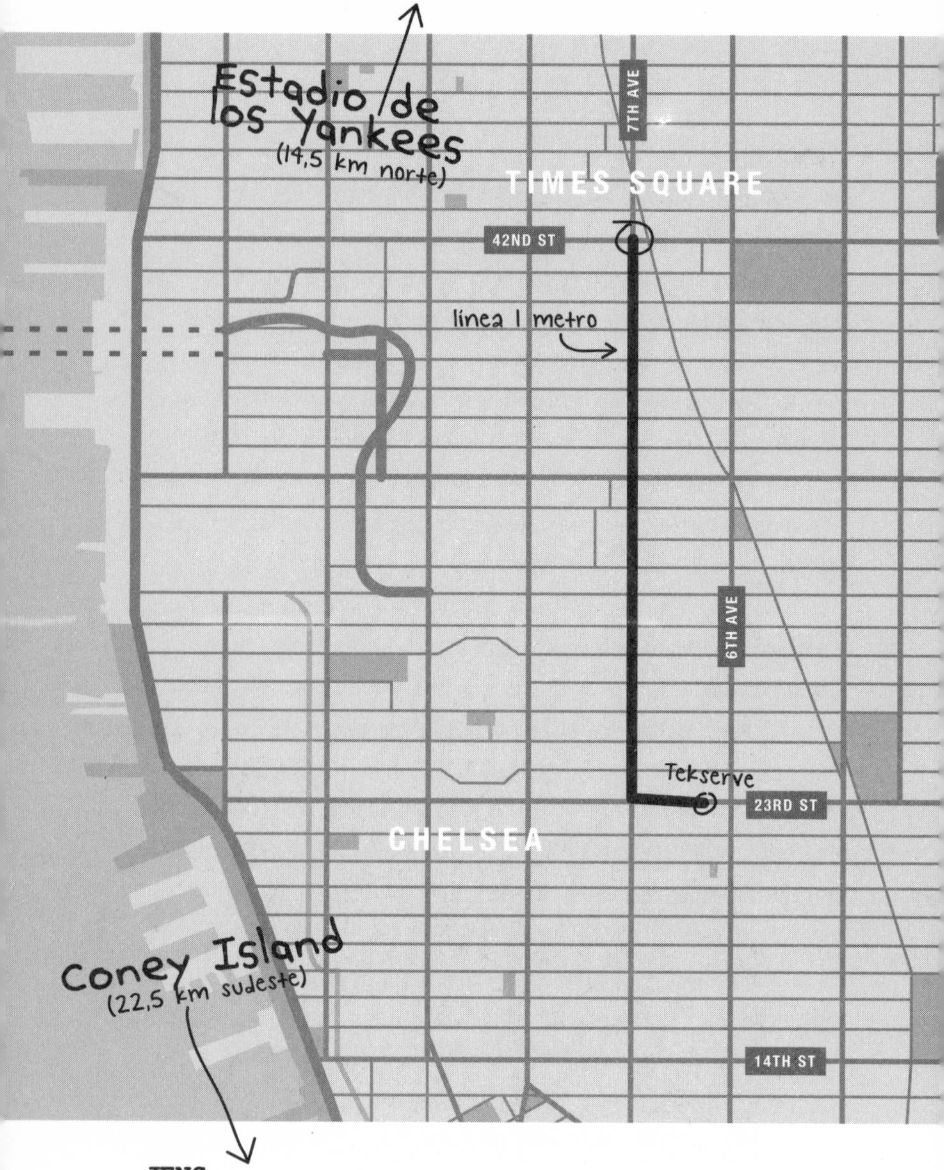

JENS

Me interesaba mucho probar ese restaurante llamado Katz's.

CLAUDIA

Yo le dije a Jens que eso era ridículo, y que podía beberse toda la Coca-Cola de la máquina de 5 centavos (3 puntos) y QUIZÁ si encontrábamos algún sitio con pizza a 99 centavos (4 puntos), nos quedaría tiempo para comprar una porción, pero que PARA NADA íbamos a perder tiempo sentándonos a comer, y menos en un sitio como Katz's Delicatessen (5 puntos), que los sábados por la tarde está a petar de turistas.

Y de no turistas también, porque los sándwiches de Katz's son totalmente increíbles.

Katz's Deli: probad el bocadillo de pastrami (ALUCINANTE)

Pero eso no se lo dije a Jens, porque aún habría insistido más en ir.

JENS

Estabas muy estresada. Por eso dije: «¿Por qué no nos relajamos, lo pasamos bien y no pensamos en ganar?».

Y eso te hizo enfadar. Dijiste: «¡No se trata de divertirse, sino de hacer justicia!».

CLAUDIA

Lo pensaba en serio. No es que fuéramos a perder, ¡es que íbamos a perder ante las FEMBOTS, que estaban haciendo trampas a saco!».

Y yo no era una simple participante ¡era la creadora de la caza del tesoro! Y si al final resultaba que la única forma de ganarla era actuando con perversidad absoluta y saboteando a todo el mundo, eso significaría que yo había creado un monstruo.

Y, por mucho que recaudáramos para el Banco de Alimentos de Manhattan, la moraleja de la caza sería que la única forma de ir por delante en la vida es siendo perverso. (y rico)

Y eso sería muy muy nefasto, no solo para esta caza en concreto, sino para las generaciones futuras.

O sea que había MUCHO más en juego que un simple «Divirtámonos y vayamos a comer un sándwich de pastrami con pan de centeno y con pepinillos gigantes». aunque hubiera sido delicioso (sobre todo en Katz's)

Y cuando le expliqué todo esto, Jens cambió completamente de actitud.

JENS

Yo pensé: «¿Cómo podemos dar la vuelta al juego para ganarlo?».

Miro la lista otra vez. Y está claro.

Si hacemos foto con Deondra, sacamos 500 puntos. Y nadie nos puede ganar.

CLAUDIA

Al principio le dije: «Jens, lo del beso de Deondra era una BROMA. ¿No conoces la canción?».

Porque cuando se celebró la caza del tesoro, la canción de Deondra «Beso de Gato» era LO MÁS. Imagino que por eso Akash lo puso en la lista.

10 PRINCIPALES SEMANA 6-10 OCT 14

1 BESO DE GATO, Deondra

2 TÚ PUEDES HACERLO, Miranda Fleet

3 HIBBITY BIG, Fiddy K

AKASH

¡POR SUPUESTO que por eso lo puse en la lista!

¿ES QUE NO HAY NADIE EN ESTE COLEGIO QUE TENGA SENTIDO DEL HUMOR?

JENS

Yo dije: «Sí, vale, es broma. Pero está en la lista. Si hacemos una foto con Deondra besando al gato, tenemos 500 puntos».

CLAUDIA

No entiendo cómo no se me ocurrió a mí antes. Pero estaba tan emocionada con la idea de Jens que lo habría podido besar allí mismo en el metro.

¡Que no digo que lo BESARA! En cualquier caso no es asunto de nadie, así que ni niego ni confirmo. Y recuerda que TÉCNICAMENTE NO es mi novio

Lo importante es que estaba superemocionada. Y aliviada, porque, para ser sincera, hasta ese momento Jens no había puesto mucho de su parte.

En cuanto salimos del metro, llamé a Parvati para decirle que teníamos que concentrar todos nuestros recursos en encontrar a Deondra.

PARVATI

Cuando llamaste, Carmen y yo estábamos con tu madre esperando en la cola para hacer el vídeo del piano de FAO Schwarz. Y, en cuanto mencionaste lo de buscar a Deondra, yo dije: «¡Madre mía! ¡Es una idea GENIAL! Y no puedo creer que no lo pensara yo antes. Además, soy la persona idónea para encontrarla porque llevo obsesionada con Deondra desde los once años, y conozco todas las webs que nos pueden ayudar a localizarla».

Colgué enseguida y me puse a buscar.

CLAUDIA

Mientras tanto, Jens y yo fuimos a Tekserve, que resultó ser una tienda de informática muy guay.

TEKSERVE
(merece una visita)
(¡y a solo una manzana de Doughnut Plant!)
(que también merece una visita)
(si te gustan los dónuts)

En mitad de la tienda había una máquina antigua de Coca-Cola, y un chico con la camiseta de Tekserve estaba abriendo la puerta de la máquina justo cuando llegamos.

Me asusté. Pero cuando le pregunté: «¡Hola! ¿Queda alguna Coca-Cola?», me contestó: «Sí, las estoy reponiendo».

Y añadió: «Ha venido una chica y ha vaciado la máquina. Muy raro, ha comprado todas las botellas, las ha dejado tiradas en la fuente de agua y se ha llevado las chapas. Cuando se ha ido he tenido que subir dos cajas enteras del almacén».

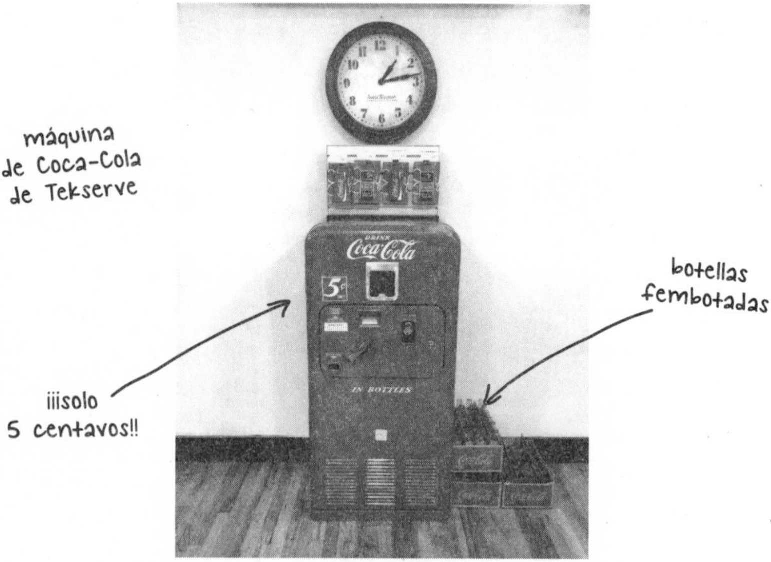

chapa de Coca-Cola de 5 centavoss

Saber que un intento de sabotaje de las fembots había quedado frustrado me hizo pensar que a lo mejor nuestra suerte iba a cambiar. Cuando Parvati me llamó con las noticias sobre Deondra, mis esperanzas crecieron.

PARVATI

Vale, pues primero miré la web Deondra Online para comprobar que no estaba de gira, ni rodando una peli ni grabando un álbum en Francia o qué sé yo. Y no. Todo en orden.

Luego fui a la web de Fiddy K para comprobar que ÉL no estaba de gira, porque, claro, están casados y tal, y se respaldan mucho profesionalmente. Si él hubiera estado de gira, es bastante probable que ella estuviera con él.

Pero Fiddy K tampoco estaba de gira. Todo en orden también por ahí.

Luego fui a la web ¡OMG, Famosos Sueltos!

para ver si alguien había visto recientemente a Deondra por alguna parte. Y la última foto que había de ella era en una cafetería de Miami. Pero de eso hacía quince días. Así que pensé que aún SEGUÍA todo en orden.

Luego visité la web Alfombra Roja 24H y AHÍ descubrí que la noche anterior ella y Fiddy K habían ido a una gala benéfica por el autismo celebrada en el Waldorf.

Y pensé: «OMG, esto es GENIAL. Porque seguro que se acostaron tarde, y que han dormido mucho, y, en el libro *Yo, Deondra*, leí que lo que más le gusta hacer los fines de semana es pasear a su perro y/o ir con su marido y como mucho un par amigos íntimos a almorzar en plan superdiscreto».

(autobiografía de Deondra)
(para ser sincera, no tan buena como *Fleeting*, de Miranda Fleet

Y te dije: «Claudia, TIENES que ir YA MISMO al edificio donde vive Deondra y esperar a que salga a pasear el perro o a almorzar».

CLAUDIA

Estaba muy impresionada con la labor de detective de Parvati. Solo tenía una pregunta: «¿Dónde narices vive Deondra?».

PARVATI

Y yo contesté: «¡Pues en el número 511 de Leonard Street de TriBeCa! ¡Si eso lo sabe todo el mundo!».

Por supuestísimo habría ido yo, pero llevábamos veinte minutos haciendo cola para aquel piano de suelo. Y NO quería ceder nuestro puesto, sobre todo porque justo detrás teníamos a Colin Hartley, del equipo Gingivitis.

CLAUDIA

Jens y yo buscamos la dirección en Internet y al cabo de dos minutos estábamos otra vez en la línea 1 en dirección a TriBeCa.

Por cierto, igual que «SoHo» es una abreviatura de «SOuth of HOuston Street» (sur de Houston Street), «TriBeCa» lo es de «TRIangle BElow CAnal Street» (triángulo por debajo de Canal Street).

Aunque para nosotros, en esos momentos, significaba más bien «**TRI**turemos a las **BE**llacas en la **CA**za».

Y, para mi padre, que en esos momentos estaba muy cerca de allí, era «**TRI**bulaciones y **BE**rrinches de un **CA**ballero que ha perdido a James Mantolini».

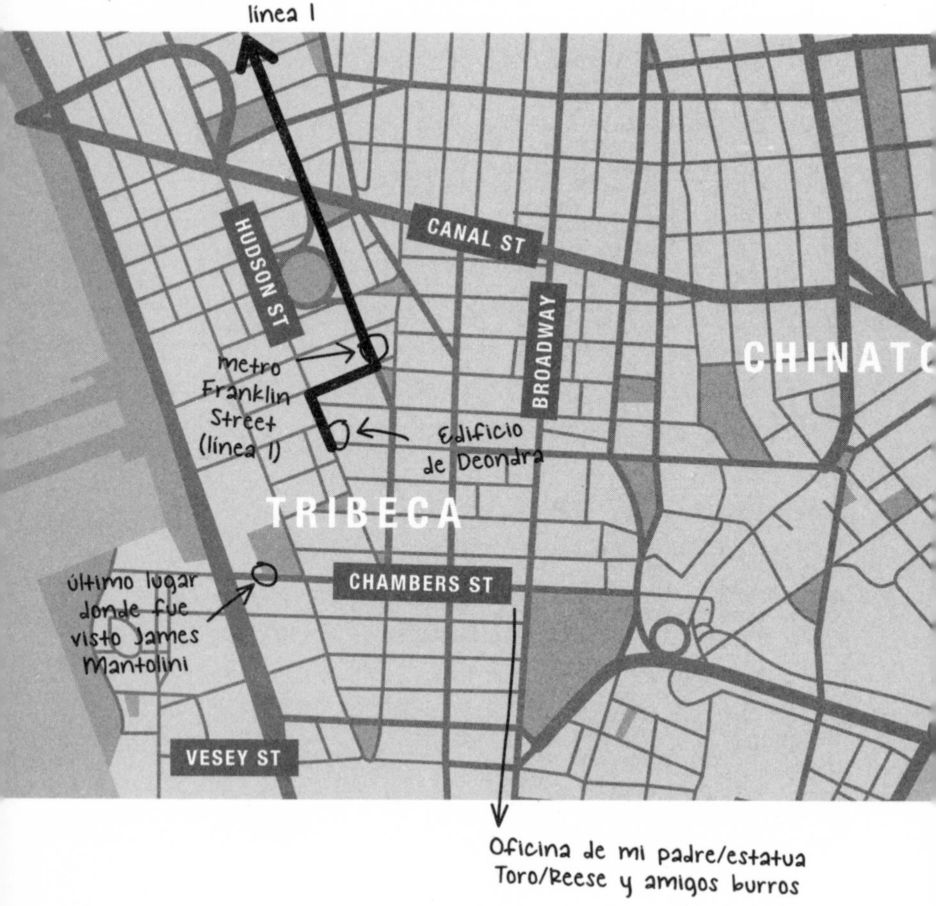

CAPÍTULO 19
EL EQUIPO DE MI HERMANO CAE AÚN MÁS BAJO

REESE

Cuando volví a la estatua del Toro, mi padre y Wyatt ya estaban allí. Mi padre estaba estresado que te mueres por haber perdido a la mitad del equipo, y lo primero que hizo fue llevarnos de vuelta al bar Hooligans para recoger a Xander. Wyatt y yo nos escondimos en la esquina para que ningún hincha del Liverpool volviera a intentar matarnos mientras mi padre sacaba a Xander a rastras.

XANDER

Man, diez puntos para Superpapi Tapper por costear las alitas.

REESE

Después de eso nos preguntamos: «¿Qué más hay en la lista?».

Y mi padre: «¡Encontrar a James Mantolini! ¿Qué número tiene?».

Y nosotros: «¿No te lo ha dado al principio?».

Y mi padre: «Sí, pero era falso. ¿Cuál es el de verdad?».

Y nosotros: «Ni idea».

Porque nadie había llamado nunca a James. Pero sí que tenía su e-mail, porque estaba entre los destinatarios del grupo de refuerzo de mediodía de la clase de mates de la señora Santiago.

Total, que le envié un mail, aunque supuse que no me contestaría nunca.

REESE (Mail dirigido a James)

JAMES DONDE ESTAS???????

De: monstruoflipao@gmail.com
Para: soi_batman_ytuno@yahoo.com
Fecha: 25/10/14 12:54:33
Asunto: JAMES DONDE ESTAS???????

MI PADRE MEGAPREOKUPADO, LLÁMALE
[redacted]

número de tel. tachado por privacidad

REESE

Luego dijimos: «Papá, no te preocupes, seguro que está bien».

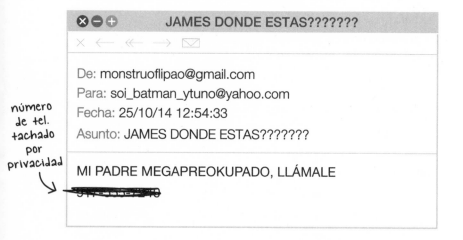

Y mi padre dijo: «Yo soy el acompañante. TENGO que garantizar la seguridad de todo el mundo».

Y eso, teniendo en cuenta que era él el que nos había dejado solos era, er... ¿cómo se dice? ¿Cuando alguien dice algo y es casi lo contrario de lo que esperarías?

CLAUDIA

Una ironía.

DICCIONARIO

ironía

ironía: f.
Expresión que da a entender algo contrario o diferente de lo que se dice, generalmente con burla disimulada.

REESE

Exacto, eso. Y además era flipador intentar encontrar a James. No solo porque Nueva York es megagrande, sino porque estábamos en mitad de la caza del tesoro.

Y todos saltamos: «¿Por qué no volvemos a separarnos?».

Y mi padre nos cortó: «¡Por encima de mi cadáver! ¡Aquí NO se separa nadie!». Y eso también era... ¡Ostras, ya se me ha olvidado la palabra!

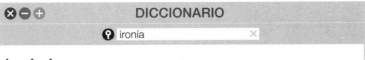

CLAUDIA

Una ironía.

REESE

Eso. Perdona.

Y Wyatt y Xander, en plan: «¡No podemos abandonar la caza ahora! ¡Estamos ganando! ¡Tenemos el crónut!».

Y tuve que decirles que me lo había comido.

WYATT

A mí eso me mató bien muerto. Me metéis en el ferry solo y, mientras tanto, ¡¿OS COMÉIS EL CRÓNUT?!

REESE

Fue un error frikante, tío.

EPNE

XANDER

¡Qué débil, man! LOOSER.

REESE

¡Lo sé! ¡Lo siento!

Total, que mi padre nos puso a recorrer Broadway, hacia el lugar donde habíamos visto a James por última vez. Dijo: «Si fuerais James, ¿adónde iríais?».

XANDER

Yo dije: «Al talego». Porque te digo que Jotaemo acabará ahí de cajón si no se gobierna.

Y Superpapi Tapper dijo: «Ahí ya miraremos luego».

WYATT

Y luego yo propuse: «¡Dunkin' Donuts!».

Y tu padre: «¿A James le gustan los dónuts?».

Y yo: «No lo sé, pero ahí hay un Dunkin' Donuts. ¡Podemos comprar un dónut y hacerlo pasar por un crónut!».

REESE

Era una idea guay, porque, aunque me había comido el crónut, había guardado la caja.

De manera que fuimos corriendo a comprar el dónut antes de que mi padre pudiera discutirlo o con nosotros.

Elegimos uno con cobertura de fresa porque se parecía al crónut que me había comido, pero, como este era un poco ovalado, mordisqueé los bordes para acronutarlo.

Luego lo metimos en la caja. Lo que pasa es que dentro había estado la cabeza de

Calvin, así que la caja estaba un poco mojada con el agua nabusunda de las cloacas.

CPNEPNE: Casi Pero No. Esta Palabra No Existe

CLAUDIA

Dime por favor que nadie se llevó a la boca aquel dónut mordido que había estado en aquella caja nauseabunda.

EPSE: Esta Palabra Sí Existe

esto es DEMASIADO REPUGNANTE

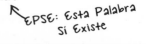

REESE

Sin comentarios.

El caso es que, cuando ya teníamos el crónut de recambio, mi padre dijo: «Mira el mail a ver si ha contestado James».

Y yo le dije: «Papá, James no va a… ¡ostras, sí que ha contestado!».

JAMES (Mail dirigido a Reese)

RE: JAMES DONDE ESTAS???????

De: soi_batman_ytuno@yahoo.com

Para: monstruoflipao@gmail.com

Fecha: 25/10/14 13:02:33

Asunto: RE: JAMES DONDE ESTAS???????

El 25 de octubre de 2014 a las 12:54, Reese Tapper <monstruoflipao@gmail.com> escribió:

MI PADRE MEGAPREOKUPADO, LLÁMALE

[redacted]

Estoy solo y asustado venid a buscarme Flatbush esquina Atlantic

REESE

Le enseñé el mail a mi padre, que dijo: «¿Flatbush esquina Atlantic? ¿Cómo ha ido a parar a Brooklyn?».

Y luego dijo: «Tenemos que ir a buscarlo».

Y los demás saltamos: «¡Pero entonces

nunca ganaremos la caza del tesoro! ¡Ya quedan muy pocas horas!».

WYATT

Y tu padre, en plan: «Chicos, voy a ser sincero: YA no tenéis la menor posibilidad de ganar. Pasa de la una del mediodía y lo único que tenéis es un recibo de taxi, unas patas hechas polvo delante de la Estatua de la Libertad y un dónut mordido.

»Os van a MACHACAR, así que venid conmigo a buscar a James para que al menos todo el mundo vuelva a casa sano y salvo».

XANDER

Eso fue un palo, man. Superpapi Tapper nos dio un zasca de narices con lo que nos dijo.

Pero a mí eso no me rompía. Porque maquinaba un plan secreto para ganar.

REESE

Xander le preguntó a mi padre si podíamos ir los tres en taxi a su casa —que está a un par de manzanas del colegio— para esperar allí mientras él iba a Brooklyn a buscar a James.

Wyatt y yo le dijimos: «¿Para qué vamos a ir a tu casa?».

Y Xander: «Plan secreto, man».

Y nosotros: «¿Qué plan secreto?».

Y él: «Dos palabras: Photoshop».

CLAUDIA

«Photoshop» es una palabra.

REESE

¿En serio? ¿No es «Photo» y «Shop»?

CLAUDIA

No. Es «Photoshop».

la lista de cosas que Xander no sabe es tirando a LARGA

REESE

Ah. Pues no creo que Xander lo sepa. En fin, a mi padre no le gustaba mucho la idea de que nos volviéramos a separar. Pero le juramos y perjuramos que iríamos directos a casa de Xander y no nos moveríamos de allí bajo ningún concepto, a no ser que se quemara la casa.

Y entonces mi padre preguntó: «¿POR QUÉ iba a quemarse la casa de Xander?».

Y nosotros: «¡No va a quemarse! ¡Solo era un ejemplo!».

Y él: «PROMETEDME que no vais a quemar nada».

Y nosotros: «¡CLARO QUE NO!».

Al final nos metió en un taxi en dirección norte y él se fue hacia Brooklyn a buscar a James. Creo que tenía que haberle recordado lo mentiroso que puede llegar a ser James y lo probable que era que no estuviera en Brooklyn. Pero estaba tan emocionado con el plan secreto de Xander que, bueno, digamos que lo olvidé.

otra decisión arriesgada de mi pad
(pero que no acabó e
incendio)

Y ahí la cagué.

CAPÍTULO 20
PARVATI HABLA UN POCO DEMASIADO ALTO

CLAUDIA

Resulta que ser tan famosa como Deondra tiene su lado negativo: cuando estás en casa siempre hay unos tipos con mala pinta y cámaras enormes rondando la puerta de tu edificio para hacerte fotos y/o seguirte cuando salgas.

tipos con mala pinta y cámaras (también llamados paparazzi)

La palabra oficial para ellos es «paparazzi», que creo que significa «fotógrafo molesto» en italiano. Frente al edificio de Deondra había cuatro cuando llegamos. No creo que ninguno fuera italiano de verdad, de hecho había uno que era francés. Y, aunque tenía mala pinta, resultó ser muy enrollado.

JENS

El francés era un buen tipo, es verdad.

CLAUDIA

Se llamaba Jacques. Cuando Jens y yo nos paramos delante del edificio, nos preguntó: «¿Estáis buscando a Deondra?».

Yo contesté: «¡Sí! ¿Sabes si está dentro?».

Jacques dijo: «Creo que sí. Un asistente ha salido a pasear al perro. O sea que el perro está. Normalmente, si el perro está, Deondra también».

«¿Qué raza de perro es?», le pregunté.

«Un rottweiler», me contestó. Lógico. Si yo tuviera a una pandilla de tipos con mala pinta rondando constantemente mi casa, también tendría un rottweiler.

Rottweiler: perro ideal para famosos con problemas con los paparazzi

Luego dijo: «¿Queréis conocerla?».

Y yo respondí: «No exactamente... Necesitamos hacerle una foto dándole un beso a este...», y le enseñé a nuestro Gato Calvin. Como puso cara de extrañado le explicamos lo de la caza del tesoro.

JENS

Yo le pregunté al tipo francés: «¿Crees que nos hará ese favor?».

Y me contestó: «Quizá. Para ser tan famosa, es bastante enrollada. Pero mejor que el perro no esté con ella».

Y yo dije: «¿El perro no es enrollado?».

Y contestó: «El perro es un auténtico _____». Yo esa palabra no la conocía. Luego pensó un poco y dijo: «Pero a lo mejor al perro no le gustan los fotógrafos».

no puedo decirlo (pq taco gordo)

CLAUDIA

Durante un rato no pasó nada, excepto que Jacques nos contó historias de paparazzi. Algunas eran bastante alucinantes. En un momento determinado nos enseñó una cicatriz que tenía en el antebrazo, y nos explicó que era de cuando una estrella del cine muy famosa le mordió a la puerta de un restaurante.

mi padre dice que no pue poner el nombre pq me demandarían

No estoy cien por cien segura de que fuera cierto, pero la cicatriz tenía forma de mordisco. Y, teniendo en cuenta lo que he leído en Internet sobre esa estrella de cine en concreto, parece creíble.

En ese momento se abrió la puerta del garaje del edificio de Deondra y salió un gran monovolumen.

gran monovolumen (no el de Deondra)
(pero se parecía a este)

Todos los paparazzi se fueron corriendo a sus vehículos —dos tenían motos grandes; otro, una bici de montaña, y Jacques llevaba una Vespa— y desaparecieron tras el monovolumen.

«¿Adónde van?», gritamos a Jacques.

«¡No lo sé!», nos gritó él. Pero antes de salir disparado, nos dio su tarjeta y nos dijo que, si le mandábamos un mensaje de texto, nos diría dónde había ido Deondra.

al número local (seguro que env
un mensaje a alguien en Franc
es carísimo)

Así que le mandamos un mensaje al número que salía en la tarjeta y, cinco minutos después, nos contestó.

MENSAJES DE MÓVIL (Claudia y tipo francés con mala pinta pero enrollado)

Hola, Jacques! Soy la fan d Deondra q acabas de conocer. Si me puedes mandar su ubicación, sería alucinantemente increíble, y t estaría muy agradecida

Zoso en West Village

CLAUDIA

Como no tenía ni idea de lo que era Zoso, tuve que buscarlo en Internet.

PARVATI

NO puedo creer que nunca hayas oído hablar de Zoso. Es, no sé… EL restaurante más *fashion* de todo Manhattan.

CLAUDIA

¿Tú has estado allí?

PARVATI

¡Claro que no! Es como imposible conseguir una mesa si eres un ser humano normal. Tienes que ser rico o famoso o ambas cosas.

CLAUDIA

Zoso es tan exclusivo que ni siquiera tiene web, así que tuvimos que sacar la ubicación exacta (Grove Street) de un artículo de la web ¡OMG, Famosos Sueltos! sobre una estrella de cine que vomitó sobre un coche aparcado a la puerta del restaurante.

NO la misma que mordió a Jacques

Cogimos un taxi —que me costó casi todo el dinero que llevaba, pero no quería correr riesgos— y fuimos hasta Grove Street, que es una de esas calles secundarias monísimas del West Village que parecen el decorado de una peli.

calle monísima del West Village

Por el camino llamé a Parvati —que seguía haciendo cola para el piano de FAO Schwarz—, porque era un momento muy grande para el Equipo Revoltijo. Y quería felicitarla por su increíble labor detectivesca.

Por desgracia, llamar a Parvati resultó ser un error épico.

PARVATI

Solo una cosa: ¡lo que pasó NO fue culpa mía!

CARMEN

¿Cómo no va a ser culpa tuya? Gritaste: «¡CLAUDIA HA ENCONTRADO A DEONDRA! ¡ESTÁ ALMORZANDO EN ZOSO!» tan alto que lo oyó toda la tienda.

PARVATI

¡Tú fuiste la que me preguntó por qué estaba dando tantos saltos!

CARMEN

¡No sabía que ibas a gritar a los cuatro vientos una información tan increíblemente delicada! ¡SOBRE TODO teniendo a Colin Hartley a medio metro de distancia!

PARVATI

Lo siento, pero ¿te imaginas haberte pasado toda TU vida adorando a Deondra y todo lo que hace? ¿No se te iría también la olla si descubrieses dónde ha ido a almorzar?

Hablando de irse de la olla, lo de Colin anunciándolo en ClickChat fue la idea más estúpida del mundo. Una cosa es ir a Zoso a hacerle la foto de Deondra, pero decirle a TODOS los que participan en la caza dónde estaba era el colmo de la estupidez.

CLAUDIA

Zoso no tiene ningún cartel ni la carta expuesta en la entrada, así que cuando llegamos a Grove Street, no hubiéramos sabido dónde estaba si no fuera por todos los paparazzi que había en la acera de enfrente.

A
Zoso
(tan moderno que ni siquiera sabes que es un restaurante)
(si no fuera por la autorización sanitaria que tiene puesta en la ventana)
entrada principal
(escondida bajo las escaleras)

Le dimos las gracias a Jacques por avisarnos y fuimos hacia la puerta, pero no pudimos ni poner el pie, porque los recepcionistas (o los *maîtres* o los de la puerta o como se llamen) nos pararon. Eran un tipo alto y superflaco con un corte de pelo megacaro y una tipa rubia aún más alta, más flaca y con un corte de pelo aún más caro, los dos vestidos de negro con jerséis de cuello cisne a juego.

JENS

El hombre dijo: «¿En qué puedo ayudaros?». Pero lo dijo de una forma que se veía que no quería ayudarnos.

Y, cuando tú dijiste: «Una mesa para dos, por favor», la mujer hizo un ruido raro con la nariz.

CLAUDIA

Eran un par de creídos. Nos dijeron que no había mesas libres y de repente apareció un matón gigantesco.

JENS

Creo que el matón llevaba todo el tiempo ahí, pero que, hasta que no se movió, yo creía que era un mueble. Como una librería.

CLAUDIA

Nunca había visto a un ser humano tan grande. No entiendo cómo encontraron un cuello cisne de su tamaño.

Dos segundos después ya estábamos otra vez en la calle. Pero supusimos que tampoco hacía falta entrar dentro, que bastaba con esperar a que Deondra acabara de almorzar y pedirle la foto con Calvin cuando saliera.

Así que nos sentamos en los escalones de una casa de ladrillo de dos números más abajo y nos pusimos a esperar.

Fue entonces cuando aproveché para mirar ClickChat y vi que las cosas se iban a salir de madre.

POSTS EN EL MURO PÚBLICO DE CLICKCHAT «CAZA DEL TESORO DE CULVERT»

Daniella R. (Las Fieras)

daniR Pero, si mide 8 cm ¿nos das al menos 2 puntos?

Akash

ZarDeLaCaza No hay créditos parciales. Una estatuilla del Empire State de máx. 7 cm da 5 puntos. Cualquier otra cosa es cero puntos.

Colin (Gingivitis)

HartAttackK01 HAN VISTO A DEONDRA EN ZOZO

daniR K?????!!!!!!

daniR K es ZOZO?

Natasha (Los Olakease)

tasha_manda T refieres a Zoso? El restaurante?

HartAttackK01 Sí

ZarDeLaCaza Lo de Deondra es BROMA! Olvidadlo ya, de verdad!

HartAttackK01 Sí, pero está en lista. O sea k si conseguimos foto son 500 p. verdad?

HartAttackK01 Verdad? 500 p. por Deondra besando a Calvin

HartAttackK01 Verdad, Akash???

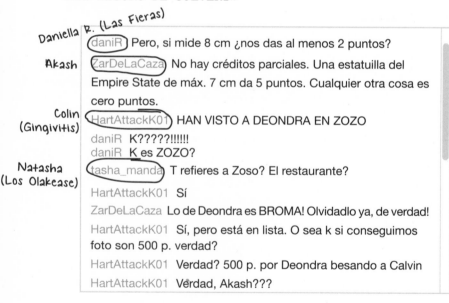

HartAttackK01 VERDAD??????

ZarDeLaCaza Un momento. Hablando con sra. Bevan

ZarDeLaCaza Técnicamente es así.

tasha_manda OMG! Voy a Zoso ahora mismo. Grove Street en West Village

HartAttackK01 No t molestes. JKopp ya casi está allí y nosotros nos llevaremos los 500 p. antes

tasha_manda K más da quién lo haga antes? TODOS podemos ganar los 500 p

AidanTheGrif Ya voy para allá.

namber_uan TIRA TIRA!!

BritSeavs ESTO ES FLIPANTE!!!!

Aidan
illers)
ucker
obos)
ittany
s Fieras)

CLAUDIA

Lo primero que vi cuando levanté la vista del móvil fue a Josh Koppelman, del equipo Gingivitis, corriendo a toda pastilla hacia nosotros por Grove Street.

Cuando se paró a preguntar dónde estaba el Zoso, Jens y yo nos hicimos los tontos. Pero se lo imaginó y se lanzó directo.

Cinco segundos después salía de allí también en lanzamiento directo. Y con cara de asustado. Probablemente por el matón.

JENS

Josh, grandullón de dos cursos más, de

pie entre nosotros y el restaurante. Si Deondra sale, él está antes.

CLAUDIA

Si esto parecía que iba a ser un problema, lo que vino después fue MUCHO peor. Porque al cabo de un minuto Ella Daniels, de Las Fieras, apareció corriendo por la calle.

Seguida muy de cerca por Natasha Minello, de Los Olakease.

Y por Luke Schwartz, de Los Molones.

Al que seguían Dimitri y Toby, de Los Caballeros de la Mesa Cuadrada.

Y después un montón de gente de los equipos Killers… Las Guapis… TQTC… Los Megaguays de Manhattan… Brigada Cuatro… Los Caballeros Oscuros… Lobos… y prácticamente todos los equipos participantes en la caza del tesoro.

Más un montón de turistas y de gente suelta que vio la multitud y, suponiendo que pasaba algo, se quedaron rondando por allí.

A los diez minutos, había tanta gente a la entrada del Zoso que empezó a haber problemas de tráfico.

Entonces aparecieron Athena Cohen y su madre, y ahí sí que empezaron los problemas.

El coche de alquiler de Satán
(en verdad, de Athena)
(no es el mismo que utilizó ella)
(pero se parece mucho)

CAPÍTULO 21
PESADILLA EN GROVE STREET

CLAUDIA

En cuanto vi que ese estúpido coche de alquiler con chófer doblaba la esquina, supe que eran Athena y su madre.

Se detuvo justo delante del Zoso, y se montó tal remolino de gente mientras el chófer les abría la puerta que parecía que estuvieran llegando a un gran estreno cinematográfico.

Ahora, el matón gigante estaba protegiendo la puerta de entrada del restaurante. Y los recepcionistas flacos estaban como encogidos detrás de él, creo que muertos de miedo ante tanta gente.

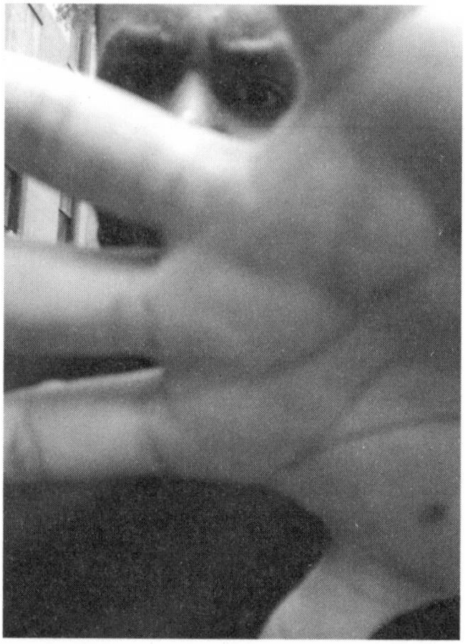

matón enorme (NO le gustó que le hicieran una foto)

Athena y su madre fueron directamente hacia la puerta y por un momento me emocioné y todo, porque supuse que les iban a echar como a todos los demás, y que sería totalmente humillante.

Por eso lo que pasó después fue para mí un chasco espantoso.

JENS

Creo que quizá mamá de Athena come mucho en Zoso. Porque chico recepcionista sonrió mucho y dijo: «¡ME ALEGRO DE VOLVER A VERLA!».

Y hombre gigante abre la puerta para que entren.

Cuando hizo eso, toda la gente se quedó… ¿cómo se dice? Ah, sí, «bocaabierta».

Jens aún no domina el idioma (pero suena adorable)

CLAUDIA

«Boquiabierta». Nos quedamos todos boquiabiertos.

JENS

Sí. Y luego Athena movió la mano. Y todo el mundo muy enfadado.

CLAUDIA

Antes de desaparecer en el interior, Athena se dio la vuelta y nos saludó con la mano.

Era básicamente su forma de decirnos: «¡JA, JA, JA! ¡MIS PADRES SON TAN RICOS Y TAN ENROLLADOS QUE PODEMOS TENER MESA EN EL ZOSO MIENTRAS TODOS VOSOTROS ESPERÁIS FUERA COMO PUEBLERINOS!».

Era el saludo más perverso y engreído que he visto en toda mi vida.

Y todo el mundo pensó lo mismo.

JOSH KOPPELMAN, miembro de Gingivitis

Yo me quedé PASMADO. ¿Cómo se llama esa chica? ¿Athena? ¡Pues menuda malcriada!

NATASHA MINELLO, miembro de Los Olakease

Yo básicamente quería estrangularla.

LUKE SCHWARTZ, Los Molones

Si tuviera que describir lo que sentía en ese momento en, por ejemplo, dos palabras, diría: «furia ciega».

CLAUDIA

Pero, por muy enfadados que estuviéramos, es MUY importante que quede clara una cosa: digan lo que digan los idiotas del *New York Star*, NO montamos ningún disturbio.

Si quieres, y apurando mucho las cosas,

puedo aceptar que montamos medio disturbio: justo después de que el saludito de Athena encendiera a la multitud. Y la gente empezara a amontonarse/agolparse contra la puerta del restaurante.

Pero entonces el matón levantó las manos y gritó: «¡HEY! ¡NI UN PASO MÁS U OS METO UNA GALLETA!».

NOTA: no es exactamente la palabra que utilizó

Al oír eso, todos retrocedimos porque no queríamos una galleta de ese hombre. Porque era muy grande, y respetábamos su autoridad.

En resumen, toda la multitud se portó muy bien.

O sea, que no había ninguna razón para que apareciera la policía. Y menos seis de ellos.

AKASH

Tuvisteis mucha suerte de que la señora Bevan no se enterara de que fue la policía hasta que la llamó aquel periodista cuatro horas después.

CLAUDIA

NO me menciones al periodista. Casi todo lo que dijo en su artículo era pura mentira. Ni siquiera lo voy a reproducir todo de tan ridículo que era. Pero, para que quede constancia, pongo un trozo:

UNA CAZA DEL TESORO ESCOLAR ACABA EN DISTURBIOS

Alumnos y padres de colegio de pago montan una algarada durante recaudación benéfica

A los disturbios que Nueva York ha vivido a lo largo de su historia (los del Reclutamiento y los de Stonewall) habrá que añadir ahora el o Disturbio de los Preadolescentes.

El sábado pasado, una panda de adolescentes de uno de los colegios más elitistas de la ciudad se plantó ante el Zoso, en el West Village. prendieron fuego a un contenedor, y al parecer un grupo de lo que parecían jugadores de polo púberes hicieron bajar al conductor de un coche que intentaba pasar la calle al grito de «¡Vamos a comer gente!», «¡Dale a tope!» y otras amenazas. asientos de primera fila en el Madison!» dice emocionado Dimitri Sharansky, de trece años. «¡Yo pasaría por encima de quien haga falta!».

«¡Todos lo haríamos!», añade su compañero Toby Zimmerman. «En el colegio Culvert somos supercompetitivos

Guerra Civil EE.UU.

derechos de los gáis

Ja, ja, me parto... (pues NO)

NADA de todo eso es cierto. Excepto lo que dijo Toby sobre lo supercompetitivos que somos en Culvert.

AKASH

¿Estás SEGURA de que no es cierto nada de eso? ¿Seguro que nadie prendió fuego a un contenedor?

CLAUDIA

¡Claro que no! Creo que un paparazzi arrojó una colilla y se empezó a quemar una servilleta o algo. Pero nada más.

AKASH

¿Y nadie hizo bajar a un tipo de su coche?

CLAUDIA

¡No! Ese tipo bajó por su propio pie del coche y empezó a gritarnos a todos porque cerrábamos la calle.

Y, como fue bastante borde, algunos de los más mayores del cole le dirigieron algunas palabras.

Pero entonces él les llamó «gamberros», subió al coche y se fue.

AKASH

¿Y no cantaban «¡Vamos a comer gente!»?

CLAUDIA

¡CON COMA! «¡Vamos a comer, gente!».

AKASH

¿Y qué me dices de lo de «¡Dale a tope!»? Me han dicho que la gente coreaba: «¡Dale a tope! ¡DALE A TOPE!».

CLAUDIA

¡Madre mía, qué sordera! Lo que decían era «¡Kale a tope! ¡Dadnos KALE A TOPE!».

Porque al parecer la ensalada de col kale es el plato estrella del Zoso. Y supongo que a los chicos del equipo Gingivitis les pareció especialmente graciosos corear eso.

ensalada de col kale
(no exactamente la de Zoso)
(pero seguro que se parece)
(aunque quizá no lleva manzanas)

AKASH

Pero entonces, si nunca se produjo un disturbio, ¿por qué fue la poli?

CLAUDIA

De verdad que no lo sé. Bueno, yo imagino que los llamó el flaco del cuello cisne.

En cualquier caso, para cuando llegó la poli la cosa ya había acabado. Porque el tipo flaco salió y gritó: «¡DEONDRA YA SE HA IDO! ¡HA SALIDO DEL EDIFICIO POR LA PUERTA DE ATRÁS!».

Al principio nadie se lo creyó, pero

cuando vimos que no quedaba ningún paparazzi, supusimos que era cierto.

Encima, para entonces Athena ya había colgado su absolutamente repulsivo mensaje en el muro de ClickChat, que fue la gota que colmó el vaso.

POSTS EN EL MURO PÚBLICO DE CLICKCHAT «CAZA DEL TESORO DE CULVERT»

Athena (el Mal)

diosastupenda Acabo d hacer UNA FOTO INCREÍBLE a Deondra con el Gato Calvin. La colgaré en cuanto sume los 500 puntos!

diosastupenda Es la mejor. TAN maja! K lástima k no la hayáis visto. Ha salido por detrás para evitar la muchedumbre.

diosastupenda Por cierto, la ensalada d kale está de muerte. No creo que me la pueda acabar. ¿Alguien quiere mis sobras?

CLAUDIA

Cuando ya nos íbamos a ir, aparecieron Parvati, Carmen y mi madre.

CARMEN

Nunca te había visto tan triste. Estabas incluso peor que aquella vez que te hiciste un esguince en gimnasia.

voleibol = más peligroso de lo que parece

CLAUDIA

La verdad es que me dolió bastante más que aquel esguince.

Vale, fue un dolor diferente. Pero definitivamente peor.

PARVATI

Yo aún no puedo creerme que me lo perdiera todo. Ya sé que nadie, excepto Athena, llegó a VER a Deondra. Pero ¿y el honor de estar en la misma manzana de casas que ella?

CLAUDIA

Ya eran casi las tres de la tarde. Y, como sabíamos que había triunfado el mal, no íbamos a matarnos ahora por conseguir más puntos antes de las cuatro, que era cuando terminaba la caza.

Así que comimos en plan superdeprimente en una pizzería de raciones de 99 centavos (4 puntos, ¡viva!) y volvimos en metro hacia el cole.

<<viva>> sarcástico

Por cierto, la relación calidad-precio de esa pizza a 99 centavos es muy clara: lleva 10 centavos de queso y 5 de salsa de tomate (que ni siquiera llega a cubrir toda la porción). En el fondo es como una corteza de pan con sabor a pizza.

JENS

Por favor, di gracias a tu madre otra vez por pagar comida.

CLAUDIA

Solo costó 3,96 $ los cuatro. (sin bebida) Pero vale.

CAPÍTULO 22
ESCUADRÓN BESTIAL: LA HUMILLACIÓN FINAL

CLAUDIA

A esas alturas, las cosas pintaban fatal para cualquiera que no fuera una fembot.

Pero sobre todo para el Escuadrón Bestial.

Tres de los cuatro miembros del equipo de Reese (James Mantolini seguía desaparecido en combate) estaban metidos en casa de Xander en Park Avenue, trabajando en su «plan secreto», consistente en colocar —con ayuda de Photoshop— a su Gato Calvin en fotos bajadas de Internet.

La idea tenía pocas probabilidades de éxito INCLUSO si hubieran sido expertos en Photoshop.

Pero es que además no lo eran.

Y su Calvin daba más asco que nada.

REESE

Intentamos lavar a Calvin en el fregadero de la cocina, pero las manchas no se fueron. Al menos no olía tan mal como antes, así que tampoco fue un fracaso total.

Luego quisimos coserle las patas y cerrarle la cabeza con grapas. Pero nadie sabía coser y no conseguíamos que la grapadora funcionara. Así que utilizamos celo. Pero el celo no se pegaba. Así que pusimos un trozo sobre el otro, lo aguantamos como pudimos y le hicimos una foto.

PENOSO
ES
POCO

Luego nos pusimos a photoshopear. Bueno, antes Xander y Wyatt se pelearon para ver quién manejaba el ratón.

WYATT

Sin ánimo de ofender, pero Xander NO tenía ni idea de lo que hacía. Hombre, yo no soy ningún experto en Photoshop, pero al menos lo he usado alguna vez. No creo que él lo haya abierto en su vida.

XANDER

Abre las orejas, man: MI idea. MI Photoshop. MI mano en el ratón.

Y MIS ganchitos.

WYATT

Cuando Xander se puso a chuparse los dedos para limpiarse el polvillo de los ganchitos y el ratón se empezó a cubrir de grumos mojados de color naranja yo me rendí: «Es igual, paso. ¡Yo esto ya no lo toco ni muerto!».

REESE

Empezamos con una foto de Deondra, claro, por lo de los 500 puntos.

Pero era superdifícil. Primero nos costó un montón encontrar una foto de Deondra en la que estuviera besando a alguien. Y nos costó aún más cambiar luego a ese alguien por Calvin.

CLAUDIA

Creo que es lo más patético que he visto en mi vida.

Sin contar vuestros otros montajes.

REESE

No eran TAN malos.

WYATT

Eran espantosos. Cuando vi lo mal que había quedado la foto de Deondra, me rendí y me fui a jugar con la Xbox mientras Xander y Reese se curraban las otras fotos.

REESE

A mí la del Flubby me pareció buena.

CLAUDIA

Si no fuera porque parece que Calvin mide tres metros de alto en lugar de un palmo.

WYATT

En serio. Parecía Godzilla Calvin arrasando Times Square.

REESE

¡Qué va! No parecía TAN grande. En todo caso, si hay que elegir un Godzilla Calvin, sería el del Cyclone de Coney Island.

WYATT

Bueno, es que esa ya era de llorar. Parecía que Calvin se iba a tragar la montaña rusa.

REESE

La del estadio de los Yankees estaba bien.

CLAUDIA

Depende de lo que entiendas por «bien».

WYATT

Parecía un superhéroe Calvin volando sobre el estadio. Un superhéroe que acababa de ser succionado por el motor de algún avión, claro.

REESE

Es que para esa nos quedamos sin tiempo, porque mi padre llamó diciendo: «Son casi las cuatro. ¡Nos encontraremos en el colegio, corred!».

Yo le pregunté: «¿Has encontrado a James?».

Y mi padre suspiró profundamente y contestó: «No... ¿Ese chico tiene algún problema?».

Y yo: «Todos. ¿No te lo había dicho?».

Y mi padre: «No, no me lo habías dicho».

Así que me disculpé con mi padre por no haberle avisado sobre James antes de que fuera hasta Brooklyn a buscarlo.

Y él me dijo: «Brooklyn ha sido solo la mitad de la historia. Ahora estoy volviendo de Queens».

JAMES Y MI PADRE (Intercambio de mails)

RE: VOY A BUSCARTE

De: soi_batman_ytuno@yahoo.com
Para: eric.steven.tapper@gmail.com
Fecha: 25/10/14 13:23:16
Asunto: RE: VOY A BUSCARTE

El 25 de octubre de 2014 a las 13:14, Eric Tapper
<eric.steven.tapper@gmail.com> escribió:
James, soy el padre de Reese. ¿Sigues en Flatbush esquina Atlantic? Si estás ahí, espérame que voy a buscarte. En cualquier caso, mándame un mensaje a [redacted] cuanto antes y dime dónde estás.

Vale, pero deprisa, hay unos tipos de una secta que me quieren meter en su furgoneta

RE: ¿DÓNDE ESTÁS?

Re: ¿Dónde estás?
De: soi_batman_ytuno@yahoo.com
Para: eric.steven.tapper@gmail.com
Fecha: 25/10/14 13:42:11
Asunto: RE: ¿DÓNDE ESTÁS?

El 25 de octubre de 2014 a las 13:37, Eric Tapper
<eric.steven.tapper@gmail.com> escribió:
Estoy en Flatbush esquina Atlantic. ¿Estás aquí? Llámame o mándame un mensaje a [redacted] cuanto antes

Sí lo siento chicos d la secta me han ofrecido caramelos y me he ido con ellos. Ahora hacia Queens en su furgoneta a jugar a una batalla d láser.

Flatbush esquina Atlantic
(James nunca
estuvo aquí)

RE: HAZ EL FAVOR DE IR AL COLEGIO ANT...

De: soi_batman_ytuno@yahoo.com
Para: eric.steven.tapper@gmail.com
Fecha: 25/10/14 13:52:54
Asunto: RE: HAZ EL FAVOR DE IR AL COLEGIO ANTES DE LAS 16:00

> El 25 de octubre de 2014 a las 13:47, Eric Tapper <eric.steven.tapper@gmail.com> escribió:
> He empezado a sospechar que no estás hablando en serio. Haz el favor de presentarte en el colegio Culvert antes de las 16:00. Soy personalmente responsable de tu seguridad.

Perdón. Lo d la secta era broma, pero lo d los tipos de la furgoneta no. Cuando hemos llegado al local de la batalla de láser me han quitado todo el dinero y se han largado. ¿Puede venir a buscarme? No puedo volver a casa y solo me queda un 3% de batería. Avenida 47 y Van Dam

RE: RE: RE: HAZ EL FAVOR DE IR AL COLEGIO...

De: soi_batman_ytuno@yahoo.com
Para: eric.steven.tapper@gmail.com
Fecha: 25/10/14 14:37:54
Asunto: RE: RE: RE: HAZ EL FAVOR DE IR AL COLEGIO ANTES DE LAS 16:00

> El 25 de octubre de 2014 a las 14:36, Eric Tapper <eric.steven.tapper@gmail.com> escribió:
> Estoy en la puerta del local de las batallas de láser y empiezo a estar muy enfadado. Los tipos de la furgoneta no existen, ¿verdad?

¡YA VOY! Estoy en 5 min. 1% batería. ¡NO SE VAYA!

local de las batallas de láser (James tampoco estuvo nunca aquí)

RE: RE: RE: RE: RE: HAZ EL FAVOR DE IR...

De: soi_batman_ytuno@yahoo.com

Para: eric.steven.tapper@gmail.com

Fecha: 25/10/14 14:53:02

Asunto: RE: RE: RE: RE: RE: HAZ EL FAVOR DE IR AL COLEGIO ANTES DE LAS 16:00

> El 25 de octubre de 2014 a las 14:45, Eric Tapper <eric.steven.tapper@gmail.com> escribió:
> James, ¿no te das cuenta de la poca gracia que hace esto? Me temo que voy a tener que llamar a tus padres.

Bueno, pero seguro k le sale el contestador.

CAPÍTULO 23
A PAPÁ LE CANTAN LAS CUARENTA

CLAUDIA

Cuando llegamos al auditorio de Culvert hacia las 15:50, Akash y la señora Bevan estaban sentados a una mesa sobre el escenario, sumando los puntos de los equipos que iban llegando.

Había ya unos cuarenta alumnos y se respiraba mal ambiente. Cuando entraron las fembots —Athena y su madre contoneándose por el pasillo como la Princesa Maldad y la Reina del Hielo, con su séquito de las perversas hermanastras Ling, Meredith y Clarissa—, se oyeron algunos abucheos.

CARMEN

Yo, personalmente, agradecí los abucheos. Sentaba bien saber que, aunque las fembots hubieran ganado, todo el mundo las odiaba por ello.

CLAUDIA

A mí eso también me animó, aunque poco.

Los del Equipo Revoltijo fuimos a que nos contaran los puntos. Akash y la señora

Bevan aún no estaban anunciando las puntuaciones, pero calculamos que teníamos 76 puntos, lo cual no era malo, pero definitivamente no era suficiente para vencer a las fembots sin contar siquiera su estúpida foto de Deondra de 500 puntos.

cosas varias que Carmen, Parvati y mi madre recogieron mientras Jens y yo acosábamos a Deondra

Por otro lado, multiplicando los 76 puntos por las cantidades aportadas por punto, salían 436,20 $, todos para el Banco de Alimentos de Manhattan, y eso era alucinante.

Así que decidí centrarme en eso en lugar de pensar que iban a ganar las fembots, que la vida era totalmente injusta y que yo había creado un monstruo en forma de caza del tesoro.

Fue entonces cuando apareció mi padre con tres cuartas partes del Escuadrón Bestial, y subieron a que les contaran los puntos.

REESE

Estábamos mitad y mitad, no sé, preocupados y esperanzados. Porque lo del Photoshop no parecía tener muchas posibilidades.

¡Pero teníamos un crónut de 30 puntos! Más o menos. la verdad es que no

WYATT

El caso es que eran casi las cuatro y sabíamos que, si James no aparecía en cinco minutos, quedaríamos descalificados.

A tu padre se le veía bastante estresado con eso. No con lo de que nos descalificaran, pero sí con lo de haber perdido a una persona entera.

AKASH

Doy las gracias a Shiva por permitir que Reese y los imbéciles de sus amigos existan, porque llevaba seis horas seguidas a solas con la señora Bevan, que se ponía histérica por todo. Necesitaba desesperadamente reírme un rato.

Y con ellos lo conseguí, y a fondo.

CLAUDIA

Lo primero que hizo Reese fue entregarle a Akash la caja amarilla de la pastelería de los crónuts, empapada. Al abrirla, Akash se echó a reír y ya no paró.

AKASH

Me traen esta caja de la pastelería de Dominique Ansel, que debieron de dejar caer en alguna alcantarilla o algo, porque tenía unas manchas muy raras y un olor NADA bueno.

Y voy y miro dentro y había un dónut con cobertura de fresa —que estoy casi seguro de que era de Dunkin' Donuts— que habían mordido por los bordes para darle una forma vagamente parecida a la del crónut.

Pero en realidad solo parecía un dónut mordido y asqueroso. Espolvoreado con algo.

Les dije: «¿Qué narices es esto?».

REESE

Le contesté: «Es un... er... ¿crónut?». Pero me costó mucho. Porque NO sé mentir.

Cierto. Reese miente FATAL

AKASH

Era para flipar. Es que, precisamente... ¡yo soy experto en crónuts! ¡Los distingo con los ojos cerrados!

Hasta la señora Bevan, que es una negada total en cuestión de crónuts, dijo: «A mí NO me parece que eso sea un crónut».

REESE

Entonces les dije: «Es que... TENÍAMOS un crónut. Pero me lo he comido».

AKASH

Yo ahí ya no podía parar de reír para hablar. Pero la señora Bevan le preguntó: «¿Por qué te has comido el crónut?».

REESE

Y yo contesté: «Porque James y yo estábamos atrapados en un camión».

Y ella: «¿CÓMO os habéis quedado atrapados en un camión?».

Y yo: «Es que nos perseguían unos hinchas de fútbol. Porque hemos ido a un bar, y...».

WYATT

Cuando Reese dijo «bar», a la señora Bevan se le salieron los ojos de las órbitas.

Y se dio la vuelta para mirar a tu padre. Que tenía una cara de preocupación, el pobre…

XANDER ← apodo de Xander para la señora Bevan (creo)

Yo vi que Beuve estaba a punto de saltar al cuello de alguien.

Y dije: «Bro, ¡hay que cambiar de tema YA!». Y saqué las fotos.

AKASH

Y entonces va el burro de Xander y me planta el móvil en las narices diciendo: «¡MAN, MIRA QUÉ FOTOS!».

Y yo miro y… ¡madre mía!… supongo que era su Gato Calvin, pero parecía que se lo hubiera comido un oso y lo hubiera vomitado, una y otra vez, y lo habían retocado con Photoshop volando sobre el Estadio de los Yankees y…

Y no pude aguantar más.

CLAUDIA

Básicamente, Akash tuvo un ataque incontrolable de risa sobre el escenario. Estaba doblado sobre la silla, con la cara roja.

Sin embargo, la señora Bevan no se reía, para nada.

REESE

La señora Bevan dijo: «Sr. Tapper, ¿podemos hablar un momento en privado?».

Se llevó a mi padre a un rincón del escenario y básicamente se lo comió crudo.

No se oía todo lo que decían, pero sí que en un momento dado el tema dejó de ser el bar y pasó a ser cómo mi padre había perdido a James. La oí decir: «¿Lleva móvil?» y «¿DÓNDE lo ha visto por última vez?».

CLAUDIA

Posiblemente, la señora Bevan TODAVÍA estaría sobre aquel escenario echándole la bronca a mi padre si no fuera porque justo entonces James Mantolini entró a saco en el auditorio. Estaba empapado en sudor y le faltaba el aire, pero gritó «¡TRES CINCUENTA Y NUEVE!». (es decir, que faltaba 1 minuto para la hora tope, las 16:00)

Luego se desplomó. No porque se hubiera

desmayado, sino haciendo cuento en plan melodramático y como si acabara de terminar un maratón.

La señora Bevan lo llamó al escenario y, después de interrogarlo —y de que él le enseñara a ella y a Akash algo del móvil—, le dijo al Escuadrón Bestial que se sentaran a esperar.

REESE

Nos sentamos y dijimos todos a la vez: «James, ¿dónde estabas?». Y «¿qué tienes en el móvil?».

Y James contestó: «Sin comentarios».

JAMES

Me gusta dar la información estrictamente necesaria en cada momento. Y esta no lo era entonces.

(ni le faltaran partes del cuerpo)

CLAUDIA

El hecho de que James no estuviera muerto básicamente sirvió para que mi padre se librara de la señora Bevan.

Pero no de mi madre, que se pasó el resto del fin de semana echándole la bronca por: A) ser el peor acompañante de la historia, y B) mentirle al respecto.

De hecho, aún no lo ha superado:

NUESTROS PADRES (Mensajes de móvil)

DOS SEMANAS DESPUÉS DE LA CAZA DEL TESORO:

MI PADRE → Después del partido me llevo al equipo d fútbol de Reese a comer una pizza

INTENTA NO PERDER A NINGUNO ← MI MADRE

TRES SEMANAS DESPUÉS DE LA CAZA DEL TESORO:

En pescadería. El salmón tiene mejor pinta q el atún. Compro para cenar?

Cómo sé q no me mientes sobre el salmón?

El pescadero me apoyará

CUÁNTAS MENTIRAS LE HAS CONTADO AL PESCADERO, ERIC?

SEIS SEMANAS DESPUÉS DE LA CAZA DEL TESORO:

En el trabajo. Salgo tarde

Demuéstralo

En serio?

Sí. Envía una foto donde se t vea en la oficina con un ejemplar del periódico d hoy

Y además declaraciones juradas d colegas

No te cansarás nunca d la bromita?

La confianza no se da, Eric. Se gana.

CAPÍTULO 24
FOTO FINISH

CLAUDIA

Cuando el Escuadrón Bestial bajó del escenario, ya pasaban de las cuatro, así que Akash y la señora Bevan cerraron las puertas del auditorio y pasaron lista.

Seis equipos fueron descalificados porque no estaban todos los miembros. Supongo que los que faltaban no estaban dispuestos a ver cómo las fembots ganaban asientos de primera fila en el Madison Square Garden simplemente por ser perversas.

PARVATI

Solo una cosa: entiendo muy bien a los que se lo saltaron. Chica, ¡todos estábamos MÁS QUE seguros de que ganarían las fembots!

Y durante todo el recuento, Athena Cohen NO paraba de restregárnoslo por la cara.

CARMEN

Athena se pasó mil pueblos de tan odiosa. No paró de hacer comentarios en voz alta, a las demás fembots, diciendo: «No sé si deberíamos utilizar los asientos de primera fila para un concierto de Deondra. Es que LA ACABO DE VER a dos palmos de distancia, me entendéis, ¿no? ¡Qué pena que haya sido yo la única…». Era totalmente insultante.

CLAUDIA

Al final, la señora Bevan se puso en pie para anunciar el nombre de los ganadores.

Primero nos agradeció a todos nuestra participación y volvió a recordarnos que la caza del tesoro era benéfica y que lo verdaderamente importante era que todos habíamos contribuido a recaudar mucho dinero para el Banco de Alimentos de Manhattan.

Es un orgullo poder decir que la gente aplaudió mucho el comentario.

Luego dijo: «Antes de anunciar los tres equipos vencedores, recordad: no importa cuántos puntos tengáis, TODOS habéis ganado».

Y Athena Cohen soltó: «¡Pero sobre todo nosotras!». Lo dijo lo bastante alto como para que lo oyera la señora Bevan.

En condiciones normales, esa conducta suele hacer que la señora Bevan interrumpa

<<momento pedagógico>> = sermón de 5 minutos (como mínimo)

lo que sea para tener un «momento pedagógico» sobre por qué no hay que ser malas personas.

Por eso nos sorprendió un montón cuando calló un momento y se mordió el labio como si intentara no sonreír.

Y NOS SORPRENDIÓ INCREÍBLEMENTE MUCHÍSIMO MÁS cuando dijo: «En el tercer puesto: ¡Diosas y Cía.!».

Durante un par de segundos, el auditorio entero se quedó en silencio.

Luego empezaron a oírse risas.

Seguidas de gritos de entusiasmo.

CARMEN

De verdad, de verdad que ese tercer puesto para las fembots fue el momento más grande de la historia de… todo. Del mundo. De todos los siglos. ¡Fue TAN bueno!

PARVATI

Yo casi me desmayo, en serio.

Bueno, creo que SÍ que me desmayé. Un segundo o así.

REESE

Fue bastante alucinante. Yo personalmente no tengo nada especial contra

Athena, Ling y las otras. Pero se habían estado burlando de todos en plan muy bestia. Se lo merecían totalmente.

CLAUDIA

Primero las fembots se quedaron con la cara a cuadros. Luego se enfadaron.

La señora Bevan alzó en el aire uno de los estuches de lápices y dijo: «¡Venga, chicas!».

estuche de lápices del colegio Culvert (normalmente la cremallera se rompe a la quinta vez que se usa) (además, el plástico es tan malo que ha habido casos de eczemas)

Entonces se produjo una breve e intensa discusión en voz baja entre Athena y su madre, porque Athena claramente NO quería subir al escenario.

Pero, al final, la señora Cohen las hizo subir a todas.

No hay duda de que lo mejor de la caza del tesoro fue recaudar todo ese dinero para el Banco de Alimentos de Manhattan.

Pero lo mejor después de eso, DEFINITIVAMENTE, fue ver la cara de Athena Cohen cuando la señora Bevan le hizo entrega de su estuche de diez centavos a cambio de los millones de dólares que se había gastado para comprarse la victoria.

cifra no real (sería más exacto decir «cientos» o incluso «miles»)

Mientras las fembots regresaban como podían a sus asientos, Parvati me dio un codazo y dijo: «¿Quiénes crees que han hecho las otras dos fotos de Deondra?».

Yo imaginaba que tenían que ser gente con padres forradísimos o superbién colocados, porque solo esa gente tiene acceso a Deondra.

Por eso me quedé bastante sorprendida cuando la señora Bevan dijo «En el segundo puesto… ¡los Avada Kedavras!».

Con toda sinceridad, me alegré mucho por Kalisha y su equipo. Aunque solo se llevaran un vale regalo de Starbucks.

PARVATI

Pues no lo demostraste mucho.

CLAUDIA

Quizá porque te pusiste a darme codazos en las costillas murmurando: «¿Lo ves? ¿LO VES?».

PARVATI

Porque, insisto, si Kalisha hubiera sido de nuestro equipo, podríamos haber quedado segundas.

CARMEN

De acuerdo total. Dirigió genial a su equipo.

CLAUDIA

Vale, vale. Cualquiera diría que Kalisha ganó la caza del tesoro.

PARVATI

DEBERÍA haberla ganado.

CARMEN

Pues claro. Yo todavía flipo con los ganadores.

CLAUDIA

Todos flipamos.

En serio, no sé cómo explicar lo que viene ahora. Me limitaré a reproducir las palabras exactas de la señora Bevan:

«Los vencedores de la Primera Caza del Tesoro Benéfica del Colegio Culvert son: ¡ESCUADRÓN BESTIAL!».

CAPÍTULO 25
SORPRESA Y CONFUSIÓN (Y PLEITOS)

REESE

¿QUIÉÉÉÉÉÉÉEN? ¿QUIÉÉÉÉÉÉÉÉÉÉN?
¿QUIÉÉÉÉÉÉÉÉÉÉN?

WYATT

¿Crees en los milagros? ¿CREES EN LOS MILAGROS?

XANDER

¡OOOOHHHHH, SÍÍÍÍÍÍ!
¡EL PLAN SECRETO, CHAVAL!

CLAUDIA

Vale, no. ESO es ridículo. La victoria del Escuadrón Bestial no tuvo absolutamente NADA que ver con los espantosos montajes de Photoshop de Xander.

En el fondo sigo creyendo que los deberían haber descalificado por hacer trampa.

AKASH

Algo de razón tienes. Pero no creo que

se pueda descalificar a nadie por intentar hacer trampa de una forma tan incompetente que no engañarías ni a un muerto.

Además, el crédito al que le corresponde: el que lo consiguió fue James Mantolini.

JAMES

Creo que mi obra habla por sí misma.

CLAUDIA

Dejadme retroceder un poco a ver si explico lo que pasó al final, porque es bastante confuso. también TOTALMENTE SURREALISTA

En cuanto la señora Bevan acabó de hacer entrega a Reese y a los burros de sus amigos de sus entradas de primera fila al Madison Square Garden, la madre de Athena subió corriendo al escenario a exigir que se repitiera el recuento.

Yo aún estaba en estado de shock —de hecho todos los presentes lo estaban bastante—, pero cuando vi levantarse a la señora Cohen supe que habría pelea.

Y decidí que, como fundadora y coorganizadora de la caza del tesoro, yo debería estar presente. Así que también subí al escenario.

Y me siguió medio colegio. Fue básicamente el caos.

REESE

Al principio no me di cuenta de que era la madre de Athena. Solo sé que vi una señora en el escenario chillando: «¡¿QUIÉN HA AUDITADO ESTOS RESULTADOS?!».

Y yo dije: «NO sé lo que significa eso, pero, por si acaso, me voy a meter la entrada de primera fila dentro de los pantalones para que nadie me la quite». Pufff

WYATT

La señora Cohen dijo: «¿CÓMO DEMONIOS HAN PODIDO GANAR ESTOS CHICOS?».

Y yo le solté: «Sí... ¿CÓMO es que hemos ganado?».

Porque, en cuanto me paré a pensarlo, no le veía mucho sentido.

AKASH

Yo soy un profesional, eso no me lo discutiréis. Los números cantaban: Diosas y Cía. tenían 216 puntos, los Avada Kedavras, 218, y el Escuadrón Bestial, 511 y medio.

CLAUDIA

O sea que el Escuadrón Bestial tenía una foto de Deondra de 500 puntos y… ¿básicamente nada más?

AKASH

Más o menos. Tenían una foto de Deondra, un recibo de taxi y la mitad de la puntuación por las fotos del Toro de Wall Street y la Estatua de la Libertad. Porque en cada una solo había medio Calvin.

CLAUDIA

¿Y al final las de Diosas y Cía. no tenían una foto de Deondra?

AKASH

Sí que la tenían. Pero fue descalificada porque en la lista indicaba específicamente «foto del Gato Calvin recibiendo un BESO de Deondra».

Y en la foto que trajeron salía Deondra ABRAZANDO al Gato Calvin.

FOTO DE DEONDRA ABRAZANDO A CALVIN
(debería ir aquí, pero Athena no me deja utilizarla si no le pago 500 $)

ATHENA COHEN, fembot/miembro del equipo Diosas y Cía. (le tuve que pagar 20$ por esta entrevista)

Vale, perdona, a ver… es que, lo siento, pero AÚN estoy sin habla. Porque todo es ¡TAN INCREÍBLEMENTE RIDÍCULO!

O sea, ¿has CONOCIDO alguna vez a alguien tan importante y famoso como Deondra?

Seguro que no. Pero yo SÍ, a muchos, ¿vale? Y con la gente famosa pasa una cosa: tú no les dices lo que tienen que hacer.

¿Vale?

O sea que si tú dices: «Disculpe, señorita Deondra, pero soy una gran fan y le agradecería mucho que dejara de comer su ensalada de kale y le diera un beso a este peluche para una foto».

Y va ella y dice: «Sí, vale». (Lo que, por cierto, ya es un GRAN logro, porque ninguno de los otros participantes de esa estúpida caza llegó a pisar el mismo suelo que Deondra, ¿vale?).

Pero entonces, a ver, Deondra coge tu Calvin y lo ABRAZA y tú estás a punto de decirle: «¿Podría mejor darle un beso?», pero va su guardaespaldas o quien sea y te dice «¡HAZ YA LA FOTO, NIÑA!».

Y luego va Deondra y te devuelve a Calvin y te dice: «¡Que tengas un buen día!», y vuelve a coger el tenedor, pues... FIN DE LA HISTORIA...

Lo siento, pero cuando pasa eso no puedes ponerte en plan: «Esto... Deondra, ¿me lo repites otra vez todo, pero con beso?».

CON LOS FAMOSOS LAS COSAS NO FUNCIONAN ASÍ.

Claro que qué vais a saber vosotros.

CLAUDIA

Oh, Athena, siento MUCHO lo que te pasó.

↑
(sarcasmo)

ATHENA

Déjalo, Claudia. No tienes ni idea. ¿Por qué no te tiras por un precipicio con tu patinete rosa?

CLAUDIA

Total, que cuando Akash le dijo por qué había descalificado la foto de Deondra, la señora Cohen empezó a gritar: «¡Esto es absurdo! ¿Qué diferencia hay entre abrazar y besar?».

AKASH

Y la señora Bevan —que estaba poniendo

su voz suave especial para padres enfurecidos— dijo: «Creo que hay una diferencia pertinente».

Y la señora Cohen soltó: «¿Una diferencia PERTINENTE?».

Y entonces James Mantolini —quien, por cierto, está definitivamente loco para enfrentarse cara a cara con la señora Cohen, porque esa mujer es FEROZ— va y dice: «Hay DEFINITIVAMENTE una diferencia entre abrazar y besar. Déjeme que le ponga un ejemplo…».

JAMES

Me limité a señalarle que Xander me acababa de abrazar delante de todo el colegio. Y que a mí me había parecido normal…

XANDER

¡Fue un abrazo machote! ¡JOTAEMO ES MI NENE!

JAMES

Pero, si me hubiera BESADO delante de todo el mundo… eso hubiera sido extraño. Sobre todo en la boca.

XANDER

¡Vaya…!

AKASH

La señora Cohen dijo: «¡Ahórrate el discurso, niño!».

Y entonces fue a por James: «Y supongo que en TU foto de Deondra sí que hay beso, claro».

JAMES

Yo contesté: «Pues, ya que lo pregunta, sí lo hay».

Y ella dijo: «Pues me gustaría mucho verla».

Aunque por su tono de voz sonaba más bien a «Pues me gustaría mucho abrirte en canal y sacarte las entrañas». entrañas = tripas

Y yo le dije: «Faltaría más». Y le enseñé mi foto de Deondra.

AKASH

Y ESO provocó el desmadre total.

CLAUDIA

La madre de Athena miró la foto y gritó «¡ESA NO ES DEONDRA!» tan alto que me hizo daño en los oídos.

Y tenía algo de razón. Porque definitivamente NO era una foto de la superestrella mundial del pop Deondra Williams.

JAMES

Eso no lo discuto. Y ya me esperaba algo de controversia sobre eso. Por eso hice la segunda foto.

Se llama Deondra Anthony. Trabaja con mi padre, y es muy enrollada. Le debo un gran favor. O mejor se lo debe mi padre. Por eso me obligó a hacerle la tercera foto.

¡ME DEBES una, GARY!
(Gary = Padre de James = Gary Mantolini)

CLAUDIA

Ver la placa con el nombre de Deondra Anthony NO calmó el enfado de la señora Cohen.

De hecho, lo empeoró.

Se puso a gritar: «¡ESO NO CUENTA! ¡Tiene que ser Deondra en mayúsculas, la famosa! ¡No te pueden dar 500 puntos por la primera Deondra que te encuentres en la calle!».

AKASH

La señora Bevan —que creo que lo estaba disfrutando— esperó a que la madre de Athena parara para respirar.

Y dijo: «Si me permite la interrupción… la lista no especificaba QUÉ Deondra tenía que ser. Decía simplemente "Deondra". Así que, técnicamente, podía ser CUALQUIER Deondra».

CLAUDIA

Esto último puso básicamente a la señora Cohen en modo rabia perruna. Se puso a gritar cosas como: «¡OH, ESO ES ABSURDO!» y «¿NO LO DIRÁ EN SERIO?». Y mi favorito: «¡LAS MAYÚSCULAS ESTÁN IMPLÍCITAS!».

Y entonces James soltó lo que todo el mundo pensaba, pero nadie se atrevía a decir a la cara de la señora Cohen.

JAMES

Dije: «Perdone, señora, yo no estoy licenciado en Derecho por Harvard como usted, pero sé leer. Y me temo que aquí tiene poca razón».

AKASH

Aquello fue precioso y aterrador. Desde luego, Mantolini FOR PRESIDENT.

Después de eso, ya no hubo más que gritos. Y amenazas de pleito. Que está claro que la madre de Athena no cumplió porque, de lo contrario, a estas alturas yo ya habría recibido una citación.

DICCIONARIO

citación

citación: f. Der.
Acto de la autoridad judicial o administrativa por el que se convoca a una persona para una comparecencia.
(que puede estar asociada o no a las fembots)

CLAUDIA

Creo que ayudó mucho que las fembots ni siquiera hubieran quedado en el segundo puesto, porque, aunque la señora Cohen hubiera conseguido que descalificaran la foto de James, el que habría ganado entonces hubiera sido el equipo de Kalisha.

REESE

Yo no seguí muy bien la discusión. Iba bastante perdido. De lo único que estaba seguro era de que dentro de los pantalones aún tenía una entrada de primera fila para el Madison Square Garden.

¡¡¡¡Y ESO ERA ALUCINANTE!!!!

CLAUDIA

Yo creo que las verdaderas víctimas en esta historia fueron Kalisha y los Avada Kedavras, que habían vencido a un equipo que tenía cuatro coches con chófer y una cantidad de dinero ilimitada. Eso sí que fue una hazaña.

KALISHA

La clave estaba en el crónut. Supongo que Diosas y Cía. creían que si enseñaban muchos billetes, la pastelería les vendería uno. Pero el caso es que solo hornean una vez al día. Cuando se acaban, se acaban. Y entonces ni con todo el dinero del mundo puedes comprar un crónut.

CLAUDIA

¿Y vosotras cómo lo conseguisteis?

KALISHA

Lo reservamos una semana antes.

CLAUDIA

¿CÓMO? ¿Y cómo sabíais que estaría en la lista?

KALISHA

Psicología elemental. Sabíamos que la lista la estaba preparando Akash, así que nos pusimos en su lugar para prever qué pondría.

Lo que no es nada difícil en el caso de Akash, porque tiene unos gustos muy claros y no los esconde.

AKASH

Eso es cierto. Mi obsesión por los crónuts es un asunto de dominio público.

KALISHA

Pero los crónuts no fueron lo único. También reservé un montón de cosas que luego no utilizamos. Entradas para la Estatua de la Libertad, un almuerzo en la tienda American Girl, una exposición especial del MoMA...

CLAUDIA

Pero ¿cómo pudisteis ganar a un equipo que llevaba CUATRO coches?

KALISHA

Logística. Dividimos la lista geográficamente según las líneas de metro.

Es lo bueno de Nueva York, que no tienes que ir en coche. El metro es perfecto.

CLAUDIA

¡Vaya, me quito el sombrero!

Aunque, ya puestos, me sorprende que no pensaras en lo de hacer una foto a una Deondra no famosa. Digo yo, con lo lista que eres…

KALISHA

Ah, pero es que sí que lo PENSÉ. Simplemente, no conocía a ninguna Deondra. ¿Tú sí?

CLAUDIA

Pues ahora que lo pienso… sí. Hay una Deondra en mi edificio.

Es que, er… no se me ocurrió.

KALISHA

Oh, vaya. Qué pena no haber estado en tu equipo. Las dos juntas habríamos, ya sabes…

CLAUDIA

Sí.

KALISHA

Pero no estoy enfadada. Me gustó mucho el Moca Latte que me tomé con nuestro vale de Starbucks. Y vuelve a felicitar de mi parte a tu hermano por ganar.

CLAUDIA

Sí.

REESE

¿QUIÉÉÉÉÉÉÉÉÉÉÉNNN?

CLAUDIA

Corta ya, Reese. En serio.

EPÍLOGO
UN MONTONAZO DE LECCIONES APRENDIDAS

CLAUDIA

Además de servir para recaudar mucho dinero para una buena causa, la caza del tesoro fue una experiencia de aprendizaje importante. Y no solo para mí.

Por ejemplo, creo que todos aprendimos que no podemos confiar en los medios de comunicación, que pueden exagerarlo todo. Así que, si algún día pasa algo y tú has tenido algo que ver, NO HABLES CON LOS PERIODISTAS.

DIMITRI SHARANSKY, miembro del equipo Los caballeros de la mesa cuadrada

¡Salí en el periódico!

TOBY ZIMMERMAN, miembro del equipo Los caballeros de la mesa cuadrada

¡Yo también! ¡Fue bestial!

CLAUDIA

Pero, chicos, ¿no os dais cuenta de que ese artículo destruyó él solito toda la caza del tesoro? ¿De que vuestras declaraciones al periodista costaron básicamente al Banco de Alimentos de Manhattan millones de dólares en futuras donaciones?

DIMITRI

Glups. Eso no lo había pensado.

CLAUDIA

Además, por debajo de los sesenta y cinco años ya nadie lee un periódico.

TOBY

¡Buf! ¡Ya te vale hacernos sentir tan mal, Claudia!

CLAUDIA

Solo quiero que todos aprendamos de nuestros errores, Toby.

Personalmente, yo aprendí que cuando se monta un equipo es muy importante elegir a la persona ABSOLUTAMENTE MEJOR para el puesto.

Y la persona mejor PUEDE ser alguien con quien estás saliendo.

Pero no necesariamente.

JENS

Yo aprendí que los chicos de Nueva York

pueden hacer un juego divertido muy, muy serio. A veces, hasta demasiado serio.

También, que si vas a una caza del tesoro mejor no llevar zapatos buenos.

CARMEN

Yo aprendí que si tu amiga te intenta enredar con una mala idea, debes mantenerte firme y negarte por completo a que traiga a su novio a vuestro equipo de la caza del tesoro.

¡NO es mi novio! (POR ENÉSIMA VEZ)

PARVATI

¡OMG! ¡Es EXACTAMENTE la misma lección que aprendí yo!

También aprendí que Kalisha Hendricks es DEFINITIVAMENTE la persona más lista de clase.

CARMEN

¡Vaya coincidencia! ¡Yo también aprendí eso!

CLAUDIA

Vale, muy bien, avancemos.

JAMES

Yo aprendí que siempre hay que leer la letra pequeña.

Y que no hay que subir a la parte de atrás de un camión.

CLAUDIA

Hablando de letra pequeña, yo también aprendí —aunque creo que es más importante que CIERTAS personas aprendan esta lección en concreto— que siempre hay un momento y un lugar para el humor. Pero no cualquiera.

Por ejemplo, «en mitad de la lista de objetos de una caza del tesoro» NO es un buen lugar para el humor.

AKASH

Yo aprendí que la gente es tonta y no sabe distinguir una broma.

¿Qué?

No me mires así, Claudia. No me arrepiento de nada.

MI PADRE

Yo aprendí La importancia de decir siempre la verdad. Sobre todo en los mensajes de móvil a tu mujer.

Mi padre también está «reflexionando sobre el equilibrio trabajo-vida» (es decir, quiere dejar su trabajo)

REESE

¿Quieres saber qué he aprendido? Que por muy mal que estés, nunca, nunca debes rendirte.

¡Porque puedes conseguirlo! ¡TÚ PUEDES SER EL MILAGRO!

Solo tienes que creer en ti mismo.

CLAUDIA

Tú ya sabes que no tuviste absolutamente nada que ver con ganar esas entradas, ¿verdad, Reese?

REESE

¡Ay! Parece que también he aprendido que hay gente que no sabe perder.

CLAUDIA

Reese: sin contar la foto de Deondra, teníais once puntos y medio. De un total posible de doscientos cincuenta.

Tuviste un objeto de treinta puntos en las manos... ¡Y TE LO COMISTE!

REESE

Si te pica, te rascas, Claude.

Pero ¿quieres saber una cosa? Y te lo digo en serio, ¿eh? Sin bromas.

Lo que hiciste estuvo muy bien, lo de crear la caza del tesoro. Trabajaste muy duro en ello.

Y es verdad que hubo un poco de caos, pero conseguiste recaudar un montón de dinero para una causa muy importante. Y SÉ que ese dinero ha mejorado la vida de gente de verdad.

O sea que deberías estar orgullosa de ti misma. Yo, desde luego, lo estoy.

CLAUDIA

Vaya… Gracias, Reese.

REESE

De nada, faltaría más.

¿Y sabes otra cosa? Aunque lo único que hiciste fue hablar mal de mi equipo y repetir lo patéticos que éramos, que no teníamos ninguna posibilidad de ganar, etcétera, a cambio de tanto trabajo duro que hiciste te mereces mi asiento de primera fila. Te lo cedo.

CLAUDIA

¿En serio?

REESE

No.

¡Madre mía, la cara que has puesto cuando creías que te lo iba a regalar! ¡De partirse la caja!

CLAUDIA

Primero cerraré la aplicación de notas de voz.

Luego contaré hasta cinco.

Y luego te mataré.

REESE

¡ME PIRO VAMPIRO!

(salió corriendo)

(se encerró en la habitación)

(suplicó a nuestra madre que viniera a salvarlo)

(algún día me las pagará)

FIN

AGRADECIMIENTOS

Trevor Williams, Yvette Durant, Alec Lipkind, Fernando Estevez, Rahm Rodkey, Dafna Sarnoff, Tal Rodkey, Ronin Rodkey, Jesse Barrett, Anna Rose Meisenzahl, Kai Nieuwenhof, Mustafa the Tailor, Liz Casal, Lisa Clark, Chris Goodhue, Russ Busse, Andrea Spooner, Josh Getzler y La Mejor Ciudad del Mundo.

RIP

La juguetería FAO Schwarz situada en el número 767 de la Quinta Avenida (1986-2015). Probablemente la sustituirán por una farmacia Duane Reade. (véase pág. 132.)

CRÉDITOS DE LAS FOTOGRAFÍAS

Copyright © Geoff Rodkey, 2015 para todas las fotografías salvo las siguientes, reproducidas con autorización.

pág. 20: Currier & Ives N.Y.

pág. 28: pop_jop/iStock

pág. 141, 142, 146, 147, 148, 149: Jesse Garrett

pág. 189: dageldob/iStock

pág. 215: imagen del fondo: wavebreak/iStock

CRÉDITOS DE LAS ILUSTRACIONES

Liz Casal: págs. iii, 1, 2, 6, 8, 13, 22, 26, 33, 35, 37, 46, 53, 60, 61, 68, 76, 88, 100, 108, 110, 114, 126, 138, 151, 154, 165, 169, 174, 177, 187, 196, 197, 202, 206, 212, 223, 233, 239, 250, 255, 261

Lisa Clark: págs. 11, 15

Chris Goodhue, mapas: págs. 6, 31, 69, 77, 95, 101, 127, 138, 157, 166, 176

El autor

GEOFF RODKEY

Ha trabajado como guionista en cine y televisión, y ha escrito libros, aunque también revistas, monólogos humorísticos para teatro y hasta discursos para dos senadores norteamericanos. Su experiencia como guionista de películas cómicas, episodios para *Beavis y Butt-head* o series de Disney Channel, le da un punto de humor a toda su obra, que le ha valido una nominación a los premios Emmy. *Los gemelos Tapper* es la segunda serie de libros que escribe para niños.

Títulos de la colección

LOS GEMELOS TAPPER

Próximamente

volverán

LOS GEMELOS TAPPER

Nuestra tercera aventura

Claudia Tapper quiere convertirse algún día en presidenta de Estados Unidos. Ella es la actual delegada de su curso, y tiene todos los números para ser reelegida. A Reese Tapper no podía preocuparle menos ese cargo... hasta que se entera de que con él podría abolir una nueva y odiosa norma del colegio. En medio de un lío de asesores geniales y malvados, amigos entrometidos, campañas de desprestigio y divertidísimas meteduras de pata, ¿quién acabará imponiendo su ley en Culvert?

¡La campaña electoral más divertida de la historia!

THE THUNDER OF THE GUNS

A Century of Battleships

By the same author:

U-BOAT KILLER

JUTLAND

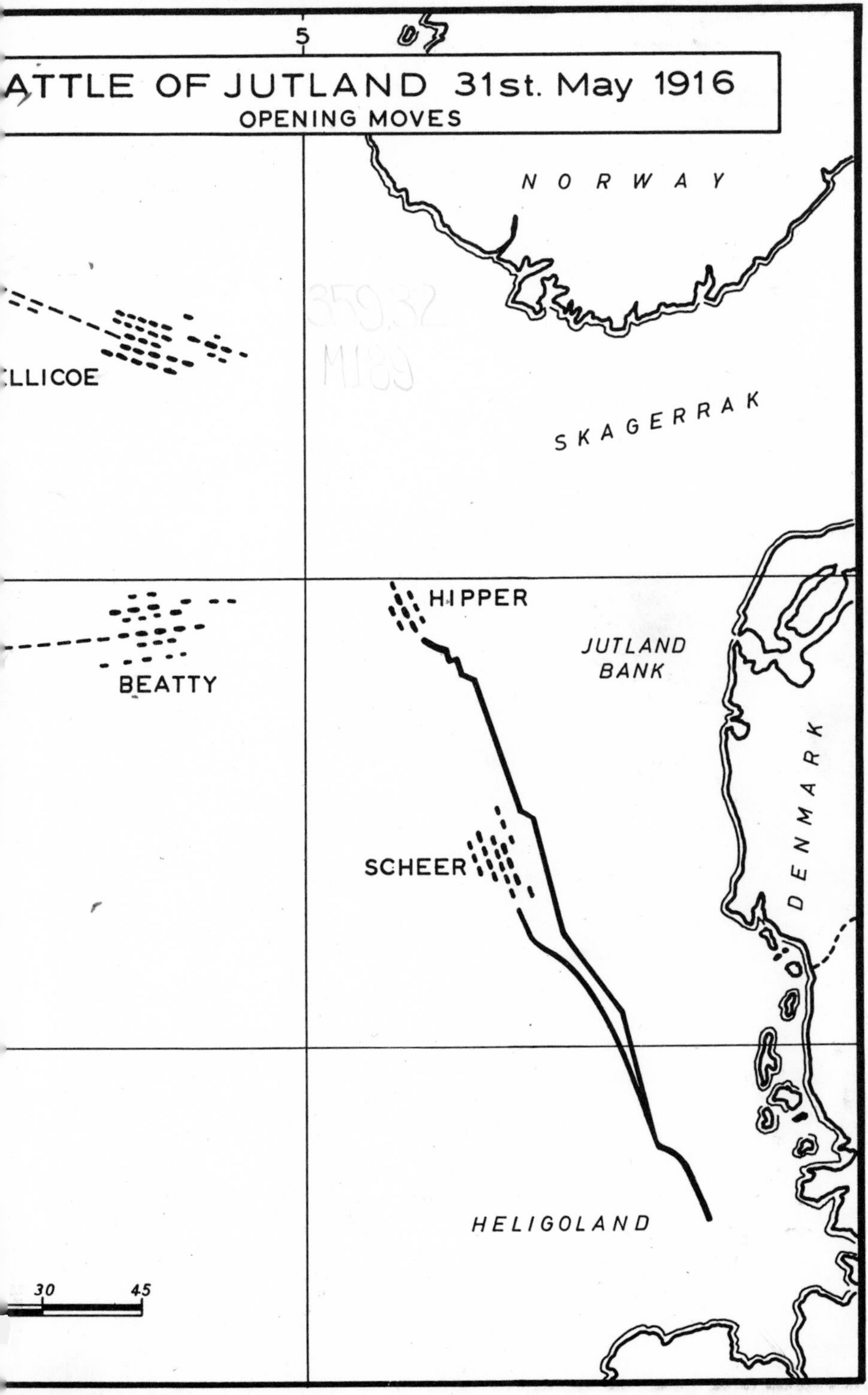
5
ATTLE OF JUTLAND 31st. May 1916
OPENING MOVES
NORWAY
SKAGERRAK
LLICOE
HIPPER
JUTLAND
BANK
BEATTY
DENMARK
SCHEER
HELIGOLAND
30
45

THE THUNDER OF THE GUNS

A Century of Battleships

by

CAPTAIN
DONALD MACINTYRE

New York · W·W·NORTON & COMPANY · INC·

FIRST AMERICAN EDITION 1960

Library of Congress Catalog Card No. 60-6276

PRINTED IN THE UNITED STATES OF AMERICA

1 2 3 4 5 6 7 8 9

Contents

Illustrations in the Text

Plates

between pages 176 and 177

I

The Origin of the Modern Battleship

THE term "battleship" is one of comparatively recent origin. Since the latter years of the 19th century it has evoked the vision of a great, broad-beamed, steel Leviathan built to mount the largest guns in existence and armoured against penetration by the heaviest armour-piercing shells, which have comprised the hard core of war fleets of the age of steam. The battleship and its function, however, have existed for as long as there have been organised fleets of warships. Any ship forming one of a fleet's main fighting formation could strictly be termed a battleship.

But it was not until wide-ranging sailing-ships superseded the oared galleys, and were built to mount cannon of ever-increasing weight and number, that warships began to vary widely in size and function. Within limits, the fewer the guns to be mounted, the faster and more handy were the designs; but unless the ships were armed with a certain minimum number of cannon according to the size of the principal ships of the enemy, they could not fairly be asked to take their place in the line of battle.

Thus warships came to be divided into classes or "rates". The main division was between those fit to take their place in the line—"line-of-battleships"—and the remainder, named variously corvettes, sloops or frigates. Such a division had long existed, but with no clear rule as to the lower limit of ships of the line, when Admiral Anson, in the middle of the 18th century, laid down that in the British fleet only ships mounting seventy-four guns or more could be so classified. Thus for the first time a clear distinction was drawn between the battleship and all other warships.

However, the waters again became muddied in the middle years of the 19th century, when the early warships driven by steam first joined the fleets of the world. The British Admiralty, loath to abandon faith in the old wooden ships of the line which still formed the backbone of the fleet, called these new-fangled contraptions "steam frigates", thereby classing them as unfit to take their place in the line of battle—though in fact, with their ironclad sides and high speed in any direction, they could face and make rings round any battleship of the day. Neither were they any smaller than the biggest three-decker sailing-ships; often, indeed, they were considerably larger.

Similarly with the development of guns of large calibre firing explosive shells, the number of guns mounted could no longer be a criterion of fitness "for the line". The destructive power and range of a few big guns could comprise a more powerful armament than a large number of guns of lower calibre, though expert opinion was by no means always unanimous in this matter, owing to the development of smaller guns with a great rate of fire.

In spite of official nomenclature, the line of descent of the modern battleship must therefore run direct from the two- and three-decker wooden sailing-ships down to the steam ironclads of comparable size. The modern sub-division of capital ships into battleships and battle-cruisers must also to some extent be ignored, the latter differing from the former not in size but in the sacrifice of some measure of armour and number or calibre of guns for the sake of speed. Battle-cruisers have usually been capable of facing contemporary battleships. The histories of the two types are interwoven, and will here be considered as one.

* * *

The sea battles of the century of almost continuous war from 1714 to 1815 established the position of the wooden line-of-battle sailing-ship as the mistress of the seas. A naval power wishing to control any particular sea area in support of its land campaigns, or to protect its merchant ships on the trade routes, had sooner or later to face the enemy's battleship fleet with a fleet of similar vessels. The victor could thereafter protect his convoys of troopships or merchantmen with certainty, for with the enemy's battleships eliminated, only frigates were left to him—and frigates could not face battleships. The loser, escorting his convoys with frigates, was liable to be overwhelmed by the arrival of a few battleships.

Actions between frigates there were in plenty, but they were minor events of the war at sea. The squadrons of stately First- and Second-Rates were the ultimate arbiters of victory or defeat; so that when peace at last settled down over Europe in 1815, leaving Britain unquestionably the leading naval power, it was to her huge fleet of "wooden walls" that she looked to retain for her her maritime supremacy. She had the ships, and she had also the large reserve of men trained in the art of handling yards and sails.

But the very hundred years during which the wooden ship-of-the-line was deciding the fate of Europe and America saw also the invention and development of the steam-engine, which was eventually to drive the sailing-ship from the oceans of the world. Though the application of steam power to driving ships was to lag far behind its other uses, a small paddle-steamer had been built before the 18th century was out, and successfully navigated by William Symington on a lake in Scotland. In 1801 Symington produced the first steamer to be put to practical use, the paddle-tug *Charlotte Dundas*.

From this time the development of steamships made slow but steady progress. The centre of activity moved for a time to America, where the name of Robert Fulton soon gained fame as the foremost inventor and designer. His renown is well-deserved, even though he quite openly borrowed the basic ideas for his steamboats from the British engineers whose work he had studied. He first offered his services and proposals to the British Admiralty, but the Sea Lords, who had just seen the triumph of the well-tried sailing ship-of-the-line at Trafalgar, could not yet bring themselves to support a development which might soon make such ships obsolete.

It was to America, therefore, that Fulton turned—to receive an encouragement already typical of the restless, ranging minds of the New World. It was in America, during the war of 1812, while British and American sailing-frigates fought ferocious duels off the American coast, that Fulton designed and built the first steam man-of-war. It was completed too late to see service in the war, but a seed had been planted in the naval minds of all nations, where it was to germinate, slowly and painfully, until with many backward looks and doubtful heart-searching, yards and sails were finally discarded. Before that day came there were many intermediate steps to be taken, each one in defiance of the old school of thought.

In the face of the discouraging naval attitude of the day, it was a commercial incentive which led to the first noteworthy steps. Fulton's famous pleasure-steamer *Clermont* soon found imitators in Britain, the first being the *Comet*, built on the Clyde in 1812. By the 1820's ships with steam-engines were making long ocean voyages; but they still relied upon a full rig of sails for the greater part of their journeys, turning only to their engines when winds were contrary, or to enter and leave harbour. By this time also the Royal Navy had begun to acquire a few small steam-tugs to assist the line-of-battleships in and out of harbour.

But this was a long way from mounting engines in warships. The very idea was looked upon with horror by the Board of Admiralty. A successful design of steam-warship could make the whole British fleet obsolete overnight. As Lord Melville, First Lord of the Admiralty, wrote in 1828: "Their Lordships feel it their bounden duty to discourage to the utmost of their ability the employment of steam vessels, as they consider that the introduction of steam is calculated to strike a fatal blow at the naval supremacy of the Empire."

This ostrich-like attitude to the problem could not long be maintained. Across the Channel, the French, with far less to lose by a revolution in naval ship-design, were listening to the urgings of a General Paixhans to start afresh with a steam navy. Stealing a march on the hesitant British, they might easily find themselves in a position to reverse the decision of Trafalgar.

In the face of this threat, during the next ten years or so, the

British Admiralty—under more enlightened leadership than that of Melville—accepted the proposition that if possible, its warships should be given steam-engines. The change agreed in principle, its practical application came up against a seemingly insuperable difficulty in so far as the larger ships of the fleet were concerned. The only method of propelling a steam-ship which had been devised up to that time was by means of paddle-wheels. Not only were these wheels extremely vulnerable to cannon fire, but their huge paddle boxes occupied the space required for a large proportion of the ships' own cannon. The broadside of tiers of heavy, smooth-bore cannon firing solid shot was still the armament of ships of war. Primitive round shells had been experimented with for some time, but until the advent of the rifled gun and the cylindrical shell, at a later date, they were to prove little more destructive and a great deal more dangerous to the user than the solid shot. If half the armament were to be sacrificed to install so fragile a device as a paddle-wheel, the value of steam propulsion was doubtful, to say the least.

Given the need for some method which would not interfere with the broadside, inventive minds got to work to adapt the steam-engine to drive a screw, a method of propulsion which had been appreciated since classical times, but which had never before been put to practical use. A Swedish engineer named John Ericsson working for the United States Navy, and Sir Francis Pettit Smith for the Royal Navy, produced successful screw-propulsion installations at about the same time.

It was not without a convincing demonstration, however, that the overall superiority of the screw over the paddle was generally accepted. When arguments for and against both methods had reached deadlock, the Admiralty staged a test which appealed to good sense and the public love of a sporting event. In May 1845 the steam-sloop *Rattler*, screw-driven, was put to compete with the paddle-sloop *Alecto*, of similar power and size.

Amidst great excitement the two ships first ran races in various weather conditions, which the *Rattler* won with ease. Crestfallen supporters of the paddle then fell back on assertions that at least for towing purposes it was superior. Thereupon the two ships were connected by a tow rope stern to stern, and a tug-of-war began. The *Alecto*'s paddles pounded the water bravely. Round the *Rattler*'s stern the sea boiled and foamed. But at first neither ship gained any way.

Then it was seen that the *Rattler* was inching forward. Her way slowly increased until finally the *Alecto*, her paddles still wildly thrashing the water, was being towed stern first at some 2½ knots. The screw had conclusively won the day.

Now the last obstacle to an all-steam navy was seemingly overcome. Such an assumption, however, would ignore the overwhelming influence in that era of the great body of sea-going officers, brought up in sail, mistrustful of the reliability of the new-fangled steam-engines and dismayed at their dependence on frequent supplies of coal to keep functioning. They resented the smoke and dirt which befouled their snowy decks and shining paint, and were contemptuous of the humble origins of the engineers, whom they had to accept as fellow officers—though not for a long time as mess-mates. The thought of depending solely on such machines and men for mobility was abhorrent to them. Though the first British battleship to be designed and built with steam-engines, the *Agamemnon*, was launched in 1832, she was still essentially a typical sailing ship-of-the-line, full rigged for sail.

Now we must consider the other great innovations of the mid-19th century in the design of warships—the introduction of armour protection, the development of the rifled, shell-firing gun and its mounting in revolving turrets, and the transition from wood to iron in ship construction. These developments are closely interlocked, the introduction of one giving rise to the necessity for another, each progressing to overcome the effect of the other in leap-frog fashion.

Armour protection for ships may be said to be as old as sea warfare, an example being the Viking shields fixed along the bulwarks of their galleys. It is from the Far East, however, that the first record comes of a ship armoured, as we use the term, with iron plates—as long ago as the 16th century. At that time

Korea and Japan were at war, and the Japanese efforts to invade Korea were being prevented by the Korean Navy led by a remarkable seaman, Yi-sun-sin. The Korean Admiral was a tactician of masterly skill, and he also displayed great technical ingenuity by constructing what he called his "Tortoise Boat". This, with its domed deck of iron plates studded with spikes, was immune to the missiles of the day, and was impossible to capture by boarding.

In Europe the use in ship construction of heavy timbers of seasoned oak, to a great extent resistant to penetration by solid roundshot, made the complications of adding an iron skin not worth while. In the latter part of the 18th century, both in France and England, experiments were, however, being made with explosive shells. Though this "ungentlemanly" form of warfare soon became common on land, it did not at first commend itself to seamen, for several reasons. A spherical shell was not very effective against the solid oaken sides of ships, and it was difficult to load safely into the old muzzle-loading cannon. To be efficient in a sea-fight the shell had to be cylindrical and pointed, to give it penetrative power. But such a projectile fired from a smooth-bore gun turned somersaults as it flew through the air, so that it could be relied upon neither to land where it was aimed nor to hit nose-first when it arrived.

With such disadvantages to shell-fire, the school of thought which condemned such a form of warfare as "inhuman" held the field for many years after enthusiasts such as the French General Paixhans had begun to press for change. By 1839, however, all navies were beginning to introduce a proportion of shell-firing guns into the armament of their ships. In a world at peace, no practical tests between the two forms of projectile were possible. Everything depended upon pure theory.

Then in 1853, Russia and Turkey went to war. In November a large Russian fleet armed for the most part with smooth-bore, shell-firing guns, attacked a small squadron of Turkish ships in the harbour of Sinope. The odds against the Turks were overwhelming—six ships-of-the-line, two frigates and three steamers against seven frigates, three corvettes and two steamers. The result would have been a foregone conclusion in any case, but the fact that the Turks had no shell-firing guns, and the speedy massacre which resulted, was ascribed largely to the results of shell-fire upon wooden ships.

The effect on naval opinion everywhere was to make the necessity for armour imperative. The day of the ironclad had dawned. Yet even now it was not primarily for the purpose of ship-to-ship fights that armour was introduced. The Crimean War was not to any great extent a naval war. The function of the French and British fleets was to support their land forces; their task was to reduce forts on the shore.

It had long been an established truism of naval strategy that ships could not successfully engage forts; but now, for a short period of history when the development of guns was at a standstill prior to the introduction of the rifled barrel, this principle no longer held good so long as the ships were armoured.

The Crimean War demonstrated the superiority of the screw-driven line-of-battleship over the sailing-ships which still composed the greater part of the British fleet. At the bombardment of Sevastopol in 1854, out of the whole fleet taking part it was only the two screw battleships, one of which was the flagship *Agamemnon*, which proved effective in the slightest degree. Now the same war was to show that the day of the "Wooden Wall" was over.

The French were the first to react to the lessons of Sinope. By 1855 they had constructed and brought to the Black Sea three armoured floating batteries. Flat-bottomed for operation in shallow water, they were bad sea-boats, and could not in any way be considered as ships-of-the-line. Steam-driven and of wooden construction, their armour consisted of $4\frac{1}{2}$-inch iron plates backed by 17 inches of wood.

On 17th October 1855 these ships, *Dévastation*, *Lave* and *Tonnante*, went into action as part of a combined Anglo-French squadron entrusted with the task of reducing the Russian fort at Kinburn at the mouth of the Dnieper. While the old-fashioned wooden ships gave supporting fire and engaged some outlying s the lessons of the Crimean War which finally broke down osition. Steam propulsion, armour and shell-firing guns en shown to be essential features of any warship. The in-g size and weight of the whirling, cumbrous engines of days was becoming too much for wooden hulls to support. ncreasing thickness of the armour required to withstand the ing destructiveness of shells was too great a burden for the den side-planking to which it was secured. Finally, the weight shock of the big pivot shell guns which were being intro-ed were setting up stresses and strains which only an iron hull ld absorb. The time was at last ripe for the emergence of the iron-built battleship.

Yet even now it required one final incentive before the British miralty took the decisive step. In 1859 the French launched the *oire*, the first of a class of large armoured frigates. There was othing particularly revolutionary in her design, which was that a conventional two-decker with the top deck removed. The eight thus saved was put into an armoured belt 4·7 inches thick. he was full-rigged for sail, but a single-screw steam-engine gave er a speed of 13 knots. Her armament consisted of thirty-four 56-pounders and two of the new, heavy pivot-guns firing shells of 86 lb. weight. Her displacement was 5,600 tons.

The *Gloire* was fast, and she was powerful. To maintain naval supremacy, Britain was bound to provide an answer. Thus it was that in the same year the famous *Warrior* was launched, the first all-iron battleship-of-the-line in the world.

She and her sister-ship, *Black Prince*, were very large ships for their day with a displacement of 9,210 tons. Their armour was 4½ inches thick. They had a speed of 14½ knots. Their gun batteries were most formidable and, with the development of rifled guns, were altered from time to time to keep them up to date. Yet revolutionary as was their design, these ships cannot be looked upon as the prototype of the modern battleship, for they still lacked some of the essential features of such a ship.

First, in spite of engines which could drive them along at over 14 knots and which, for the first time, were looked on as the

batteries, the ironclads stationed th
from the fort, and opened fire.

Within four hours, during which th
as well as shells at the French ships, the fo
after losing 45 men killed and 130 w
floating batteries had suffered only triflin
The Russian roundshot, bouncing off the
exploding harmlessly on impact, made it
that armour had come to stay.

The British Navy was not slow to follow t
first four ironclads were frank copies of the F
were followed by four more ships, *Thunderb*
Erebus, which, though they were not in any w
took a further important step towards the d
modern battleship. For they were constructed th
the first steam-warships so to be built in the wo

The fighting navies had been very slow to tak
back as 1832, despite a storm of criticism, the E
Brunel had designed and built the first large ir
liner, the *Great Britain*. To the astonishment of her
was an immediate success. When, on her fourth
aground off Ireland, she gave unwittingly an eve
vincing demonstration of the advantages of iron.
nearly a year while repeated efforts were made to sa
was finally refloated to show, on examination, astonis
damage after her long ordeal.

But governments dependent upon an annual parliame
for every penny they spent on the navy had to persuade
uninformed members of the rightness of any such revol
ideas as the change from wood to iron. In 1843 the
Admiralty proposed to lay down a flotilla of iron frigat
opposition was so fierce and so prolonged that the Admiral
forced to cancel the order. Even in naval circles there was a
siderable body of die-hards unconvinced on this vital issue, o
the chief objections being the appalling storm of jagged splin
which resulted when a shot tore through the iron side-plating

It wa
all opp
had be
creasin
those
The i
grow
woo
and
duc
cou
firs

Ad
G
no
of
w
S

primary means of propulsion, they were still given the masts, yards and sails of a full-rigged ship. Sail drill was still a major preoccupation of ships' companies; "Down funnel, Up screw. Make all plain sail" the order on getting to sea. It is often in contemptuous terms that the British Admiralty's dogged retention of masts and sails in this era is discussed. "Obstinate conservatism" sums up the verdict of the majority. Viewed from this machine age, it is easy to concur in this view.

But it must also be remembered that the Royal Navy's commitments in that age were world-wide. In every ocean of the world it was ships flying the White Ensign which played the principal and often the solitary part of policeman and law-enforcer. Such ships needed to be capable of long voyages and extended cruises in areas where coaling-stations were few and far between. It was not surprising, therefore, that naval officers of the "Up funnel, Down screw" days were reluctant to discard the well-tried and sure methods which had served their fathers in the hey-day of British naval supremacy, in favour of engines which might break down and boilers which required fuel which might not be available at the vital moment.

Coaling-stations were established throughout the world, and machinery gained steadily in reliability until these arguments were no longer valid. However, it was not until the increase in armament and armour reduced the stability of warships to such an extent that they could no longer safely carry the top-weight involved in masts and yards, or take the heeling moment of a spread of canvas, that sails were at last abandoned. A tragic disaster hastened the decision.

The other major development which the *Warrior* lacked, and which had to come before the modern battleship could be said to have been born, was the replacement of the broadside of fixed guns by the revolving turret. In the natural sequence of events, this would have had to await the advent of the iron ship which alone could support the monstrous weight of the armour, the big guns and the revolving machinery. But in fact it was in a ship of basically wooden construction that the turret was first mounted—the American *Monitor*, designed by Ericsson. Yet together with her armour, the heavy timbers necessary made the *Monitor* barely sea-worthy. Neither she nor her successors which fought in the American Civil War can therefore be considered as ocean-going warships; but as the first exponents of turret mountings, their operations will be studied later.

While the idea of mounting a few large guns in turrets was coming to the fore, instead of the broadside of smaller guns, important developments in the design of the guns themselves were also taking place. As we have noted before, the early supporters of explosive shells were disappointed with their inaccuracy and lack of penetrative power. The system of giving gun-barrels twisted internal grooves or rifling had long been understood, and was used in small-arms to give the bullet the spinning flight which so greatly increased its accuracy. A round bullet from such a gun, however, lost much of its range, so the next step was to make an elongated, cylindrical bullet. Rifles then achieved a performance which finally abolished the smooth-bore musket.

The same process was now applied to the cannon; to field-guns at first, and then to the heavy ship-borne cannon. By the middle years of the 19th century most warships had included some rifled guns in their broadsides. In the Royal Navy, the type which finally became the standard weapon was one developed by Sir William Armstrong and Sir Joseph Whitworth. It had grooved rifling, and fired an elongated shell with excellent accuracy and range for its day; but in default of a really safe type of breech, it was a muzzle-loader, the shells being awkwardly eased down the spiral grooves of the rifling.

At the time, this was not such a disadvantage as might appear at first sight, for guns were still comparatively short-barrelled and could be run back inside a turret or behind armour to be loaded. It was not until new propellant powders were invented, giving greatly increased range if used in guns with long barrels, that the need for breech-loading became imperative. By that time the discovery by the French of the principle of the "interrupted thread" brought a safe form of breech into existence, and the naval cannon assumed all the essential features of the big gun as we know it today.

Thus the early years of the second half of the 19th century saw great changes in the world of naval construction and armament. The abolition of sail, the application of armour, the change from solid shot to shell and the transition from broadside to turret were all matters of hot dispute, disputes which would finally be resolved in 1873 by the emergence of the true progenitor of the modern battleship, H.M.S. *Devastation*.

Before this, however, the die-hard, "Up funnel, Down screw" school had to be converted by a notorious calamity, the loss of the British battleship *Captain*.

The *Captain* was the brain-child of a brilliant English inventor, Captain Cowper Coles, R.N. At about the same time as Ericsson, Coles had invented the turret, and had also been responsible for other ideas which eventually became incorporated in every battleship design. His reputation was high, and when he proposed to build a ship mounting turrets, driven by steam but retaining a full sailing rig, he prevailed upon the Admiralty to allow him to do so, in spite of strong expert criticisms and fore-warnings inside and outside of Parliament.

Coles' ship was smaller than the *Warrior*, displacing 6,900 tons. By the time four 25-ton guns in two turrets with 13-inch armour and an armoured belt 6 to 8 inches thick had been added to her hull, her freeboard, designed to be unusually low at 8 feet 6 inches, proved in fact to be only 6 feet 8 inches. Towering over this low-lying hull were three tripod masts and the yards of her full rig of sails, their rigging coming down to a flying deck from which the sails were worked.

In spite of this, everyone except a few head-shaking experts had confidence in the *Captain*. True, her constructors, Laird's of Birkenhead, were somewhat uneasy about her after her trials, and recommended that the Admiralty should give her an inclining test for stability. The test showed her to be reasonably stable, but, disturbed by her abnormally low freeboard, calculations were set afoot by the Royal Corps of Naval Constructors. These, when completed, raised serious doubts as to her safety, not so much on the score of straightforward stability but on account of the fact that a heel of more than 14 degrees put her lee deck under water. There seemed a danger, therefore, that with the leeway induced by a press of sail, this weight of water might increase the capsizing force of a beam wind and sea.

These calculations took some time. The conclusions had not been confirmed when the *Captain* joined the Fleet under the command of Captain H. T. Burgoyne, an officer with the reputation of a fine seaman. In her first two cruises with the Channel Fleet the ship won golden opinions from all who sailed in her or watched her performance under sail or steam.

Admiral Symonds, after seeing her fire her guns and make good practice in heavy weather reported: "She is a most formidable vessel and could, I believe, by her superior armament, destroy all the broadside ships of the squadron in detail."

Opinions on the *Captain* were by now almost unanimously favourable. Survivors from her crew were later to testify that they had believed they were serving in the finest warship afloat. If she had been inherently unstable, the fact would surely have revealed itself to them.

The squadron under Admiral Milne had crossed the Bay of Biscay, and on 6th September 1871 was off Cape Finisterre. A moderate sea was running, but not sufficient to prevent the Admiral from visiting the *Captain* to observe her behaviour. Under sail, with steam up ready to be used if required, the ship was rolling at times as much as the 14 degrees which put her lee deck under the water. The Admiral remarked to Captain Coles, her designer, who was also aboard, that "he could not reconcile himself to such conditions", but he was assured by Coles that "there was no danger" and that conditions were not abnormal for the ship. Both Coles and Burgoyne urged the Admiral to stay on board for the night, which is proof of their complete confidence, but fortunately for himself Milne decided to return to his flagship.

Around midnight a rapid fall of the barometer brought with it a sudden furious gale. In the flagship her square sails were first close-reefed and then furled, and she was thereafter kept with her bow to a heavy cross-sea with the aid of her screw and after trysails.

In the *Captain* the sudden onset of the gale, accompanied by savage squalls, found her with her three topsails set but double-reefed. The starboard watch had just been mustered when the ship gave a heavy lurch. As she slowly recovered, there came the urgent commands from Captain Burgoyne: "Let go topsail halliards" and then "Let go fore and main topsail sheets."

As the ship began a second lurch, the men rushed to obey; but the list was rapidly increasing. Before they could reach the sheets and cast them off, they were thrown from their footholds, and many were washed overboard. Meanwhile on the poop, in answer to a question from Burgoyne, a voice was calling the rapidly increasing angle of heel. At 28 degrees she was past recovery, and every sea which hit her was forcing her farther over on to her beam ends. She was capsizing.

Trapped below were the men of the port watch, as well as the stokers and engineers. Glowing coals cascaded out of the athwartships fired furnaces of the port boilers in a deadly stream on to the wretched men flung by the list on to the fronts of the starboard boilers. Their agony must have ended when the sea came rushing down the funnel and the boilers exploded. The *Captain* had gone, leaving a launch with a few survivors and a pinnace, bottom up, to which clung a further few—including Burgoyne.

The crew of the launch brought their boat near to the pinnace, and some of the men were able to jump to safety; but Burgoyne failed to do so, and as the launch could not be brought close alongside the pinnace in the wildly leaping seas, he had to be abandoned.

Eighteen men in the launch were all who survived the wild night, eventually reaching shore to tell the tale of the last minutes of their ship.

The findings of the court-martial which, according to custom, sat to try the survivors, took pains to make it clear that the Board of Admiralty had had no hand in the design of the *Captain* and that public opinion had forced it, against its better judgement, to permit an amateur in the art of ship-construction to have a free hand. Such a thing would never be allowed again.

But in spite of Captains Coles' failure in that difficult field, for which he paid with his life and that of 472 men, he had at least convinced everyone that turret mountings had come to stay. If either turrets or a full rig of sail had to go, it must be the latter. The way was at last clear for the first true prototype of the modern battleship. In 1873, H.M.S. *Devastation*, a turreted battleship, screw-driven, armoured, but with a solitary signal mast only, joined the Fleet.

2

Turret and Ram

WHILE the great transformation of battleship-design was proceeding in Europe, its pace adjusted to a process of trial and error in the slow-moving times of peace, in America the latest fashions in warship-design were being put to the test in actual warfare.

In 1861, at the opening of the American Civil War, the dividing-line between Northern and Southern territory on the east coast ran through Hampton Roads, the broad estuary formed by the junction of the James, Elizabeth and Nansemond rivers. On the south side, a few miles up the Elizabeth River, was the Confederate naval base of Norfolk, with fortifications on the southern shore of the Roads, of which the principal strong-point was at Sewell's Point, commanding most of the waters of the estuary. The far side was in Federal hands, and ships of the Northern navy could therefore lie in safety close in shore under the protection of the batteries at Newport News and of Fortress Monroe at the mouth.

At the opening of the war the United States Navy was a small force composed largely of obsolete wooden sailing-ships with a few steam-and-sail ships, most of which were on foreign stations. None of its ships was armoured. The Confederates, however, were even worse off. They possessed a much smaller ship-building capacity, especially in iron, with which to even the odds. The Federal ships stationed at Newport News to guard against any excursion by Confederate warships up Chesapeake Bay and the Potomac against the capital city of Washington seemed therefore in no great danger of attack.

But across the water, work was going on which was to alter

the situation. A wooden frigate of the United States Navy, the *Merrimac*, had been burnt and scuttled at Norfolk when the naval base was occupied by the Confederate forces. The hull was raised, and was found to be little damaged, while the engines also were capable of repair. Ingenious hands at once set to work to convert her into the first armoured American ship and the first warship to discard masts and sails.

The hull cut down, and a heavy timber deck was laid over the existing berth deck. On this was erected a casemate with sides sloping inwards to support a strong flat deck 20 feet wide. The walls were of 12-inch timbers covered by oak planks 4 inches thick and armoured with two layers of iron plates, each layer 2 inches thick. These walls projected down and out over the sides of the hull, like the eaves of a house, to protect the hull—which was itself plated with 1-inch iron for two feet below the deck.

Through ports in the casemate walls on each side grinned the muzzles of three 9-inch, smooth-bore guns and a 6-inch, rifled pivot-gun, all firing explosive shells, while fore and aft were two more 7-inch, rifled guns which could be trained on the keel-line or on to either beam. As a final weapon of offence, a cast-iron ram was bolted to her prow, projecting a distance of 2 feet below the water-line.

Though the ingenious adaptors of the *Merrimac* took the bold step forward of relying solely on steam-engines to propel her, it is unlikely that they ever envisaged her as a sea-going craft. Her reconditioned engines were incapable of driving her at more than 2 or 3 knots. Whether with more powerful engines she could have faced the open sea is open to doubt, but actually she was never called upon to make that attempt.

News of this Confederate naval activity soon reached the United States Navy Department. The old-fashioned wooden ships in Hampton Roads guarding the capital would never be able to stand up to such a ship as the *Merrimac*. In great haste, John Ericsson was commissioned to design and build a ship which could do so.

Ericsson was an early supporter of the turret idea, and so the ship which he designed, the *Monitor*, was naturally built round such a mounting. Like the *Merrimac*, she relied solely upon a steam-engine driving a screw. This gave her a speed of some 5 knots. Her low wooden hull was armoured down to the waterline with five layers of 1-inch iron plate, projecting out from the hull as protection against being rammed. But there the similarity ended.

On her heavily timbered and iron-shod deck was mounted a single revolving turret containing two 11-inch, smooth-bore guns firing solid shot weighing 170–180 lb. Made of eight layers of 1-inch iron, the turret was 20 feet inside diameter and 9 feet high. Except for her funnel and ventilating tubes, which could be unshipped for battle, the only other projection above the *Monitor's* deck was a pilot house or conning tower made of 9-inch iron logs and built in the manner of a log cabin, with ⅝-inch eye-slits for captain and steersman.

With a freeboard of barely 1 foot the *Monitor* resembled nothing so much as a steam-driven raft, and it was not surprising that her sea-keeping qualities were low. But the threat which she was built to meet was one which was likely to deploy only in the sheltered waters of rivers and estuaries as the navies of North and South brought support to their land forces. There was no possibility of blue-water fights between the opposing fleets. Furthermore, the threat was an urgent one. Speed in completion of the *Monitor* was paramount if the *Merrimac* were not to achieve a domination of the Chesapeake Bay area and menace the capital.

Owing to bureaucratic delay, it was not until October 1861 that the contract with Ericsson was finally signed, but from that moment the work of construction was pressed with feverish energy. The hull was launched on 30th January. On 6th March 1862, the *Monitor* sailed from New York for the south, in tow of a tug.

It was none too soon; for even as the *Monitor* was experiencing her first alarming encounter with the open sea, final preparations for the *Merrimac's* first sortie were being made at Norfolk. At noon on 8th March, look-outs in the Federal warships anchored along the north shore of Hampton Roads reported a dense column of smoke to the southward, evidently from steam-ships emerging from the Elizabeth River.

The Federal ships concerned were the steam-frigates *St. Lawrence*, *Roanoke* (flagship of Admiral Marston) and *Minnesota*; the sailing-frigate *Congress* and the sloop-of-war *Cumberland*, anchored in that order at wide intervals along the edge of shoal water between Fortress Monroe and Newport News.

The *Merrimac* was on her way out with orders to carry out steam trials only; but Captain Franklin Buchanan, in command, and his excited crew were determined not to miss such a golden opportunity to strike a blow for their cause. The sloping sides of the great ironclad casemate had been slushed down to assist in the deflection of enemy shot, and all was ready for battle. Buchanan therefore steered directly for Newport News and the *Congress* and *Cumberland* anchored one each side of the point.

At the majestic pace which was all she was capable of, with black smoke pouring from her funnel, the *Merrimac* crept forward. As she drew abreast of the *Congress*, smoke erupted all along the side of the Northern frigate as a broadside crashed out. A moment's pause as the solid cannon-balls flew through the air was followed by a rattle as they struck the *Merrimac*'s casemate. The slush sizzled and smoked but the shots flew harmlessly off. Then it was the *Merrimac's* turn. At point-blank range every shell from her broadside struck home in the wooden hull of the *Congress*. Satisfied for the moment with the damage done, and while his guns were being reloaded, Buchanan steamed steadily on to engage the *Cumberland*, which had been making ineffectual efforts to damage the *Merrimac* with her heavy pivot-guns.

A broadside into the little *Cumberland* and then Buchanan turned his ship until she was heading straight at her. A shell from his bow rifled gun killed or wounded most of the crew of the *Cumberland*'s after pivot-gun. Buchanan was impatient to make an end; ponderously the *Merrimac* drove on, and thrust her ram into the *Cumberland*'s side.

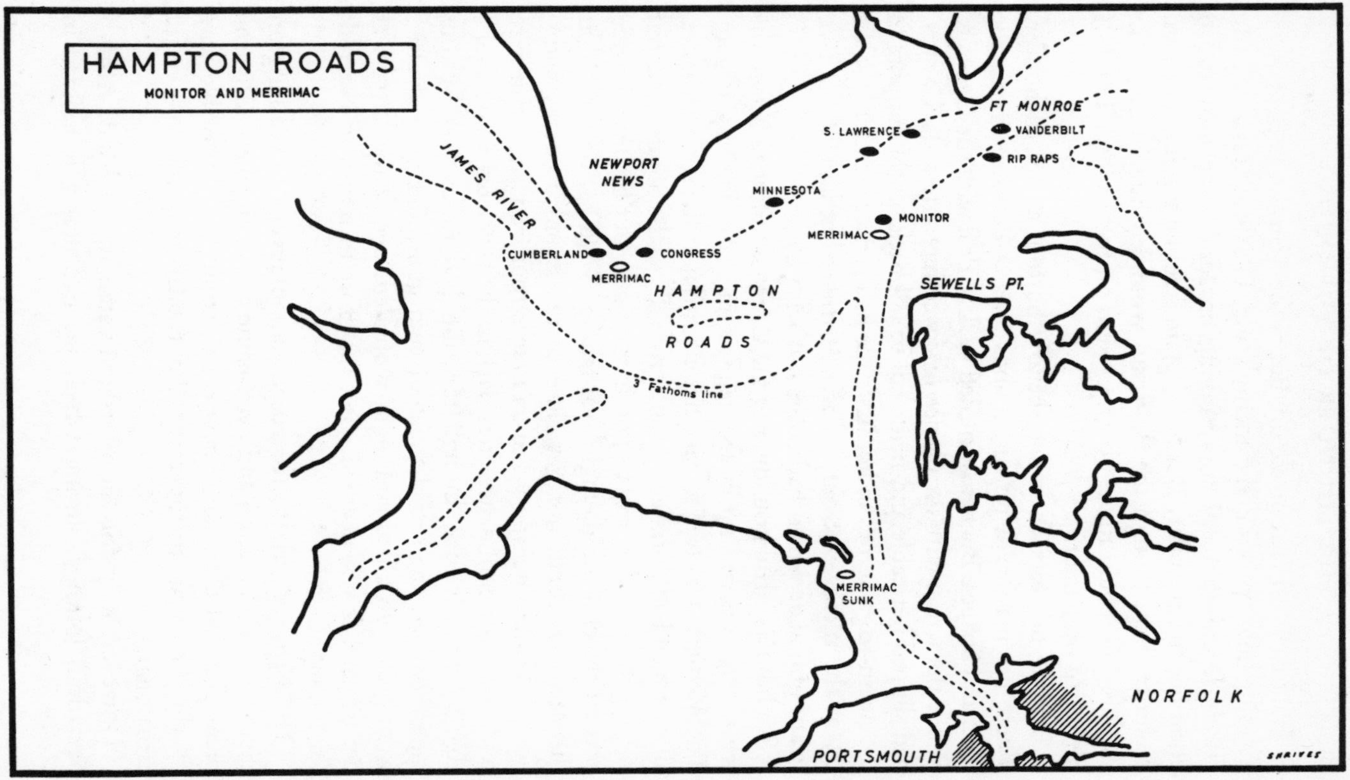
HAMPTON ROADS
MONITOR AND MERRIMAC
JAMES RIVER
NEWPORT NEWS
CUMBERLAND
MERRIMAC
CONGRESS
MINNESOTA
S. LAWRENCE
FT MONROE
VANDERBILT
RIP RAPS
MONITOR
MERRIMAC
HAMPTON
ROADS
3 Fathoms line
SEWELLS PT.
MERRIMAC SUNK
NORFOLK
PORTSMOUTH
SHRIVES

The makeshift ram broke off, but as the *Merrimac* backed away a gaping hole was left in the enemy's side. The sloop was obviously doomed, and after one more raking broadside Buchanan called upon her to surrender. But her captain resolutely refused to haul down his flag, though the dead and wounded littered his decks and his guns could make no impression on the armoured hull of his weird opponent.

Leaving her to sink to the shallow bottom at her anchorage, where her mastheads remained above water defiantly flying the Stars and Stripes, Buchanan turned back to deal with the *Congress*. While the action with the *Cumberland* was in progress, the *Congress* had slipped her cable and made sail to fall back on the support of the steam-frigates, but in her haste she had run aground. Now she lay at the mercy not only of the *Merrimac* but also of the two steam-gunboats which had come out with her.

An hour's fearful pounding of the *Congress* followed before the white flag was run up in the helpless and now burning frigate. The *Merrimac* was free to turn her attention to the steam-frigates, all of which had "prudently run aground", as the Southerners put it, on getting under way to join in the fight. But by now the tide was on the ebb and daylight was fading. With her deep draught the *Merrimac* could not get close to the stranded enemy ships, nor could the underpowered and cumbrous ironclad manœuvre with sufficient confidence after dark in the restricted water available to her. Besides, though the ship had suffered no serious injury beyond the disablement of two guns, and her casualties were only two killed and eight wounded, one of the latter was her captain. It was deemed wiser therefore to return to Norfolk for the night.

The *Merrimac*'s trial run had been a notable event. In Washington there was consternation and even panic as the Northern Government pictured the strange new craft making her irresistible way to the Potomac to overawe the capital with her powerful armament.

However, help for the Northern cause was at hand. After a hazardous journey, during which she had nearly foundered in heavy weather, the *Monitor* had rounded Cape Henry at 4 o'clock that afternoon; and hearing the distant thudding of the guns, her commander, Captain J. W. Worden, had hurried on to Hampton Roads. It was by the light of the flames of the burning *Congress* that Admiral Marston had his first sight of the strange craft that was to save his squadron from destruction—destruction which had seemed inevitable.

The Confederates also saw the new arrival. When Lieutenant Catesby Jones took the *Merrimac* out the following morning to renew the fight, he was under no delusion that he was going to have things all his own way. His first objective was the steam-frigate *Minnesota*, aground to the eastward of Newport News; but hardly had he had time to hurl a couple of broadsides at her when the *Monitor* arrived and ranged up alongside her much larger opponent.

Placing his ship with great deliberation at point-blank range, Worden gave the order to Lieutenant Greene, his executive officer in charge of the turret, to open fire. So began a strange, slow-moving fight which was to continue until well into the afternoon. Every seven or eight minutes one of the *Monitor*'s huge 11-inch guns spoke out and sent a solid ball slamming against the *Merrimac*'s sloping casemate; but though they split and broke some of the iron plates, they bounced off without penetration. At intervals of a quarter of an hour the *Merrimac* in return, manœuvring ponderously to bring her guns to bear on her circling opponent, would send a broadside of explosive shells which burst harmlessly on the *Monitor*'s armour.

Weaknesses in the design of each ship soon came to light. The *Merrimac*, her funnel shot away and steam-pipe riddled, could not keep steam pressure for her engines, and twice drifted aground—while her lighter draught opponent steamed round her, seeking in vain to find a weak point in her armour. In the *Monitor*, Lieutenant Greene found that the training engine for the turret was hard to start and harder still to stop at the right moment, so that he was forced to fire as the gun was swinging across the target.

Captain Worden steered the more manœuvrable *Monitor* to ram the *Merrimac*, but failed by a bare 2 feet to strike her stern. Jones, equally frustrated by his inability to damage the *Monitor* by gunfire, retaliated with a similar manœuvre. He proved more skilful than his antagonist, but at the last moment the *Monitor* was slewed so that she received only a glancing blow which did her no damage, while the sharp edge of her armoured belt cut into the *Merrimac*'s bow, starting a bad leak.

While the two ships were actually touching one another, Lieutenant Greene got away a round which broke the armour plate of the *Merrimac* and bulged the wood backing inwards; but still the ball did not penetrate. Except for the misfortune of her torn bow, which was temporarily plugged, the *Merrimac* could be said to be having the better of the fight, for while engaging the *Monitor* with one broadside she was still able from time to time to use her other broadside to do considerable damage to the grounded *Minnesota*.

Now there came a lull. In the *Monitor* the ammunition in the turret was exhausted, and Worden therefore drew off into shoal water where the Confederate ship could not follow, while a fresh supply was hoisted up from the magazine. The Southerners were astonished and jubilant, thinking that their opponent had given up the fight and retreated; but an hour later they saw the *Monitor* steaming back to renew the action.

However, the interval had given Catesby Jones time for thought. As his enemy came into range again, he ordered his gunners to concentrate on the *Monitor*'s conning tower. Almost at once, a shell striking square on to the eye-slit through which Captain Worden was looking wounded him fearfully in the face and temporarily blinded him. Though stunned and in terrible pain, Worden managed to give the order to sheer off until Lieutenant Greene could take over command from him.

Once more this strange fight ceased. This time each side believed the other had given up, and before the *Monitor* could get back into action the *Merrimac* had turned for Norfolk to patch up her injuries.

In spite of the prolonged bombardment each had endured at point-blank range, neither had suffered serious damage. Forty-one times the 11-inch shots of the *Monitor* had slammed against the *Merrimac*. All her boats were shot away and her funnel and steam-pipes riddled; but she was still fit to fight, and had only eleven men wounded. The *Monitor*, a smaller and more difficult target, had received twenty-two shell hits, but was virtually unharmed, and had had only half a dozen casualties.

The battle had been inconclusive, and was never renewed because on the two latter occasions when the *Merrimac* came out to fight, the *Monitor* refused action on strict orders from Congress. The orders were probably wise. The *Monitor* was all that stood between the apparently irresistible *Merrimac* and the United States capital. While the Northern ironclad remained fit for action, the *Merrimac* was pinned down in Hampton Roads.

The brief but notable careers of both ships had not long to run. On the evacuation of Norfolk by the Southern forces in May of the same year, the *Merrimac* had once again to be scuttled and burnt to prevent her falling into the hands of the enemy. The *Monitor* survived until the following January, when she foundered while on passage under tow to Beaufort in North Carolina. She was followed, however, by several similar craft of improved design which played an important part in the naval operations of the Civil War.

These ships were never to be pitted against anything so formidable as the *Merrimac*, but the battle of Hampton Roads was to have a great influence on naval construction and tactics throughout the world. The imperviousness of armour to both the shot and shell of the day, whether fired from smooth-bore or rifled guns, gave a strong impetus to the search for improved weapons, and hastened the retirement of wooden men-of-war everywhere.

Perhaps the most noteworthy result of the battle was the emergence of a belief in the importance of the ram, which was to dominate the tactics followed in a famous sea-fight four years later. Given the short effective range of the guns of the 1860's and the difficulty of inflicting serious damage on armoured ships with them, the tactics of ramming were to prove sound when put to the test on that occasion.

* * *

The battle in which the new tactics of the ram were to be effectively demonstrated took place in 1866 off the island of Lissa in the Adriatic. As it was the only large-scale sea-fight of the steam age in which the protagonists deliberately sought to ram each other, it merits study in some detail.

In 1866 Bismarck's Prussia had gone to war with Austria-Hungary. As she was to do again in 1915 and 1940, Italy had joined the side which she believed could help her to satisfy her territorial ambitions—in this case the acquisition of Venice from Austria. Control of the Adriatic thus came to be disputed between the Italian and Austrian navies.

The Italian fleet was a great deal more powerful than its opponent. Its armoured squadron consisted of twelve ships, mostly quite new, and was backed by seven wooden screw-frigates and some smaller craft. Of the armoured squadron, the two largest, the *Re D'Italia* and the *Re Di Portogallo*, which had recently been acquired from their American builders, mounted two 8-inch and two 10-inch Armstrong rifled guns respectively, as well as batteries of fifteen 6·3-inch weapons of the same type on each broadside. Five further armoured ships, *Maria Pia*, *Castelfidardo*, *Ancona*, *San Martino* and *Principe Carignano* had broadsides of 6·3-inch rifles, and there were two smaller armoured ships, *Palestro* and *Varese*.

There were three further armoured ships, designed in the light of the lessons learnt from the *Monitor-Merrimac* battle. Each had a built-in ram. Two, the *Formidabile* and the *Terribile*, were small ships with central batteries of sixteen 6·3-inch rifles behind armour. The third, the *Affondatore*, designated a "turret-ram", of 4,070 tons, was still on her way from the builders in England, but was daily expected to join the Italian fleet lying at Taranto.

The Austrian armoured squadron also contained two new ships, *Erzherzog Ferdinard Max* and *Hapsburg*, but the big Krupp breach-loading rifles which they were designed to mount had not been delivered when war broke out, and the Prussians had naturally held them up. In their place the Austrian ships had to make do with an old-fashioned broadside of 56-pounder, smooth-bore cannon, almost useless against armour. The remainder of the squadron consisted of five smaller broadside ships with a mixed armament of Krupp 64-pounder, breech-loading rifles and 56-pounder smooth-bores.

As in the Italian fleet, besides these armoured ships there were a number of old, screw-propelled wooden ships, small gunboats and steamers. On the face of it, the odds against the Austrian fleet were crippling, and the consequences of an encounter with the Italians a foregone conclusion. However, the inequality in material strength was compensated for by the lack of resolution of the elderly Italian admiral, Count Carlo Pellion di Persano, who was facing the young and energetic von Tegetthoff, in command of the Austrian fleet. Tegetthoff had already proved himself a fearless and thrusting sea-commander in the war against Denmark two years earlier.

Both admirals were imbued with a belief in the principle of the close-pressed attack and the use of the ram. Indeed, with the weapons and armour of the day, no other tactics could hope to achieve much. But whereas Tegetthoff, though his ships were not built with a ram, had the resolution to force such tactics and the determination to use them, Persano favoured them in theory but was too indecisive to put them into practice.

Ordered to sea to seek out and engage the Austrian fleet, Persano simply moved his fleet from Taranto to Ancona, where he sat down to await the arrival of the *Affondatore*, without which he deemed it imprudent to seek battle. Even when Tegetthoff appeared off the port offering battle with his weaker fleet, Persano refused to be drawn.

By July, the end of the war was in sight; Prussia had decisively defeated Austria at the battle of Sadowa on the 3rd. Italy had played an inglorious part in the war on land, being soundly beaten by the Austrians at Custozza. Prestige and the desire for an honourable place at the peace conference both demanded a victory at sea, for which the Italians seemed well-equipped.

Unable to induce their chosen admiral to force a pitched battle with the Austrian fleet, the Italian Government decided to send their fleet to capture the small island of Lissa off the Dalmatian coast. Persano accordingly put to sea on 16th July with the whole of his armoured force except the missing *Affondatore*, escorting a convoy consisting of his wooden ships and a mixed force of gun-boats and transports carrying the troops for a landing.

Though the attack on Lissa was very sure to bring Tegetthoff pounding south from Pola to engage the Italian fleet, an eventuality for which Persano had shown himself to have no relish, the Italian admiral could not bring himself to act with the vigour necessary to complete the capture quickly. A leisurely bombardment on the 18th failed to silence the Austrian forts, and no attempt to land the troops was made. By the end of the next day, during which the much-prized *Affondatore* at last joined Persano, both ammunition and coal were running short in the Italian ships. Preparations were, however, made to land the troops on the following day.

At 8 o'clock on the next morning, the look-out vessel *Esploratore* came tearing into sight of Persano's fleet, which was dispersed along the coast ready to renew the bombardment. A string of flags was whipping at her mast. As she drew nearer the signal was read, "Suspicious vessels west north-west." That they were the Austrian fleet was in no doubt, for the Italian admiral had had warning that Tegetthoff had promised the garrison of Lissa that he would come to their aid. Persano found himself committed to a battle he did not want, with his fleet in disarray and his retreat to the west cut off.

Persano lacked almost every attribute of the successful sea-commander in war except personal courage. Setting a bold face on things he called on his armoured ships to join him, and bore away towards the approaching enemy. By 9 o'clock nine of them were in line ahead, with the flagship *Re D'Italia* leading the centre division of three ships, *Re D'Italia Palestro* and *San Martino*.

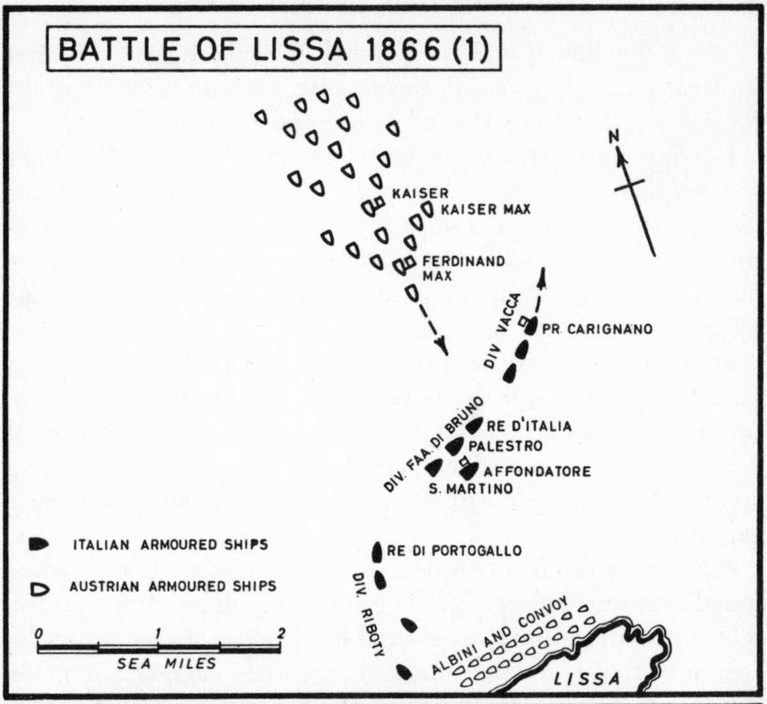
BATTLE OF LISSA 1866 (1)
N
KAISER
KAISER MAX
FERDINAND MAX
DIV VACCA
PR. CARIGNANO
DIV. FAA. DI BRUNO
RE D'ITALIA
PALESTRO
AFFONDATORE
S. MARTINO
ITALIAN ARMOURED SHIPS
AUSTRIAN ARMOURED SHIPS
RE DI PORTOGALLO
DIV. RIBOTY
ALBINI AND CONVOY
0
1
2
SEA MILES
LISSA

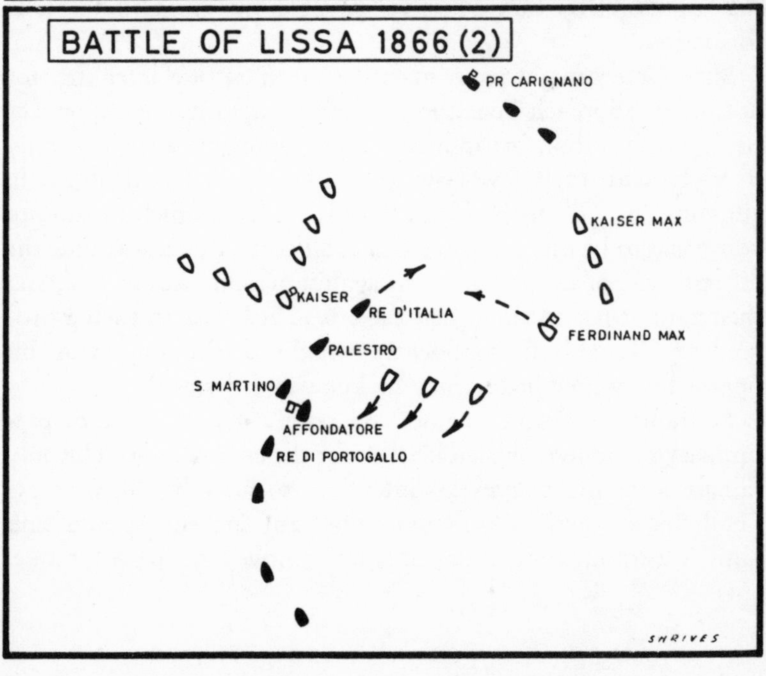
BATTLE OF LISSA 1866 (2)
PR CARIGNANO
KAISER MAX
KAISER
RE D'ITALIA
FERDINAND MAX
PALESTRO
S. MARTINO
AFFONDATORE
RE DI PORTOGALLO
SHRIVES

Leading the line was Rear-Admiral Vacca's division, *Principe Carignano*, *Castelfidardo* and *Ancona*; bringing up the rear were the *Re di Portogallo*, *Maria Pia* and *Varese* under Captain Riboty.

Having been given no station in the organisation, *Affondatore* was keeping pace with and abreast of the centre division. Of the two remaining armoured ships, the *Terribile* was some way astern trying to catch up, while the *Formidabile*, almost out of ammunition, had steamed away home to replenish and to repair damage suffered at the hands of the forts.

It was in this formation that the Italian fleet was waiting when the enemy hove over the horizon. At this moment the Italian admiral suddenly decided to transfer his flag to the *Affondatore*. As the *Re D'Italia* stopped engines for the purpose, the leading division failed to conform and drew somewhat away, leaving a gap in the Italian line.

Meanwhile the Austrian fleet drew plainly into sight, heading straight for the Italian centre. Tegetthoff's cruising formation was with his ships in three arrow-head lines astern of each other, his armoured ships in the first line. As he wanted a close-action mêlée, making use of the ram whenever possible, this was also his battle formation.

Such tactics might seem suicidal to seamen of a later age, for during the approach Tegetthoff's leading ships must be exposed to fire from the whole broadsides of their opponents while able only to reply with their few bow guns. He was in fact deliberately allowing his "T" to be crossed, a proceeding which in time to come was to be one to be avoided at all costs. But at this time the effectiveness of most naval guns against armour was so low, and their rate of fire so slow, that there was little risk in such a proceeding. Tegetthoff confidently sought a decision with his opponents, whose inefficiency he knew and despised.

Without a moment's pause, and with a total absence of preliminary manœuvre, he led his fleet for the enemy's line. The only signals needed to convey his intentions to his subordinates were "Full Speed" and "Armoured ships ram the enemy and sink him". Steamships of that day invariably moved in a pall of smoke, and no doubt Tegetthoff did not at first see the gap which had opened in the enemy line, although Baron Sterneck, his flag-captain, had climbed into the shrouds of the flagship *Ferdinand Max* to con her into action. When Tegetthoff did see the gap it was too late.

His armoured squadron thus passed ahead of the *Re D'Italia* without seriously joining action. Three of his ships swung round to engage the Italian centre on the far side on opposite courses. Tegetthoff himself, seeing the leading Italian division haul round to port to attack the Austrian wooden ships in the rear, turned back with the flagship and the *Kaiser Max*, *Salamander* and *Hapsburg* to counter this move.

On completion of his turn, however, he found himself abreast the *Re D'Italia* and *Palestro*. Charging into the fray he made two attempts to ram, but succeeded only in delivering glancing blows to each of them. As he drew off for a further attempt, a shell from an Austrian ship got home in the stern of the *Palestro*, starting a raging fire and forcing her to quit the line while efforts were made to master it. At the same time the steering gear of the *Re D'Italia* was damaged and she swung round out of control. As she did so, her captain, Count Faa di Bruno, saw an Austrian armoured ship across his path through the smoke pall ahead of him. On his beam was the *Ferdinand Max* steering straight for him.

What passed through di Bruno's head at this moment will never be known. It would seem that he was not conditioned to an instinctive use of the ram when opportunity offered, and shrank from collision with the ship ahead of him. He rang his engines to go astern, and brought his ship to a standstill. As she lay motionless, a sitting target, the *Ferdinand Max*, moving at a speed of $11\frac{1}{2}$ knots, drove her stem with a destructive crash into the Italian's engine-room on the port side, rolling her far over to starboard.

The *Ferdinand Max* backed away, and as the *Re D'Italia* rolled back again to port, the water poured into her gaping wound and she sank like a stone with 381 out of her crew of 549.

Elsewhere in the battle there was wild confusion. Where armoured ship met armoured ship, neither was able to inflict much damage on the other. In spite of much sound and fury, the Austrian ships were so little damaged that the Austrians were of the opinion that the excitable Italians forgot, as often as not, to insert the shells into their muzzle-loaders before firing. Persano, who had placed such faith in the *Affondatore*, had been steaming aimlessly through the mêlée and had found no opportunity to use her formidable ram. But in the rear of the Italian line the Austrian wooden ships had been boldly attacking Riboty's armoured division.

In the *Kaiser*, an old-fashioned screw-driven two-decker, Commodore Petz, well imbued with his admiral's offensive spirit, had gone fearlessly in to ram the *Re di Portogallo*. Striking at an acute angle, the Austrian tore away the Italian's boats and gun-port lids and displaced some 60 feet of her armour; but as the *Kaiser* lay close alongside, the full broadside of the *Re di Portogallo* crashed into her, setting her on fire and bringing down her bowsprit and foremast in a tangle of wreckage across her funnel. The *Kaiser* managed to withdraw, steam pressure for her engines failing.

While Commodore Petz was in this unhappy state, the *Affondatore* loomed out of the smoke, Persano gave the order to ram, but in two successive attempts her captain failed to do so. The ram was not proving so simple a weapon as had been expected. At the third attempt the Italian had more success, and the *Kaiser* lay athwart his bows at his mercy. But at the last moment Persano turned deliberately away, the *Affondatore* having meanwhile taken several shells through her deck starting a fire below.

Commentators on the battle of Lissa all lay stress on the personal courage and kindly nature of the Italian admiral. His chivalrous refusal to attack a helpless enemy cannot but endear him to us. But it cannot hide the fact that so long as the Austrian flag flew in the *Kaiser* his duty was to attack and sink her, and he does not seem to have continued to engage her even with his heavy guns which could have made short work of the wooden ship. It is not surprising, therefore, that the old gentleman was subsequently tried by the Italian Senate, found guilty of negligence and incapacity, and disgraced.

At midday the two fleets disengaged and formed up in line. Tegetthoff, his first ardour dimmed, was well satisfied with his success. The enemy's biggest ship had been sunk; another, the *Palestro*, was still burning furiously and was soon to blow up in full view of both fleets. However, the Italians had still a superiority in armoured ships. Persano, indeed, with a Latin fondness for dramatic gesture, signalled "General Chase" and "Closer Action" and even the flamboyant message, "The ship which is not in action is not in her station." But he had no way nor any real inclination to renew the battle unless the enemy met him half-way. At dark he withdrew his fleet to the shelter of Ancona, leaving the Austrian in possession of the field and Lissa still in Austrian hands.

The Battle of Lissa, fought for reasons of prestige when the war was virtually over, was not a decisive battle; nor was it important except from the point of view of its effect on warship-design and naval tactics. The sinking of the *Re D'Italia*, pictured with varying degrees of accuracy and dramatic effect in illustrated journals, advertised the effectiveness of the ram at a time when armour had won an ascendancy over the gun. The success of the ram and the head-on approach it necessitated emphasised the importance of a clear field of fire directly ahead for the main armament. This gave an added incentive for the abolition of sailing rig.

But though the ram in its brief span of popularity helped to hasten these two developments in battleship-design, its own reign was brief. Improvement in guns soon redressed the balance between armour and gunfire, and made it impossible for ships to get close to each other without suffering mortal damage. The ram, however, remained a feature of most battleships long after its use had become impossible.

It was overtaken by the incessant and rapid advance in weapons, with the consequent change in ship-design and tactics which have been a feature of the machine age. An example was taking place even as the ram was gaining its reputation at Lissa in 1866. For Robert Whitehead's self-propelled, submersible torpedo, the model from which all modern torpedoes have sprung, was making its first dubious trials.

3

Quick-firing Gun and Torpedo

FOR nearly thirty years after the Battle of Lissa, no actions between any of the major fleets of the world took place which could apply the acid test to the many innovations and improvements being made in warship-design and armament. Off South America several minor actions were fought, clearly showing the difficulty of successfully using either the ram or the Whitehead torpedo, in its form at that time, against fully mobile ships in the open sea.

The first attempt to torpedo a ship at sea was made in 1877 by a British cruiser, the *Shah*, in which Rear-Admiral de Horsey was trying to subdue a rebellious Peruvian ironclad, the *Huascar*, which had been operating in a piratical fashion off the coast of Peru. The *Shah*, an unarmoured cruiser of 6,250 tons with a mixed armament of 9-inch and 7-inch rifles and 64-pounders, in company with the *Amethyst*, a smaller ship with a broadside of 64-pounders only, fought the *Huascar*, an improved vessel of the *Monitor* type, heavily armoured and mounting two 10-inch guns.

For two hours the British ships had some good practice, but out of sixty hits only one succeeded in penetrating the *Huascar*'s iron hide, while the Peruvian tried in vain to hit the fast-moving British ships at all. Guns and armour were still in a state of stalemate, it seemed. When the *Huascar* at one stage steered for the *Shah*, apparently intending to ram, the *Shah* made history by discharging the first Whitehead torpedo to be fired in earnest. But eleven years of development had given the new weapon only a speed of 9 knots and a range of 600 yards, so that it was easily avoided. The fight came to an end when the *Huascar* steamed away to surrender to the Peruvian authorities.

In those days the Republics of South America were in a state of chronic ferment, and when not fighting each other were indulging in revolutions and civil war in which opposing warships fought a number of spirited actions. In 1879 Peru and Chile went to war. During the sea-fights which took place between their navies, repeated attempts were made to apply the lessons of Lissa by ramming; but except for a small Chilean gunboat sunk by the *Huascar* by this method, at her third attempt, it was found that it was by no means easy to bring off such an attack in action. It began to be realised that Tegetthoff's good fortune in finding the *Re D'Italia* stopped had had much to do with his spectacular success. In the heat of battle, ships charging at each other had narrow escapes from colliding with others of their own side. A Peruvian warship similarly engaged missed her target, struck a reef and became a total loss. Consequently the reputation of the ram began to lose much of its glitter.

Minor actions between the smaller navies of the world gave food for thought to students of naval warfare, but did not greatly affect the type of ships being built by the greater maritime powers, of which Great Britain was incomparably the foremost at that time. The advances being made by engineers and armament manufacturers were in any case so rapid that design could not crystallise sufficiently for standard classes of ships to emerge.

The prime example of experimentation of this epoch was undoubtedly the round battleship *Admiral Popov* designed for the Imperial Russian Navy. This astonishing craft, like several others of her type built about 1875, had a circular hull, the idea being to provide a steady gun platform even in a seaway.

Fitted with six propellers driven by two-stage expansion reciprocating engines, the *Admiral Popov* was armed with two fixed 12-inch guns. To train them on the target the ship itself was slewed. The diameter of the hull was 121 feet, and it had a draught of 13 feet. The ship's displacement was 3,533 tons. Her top speed was 8 knots.

Bearing in mind the Russian attitude to their Navy, which was

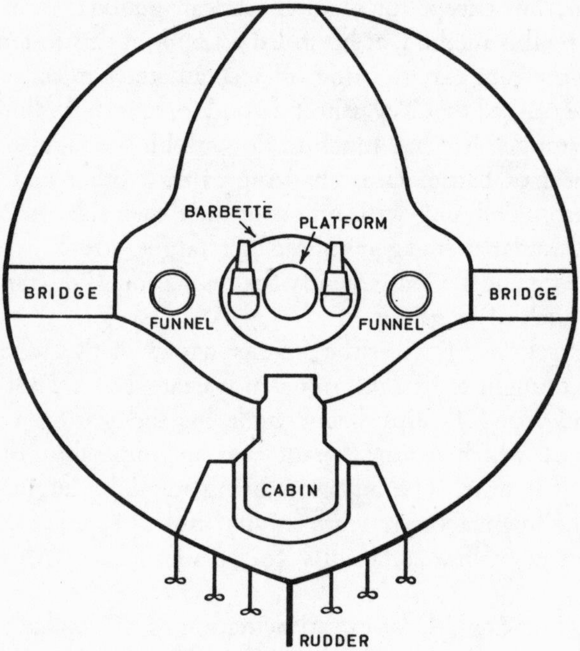

DECK PLAN OF RUSSIAN BATTLESHIP
ADMIRAL POPOV BUILT 1875.

SHRIVES

primarily required to act in support of her land armies, the round battleship was not unsuccessful. Up to a point it *was* a steady gun platform in seas which would set the conventional ship rolling. But it was perhaps just as well that it was confined to the Black Sea, and did not have to brave an ocean swell.

As can be imagined, the flat dish-shaped bottom was subjected to severe buffeting by the waves, while the upper deck was almost permanently awash. Life aboard her in anything but a flat calm was uncomfortable, to say the least.

A glance at the heterogeneous collection of ships which formed the Mediterranean Fleet which went into action to bombard the forts at Alexandria in 1882 also illustrates the incessant evolution of warship-design at this time. No two of the armoured ships were even approximately alike in size, armour, gun-power or speed. Two of them were turret ships, the remainder having central batteries.

To understand the reason for this we must turn to technicalities. Let us look first at the progress made in the engines of warships, which had advanced from those in the old sailing battleships converted to steam—where the Indicated Horse Power was little more than 1,000, and the steam pressure 12 lb. per square inch—to the 8,000 horse power of the *Inflexible* launched in 1881. In the process, engines and boilers had altered out of all recognition. The massive, slow-moving machinery adapted from the beam-engines in use ashore were replaced first by engines with oscillating cylinders, which did away with the space-wasting beams and connecting rods. Then, about 1843, came the horizontal, direct-acting engines.

By 1860 the idea of compound engines, in which the steam introduced first to a high-pressure cylinder passed on to a lower-pressure cylinder where its residual power could be used, was coming into fashion. The consequent demand for higher pressure steam had its effect on boiler-design also. About 1850, the old type of flue boiler was superseded by the tubular boiler in which the hot air and flame from a combustion chamber at the back of the furnace was conducted through a nest of fire-tubes, around which the hot water circulated, and thence to an up-take chamber and on up into the funnel. Then, to give greater strength, the boiler from being box-shaped became cylindrical.

The next development in boiler-design arose from the need for flexibility of performance in the little, high-speed torpedo-boats which were joining the fleets in the 1890's. The fire-tube boiler described above was simple to construct and reliable in operation; but to raise steam in it was a slow process, perhaps six hours or more from cold. Then when a ship was making complicated manœuvres, such as leaving or taking up its berth in harbour, sudden calls for steam would probably be made on the boilers; pressure would drop and it would take some time to restore it. Violent changes of speed at sea would have the same effect.

The boiling process was therefore reversed. The water was made to circulate in nests of small-bore tubes, and the furnace flame played around on the outside of them. In these water-tube boilers steam could be raised in a fraction of the time, and pressure could be quickly restored during manœuvring.

In combination with these boilers there was introduced the system of forced draught. Powerful fans forced air into the hermetically sealed boiler-rooms, where its only outlet was by means of the boiler furnaces and thence up the funnel. In this way furnace temperatures were raised and made more simply adjustable to take care of the varying calls for steam by the engines. So successful were these boilers and the forced-draught system that eventually all warships were equipped with them.

Up to the time of the compound engine, sea-water in the boilers was quite satisfactory to give the low steam pressures required; but now it became necessary to use fresh water, which meant that condensers had to be used to turn the steam back into water to conserve the limited supply.

Between 1875 and 1880 engines began to be designed with the cylinder upright and above the crankshaft, and so began to have the appearance which marine reciprocating engines have retained ever since. Everything combined in that amazing half-century to revolutionise engineering; not least was the advance in the strength and malleability of steel, which permitted higher steam pressures and far greater engine speeds. From simple compound engines designers moved on to triple- and quadruple-expansion engines taking steam at 150 lb. per square inch, their crankshafts revolving at more than 300 revolutions a minute.

Thus whereas at the Battle of Lissa full speed was in the region of 9 knots, thirty years later the biggest warships had a speed of 20 knots, while torpedo-boats were streaking through the water at 30. Horse-power in the former was up to 20,000, and in the latter some 3,000

This rapid development in engine power was alone enough to make any standardisation of type impossible. Added to it, however, there was an incessant redesign, improvement and fresh invention in the weapons available. Hardly had a ship joined the fleet than she was outmoded by some revolutionary discovery in gun manufacture. At the same time the torpedo was growing in reliability, range and destructive power, and obviously would in time force the adoption of guns of long range and accuracy great enough for fleets to engage without exposing themselves to the enemy's torpedo fire.

We have already seen the smooth-bore gun giving way to the rifle. The change from clumsy muzzle-loading to breech-loading was for a long time held up by the failure to find a safe method of closing the breech. The change was finally forced by the invention of more efficient forms of propellant powder. Instead of the rapid-burning black powder, which had held the field for centuries and which expended its force in one instantaneous burst, there came into use a comparatively slow-burning "cocoa" or brown powder. The former gained nothing from being used in a gun with a long barrel. Its energy was expended at once; the sooner the ball or shell was on its way and free of friction in the barrel, the further it would go. The latter, however, continued to develop power as the projectile moved along the barrel, increasing in velocity as it moved. From "cocoa" powder the explosive experts moved on eventually to produce cordite, a form of nitro-glycerine which was not only relatively smokeless but was even more powerful and slow-burning. Within limits, therefore, a longer gun gave increased range as well as accuracy.

Such a gun became impossible to load from the muzzle, particularly if it were mounted behind armour or in a turret. Fortunately the invention by the French of the principle of the "interrupted thread" came to the rescue of the gun-designers, and from that time muzzle-loading rapidly vanished from naval armament.

With the breech-loading principle established, armament designers addressed themselves to the problem of increasing the rate of fire. In the big turret guns this took the form of hydraulic machinery to hoist the massive ammunition from the magazines to the gun-house and load it into the guns. At the same time there arose a clear need for smaller, quick-firing guns. Even before the advent of the fast-moving, highly manœuvrable torpedo-boat, there was a school of thought which believed that a number of small, rapid-firing guns was more effective than a few huge cannon.

For these smaller guns the powder was made up in brass cartridge cases, and in some cases shell and cartridge were made up in one piece. The act of thrusting the cartridge into the gun released a spring-loaded breech-block which automatically closed the breech. After firing, the opening of the breech ejected the empty cartridge and the gun was ready for the next round. On this system guns of as much as 6-inch calibre were designed.

When it is realised that the heavy cannon of the later years of the 19th century could get away only one round every five minutes, while the 4·7-inch quick-firer could shoot as fast as fifteen rounds a minute, it will be seen that there was much to be said for the arguments of the quick-firing school.

It is an axiom of naval warfare that the weapon governs tactics. It also governs warship-design. It is not surprising, therefore, that in that period of rapid advance and change in ordnance, controversy and uncertainty should arise with regard to both. Ships and their armament were of all shapes and sizes. Tactical teaching varied from the head-on approach and the use of the ram to the line ahead and deliberate broadside cannonade. The various theories were to be put to the test to some extent in 1894, when the Japanese and Chinese fleets met in battle off the Yalu River.

Before we examine that action, however, we should note the progress being made with the weapon which, in the long run, was to come to dominate sea-warfare; to prevent the battleship from facing the open sea without the escort of a screen of destroyers, or even to rest easy in harbour unless its entrances were blocked by impenetrable net defences.

After two years of trials and tests, Robert Whitehead had developed his little torpedo while working for the Austrian Government at Fiume. By 1868 it had become quite a workable weapon, though its scope was still very limited. It could carry an explosive charge of 18 lb. of dynamite some 400 yards at 6 knots, running at a depth between 5 and 15 feet. Difficulty in keeping it to its set depth was then overcome by the incorporation of a hydrostatic valve connected to horizontal rudders. At the same time, by giving it a stronger air-chamber in which a pressure of 1,200 lb. per square inch could be stored, its performance was increased to give it a range of 700 yards at 8 knots.

At this stage the Austrian Government, not realising what a revolutionary weapon was being put at its disposal, withdrew its financial backing to the project. The British Admiralty, unusually forward-thinking, took action. After a committee of officers of the Mediterranean Fleet had reported enthusiastically on the new weapon, Whitehead was invited to bring two of his torpedoes and their launching apparatus to England. He accepted, and in 1870 he was installed at Sheerness, where exhaustive trials took place, a submerged torpedo-tube being fitted for the purpose in H.M.S. *Oberon*.

When the committee produced a report on these trials, containing the statement "that it was unanimously their opinion that any maritime nation failing to provide itself with submarine locomotive torpedoes would be neglecting a great source of power both of offence and defence", the British Government acted with commendable promptitude. It bought the rights of manufacture for £15,000, and provided a workshop for Whitehead at Woolwich Arsenal.

Though the torpedo was still an unreliable, chancy weapon—it was not until 1895 that a trustworthy method of keeping it running straight, by installing a gyroscope, was discovered—it began at once to be given a high degree of consideration. In 1877 the first torpedo-boat, H.M.S. *Lightning*, was built to carry a single Whitehead torpedo. Soon all warships were being equipped with torpedo-tubes, either mounted on the upper deck or below the water-line. The torpedo, though still looked on as a poor relation of the gun, had become an indispensable weapon.

In the distant future, the torpedo was in fact to become the weapon which above all others was to revolutionise naval warfare, for it was the perfect armament for the submarine. As far back as 1578 the first submersible boat had been built by an Englishman, William Bourne. Thereafter at intervals inventors had devised similar craft with varying degrees of success, and in 1776 an American, David Bushnell, produced the first submarine to be used in war—a manually-operated, screw-driven craft in which an attempt was made to sink H.M.S. *Eagle*, the flagship of Admiral Lord Howe, by attaching a delay-action explosive charge to the ship's bottom.

The attempt failed only because the craft was sighted and chased away; an idea had been born which not unnaturally appealed to the fertile brain of Robert Fulton twenty-five years later. His ingenious craft, the *Nautilus*, was successfully demonstrated to Napoleon in 1801, but it was not until the war of 1812 between Britain and the United States that it was used. Then it was Commodore Hardy's flagship *Ramillies* that was the intended victim, and only by the narrowest margin did the attempt to sink her fail.

Technically successful as these craft were—and, given the element of surprise, reasonably effective—submarines still lacked two essentials to make a serious contribution to naval warfare. These were an engine and a mobile torpedo. The former was first provided by the use of compressed air in a boat built in 1861 by a

Frenchman, Charles Brun, a submersible to which he gave the name *Plongeur*. In 1864 a boat of a similar type achieved the first submarine success in action when, during the American Civil War, the Confederates sank a Federal warship, the *Housatonic*.

However, the submarine was also itself lost, and indeed the risks involved in having to attach the explosive charge to the hull of the victim made such attacks virtually suicidal. Whitehead's torpedo was thus the one thing needed to set the submarine on a course of development which was eventually to make it the most deadly of all warships, twice coming within a short distance of wresting command of the sea from the greatest maritime powers. At the present day it bids fair to make the surface of the sea untenable in war.

Thus even as the battleship was undergoing the metamorphosis which would change it from the wooden wall of Nelson's day into the steam-driven, ironclad mistress of the seas of the last years of the 19th century, the seed had been sown which, in the fullness of time, would grow into the means of eliminating the battleship from the world's navies.

However, it was not until the Great War of 1914–18 that the submarine progressed from a short-range, coastal craft of very limited effectiveness into an ocean-going threat which raised it to an equal partnership with other ships of war. On the other hand the torpedo, mounted in surface ships, began to influence the armament and therefore the design of battleships somewhat earlier.

Yet in 1894, when there took place the next fleet action which influenced battleship design, torpedo-boats already formed part of all modern navies, but their rôle was still limited to sneak attacks by night on ships in harbour or sheltered waters. The gun was still the only battle winner, as was clearly shown in the Battle of the Yalu of that year.

The Sino-Japanese War arose ostensibly from a dispute over the status of Korea. More fundamental causes moved beneath the surface. The newly awakened, ambitious Japanese nation, its old isolation abandoned, was seeking to expand at the expense of the decaying Chinese Empire. Korea, nominally a tributary State of that Empire, separated from Japan by only 120 miles of sea, could be either a pistol pointed at Japan's heart or else a convenient stepping-stone to continental expansion.

By a treaty concluded in 1885, Korea had become a no-man's-land to which either China or Japan might send troops provided due notice were given to the other. It was a situation out of which it was easy to pick a quarrel. When China sent 1,500 troops to Asan on 8th June 1894, proper notice being given, Japan replied with a force of 5,000 and refused to withdraw them when called upon by China to do so. China sent reinforcements, and matters quickly developed into a state of war.

The armies of both sides were completely dependent upon sea communications for their supplies. The war would be won or lost at sea. At first sight it would appear that the odds against Japan were severe. But though China possessed a much larger fleet than that of Japan, the Empire was falling apart; and of the four squadrons into which the Chinese fleet was divided, only the northern squadron, based on Port Arthur in the Gulf of Pechili and Wei-hai-wei on the Shantung Peninsula, was under the control of the Central Government and so could be employed in the war.

Even so, the eyes of supporters of the big-gun school held that the Chinese squadron was on paper more powerful than the Japanese fleet. The Chinese Admiral Ting had two battleships, the *Ting Yuen*, his flagship, and *Chen Yuen*, each of 7,400 tons displacement, protected by an armoured belt 14 inches thick and mounting four 12-inch guns, besides eight cruisers mounting guns varying in calibre from 10·2-inch to 5·9-inch.

The Japanese fleet under Admiral Ito was divided into a Main Squadron under his personal command and a fast Flying Squadron under Rear-Admiral Tsuboi. The biggest ships of the Japanese Main Squadron were three unarmoured cruisers, *Matsushima* (Ito's flagship), *Itsukushima* and *Hashidate*, which mounted but one 12·6-inch gun each. The remainder of the squadron consisted of two cruisers *Fuso* and *Hiyei*, ancient veterans built seventeen years before, carrying a few antiquated guns, and one, the *Choyoda*, armed with nothing bigger than 4·7-inch guns, but of the quick-firing type.

Rear-Admiral Tsuboi's flag flew in the cruiser *Yoshino*, a fine modern ship of 4,150 tons with 6-inch and 4·7-inch quick-firers. With him were three other fast cruisers; *Takachiho* and *Naniwa*, mounting two 10·2-inch guns and six 6-inch each, and the *Akitsushima* which, like the *Yoshino*, carried only quick-firing guns of 6-inch and 4·7-inch calibre. None of these ships was armoured, but even the slowest could make nearly 19 knots, a good speed at that time.

So far it might seem that the Japanese fleet was much too weak to think of facing the heavy guns of the Chinese. On the other hand all the Japanese ships except *Takachiho*, *Naniwa*, *Fuso* and *Hiyei* carried between ten and twelve quick-firing guns, either 6-inch or 4·7-inch. A meeting between the two fleets might show which of the rival theories was right—that of the believers in the massive blow of a few big guns, or the contrary theory that many quick-firers would smother the slow-firing, big-gun ships before they could score many hits.

When the time came, however, the test was not to be so clear-cut. There were several reasons for this. The Japanese fleet was a highly trained and skilful force, whereas the Chinese, who a few years previously had achieved a high state of efficiency under the guidance of Captain W. M. Lang of the British Navy, had reverted on his departure to the condition of glossed-over incompetence usual in the armed forces of the Empire. The ships were kept outwardly smart and well-painted, but behind this façade there were half-empty magazines and unpractised gunners. Troubles in the shell factories had led to indifferent bursting charges, or even cement and coal dust inserted in their place.

Furthermore, Admiral Ting's study of fighting tactics had left him an admirer of Tegetthoff's frontal, line-abreast attack as displayed at Lissa. The fact that the big guns of his two battleships could all fire ahead increased Ting's faith in such a method. He had completely overlooked the fact that guns had greatly increased in range and effectiveness since Lissa, so that a fleet which awaited such an onslaught in line ahead would have a considerable gun advantage for a long period during the approach. The ram had ceased to be a practical proposition, but Ting's favoured tactics were based on its eventual use.

Although hostilities at sea had opened as early as 25th July, when the Japanese Flying Squadron had attacked two smaller and weaker Chinese ships, heavily damaging one and destroying the other, the opposing fleets did not at first seek battle with each other, confining themselves to escorting their troop convoys to Korea. Then, on 16th September, both fleets having successfully delivered a convoy to its destination, the mouth of the Yalu for the Chinese and the Pingyang Inlet for the Japanese, Admiral Ito decided to reconnoitre towards Port Arthur in the hope of finding the enemy.

Ting, his task temporarily completed, had, however, anchored for the night off the mouth of the Yalu with his whole squadron except two small ships which, with two torpedo-boats, had accompanied the transports into the river. In consequence Ito, finding Port Arthur empty, had searched eastwards, and early on the morning of the 17th had found the harbour of Haiyun Island in Korea Bay similarly vacant. His next cast, north-east to Talu Island, was to bring him the contact he wanted; for at 10 a.m. the look-outs on Ting's flagship sighted a cloud of black smoke to the south-west which could only be from a fleet. Steam was hastily raised, and by 11.30 the Chinese squadron was steering forth to battle.

Ito was between the Chinese and their bases. There was no avoiding battle even if Ting had wanted to do so, which was certainly not the case. With the overweening self-conceit of the Chinese of the old Empire, Ting had the greatest contempt for the upstart race of islanders. The Japanese were equally confident in their knowledge of the perfect state of their training and technical efficiency.

So the two fleets steered for each other; the Japanese at about 10 knots, which was the best that *Fuso* and *Hiyei* could achieve, the Chinese at a knot or two faster. Ito's fleet was in line ahead with the Flying Squadron in the van. Besides the major units there were present two ships of little or no fighting value, the gunboat *Akagi* and an armed merchant steamer *Saikio Maru*, which were to prove an embarrassment to Ito. It is not clear why the Japanese admiral did not send such vulnerable ships away to the southward where they would have been clear of the battle. Instead he stationed them on the port side of his Main Squadron, the side away from the enemy.

Meanwhile Ting's squadron was approaching on a south-westerly course in a formation somewhat similar to Tegetthoff's at Lissa, with the two big ships in the centre. But owing to tardiness in getting under way, the two starboard wing ships were lagging, while on the other wing one of the Chinese cruisers, the *Tsi-Yuen*, was well behind and unable to get up into station. In fact, viewed from the Japanese ships, the Chinese squadron seemed to be in considerable disorder.

The tactics of the two admirals were soon evident. At the long range for those days of 6,000 yards, the Chinese opened fire with their big guns. With calm confidence the Japanese held their fire, and indeed they could well afford to do so; for with the rapidly changing range making shooting difficult, the unpractised Chinese gunners failed to score a single hit during the approach.

The Japanese line drew steadily across the Chinese front until the Flying Squadron was able to pass round the starboard wing, and at a range of 3,000 yards open a withering fire from their quick-firers on the wing ships of the Chinese formation. Their Main Squadron now came into action, passing close ahead of Ting's flagship and the *Chen-Yuen*, which bore down as though to ram, both battleships being heavily shot-up in the process. The whole of Ito's squadron except the *Hiyei*, the rear ship, passed safely round the northern flank of Ting's line, and Ito then led round to starboard, circling the now completely disorganised Chinese fleet and keeping up a punishing fire to which only a feeble reply was made.

Indeed the Chinese had more than the enemy's fire with which to reckon. Dense funnel smoke, increased by that from a hundred guns, enveloped the whole scene. The laggard *Tsi-Yuen*, coming up at last, plunged into the smother and ran amok, colliding with two ships of her own side, sinking one and so damaging another that it steamed away blazing to be beached. The *Tsi-Yuen* herself then withdrew to Port Arthur, where her captain subsequently paid for his actions with his head.

Meanwhile the *Hiyei*, unable to follow the Japanese Main Squadron round the Chinese flank, boldly turned to pass through the Chinese. Avoiding two torpedoes fired at her and which strangely enough hit nothing in spite of the milling throng of ships the *Hiyei* won through, though suffering considerably in the process.

The two weak Japanese ships, *Akagi* and *Saikio Maru*, also cut off, kept on across the Chinese front, the former being badly battered. Seeing this, Rear-Admiral Tsuboi led the Flying Squadron round to port to come back and cover them. This brought a temporary relief to the Chinese ships, but by the time Tsuboi had completed his turn the Chinese found themselves between two fires, Ito to the eastward and the Flying Squadron to the north-westward.

By now Ting's squadron was in desperate straits. Apart from the victims of the *Tsi-Yuen*'s wild career, two other cruisers, smothered by the rapid fire of Tsuboi's 6-inch and 4·7-inch guns, had gone down. Yet another had struggled away burning furiously, ultimately to be run aground near Port Arthur. Ting was thus left with only four of his original ten ships, all of which had suffered severely and had shot away nearly all their ammunition.

Complete annihilation of the Chinese squadron was in Ito's grasp. The Japanese had not achieved this without damage to themselves, however; in particular Ito's flagship *Matsushima* had been hit twice by 12-inch shells, once by a 10·2-inch, suffering more than 100 casualties and had been set on fire. By the time Ito had transferred his flag to the *Hashidate* and despatched the *Matsushima*, *Hiyei*, *Akagi* and *Saikio* to base for repairs, the sun was sinking low; and as dusk fell, the two fleets disengaged and formed up on parallel courses in line ahead.

A renewal of the fight might now have wiped out the Chinese

force, but a new element had entered the situation. The two torpedo-boats of Ting's squadron had joined him from the Yalu. Not for the last time in our story, an admiral with an enemy fleet ripe for destruction in view was made to pause by the incalculable threat of Whitehead's sinister weapon. Ito decided to await the dawn before completing the enemy's annihilation.

In the night Ting slipped away with his surviving ships, which included his two battleships. Nevertheless the Japanese had won a considerable victory, and had secured control of the disputed sea area. The action was studied with great interest by the naval experts of every nation. Controversy raged furiously as to the lessons to be learnt from it. The supporters of the fast, multi-gun ship claimed that their views had been justified by the Japanese victory. Too much weight was being put into armour, they insisted, which would be better allocated to guns.

Their opponents objected that the test had not been a fair one in view of Ting's faulty tactics and the incompetence of the Chinese gunners. The fire of the Japanese quick-firers had not succeeded in doing vital damage to either of Ting's armoured ships. On the other hand, only three hits from big guns—one of them a solid shot which passed straight through the ship doing little damage, and another a shot which broke up on impact, spewing cement instead of a bursting charge—had been sufficient to put the *Matsushima* out of action.

The arguments could not be conclusive, for while the protagonists were fulminating against each other, the weapons on which they based their views were being rapidly improved upon. Ten years after the Battle of the Yalu, the big naval gun had become a weapon of such precision and destructive power at ranges hitherto undreamed of that a ship mounting only the smaller, quick-firing guns would have been hopelessly outclassed and quite unable to engage a big-gun battleship. The era of the dreadnought had come.

But before that day dawned two naval campaigns were to be fought by ships armed and designed in the heterogeneous fashion of the pre-dreadnought days of swift transition and technical development. In the first, that of the Spanish-American War, the overwhelming preponderance of strength of one side over the other militated against any useful lessons being drawn by the naval constructors or tacticians. The second war, that between Russia and Japan, was to culminate in a battle in which fleets composed of battleships in the final stage of development prior to the dreadnought epoch were to meet in a pitched battle—the first of its kind since Trafalgar, a hundred years before.

4

Steam Comes of Age

THE comparatively sudden transformation of the man-of-war from the three-masted, wooden sailing-ship whose limitations, handling characteristics and sea-worthiness had been familiar to generation after generation of seamen, into the floating steel fortress driven by steam, brought problems and dangers as well as advantages.

Though steam power released seamen from dependence on the wind for mobility, took away much of the danger of the lee-shore and eliminated the embarrassment of the calm, the low-powered steamships of the 19th century had drawbacks of their own.

Their deep-draught, massive bulks were in some ways less manœuvrable than sailing-ships in the hands of well-trained crews. The speed of a sailing-ship could be adjusted by a judicious spilling of the wind from a sail here, the backing of a topsail there; moreover, the ship could be brought to a standstill by luffing up into the wind. The speed of a steamship could indeed be varied by a turn of a valve increasing or shutting off steam to the engines, but this took some time to have any effect on the momentum of the great mass of steel ploughing through the waters. To stop it reasonably quickly the engines had to be reversed—a cumbersome procedure with the early engines—and even so the ship's way would not be halted at once.

On the other hand the ability to move in any direction irrespective of the wind, and to maintain a steady course at all times, naturally meant that warships tended to adopt formations of closer order, and to indulge in drill manœuvres of greater nicety and complexity. Risks of collision were thus greatly increased.

There was little room for error, and a mistake could not quickly be rectified.

The result of collision was far more destructive and dangerous than with the old wooden ships. The sharp prow of an ironclad, often fitted with a projecting ram below the surface, could cleave through the iron or steel plates of a ship's hull, tearing a jagged hole almost impossible to plug and make watertight. The sea would pour in; the small balance of buoyancy of an iron ship would vanish, and she would sink very rapidly.

This danger was, of course, appreciated. To offset it, the system of watertight sub-division—copied, incidentally, from the age-old practice of the builders of Chinese junks—was introduced, though for a long time to a degree barely sufficient to take care of the risks of collision and quite inadequate for use in war, when shell bursts on the water-line and torpedo hits below it were to be expected.

As the system developed, not only was the ship divided into a number of transverse watertight compartments—the number increasing continually as time went on—but also the hull below the water-line was given an inner shell, a space being left between the inner and outer skin, which could be left empty or used to store coal or fresh water. This was known as a double bottom.

Nevertheless, it was only after a number of calamitous collisions that the system of watertight sub-division was applied with sufficient thoroughness to prevent a simple collision from having fatal results. The first of these collisions occurred in 1875, and is described here not only to illustrate the consequences of collision in an early ironclad, but also to show how the handling of ships and squadrons under steam introduced new hazards to which ships under sail were not exposed. Once steam "caught on", senior officers were apt to assume that the restrictions on manœuvre accepted in a sailing-ship had all been swept away. A turn of the wheel would swing their ships to any new heading, a ring to the engine-room bring an alteration of speed.

But these advantages brought added responsibilities which were not always appreciated. An alteration of course or speed made without a warning signal to a neighbour could bring about a most dangerous situation. The neat cruising formations possible could easily become an embarrassment when navigating in busy sea areas.

On 1st September 1875, four battleships of the British Channel Squadron, *Warrior*, *Hector*, *Vanguard* and *Iron Duke*, which had left Dublin Bay early that morning, were heading south through the St. George's Channel in line ahead. Though the weather held a threat of fog, Admiral Tarleton, leading in his flagship, *Warrior*, ordered the ships to assume formation, "Divisions in line ahead, columns disposed abeam to port", or in other words a rectangle with *Warrior* and *Vanguard* leading *Hector* and *Iron Duke* respectively.

Captain Dawkins of the *Vanguard* had accordingly signalled for *Vanguard* and *Iron Duke* to turn together to port and, when they had thus side-stepped the necessary distance, to turn back to the course of the squadron. Increasing speed a couple of knots, *Vanguard*'s division then crept slowly ahead to take up its station abreast *Warrior* and *Hector*. So far all was well. By 12.30 the manœuvre had been almost completed, and the speed of *Vanguard* and *Iron Duke* had been reduced to that of the squadron, 8 knots.

At this moment the ships plunged into a dense fog, with visibility 50 yards. At once the hazard of such a formation in fog became apparent, as did the inexperience and lack of confidence of everyone concerned. Fleet orders for conduct in a fog laid down that speed should not exceed 3 or 4 knots, but there was no means of signalling a reduction other than by steam-whistle—which, as events showed, could not be heard at more than a few hundred yards at most.

Captain Dawkins, his unwieldy ship thrusting blindly forward in a busy traffic lane at 8 knots, correctly decided that he must take steps to reduce the speed of his division, irrespective of any action taken by his Admiral, nearly a mile away and out of touch. However, he also had the *Iron Duke* astern of him to consider. Unfamiliar with the signal books, Dawkins consulted his Yeoman of Signals, and both came to the conclusion that the ship's pennants in Morse code on the steam-whistle followed by a prolonged blast would give the *Iron Duke* the necessary warning. Engine revolutions for 6 knots were therefore ordered, and the siren sounded.

From the look-out placed in the "eyes" of the ship there came a sudden shout: "Ship right ahead!" At this, Captain Dawkins shouted "Stop her!" to the officer of the watch, and rushed down to the forecastle to see for himself. The officer of the watch ordered "Stop Engines," and at the same time had the wheel put over to port to sheer away from the danger ahead.

When the fog came down the *Iron Duke* had lost sight of the *Vanguard* completely. The officer of the watch in the *Iron Duke*, nervous at the thought of following close in the wake of the invisible ships ahead, had sheered out of the line to port. Captain Hickley of the *Iron Duke*, coming on the bridge and discovering this, had ordered the officer to get the ship back into the line. No sound of the *Vanguard*'s fog signals had been heard; the *Iron Duke* was still doing 8 knots and swinging back to starboard to her station when out of the fog, 50 yards ahead of her prow with its menacing ram, loomed the shape of the *Vanguard*, making an angle of 45 degrees across the *Iron Duke*'s course.

Having seen the sailing-ship which had caused the alarm pass safely across his bow, Captain Dawkins in the *Vanguard* had just turned aft to call "Full speed ahead" to the bridge when he, too, saw the *Iron Duke* and knew that collision was imminent. With a rending crash the *Iron Duke*'s prow struck the *Vanguard* on her port quarter.

The *Vanguard* was divided by bulkheads below the main deck into eight watertight compartments. It had been calculated that the flooding of any one compartment could be suffered without fatal effects. Unhappily, the collision had occurred exactly on the bulkhead between engine-room and stokehold. The water rushed in, quickly filling not only both these large compartments but also drowning out the boilers, leaving the pumps without steam. Though watertight doors were at once closed, little else was attempted in the way of attempting to cover the hole with collision mats or sails, and in any case it is doubtful if such action would have had much effect. The ship was clearly doomed, though it was not until one and a quarter hours after the collision that she went down. In the meantime the whole of the crew had been rescued.

The loss of the *Vanguard* clearly showed that there was much to be learnt by seamen if steam navigation were to be made safe, particularly where squadrons of warships in company were concerned. A similar calamity in the Imperial German Navy three years later, though in clear weather and accompanied by heavy loss of life, gave a further example.

On a fine day in May 1878, the armoured sail-and-steam-ship *König Wilhelm*, flagship of Admiral von Batsch, was steaming down channel in company with the *Grosser Kurfürst* and the *Preussen*. The *Preussen* was in line astern of the flagship, but the *Grosser Kurfürst* had been stationed to starboard of the *König Wilhelm*, slightly abaft the beam and very close—only 110 yards.

It was an astonishing formation to adopt at any time or place, but in the busy traffic lane of the English Channel it was extremely hazardous. The Rule of the Road at sea demanded that a steamship meeting another vessel must alter course to starboard to keep clear. To do this in safety the German admiral would have first to signal the *Grosser Kurfürst* on his starboard hand, so that she would know his intentions and also alter to starboard. In an emergency there might be no time for this, and danger of collision would be immediate.

In spite of this dangerous situation, the bridge of the flagship had been left to a junior watch officer, while at the wheel was a petty officer of no experience. Admiral and captain were still below when two sailing-ships were seen to be steering to pass close across the bows of the squadron.

Seeing that an alteration of course to give way to the sailing-ships was inevitable, the captain of the *Grosser Kurfürst* very prudently swung his ship to starboard without waiting for a signal from the flagship. Having cleared the sailing-ships and seeing that the flagship was holding her course, he then altered back to port to regain his station.

In the *König Wilhelm*, the officer of the watch, hesitating to take action in the absence of his seniors, had held on in hope of being able to pass ahead of the sailing-ships. At the last moment, however, he realised this was impossible. Too preoccupied with his own difficulties to give thought to the *Grosser Kurfürst*, he turned to starboard, and only then appreciated the peril of the situation.

He at once ordered the wheel to port to turn back parallel to the *Grosser Kurfürst*, but in the stress of the moment the inexperienced helmsman put it the opposite way. Collision was now unavoidable, but in the *Grosser Kurfürst* the captain did what he could to try to avert it. He called first for full speed ahead in the hope of getting clear across the flagship's bows. When he saw that was impossible, he put his wheel to starboard to take the blow at as acute an angle as possible; but it was too late for this to have much effect. Though the *König Wilhelm*'s engines were by now going astern, she was still moving ahead at 6 or 7 knots when her ram crashed into the *Grosser Kurfürst*'s side, peeling off the armour, thrusting on through the ship's side into the stokehold.

The *Grosser Kurfürst* was forced bodily to starboard. Her way took her grinding on across the *König Wilhelm*'s bow, breaking off the ram, so that as the flagship backed away the water poured into the great rent in the *Grosser Kurfürst*'s side, flooding the furnaces. As the stokehold filled, the ship listed to port till she was on her beam ends, and within five minutes of the collision she had sunk; 281 out of her crew of 497 were lost with her.

It is a sorry story, serving only to show how the transition from sail to steam raised problems of ship and squadron handling which were not readily solved by men brought up in sail. No experienced seaman of a later date would station another ship close on the starboard quarter of his own when navigating a traffic lane.

* * *

The ability to perform precise manœuvres with large bodies of ships was one of the qualities which the steam age demanded. The practice of them developed the art of ship handling and the "seaman's eye" amongst the officers of a fleet. Familiarity with them and with the signal codes by which they were ordered was calculated to develop the flexibility of manœuvre so essential to a fleet in battle.

The Mediterranean station had always been the premier training-ground of the Royal Navy. There, in the generally fair weather conditions and uninterrupted by the periodical leave periods which divided the squadrons of the Home Fleet up amongst the three home ports, fleet manœuvres reached their peak of smooth efficiency and drill. In 1893 the commander of the Mediterranean Fleet was an admiral universally looked upon as a veritable master of precise manœuvre, Vice-Admiral Sir George Tryon.

Though greatly liked and respected, Tryon was held in considerable awe by his subordinates, and was known as a strict disciplinarian. He delighted in bringing off spectacular drill movements with large formations of ships, and never more so than when bringing the fleet to an anchorage. The final approach had to be made with every ship in exact station; every anchor must splash into the water at the same moment. So it was to be when the fleet of eight battleships and three cruisers entered the harbour of Tripoli on the afternoon of 22nd June 1893.

The berthing plan called for the ships to anchor in two lines, and the final approach would be made with six ships in line abreast followed at anchoring distance—500 yards—by a second line abreast. To achieve this the fleet would advance in two divisions in line ahead, until at the right moment all ships would be ordered to turn 90 degrees together, bringing them into their line-abreast formation.

So far there was nothing out of the ordinary about Tryon's plan, though it would make a smart piece of drill. But in order to give all ships a good long run in line ahead during which they could get themselves accurately into station before the final turn into line abreast, Tryon intended first to lead the fleet seawards in two columns. Leading the starboard column would be his flagship *Victoria*, while the *Camperdown*, flagship of Rear-Admiral A. H. Markham, would be leading the other line. When he had gained sufficient sea-room, he would then reverse course.

With his love for something spectacular and out of the general run, Tryon decided to do this by ordering the two columns to wheel inwards in succession—leading ships together and the remainder following—on completion of which, provided the two columns had started at the right distance apart, they would be at the 500 yards distance apart required by the anchoring plan, and also on the desired course for the harbour.

His plan settled, the admiral sent for the flag-captain, the Hon. M. A. Bourke, and the staff navigating officer, Commander T. H. Smith, to explain it and to give the order to get the fleet into the necessary two columns, which he directed should be 6 cables (1,200 yards) apart.

The navigating officer at once pointed out that this distance apart was insufficient for the manœuvre, and suggested 8 cables (1,600 yards), to which the admiral agreed. Even this distance was not really enough; yet when the flag-lieutenant arrived in answer to a summons he was told to signal for 6 cables, and so the fleet was formed up.

By this time the navigating officer had gone back to the bridge, but Captain Bourke was still in the admiral's cabin, and he pointed out that the diameter of the *Victoria*'s turning circle using normal manœuvring helm was 800 yards. There could obviously therefore be no room for the intended manœuvre. Confident that his admired chief, the "master-mind" as he was later to call him, had some plan of his own to take care of the difficulty, Bourke then went on the bridge.

One further warning was given when the flag-lieutenant, told by the navigating officer that 8 cables had been agreed on, checked again with Tryon. "Leave it at 6," he was told, and so the fatal scene was set. At 3.25, at the Commander-in-Chief's order, the flags ran up giving the order: "Second division alter course in succession 180 degrees to starboard preserving the order of the fleet. First division alter course in succession 180 degrees to port, preserving the order of the fleet"—in other words, "Reverse course by wheeling inwards."

As the meaning of the flags was read out on the bridges of the various ships, every captain in the fleet realised that the manœuvre was an impossible one. The two leading ships were those most immediately concerned. In the *Camperdown*, Rear-Admiral Markham said to his flag-lieutenant: "It is impossible, as it is an impracticable manœuvre," and gave the order for his flag hoist to be kept at the dip, indicating that the signal was not understood. At the same time he drafted a message to be semaphored asking for a clarification.

Before it could be sent there came from the fleet flagship a message betraying the Commander-in-Chief's impatience: "What are you waiting for?" Then at the *Victoria*'s yard-arm could be seen the *Camperdown*'s pennants at the dip, sure signal of the great man's displeasure at the delay, visible to the whole fleet.

In the face of such utter confidence on the part of so infallible an authority, Markham gave in and hoisted his signal close up, comforting himself with the thought that Tryon must be intending to give the executive signal for the turn first to the second division, and after an interval to the first division, so that the two columns would thus circle round each other, exchanging station.

But it was only too true that some strange mental aberration was blinding Tryon. In spite of every warning, he persisted; and as the fatal signal came down with a run, the two battleships began their ponderous turn towards each other. In each ship the anxious captain watched the cone-and-flag indicator in the other which showed how much helm was being applied. In each ship the indicator showed that full helm was being held on. At about the same time in both *Victoria* and *Camperdown* the captain ordered the inner screw to go astern to tighten the turn. At about the same moment each saw that collision was imminent, and ordered full speed astern on both engines.

Both captains, fearing the wrath of their revered Commander-in-Chief, had left it too late. Once set on their fatal courses, the clumsy ironclads could not easily be deflected. The *Camperdown*'s ram plunged through the *Victoria*'s side, through a coal-bunker and into the big compartments below. A petty officer on the mess-decks saw the *Camperdown*'s bow crashing in amidst a cloud of coal-dust. Then, as the two ships drew apart, the sea flooded in. One minute before the collision, orders had been given to close watertight doors, but it was not sufficient time for the many openings to be shut before the inrush of water drove the men up on deck. As the list increased, ventilators and scuttles which had been left open became submerged. A final lurch to starboard, and the *Victoria* plunged to the bottom, her screws still slowly revolving as she threw her stern into the air. The admiral, who was heard in the last moments grimly confessing "It is all my fault", was never seen again.

That he was primarily to blame must be conceded. But a system of discipline under which officers of great experience and seniority could not or dared not bring home to an admiral that an order was impossible to obey without disaster must share the responsibility. The rigid code under which the Royal Navy lived, the exaggerated awe of seniority and an insistence on unquestioning obedience of orders, was fatal to initiative in the presence of a senior; on the other hand, they encouraged in an admiral such a god-like confidence in his own infallibility that it was not until a much later date that fleet commanders would tolerate a proper staff to assist them.

The bitter lessons from the loss of the *Victoria* may have brought a healthier atmosphere for a time, but twenty-three years later, at the Battle of Jutland, one of the Royal Navy's most vital engagements, the same defects were to rob it of a great and decisive victory.

Across the Atlantic, a disaster of a very different kind to a battleship of the United States Navy became one of the causes of war between that country and Spain. Relations between the two were already strained on account of the situation in Cuba, where a republican insurrection against Spanish rule had for three years defied a large Spanish army to repress it. To give protection to

United States citizens who were believed to be in danger, the battleship *Maine* was sent to Havana on 25th January 1898.

While she lay at her anchor berth in the harbour during the next three weeks, precautions were taken against any attempt at sabotage being made against her by boat. Yet when on the evening of 15th February she was rent by a shattering explosion, it was at once assumed that she had been mined by Spanish treachery. There was a tragically heavy loss of life, and the *Maine* sank by the bow to the bed of the harbour, leaving her after-part above water.

On evidence supplied by divers who examined the wreck, an American court of inquiry decided that a mine had been exploded under the forward part of the ship, and that this had caused the partial explosion of some of her forward magazines. The finding was undoubtedly an honest one, as was that based on a further and more detailed examination in 1911—which came to a similar conclusion, though it deduced a different point of explosion from that of the first.

The evidence upon which both findings were based was the appearance of the ship's bottom after the explosion and the form which the damage had taken. No concrete evidence of a mine has ever emerged, however, and only insanity could have led the Spanish to connive at such an act which would involve them in war with the far stronger United States—a war which they could not hope to win. On the other hand, many examples of spontaneous explosion of warship magazines occurred in various navies over the next twenty years, and went on until precautions against the instability of the explosives of the day were taken. The one certain fact about the *Maine* disaster was that the forward magazines had exploded.

In the largely naval war that followed, the battles of Manila Bay and of Santiago were the principal events. In both the disparity of force of the opposing sides was so great that little of tactical or technical interest emerged. In the former, not only were the Spanish ships smaller and weaker than those of the United States Asiatic Squadron of cruisers under Commodore Dewey, but also their crews were ill-trained, and their fitness for sea was so low that it was at anchor in the Bay of Manila that they awaited the American onslaught on 1st May 1898.

A two-hour cannonade was sufficient to reduce the Spanish squadron to desperate straits, with heavy casualties, while not a man in Dewey's squadron had been wounded, and his ships had been scarcely touched. Withdrawing at this stage to hold a conference of his captains and to send his ships' companies to breakfast, Dewey returned three and a half hours later to complete the destruction at his leisure.

The preponderance of American force was even greater at Santiago. The action there could be likened more to shooting bolting rabbits forced into the open by ferrets than to a pitched battle. On 3rd July 1898, an American squadron under Rear-Admiral W. T. Sampson lay waiting outside the harbour. It consisted of three modern battleships, *Indiana*, *Oregon* and *Iowa*, ships of more than 10,000 tons, armed with four 13- or 12-inch guns each, eight 8-inch as well as smaller guns, and stoutly armoured; a second-class battleship with two 12-inch guns, the *Texas*; and two armoured cruisers with 8-inch guns for their main armament.

The prey for which they were waiting was a Spanish squadron under Rear-Admiral Pascual Cervera y Topete, which had taken refuge there on 19th May after arriving in the West Indies with orders from the Spanish Government "to protect Puerto Rico". The four armoured cruisers of which it was composed, *Infanta Maria Teresa*, *Almirante Oquendo*, *Vizcaya* and *Cristobal Colon*, together with two small destroyers, comprised the whole naval force available to Spain at this time. Such was the state of unpreparedness of the Spaniards for this war, which they were accused of having deliberately provoked by the sinking of the *Maine*, that there had been no arrangements for stocks of fuel and ammunition in the West Indies, and little or no effort made to build or buy a fleet which could face the powerful United States Navy with the slightest confidence.

Now, with a complete misunderstanding of the basic facts of naval strategy, the Spaniards had sent their entire force out where, far from its bases and sources of supply, it must either face certain annihilation or consent to be bottled up in harbour. Their chosen Admiral, Cervera, had warned the Minister of Marine in bitter, passionate words that the disorganisation of naval affairs could only lead to disaster.

> For these reasons [he wrote] I hesitated exceedingly before accepting my command, but having accepted it I will face all the consequences which it involves and, as I have said, I will do my duty. Yet shall I bear in mind the words of Our Lord Jesus Christ and say, not so much for myself as for helpless Spain, "Father, if it be possible, let this cup pass from me"!

The Spanish admiral, driven on by his fierce sense of duty to obey the crazy orders of his Government, was to drink the cup to its bitter dregs. Arriving in the West Indies with his bunkers almost empty, he made first for the Dutch island of Curaçao, where he had hoped to find colliers awaiting him. Disappointed in this he made for Santiago de Cuba, the only port which he could reach without meeting the United States fleet, and there he arrived on 19th May, short of fuel, supplies and ammunition.

The Americans were slow to discover that he was there, and it was not until 29th May that a force under Commodore W. S Schley, with his flag in the armoured cruiser *Brooklyn*, established a blockade. On 1st June they were joined by the remainder of the North Atlantic Squadron under Sampson, who assumed command of the operations. Had coal been readily available, Cervera might have got clear away to Havana and relative safety; but Spanish ineptitude was revealed by the fact that though 2,300 tons of Welsh coal was stored in the naval depôt at Santiago, there were no baskets or sacks for loading it, so that it could be taken on board only slowly and in small quantities at a time. In fact, Cervera's squadron never succeeded in filling its bunkers during its entire stay.

With the arrival of Sampson's battleships, the fate of the Spanish squadron, already virtually hopeless, was finally sealed. Though they were safe from attack so long as Santiago held out against the military operations launched to capture it, any attempt to break out could be only suicidal. The narrow and intricate entrance channel, made even more so by the sinking of an American block-ship, would allow only one ship at a time and at long intervals to emerge. Each would then have to face the concentrated fire of the whole American squadron.

Cervera, a man of great personal courage, had no doubt whatever that so long as the decision lay with him he would never sanction such a useless waste of lives. When therefore the town of Santiago was seriously threatened by the United States expeditionary force and General Blanco, Captain-General of Cuba, requested him to go out, he firmly replied:

> I, a man of no ambitions, with no mad passions, say most emphatically that I shall never order the horrible and useless hecatomb which can be the only result of attempting to force a passage out. I should hold myself responsible in the sight of God and of history for lives thus sacrificed on the altar of vain glory and not in the legitimate defence of our country.

That Cervera was right cannot be doubted. Even if his ships had been in fighting trim, a sortie would have been fatally disastrous, but some damage might have been inflicted on the enemy before their own destruction was complete. As it was, the neglect and disorganisation of which he had complained had left his heavy guns defective and the ammunition for his quick-firers unreliable. The *Cristobal Colon*'s deep draught gave her so little clearance over rocks in the channel that in any but perfectly calm weather her pitching would cause her to strike on them. The *Vizcaya* was so long out of dock that her foul condition reduced her to 13 knots. A suggestion that the squadron should slip out at night was vetoed by Cervera, because the glare of American searchlights in the pilots' eyes would make safe navigation of the twisting channel impossible.

But Cervera had said "I will do my duty", and when at last direct orders came to him to take his squadron to sea, he decided that his duty was to obey. It may be argued that a greater man than Cervera, holding the views he did, would have refused, accepting the charge of cowardice and mutiny which would have been brought rather than lead his men to their deaths. But for all his physical courage, Cervera had not the moral fortitude for that.

Calling his captains together, he informed them that he would lead them forth in the *Maria Teresa* at 9 o'clock on the morning of 3rd July. As they left to prepare their ships for battle, each solemnly clasped his commander's hand in farewell.

The rest of the story can be briefly told. As the Spanish ships emerged one at a time, their red and yellow battle ensigns making a superb but pathetic show of defiance, they were quickly overwhelmed, their wooden decks set ablaze, their power to steam destroyed. All except the destroyer *Furor*, which blew up and sank, were run ashore at the last minute before sinking, thereby saving many lives; but even so 323 were killed and 151 severely wounded. The American losses were 1 killed, 10 wounded.

Cervera himself survived the destruction of his flagship and was taken prisoner, arriving naked aboard the armed yacht *Gloucester*, having stripped to swim ashore. When he was taken later to the battleship *Iowa*, her commander, Captain Evans, greeted him with all the ceremony and respect due to his rank, a marine guard presenting arms and bosuns' pipes trilling as he stepped aboard. The ceremony over, the crew of the *Iowa* broke into a storm of cheers in tribute to his courage.

Though the cost had been grievous, the sacrifice useless and needless, such gallantry, however ineffective, cannot help but add a golden page to naval history.

5

The Rising Sun

THE last years of the 19th century saw a restless ferment among the nations of the world. The United States of America, recovered from the devastation and ruin of the Civil War, the Union at last commanding the respect and loyalty of the whole country, were feeling their new strength and going through the brief expansionist phase which brought them the acquisition from Spain of the Philippines and Puerto Rico. However, they did not yet aspire to a place in the front rank of naval powers. With few overseas commitments, and their homeland separated from the quarrelsome countries of Europe by thousands of miles of ocean on which the Royal Navy rode supreme, they had no reason to do so.

In Europe the ninety-year-old unchallenged naval ascendancy of Great Britain was still unassailable. Maintaining only a small regular army, Britain, at the height of her prosperity, could afford to build and maintain a fleet as powerful as any two of her European neighbours. Russia and France, burdened with the upkeep of huge standing armies, were forced to accept this position which had been a potent factor in the balance of power and the maintenance of peace since 1871.

But a new and vigorous power had arisen as a result of Bismarck's unification of Germany, a power which, under the ambitious, unbalanced young ruler who had come to the imperial throne in 1888, was to embark upon a course of deliberate challenge to Britain's naval supremacy.

Such a challenge, though doomed to failure in face of Britain's long start in the race, was to force a reappraisal of that country's assumption of world-wide naval responsibility. The threat near

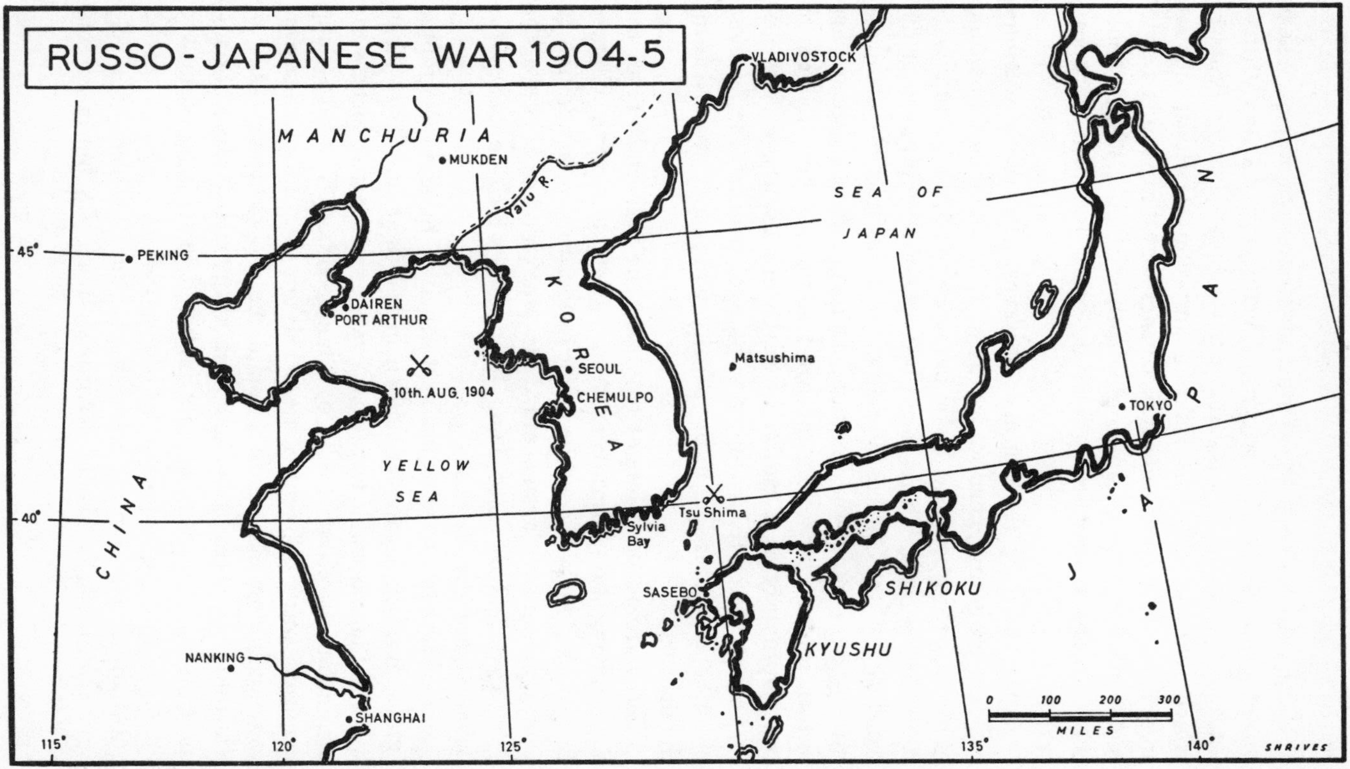
RUSSO-JAPANESE WAR 1904-5
MANCHURIA
MUKDEN
Yalu R.
VLADIVOSTOCK
SEA OF JAPAN
JAPAN
PEKING
DAIREN
PORT ARTHUR
KOREA
SEOUL
CHEMULPO
10th. AUG. 1904
Matsushima
TOKYO
YELLOW SEA
CHINA
Tsu Shima
Sylvia Bay
SASEBO
SHIKOKU
KYUSHU
NANKING
SHANGHAI
45°
40°
115°
120°
125°
135°
140°
0
100
200
300
MILES
SHRIVES

at home had to be met by a reduction of strength abroad, which meant primarily in the Far East. There, largely under British tutelage, a new naval power had emerged, the Japanese Empire, which might restrain the vaulting ambitions of Russia in that area. A steady encouragement of Japanese naval expansion was to be followed in 1902 by an Anglo-Japanese alliance which would allow Britain's main strength to be concentrated in European waters.

At the turn of the century, however, Germany's warship-building programme had some way to go before it could become of immediate importance. It was in the Orient that rival ambitions were first to clash. There, Japan had emerged triumphant at the conclusion of the Chinese War. In her first war since the abandonment of her century-old isolation, she had decisively defeated her historic enemy, by whom she had traditionally been looked on contemptuously as a nation of barbarous dwarfs. It was not surprising, therefore, that in their hour of triumph the Japanese overreached themselves in the penalty which they exacted from the defeated.

The war had been fought to obtain the independence of the Korean King and Government from the suzerainty of the Chinese Emperors. This was conceded; but further to this, in addition to a large indemnity, Japan claimed the annexation of Formosa, the Pescadores and the Liao-Tung Peninsula, which contained the naval base of Port Arthur.

Formosa and the Pescadores formed a natural geographic extension of the Japanese island chain and their transfer to Japan was a not unreasonable territorial arrangement, particularly as the inhabitants were not wholly of Chinese blood. The Liao-Tung Peninsula was a different matter. Though the European powers were gathering like vultures round the dying China, ready to tear outlying pieces from the corpse in the sacred name of commerce, some of them were not prepared to see a newcomer to the feast snatch so important a limb as that.

Britain and the United States, whose interests were genuinely only commercial and not territorial, made no objection; but land-hungry Germany and Russia, late-comers in the colonial field, saw their ambitions threatened—particularly Russia, who already had a predatory eye on Manchuria and on Port Arthur as an ice-free port. With the backing of France, these two objected to the transfer of the Liao-Tung Peninsula. Faced by their combined front, Japan was forced to give way on this point.

Such a confiscation, as she saw it, of her legitimate spoils of war was an injury which Japan was neither to forgive nor forget. Formosa and the Pescadores she was allowed to keep, but even the war indemnity was to react against her interests; for in order to pay it, China was driven into the only too willing arms of Russia.

Obtaining first a concession to take the Trans-Siberian railway to Vladivostock through Manchuria, Russia then demanded the right to station troops there to protect it. But Russia has always been anxious to obtain ice-free ports for her vast, sprawling continental territories. Vladivostock is closed by ice for many months of the year, but this is not the case with the harbours of the Kwantung Peninsula, the seaward tip of the Liao-Tung Peninsula, Port Arthur, Dairen and Talien-wan. In December 1897, taking advantage of the prostrate Chinese Empire, Russia sent a squadron of warships to Port Arthur, and by March of the next year had obtained agreement to a twenty-five-year lease of the Kwangtung Peninsula and the right to connect it by railway with the line to Vladivostock. To protect the line and the Russian employees, troops could be stationed where necessary.

All this was galling enough to the Japanese; they had been forced to give up Port Arthur, which they had captured from the Chinese at a heavy cost in blood and treasure, and now they saw it pass into the hands of Japan's most serious rival. In addition, after all the high-minded arguments by which the spoils of war had been filched from her, she saw Germany annexe the port of Kiao-Chow in 1897, while France obtained a lease of Kwangchow in the south, and Britain a lease of Wei-hai-wei and the New Territories of Hongkong.

In her still comparatively weak and poverty-stricken condition,

Japan was forced to accept these facts while biding her time and building her strength. But her position in Korea was a matter on which her security absolutely depended, and it brooked no compromise. On no account could she allow a foreign power to dominate that country, let alone secure naval bases in it.

Yet this is just what Russia went on to try to do. Already she had inherited the Chinese position in Korea, and in 1896 secured Japanese agreement to an equal division of influence and rights, particularly those of stationing troops in Seoul, the capital. Now her naval experts were pointing out that Port Arthur was useless as a base, being separated from Vladivostock by a long sea passage through the narrow Korean Straits dominated by the Japanese Navy.

Pressure was brought to bear on the Korean Government, and in May 1899 a Russian squadron arrived at Masanpo on the south coast of Korea to establish a base in Sylvia Basin, a first-class, land-locked fleet anchorage. Though Russian plans were temporarily halted by the purchase by a Japanese subject of the site selected, diplomatic pressure, backed by the threatening presence of Russian cruisers at Chemulpo, the port of Seoul, was renewed in the following year. In reply, Japan made open preparations for war and at last it became clear to the Russians that a base on the Straits of Korea could only be obtained by fighting for it. Russia was not prepared to fight, and so was forced to accept the unsound strategic position which she had brought upon herself by her acquisition of Port Arthur.

The Boxer Rebellion in China, essentially an anti-foreign rising fostered by "nationalist" elements in protest against the annexations of Chinese territory by foreigners, meant that all countries with a stake in China combined to restore order. These countries naturally included Japan. With her expeditionary force which fought alongside those of European countries and America, Japan demonstrated the high state of training and efficiency her army had achieved under German guidance. Her troops made a great impression upon all who saw them.

Russia, blindly pursuing her course of aggrandisement at the expense of China, used the Boxer Rebellion as a pretext to station as many as 100,000 troops in Manchuria, and on conclusion of the troubles it became clear that the Russians intended to make such an arrangement permanent. Furthermore, by means of a Russo-Chinese Bank, she planned to gain control of the whole of the finances of the Empire.

By now Russia's ambitions were antagonising and alarming all the powers. America came down firmly against the proposed financial agreement. Then, on 30th January 1902, as a result of negotiations which had been held in strict secrecy, England and Japan announced the conclusion of an alliance whose object was the preservation of the independence and integrity of China and Korea and equal opportunities in those countries for the commerce and industry of all nations. The terms of the alliance laid down that if either party had to go to war with a third power in defence of its interests in the Far East, the other would maintain strict neutrality and use its efforts to prevent other powers from intervening against its ally; and if any such power did intervene, then the neutral party would come to the assistance of its ally, and give actual military assistance.

At last it was borne in on Russia that she would be completely isolated in any dispute with Japan, and that the sympathies of Europe and America were ranged against her. She bowed to the storm. On 8th April 1902 she signed a treaty with China, by the terms of which Russia would evacuate Manchuria in three stages of six months each, leaving China to take responsibility for the safety of the railway and the protection of Russian subjects and establishments in the province.

It was a complete and startling change of front on the part of Russia. Though she retained her hold on the Kwantung Peninsula, it was quickly apparent that the men in power in Russia had genuinely abandoned all plans for adventurous military expansion.

Japan met the new Russian attitude half-way with proposals for a formal understanding about Korea. Both powers would undertake not to use any part of Korea for military or strategic purposes;

both would mutually guarantee the integrity of China and Korea. In return for a recognition by Russia that Japan had exclusive interests in Korea, Japan would acquiesce in the Russian possession of the Kwangtung Peninsula, and recognise her right to take any action necessary to protect her railway.

It began to look as though a solution to Far Eastern tensions might be in sight. While negotiations were in progress, the first six-month period in the promised evacuation of Manchuria expired, and in October 1902 Russia faithfully honoured her obligations to withdraw her troops from the southern part of the province. There was further evidence of Russia's good faith in the fact that no efforts were made to improve the defences or facilities of the naval base at Port Arthur, whereas vast sums were expended on the purely commercial harbour of Dairen. Indeed, Port Arthur necessarily ceased to be of great value if the occupying power did not have control of the hinterland or any good landward communications.

But for all the honeymoon atmosphere, neither side altogether trusted the other. Japan had been devoting a great proportion of her limited resources to building up her armed forces, the naval share of the increase being represented by a building programme which would bring the fleet by 1903 up to six new battleships, six armoured cruisers as good as any of their class anywhere, and eight light cruisers. However, there were no further additions to be expected, so that if war had to come, it would suit Japan for it to come not later than 1904.

During 1903 the Russians, appreciating this, despatched sufficient ships to match those of the Japanese fleet—in numbers, at any rate. These comprised three battleships, one armoured cruiser, seven cruisers, two light cruisers and seven destroyers. Two further battleships, two cruisers, one old armoured cruiser and seven destroyers from the Mediterranean were also under orders for the Far East at the the end of 1903.

Meanwhile, the Russo-Japanese negotiations in St. Petersburg were not going too smoothly. Though the three chief Ministers of the Russian State, Count Lamsdorf (Foreign Minister), Witte

(Minister of Finance) and General Kuropatkin (War Minister), were at one in a desire for peaceful development in the Far East, each for good reasons of his own, a combination of political force was rising which was to overwhelm them. It was a strange alliance of the semi-religious devotion to "Holy Russia" of the Tsar and his entourage, and the self-interest of a group of ambitious financiers.

The former, observing Japan's increasing influence with the Chinese Government, became obsessed with the idea of the Yellow Peril, which was having a vogue in certain European circles at that time.

The latter was under the leadership of a M. Bezobrazov, who had acquired from the original concessionaire, a Vladivostock merchant, the right to cut timber in a huge stretch of country covering the whole length of the Korean side of the border from sea to sea. The promised evacuation of Manchuria would leave this immensely valuable concession void of any Russian protection, and in the unsettled condition of the country it could not be exploited. Representing this to be a great blow to Russian national aspirations, Bezobrazov obtained the support of the grand dukes and the court. He then went further, and obtained from the local Chinese governor a similar concession on the Manchurian side of the border.

In spite of this, the power of the three ministers was for a little while unshaken, and preparations for the second stage of the evacuation of Manchuria went ahead. Kuropatkin, visiting Tokyo in July to get the feel of the situation for himself, was vastly impressed by the progress of Japanese armed strength. He reported that Japan was no light adversary to provoke, and that Russian intrigues on the Korean border were being taken very seriously.

But Kuropatkin's absence from the capital was fatal to the peace party. By the time he got back to St. Petersburg he found that the court had fallen under the sway of the "patriotic" clique headed by M. Pleve, the rival of M. Witte for power. From this time onward matters drifted inexorably towards war, though Japan offered concessions. Behind the backs of Lamsdorf, Witte and Kuropatkin, still officially the chief ministers, it was suddenly announced that the whole Far East had been constituted into one province with Admiral Alexeieff, a leader of the "patriotic" clique and Governor of Port Arthur, as Viceroy.

Kuropatkin at once asked to be relieved of his duties, and Witte was replaced by Pleve. It became clear that Russia was bent on defying Japan and proceeding with her policy of expansion in Manchuria. Only blind ignorance of the realities of the naval situation can have led her to such a course. Her Far Eastern squadron was not only still weaker in numbers than the Japanese, but also its ships were a mixed force, unaccustomed to working together; its crews were ill-trained, and morale was low under the uninspiring leadership of its commander, Vice-Admiral Stark. On the other hand Japan's fleet, with its six battleships and six armoured cruisers of homogeneous design and its greatly superior torpedo-boat force, was in all respects ready for war; under its able and energetic leader Admiral Togo, it was only too ready for a fight.

Moreover, the whole strategic position was in Japan's favour. So far as Russia was concerned, the two "bones of contention", the Kwangtung Peninsula and Korea, were isolated at the end of interminable, primitive lines of communication. The two Russian naval bases, Port Arthur and Vladivostock, were similarly cut off from each other by land, and their sea communications blocked by the Japanese-dominated Straits of Korea. Furthermore, to defeat Japan the Russians would have to invade the island empire, whereas the occupation of Korea and the Kwangtung Peninsula would gain the Japanese their objective.

Thus success for either side would depend absolutely upon command of the Yellow Sea in the early stages, when Japan could be expected to be landing her armies in Korea and on the Liao-Tung Peninsula. In the long run command of the Sea of Japan would also be necessary if Russia wished to send her armies across to Japan. But unless the Russians divided their fleet between Port Arthur and Vladivostock, the Japanese would be left a free hand to attack one or the other. In any case, Port Arthur lacked facilities to base more than a portion of the Russian Far Eastern squadron.

The Russians were therefore forced back on the conception of keeping a "fleet in being" at Port Arthur, which though it could not hope to wrest command of the Yellow Sea from the Japanese, could hold it in dispute sufficiently to limit Japanese landings to the southern half of Korea, so delaying their advance on Manchuria long enough to allow Russia to gather her armies for the defence of Port Arthur. Meanwhile the presence of a diversionary force of three armoured cruisers and one protected cruiser at Vladivostock would prevent any Japanese military threat in that area. Finally, Russia's Baltic Fleet would be despatched to the Far East, its combination with the Port Arthur squadron making a fleet far superior to anything which the Japanese could muster.

Yet in spite of the difficulties from which Russian plans suffered owing to her lack of sufficient naval force in the Far East, the despatch of reinforcements was put in train with a lack of energy and administrative efficiency only too typical of the Tsarist Russian Navy. A battleship, two cruisers and seven destroyers were still in the Mediterranean area when war finally broke out.

By the beginning of January 1904, it was clear to the Japanese that the Russians were simply dragging out negotiations in order to gain time to improve their military situation. The Japanese therefore went ahead with final preparations for a landing in Korea. But they, too, wished to delay the final outbreak of war, for in the Mediterranean a strange comedy was being played out.

At Genoa were lying two armoured cruisers recently completed for the Argentine Navy and which Japan had bought, renaming them the *Nisshin* and *Kasuga*. At the same time a Russian squadron consisting of the battleship *Oslyabya*, flagship of Rear-Admiral Virenius, the armoured cruiser *Dmitri Donskoi*, the protected cruiser *Aurora* and seven destroyers was passing through the Mediterranean. So when the *Nisshin* and *Kasuga*—flying the Japanese naval ensign, though commanded for the passage by

British naval reserve officers—arrived at Port Said, they found the whole Russian squadron in harbour there, except for the *Dmitri Donskoi*, which had already entered the Suez Canal.

The situation was not without piquancy. Had the Russian admiral possessed a spark of initiative, he could have taken the rest of his squadron through the Canal in time to shadow the Japanese cruisers and hold himself ready to attack them if war should break out. But it was not until six days later that the last of Virenius' squadron mustered at Suez, and then they loitered for the next few months in the Red Sea, not daring to face the risk of being intercepted on passage to Port Arthur or Vladivostock.

By 2nd February *Nisshin* and *Kasuga* were at Singapore under orders to sail not later than the 6th. The last obstacle to the opening of hostilities had been cleared from the Japanese path. The troops for the landing on the west coast of Korea at Chemulpo were already embarked in their troopships. The fleet was concentrated at Sasebo. Sealed orders were held by General and Admiral and on the afternoon of 5th February 1904, the two commanders received instructions to open the orders.

So the die was cast. As the squadrons filed out of Sasebo harbour in line ahead the following morning, to the "Banzais" of an enthusiastic population ashore, a war had begun which was to take Japan, a brief fifty years after her awakening from medieval slumber, into the front rank of world powers. In St. Petersburg, however, negotiations still went on in desultory fashion and an absence of good faith on either side, so that it was not until 8th February that the Japanese ambassador finally asked for his passports and announced that his mission would leave on the 10th. Before that time had come, guns and torpedoes had proclaimed the outbreak of war without benefit of formal declaration.

The Japanese naval staff plan for the opening moves of the war had originally visualised a bold attack, using the whole Japanese fleet, on the Russian squadron in Port Arthur. They expected the Russian ships to come out and offer battle in an attempt to gain control of the Yellow Sea, which was of such vital importance to both sides. The movement of the expeditionary force would await the outcome of this battle. Togo, however, saw clearly that by using his main fleet as a covering force for the troop convoy, the landing could be proceeded with at once without risk, particularly as he correctly judged that the Russian squadron would not, in fact, seek a decisive battle while their paper strength was no greater than that of the Japanese.

Having seen the convoy safely on its way, Togo proposed to press on to Port Arthur, where the war was to open with a surprise torpedo attack by his flotillas, under cover of darkness, on the Russian fleet which he expected to find lying in the Roads. Togo's plan was accepted, and it was on this basis that the various squadrons made their way northwards. The actual close escort of the troop convoy was undertaken by Rear-Admiral Uriu's division of cruisers, the armoured cruiser *Asama* and eight torpedo-boats.

With the first shots of the war about to be fired, it is a convenient moment to examine the relative strength of the opposing fleets. The Japanese were divided into three squadrons, of which the first two, under the supreme command of Admiral Togo, sailed north to cover the troop convoy and subsequently to challenge the Russian fleet in Port Arthur.

They consisted of the following ships:

FIRST SQUADRON

First Division. Battleships *Mikasa* (Flag of Vice-Admiral Togo, Commander-in-Chief), *Asahi*, *Fuji*, *Yashima*, *Shikishima* and *Hatsuse* (Flag of Rear-Admiral Nashiba). Main armament of each, four 12-inch. Secondary armament ten or fourteen 6-inch.

Third Division. Cruisers *Chitose* (Flag of Rear-Admiral Dewa), *Takasago*, *Kasagi* (each two 8-inch and ten 4·7-inch); *Yoshino* (four 6-inch and eight 4·7-inch).

Three divisions of four destroyers each mounting two 18-inch torpedo-tubes, two 12-pounders and four 6-pounders.

Two divisions of four torpedo-boats each mounting three 18-inch torpedo-tubes.

SECOND SQUADRON

Second Division. Armoured cruisers *Idzumo* (flag of Vice-Admiral Kamimura), *Adzumo, Asama, Yakumo, Tokiwa* and *Iwate* (Flag of Rear-Admiral Misu). Each mounting four 8-inch and twelve or fourteen 6-inch guns.

Fourth Division. Cruisers *Naniwa* (Flag of Rear-Admiral Uriu), *Takachiho* and *Niitaka* mounting six or eight 6-inch and *Akashi*, two 6-inch and six 4·7-inch guns.

Two destroyer divisions of four boats each, with two 18-inch torpedo-tubes, two 12-pounders and four 6-pounders.

Two divisions of torpedo-boats as in 1st. squadron.

The third squadron, composed of the oldest ships of the fleet, formed an independent command under Vice-Admiral Kataoka, charged with holding the Straits of Korea against the Vladivostock section of the Russian fleet should it attempt to join the Port Arthur squadron. It was made up as follows:

THIRD SQUADRON

Fifth Division. Second Class Battleship *Chinyen* (ex-Chinese); cruisers *Itsukushima* (Flag of Vice-Admiral Kataoka), *Hashidate, Matsushima.*

Sixth Division. Light cruisers *Idzumi* (Flag of Rear-Admiral M. Togo), *Suma, Akitsushima, Chiyoda.*

Seventh Division. Third Class Battleship *Fuso* (Flag of Rear-Admiral Hosoya), two coast defence vessels, seven gunboats and one despatch vessel.

Three divisions of four torpedo-boats each.

The Russian fleet was divided into two sections also. At Port Arthur under Vice-Admiral Stark there were the following:

Battleship Division. Petropavlovsk (Flag of Vice-Admiral Stark), *Tzesarevitch, Retvizan, Sevastopol, Peresviet* (Flag of Rear-Admiral Prince Ukhtomsky), *Pobieda* and *Poltava.* Main armament four 12- or 10-inch. Secondary eleven or twelve 6-inch.

Cruiser Division. Askold (Flag of Rear-Admiral Reitzenstein), twelve 6-inch. *Bayan* two 8-inch, eight 6-inch. *Diana* eight 6-inch. *Pallada* eight 6-inch. *Boyarin* six 4·7-inch. *Novik* six 4·7-inch.

Two torpedo-gunboats and twenty-five destroyers mounting two or three 18-inch torpedo-tubes, one 12-pounder and three or five 3-pounders.

At Vladivostock there were the three armoured cruisers *Gromoboi* (Flag of Rear-Admiral Stakelberg), *Rossia* and *Rurik*, mounting four 8-inch and sixteen 6-inch guns, the protected cruiser *Bogatyr*, twelve 6-inch, and seventeen torpedo-boats.

* * *

At first sight the two fleets were well matched. Though the Japanese had a superiority in cruisers, they were unlikely to be found concentrated at the moment of battle owing to their escorting and patrolling commitments. The Russians had a superiority of one in the main battle line.

The Russian fleet was strong enough on paper to make Togo, commanding Japan's only fleet, anxious to reduce its strength before meeting it in battle. He could not even afford to lose ships in a drawn fight, for at the other end of the world Russia's other fleet was being prepared for the Far East. Its arrival and junction with the Port Arthur squadron could decisively alter the balance in Russia's favour.

Quantity alone in ships and guns is no sure guide to relative strength, however. To the Japanese homogeneous squadron of fast battleships, each capable of 18 knots, each mounting four 12-inch guns, the Russians opposed a squadron limited by the speed of two of them to a maximum of 16 knots, their armament varying between 10- and 12-inch guns. The Japanese crews were well-trained and enthusiastic; the Russians were demoralised, unpractised and badly led. There were already signs of the revolution which was to break out the next year.

It is of interest therefore to speculate as to what might have happened if Togo, in his encounters with the Port Arthur squadron, had had sufficient confidence in the moral and technical superiority of his fleet to attack with less caution, aiming at annihilation. Had he achieved this, it is unlikely that the Baltic squadron would have been sent on its mission of reinforcement, and the naval side of the war might have been concluded much sooner.

As we have seen, it was inevitable that the Russians should divide their fleet in some way; but whether they ought to have done so in the proportion which they actually did, is open to question. So knowledgeable a student of naval war as the late Sir Julian Corbett has criticised them for a false interpretation of the strategy of the maintenance of a "fleet in being". If they had no intention of challenging the Japanese fleet in pitched battle, Corbett considered, they should not have allowed such a strong force to be pinned down in a harbour so easily blockaded, so devoid of facilities for a fleet and of adequate defences, and so liable to be cut off from the hinterland by a land expedition. A smaller force employed would still have been able to threaten the Japanese control of the Yellow Sea sufficiently to require them to keep the modern portion of their fleet there. At the same time the Vladivostock squadron, strengthened by the addition of some battleships, would have posed a serious threat to the Japanese homeland. Instead, Togo was able largely to ignore Rear-Admiral Stakelberg's division unless he should come south to join the main body, in which case the Japanese fleet was itself well placed to concentrate.

Indeed the naval strategy of Admiral Alexeieff, supreme commander in the Far East and Viceroy, advised by Rear-Admiral Vitgeft, his Chief of Staff, was as inept as the tactics and administration of the fleet commander, Vice-Admiral Stark. Though the Russian naval attaché in Tokyo had given clear warning that Japanese operations were to be expected immediately, the Port Arthur squadron lay at anchor in the Roads on the 8th February in three lines running east and west, some engaged in coaling. Admittedly Stark had proposed to Alexeieff that precautions should be taken against a sudden attack; but on being discouraged by the supreme commander, who was at Port Arthur, Stark

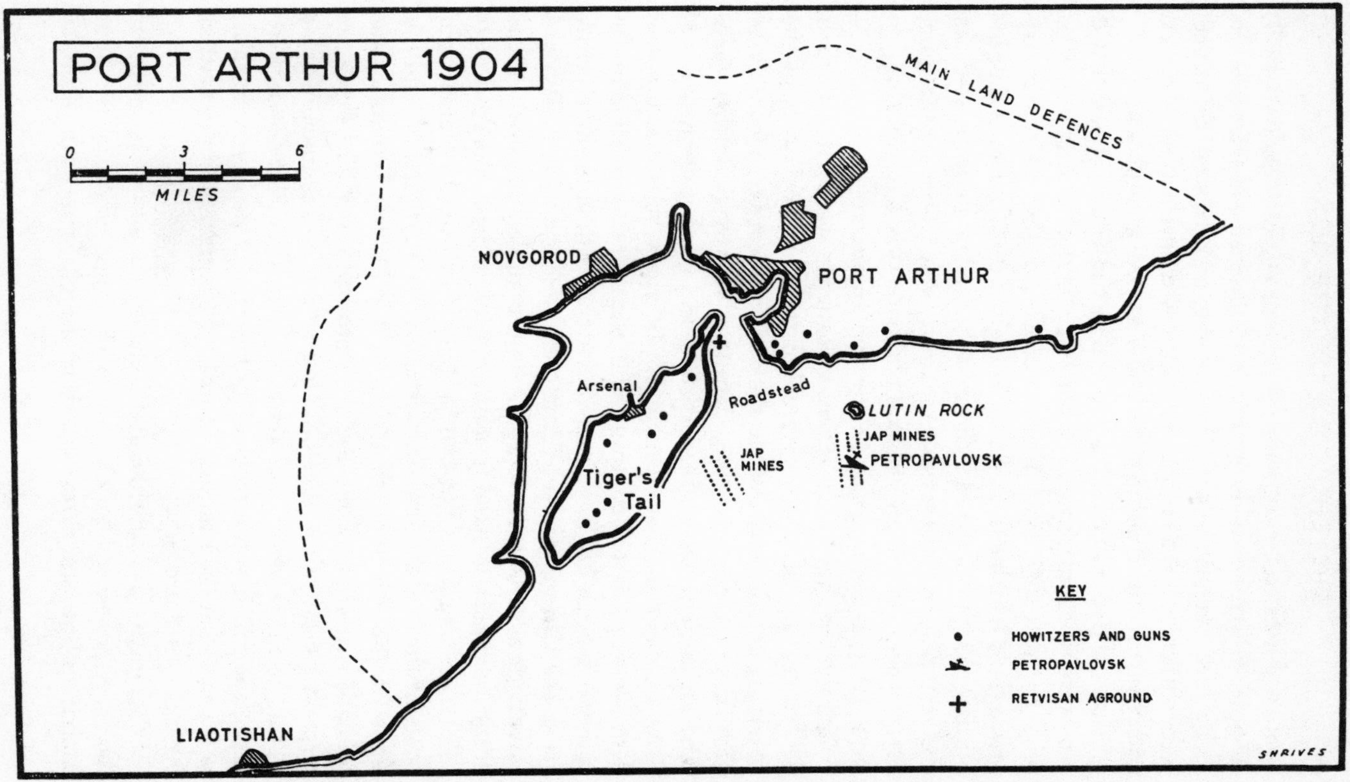
PORT ARTHUR 1904
0
3
6
MILES
MAIN LAND DEFENCES
NOVGOROD
PORT ARTHUR
Arsenal
Roadstead
LUTIN ROCK
JAP MINES
PETROPAVLOVSK
JAP
MINES
Tiger's
Tail
KEY
HOWITZERS AND GUNS
PETROPAVLOVSK
RETVISAN AGROUND
LIAOTISHAN
SHRIVES

contented himself by signalling "Prepare to repel torpedo attacks", an order which was taken by his unenlightened and inert captains to be "for exercise" only. As warning pickets, two destroyers were sent to patrol 20 miles to seaward with instructions to return and report to the flagship if they saw anything suspicious.

Alexeieff had, indeed, been ordered by the Tsar to ensure that if war were to come it should be the Japanese not the Russians, who fired the first shot. But it was a careless neglect of elementary precautions which left the fleet that night with all its normal lights burning, its guns unloaded, the crews turned in on the mess-decks and no arrangements for challenging any vessels seen approaching. Furthermore, the Liao-ti-shan lighthouse was left working, to send out its beam to guide an enemy's approach.

Ashore, the guns of the defensive batteries were left with their winter coating of heavy grease and the recoil cylinders of the 10-inch guns drained. While the Russian fleet lay heedlessly in such a defenceless posture, Japanese destroyer flotillas were slipping through the night, torpedoes and guns at the ready.

At 6 o'clock on that evening, 8th February 1904, the Japanese destroyers had parted company with the fleet to the sound of the rousing "banzais" of their comrades in the battleships and cruisers. From the Commander-in-Chief had come the order: "Proceed and attack as arranged. I pray for your complete success." As the fleet turned back to stand to seaward until daylight, the destroyers —little craft of some 350 tons in those days—went on alone; ten boats of the 1st, 2nd and 3rd Divisions for Port Arthur, and the eight of the 4th and 5th Divisions for Dairen, where it was believed that some of the Russian ships had gone. The first mass torpedo attack, of the type which was later to become a regular feature of naval tactics, was about to be made. Great things were expected of it. It was soon clear, however, that there was much to be learnt about the handling of darkened flotillas at night, even in the highly trained Japanese fleet.

First, in the darkness the 2nd Division cut across the bows of the 1st Division led by Captain Asai, senior officer of the Port Arthur section, and threw it into confusion for a time. Then, as the re-formed flotilla pressed on to raise the Liao-ti-shan light, the lights of the Russian destroyer patrol were sighted heading straight for them. Though by an alteration of course and the dowsing of their dimmed sternlights the Japanese escaped detection, the Russian boats passed through the line, ahead of the 2nd Division, whose leader was forced to go dead slow without signal. The next boat, the *Oboro*, came charging up to collide with her leader the *Ikadsuchi*, suffering considerable damage. The *Ikadsuchi* was able to carry on, but lost touch with the remainder of the division and found herself alone. The *Inadzuma*, third ship of this division, returned to stand by the damaged *Oboro*. Meanwhile the 3rd Division also had been forced to stop, and by the time the Russians had passed clear, had lost touch with the remainder. Its rear ship, the *Sazanami*, actually formed up astern of the Russian destroyers for a time before realising her mistake, when she too hurried on alone for the objective.

The *Inadzuma* returned to her place with the 3rd Division, having seen that the *Oboro* was not in serious danger. Thus reconstituted as a unit of three, the 3rd Division again set course for Port Arthur.

Already the mass attack had been broken up into several un-co-ordinated groups. Captain Asai was well ahead with four boats, followed at an interval by the three of the 3rd Division, while the *Oboro* was desperately patching up her injuries and the *Sazanami* and *Ikadsuchi* were coming on by themselves, determined not to be left out of the fight.

In the Russian fleet two ships, *Retvizan* and the cruiser *Pallada*, had been detailed as searchlight guards, and the blue-white, dazzling beams of the lights swept back and forth to seaward. *Askold* and *Diana* were the duty cruisers, and lay with steam on their main engines. In the rest of the Russian fleet there was steam only for auxiliary purposes, pumps and dynamos. In the *Petropavlovsk*, Admiral Stark was entertaining the Chief of the Staff and the Port Commandant, who had come on board the flagship for a conference.

By midnight the Russian searchlights were plainly in view from the Japanese destroyers, and Captain Asai was steering for them at slow speed. Suddenly the beams were held steady, full into the eyes of the approaching Japanese. It seemed certain that they had been detected; but then, amazingly the searchlights resumed their unhurried sweeps.

Asai realised that the moment for action had come. Signalling for the attack, he led directly for the clustered lights of the unsuspecting Russian ships. Soon the silhouettes of the ships could be made out in spite of the dazzle of the searchlight-beams, and the Japanese picked as targets the two searchlight ships and the battleship *Tzesarevitch* at the end of the second line of ships.

As the estimated range dropped to 700 yards, Asai swung his ship to port to bring his torpedo-tubes to bear, and reduced speed to dead slow to take careful aim. As the torpedoes leapt from each of his two tubes, he rang for full speed and sped away into the darkness. The three boats with him followed his example, and five more torpedoes were soon streaking for the mass of shipping.

Now at last the alarm was raised in the Russian fleet. At half an hour after midnight the officer of the watch in the *Retvizan* sighted two destroyers in the beam of the *Pallada*'s searchlight. He at once ordered "Repel Torpedo Attack", but the sleeping gun-crews had to be roused from their hammocks and sent stumbling dazedly to their action stations. Long before they were ready to open fire, a torpedo had exploded against the port side, plunging the ship into darkness and causing her to list heavily.

From the *Pallada* nothing was seen until 12.41, when the alarm was sounded. Even when the guns were made ready her captain feared to give the order to open fire, uncertain whether the destroyers were friend or foe. Only when the track of a torpedo was seen approaching was he sure, and then it was too late. In quick succession three torpedoes exploded, that on the *Retvizan*, one against the *Pallada* and one on the *Tzesarevitch*.

At last the guns came uncertainly into action, but the Japanese 1st Division was already retiring at high speed. Though some ships of the Division were hit, the damage was not serious. Following close behind the 1st Division had come the *Ikadsuchi*, which, meeting the ever-growing storm of shells, turned and fired her torpedoes at somewhat longer range. Though she got away unhit, her torpedoes failed to find a target.

Next came the three destroyers under the leader of the 3rd Division. By the time they arrived the situation was not nearly so favourable for them. The Roads were a blaze of searchlights; guns from every ship were firing furiously, if wildly. When the range had fallen to an estimated 1,600 yards just inside the extreme range of the torpedoes of those days, the destroyers turned and fired. They escaped almost untouched, but once again no hits were scored on the Russian ships. Lastly the *Sazanami* came gallantly in for her solitary attack. Though continuously in the searchlight-beams, she closed to within 800 yards before firing two torpedoes; yet even so both missed.

As the *Sazanami* slipped away into the darkness, the gunfire died away, only to break out again an hour later with redoubled fury from the now thoroughly aroused Russian ships. The little *Oboro*, her damaged bow patched up, had got under way again; and taking advantage of the lull, she crept in to 1,300 yards to fire both her tubes. But though the concentrated fire of the whole fleet failed to damage her, her boldness went unrewarded, for neither of her torpedoes hit.

So the first operation of its kind came to an end—for the flotilla allocated to Dairen found that harbour empty. Great hopes had been pinned on the attack. The Japanese torpedo-men were looked on as something of a "corps d'élite", highly trained and well practised. Yet in fact the results were paltry considering the favourable conditions under which the attack was made. An unalerted, anchored fleet, its lights burning, its guns unready, full navigational facilities available to the attackers, no boom or net defences; yet out of nineteen torpedoes fired, only three took effect and not one of the ships hit was sunk.

Not for the last time by any means, the effectiveness of the torpedo mounted in surface ships had been greatly exaggerated. Theoretically every torpedo fired which ran correctly should have been a certain hit, but theory did not take into account the blinding effect of the searchlights stabbing through a particularly black night; the bitter cold, accentuated for the destroyer officers and control personnel by the icy wind sweeping across the exposed bridges, blurring vision and numbing thought; the intimidating leap of a forest of shell splashes, and the shock of an occasional hit.

The first division to attack achieved almost complete surprise, pressed in to close range and scored three hits out of seven torpedoes fired. The remainder, coming against an alerted defence, were forced to fire at longer range, their target hidden in the dazzle of the searchlights. It is possible they did not even close to the maximum range of their torpedoes. Of the twelve torpedoes fired under these conditions, not one hit.

Meanwhile in the Russian fleet all was bustle and flurry at long last. Smoke belched from funnels as steam was hastily raised, though only one ship, the cruiser *Novik*, sailed in chase, returning some hours later empty-handed. The *Retvizan* and the *Tzesarevitch* were got under way, but were so deep in the water through extensive flooding that they both grounded, the *Tzesarevitch* in the inner harbour and the *Retvizan* in the narrow entrance. The *Pallada* steamed to shallow water close inshore and again anchored.

Disappointing as the results of the attack were to the Japanese, a serious blow had been struck at the Russians, psychologically as well as physically. Two of their best battleships were out of action, and there was no dry dock in Port Arthur which could take them in their deep-draught, damaged condition. To a squadron already in low spirits and poor heart under the inept leadership of Admiral Stark, it was a disaster. The dismay was heightened by the news which now reached them of the destruction of the light-cruiser *Variag* and a gunboat which had been foolishly left at Chemulpo to be overwhelmed by Rear-Admiral Uriu's squadron escorting the Japanese troopships to that port.

So the first naval war of the ironclad age between fleets roughly equal in initial strength began with a limited though important success to one of them even before war had been formally declared. It set the pattern for the rest of the war, but fortune was not always to smile on the Japanese, who also would have to face calamity in due course.

6

Mines and Close Blockade

GREAT as had been the expectations of success for the Japanese torpedo attack, the Commander-in-Chief had made no plans to exploit it vigorously without delay. It would seem that it had not occurred to him that Russian lack of preparedness could be so absolute. Togo had no desire to risk his irreplaceable battleships in an attack which would expose them to the fire of the powerful shore batteries as well as that of the Russian fleet. He knew and agreed with the naval dictum that ships could not assault forts with advantage.

At the same time, Togo's primary task of covering the landing operations at Chemulpo embraced the necessity of engaging the Russian fleet if it should come to sea. During the night of the torpedo attack he had cruised in the offing, therefore, ready for any eventualities, and at daylight Rear-Admiral Dewa's cruiser division was sent in to reconnoitre.

By 9 o'clock on 9th February Dewa was close enough to distinguish individual Russian ships through the morning mist. Three or four ships, he could see, were listing badly and seemed to be ashore, while the remainder were huddled together without order. No notice seemed to be taken of him, so he closed to within 8,000 yards. Still not a shot was fired at him. Convinced that the whole force was thoroughly demoralised and disorganised, Dewa turned away at high speed to carry the news to his Commander-in-Chief.

Russian accounts disagree with Dewa's conclusions. The fleet was ready for action, they claim. Steam was on the engines, battle ensigns at the mastheads and anchors aweigh when the Japanese squadron was seen to turn and make off to seaward. Be that as it may, the failure to engage Dewa's squadron when it closed to $3\frac{1}{2}$ miles displayed little offensive spirit, and the Japanese admiral was justified in informing Togo that "they have very little spirit left, and I consider that an attack delivered at once would be very effective".

So undoubtedly it would have been, if "delivered at once", that is to say at first light, when disorganisation still reigned amongst the Russians and the heavy guns of the forts were still being got ready. But it was not until 10 o'clock that Dewa was within wireless range and able to get his message through, and another hour before he rejoined the fleet and renewed his urging of an immediate assault.

Meanwhile three hours of precious daylight had gone by, during which the Russian fleet was pulling itself together and the garrison gunners were hurriedly preparing their guns for action.

By 11 o'clock Togo had been convinced by Dewa's enthusiastic signals that an opportunity for a decisive blow had come, even if it meant accepting the fire of the shore batteries. Directing Dewa to form his division in line astern of the armoured cruisers of the 2nd Division, he led the way for Port Arthur with the battleships in the van, and sent all crews to their dinners.

Shortly before noon, the cruiser *Boyarin* was sighted, and opened fire at extreme range as she fled back to harbour to give the alarm. In Togo's flagship *Mikasa*, the signal for action was run up to the yard-arm. The great battle ensigns were unfurled at the mastheads of the long line of ships. Down the line was passed the admiral's encouraging though ill-judged message: "Victory or defeat will be decided by this one action. Let every man do his utmost."

In spite of clear warning given by the early morning appearance of Dewa's division, the moment of alarm found the Russian Commander-in-Chief ashore, "receiving instructions" from Alexeieff. Though the Chief of Staff took it upon himself to order the fleet to weigh and form single line ahead, it was still in considerable disorder when the Japanese ships were sighted.

There is some doubt, indeed, whether the Russian ships moved from their anchor berths during the ensuing action. The Japanese account states that only the outer line of cruisers, *Bayan*, *Askold* and *Novik*, made any move to come out, and of these only *Novik* was handled with courage, miraculously escaping destruction as she was steered boldly through heavy, concentrated fire to loose two torpedoes at a range of 3,000 yards.

The Russian account claims that the fleet advanced towards the enemy in line abreast before turning together to the eastward into line ahead, passing the Japanese fleet on opposite courses. But certainly they did not go far before turning back 180 degrees; by then the Japanese were withdrawing, and the Russian ships returned to their anchorages.

While this was going on Togo was leading his line on a westerly course, the range coming down from 8,700 yards, when the first shot flashed out from the *Mikasa*, to less than 7,000 yards as the two fleets drew abreast of each other. At this range, 6-inch and even 12-pounder guns came into action, and soon the Russian fleet was so smothered in smoke from bursting shells and from the discharge of its own guns that it became impossible for the Japanese to spot the fall of shot with any confidence.

For a time hits were being scored on the Russians at a great rate, but the majority were on the four cruisers, *Bayan*, *Askold*, *Diana* and *Novik*, which, being nearest to the enemy and seen to be under way, drew most of the fire. Some of the battleships received hits—the *Pobieda* had fifteen—but none penetrated their armour, and they were not seriously damaged.

At the same time, not only did the Russian fleet prove by its good shooting that it was less demoralised than had appeared to Dewa during his morning reconnaissance, but Togo found that his reluctance to expose his ships to the fire of the shore batteries had been well founded. After some wild firing in the opening minutes the Russians found the range, and within five minutes the flagship *Mikasa* had been struck three times by heavy shell. Four out of six of the Japanese battleship division suffered hits and casualties.

The exchange was too level for Togo to accept. As the Japanese line drew across the front of the Russians and the range from the

Mikasa opened, he came under heavy fire from the western shore batteries—a fire to which he could make no effective reply. He accordingly led round 90 degrees to port on to a southerly course, to withdraw out of range. The Russian gunners then shifted their aim to the 2nd Division of armoured cruisers, which had to follow round through a sea leaping with shell splashes. Somehow the Japanese ships escaped serious damage, but Togo could not risk exposing Dewa's light cruisers to a similar concentration, and he ordered them to withdraw by the quicker method of a 90-degree turn away, all ships together.

So after some forty minutes of furious cannonade the firing died away and Togo had leisure to consider the results of his assault, an assault which had only been made on the assumption that the Russian morale and preparedness were at a low ebb, as reported by Dewa. But the fatal delay of four hours had entirely altered the situation as seen from Dewa's bridge in the light of early morning. It had not been Togo's original intention to risk his invaluable, irreplaceable ships unless the Russians came to sea to dispute the control of the Yellow Sea and threaten the safe passage of Japanese armies to Korea. Dewa's enthusiasm had encouraged him to change his plans. Had he been in position to implement Dewa's urging at once, the boldly improvised attack might well have brought the Japanese a decisive naval victory which would have delivered Port Arthur into their hands and made unnecessary the long and costly naval campaign of the next fifteen months.

But the great opportunity had slipped by, never to return. Togo saw this clearly, and decided to leave well alone. In spite of protests from Admiral Kamimura, who pointed out the practically undamaged condition of his armoured squadron and urged a further attack the next morning, the Commander-in-Chief, with considerable moral courage, held to his decision to withdraw. By the next day he was at his forward base of Asan.

Perhaps the most telling point to emerge from this action was the surprisingly little damage done to either side in forty minutes of furious gunfire at what was soon to be looked upon as almost point-blank range. In the Japanese battleship division, twenty-four 12-inch guns and thirty-five 6-inch, as well as a large number of 12-pounders, were in action. The armoured division brought forty 6-inch guns as well as a smaller number of 8-inch to bear, while Dewa's light-cruisers added the rapid fire of a great many 4·7-inch. Yet the Russian casualties were only 21 killed and 101 wounded; their battleships were very little damaged, and none of the cruisers, on which much of the fire was concentrated, were put out of action.

The Japanese, attacked by the heavy guns of the shore batteries as well as those of the whole Russian fleet, suffered only superficial damage and even fewer casualties. Without doubt two principal causes for the ineffectiveness of the gunfire were the flat trajectory of projectiles at such short range, which caused most hits to waste their energy on heavy side-armour which they failed to penetrate, and the difficulty of determining the fall of shot amongst the almost continuous plunge and splash of shells from every calibre of gun being fired independently and individually.

Range-finders could give a fairly accurate range of a target, but the many small errors which could affect the application of the range to a gun necessitated spotting corrections to obtain a hit. Unless each individual splash could be identified, it was impossible to apply such corrections. With guns of various calibres all firing simultaneously and independently, no such identification could be secured. It could have been done only with guns of similar size and performance, firing approximately together in salvoes.

In the navies of Europe and the United States this conclusion had already been reached theoretically. Furthermore the big gun, gaining steadily in range and accuracy, had been recognised as the battle-winner of the future. Therefore it was considered a waste of armament, tonnage and space to fit smaller guns which could never come into action against a ship which stood off at long range and relied upon her big guns.

Lieutenant-Commander W. S. Sims, the brilliant gunnery expert of the United States Navy, had for long advocated the introduction of the all-big-gun battleship. Admiral Sir John

Fisher, the Royal Navy's great reformer and innovator, was even then studying designs for a similar ship which was to burst upon a startled world in the following year as H.M.S. *Dreadnought.*

That great revolution in battleship-design and all its implications will be examined in a later chapter. Meanwhile the naval battles of the Russo-Japanese War were to give practical example to support the ideas of the theorists elsewhere. The big gun was not the only new weapon which was to be given the test of war. The torpedo was to come to the fore, though with disappointing results, and the moored mine was also to play a big part.

* * *

The fleet action of 9th February 1904, indecisive as it was, had achieved for the Japanese their principal objective, the temporary local control of the Yellow Sea and the safe passage of their armies to Korea. The Russians had withdrawn their ships into the inner harbour with the exception of the *Retvizan*, still aground at the entrance, and it was clear that for the time being their squadron would not venture to sea; yet so long as it was "in being" and able to come out, it was necessary for the Japanese to retain the whole of their modern fleet in the area, which left the Russian Vladivostock squadron unwatched and free to threaten the northern coasts of Japan.

On the other hand the state of unpreparedness of the Port Arthur garrison was such that, as the Russians themselves admitted, had the Japanese taken immediate advantage of their temporary naval supremacy to land an army and take the defences in the rear, the base must have quickly fallen. But this was beyond the limited resources of the Japanese, who were still in process of mobilising their main armies, and it would have called for a skilful improvisation of plan of which the Japanese Imperial General Staff was not capable.

Instead, the carefully prepared war plan with its cautious time-table was adhered to. The Japanese Army was thus condemned to the long siege and bloody assaults which would eventually be necessary to reduce Port Arthur. For the next six months both fleets were committed to a course of skirmishing, during which serious losses were suffered by both sides, chiefly from mines. On several occasions the Japanese attempted to block the harbour exit by sinking merchant ships in the channel, and they sent in their destroyers to make night torpedo attacks. None of these operations succeeded.

The Russians laid extensive minefields in an attempt to embarrass the blockade and to prevent Japanese landings in Talien Bay and elsewhere. The first victims of these, however, were the ship which had laid the mines and the cruiser *Boyarin* which went out to her assistance—both of which were sunk, the former with heavy loss of life. Russian blundering also cost them a destroyer cut off and sunk, two more badly damaged through grounding in a snowstorm, and damage to the cruisers *Bayan*, *Askold* and *Novik*, which were caught outside the harbour and engaged as they ran for shelter.

Russian morale was at its lowest ebb when, on 8th March, a new spirit was infused into the fleet by the arrival of Vice-Admiral Makaroff to assume the command. He at once roused the squadron from its lethargy. The *Retvizan* was refloated and towed into the harbour, where repairs were pressed ahead with her and the *Tzesarevitch*. Unable to enter the dry dock in their damaged condition, they were fitted with cofferdams, large close-fitting box-like structures sunk against the side of the ship, and then pumped out to enable work to be done on damage below the water-line.

Makaroff instituted strong destroyer patrols to seaward by night, which brought on a brisk destroyer action on his second night in command. Four Japanese and six Russian boats clashed in a wild, scrambling mêlée in the darkness, during which collisions were narrowly avoided, guns sent shells repeatedly into enemy hulls at ranges so close that grenades could be hurled from one ship to another, and a Russian destroyer was disabled by a torpedo from one of her comrades. Both sides were so damaged that they were barely able to retire to seek support.

The action was a tonic to the drooping morale of the Russians;

but at daybreak, two other Russian destroyers allowed themselves to be cut off by the enemy and one was quickly disabled. The admiral himself put to sea in the *Novik* to rescue them and, though he was driven off and failed to save the disabled boat, his example, in marked contrast to his predecessor's inactivity, dispelled the disheartening sense of inferiority which had permeated the Russian crews.

The Japanese followed up the night's activities by an ineffective long-range bombardment of the harbour, which failed to prevent Makaroff from leading the squadron to sea on the following morning to give them much-needed practice in steam tactics. The sad lack of skill on the part of the Russians was demonstrated when the *Sevastopol* collided with the *Poltava*, fortunately without causing serious damage.

The distressing incompetence of the officers of the Port Arthur squadron was not the least of the new Commander-in-Chief's worries. When on the next occasion of going to sea the *Sevastopol* was again in collision, this time with the *Peresviet*, the captain was relieved of his command; but at all levels the same lack of seamanlike skill was evident. Allied to his harassing strategic problems, it made a burden almost too heavy for even such an outstanding personality as Makaroff.

To counter any further attempts at blocking operations or night torpedo attacks, Makaroff had two merchant ships sunk and a timber boom fixed between them. Backing it was a line of gunboats, while the cruisers *Askold* and *Bayan* were stationed in the harbour entrance where their guns and searchlights could dominate the channel.

Thus when eight Japanese destroyers attempted an attack on the night of 21st March, they received a hot reception and were driven off. When Togo appeared off the port the next morning and detached the battleships *Fuji* and *Yashima* to bombard the harbour, Makaroff led his battleships out and, ranging them within supporting distance of the shore batteries, challenged the Japanese to action, a challenge which they refused even though they had twelve armoured ships to Makaroff's six.

The new spirit in the Russian squadron was apparent to the Japanese, and drove them to a fresh attempt to block the harbour during the night of 26th March. Though the four blockships were duly sunk near the entrance, they failed to obstruct the channel, and at daylight the mortified Japanese saw the Russians steaming out of harbour.

Yet the operation had very nearly succeeded, and Makaroff appreciated that fresh attempts were bound to be made. With all haste he had further booms stretched and two triple rows of mines, so laid that a direct approach to the harbour was not possible without fouling one or the other.

For all their early successes—to some extent the fruit of treachery—the Japanese were finding that their failure to follow them up promptly was costing them dearly. Togo was forced to employ his fleet in blockade, a form of warfare which was becoming daily more hazardous as the Russians extended their defensive minefields.

The Japanese Commander-in-Chief's anxieties were greatly increased by the Imperial General Staff's somewhat belated decision to land an army on the Kwangtung Peninsula. The area for the landing, Yentoa Bay, was a bare 53 miles from Port Arthur. A brief sortie by the Port Arthur squadron during one of the necessary absences of the Japanese battleship division for coaling or maintenance might spell disaster. The need to block the harbour was more vital than ever, and Togo asked for twelve merchant ships to be allocated for the purpose. The General Staff, already desperately short of shipping for troop movements and supply, was unwilling to grant the admiral's request.

While Togo pressed his demand and planned the fresh blocking operation for 3rd May, he also decided to take a leaf out of the Russian book by planting two minefields athwart the usual routes taken by the Russian ships on coming to sea, one at the south-western and one at the south-eastern limit of the roadstead in which the Russians usually manœuvred under the protection of the shore batteries. He hoped then to lure the Russians into an incautious sortie.

During 11th April, Makaroff had taken the squadron for a training cruise along the coast to the eastward. On his return he had sent a force of destroyers to reconnoitre the off-shore islands, with orders to return to harbour at daybreak. He had then led the remainder back into Port Arthur.

That evening two Japanese destroyer divisions and a minelayer set out in pitch darkness and a drizzling rain to lay the planned minefields. As they drew near Port Arthur, searchlight activity showed them that the Russians were fully alert. The tireless, indefatigable Makaroff was indeed fully expecting some form of attack that night, the first calm night after a period of heavy gales, and he had himself gone aboard the *Diana*, the guard cruiser, in the narrows of the entrance.

Around midnight his premonitions had taken him restlessly touring the *Diana*'s gun quarters and control positions to see that all was ready, everyone on the alert. As he stood by the captain, a sweeping searchlight steadied and, through the obscuring rain, dimly illuminated some objects to the south-eastward of the harbour entrance. The captain asked permission to open fire, but the ill-served admiral could not be sure that the objects were not his own destroyers returning prematurely to the Roads owing to some all-too-probable calamity. He contented himself with arranging for the position to be carefully noted with the object of searching the area at daylight.

The rest of the night was apparently uneventful, and at 4 a.m. Makaroff returned to his flagship *Petropavlovsk*. But in the dark, dripping night the Japanese minelayers had fulfilled their task to the letter and slipped away undetected.

Meanwhile Makaroff's incompetent destroyer captains had indeed got themselves into the sort of trouble he had feared. Three of the eight boats sent on the mission of reconnaissance lost touch with the remainder. Two of them thereupon made for home, slipping unsighted in the darkness past a Japanese patrolling destroyer division, and at first light were nearing harbour. The third, however, the *Strashni*, sighting the Japanese division, took them for her consorts and followed them unsuspectingly while darkness held. Then as the light began to make, the Russian captain realised his terrible mistake. At his utmost speed he turned to escape; but the four Japanese were after him at once. In spite of a gallant resistance, during which she got off a torpedo which closely missed one of the enemy the *Strashni* was overwhelmed. The end came when a shell hit her other torpedo still in its tube and exploded it. Brought to a standstill, on fire and settling by the stern, all resistance was at an end, and the Japanese tried to take her in tow.

But now the *Bayan* was seen to be tearing out of harbour to the rescue, and the Japanese were forced to make off though they saw the *Strashni* sink before they left the scene. Togo had anticipated something of this sort. Now his plan to lure the Russian fleet out, either to fight or on to the new minefield, went smoothly into action. As the *Bayan* chased the destroyers to seaward, the masts of Rear-Admiral Dewa's light-cruisers were seen coming up over the horizon. The Russian ship was forced to fall back on the support of her consorts, *Novik*, *Askold* and *Diana*, which were now coming out in their turn. Following them were the flagship *Petropavlovsk* and the *Poltava*.

Following his instructions, Dewa turned away to the south-west to lure the Russians in the direction of the westerly of the two minefields; but so far Makaroff was concerned solely with trying to save as many survivors as possible from the *Strashni* and to cover the return of the remainder of his destroyers. He therefore continued in an easterly direction, by pure good fortune clearing the other Japanese minefield as he did so.

The Russian Commander-in-Chief, who had been up all night, apparently unable to delegate any responsibility to his untrustworthy subordinates, had flown into a frenzy of anger when he heard of the latest escapade of his destroyer captains and the loss of the *Strashni*. All thought of the mysterious incident during the night had gone out of his head. Fuming with rage, he had led his battleships out of harbour without taking his usual precaution of having the channel swept before them.

Fog and smoke were by now obscuring the scene; and Dewa,

finding the Russians had not followed him, turned back to try again. As he reapproached the eastern end of the roadstead, Makaroff's ships suddenly loomed out of the murk at short range. The guns on both sides roared out. But it was no part of the Japanese plan for Dewa's light-cruisers to be opposed to the Russian armoured ships. Turning hastily away, Dewa signalled to Togo to tell him that his plan of enticement was working and that action with the Russian fleet awaited him if he would come on. Togo was ready, and within fifteen minutes was in sight of the Russian ships, his battle flags hoisted.

However, Makaroff had still only two battleships and four armoured cruisers with him. The remainder of the battleships were still filing out of the harbour, and so he declined to be drawn. Falling back under the protection of the shore batteries, he picked up his other battleships and formed line on a north-easterly course, ready at last to engage.

Now it was Togo's turn to stand off, for Makaroff was leading his whole squadron unsuspectingly across the freshly laid mines. In breathless suspense the Japanese watched and waited as the Russian ships moved majestically forward into the danger zone.

The *Petropavlovsk* reached the eastern end of the roadstead. Surprisingly, the Russian ships were still unscathed as the signal for a 180-degree turn back in succession was hoisted. The flagship began to lead round. Suddenly there came a muffled explosion under her, followed by two more, far more terrible, enveloping the flagship in flame, steam and smoke as her magazines exploded. Hurtling upwards could be seen her mizzenmast and funnel, a complete turret and her bridge. In less than a minute her stern had risen high out of the water and the flames were suddenly quenched as she slid to the sea bottom. Even the watching enemy recorded that "the sight was a most appalling one".

How much more so must it have been for the Russians. Yet something of their dead commander's personality—he was never seen again—must have continued to hover over the scene; for admirable calm discipline prevailed in the fleet. Boats were smartly lowered for rescue work. The ships held to their ordered formation, and Rear-Admiral Prince Ukhtomski had only to signal "Follow me" and lead off on the south-westerly course that Makaroff had ordered. But now the line was heading for the more westerly of the two Japanese minefields. Once again, as they entered it, it became time to turn back, and the *Peresviet*, flagship of Prince Ukhtomski, led round. She had just steadied on the new course when an explosion shook the *Pobieda* astern of her. The mine had exploded abreast a coal-bunker which absorbed much of the shock, but a group of boilers was put out of action, and the flooded compartments gave the *Pobieda* a considerable list.

This second catastrophe was too much for the already shaken Russian nerves. A wild panic broke out. Submarines were reported; as the ships turned this way and that and all order vanished, guns were fired at random into the water, the shore batteries adding their quota to that of the ships; there were narrow escapes from collision; shell splinters were flying everywhere. Even when the officers pulled themselves together and ordered the "Cease Fire", it was only by pulling the crazed sailors bodily away from their guns that they could get the order obeyed.

Fortunately for the Russians all this was hidden from the enemy in the murk. By the time they came in sight again, Ukhtomski had succeeded in reducing them to some order, and behind the crippled *Pobieda* was leading them into harbour.

It had been a calamitous day for the Russians. The one man who might have brought them to fighting pitch had gone, and the new spirit that had been growing died with the *Petropavlovsk*. In addition their battle squadron was reduced to three ships, *Peresviet*, *Sevastopol* and *Poltava*, though repairs to the *Tzesarevitch* and *Retvizan* were well advanced and the *Pobieda* was at once taken in hand.

At the news of the loss of Makaroff, the Viceroy, Admiral Alexeieff, placed himself in command, hoisting his flag in the *Sevastopol* and appointing his Chief of Staff, Rear-Admiral Vitgeft, as second-in-command. Togo, rightly judging that for the time being the Russian fleet was eliminated, returned to his base to prepare for the large-scale landing operations which were planned.

He still felt, however, that only a complete blockage of the harbour entrance could absolutely ensure the safe passage and disembarkation of the troops. Plans went ahead, therefore; and on the night of 2nd May the desperate attempt was made, with the greatest gallantry.

A gale of wind which rose suddenly after dark scattered the twelve blockships; but orders for a postponement failed to get through, and in wild weather the ships struggled on, through minefields and booms, blinded by searchlights and smothered by a storm of fire. For all their heroism, not one of the Japanese captains succeeded in reaching the fairway before his ship sank. At a cost of more than half of the crews engaged, the operation was a complete failure.

Yet when the few survivors who got back were interrogated, they were confident they had succeeded. Added to the fact that not a single Russian ship had come out, it was enough to convince Togo that at last the Russian fleet was securely penned in. The safe landing of the troops seemed assured, and early on 4th May the convoy and escort set forth on the great enterprise which was to cut Port Arthur off from its hinterland and communications.

Though based on the false assumption that Port Arthur was securely blocked, Togo's belief that the troop convoys were safe from interference was justified. The landing went ahead with perfect smoothness interrupted only by bad weather. The morale of the Russian squadron had in fact received such a shock that there was no question of any of its ships venturing beyond the roadstead. Even so, Togo was determined to take no chances, and a close blockade was instituted, Dewa's division alternating by day with the battleship division which had been entrusted to Rear-Admiral Nashiba, while the Commander-in-Chief was occupied with the supervision of the amphibious operations. By night, destroyer divisions took over the patrol. The whole arrangement worked in a regular routine, a routine which the Russians were forced to watch in angry frustration until 14th May, when a fog came down to veil the whole scene in obscurity. This fog was to be the basic cause of a day of fearful calamity for the Japanese.

Amongst the Russian squadron was a minelayer, the *Amur*, whose captain had long fretted at the limitations put on his weapons. Time and again he had watched the Japanese squadrons manœuvring in the same stretch of water some ten miles south-east of Liao-ti-shan, whence they could observe the entrance and inner harbour of Port Arthur. Frequently he had begged permission to sow a minefield in the area, but it was outside territorial waters, and it had never been considered within the bounds of civilised warfare to make such indiscriminate use of these treacherous weapons, exposing innocent neutral shipping to danger.

Admiral Stark had consistently vetoed it. Vitgeft was now in command, Alexeieff having left Port Arthur when the Japanese landings threatened to cut it off from the remainder of his dominions. Like Stark, Vitgeft had at first set his face against the laying of mines in the open sea, but the rapidly deteriorating situation now led him to give way. So through the fog on 14th May the *Amur* stole out and laid a line of forty mines, 50 to 100 feet apart, and slipped back into harbour undetected.

During that day the coastal fog had kept Dewa's division, consisting of his flagship *Chitose*, the light-cruiser *Yoshino*, the battleship *Fuji* and the armoured cruisers *Yakumo* and *Kasuga* 20 miles out to seaward where the weather was not so thick. At nightfall he had withdrawn as usual, with the intention of being back on station at dawn. At 1 a.m. he was still steering to seaward and intending to alter back towards the land in half an hour's time when his division ran into an area of dense fog.

The *Kasuga*, caught somewhat astern of station, lost touch with her next ahead and increased speed to regain it. For a time she went blindly on while all eyes peered ahead hoping to sight a wake or a stern-light. At last at about 1.40, a dim shape loomed up. But at this very moment Dewa's line was turning in succession to reverse course. Instead of the stern of the ship next ahead, steering away on the same course, it was the *Yoshino* which had come into sight athwart the *Kasuga*'s bows. In the violent collision which followed, the *Yoshino* was holed below the water-line. It was quickly evident that there was no hope for her. The order to abandon ship was given, but not until the portrait of the Emperor had been fetched on deck, saluted by the assembled ship's company and reverently borne away to a cutter, were the remainder of the boats lowered and the crew permitted to man them.

The ceremonious delay was to cost the Japanese dearly. With the boats still alongside, the *Yoshino* suddenly heeled over and plunged to the bottom. The boats were dragged down with her and a great many of the crew with them. Boats from the *Kasuga* searched in the darkness and fog for survivors; but from her complement of 410 officers and men, 30 officers, including her captain, and 287 men were not seen again.

The *Kasuga*, her ram bent at an angle of 29 degrees and badly flooded forward, withdrew to base and thence to Japan for repairs.

This was a terrible start to 15th May, but worse was in store for the Japanese, who had not previously lost a single major war vessel. While the disaster to the *Yoshino* was unfolding, Admiral Nashiba's division was making through the night for the routine take-over from Dewa's division. Besides his flagship, the battleship *Hatsuse* he had with him the battleships *Shikishima* and *Yashima* and the cruiser *Kasagi*.

At dawn the *Kasagi* was sent in close to the harbour to reconnoitre, and on her return with a report that all was quiet, Nashiba led away on the customary off-shore patrol, straight into the *Amur*'s line of mines. At 10.50 the *Hatsuse* was shaken by an explosion and heeled over with her port engine-room and steering engine compartment flooded. Nashiba at once signalled for the squadron to turn 90 degrees together away from the danger area; but before the order could be obeyed, his rear ship *Yashima* had also been struck.

It was the turn of the Japanese to be stupefied. As with the Russians, submarines were suspected, and the *Shikishima* began firing into the water. The admiral kept his head, however. Calling up the cruiser *Takasago*, which was in the offing, to go to the *Yashima*'s aid, he ordered the *Kasagi* to take the *Hatsuse* in tow;

but even as the cruiser was hauling the tow rope aboard, the *Hatsuse* disintegrated in another shattering explosion as a second mine detonated her magazines. In a cloud of yellow smoke, the battleship's funnels and masts were seen to fall and her upper deck to leap into the air. Then she was gone. Though the admiral and captain, 21 officers and 313 men were rescued, 38 officers and 458 men went down with her. Meanwhile the *Yashima*, her pumps barely able to keep her afloat, was trying to withdraw.

As efforts to rescue the survivors of the *Hatsuse* were going on and laden boats dotted the sea, the Russian destroyers were seen to be coming out. For a time things looked ugly for the Japanese, but when first the *Kasagi* and then the cruisers of Rear-Admiral Togo's division, which was passing on a separate mission, came to the rescue, the destroyers were driven off.

As the flotilla retired on the harbour, the Russian cruiser *Novik* was seen coming out, and for the first time the Japanese realised that the harbour was not blocked as they had thought. It was news of the utmost gravity; for if the Russians brought out their armoured ships at once, they could catch the Japanese in a position of great disadvantage, their ships scattered, their numbers reduced and handicapped by the need to stand by the crippled *Yashima*.

But Vitgeft was no Makaroff. Nothing was ready. The battleships lay without steam. The channel had not been swept. A dread of mines lay over the admiral's mind, and so the opportunity to wrest control of the Yellow Sea from the Japanese slipped by. Yet it had been a black day for the Japanese. In spite of heroic efforts to keep the *Yashima* afloat, they were finally forced to abandon her, and during the night she sank. In one day the Japanese slender excess of battleships had been converted into a deficiency of two. As soon as their battleships were repaired, the Russians would be in a position to challenge Togo with six to four. No replacements of the Japanese ships could be looked for, while from the other side of the world reinforcements for the Russians were assembling in the Baltic under Rear-Admiral Rozhestvenski.

Thus Togo's anxieties for the safety of the army's sea communications were once again acute. Only the efficiency and fighting spirit of the Japanese Navy, fostered by constant activity at sea, compared with the demoralisation and incompetence of the harbour-bound Russians, could give him any confidence. The relative strength, moral and material, was soon to be put to the test.

7

Sound and Fury

So far the naval side of the Russo-Japanese War had provided a classic demonstration of a basic principle which is often forgotten—that the prime function of a navy in war is the protection of its own country's merchant ships and transports, and the elimination from the sea of those of the enemy. The destruction of the enemy's main fleet in battle simplifies the task, but is not essential.

The enemy with the weaker fleet will naturally refuse action. By remaining behind secure defences, yet ready to emerge at its own good time if a suitable occasion arises, it can tie up the whole of its opponents' main fleet, which, obliged to keep the sea constantly, ready to face any sortie by the enemy, exposed to damage by weather, liable to attrition by submarine or air attack or mine-laying, can rarely be assembled at full strength.

Thus Togo's situation at the beginning of the war had been by no means a comfortable one, even though the damage to the *Tzesarevitch* and the *Retvizan* had given him a small superiority in capital ships. An active policy on the part of the Russian admiral could have kept the Japanese at full stretch, and would have made the transport of their armies a highly hazardous undertaking.

If at the same time the Vladivostok division had been boldly handled to threaten the shipping passing between Japan and Korea, it would hardly have been possible for the army in Korea to have been supported, or the landings on the Kwangtung Peninsula to have been undertaken at all. Fortunately for the Japanese, it was not until the arrival of Makaroff that the apathetic Russian naval command took up the posture of instant readiness so essential for the strategy of the "fleet in being" to function with effect.

With Makaroff's arrival, not only did the activity to which he spurred the Port Arthur squadron create fresh anxieties for Togo (who, it must always be remembered, had all his assets in the front window with no reserves whatever), but by instructing the Vladivostok squadron similarly to hold itself in readiness for a sortie simultaneously with one by the Port Arthur squadron, Makaroff was making plans which could have led to a battle which, short of a decisive win for the Japanese, would have upset the whole Japanese war plan.

Then came the loss of the *Petropavlovsk* and the death of Makaroff. Once again the spirit went out of the Russian fleet, and its material strength was so reduced that not only could the landings on the Kwangtung Peninsula be proceeded with, but Togo was able to detach Kamimura's 2nd Division of armoured ships to take over the guarding of the Tsushima Straits, so preventing a concentration of the two sections of the Russian fleet.

Once again the material situation was reversed by the events of the disastrous 15th May. But by then, under the irresolute, uninspiring command of Vitgeft, all desire to seek a decision at sea had left the Port Arthur squadron. As the Japanese armies closed round the port, a great many of the 6-inch and smaller guns had been landed from the ships to aid in the defence. The Russian land-dominated mind failed to see that the real defence of Port Arthur lay on the sea. Unless the sea communications of the Japanese armies were secure, their whole plan of operation was in jeopardy, their very existence endangered.

Without risking their battle strength, but simply by constant activity and demonstration of their readiness, the Russians could have kept Togo in a state of anxious suspense, unable to assist the army or to ensure the safety of its communications. Such was the meaning of the maintenance of a "fleet in being" as understood by Makaroff. In Vitgeft's hands, the fleet was virtually in a state of suspended animation.

Altogether, Vitgeft was not the man for the task. On being

given the command, he had told his assembled captains with devastating candour, "I am no leader of a fleet." As the position of Port Arthur became more precarious, it was the general commanding the garrison who insisted that it was the fleet's function to assist the defence by operations against the enemy's communications; it was the admiral who shamefully pleaded that the fleet was unready to fight, lacking gunnery practice or general training, and that he himself was unfit to lead them.

The result was that in spite of the losses of 15th May 1904, Togo felt that he could continue to spare Kamimura's armoured division to hold the Tsushima Straits against any sortie by the Vladivostok division. By early June, however, as the *Tzesarevitch*, *Retvizan* and *Pobieda* completed their repairs, giving the Russians a battleship strength of six ships again, more and more pressure was being brought to bear on Vitgeft to take the fleet to sea. A wrangle between Vitgeft and the garrison general was finally brought to an end by orders from Alexeieff for the squadron to put to sea, though with no clear indication of the purpose of the sortie.

So it was that the decision was finally reached to go out on the morning of 22nd June. Sweeping operations were put energetically into operation, and destroyers were out every night to drive off any attempts by Japanese minelayers. At last a channel 700 feet wide was reported clear, as well as an anchorage in the roadstead.

The purpose of the sortie was stated to be to put to sea for a three-day cruise to examine the Japanese advanced base in the Elliot Islands, and to engage the enemy should he be met with "in suitable force". A "suitable force" would have to be something far less than a concentration of Togo's armoured divisions, for Vitgeft was not at all happy about the state of his ships. They were still short of eighteen 6-inch guns and a great many smaller; they were also short of 600 skilled men to serve them, and the ships' companies were made up from the naval barracks and reserve. One of the *Sevastopol*'s 12-inch guns was permanently out of action owing to damage to its mounting. A new Chief of Staff, Rear-Admiral Matsusevich, had just taken up his appointment. At the last minute the captain of the *Pobieda* was taken ill and had to be relieved, causing the operation to be postponed until the next day.

During the night of the 22nd, steam was raised in all ships, and at daybreak on the 23rd Vitgeft gave the order to weigh. By 6 o'clock the Japanese destroyers watching the entrance could see the first ship coming through the Narrows. Being without wireless, it was necessary for one of them to speed away to pass the important news to Rear-Admiral Dewa in the offing, but as the messenger ship naturally left at the first alarm, she was unable to know that bringing up the rear of the Russian line were the three battleships last heard of as being under repair and unfit for sea.

Thus when Togo first received the alarm by radio at 8.20, he presumed that there would be only three battleships in the Russian force, which would not give him much cause for anxiety. It was 10.30 before he got under way from his base in the Elliot Islands, and it was at 10 knots only that he headed for Port Arthur while he gathered his scattered forces together.

There was in fact little need for haste, for the Russian sortie was proceeding at solemn pace and with the utmost caution. The squadron first anchored in the carefully swept anchorage, only to discover from mines which broke adrift that it was in the midst of a freshly laid minefield. Not until the area had been swept, a delay of some hours, could the squadron get under way.

At last, shortly before 3 o'clock in the afternoon, a screen of minesweepers and destroyers going slowly ahead of them, the Russian line formed on a south-easterly course. As the ships drew clear of the shore defences, Japanese destroyers swooped down on the minesweepers. Then the *Novik* and Russian destroyers moved out in their defence, and drove off the Japanese. But as they chased to seawards and the Russian line moved majestically forward mastheads of Japanese ships began to appear over the horizon from every point of the compass as they concentrated on their Commander-in-Chief.

Almost simultaneously the Russians realised that there was no possibility of slipping out without engaging Japanese battleships supported by a strong force of cruisers and destroyers, and Togo appreciated that there were six Russian battleships instead of the three which he had expected. To all outward appearances the two sides were fairly evenly balanced, the Japanese superiority in light forces making up for their inferiority in capital ships. In fact, each side thought the other stronger.

It was inevitable, therefore, bearing in mind Togo's preference for blocking the Russian fleet in harbour rather than unnecessarily risking his precious battleships, and Vitgeft's knowledge of his own shortcomings and his fleet's inefficiency, that neither should press the issue to battle. But whereas Vitgeft's objection to battle was absolute, Togo was prepared to fight if the Russians continued to seawards aiming to escape from Port Arthur.

So as Vitgeft steamed on, Togo steered to and fro across his line of advance and awaited the outcome. As dusk fell it was clear that a night action must follow if Vitgeft held on, an eventuality which could only be disastrous for the ill-led, unpractised Russian crews against the seasoned Japanese veterans, and which would give the Japanese torpedo craft the opportunity for which they had long waited.

At the last moment before darkness overtook him, Vitgeft turned back for the roadstead. At once Togo unleashed his destroyer flotillas to the attack. Vitgeft fled for harbour at high speed by the most direct route, all thought for mines driven from him. His apparent recklessness paid him off very well, for it surprised many of the Japanese destroyer divisions. Expecting longer in which to develop their attack, they delayed, waiting for the moon to set. Others failed at first to find their target. Thus only a few got their attacks home before the Russian ships had come to their anchors and spread their anti-torpedo nets.

The remaining divisions, coming in one at a time to deliver their attacks, were caught in the beams of the shore searchlights, and were received by a concentrated storm of fire from every gun from 12-inch downwards that could be brought to bear. Blinded by the glare, dazzled by the shining fountains of water leaping all around them, dazed by the bedlam of noise, the Japanese destroyer-men could neither see to judge their distance, nor pass coherent orders to the tube crews. It was as much as they could do to fire their torpedoes at random and get away in safety into the darkness.

Yet when it is considered that no less than forty destroyers or torpedo-boats attacked during the night, firing sixty-seven torpedoes at a range of between 500 and 1,500 yards, the miraculous nature of the complete Russian immunity is only equalled by the almost unscathed escape of the Japanese. Not a Russian ship was hit, while of the Japanese only four boats received minor damage and a total of eight casualties.

Vitgeft had not escaped entirely scot-free, however. His disregard for possible mines during his hasty retreat was astonishingly successful, and might have avoided all penalties had not one ship, the *Sevastopol*, edged out of the line during one of the early attacks while she was still under way. A mine exploded under her bow, tearing a large hole in her hull and flooding two compartments. However, she was in no danger of sinking, and at daylight she passed into the inner harbour, with the rest of the fleet.

It is not to be wondered at that the disappointment of the Japanese was intense when they approached the following morning ready to make further attacks on the disabled ships they expected to find, only to discover the roadstead empty. The dreary round of the interminable blockade had to be resumed. Little or nothing had been achieved out of the long-awaited opportunity. Indeed, the whole incident assumed the shape of a serious strategical set-back to the Japanese. The parlous condition of the Russian ships, their lack of training and low morale was not realised. All the Japanese knew was that the damaged battleships had been repaired while the two Japanese ships which had been mined were at the bottom, and that the repeated blocking operations had been entirely unsuccessful. They at once feared for the safety of the troop and supply convoys upon which the whole of the military strategy depended.

The great troop movements which had been ordered in an

attempt to lead to an advance into Manchuria were postponed indefinitely. Knowing the state of the Russian fleet, it can be seen that the Japanese were unduly nervous, but the General Staff was no doubt influenced by events which had taken place in the Korean Straits at about the time that the Port Arthur squadron was making its sortie. The Russian Vladivostok division under its new commander, Rear-Admiral Bezobrazov, had suddenly appeared on the shipping route between Japan and Korea. There they found and sank two transports carrying troops and stores as well as eighteen 11-inch howitzers destined for the seige of Port Arthur; a third ship was torpedoed, but got back to port. Then after a cruise up the Japanese coast, during which he captured or sank further merchant ships, Bezobrazov, aided by thick weather, had escaped unharmed back into Vladivostok.

However exaggerated may have been the respect with which the re-vitalised Port Arthur squadron was regarded, the fact that it was once more mobile and at nearly full strength forced Togo to keep his fleet concentrated and ready to engage it should the Russians again attempt a sortie. And indeed such an event was impending. All through July the Viceroy urged Vitgeft to go out and fight, while Vitgeft continued to protest the unpreparedness of his ships and his own unfitness to lead them into battle. Only the imminent fall of Port Arthur could justify him in taking them out on a forlorn hope, he believed.

So the deadlock continued, until the matter was resolved at the end of July by a personal order from the Tsar that the squadron should go out. Reluctantly the Russians set about preparing for sea. By 9th August they were as ready as they could be in the absence of tactical training or target practice. As black smoke pouring from the funnels told of steam being raised, the unhappy Vitgeft was bidding his friends farewell with the discouraging prophetic phrase: "We shall meet in another world."

At first light on 10th August the signal was made to weigh anchor. As usual, the ubiquitous *Novik* led the way out, accompanied by the minesweepers and their gunboat escort. As the bigger ships were seen following them the news was flashed by radio to Togo, who, with his division of four battleships, was patrolling some 50 miles to the south-eastward.

Plans for the conduct of the Japanese fleet had been drawn up to cover any of the several courses open to the Russians. They might be coming out in support of their armies either to east or west of Port Arthur or they might be attempting to escape to Vladivostok. But until their intentions were clear, Togo could but watch and wait. What with the usual delay caused by the Russians' awkward unpractised manœuvres to form line, and the necessity to follow the minesweepers until clear of coastal waters, it was not until nearly noon that Togo could come to any conclusion, and then it was to the effect that Vitgeft was heading westward along the coast, intending to pass into the Gulf of Pechili.

This was the one direction not catered for, and it left the Japanese divisions far behind with the prospect of a long stern chase before them. It seems, however, to have been only an attempt to deceive and throw out the Japanese deployment. Hardly had Togo signalled his conclusions to his subordinate admirals, than the Russians were seen to turn south and then south-east on to their true course for an escape seawards. At once all Togo's outlying squadrons steered to join the battleship division. While they raced to try and take up the battle stations allotted to them, Togo manœuvred to and fro across the Russian line of advance, in a position to bring off his favoured tactic of crossing the enemy's "T" and bringing a concentration of fire upon his van.

In the battle line with the Russian battleships were the three cruisers under the command of Rear-Admiral Reitzenstein, with his flag in the *Askold*. Thus the Russian force as seen from Togo's bridge was a formidable array. Vitgeft's flagship *Tzesarevitch* led the way, followed by *Retvizan*, *Pobieda*, *Peresviet* (flag of Rear-Admiral Prince Ukhtomski), *Sevastopol*, *Poltava*, *Askold*, *Pallada* and *Diana*. With the eight Russian destroyers stationed on the landward side of the line were the *Novik* and a hospital ship, *Mongolia*.

Togo's 1st Division, reduced by the loss of the *Hatsuse* and *Yashima* to four ships (*Mikasa*, *Asahi*, *Fuji* and *Shikishima*), had been made up to six by the inclusion of the armoured cruisers *Kasuga* and *Nisshin*, in the latter of which was the flag of Rear-Admiral Kataoka. His total force, which included Rear-Admiral Dewa's 3rd Division comprising two armoured cruisers and three light cruisers, the 6th Division of five elderly cruisers under Rear-Admiral Togo and a (reserve) 5th Division of even older ships under Rear-Admiral Yamada, was ostensibly greatly superior to the Russians'.

But an old lesson from the days of sail navies was shown still to apply in the course of the battle to follow, in that it was soon apparent that once battle was joined it was the capital ships, the ships "fit to stand in the line", which decided the issue. Though the 3rd Division was in company with the 1st from the start, Dewa found himself so busy keeping clear of the fire of his own battleships, or having to retreat in the face of fire from the heavier ships of the enemy, that in the early stages he was of little account. The 6th Division, which soon joined from the eastward and manœuvred to take up its battle station 5 miles astern of the 1st, eventually found itself as much as 8 miles behind, while the 5th Division was unable to join in at all.

Nevertheless, it was no doubt in order to await the concentration of his scattered forces that Togo showed himself in no hurry to engage. Keeping out of range, he weaved to and fro across the path of the Russians to head them off from their desired escape route to the south-east, while Vitgeft turned this way and that trying to get away round Togo's stern. In the course of the mutual feints it was Togo who was finally outmanœuvred.

Soon after one o'clock, Togo had turned his line about to the north-eastward to cut off Vitgeft's latest circling movement around the Japanese rear. Vitgeft thereupon altered sharply to the southward, aiming to pass behind the Japanese on their new course. By now the distance between the two fleets was inside the extreme range of the big guns, and the first shots of the battle flashed out as first the *Nisshin*, leading the Japanese line, and then the remainder of the 1st Division began a deliberate fire at a range of more than 14,000 yards. But the chances of a hit under the fire control systems of the day were very small, and Vitgeft's line completed its turn without a single shell striking home.

The two lines were now steaming past each other on almost opposite courses. To head the Russians off again, Togo once more turned his ships together 180 degrees. Now it was the turn of the Russians to make undisturbed practice on the enemy as he turned. They at once showed that whatever their other shortcomings, at this form of action they knew their business. As the *Mikasa* swung round under helm, two 12-inch shells smashed aboard, one wrecking the wireless gear, the other plunging through her deck at the foot of the mainmast and causing a number of casualties.

First blood was to the Russians. With his constant preoccupation with the need to preserve his country's battleships against the eventual arrival on the scene of the Russian reinforcements from the Baltic Fleet, it must have given Togo much food for thought. For all its misfortunes, lack of inspired leadership and long inactivity, the Port Arthur squadron had by no means had its fangs drawn. Togo's intention to fight at long range, relying upon his superior gunnery to decide the issue, was not working out well.

On the other hand, time seemed to be on Togo's side from the point of view of the attainment of his strategical object. His far-sighted mind told him that the destruction of the enemy fleet was not the aim if it entailed heavy losses on his own part. The Russians had a fresh battle squadron in reserve assembling in the Baltic; the Japanese had none, therefore the enemy must either be driven back to Port Arthur or else destroyed piece-meal during the long voyage to Vladivostok. Mutual destruction at point-blank range might bring Togo a tactical victory, but would lose him the strategical object.

The day was more than half gone. With the night Togo's greatly superior torpedo forces could go into action. By the next day the scene of battle would perhaps have shifted to the Korean Straits, where Rear-Admiral Kamimura's squadron of armoured ships could come to swell the Japanese strength. There was no immediate hurry.

Meanwhile Togo's line had completed its turn and was once more heading to cross Vitgeft's "T". Yet again the Russian admiral turned to the eastward to circle the Japanese rear. A turn, all ships together, such as the Japanese had twice performed, was too difficult a manœuvre for the unpractised Russians. The long process of a turn in succession was necessary; while it was taking place the Japanese concentrated their fire on the turning-point, and now at last they drew blood. The *Tzesarevitch* and the *Retvizan* were seen to be hit and on fire.

But this success led Togo into a tactical mistake. Instead of turning back in good time once more to head off the Russians from their escape route, a temporary confusion in the Russian line as they turned in their customary unhandy fashion tempted him to make the most of the advantage. The range was now down to less than 8,000 yards. As he circled the enemy's rear, every gun from 6-inch upwards came into action. The Russian ships were hidden in a forest of shell splashes and seemed to be veritably overwhelmed.

Yet with the completion of their turn the Russian line was seen unbelievably to be steaming away in good order, little damaged and returning the fire in great style. As in the previous action of 9th October, it was shown that with indiscriminate fire from guns of many different calibres making spotting impossible it became a matter of luck to score hits.

Togo had now sacrificed his commanding position across Vitgeft's escape route, and all for nothing. Realising this, he led round to the south-east. By the time he was steering a parallel course to the enemy, his flagship, leading the line, was only just abreast of the enemy's last ship, the rear ships of the Japanese line being so far astern that they were out of range and forced to cease fire. Furthermore at his battle speed of 14 knots, Togo was surprised to find that he was not gaining on the Russians, who were doing much better than he had expected considering they had one ship, the *Poltava*, which had made only 16·2 knots at her original full-speed trials.

The Russian cruisers were now bearing the brunt of the Japanese

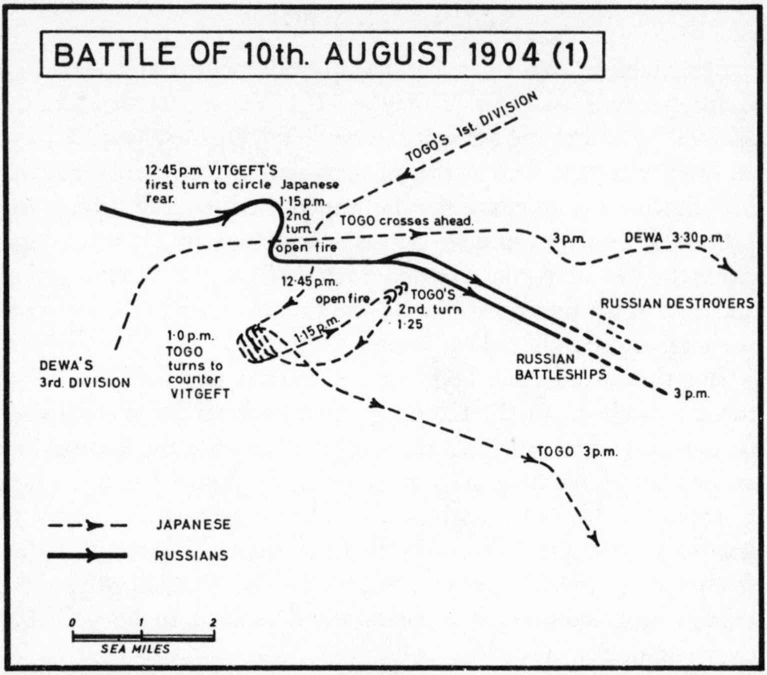
BATTLE OF 10th. AUGUST 1904 (1)
TOGO'S 1st. DIVISION
12·45 p.m. VITGEFT'S first turn to circle Japanese rear.
1·15 p.m. 2nd. turn
TOGO crosses ahead.
open fire
3 p.m.
DEWA 3·30 p.m.
12·45 p.m.
open fire
TOGO'S 2nd. turn 1·25
RUSSIAN DESTROYERS
1·15 p.m.
1·0 p.m. TOGO turns to counter VITGEFT
DEWA'S 3rd. DIVISION
RUSSIAN BATTLESHIPS
3 p.m.
TOGO 3 p.m.
JAPANESE
RUSSIANS
0
1
2
SEA MILES

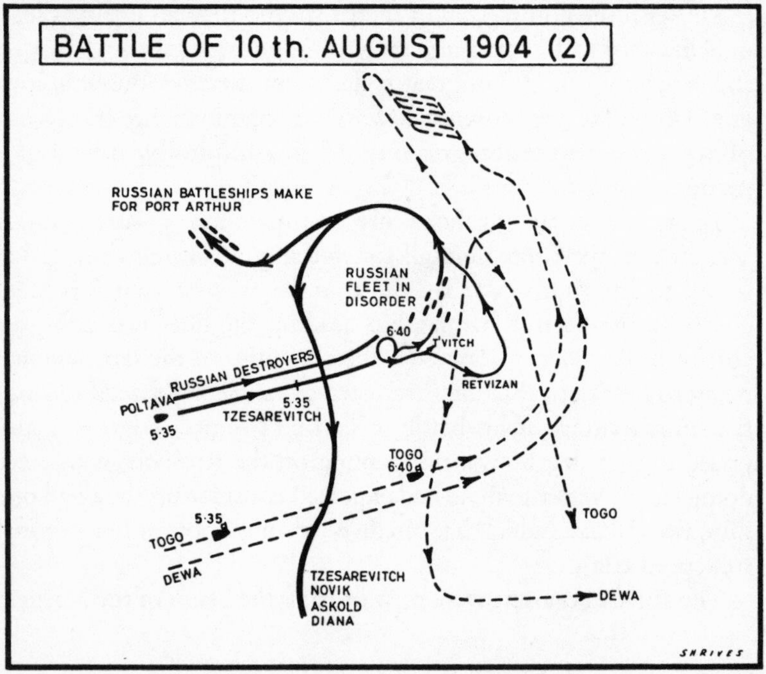
BATTLE OF 10 th. AUGUST 1904 (2)
RUSSIAN BATTLESHIPS MAKE FOR PORT ARTHUR
RUSSIAN FLEET IN DISORDER
6·40
T'VITCH
RETVIZAN
RUSSIAN DESTROYERS
POLTAVA
5·35
5·35
TZESAREVITCH
TOGO 6·40
TOGO
5·35
TOGO
DEWA
TZESAREVITCH
NOVIK
ASKOLD
DIANA
DEWA
SHRIVES

fire. Vitgeft therefore ordered them to turn away to port out of range, while to shelter them he turned his battleship division 45 degrees to starboard together, for a short while, and so once more came within range of Togo's battleships. However, the gunnery advantage by no means lay with the Japanese. Togo's van was exposed to a concentration of fire—the reverse of the position which the Japanese admiral had always hoped to achieve with superior speed.

At 2.50 p.m. the *Asahi*, second in the line, was heavily hit. Ten minutes later the *Mikasa* was hit on the water-line, and again below the quarter-deck at 3.5. The only apparent effect on the Russians of the exchange of fire was that the *Poltava* was seen to be dropping astern. Actually, this was due to the high speed which she had been forced to maintain; her racing reciprocating engines were unable to take the strain of the prolonged run at full power and were beginning to fail.

Two alternatives now faced Togo. He could either close on the last two ships of the enemy line, the slow *Poltava* and the *Sevastopol*, and let the remainder escape for the time being, or else he could disengage, and by using his maximum speed circle out of gun range until he could come in again from such an angle that he could concentrate on the enemy's van and head him off from his escape route. The briefest consideration showed the first to be unthinkable. The two rear ships were the least valuable. The remainder, if they got away to Vladivostok and joined the armoured cruisers there, would constitute a force capable of engaging the whole Japanese fleet. The arrival of the reinforcements from Europe would give them an overwhelming superiority.

So at 3 o'clock in the afternoon Togo led his ships on a south-easterly course diverging from that of the Russians, and increased to his maximum sustained speed of 15 knots. As the range opened, the firing died away, but not before the *Mikasa* had received two further hits.

It was just at this time that Dewa's 3rd Division, which had been circling the Russians to the northward, turned in response to an order from the Commander-in-Chief, and ran down towards the Russian cruisers to attack them. Unfortunately for him it was at this moment also that the Japanese battleships drew out of range. The 12-inch guns of the Russians were free to swing round on Dewa's flagship, and in the sudden concentration of fire to which his 8-inch guns could make no reply the *Yakumo* was badly hit. The odds were too heavy, and Dewa turned away again out of range. Soon afterwards he decided to circle astern of the Russian fleet in order to regain his assigned battle station on the disengaged quarter of the 1st Division.

Thus with the afternoon well advanced Togo was left committed to a long chase. Only with agonising slowness was he gaining on the enemy. The sun was sinking low. It seemed that contrary to all expectations, even on the part of the Russians, they were going to get away at least for that day; but at 4.30 the bearing of the enemy began to drop fast. The *Poltava*'s desperate efforts to keep up had come to an end as one set of her engines broke down, leaving her to struggle along on the other. The remainder had for a time reduced speed to stay with her.

At last Togo could turn to close the range again. At 5.35 the lagging *Poltava* at a range of less than 9,000 yards, was set upon by the whole Japanese line; but she replied with splendid spirit, giving back at least as good as she got and perhaps better. The tornado of fire and the impenetrable wall of splashes made the Japanese fire control a matter of guesswork, as had been the case earlier in the action. Moreover, Togo's flagship came once again under concentrated fire from the Russian battleships. Vitgeft had been forced to leave the *Poltava* to her fate, and pressing on again at 14 knots he had prevented Togo from getting as far ahead as the Japanese admiral had hoped. For the next hour a furious cannonade continued, during which misfortune piled on misfortune in the Japanese battleships.

The *Mikasa* was repeatedly hit, her after turret being put out of action and almost destroyed. In the *Shikishima* one of her fore barbette guns burst, and one of her 12-inch guns was disabled for a time. The *Asahi* had bursts in both her after turret guns due to overheating of the barrels. Out of sixteen turret guns in the Japanese battleships, five were out of action, and still the Russians sailed on apparently unaffected by the Japanese fire.

At 6.30 the situation must have seemed calamitous to the Japanese Commander-in-Chief. Sunset was only half an hour away. His flagship was shuddering under blow after blow from 6-inch and 12-inch shells. Her casualties were severe. On her starboard side a huge hole gaped a bare two feet above the water-line. Except for a disarrangement of the Russian line, there was little sign that the Japanese gunners were achieving comparable results.

Then suddenly, at 6.40, the whole picture was changed. The *Tzesarevitch* was seen to swerve out of the line to port, with a heavy list. Pouring smoke, she continued in a wide circle until she charged through her own line ahead of the *Sevastopol*, the rear ship except for the *Poltava*, now far astern and disabled. Her engines were then stopped.

The two 12-inch shells which were the cause lost the day for the Russians. The first, bursting near the foot of the mainmast, had at one stroke killed the Commander-in-Chief and sixteen others, and wounded and knocked senseless the Chief of Staff and the Flag Captain; the second hit the conning tower and killed or stunned every man in it. The flagship was bereft of all control, its wheel jammed hard a-port. The fleet was without a leader.

In the best regulated fleet such a calamity would have led to some confusion. To the Russians it spelt an end of all order, but not of the gallantry with which their ships had been so far handled. The captain of the *Retvizan* who had followed the *Tzesarevitch* round, not at first realising she was out of control, steered boldly for the enemy to draw the fire away from the disabled flagship. He was followed by the *Pobieda*.

When Togo saw the Russian line dissolve into a milling throng, he had begun to circle and close for the kill; but this movement of the *Retvizan* and *Pobieda* was so threatening that he was forced to give ground. Onwards the *Retvizan* came, her captain bent on trying to ram the *Mikasa*. Every Japanese gun was concentrated on her until she was completely hidden by smoke and spray, so that the *Mikasa*'s gunlayers were forced to cease fire for want of a point of aim. It seemed that nothing could stop the great ship in her desperate ride, but when she had got to within a mile and a half of the *Mikasa* a 12-inch shell at last got home. A splinter struck the *Retvizan*'s captain. Suffering excruciating pain, he was only able to gasp out instructions to take the ship back to join the squadron before he collapsed.

Yet his audacity, coupled with Togo's unwillingness to close to point-blank range for a fight to the finish, probably saved the Russian squadron from annihilation. After remaining motionless for twenty minutes the *Tzesarevitch* got under way again. Steering on her engines she staggered away with the remainder to the north-west. Though Prince Ukhtomski had tried to take over the command and make the signal "Follow Me", both topmasts of his flagship, the *Peresviet*, had been shot away and his signal was not readable. In complete confusi)n the Russian ships fled, firing wildly all the while at the circling Japanese battle squadron.

All that Togo needed to annihilate his defeated enemy was a period of daylight, but this was denied him. Darkness was now closing quickly. The waste of time, first in fruitless manœuvring ahead of the Russians at midday and secondly in the long chase which had been imposed by his tactical error later, was now to exact its toll. As night fell he held back, allowing the Russians to draw away. In spite of the repeated failure of torpedo attack in the past, he feared to expose himself to it, and at the same time he unleashed his own destroyers.

Through the night, as the main body of the Russians made their straggling way back to Port Arthur, the Japanese destroyers and torpedo-boats made attack after attack; but not a single torpedo found a billet. By daybreak the five battleships, *Retvizan*, *Peresviet*, *Pobieda*, *Sevastopol* and *Poltava*, the cruiser *Pallada* and three destroyers, were in the roadstead and passing into the inner harbour.

Of the remainder, the *Tzesarevitch* had been unable to keep up with the main body. The surviving officers decided to try to make for Vladivostok. It was soon found, however, that her damaged funnels induced such an enormous rate of fuel consumption that she could never get there. Together with the *Novik* and three destroyers she made for the neutral German port of Kiao-chao, where she and the destroyers were interned. The *Askold* and another destroyer suffered the same fate at Shanghai, while the *Diana* went to Saigon.

Only the *Novik*, after coaling at Kiao-chao, kept her gallant record to the last and set forth to make the circuit of the Japanese islands to reach Vladivostok. Reaching the island of Sakhalin far to the north, she was cornered while coaling at the Russian port of Korsakovsk, by the cruiser *Tsushima.* Though the *Novik* could oppose only four 4·7-inch guns to the *Tsushima's* four 6-inch, she came boldly out to fight. In the action that followed the *Novik* was almost destroyed, having five hits on the water-line; but before escaping to harbour, where her crew scuttled her, she had driven her powerful opponent off with a hole on the water-line and a dangerous list.

So ended the battle of 10th August 1904, and the last sortie of the Port Arthur squadron.

Tactically it had been indecisive. Had Togo at once closed on the Russians as they dissolved into chaos he might have achieved annihilation, but that was just what he felt he could not afford to do. The shadow of the Baltic Fleet lay over him. His precious battleships must be preserved against the time of its appearance in Pacific waters. His strategic object had been secured when the Russians turned back in flight for Port Arthur. Once again the Japanese Army's sea communications were safe, and the navy was fulfilling its primary function. The destruction of the Port Arthur Squadron would have been a bonus for the attainment of which Togo would have had to take risks which seemed to him unjustifiable.

Before we leave the Port Arthur squadron to its ignominious fate at the hands of the howitzer gunners of the Japanese Army, it is perhaps of interest to see how much damage each side inflicted on each other in the course of the long and furious battle.

To take the defeated side first, the Russian flagship *Tzesarevitch* was hit fifteen times by 12-inch shells alone besides many of smaller calibre. She lay stopped for twenty minutes within 8,000 yards of the Japanese line. Yet although she presented a shattered appearance with her after funnel destroyed and her upperworks riddled, no really vital damage had been inflicted, and she was never in any danger of sinking.

The *Poltava* had at various times been the target of every Japanese battleship and cruiser, and had been isolated and cut off, yet she made her way safely back to base. So it was with all the Russian ships.

In the Japanese fleet the *Mikasa* had suffered the most, with no less than twenty-two heavy hits, and was tremendously battered. Yet although the mishap to her after turret was not immediately repairable, in all other respects forty-eight hours of emergency repairs were sufficient to make her, as well as the remainder of the Japanese fleet, fit for action again.

As for casualties, the Russians suffered 74 killed and 394 wounded; the Japanese lost 69 killed and had 131 wounded, more than half the casualties being in the *Mikasa*.

It is clear, therefore, that at this stage of the development of the battleship, armour was still in the ascendancy over the destructive power of the guns at the short ranges at which hits could be obtained by the slow-firing big turret guns. Before the gun could reach the vitals of a well-armoured ship it would need to be able to score hits at long range, the shell then arriving at a steep, plunging angle. But to do this two things were necessary—salvo firing from a number of guns of the same calibre fired nearly simultaneously so as to make long-range spotting easier, and an improved system of fire control. Both these things were to come with the Dreadnought era.

8

Round the World to Disaster

By his repulse of the Russian Port Arthur squadron on 10th August 1904 on their attempt to break out for Vladivostok, Togo had achieved his strategic aim so far as it could be done without too much risk to the battleships which were so vital for Japan's continuance of the war. The Russians were once again bottled up, their numbers further reduced by the ships which had fled to neutral ports.

What the Japanese could not know was that to all intents and purposes the Russian squadron was as much eliminated as if it had been sent to the bottom. Any possibility of a further naval action was out of the question. On 19th August a council of war called by Prince Ukhtomski unanimously decided that there could be no possibility of a further break out by the squadron, and that every gun and every man not required to fight a defensive action at anchor should be landed to assist the garrison in defending the fortress.

Had this been known to Admiral Togo it would have saved him much anxiety, and his fleet would have been spared the wear and tear of the arduous duty entailed by close blockade and the inevitable losses from mines, which were already making this form of warfare hazardous and expensive. In September a destroyer and an old armoured coast defence ship were lost from this cause with heavy loss of life. In October the battleship *Asahi* was damaged by a floating mine. So it went on, a steady attrition which the Japanese could ill afford. At the end of November the cruiser *Saiyen* was lost; during the next month the *Takasago* went down with 274 officers and men, and the *Akashi* was severely damaged.

At last, on 2nd January 1905, the long and bloody siege of Port Arthur came to an end with its surrender. Only one ship, the *Sevastopol*, had survived the bombardments, and she was taken out and scuttled. For the time being the Pacific was cleared of Russian ships, for the Vladivostok squadron had been brought to action by Kamimura on 14th August, the *Rurik* being sunk and the other two cruisers being heavily damaged. Then the *Gromoboi* ran aground, and was wrecked just after her repairs had been completed. Only the flagship *Rossya* remained, unlikely to operate on her own and hemmed in by extensive Japanese minefields.

The breathing-space granted to the Japanese was put to good use. Their growing ship-building industry was set to work to recondition, refit and rearm the battle-damaged and work-worn ships. Plans were perfected to meet the new threat from the Baltic Fleet, or the 2nd Pacific Squadron as it had been renamed, which was making its slow and misfortune-studded voyage to the Far East under the flag of Rear-Admiral Rozhestvenski.

The decision to send reinforcements to the Russian Pacific Squadron had been taken as long ago as April 1904. On the face of it, if the Russian building programme could be relied upon to progress as planned, a useful force of new first-class battleships could be ready by the autumn. There was firstly the *Oslyabya*, the ship which had been on its way to the Far East when war broke out and which, after a long wait in the Red Sea, had been recalled. Another, the *Imperator Alexandr III*, was completed and ready at Cronstadt. Her sister-ships *Borodino* and *Kniaz Suvorov* were expected to be completed in the late summer, while another of the same class would be ready in the autumn.

Four older battleships, the *Sisoi Veliki*, *Navarin*, *Imperator Nikolai I* and *Imperator Alexandr II*, were undergoing refits which would be completed during the summer. In addition there were three modern light cruisers, *Aurora*, *Zhemchug* and *Izumrud*, as well as a number of older cruisers and some thirty torpedo craft.

So long as Port Arthur held out and the Pacific Squadron

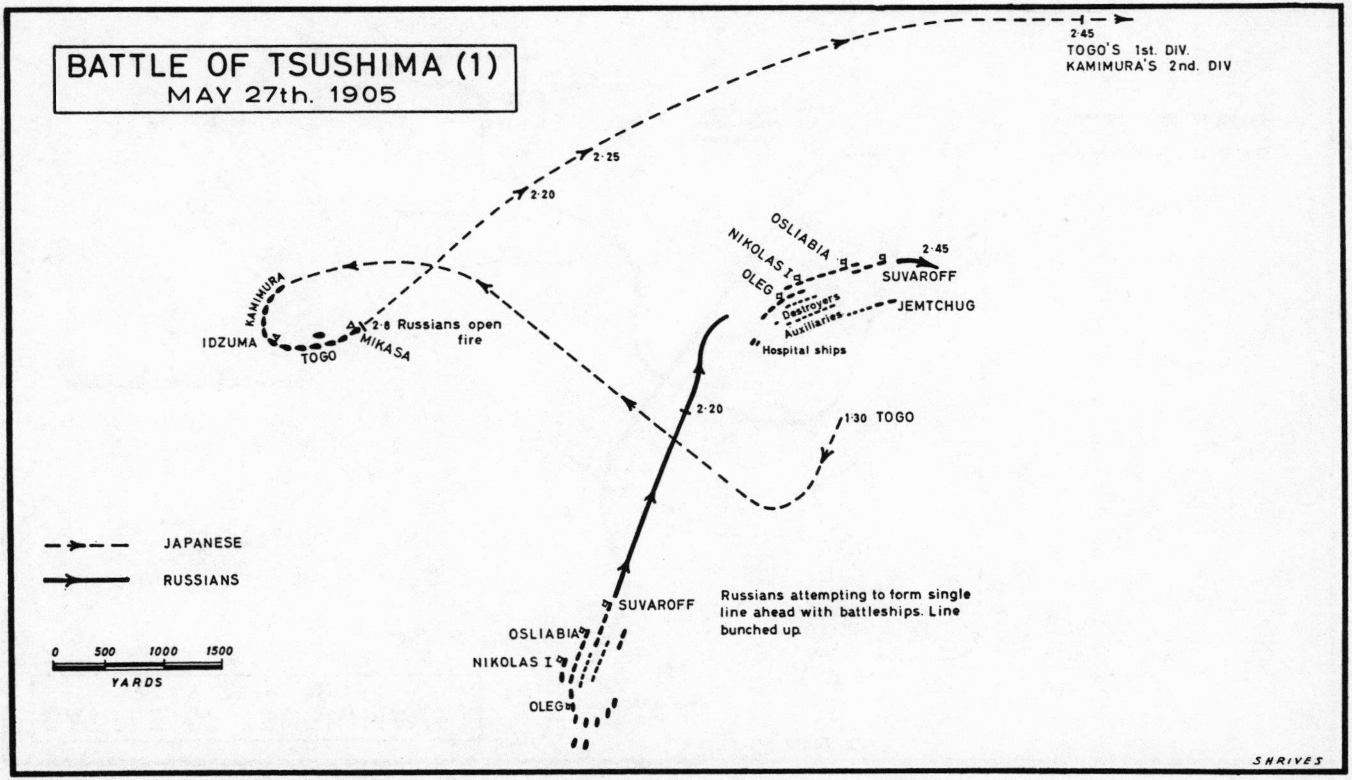
BATTLE OF TSUSHIMA (1)
MAY 27th. 1905
2·45
TOGO'S 1st. DIV.
KAMIMURA'S 2nd. DIV
2·25
2·20
OSLIABIA
NIKOLAS I
OLEG
2·45
SUVAROFF
Destroyers
Auxiliaries
JEMTCHUG
Hospital ships
KAMIMURA
IDZUMA
TOGO
MIKASA
2·8 Russians open fire
2·20
1·30 TOGO
JAPANESE
RUSSIANS
SUVAROFF
Russians attempting to form single line ahead with battleships. Line bunched up.
OSLIABIA
NIKOLAS I
OLEG
0 500 1000 1500
YARDS
SHRIVES

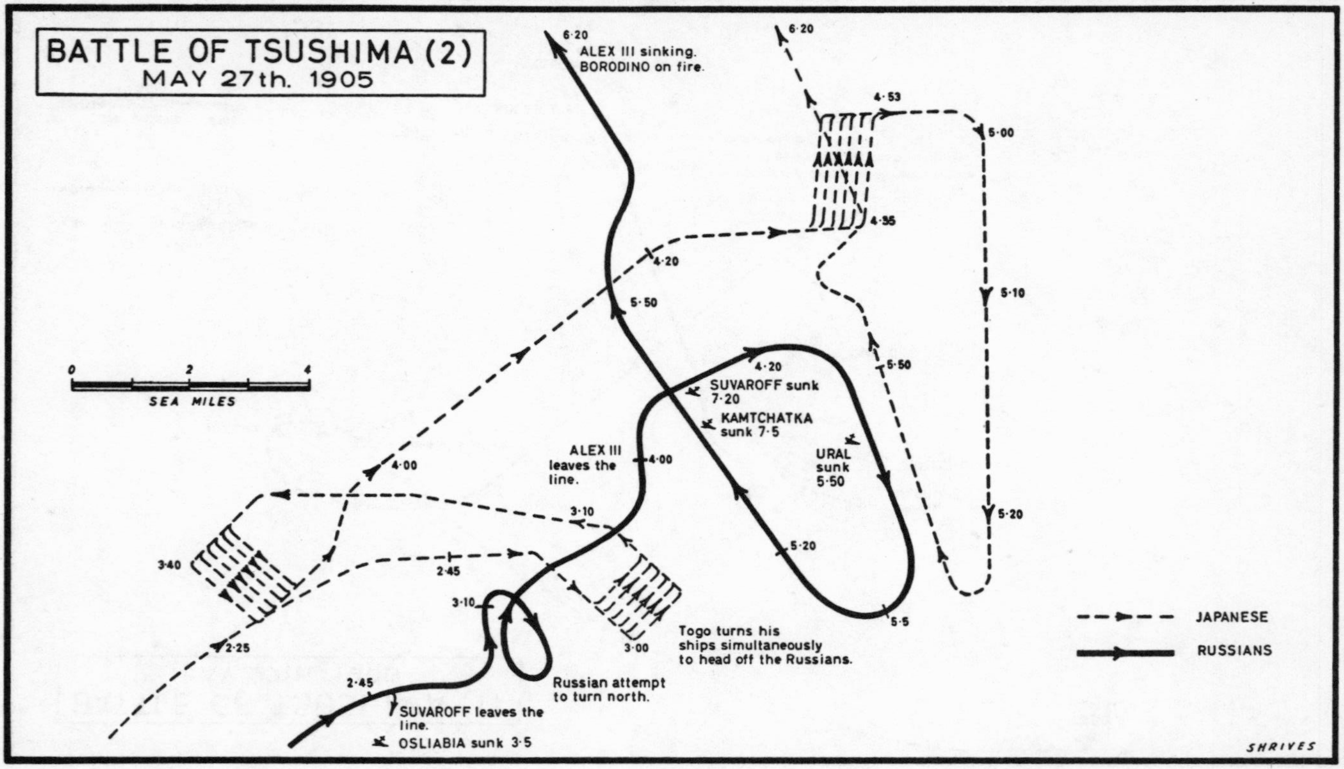
BATTLE OF TSUSHIMA (2)
MAY 27th. 1905
0
2
4
SEA MILES
6·20
ALEX III sinking.
BORODINO on fire.
6·20
4·53
5·00
4·35
4·20
5·50
5·10
4·20
SUVAROFF sunk
7·20
KAMTCHATKA
sunk 7·5
5·50
URAL
sunk
5·50
ALEX III
leaves the
line.
4·00
4·00
3·10
5·20
5·20
3·40
2·45
3·10
3·00
5·5
2·25
Togo turns his
ships simultaneously
to head off the Russians.
JAPANESE
RUSSIANS
2·45
Russian attempt
to turn north.
SUVAROFF leaves the
line.
OSLIABIA sunk 3·5
SHRIVES

remained "in being", it could be argued that the addition of an effective new squadron, its arrival timed to coincide with a sortie from Port Arthur and Vladivostok, could completely upset the naval balance of power, and with it the whole Japanese war plan. It has been seen how even the distant threat had prevented Togo from using his battleships with the vigour which would have turned his partial successes into annihilating victories.

Even to grasp so great a prize, however, there were grave difficulties to be overcome in sending a squadron of those days some 19,000 miles over a route devoid of friendly naval bases. The pounding reciprocating engines of battleships of the pre-dreadnought era were liable to constant defects if run for long periods at anything but slow speeds. Boilers required frequent cleaning, a horrible task for white men in the tropics. The high-grade Welsh coal for their furnaces would need repeated replenishment, which could be procured only by a system of colliers organised in advance to meet them at sea—for legally a neutral might not allow coal to be embarked in its ports by a belligerent. At the end of the voyage the ships would have to go into action needing refit and docking, their bottoms foul after cruising in tropical waters, with only a fraction of their speed available.

Nevertheless the Russian Admiralty decided to undertake this hazardous plan. Rear-Admiral Rozhestvenski, one of their best officers, was appointed to command the force. Difficulties of every sort were encountered during the fitting out of the various ships, owing to a dearth of skilled workmen, the majority of whom had been sent off to Port Arthur and Vladivostok. Trained crews were equally scarce; nor was there time to mould the rough human material available into efficient ships' companies.

However, by 11th September Rozhestvenski's 2nd Pacific Squadron had assembled at Libau, its last Russian port of call. It comprised seven battleships, *Suvorov*, *Alexandr III*, *Borodino*, *Orel*, *Oslyabya*, *Veliki* and *Navarin*, two old armoured cruisers, *Admiral Nakhimoff* and *Dmitri Donskoi*, four light cruisers, *Aurora*, *Svietlana*, *Zhemchug* and *Almaz*, seven destroyers, and nine transports. Sailing on 15th October, the squadron arrived at the southern entrance to the Great Belt between Denmark and Sweden two days later.

Its quality, moral and material, was at once revealed, as well as the awe in which the Russians held their enemy and the incompetence with which they were equipped to meet him. Fantastic rumours that the Japanese were intending to mine the waters through which the Russians would have to pass, and that they had sent a torpedo flotilla to Europe to attack the squadron, were taken seriously.

Before Rozhestvenski would risk the narrow waters leading out of the Baltic, some of his auxiliary craft were set to sweeping the channel; but after vain efforts to make their sweeping gear function they were forced to give up, whereupon the squadron ventured the passage, arriving safely off the Skaw and anchoring on 20th October.

It was planned for the squadron to get under way again in six groups on the following day, each group travelling independently as far as Tangier. The battleships too deep in the water for the Suez Canal would then take the long route round the Cape of Good Hope, the remainder passing through the Mediterranean. All would eventually rendezvous in Madagascar.

Hardly had the squadron anchored when reports reached the admiral from the captain of one of his transports that suspicious-looking craft resembling torpedo-boats had been seen during the night. The alarm was passed to all ships, and orders were given to sail at once.

At 4 o'clock in the afternoon the destroyers, in two groups each with a transport, set off, followed by a division composed of the *Svyetlana*, *Zhemchug* and *Almaz*. At 5 p.m. *Aurora* and *Donskoi*, with the armed merchant cruiser *Kamchatka*, set out. Twenty-five miles astern of them came a battleship division comprising *Oslyabya*, *Veliki*, *Navarin*, *Admiral Nakhimoff* and two transports, followed at 10 p.m. by the four remaining battleships led by the *Suvorov*, Rozhestvenski's flagship.

Throughout the squadron there was a state of the utmost

tension. Through the dark, misty North Sea night the ships steamed with the crews at action stations. Anxious eyes peered through the darkness on the look-out for the mythical Japanese torpedo-boats. In the *Kamchatka*, a converted passenger liner particularly vulnerable to torpedo attack, nerves were at full stretch. She had lost touch with her division soon after getting under way. When dim shapes loomed up near by, albeit showing normal navigation lights, they were at once taken for the enemy, and guns' crews leapt into action. First the Swedish steamer *Aldebaran*, then the French sailing-ship *Guyane* and a German trawler came under their fortunately wild and inaccurate fire.

None of them were hit, but the *Kamchatka*'s reports made the Russians all the more convinced that an attack was imminent. Already their organisation was breaking down, and the various divisions were bunching up on each other. So it was that when at around midnight the battleships caught up with the *Aurora* and *Donskoi* just as they ran in amongst the British fishing fleet off the Dogger Bank, wild alarm spread. Guns opened fire in every direction, not only at the unfortunate trawlers but at the two Russian cruisers also.

The British trawler *Crane* was sunk, five others hit and many damaged by splinters from near misses. Two fishermen were killed and six wounded. The *Aurora* was hit five times, her chaplain being mortally wounded. Finally the firing died away as the victims were left astern. The battleship divisions steamed on amidst mutual congratulations at the successful repulse of a dangerous attack.

Relations between the British and Russian Governments were not unnaturally strained to the limit by this astonishing affair, but apologies and an agreement to refer the matter to an International Commission prevented an open breach. The disorganisation and lack of training which the incident revealed set the pattern for the rest of Rozhestvenski's ill-starred venture. His halting, uncertain progress round the world continued at a funeral pace haunted by the constant uncertainty of fuel supplies. Indeed had not the neutral countries, particularly France, winked at the breaches of international law involved in permitting long stays in their harbours and the supply of coal to the Russian ships, the 2nd Pacific Squadron would very quickly have had to revert to its previous rôle of Baltic Fleet.

To reduce the halts for refuelling so far as was possible, coal was piled high on the decks, so that not only were the ships permanently bedraggled and filthy with coal-dust, but also the systematic training which the crews so badly needed became impossible.

When Port Arthur capitulated to the Japanese in January 1905, Rozhestvenski's force had reached Madagascar, where it had been lying for nearly a month while fresh contracts for the supply of coal were being negotiated. The British Government had stopped the shipment of Welsh coal for the Russian squadron, the German Hamburg-Amerika line colliers had refused to accompany it into the war zone. Not until the middle of March 1905 would Rozhestvenski be able to set forth again.

Meanwhile the state of affairs which had led to the decision to send reinforcements to the Pacific had entirely changed. With the fall of Port Arthur and the elimination of the 1st Pacific Squadron, Rozhestvenski's untrained, disheartened, apprehensive and periodically mutinous squadron would have to face the whole of Japan's freshly refitted fleet manned by war-experienced, supremely confident veterans. Even if the Russians could succeed in brushing aside the Japanese opposition, there was only the port of Vladivostok with its limited facilities for warship maintenance to receive them. Furthermore the supply of steam coal for such a large force presented an almost insoluble problem.

As the Russian admiral lay at Nossi Bé in Madagascar, he and many of his officers and men in ill-health owing to the tropical climate, the question of coal supplies was still unsolved. The Government, with an astonishing lack of comprehension of maritime affairs, telegraphed to point out to him that the task of securing command of the sea now lay in his hands alone, offering to send him reinforcements from amongst the ancient and quite unbattleworthy warships still in the Baltic.

It is impossible not to sympathise with the sorely tried Rozhestvenski when he replied in terms reminiscent of the unfortunate Cervera in the Spanish-American War:

"I have not the slightest prospect of recovering command of the sea with the force under my orders. The despatch of reinforcements composed of untested and in some cases badly built vessels would only render the fleet more vulnerable."

Rozhestvenski concluded this frank expression of opinion with a request to be relieved on account of ill-health. Ignoring his request and his warning alike, the Russian Government sent the reinforcements on their way on 15th February; museum pieces such as the obsolete battleship *Nikolai I*, an old armoured cruiser *Vladimir Monomakh*, and three small coast defence ships *Admiral Apraxin*, *Admiral Seniavin* and *Admiral Ushakoff*, as well as seven auxiliary vessels. Under Rear-Admiral Nebogatoff they caught up with the main squadron on 9th May at Van Fong Bay in French Indo-China, to embarrass the unhappy Commander-in-Chief with their slow speed and lack of armament.

From this point onwards the story of Rozhestvenski is dominated by an air of inevitable doom. The only practicable route for the squadron was through the Korean Straits, and there the Japanese fleet lay, tensed and waiting at their base in Sylvia Basin, trained to a hair and superbly confident. The Russians coaled for the last time off the coast of China on 23rd May, on which day Rozhestvenski's second-in-command, Rear-Admiral Folkersam, at last died from the illness which had overtaken him during the voyage. To avoid such an omen further depressing the spirits of his already demoralised crews, Rozhestvenski kept the news from all but Folkersam's flagship, *Oslyabya*, where he ordered the admiral's flag to be kept flying. Again getting under way, the squadron—complete with its embarrassing tail of auxiliaries, including hospital ships—steered to pass through the Straits of Tsushima to the eastwards of the island of that name.

The force was organised in four divisions. The 1st was composed of Rozhestvenski's flagship *Suvorov* and the battleships *Alexandr III*, *Borodino* and *Orel*. The 2nd comprised the *Oslyabya*, *Sissoi Veliki*,

Navarin and *Admiral Nakhimoff*. The *Nikolai I*, in which Nebogatoff flew his flag, led the *Apraxin*, *Seniavin* and *Ushakoff* to form the 3rd Division, while the eight cruisers formed a separate division under Rear-Admiral Enquist with his flag in the *Oleg*.

Rozhestvenski, who lacked nothing in personal courage, whatever may have been his other qualities, had decided that battle must be accepted and even sought. Merely to evade Togo and take refuge in Vladivostok would in no way contribute towards a challenge to the Japanese control of the sea. He had at least to try to inflict some damage on the enemy. Partly for this reason and partly because he feared torpedo attack by night in the narrow waters close to the enemy bases, he adjusted his speed to enter the Tsushima Strait at daylight on 27th May.

With time in hand, he steamed at slow speed during the 26th, and spent some time exercising battle manœuvres. On account of the old, slow ships in company, all of which were foul with tropical growth and many of which had boiler defects, the battle speed was established as only 11 knots. As the daylight faded, he reformed his unwieldy squadron into its cruising order and signalled: "Prepare for action. Tomorrow at the hoisting of the colours, battle flags will be flown."

All that day and during the night the Russian wireless operators were reporting heavy Japanese signal traffic. The enemy were evidently near and in considerable force. Togo himself, with his battleship division, Kamimura's division of six armoured cruisers and Rear-Admiral Uriu's 4th Division of light cruisers, were still at anchor in Sylvia Basin. All were at short notice for steam, and awaiting the alarm from the scouting forces stretched across the straits south of Tsushima Island. These were in two lines, the outer composed of four armed merchant cruisers backed by the two old cruisers *Akitsushima* and *Idzumi*. Behind them were stretched Rear-Admiral Dewa's light cruisers *Kasagi*, *Chitose*, *Niitaka* and *Otowa*. In the harbour of Tsushima was the 5th Division of Rear-Admiral Kataoka, with those veterans of the China War, *Itsukushima*, *Chinyen*, *Matsushima* and *Hashidate*.

The last news Togo had received of the Russians was of their appearance off the Yangtse on the 25th. At their normal cruising speed they should have reached the Tsushima Strait on the evening of the next day, but no sighting reports had come in. Doubts began to plague him that his judgement that Rozhestvenski would come that way had been wrong, in which case the Russians would be keeping to the eastward of Japan and would have to be met far to the north. When night fell on 26th May the Russians had still not been located.

Togo's anxiety was soon to be allayed. At 2.45 on the misty but moonlit middle watch of the 27th, one of the armed merchant cruisers of the outer scouting line, the *Shinano Maru*, sighted lights. Closing them to investigate, Captain Narukawa discovered them to be those of a Russian hospital ship. While still investigating her, Narukawa sighted the dim shapes of many warships against the first pale gleams of dawn to the eastward, accompanied by a cloud of black smoke. The honour of the first sighting of the enemy was his. The alarm was signalled, and by 5 o'clock it had reached the Japanese Commander-in-Chief.

Togo's great moment had come. The enemy had been located where he had forecast, and were making for the Straits of Tsushima. There he would meet them. As the news spread through the ships, the orders for getting under way were received with wild excitement and enthusiasm. Proudly the admiral drafted his message to the Emperor:

"I have just received the news that the enemy's fleet has been sighted. Our fleet will forthwith proceed to sea to attack the enemy and destroy him."

All over the world the result of the impending clash of arms was being anxiously awaited. At 6.34 a.m. Togo led the way to sea, and circling to the north of Tsushima Island he steered for the little island of Okinoshima in the centre of the Straits, where he placed himself across the path which the Russian ships must follow. With him were the ships of his own division, *Mikasa*, *Shikishima*, *Fuji*, *Asahi*, *Kasuga* and *Nisshin*, and Kamimura's armoured cruisers, *Idzumo*, *Adzuma*, *Tokiwa*, *Yakumo*, *Asama* and *Iwate*.

Meanwhile, at the *Shinano*'s enemy report, the Japanese cruisers moved in to shadow. Dewa's fast squadron, arriving first, missed the Russians in the misty half-light of dawn and carried on some way to the south before realising its mistake and turning back. But at 7 a.m. the *Idzumi* from the scouting line had stationed herself 5 miles to starboard of the Russians, and there she stayed unmolested and reporting the enemy's every movement. At 9 a.m., Kataoka's 5th Division fell in on the Russians' other side.

Rozhestvenski was still in his cruising formation, his battleships in two columns with the transports between. At 10 a.m. he changed to battle formation, leading his twelve armoured ships in single line ahead and placing his cruisers transports and destroyers to starboard which he expected to be his disengaged side.

Now Dewa's division joined the shadowing force, and for the next three and a half hours the Russian squadron was thus conducted towards the Japanese main body as by some ceremonial guard of honour, or perhaps more like a line of stolid oxen to the slaughter. For a few minutes at 11.40 some of the Russian ships opened fire on Dewa's division which had impudently closed to within 9,000 yards, but Rozhestvenski, to conserve his precious ammunition for the main combat, ordered "Cease Fire" and sent his crews to dinner to prepare them for the ordeal ahead of them.

Knowing that Togo must be somewhere ahead, the Russian admiral now attempted a manœuvre designed to give him the advantage of being across the enemy's "T" at the moment of encounter. A thickening of the mist had hidden the watching Japanese cruisers, and he thought he might surprise Togo by advancing in line abreast. A simple turn together would then put him in line ahead across the path of the approaching Japanese battle divisions.

Rozhestvenski's tactical idea was beyond the capabilities of his unskilled, unpractised captains. Long before it had been completed, the Japanese cruisers had drawn into view again. Surprise being lost, Rozhestvenski cancelled the manœuvre. Thus when at 1.39 p.m. the Russians were sighted by the Japanese battle divisions at a distance of 7 miles, they were in neither one formation nor the other.

Togo had previously decided that he would attack from the enemy's port bow; so when the Russians came in sight fine to starboard, he at once led round to cross ahead of the enemy line at right angles. Then, as he reached his chosen position, he unfurled his battle ensigns and led round in a turn of more than 180 degrees to range himself on a parallel course to the Russians. It was a risky manœuvre, for his turning-point was well within range of the enemy, who at once opened undisturbed fire. The time was 8 minutes past 2 o'clock.

The Togo of this day, however, was in a different mood from that of 10th August. Not only was he confident that he had the measure of the Russians, but, with Russia's last fleet in view, he was prepared to exchange blow for blow at killing range even at some cost in ships to himself. There was no longer need to conserve his battleship strength against the possibility of another battle later. As he had signalled to his fleet on sailing, "The future of the Empire depends on this battle." He therefore deliberately risked placing himself where he could concentrate on the head of the enemy line, with his strongest ships in the lead to bear the brunt of the shell fire.

The risk had in fact been well calculated; for though the Japanese ships were surrounded by shell splashes as they followed their flagship round, hits were very few, and none of them from the bigger guns. As they settled on their course, one after the other they in turn opened a slow deliberate fire at a range of from 5,000 to 6,000 yards. For a while their shooting was indifferent as they picked their targets from the still confused Russian line. Then as they found the range, the five leading Russian ships were subjected to a violent battering.

The flagships of the two leading divisions, *Suvorov* and *Oslyabya*, were particularly singled out for punishment, and were soon set ablaze. As the fire parties struggled to control the flames they were killed or wounded by the storm of shell which swept the decks. Guns became jammed through shell fragments entering by the gun ports and lodging in the mechanism. In the *Oslyabya* the fore turret had been knocked out, and her decks were littered with dead and wounded.

In the midst of this fury of fire, the Russians, still trying to re-form their line following Rozhestvenski's ill-advised manœuvre fell into a worse confusion. The *Oslyabya* had to stop to avoid collision with the *Orel*; ships in the rear became bunched up, and also had to reduce speed or stop in consequence.

All the while, the Japanese with their superior speed were drawing ahead, and were thus able to pour a concentrated fire into the confused mass of ships at the head of the Russian formation. Soon they would be crossing the Russian "T". To prevent this and to enable all his guns to bear on the enemy, Rozhestvenski led away to starboard and brought the *Mikasa* once again on to his beam.

The Japanese had by no means gone unscathed through the early exchanges. The *Mikasa* had already suffered 54 casualties from hits by two 12-inch shells and two 6-inch. The *Asama*, last but one of Kamimura's division, had been hit by a 12-inch shell which had disabled her steering gear and caused such flooding that she had to leave the line for repairs, the first ship on either side to do so. But except for her, the Japanese line was not seriously affected, and still steamed in perfect formation at 15 knots, all guns fully in action.

Togo, standing fearlessly out on the open upper bridge of the *Mikasa*, had cause for grim satisfaction as he saw the Russian line staggering under his concentrated fire. At 2.50 the *Oslyabya*, all guns on her port side knocked out, a huge shell hole on her port side forward, listing heavily and settling down by the head, dragged herself out of the line and stopped. As the ships astern of her passed by, the crews saw the shattered ship capsize, figures clinging to her keel and bilge keels. So she stayed for fifteen minutes and then plunged to the bottom. Destroyers picked up 14 officers and 371 men out of a complement of 48 officers and 852 men.

Before all this had taken place, the *Suvorov* had also been battered almost to a wreck. At 2.55, under the unbearable pressure of the Japanese cannonade, her helm had been put over to bear away to starboard. Already the Commander-in-Chief lay badly wounded and barely conscious, with most of his staff officers killed or wounded. Now the ship's helm jammed, swinging her round more and more to starboard, throwing the Russian line into further confusion. The 2nd Division dropped back, while the 3rd, pressing on, drew up abreast of it, the fire of many of its guns masked.

The confusion, the ragged shooting, the destruction of the *Oslyabya* and now the disablement of the Russian flagship told Togo that the day was his. All that remained was to pound to wrecks the leaderless ships as they turned this way and that to avoid the merciless hail of shells. The lead had devolved on the *Alexandr III*. As soon as he realised the *Suvorov* was disabled, the captain of the *Alexandr III* led round to port to try to escape under the stern of the Japanese line now beginning to cross ahead; but there was no escape that way from Togo's fast and well-drilled squadrons. In perfect unison the six ships of his 1st Division turned 90 degrees together, and then a further 90, once more converging on the Russian line, though now in reverse order.

While the fire of Togo's ships was temporarily halted during this manœuvre, Kamimura, admirably supporting his chief, held on for a time, pouring in a devastating fire from the 8-inch and 6-inch guns of his ships at a range of less than 3,000 yards. The little despatch vessel *Chihaya* had joined Kamimura's line, finding it safer there than on his disengaged side, where she had been in the midst of the wild firing of the Russians. So close did she pass to the enemy now that she took the opportunity to fire two torpedoes at the *Borodino*, though neither hit.

As soon as Togo was round on his new course, Kamimura followed suit. With the Japanese again across his escape route, the *Alexandr III* was forced back on to a south-easterly course. By now the Russian ships were moving in a great bank of smoke from their funnels, their gunfire and the fires blazing in many of them; to their relief, they were for a time lost to sight from the Japanese armoured divisions. As the storm of shell died away, the course was once again altered to the northward towards the longed-for safety of Vladivostok.

Meanwhile the crippled *Suvorov* had got painfully under way again, and she too was moving northwards with a heavy list to port. Searching for the enemy, Kamimura's division came upon her. Circling slowly round her, they hammered her at short range.

Whatever the shortcomings of the Russians as seamen or tacticians, they were to show that they were not lacking in heroic qualities. With all hope gone, the crew of the *Suvorov* fought back valiantly against fantastic odds, replying to their tormentors with the single 12-inch gun still serviceable and a few 12-pounders. The *Chihaya* and destroyers of the 5th Japanese Flotilla joined in attacking with torpedoes, but still the *Suvorov* was by no means defenceless. In face of the fire from her 12-pounders, the torpedo craft failed to score a single hit. For a time she was left in peace as Togo and Kamimura manœuvred to seek out the main body of the Russians.

Turning his division again by a double 90-degree turn together at 3.40, putting the *Mikasa* back into the van, Togo set off north-eastward, and at 4 o'clock the Russian mass came into sight, steering to the north and passing their disabled flagship. Once again the Japanese guns opened up, the battleships dividing their fire between the *Suvorov* and the remainder. Now it was the turn of the *Alexandr III* to stumble out of the line, such as it was—for all semblance of order had left the Russians. As broadsides were poured into them at a range of barely 1,000 yards, they turned and streamed away towards the south, led now by the *Borodino*.

This again brought the desperate Russians some respite, for at this moment Togo, confident that the destruction of the enemy was assured and no longer a matter of any urgency, turned the battleships away northward to give his crews a rest in which damage repairs could be made. At the same time he loosed the 4th Flotilla to attack with torpedoes. In the confusion, amidst the drifting banks of smoke, the destroyers found only the indomitable *Suvorov*, and expended their torpedoes on her. Reduced to two 12-pounders only, the Russians still managed to upset the enemy attack so that no torpedoes reached the crippled wreck, and one of the destroyers was damaged.

As the Japanese torpedo craft drew off, the Russian destroyer *Buini* arrived to take off the badly wounded Commander-in-Chief and his staff. It was clear, however, that Rozhestvenski was in no condition to take control again, even if he could have been put aboard one of his surviving battleships. Barely conscious, he could only murmur to the destroyer captain, "Nebogatoff—Vladivostok—Course N23E." Another destroyer therefore left to seek Nebogatoff and tell him that the command had devolved upon him.

Taking advantage of the respite which Togo's turnaway had granted them, the mass of Russian ships again circled through west to north-west. Throughout the action the cruisers and auxiliaries had followed the armoured divisions in their gyrations, the cruisers intermittently in action with and giving protection to the auxiliaries from the Japanese 3rd, 4th and 5th Divisions which, in accordance with Togo's battle orders, had harried the Russian rear. In the course of these actions the auxiliary *Russ* had been sunk and the cruisers *Oleg* and *Zhemtchug* damaged and set on fire. Amongst the Japanese ships only Rear-Admiral Dewa's flagship *Kasagi* had been dangerously damaged, by a hit below the water-line. With the *Chitose* in company she had made for the Japanese coast, where Dewa was able to transfer to the *Chitose* and return to the battle.

Now, as the Russians were circling, Togo's 1st Division coming south again to seek them out found at first only these auxiliaries which were actually between it and its proper target. The Japanese armoured ships fired into the defenceless auxiliaries for a time before bearing away north-west in search of the Russian battle division. It was not until 6 o'clock that they once more gained touch with them.

The *Alexandr III* had by then rejoined the Russian main body, and with the *Borodino* and *Orel* she again came under a violent cannonade at a range of 7,000 yards. The fires so recently mastered broke fiercely out again. A huge hole gaped in the *Alexandr*'s port side forward; her stern was oddly distorted. Yet after withdrawing for a while for repairs she was brought back into the line near the rear.

Broadside to broadside the two forces steamed northwards. The sun was sinking behind the Russians, making spotting difficult for the Japanese, but their shells continued to hammer again and again into the riven hulls of the enemy. Suddenly her accumulated damage became fatal to the *Alexandr*. Hoisting a signal of distress, she turned abruptly away and then, in full view of the squadron, turned turtle and sank, leaving only four survivors out of the ship's company of 836 who had so gallantly fought to the bitter end.

By now Rear-Admiral Nebogatoff had come to know that the command had fallen on him. Hoisting the signal in his flagship *Nikolai I*, "Follow me. Course N23E", he tried to lead off in that direction; but the inexorable pressure of the Japanese gunfire forced him back to his north-westerly course. The situation for the Russians was indeed quite hopeless. The *Orel* and *Borodino* were blazing; though the Russian guns continued to fire, the aim was wild and uncontrolled.

The sun had now set, and dusk was settling down, lit by the lurid glare of the fires in the Russian ships. A night action was not part of Togo's plans. The final destruction of the enemy could be left to the torpedo craft, and if that failed he knew he could renew the action at daylight. He therefore led the 1st Division away to the northward, the firing dying slowly away as the enemy faded from view. As the Russians were almost out of sight, a last salvo from the *Fuji*'s 12-inch turrets crashed out, and a shell plunged full into the *Borodino*'s hull. There were two dull explosions in her vitals, and a sudden uprush of flame as her magazines detonated. Swerving away to starboard, the great ship rolled slowly over lay for a while bottom up and then slid below the surface. One solitary survivor was picked up three hours later by a Japanese torpedo-boat.

So the sound of the guns died away as, through the gathering gloom, the Japanese destroyers could be seen closing in for the kill. But before the happenings of the night are told, we must follow the dying *Suvorov* to the end of the trail.

At 6.30 p.m. while the remainder of the Russian battleships were being battered to wrecks by the Japanese 1st Division, Kamimura and his armoured cruisers had again fallen in with the *Suvorov* in company with the auxiliary *Kamchatka*. Steaming slowly past at the deadly range of only 1,400 yards, the Japanese let drive with every gun in their armaments, every shot hitting, before they passed on to find more worthwhile targets, leaving the Russians burning, the *Kamchatka* sinking and the *Suvorov* hastening a little more towards her inevitable end.

Yet when the cruisers of the Japanese 4th, 5th and 6th Divisions took Kamimura's place, somehow in that floating mass of twisted steel which had been the *Suvorov* devoted men kept two little 12-pounders barking a pathetic defiance. For a full thirty minutes the unequal fight went on, until at last destroyers of the 11th Flotilla delivered the coup-de-grâce with two torpedoes. The ship which had so valiantly borne the name of the great Russian hero could stand no more. With every man of her gallant company she plunged to the bottom, her long fight over.

As the night came down, the field was left clear for the Japanese torpedo craft, while Togo, ordering a rendezvous for daylight off the island of Matsushima some 200 miles to the north, rested his weary but victorious crews.

The Russians had achieved some sort of order before darkness came down. Following Nebogatoff in the *Nikolai* were the *Orel*, *Apraxin*, *Seniavin* and, at a considerable interval, the *Ushakoff*. A long way behind again were the *Navarin*, *Veliki* and *Nakhimoff*. On the *Nikolai*'s port side the light cruiser *Izumrud* had taken station. Abreast the *Navarin*'s division and to port of it were the cruisers *Oleg*, *Aurora*, *Zhemtchug*, *Donskoi* and *Monomakh*, under Rear-Admiral Enquist.

Seeing the Japanese destroyers gathering ahead of him, Nebogatoff led round to the south-west for a time and then altered back to the north-east on the course for Vladivostok. In the darkness, Enquist failed to note or perhaps ignored this last alteration and, holding on to the south-west, followed by the *Aurora* and *Zhemtchug*, vanished from the scene until he reappeared some time later in the Philippine Islands, where he delivered his ships into internment at Manila.

The remainder of the Russian ships in three separate bodies stood to the north-eastward, and for three hours the Japanese flotillas, fifty-eight boats in all, pressed their attacks in a rough sea. These fell for the most part on the rear division led by the *Navarin* and on the two remaining cruisers of Enquist's division.

Inspired by the successes of the day action in which they had been unable to play any part, the Japanese torpedo-men handled their craft with zest and enthusiasm, pressing in to close range to fire their torpedoes. The first ship to be hit was the *Navarin*, which, stopping to place a collision mat over the worst of her underwater damage, was caught immobilised and was torpedoed four times. She quickly sank, taking with her all but three of the 622 officers and men, the survivors being picked up by the Japanese after sixteen hours in the water.

Then the *Veliki* was torpedoed in the stern. In a sinking condition she made for the island of Tsushima, and went down the next morning as Japanese cruisers arrived to capture her. The *Nakhimoff* and the *Monomakh* also made for Tsushima after being hit, and were scuttled by their crews to avoid capture.

In spite of the great number of torpedoes fired, probably more than a hundred, these were the total of Japanese successes during the night. Nebogatoff's five leading ships, thoroughly darkened and prudently not showing their searchlights, slipped away undetected to the north-eastward. But there was no escape for them that way. Discovered by the Japanese 6th Division at daylight, they were soon ringed round by the whole Japanese fleet.

Hopelessly outnumbered, Nebogatoff surrendered his four armoured ships, while the *Izumrud* was able to use her high speed to get away to Vladivostok, only to be wrecked by running ashore in the neighbourhood of that port.

Of the larger ships, only the *Ushakoff* now remained in Russian hands. She had been following some way astern of Nebogatoff, and was brought to action and sunk by the cruisers *Iwate* and *Yakumo*.

The cruisers *Svyetlana* and *Donskoi* fought with gallantry when caught by greatly superior forces, but their end was inevitable—as was that of all but the cruiser *Almaz* and one destroyer, which escaped to Vladivostok by hugging the Japanese coast as they made their way north.

It only remains to record the fate of the luckless Rozhestvenski. The destroyer *Buini*, in which the grievously wounded admiral lay, found herself at daylight on 28th May in company with the cruiser *Donskoi* and the destroyers *Biedovy* and *Grosny*. Running short of coal and damaged in action, she could not hope to reach Vladivostok. Her crew were taken off, Rozhestvenski and his staff being taken aboard the *Biedovy*, and she was then sunk by gunfire.

The *Biedovy* and *Grosny* set off northwards and, when sighted by Japanese destroyers near Matsushima, the former, though quite undamaged, at once hauled down her flag and surrendered, while the *Grosny* succeeded in making her escape. Thus the unconscious Russian Commander-in-Chief suffered the shame of falling into his enemy's hands through the cowardly action of his subordinates.

The Russian fleet had ceased to exist. Of the line of battle, out of twelve ships, eight had been sunk and the remainder captured. Of the cruisers, five were destroyed and three interned. Seven destroyers were sunk during the 28th, one was captured and one reached Vladivostok. All this had been achieved by the Japanese at the cost of three torpedo-boats, one of which was sunk in collision. The Japanese had 117 killed and 583 wounded; the Russians lost 4,830 killed alone.

It was indeed annihilation. The whole world stood amazed. Even amongst those who had realised what astonishing progress the Japanese Navy had made in its short existence there were many who found it hard to believe the facts. Yet perhaps the really revealing thing about the Battle of Tsushima, and one which was to give strength to the arguments for a revolutionary change in naval armament, was the tremendous punishment which the Russian ships had endured before succumbing.

Study of the facts revealed that it was the hits by the big 12-inch guns which caused the fatal damage, while the smaller calibre guns did little more than smash upperworks, masts and bridges. The theory of the all-big-gun ship, already accepted in the navies of the West, was confirmed. The way was open to the Dreadnought era of naval history which was about to begin.

9

Dreadnought

THE Battle of Tsushima and its less decisive but more evenly matched predecessor of 10th August 1904 were naturally seized upon for study by naval experts all over the world. Tactical lessons were drawn from them and fiercely propounded. Technical details of the ships involved were closely studied to explain the relative performance of the two sides. Yet in fact almost every form of equipment in the battleships of either fleet was about to be made obsolete, the tactical conclusions thereby being given doubtful validity.

Only the revelation of the ineffectiveness of the smaller guns against armoured ships was to be of consequence. The mixed gun armament, compelling a decisive range of as little as from 3,000 to 5,000 yards, the system—or lack of it—of fire control, the propelling machinery so fallible when driven at full power, all were about to be superseded to make a new revolution in battle-ship-design.

Ever since the previous revolution occasioned by the introduction of steam propulsion and the use of armour, warships and their armament had been designed simply to be more powerful and better protected than those being added to rival navies. If the French Navy built a battleship with, say, four 10-inch guns and ten 6-inch with an armoured belt 8 inches thick, the answer by the British Navy might be a ship with four 12-inch guns or a secondary battery of 8-inch and perhaps thicker armour, on the assumption that these two ships or two lines of such ships might fight it out at short range, hammer and tongs, until one or the other was reduced to a wreck or sunk—as indeed was the case at Tsushima.

The inability to hit a target at the long range of which the bigger guns were capable of firing made such an idea not unrealistic. As late as 1903, the fighting range of battleships was considered to be in the region of 3,000 yards. At such range the whole of the large mixed battery of guns, mounted wherever space could be found for them, could be brought into action. The range once found, a high percentage of hits could be obtained by gun-layers using quite simple sights.

Such a state of affairs had long been looked on as normal by the great majority of naval experts and warship-designers; but towards the end of the 19th century voices began to be raised in opposition to the conservative majority, particularly in Britain, the United States and Italy. Some of these voices belonged to professional naval officers, such as the renowned gunnery expert of the Royal Navy, Captain Percy Scott, who brought his talents to bear to improve the accuracy and speed of naval gunnery, and his counterpart in the United States Navy, Lieutenant-Commander W. S. Sims. Others were ship-designers such as Colonel Cuniberti, Constructor to the Italian Navy, who can claim to have first publicly put forward the idea of the all-big-gun ship and to have designed one embodying that principle.

The work of the gunnery experts necessarily antedated the conception of the all-big-gun ship; for unless the big gun could deliver its projectiles accurately and quickly enough to obtain hits at ranges outside that of the next size of gun, it could be argued that a great many medium-sized guns could do as well as a few large ones.

Captain Scott was the first to shake the Royal Navy out of the complacency which accepted a shamefully low standard of gunnery efficiency and accuracy. In 1899, as captain of the light cruiser *Scylla,* he set his inventive talents to work to produce a "loader" with which his guns' crews could practise rapid loading of the 4·7-inch guns and thereby increase their rate of fire with the guns themselves. To give the gun-layers and trainers more practice than could be obtained with the limited amount of ammunition allowed for the purpose, he devised a system of "sub-calibre" firing in which 3-pounder guns were shipped inside the 4·7-inch. Firing with these at small targets exercised the layers and trainers under conditions which were similar to those of full-calibre firing, except for the size of shot used.

The results of these and other training innovations were seen when the *Scylla* achieved a phenomenal success in the annual competitive firing practices. Moving on to the armoured cruiser *Terrible*, Scott was equally successful with 6-inch and 9·2-inch guns.

At this time a remarkable personality, Admiral Sir John Fisher, was rising to the leadership of the Royal Navy. Already widely known as "Jacky" Fisher, feared and even hated by many of the old school of naval officers for his iconoclastic views and ruthless intolerance of complacency, he was Commander-in-Chief in the Mediterranean. Scott's achievements were, of course, well known to Fisher, and he himself had been demonstrating that by the use of salvo firing the fighting range of battleships could be raised from 3,000 to 6,000 yards. The idea of an all-big-gun ship had thus been born in his fertile mind. It is possible that it had been encouraged by the writings of W. S. Sims of the United States Navy, who also had been advocating such a design.

However that may be, during his tenure of command in the Mediterranean, Fisher set the Chief Constructor of Malta Dockyard, Mr. W. H. Gard, to work on designs for two such ships, a battleship which he called the *Untakeable* and an armoured cruiser, *Unapproachable*. When Fisher moved on to become Commander-in-Chief, Portsmouth, Gard soon followed him there as Manager of the Constructive Department, and plans for the new ships went ahead.

The arguments behind the idea of the one-calibre gun armament were unanswerable, and the need for it was to be demonstrated in the battles of the Russo-Japanese War. Up to this time the usual armament of a battleship consisted of two twin 12-inch turrets and as many 8-inch or 9·2-inch as could be accommodated. The slow-firing 12-inch were not expected to achieve many hits at more than 3,000 or 4,000 yards, but were there to deliver the heavy blows which could penetrate an opponent's armour plate. The smaller guns would come into action at the same time, and, being much quicker-firing, would deliver their smothering fire to smash the upperworks and gun batteries and kill the exposed crews.

But by now improved mountings were enabling the biggest guns to be fired at a greatly increased rate, and it had been shown that by firing a number of guns of the same calibre simultaneously, in salvoes, the shells falling more or less together, the splashes would be seen to be all over, all short or some over and some short. The last of these, a straddle, showed that the correct range had been applied, and a percentage of such shots would be hits.

To produce these conditions, however, at least four guns had to be fired at each salvo, and the rate of fire had to be fast enough for the range to be not greatly altered between salvoes by an alteration of course of the target. To achieve the necessary rate of fire, as well as for other reasons, the guns of a turret were fired alternately, so at least eight big-guns had to be mounted in twin turrets.

Faced by a battleship of the old model, the all-big-gun ship would be at an overwhelming advantage. She could stand off to fight at long range, at which the 8-inch or 9·2-inch guns of her antagonist could not come into action and at which the two-gun salvoes of the 12-inch would be most unlikely to score a hit.

While the idea of these new types of ships were germinating in Fisher's mind, the Italian, Cuniberti, was advocating it in his writings, and was producing designs for such ships for the Italian Navy. Thus it is clear that the idea of an all-big-gun ship was reached separately and simultaneously in several countries. But there was more in Fisher's mind than a rearrangement of the gun armament.

In order to catch an unwilling enemy and then to choose the range at which she would fight, superior speed was necessary. Speed, then, higher than anything so far attained by a battleship, must be sought, and furthermore a capability of *sustained* high speed. Already reciprocating engines were reaching the limit of power and speed possible in the space available in a warship.

Unlike the engines of a passenger liner, which, unlimited in height, could have a very long piston stroke and could so develop considerable power at moderate revolutions, a battleship's engines, cramped underneath the armoured deck had to whirl at a tremendous pace. The wear and tear at high speed was therefore much greater.

The scene in the engine-room of a pre-dreadnought battleship at speed was like an inferno. As the great piston-rods leapt wildly up and down and the connecting-rods whirled the massive cranks round, hot oil and water spurted everywhere. Sea-water from hoses playing on hot bearings sloshed in the bilges. In an atmosphere murky with steam from dozens of small steam leaks, the engineer officers would stand on the greasy deck plates, oilskins buttoned to the neck, their faces black and their clothes soaked in oil and water. Over all would be a noise so deafening that telephones could not be used. Breakdowns from overheated bearings or broken steam joints were common, and were always expected. After any prolonged period of high-speed running there would be work for the dockyard engineers.

Thus at the battle of 10th August 1904, Togo was reluctant to order a battle speed of 15 knots, though the slowest ship in the Japanese battle squadron had a top speed of 18. But coming now to the aid of the ship-designers was the steam turbine, in which all the moving parts were rotating. Instead of the shock and strain involved in reversing the direction of motion of huge pistons, piston-rods and connecting-rods with every revolution of the shaft, power flowed smoothly from the high-pressure steam on to the blades of the turbine rotor.

Fisher had the vision to realise that both the all-big-gun principle and the change-over to the turbine engine were essential features of the battleship of the future. The steam turbine was an invention of quite recent date, the first patent for a reactor turbine having been taken out by the Hon. Charles Parsons in 1884. He was followed in 1889 by de Laval, who invented an impulse type turbine. The early turbines, however, were designed to drive electric generators, which required speeds so high that reciprocating engines could not easily cope with them. It was not until 1891 that Parsons, the first in this field also, decided to adapt his invention to ship propulsion. In 1894 he patented his design and founded the Marine Steam Turbine Co. to develop it.

His company built a small ship called the *Turbina*, and at Queen Victoria's Naval Review of 1897 this ship made a great impression as she steamed up and down the assembled lines of warships. A year later the first turbine warship, the torpedo-boat *Viper*, appeared in the list of ships of the Royal Navy. Parsons' second company, the Parsons Marine Steam Turbine Co., went ahead with great strides. Besides a number of passenger ships powered by his engines, the Royal Navy had the light cruiser *Amethyst* by 1902 and the German Navy the cruiser *Lübeck*.

The change-over to turbine drive was now greatly accelerated as a result of the work of two committees. The first was known as the Merchant Cruisers Committee, which met in 1902 to consider what should be done to regain for Britain the supremacy of the transatlantic passenger service. The results were seen in the famous liners *Lusitania* and *Mauretania*, the first large ships to be powered by steam turbines. Their success was such that when in 1904 Fisher, by then First Sea Lord, appointed a Committee on Designs to decide on the details of future battleships, they had no difficulty in agreeing that the machinery should be Parsons Steam Turbines.

Naval officers have recorded their amazement on first entering the engine-room of a turbine-driven battleship under way. Gone were the black-faced, oilskin-clad engineers, gazing anxiously at doubtful bearings, the swirling steam, the spurting oil and water and the shattering noise. Instead they found the gleaming, white-enamelled turbine casings from whose bellies came nothing but a steady hum, white-overalled engineers moving placidly in an atmosphere of thoughtful calm.

But that is running somewhat ahead of our story. While still Commander-in-Chief, Portsmouth, Fisher had decided upon the broad characteristics of his new ship, but there remained some formidable obstacles to the acceptance of his ideas. First, he knew that the new type of ship was going to be so far superior to anything at that time afloat that every existing ship would be at once obsolete. This could be of perilous importance to Great Britain, who relied for her security against a jealous world upon her huge fleet of battleships, equal in strength to those of any two other major naval powers.

Such a development would have a startling effect on public opinion in Britain and would meet fierce opposition from uninformed sections of the population as well as from the old school of naval officers. Yet the new type of ship had to come. Cuniberti's writings and those of Sims were not going unheeded. If Britain did not take the great step, another nation would. Two things were essential to preserve the British naval preponderance of power; secrecy in planning and speed in execution. Telling no one but his most trusted friends, Fisher bided his time.

In October 1904 he became First Sea Lord. His opportunity had come, but even now he knew that he could not trample down criticism and opposition by force of his own personality alone. He therefore gathered together a Committee on Design in which the leading naval constructors, gun-designers, gunnery experts and scientists were to meet. Before them would be put the several varying designs which had been worked out. Ostensibly, at least, the Committee would decide upon the size of gun to be mounted, the thickness of armour, the speed, and the watertight system of sub-division.

Most of the Committee members, however, were chosen for their known agreement with Fisher's ideas. The naval members were inevitably men already earmarked by him for high rank. Besides Prince Louis of Battenberg, the greatest of a brilliant family, and currently Director of Naval Intelligence, there were Captains Henry B. Jackson, Charles Madden and John Jellicoe, all holding key positions in the Admiralty, and each one day to become First Sea Lord. There was Captain Reginald Bacon, whose career was later to be adversely affected by an alleged over-devotion to Fisher at the expense of loyalty to his immediate superiors. Civilian members included Sir Philip Watts, the

Director of Naval Construction, and of course the faithful Mr. Gard.

It is therefore not surprising that the result of the deliberations of this Committee was a design for a ship embodying Fisher's ideas—ten 12-inch guns, the next size being 12-pounders for anti-torpedo craft fire only, together with Parsons steam turbines developing 23,000 H.P., which in combination with an increase of length of some 100 feet over existing ships would give a speed of 21 knots.

The design agreed upon, no time was lost. On 2nd October 1905 the *Dreadnought* was officially laid down on the stocks in Portsmouth Dockyard, to be built under the supervision of Thomas Mitchell, Chief Constructor of the Yard. A year and a day later she sailed for her trials, and a new phase in naval history, the dreadnought era, had been born.

Two years later an even more revolutionary type of capital ship was laid down. The effect upon world opinion was much less marked, perhaps because she had been officially designated only as an "armoured cruiser". The *Inflexible*, as she was named, embodied a basic belief of Fisher and his school in the fundamental importance of speed and hitting power in defence as well as offence at the expense, if necessary, of armour. With an armour belt of only 7 inches thickness as opposed to the 11 inches of the *Dreadnought*, and an increase of horsepower to 41,000, the *Inflexible* on trials attained a speed of nearly 27 knots. Her main armament of eight 12-inch guns in four twin turrets obviously took her out of the cruiser class, and she became the first of a long line of "battle-cruisers".

The secrecy surrounding the details of the *Dreadnought*'s design, the speed with which she was rushed to completion and the keen attention focused on her by every maritime nation have been at times shrugged off as all part of Fisher's love of theatrical display and even personal glorification. But the results speak for themselves. The suddenness of the *Dreadnought*'s début left foreign competitors far behind in the race, forcing them to suspend all battleship construction while fresh designs were prepared.

Meanwhile the results of the *Dreadnought*'s trials, immensely successful as they proved to be, were already providing material to British designers for improvements in the future.

Instead of the revolutionary step forcing Britain to start level with her rivals in her effort to keep up the Two-Power standard, she set off with a two-year lead. Nowhere was this more bitterly realised than across the North Sea, where the young German Empire had embarked on a course of naval expansion which would in time add a first-class navy to her already supreme army. At one stroke not only were Germany's ships made obsolete, but even if she replaced them by dreadnoughts her fleet would be cut in two, unable to pass through the Kiel Canal between the North Sea and the Baltic.

Until deepening and widening operations were carried out, Germany's power to make war was neutralised. Anxiety was temporarily allayed in Britain, where the German naval expansion had been viewed with increasing alarm.

Under her ambitious, unbalanced, all-powerful Emperor, the process had been begun in 1897 when a brilliant but politically short-sighted naval officer, von Tirpitz, had been appointed Secretary of State for Naval Affairs. With the aid of an elaborate Press Bureau, Germany was flooded with propaganda by the Navy League, telling the vigorous, thrusting young nation that without a strong Navy Germany would never gain the "place in the sun" to which as the conqueror of France and Austria she was entitled.

During the following year the Reichstag passed the first of a series of Navy Acts authorising the construction of a fleet, the backbone of which would be a squadron of nineteen battleships, to be completed by 1903. Long before that date, in 1900, this Act was replaced by another providing for a battle fleet of two fleet flagships, four squadrons of eight battleships each and appropriate numbers of cruisers and torpedo craft.

The explanatory memorandum which accompanied this second Act, might have been composed with the sole object of setting the alarm-bells quivering in every British home:

> To protect Germany's sea trade and colonies in the existing circumstances, there is only one means; Germany must have a battle fleet so strong that, even for the adversary with the greatest sea-power, a war against it would involve such dangers as to imperil his position in the world.
>
> For this purpose, it is not absolutely necessary that the German battle fleet should be as strong as that of the greatest naval power, because a great naval power will not, as a rule, be in a position to concentrate all its striking forces against us. But even if it should succeed in meeting us with considerable superiority of strength, the defeat of a strong German fleet would so substantially weaken the enemy that, in spite of a victory he might have obtained, his own position in the world would no longer be secured by an adequate fleet.

Such a statement could only at that date be directed at Britain, with her vast, sprawling Empire spread over the surface of the globe, the security of which was utterly dependent on her supremacy at sea. The threat was implicit in the sentence "a great naval power will not, as a rule, be in a position to concentrate all its striking forces against us". To stress this truism was to bring home to the least politically minded Englishman that under no circumstances could naval parity with Germany be accepted.

At the same time it led to a reappraisal of Britain's policy of "splendid isolation". Allies were needed to enable her to concentrate her naval forces in the danger area, the North Sea. The first step to be taken in this direction was the conclusion of the alliance with Japan in 1902. In the years which followed, the sabre-rattling of the Kaiser and the naïve naval ambitions of von Tirpitz were to end a centuries-old blood feud, forming an alliance between England and France and leading to a settlement of long-standing differences with Russia.

Thus it was upon a world in which the battleship strength of the major naval powers was a political question of the utmost importance that the *Dreadnought* burst with such impact. At the same time, under Fisher's administration of the Royal Navy, the alliance with Japan and the *entente* with France allowed Britain's naval forces to be withdrawn from the Far East and the Mediterranean, and concentrated in home waters. Englishmen could sleep quietly in their beds, as Fisher was fond of assuring them at that time.

After a pause to study the *Dreadnought*'s design and to discover how successful her various features were, all other major naval powers followed Britain's lead. The United States had indeed accepted the all-big-gun principle even before the *Dreadnought* was laid down, when, early in 1905, Congress authorised the construction of the *South Carolina* and the *Michigan* with an armament of eight 12-inch guns and a secondary armament of 14-pounders. These ships as originally designed had one revolutionary feature of the *Dreadnought*—the all-big-gun armament. They were also the first ships to be designed with superimposed turrets, thus allowing all their guns to bear on either beam. Their speed, however, was only 18½ knots, and in their engine-rooms reciprocating engines were still to pound, shake and deafen. Their completion was held up until 1909.

The German Navy realised at once that dreadnoughts had superseded all earlier types. All battleship construction was held up while new designs were brought out. In March 1908 the first German dreadnought, *Nassau*, was launched. Alone amongst the Western powers, Germany also adopted the idea of the battle-cruiser, her first, the *Von der Tann*, being launched in May 1908. At the same time the Germans not only constructed dry docks large enough to accommodate the biggest dreadnoughts likely to be built, but they also set to work with feverish energy to enlarge the Kiel Canal and its locks, work which would take many years and enormous cost to complete.

These were the factors affecting the balance of naval power in the first years of the dreadnought era. The alliance with Japan, the *entente* with France, the eclipse of Russia as a naval power, the unconcern of the United States of America with European affairs, all combined to bolster Great Britain's naval supremacy—a supremacy defensive in nature having in mind her wide-spread possessions and her minute military strength. Only the restless ambitions of Germany provided a disquieting factor.

In spite of pronouncements by British politicians and naval authorities, and a steady support for them by British public opinion, making it clear that at any cost the Royal Navy's preponderance of battleship strength would be maintained, Germany continued to build warships far in excess of anything she could need unless she intended directly to challenge England's sea power. The Navy Law of 1900 was amended in 1906 and again in 1908, until it was calculated that by 1920 a German Navy would exist far stronger than anything which Great Britain had so far possessed.

For a time Britain held aloof from an armaments race. In 1905 she had built four battleships to Germany's two. The next year each built three. In 1907 Britain further reduced her programme to two, while Germany increased hers to four. In one of his speeches, the Kaiser styled himself Admiral of the Atlantic.

British fears were at last fully roused. In 1909 the First Lord of the Admiralty, Mr. McKenna, informed the Cabinet that his naval estimates would contain an item for the construction of six new battleships. His naval advisers from their study of the German programme had calculated that this was the minimum which would ensure Britain's security. The Chancellor of the Exchequer, Lloyd George, backed by Winston Churchill, who was then Home Secretary, opposed such a heavy expenditure and demanded that the number should be cut to four. McKenna, however, would not give way, and meanwhile public opinion had been thoroughly aroused in favour of the Sea Lords, whose original demand for eight had leaked out. An agitation followed, which put the slogan "We want eight and we won't wait" on everyone's tongue at public meetings all over the country. So powerful was it that far from cutting McKenna's figure of six, the Cabinet eventually increased it to eight.

In Volume I of his *The World Crisis*, Winston Churchill has a graceful admission of his error of judgement on that occasion. The Admiralty had estimated that by 1912 Germany would be ready to throw down the gauntlet. This proved to be two years wrong, and he therefore commented:

> Although the Chancellor of the Exchequer and I were right in the narrow sense, we were absolutely wrong in relation to the deep tides of destiny. The greatest credit is due to the First Lord, Mr. McKenna, for the resolute and courageous manner in which he fought his case and withstood his Party on this occasion.
>
> Little did I think, as this dispute proceeded, that when the next Cabinet crisis about the Navy arose, our rôles would be reversed; and little did he think that the ships for which he contended so stoutly would eventually, when they arrived, be welcomed with open arms by me.

From this time onwards both political parties were generally in agreement with the necessity for keeping ahead of Germany's naval expansion. "Two keels to one" became the popular cry in Britain, so that in August 1914, when war at last came, the Royal Navy found itself with twenty dreadnought-battleships to Germany's fourteen, and nine battle-cruisers against four. Even so, only by concentrating them all in Home Waters could a numerical superiority be assured over the German fleet, which could choose its own moment to come out at full strength.

* * *

Before that culminating period in the battleship era opens, we must follow the development of the ships themselves from the time when the *Dreadnought* made its dramatic entry on the scene. The basic features of the battleship in its ultimate shape were present in the *Dreadnought*, but many refinements were yet to come. The first to emerge were in the field of gunnery control.

The Royal Navy led the way in this, thanks largely to the work of Sir Percy Scott, whose early efforts have been already mentioned. When Fisher went to the Admiralty in October 1904, he gathered together a team composed of the more forward-thinking gunnery specialists, of whom Captain John Jellicoe, the Director of Naval Ordnance, was his most favoured protégé. They found ample scope for their talents.

In 1904, as a result of the shocking standard of shooting, a scandal had arisen with regard to the quality of gun-sights provided. Even when these were improved, Scott, who had been given an appointment as Inspector of Target Practice and had insisted on towed targets in place of the moored targets which had been considered adequate previously, rated the results in the fleet as "deplorable". This was not surprising when it is appreciated that the only gunnery control instruments at that date were three-foot range-finders and the simple telescopic sights at the guns themselves. Control was by means of voice-pipes from the bridge.

With the advent of the *Dreadnought* and the longer battle range which was the purpose of such ships, something more elaborate was necessary. Bigger range-finders, sometimes incorporated in the structure of the turrets, were fitted. Electrical transmission of information to the gun-sights from a central transmitting station was devised. Spotting tops, high up the masts, were constructed. Above all, salvo firing and a bracket system of finding and adjusting the range were adopted.

In all these developments other navies followed the Royal Navy's lead. The Germans, with their superlative optical industry to call upon, were soon better equipped with regard to gun-sights, range-finders and telescopes. Already their standard of shooting was higher than that of the Royal Navy. Scott, however, was busy with an invention which would make possible a great stride forward in the field of gunnery control.

He saw that so long as each turret was aimed and fired independently, the small human errors of the various layers and trainers must accumulate to make ragged shooting and large spreads both for line and for range in the fall of shot of each salvo. Furthermore, sited comparatively low down in the ship, the layers' and trainers' telescopes would often be obscured by smoke or spray. He therefore devised a gun-director, in essence a central independent telescopic sight to be mounted in a fighting top. In keeping their telescopes on the target, the director layer and trainer would automatically pass the necessary elevation and training to the sights in the turrets, by means of electrically operated pointers on a dial. A second pointer on the dials would move with the guns. When the two pointers were synchronised by the gun-layers and trainers, the guns would have the same elevation and training as the director, subject to small adjustments for the difference in height of the two positions and the distance apart of the turrets themselves.

When all the turrets were so aimed, the director layer could fire them all simultaneously. Thus theoretically all shells from a salvo should arrive together and in the same spot. In spite of these obvious advantages of Scott's invention, it failed to get Admiralty approval at first. It was pigeon-holed until 1911, when Jellicoe, by then a Rear-Admiral, commanding a squadron of the Home Fleet, insisted on its being fitted in the battleship *Thunderer*. In a competitive trial against her sister-ship *Orion*, the *Thunderer* made six times as many hits as the *Orion* on a target making 12 knots at a range of 9,000 yards. From that time onward the gun-director became standard equipment, at first for battleships and later for all classes of warships.

But it was not for some years that the work of fitting it, even in the battleships, was completed, so that even in 1916 at the Battle of Jutland not all British ships had been so equipped. The Germans, on the other hand, lagged far behind in this development, and at Jutland all their guns were still laid and fired from the turrets.

Other major developments in the design of capital ships which followed the first dreadnoughts were the introduction of reduction gearing, whereby the high speed normal in turbines could be made to drive the propeller shafts at speeds most efficient for the propellers; the increase in the size of the secondary, anti-torpedo armament to 4-inch guns and eventually to 6-inch; the introduction of 13·5-inch guns for the main armament; and the sighting of all turrets on the centre-line, with turrets superimposed one above the other.

In this last feature, the United States Navy was the pioneer from the start. Rejecting the line of thought of the school which favoured a high proportion of the armament being sited so as to be able to fire ahead, the Americans adopted the centre-line mounting and the superimposed turret for their first dreadnought, the *South Carolina*. They saw sooner than others that sea-fights inevitably developed into broadside battles and that in any case only when the target was almost directly ahead, a situation unlikely to persist for any length of time, could all three forward facing turrets of the *Dreadnought* and *Invincible* be brought to bear.

The Royal Navy followed their example with the "super-dreadnoughts" of the 1909 programme, which besides having 13·5-inch guns had eight of them mounted in four superimposed turrets on the centre-line with a fifth turret on the centre-line amidships.

In 1911 a new problem arose—one of the utmost importance to Great Britain, a decision on which must affect her national safety in the highest degree. For a long time the advantages of oil fuel over coal for the firing of ships' boilers had been appreciated. Particularly in the fast battle-cruisers, the rate of consumption of coal at high speed was at the phenomenal rate of nearly 1,000 tons a day. To keep the voracious boilers fed, huge gangs of stokers were kept continuously shovelling coal into their glowing furnaces. On return to harbour every man-jack aboard had to turn-to to replenish the coal-bunkers using shovels and sacks. Not until the Herculean task had been completed could the ship be said to be ready for action.

The vast fleets of that day necessitated the accumulation of enormous stocks of steam coal at bases around the coasts of the British Isles, as well as on foreign stations. The organisation necessary to have such supplies constantly and instantly available was intricate and delicate. When a war scare flared up in 1911, it was discovered that the Home Fleet could not sail at full strength, many ships being a thousand tons short of coal with no prospect of quickly remedying the situation.

A further disadvantage of coal was the black, billowing cloud of smoke which necessarily poured from the funnels of ships at high speed. Strategically it meant that a fleet betrayed itself to an enemy at great ranges owing to the cloud of smoke in which it always moved. Tactically, the smoke covered the battle area, blinding gunlayers and gun-controllers alike, so that a battle was bound to be fought in a murky obscurity from the time when the two sides came together.

Coal did have one advantage over oil fuel, however. Stored in bunkers around the hull, it served as additional protection against shell hits which penetrated the side armour. Oil tanks gave no such protection, and the oil itself could constitute a fire hazard in battle. Nevertheless, everything else being equal, it could not be doubted that oil fuel should be substituted for coal.

But here came the difficulty. Storage accommodation for the new fuel would be required all over the world, an immensely costly undertaking, estimated at ten million pounds immediately. Then there would be the problem of a regular supply to England from abroad, involving a vast new shipping industry the nucleus of which barely existed. A decision to change over to oil fuel once taken, any uncertainty of supply could be fatal to Britain's security.

At this time Winston Churchill was First Lord of the Admiralty. The responsibility for such a decision would be his, a responsibility which even a man of his stature could not bear alone. Churchill convened a Royal Commission on Oil Supply, calling upon Fisher, who had passed into retirement the previous year, to preside over it. The result was seen in the naval building programme of 1912, the first in which every ship was to be oil-fired.

So far as capital ships were concerned this was not to bear full fruit until the advent of the famous *Queen Elizabeth* class of fast battleships, so that in the 1914–18 War the majority of ships which fought on either side were still coal-fired. A further innovation with this class of ship was the 15-inch gun, the introduction of which was a considerable gamble on the part of the Admiralty. Up to this time no new gun or mounting, certainly no such huge weapon, with its intricate massive turret and loading machinery, had ever been installed without extensive and prolonged trials.

But already the portents of the coming storm were in the sky.

Germany's naval building programme was reaching maturity. The Kaiser was becoming steadily more wild in his pronouncements on international affairs. Already in 1911 he had very nearly precipitated a war with France, which had only been staved off by a speech by Lloyd George at the Mansion House in which he made it clear that Britain would come down on the side of France in the event of a challenge.

Now that the deepening and widening of the Kiel Canal was nearing completion, the last brake on Germany's career towards world war was about to be released. The *Queen Elizabeth*s must be there when *Der Tag*, to which German toasts were drunk, should dawn. The 15-inch turrets were therefore mounted untried. The gamble succeeded, and they proved an unqualified success.

Thus preparations went ahead for the greatest fight of the battleship era. The preliminary bouts had been disposed of at Lissa, Santiago, the Yellow Sea and Tsushima. The latest products of the naval constructor's art in the industrial age of steel were now to be tested in combat.

10

Battleship Heyday

THE international atmosphere of the years immediately preceding the Great War of 1914–18 was a strange mixture of grim foreboding and light-hearted fraternisation for the two greatest naval powers of the age—Great Britain and Germany.

Fortunately for England, her naval destinies were guided by people such as Winston Churchill as First Lord of the Admiralty; "Jacky" Fisher, although in retirement, giving his friend wise nautical advice; Prince Louis of Battenberg as First Sea Lord, a Prussian by blood and so imbued with an understanding of the German danger; and Vice-Admiral John Jellicoe, Commander-in-Chief elect of the Grand Fleet in the event of war, with an intimate knowledge of the character and ambitions of his counterparts in the Imperial German Navy and of the bellicose spirit of that service. They saw the war cloud forming when it was "no larger than a man's hand".

But for the average naval officer it was not easy to see beyond the veil of friendly professional rivalry, the easy comradeship of the sea and the natural affinity of two Nordic races which prevailed when the two navies met. Behind it lay a fierce jealousy of Britain's ancient naval supremacy and traditions.

The childish delight of the Kaiser in the ships of his High Seas Fleet with which he soothed his envy of his cousin, King George V, who was not only titular head of the British Navy but had actually served as one of its officers, was watched with tolerant good humour; but the autocratic power he wielded together with his irresponsible nature, constituted a grave threat. The naïve political outlook of von Tirpitz, who believed that Germany's increasing naval strength was actually a factor in improving relations with

Britain, kept the armaments race going. A clash was only a matter of time.

In June 1914, the tremendous task of modernising the Kiel Canal had been completed. The ceremonial opening by the Kaiser, who was to steam through it from the Elbe to the Baltic in his yacht, *Hohenzollern*, was to be the opening feature of an international Kiel Week. The Kaiser would then review his fleet and the foreign warships which had been invited to participate.

The British contingent at the review was a squadron of four super-dreadnoughts of the *King George V* class, the very embodiment of naval power with their ten 13·5-inch guns, and three light cruisers, the whole under the command of Rear-Admiral Sir George Warrender. The friendly rivalry of yacht racing and regattas, the exchange of banquets, the pageantry of balls and all the ceremonial inseparable from international naval occasions, took place in an air of happy camaraderie. The gay bunting of the ships, dressed overall day after day, the cottonwool puffs of white smoke of the innumerable gun salutes, the perfect summer weather, all combined to disguise the deadly rivalry which existed between the countries which the warships represented.

Even when festivities were brought to a sudden halt by the news of the assassination of the Archduke Franz Ferdinand, heir to the Imperial Austrian throne, at Sarajevo in Serbia, it was inconceivable that it could possibly be the first step towards war. When the review dispersed on the 30th June, and Warrender led his ships seaward, he expressed the hope of every man in them when he signalled to his late hosts: "Friends in the past; friends for ever."

Unfortunately, events were taking place which were in the near future to change the gaily decorated, spick and span warships into grim craft, seeking each other's destruction in the cold, misty wastes of the North Sea. As the Serbian mountaineers prepared to defend their country, humble men from all over the sprawling dominions of the Austrian Empire were pulling out their unfamiliar uniforms and preparing to answer the call to mobilise. The German military machine was beginning to turn with smooth, deadly efficiency. From remote villages all over the vast spread of Russia, peasants in their millions were answering the call to arms. From there the chain reaction spread to France, bound to Russia by treaty.

All Europe was in seething ferment; but to the great majority of the British people, accustomed to the long years of peace and prosperity, war was still unthinkable. They could not be affected by a remote Balkan squabble. Only in Whitehall was there genuine apprehension. There, the omens had been correctly read for some time past. Long before the assassination of Franz Ferdinand had provided a pretext to the Central Powers, the summer of 1914, as soon as the harvests were gathered on the plains of Europe, had been judged a danger period.

A test mobilisation to try out the organisation for bringing forward the ships in reserve, with full complements, had therefore been ordered for July. These consisted of two classes, the Third Fleet of ships manned normally by small care and maintenance parties, their machinery and weapons in a state of preservation, and the Second Fleet, the ships of which had half their complements aboard, sufficient to keep the machinery and armaments in good condition, to take them to sea for limited periods and to man and practise with a part of the armament at a time.

Then on 15th July these reserve fleets were to join the First Fleet of modern, fully manned ships in a Royal review in Spithead. Following the review, all ships would go to sea for a period of tactical exercises and gunnery practice, after which the Second and Third Fleets would once again revert to their reserve status.

So there, on that historic stretch of water, the greatest fleet that the steam or any other age had seen gathered together lay in review order—57 battleships and battle-cruisers besides a host of smaller ships. It was with no desire to offer a threat to anyone that the great assembly had come together. Indeed, Britain, with her bare nucleus of a professional army, numbering 100,000 men, could hardly be looked on as a menace by any of the continental powers with their troops numbered in millions.

There can have been few great powers in history less bellicose than England in 1914. Bound to no continental power in any formal alliance, led by a Liberal Government dedicated to the cause of peace, a large section of the population would not support intervention in the war looming in Europe. Only the student of the harsh facts of history knew that in the long run Britain would be forced to intervene to prevent any one power gaining the hegemony of the Continent. Fortunately there was such a man in Whitehall, where Winston Churchill ruled the Royal Navy as First Lord. Already Churchill was taking his precautions.

As the exercises following the Spithead Review came to an end on 27th July, orders went out to Sir George Callaghan, commanding the First Fleet, to keep all his ships and flotillas concentrated at Portland until further orders, instead of releasing them for the independent cruises which had been on their programme. Two days later the ships sailed, squadron after squadron, and vanished over the horizon. Far to the north, in the Orkney Islands, lay their chosen war base of Scapa Flow, and there the Fleet assembled in secret to await whatever might come.

On the Continent vast armies were on the move. On 26th July, Austria, encouraged by the German Emperor, rejected Serbia's placatory reply to her ultimatum and two days later declared war on her. Russia sprang to the aid of Serbia, whereupon on 1st August Germany declared war on Russia and two days later on France.

Britain might have held aloof from a continental quarrel in which she had no direct interest had not Germany assaulted her national honour by striking at France through Belgium. The neutrality of Belgium was guaranteed by international treaty to which both England and Germany were signatories. Such a blatant disregard of treaty obligations, and an unprovoked attack on a small and defenceless nation, provided a cause which united every shade of British opinion in favour of war. On the rejection of a British ultimatum calling on Germany to withdraw her troops from Belgium, England was at war as from 11 p.m. on 4th August.

Thus began a struggle more destructive than any the world had ever seen. At sea, the greatest fleets ever assembled were arrayed against each other, and at sea, for all the appalling shambles of the land fighting, the war was ultimately to be lost and won. For the last time in history, sea power, still unaffected by the influence of the aeroplane, was to be able to decide the issue through the inexorable pressure of blockade. The temporary loss of sea control, through the operations of the submarine, was to come within an ace of reversing the decision.

From the moment the war opened, sea power began to exert its world-wide influence. For all Germany's High Seas Fleet, commanded by its self-styled "Admiral of the Atlantic", German merchant shipping was immediately swept from the oceans of the world. In the Far East, Britain's ally Japan ruled the Pacific; in the Mediterranean the French fleet sailed unchallenged. In the North Sea, Britain's Grand Fleet was already at sea on the first of the innumerable "sweeps" by which it barred the egress of the High Seas Fleet from its home waters where it lay month after month, year by year, waiting for an opportunity to catch an inferior portion of the British fleet which would give it a chance to fight on equal terms.

Until the High Seas Fleet could do this it was condemned to the passive rôle of a "fleet in being". Though it thus posed a constant threat, tying up greatly superior forces out of which sufficient numbers must always be available to meet it, it was in insufficient strength to offer pitched battle. Thanks to the foresight of successive First Sea Lords from Fisher's time onwards, and the political skill of the First Lords who worked with them to gain national support for an immensely costly programme of battleship construction, the First World War found Britain with a great preponderance of naval power. In spite of her world-wide commitments, she was able to muster in home waters the Grand Fleet which included twenty dreadnought battleships, four battle-cruisers and eight pre-dreadnoughts as against the High Seas Fleet strength of fourteen dreadnoughts, four battle-cruisers and eight pre-dreadnoughts. In addition the Royal Navy had nineteen pre-dreadnought battleships which were formed into a Channel Fleet, while three more battle-cruisers were in the Mediterranean.

Great as this superiority may seem, two things have always to be remembered, both now and throughout the course of the war. First, it was the strength in dreadnought battleships and the battle-cruisers which mattered, for pre-dreadnoughts could not fairly be expected to face them in action. Secondly, while the High Seas Fleet was free to choose its own moment to emerge at full strength, all ships fresh from docking and maintenance, the Grand Fleet was always at reduced strength through necessary absences for refit or docking apart from the hazards of weather damage or collision inseparable from the ceaseless sea-keeping of a large and ponderous fleet. Thus in December 1914, Admiral Sir John Jellicoe, commanding the Grand Fleet, found himself with only seventeen dreadnoughts, while the High Seas Fleet could muster sixteen.

However, the outbreak of war found the Grand Fleet at sea and the control of home waters securely in British hands. Elsewhere German warships and squadrons on foreign stations were at large, and it was to take time and trouble to round them up. The commerce raiding activities of the various individual German ships and the operations to hunt them down are no part of the battleship story. But one German squadron, that in the Pacific under Vice-Admiral Graf von Spee, was to take part in the first action of dreadnought battle-cruisers.

The hard core of the German Pacific Squadron was composed of two modern armoured cruisers *Scharnhorst* and *Gneisenau*, von Spee's flag being in the former. Vanishing into the wide spaces of the Pacific at the outbreak of war and evading all search by British, Australian and Japanese squadrons, von Spee arrived on 12th October at Easter Island with the two armoured cruisers and the light cruiser *Nürnberg*. There he was joined by the light cruisers *Leipzig* and *Dresden*.

Moving on eastwards with his five ships, von Spee reached the Chilean coast on 31st October, and at the Battle of Coronel met and defeated a squadron composed of the two old armoured

H.M.S. *Warrior*, first warship to be built of iron.

German armoured ships *König Wilhelm* and *Grosser Kurfürst* in collision in the English Channel.

H.M.S. *Captain:* first, ill-fated, British ship to mount turrets.

EARLY STEAM IRON-CLADS

The illustrations in this book are reproduced by courtesy of the Imperial War Museum.

Spanish cruiser *Vizcaya.*

Spanish cruiser *Infanta Maria Teresa:* flagship of Admiral Cervera.

U.S.S. *Brooklyn:* flagship of Commodore Schley.

TYPE OF SHIPS ENGAGED IN THE BATTLE OF SANTIAGO, 1898

Spithead 1897.

rench cruiser *Formidable*,
898.

German cruiser
Deutschland, 1890.

H.M.S. *Terrible*.

Italian battleship *Andrea Doria*, 1895.

H.M.S. *Camperdown*.

EARLY TURRETED BATTLESHIPS

Russian battleship *Petropavlovsk:* flagship of Admiral Makaroff at Port Arthur.

apanese battleship *Iikasa:* flagship of Admiral Togo at Tsushima.

Japanese cruiser *Chitose:* flagship of Rear-Admiral Dewa.

PRE-DREADNOUGHTS: THE RUSSO-JAPANESE WAR

German battleship *Kaiser*.

U.S.S. *Michigan*.

H.M.S. *Dreadnought*.

DREADNOUGHT BATTLESHIPS

German armoured cruiser *Scharnhorst*: flagship of Admiral Graf von Spee at the Battle of the Falkland Islands.

German battle-cruiser *Moltke*.

A portion of the Grand Fleet at sea.

H.M.S. *Invincible* blows up.

The wreck of the *Invincible*.

German battle-cruiser *Seydlitz*, heavily damaged.

THE BATTLE OF JUTLAND

Italian battleship *Vittorio Veneto*, with (*in background*) cruiser *Duca d'Aosta*.

German battleship *Bismarck* at sea after action with *Hood* and *Prince of Wales*.

Battle-cruiser H.M.S. *Hood.*

BATTLESHIPS OF THE SECOND WORLD WAR

Japanese battleship *Kirishima*.

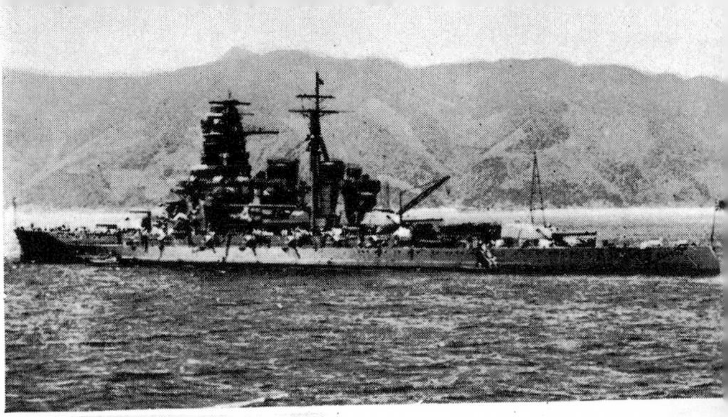

Japanese battleship-aircraft-carrier *Ise*.

U.S.S. *Washington* (*foreground*) with H.M.S. *Duke of York*.

Japanese aircraft-carrier *Shokaku.*

Japanese aircraft-carrier *Ryukaku* hit by torpedoes from American naval aircraft.

U.S. cruiser *Birmingham* assisting the burning carrier *Princeton* shortly before the latter blows up.

U.S. battleships seen from an aircraft-carrier's flight deck.

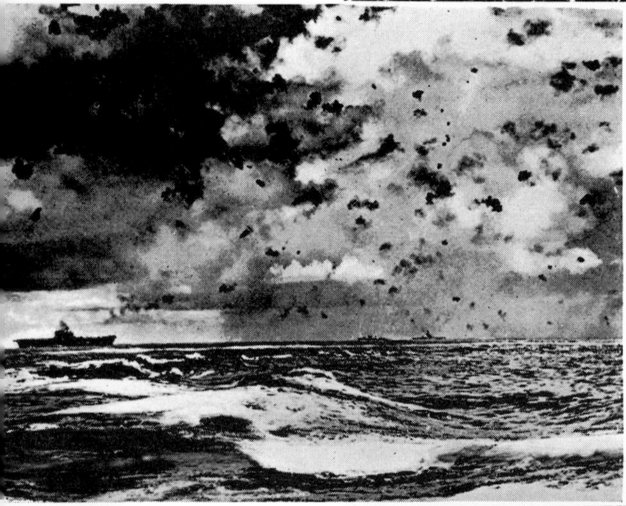

Japanese air attack on U.S. Pacific Fleet.

Japanese battleship *Musashi* under air attack.

cruisers *Good Hope* and *Monmouth*, the light cruiser *Glasgow*, and the armed merchant cruiser *Otranto*. This action, again, is no part of our story. It is sufficient to say that the ancient British armoured cruisers, manned by untrained reservists and outclassed by the *Scharnhorst* and *Gneisenau*, which were the champion gunnery ships of the German Navy, were sunk, while the *Glasgow* and *Otranto* were able to make good their escape. That the weak British squadron was thus pitted against impossible odds was owing to a combination of ill-considered Admiralty dispositions and a refusal of the courageous Rear-Admiral, Sir Christopher Cradock, to consider turning away in face of the enemy even though his own destruction was otherwise certain.

The news of the disaster reached London soon after Lord Fisher, recalled by Winston Churchill from retirement, had taken over the post of First Sea Lord. Blaming Vice-Admiral Sir Doveton Sturdee, Chief of the War Staff, for it, Fisher at once had him relieved of his appointment and sent him in command of a squadron to retrieve his mistake. Determined to leave nothing undone to bring von Spee to book, Fisher prepared to take a great risk. Jellicoe's slender margin in dreadnoughts over the enemy would be robbed to give Sturdee two of his precious battle-cruisers, *Invincible* and *Inflexible*. Furthermore, in order to have the Panama Canal adequately watched in case von Spee should break into the Atlantic by that route, a third battle-cruiser, *Princess Royal*, was to be sent.

It was a bold stroke on Fisher's part, for the High Seas Fleet had at last broken the inactivity in which it had lain since the beginning of the war, and on 3rd November had sent its battle-cruisers to raid our patrols off the English east coast. If such a weakening of Sir David Beatty's battle-cruiser squadron became known, it might lead to a further and more serious raid which would be difficult to combat.

For this reason, as well as in order to surprise von Spee, the utmost secrecy was enjoined. Speed was equally vital if the German squadron were to be caught before it again vanished into the ocean spaces before descending on some other ill-defended area. On 5th November, *Invincible* and *Inflexible* slipped out of Cromarty Firth and made for Devonport, where Sturdee's flagship, *Invincible*, was hastily docked and given some urgently needed repairs. She would be ready for sea by the 13th, the dockyard officials reported. "They are to sail not later than the 11th", came the uncompromising order from Fisher. By working round the clock and with feverish energy the order was obeyed, and on the evening of the 11th the two ships steamed out of Plymouth Sound for an undisclosed destination. On the next day the *Princess Royal* left Cromarty for her part in the wide-spread ambush.

Coaling at the Cape Verde Islands on 17th November, Sturdee pressed on to a rendezvous at the Abrolhos Rocks on the Brazilian coast with Rear-Admiral Stoddart and the force of cruisers he was commanding in the South Atlantic. There he arrived on the 26th, and took under his orders the cruisers *Carnarvon*, *Cornwall*, *Kent*, *Glasgow* and *Bristol*. By the 28th, all were on their way to the Falkland Islands.

The forces of retribution were gathering like figures of doom around the German squadron, though once again von Spee had disappeared. In the Pacific an Anglo-Japanese squadron led by the battle-cruiser *Australia* was steering for the Galapagos Islands off the Pacific end of the Panama Canal. A Japanese squadron was coming eastwards to the Marquesas Islands. Whichever way he went, von Spee must meet a superior enemy.

The German admiral indeed had few doubts that it was only a matter of time before he would have to pay the forfeit of his success at Coronel. At Valparaiso after the victory he refused to sanction any celebration by the German colony there. Triumphant German toasts to the confusion of the Royal Navy found him silent and disapproving. He was oppressed by a sense of foreboding of his end, and that of his squadron—in which his two sons were serving.

By now it was clear to the German Admiralty that further operations by their distant squadrons and ships were no longer possible in the face of the strong Allied dispositions, and consequently these ships were ordered to concentrate and try to break back to the North Sea. Von Spee had therefore been making his way southward along the west coast of South America, and on the night of 1st December he was rounding Cape Horn.

The question which he had to decide was whether he should abandon efforts to achieve further success and get away northwards as soon as possible, relying upon replenishing his coal-bunkers at the secret bases on the east coast of South America which German agents had been instructed to prepare, or to make one last blow before trying to get home. Lying athwart his route was the British colony and base of the Falkland Islands. Knowing nothing of the approach of Sturdee's battle-cruisers, he expected to find cruisers and perhaps the old battleship *Canopus* in the harbour of Port Stanley. Von Spee was confident he could defeat them, after which he could occupy the Islands and destroy the wireless station. He therefore decided to go there.

The plan was a bold one, and would certainly further reduce von Spee's chances of getting safely home. But in spite of the consensus of opinion amongst his officers against it, and particularly that of Captain Maerker of the *Gneisenau*, he persisted in his decision, perhaps persuaded that as his destruction was inevitable, he would inflict the maximum damage on the enemy before being caught.

This premonition of his approaching fate would seem to have dimmed von Spee's appreciation of the need for haste. When his light cruisers captured a British ship loaded with 2,800 tons of anthracite on the morning of 2nd December, he took her and his squadron into sheltered water and proceeded to transfer the coal to the warships' bunkers, a laborious process taking three days to complete—three precious days during which all unknown to him Sturdee's battle-cruisers were approaching Port Stanley.

In spite of the speed with which the Admiralty's dispositions had been got under way, Sturdee had been making slow progress towards the Falklands. He had been delayed for a day through a towing wire entangling a propeller of the *Invincible* during target practice, another day searching vainly for the German armed merchant cruiser *Kronprinz Wilhelm*, reported near his route, and yet another spent in a cast towards Montevideo owing to false intelligence given him by the British Chargé d'Affaires at Rio. Thus it was not until 7th December that he finally arrived off the Falklands, less than a day ahead of von Spee, who had put to sea again on the 6th.

Still lacking any sure intelligence of von Spee's whereabouts, Sturdee entered harbour and set his ships to coaling, *Carnarvon*, *Bristol* and *Glasgow* first, to be followed by *Invincible* and *Inflexible*, an order which would no doubt have been different had the admiral known that von Spee had rounded the Horn a week before. But from a study of the scanty and unreliable information available, Sturdee judged that the enemy was still on the west coast of South America. The last to coal would be the *Kent* and the armed merchant cruiser *Macedonia*, which latter was to patrol by night 10 miles from the entrance.

Bristol, *Cornwall* and *Glasgow* had engine defects, and were put at six hours notice to make them good. The remainder went to two hours notice, except for *Inflexible*, which was to act as guard-ship and keep steam for 14 knots at half an hour's notice.

Thus though Sturdee's arrangements were reasonable for a squadron which was still expecting a long voyage before meeting the enemy, he was caught in the highest degree unready for action when at 7.50 on the morning of 8th December the signal station set up ashore reported warships in the offing. They were the *Gneisenau* and *Nürnberg*, which von Spee had sent ahead to reconnoitre and, as a first step, to destroy the wireless station by gunfire.

In the midst of the grimy clatter of coaling, the alarm took some time to filter through to the flagship, and it was not until 8.14 a.m. that the general signal to prepare to weigh was made. *Glasgow* and *Bristol* could not be ready for at least two hours. The remainder—except for the *Kent* which had just taken over guard duty and the *Macedonia* anchored at the harbour entrance—could not get under way much sooner; and meanwhile the *Gneisenau* and *Nürnberg* were coming on at high speed, steering for the wireless station, while from the signal station were coming reports of further enemy ships in sight. The British squadron was in imminent danger of being taken under fire while still manœuvring to leave harbour, or as they filed one by one through the narrow entrance. Surprise was complete, and the situation perilous in the extreme.

Fortunately the old battleship *Canopus* had been settled on to the mud in the inner harbour in a position from which her 12-inch guns, directed from a control station ashore, could be brought to bear on any ship approaching the harbour. As the two German ships slowed down and prepared to shell the wireless station, the first salvo from the old veteran plunged into the sea—a long way short, but sufficient to induce them to turn away seaward for a time.

By now it was past 9.30. From the *Gneisenau* dense columns of smoke had been observed for some time rising from the harbour, but these had been assumed to be from fires burning as the British destroyed their stores and buildings. But at 9.40, as the Germans steamed across the harbour and entrance, masts and funnels came into sight and for the first time it was realised that a sizable British squadron was present.

Then came an unexpected report from a look-out in the *Gneisenau*: tripod masts were in sight! These could belong only to battle-cruisers. Fisher's trap, for which he had risked so much, had been sprung. No inkling of battle-cruisers in the area had reached von Spee. But now, as Maerker's report reached him, he knew that the situation was desperate. Recalling the *Gneisenau* and *Nürnberg* he prepared to withdraw, but with little hope of escape; for he knew that the battle-cruisers must have at least 24 knots to his 18, and by 10 o'clock they were seen to be leaving harbour. Even the weather, which—as usual in those latitudes—had plagued him with its persistent foulness, now perversely turned clear and blue with a light breeze from the north-west, withdrawing the veil of rain and snow in which he might have found shelter from the enemy's guns.

In the British squadron the *Glasgow* had been the first of those inside the harbour to report ready for sea. She was sent pelting out to join the *Kent* in keeping touch with the enemy; with her superior speed she had soon overhauled the *Kent* and was well ahead sending back reports of the enemy's movements.

By the time Sturdee's larger units were clear of the harbour, von Spee's ships had re-concentrated, and were some 13 miles from the harbour mouth, making off to the south-east at their best speed. Owing to the British squadron's unreadiness for sea, valuable time had been lost. To try to make up for it, Sturdee flew the signal for "General Chase" which released his ships from keeping station and allowed them to press on at their utmost speed.

But almost at once the drawback to coal as a fuel for warships at high speed made itself felt. As the stokers frenziedly shovelled coal into the furnaces to get every possible knot of speed out of their ships, dense, black, gritty smoke poured from the funnels, and with the following wind hung in a choking pall around the two battle-cruisers. Nothing could be seen of the enemy, and as from the *Glasgow*'s reports it was evident he was being overhauled fast, Sturdee rescinded the order for "General Chase" and reduced to 24 knots.

Even at this reduced speed, *Carnarvon* and *Cornwall* were dropping back from the battle-cruisers. To keep his squadron from getting too widely scattered Sturdee therefore further reduced speed to 20 knots at 11.30, and, confident that the afternoon would find the enemy within range, he sent his ships' companies to dinner and to clean out of their grimy coaling rig. Then at 12.20, Sturdee decided to make an end of all delay. Working up speed until the battle-cruisers were making 25 knots he left his smaller ships to follow as best they could.

He could well afford to do so, for the *Invincible* and *Inflexible* were so immeasurably more powerful than the enemy that he need not have feared even a combined attack by all five Germans. Each British ship mounted a broadside of eight 12-inch guns and eight 4-inch, and their 7-inch thick armour belt was proof against the heaviest guns in the German squadron at 14,000 yards—a range at which the British 12-inch guns were effective. *Scharnhorst* and *Gneisenau* had a mixed armament of eight 8·2-inch and six 6-inch guns each. The former had an extreme range not far short of that of the British 12-inch, but they could do little damage to the battle-cruisers at more than 10,000 yards. With their great superiority of speed, the *Invincible* and *Inflexible* could decide the range at which they would fight, and could stand off to hammer the German ships in comparative safety. Neither could there be any question of the German light cruisers joining in the action. With their armament of 4·1-inch guns, they would have to close to suicidal range to bring them into action.

As Sturdee closed in for the kill, every ship of the German squadron worked up to its maximum speed and the formation began to straggle. The *Leipzig* dropped steadily astern. In the battle-cruisers the ranges being called by the range-takers were coming down fast. The great guns were loaded, their muzzles rearing up at maximum elevation. Already the signal to engage had been made by the flagship. As a range of 16,000 yards was reported in the *Inflexible*, Captain Phillimore gave the order to open fire. The fire-gongs clanged, and the ship lurched as the first shell of the battle roared away on its 8-mile flight to raise a great white pillar of water as it fell in line with the *Leipzig*. Then the *Invincible* joined in; but the chances of a hit were small at that range, with only two turrets in each ship able to bear on the target. As the range fell, the little light cruiser was at times lost to sight amongst the tall splashes, but by good fortune she escaped a direct hit.

Nevertheless the time had come for von Spee to try to save at least a portion of his squadron. If he carried on as he was doing, his ships must be destroyed one by one. At 1.20 p.m., therefore, he gave the order to his light cruisers to scatter and try to save themselves while he himself with his two armoured cruisers turned north-eastward and accepted action with his greatly superior pursuers.

It was a gallant defiance, but fated to be of no avail, for Sturdee's light cruisers were too powerful. Turning in chase they hunted down their German opponents. All but the *Dresden* were caught and sunk. Though the *Dresden* by reason of her superior speed got away, she was finally run to earth three months later.

As for the *Scharnhorst* and *Gneisenau*, they put up a magnificent fight against hopeless odds. As the first 12-inch shells began to fall round them, they replied with their main armament at extreme elevation, but their shots fell 1,000 yards short. Von Spee turned inwards until the range was down to 13,000 yards, and at once the Germans justified their reputation for good gunnery by scoring a hit on the *Invincible*. By his manœuvre von Spee had got the range down to 12,200 yards, which enabled his 6-inch guns to join in. This did not at all suit Sturdee's book at this stage, as he wished to take advantage of his bigger guns to hit the enemy without exposing his valuable ships to damage. He therefore at 1.44 turned away 45 degrees to port opening the range so rapidly that the German fire soon became ineffective. So, however, did his own, and by two o'clock both sides had ceased fire.

Sturdee's tactics were not proving too successful. In half an hour's shooting only one or two hits had been secured on the enemy. The blanket of smoke shrouding both squadrons had made good spotting impossible for either side. A closer range would have to be accepted—one at which the German secondary armament of 6-inch guns would be in action. The theory of the all-big-gun ship would be given its first test, for the 4-inch anti-torpedo-boat armament of the battle-cruisers had a very limited effective range.

The *Invincible* led round to starboard, and both ships plunged into the cloud of their own smoke, losing sight of the enemy. When they ran clear of it, it was seen that von Spee had also turned and was now making off to the southward, and another stern chase began. By 2.45 the range had come down to 15,000 yards, and by turning some 25 degrees to port Sturdee was able to bring his full broadsides to bear and reopen fire to which the Germans were unable to reply.

For five minutes they accepted this galling position, but then von Spee once more turned at bay. Leading round through 90 degrees he charged his enemy on a course which would bring his full armament into play as quickly as possible. By now Sturdee had decided that he must accept some risk, and though he turned

65 degrees away, the courses were still converging and the range falling, until at 12,500 yards the German 6-inch guns were again in action. Sturdee manœuvred to maintain this range, and though both sides were scoring hits, the battle-cruisers were suffering but little, while their 12-inch shells were beginning to cause serious damage in the German ships.

By 3.10 the *Gneisenau* was seen to have taken a list. The *Scharnhorst* was burning, and the German fire, which had up to now kept up with admirable steadiness and volume, began to slacken. Even so the smoke interference was making really effective shooting impossible in the battle-cruisers, particularly in the *Inflexible*, which had been steaming in *Invincible*'s smoke. To get clear of it, Sturdee now turned his ships through 180 degrees together to windward, and so away from the enemy, ending up with *Inflexible* leading on a course opposite to that of the enemy. For a time the gunnery officer of the *Inflexible* rejoiced in a clear view of the target for the first time. When five minutes later course had to be altered to keep within range, the old trouble was renewed; however, 12-inch shells were still plunging home, and as both ships were now concentrating on *Scharnhorst* she was being rapidly reduced to a burning, twisted wreck.

Yet even now she could still steam, and von Spee led round to make a renewed charge towards the enemy. To the admiration and astonishment of the British, as brisk a fire as ever again came from the shattered ship. For a while the two forces were converging sharply, and the German 6-inch guns came once more into action. But under the impact of the British 12-inch shells, which were now achieving greater accuracy and rate of fire the Germans were forced to sheer away, and at the same time Sturdee turned to regain his chosen range beyond reach of the enemy's secondary batteries.

The end could not be long delayed now. For another quarter of an hour the pitiless pounding of the German flagship continued, the German gunners replying with indomitable spirit and steadiness until soon after 4 o'clock the *Scharnhorst* was seen suddenly to lurch to starboard, heading for our ships and listing heavily. With her flag still flying she rolled slowly over on to her beam ends, hung thus for a while and then slid beneath the surface. Not a soul of her company survived.

Shortly before the end, von Spee had signalled to Captain Maerker, ruefully admitting he had been wrong in not heeding his objections to attacking the Falklands and bidding him save himself and his ship if he could. When the flagship was brought to a halt, therefore, the *Gneisenau* limped away to the south-westward. But now the full fury of the fire of both battle-cruisers fell on her, and at the same time the *Carnarvon*, which had all the while been steaming along at her top speed of 18 knots to join the battle, was at last able to bring her guns into action.

Under this concentrated hail of fire, the *Gneisenau*'s speed had fallen away to 8 knots. A funnel had gone, and fires were raging fore and aft. For more than half an hour the unequal fight went on, the German gunners keeping up a defiant but ineffective fire till all their 8·2-inch ammunition had been expended.

At 5.30 the dying ship stopped and lay burning furiously, with a heavy list. The British ships would have wished to spare so gallant an enemy further agony, but from time to time a 6-inch gun still flashed out and the deliberate pounding had to go on. Then the enemy guns fell silent, and Sturdee signalled "Cease Fire". But once again defiant shots were hurled by the German gunners, and the cannonade broke out anew for another quarter of an hour. Then at last the *Gneisenau*'s end was seen to be at hand. She fell silent and heeled slowly over on to her beam ends. As the British ships were running up to rescue whom they could, the remnants of the crew could be seen walking on her side till she suddenly plunged. Her gallant but hopeless fight was over.

Of the *Gneisenau*'s complement of 850, a great proportion had been killed or wounded by shell fire, and there was no hope for the wounded in the icy waters of those latitudes. Two hundred others were picked up by the British boats, but even amongst the unwounded the shock of the bitter cold was fatal to a great many, who died after rescue.

Away to the south the last scenes of the Battle of the Falkland

Islands were being played out. First the slow *Leipzig* was caught and held in play by the *Glasgow* until the *Cornwall* could come pounding up to overwhelm the German light cruiser with her heavy broadside of nine 6-inch guns. The *Dresden*, with her high turn of speed, managed to get safely away.

The *Nürnberg* might have done the same had her machinery been in better order, for in pursuit of her went the comparatively slow armoured cruiser *Kent*, notorious for being a bad steamer. By stupendous efforts of her stokers, including feeding the furnaces with woodwork and furniture, the *Kent* was worked up to an unheard of speed of 25 knots. Yet the *Nürnberg* might still have escaped into the gathering dusk and the misty drizzle which had set in had not two of her boilers given out under the strain of continuous high speed. Her end was then certain, for she was quite outclassed by the British cruiser.

So ended the Battle of the Falkland Islands. It was hailed as a notable victory by the British, smarting under the defeat at Coronel. The laurels, however, belonged to Whitehall, where the Admiralty, largely to blame for Cradock's disaster, but re-invigorated by the vibrant leadership of Lord Fisher, had boldly taken an accurately calculated risk and acted with the speed necessary to affect the complete surprise which had proved fatal to von Spee and his squadron.

Tactically, the forces engaged were too unequal in strength for the battle to be rated a great triumph. Indeed lessons emerged which went to show that all was not well with the fire-power of the British battle-cruisers—lessons which if taken to heart might have enabled them to make a better showing later in the war. At their effective range of 14,000 yards the battle-cruisers achieved a surprisingly low rate of hitting. The need for improved fire-control and intensive target practice was indicated, but was veiled by the failure being ascribed solely to the interference by funnel smoke. Furthermore, the effects of hits by the 12-inch shells was clearly a great deal less than had been expected. For two and a half hours the *Scharnhorst* had suffered their blows before her end came. Yet two and a half years later the Germans were to gloat over and the British to bemoan their ineffectiveness in battle against armoured ships.

The strategic and tactical effectiveness of the fast dreadnoughts had been amply demonstrated. Technically, the British variety lacked the means to deliver the blow for which they were designed.

11

Dogger Bank and Dardanelles

When the huge gatherings of battleships which formed the hard cores of the Grand Fleet and the High Seas Fleet are considered, the Falkland Islands battle appears a mere outpost skirmish, important only because it marked the end of the armoured cruiser as a useful unit in a fleet. In face of battle-cruisers or fast dreadnought battleships it was, as Fisher contemptuously described the older ships in the Navy List when he became First Sea Lord in 1904, unable either to fight or to run away. However, its type was to persist in the British Navy at the Battle of Jutland in 1916, with disastrous consequences.

As 1915 dawned, an uneasy balance of power had become established in the North Sea, the main naval theatre of war. In spite of accidents, periodical absences for maintenance refits and necessary diversions to other areas, such as that of *Invincible* and *Inflexible* first to the Falklands and then to the Mediterranean, the Grand Fleet was maintained with a slight superiority of strength over that of the High Seas Fleet.

German hopes that the British fleet would expose itself to attrition by mine and submarine attack in attempting to enforce a close blockade had been shown to be vain. From its base in Scapa Flow, it could achieve the strategic objects of blockade, controlling the only practicable route by which German ships could pass to or from the outer oceans. Though it could not prevent an attack on the English east coast, a brief night's run from Heligoland by a German battleship force, it could expect to bring such a force to action before it could regain the shelter of its home waters.

Unwilling to risk his precious ships, the German Emperor

expressly forbade such adventures. However, the battle-cruisers, with their high turn of speed, could cross the North Sea by night, deliver a brief bombardment at dawn and be on their way home again before the Grand Fleet or even the battle-cruiser squadrons could get into position to bar the way. This presupposed the maintenance of secrecy up to the time they appeared to deliver their blow. Ignorant that the British Admiralty had organised a chain of wireless direction-finding stations, and that their naval codes had been broken, the Germans did not appreciate that by monitoring their radio traffic, the Admiralty knew at once when such a foray was impending.

In November and December 1914 the German battle-cruiser commander, Rear-Admiral Hipper, had led his ships on such sorties; and though on the second occasion only luck had saved him from being brought to action by a superior force sent to intercept him on his line of retreat, the unimportant damage inflicted on English east-coast towns acted as an encouragement to the German Navy, fretting under the inaction forced upon it. Furthermore it was believed, not incorrectly, that pressure would consequently be brought to bear on the British Admiralty to bring at least a portion of the Grand Fleet south. Jellicoe might thus be forced either to divide his fleet or to abandon his excellent strategic position in the north. Either would well suit the German book.

In pursuit of the same object, Hipper was again sent out on the night of 23rd January 1915. But even before his squadron of three battle-cruisers—*Seydlitz*, his flagship, *Moltke* and *Derfflinger* —and the armoured cruiser *Blücher*, with their accompanying light cruisers and destroyers, had cleared the Heligoland Bight, his plans had been revealed to the Admiralty by the patient operators reading and analysing his every radio signal. British forces were at once in co-ordinated movement to a rendezvous at dawn off the Dogger Bank.

There on the morning of the 24th, Hipper's force was discovered by the light cruisers scouting for Sir David Beatty's squadron of five battle-cruisers. Hipper at once withdrew but in a stern chase the British gradually came up with him, and by 9 a.m. Beatty's flagship *Lion* was within extreme range.

Beatty's force was greatly superior in gun power, *Lion*, *Tiger*, *Princess Royal*, *New Zealand* and *Indomitable* mounting twenty-four 13·5-inch and sixteen 12-inch guns between them to Hipper's twenty-eight 11-inch in his battle-cruisers and eight 8·2-inch in *Blücher*. With all day before them, perfect weather and a superiority of speed over the enemy, it might have been expected that the British battle-cruisers would win a notable success. But tactical mistakes and indifferent gunnery, due partly to the old enemy—funnel smoke—robbed them of the full fruits of the strategical surprise so ably brought about by the naval high command.

The rear ship of Hipper's line was the armoured cruiser *Blücher*, a ship right out of her class amongst the powerful battle-cruisers, a cod-fish amongst sharks. On her inevitably fell the brunt of the British fire, each ship opening on her as she came within range. Lacking the thickness of armour to withstand the impact of the huge 13·5-inch shells, she was soon in distress. Until 9.14 the fire of *Lion*, *Tiger* and *Princess Royal*, the only British ships within range, was concentrated on the unfortunate *Blücher*. Aim was then shifted up the line and at 9.25 a hit was scored on the *Seydlitz*. At 9.43 the *Seydlitz* was again hit, and with appalling effect. Piercing the armoured walls of the after barbette, the shell exploded in the working chamber of the turret, doing serious damage in the after part of the ship and, worse, setting fire to the ready-use ammunition waiting to be loaded into the guns. Admiral Scheer, later to be Commander-in-Chief of the High Seas Fleet, has described what followed:

> The flames rose high up into the turret and down into the ammunition chamber and from thence through a connecting door, usually kept shut, through which the men from the ammunition chamber tried to escape into the fore turret. The flames thus made their way through to the other ammunition chamber and from thence up to the second turret, and from this cause the entire guns' crews of both turrets perished very quickly. The flames rose above the turrets as high as a house.

Hipper's flagship was saved only by the extreme heroism of three of the *Seydlitz*'s crew, who grasped the red-hot valve wheels and opened the flood valves of the after magazine.

Up to this time Beatty's ships had been unscathed, except for a single hit on the *Lion* at 9.21, which had done little damage; but as both sides strained every nerve to force their ships along at greater speed, the smoke poured ever thicker and blacker from their funnels, conferring a distinct advantage on the Germans. For while they themselves were shrouded by their own smoke streaming away astern of them, the *Lion*, leading the British line, stood out, a clear target on which every enemy gun concentrated.

The devastating hit on the *Seydlitz* was the last to be suffered by the German battle-cruisers for nearly an hour, and, indeed, only one other hit—on the *Derfflinger*—was to be scored on them in the action. The *Lion*, however, began to suffer under repeated heavy blows, culminating in one a few minutes before 11 a.m. which put one engine out of action and reduced her speed to 15 knots.

As the remainder of his ships swept on, Beatty signalled to them to "attack the rear of the enemy". As he dropped out of the line, he was still signalling for an alteration of course to north-east. Beatty's second-in-command, Rear-Admiral Sir Archibald Moore, took the two signals in conjunction and read them to mean "Attack the enemy's rear bearing north-east".

It was a disastrous mistake, and the action to which it led was a deplorable example of unintelligent deduction. By then the luckless *Blücher*, shattered by a great many destructive hits, had staggered away out of the line to the north-east, abandoned by the remainder of her squadron. Moore now led the British battle-cruisers to complete her destruction, leaving Hipper to escape the fate which until that moment had seemed to be in sight.

Like the *Scharnhorst* and *Gneisenau* at the Falklands, the *Blücher* survived a prolonged battering before sinking, being seven times torpedoed by the British light forces, besides receiving more than seventy hits from heavy shells. German ability to build ships capable of taking heavy punishment was thus demonstrated at an early stage in the war. Later, British armoured cruisers caught in the fire of capital ships were to disintegrate in catastrophic explosions or be driven out of action in a near-sinking condition after comparatively few hits.

Furthermore, a lesson of the utmost importance had been given to the Germans by the calamitous fire in the *Seydlitz*. The arrangements for handling the ammunition for the big guns was similar in German and British ships at this time, but as a result of the Dogger Bank action, the Germans took steps to modify them to prevent a recurrence.

A brief description of the ammunition supply arrangements for turrets is necessary here to show the dangers against which precautions were found to be required.

Starting in the magazine, deep in the bowels of the ship, under armour and so to a great extent safe from the penetration of a shell were the cordite charges stowed in racks. From here they were passed through a hatch into the lower handing room at the bottom of the barbette, the huge fixed cylinder of armour-plate on the top end of which revolved the turret on roller bearings. From the lower handing room a hydraulic hoist delivered shell and cordite charge into the turret working chamber. The charges were by now in the revolving part of the structure, inside the "stalk" of the turret which fits inside the barbette. Here they were transferred to the actual loading cage which whisked them up, first the shell and then the charges, into position behind the open breach of the gun so that a hydraulically operated chain ram could thrust them into the breech.

These propellant charges, formed of thick bundles of sticks of cordite, were encased in silk bags. They were therefore liable to be ignited by any flash which touched them, a flash such as would be given out by the bursting of a shell in their vicinity. Even the flash from a shell bursting outside the turret might enter through the gun-ports and ignite a charge waiting in the loading cage. A shell penetrating the barbette and bursting in either the working chamber of the lower handing room could start an even more devasting conflagration, for there a great many more charges would be found. It was such an event which so nearly put an end to the *Seydlitz*.

Serious as any of these eventualities might be, a worse possibility was that flames from a single burning charge might penetrate from, say, the turret itself to the working chamber, thence to the handing room and finally to the magazine. In the *Seydlitz* this was only prevented during the Dogger Bank action by the flooding of the magazine. In the German fleet immediate steps were taken to prevent a recurrence. Anti-flash arrangements were fitted whereby flash or fire in one space could not spread to the next; metal containers were provided for all charges waiting to be loaded into the cages.

No such modifications were made in British ships. In time to come, the British Navy was to pay dearly for the omission.

* * *

The action off the Dogger Bank was hailed by the British public, somewhat unjustifiably, as a notable success. Perhaps this was not surprising when the picture of the *Blüecher*'s last moments reproduced in the *Daily Mail* appeared at a million breakfast tables. The truth of it was that a strategic success had been largely neutralised by a tactical failure.

In Germany, however, the Kaiser saw it as a warning that his navy was taking serious risks in sending detached squadrons on such minor operations, in the course of which they risked being cut off by superior forces. An order was issued forbidding any repetition. The High Seas Fleet relapsed into a demoralising inactivity.

With the dreadnoughts of the Grand Fleet in adequate strength to meet the High Seas Fleet should it come out, the British and French navies found themselves with a large force of capital ships elsewhere for which there was no employment. The fertile brain of Winston Churchill, First Lord of the Admiralty, naturally sought a way to apply it to break the deadlock reached in the land fighting. On 1st November 1914 Turkey had joined cause with the Central Powers. The Turkish capital, Constantinople, was approachable by sea, and Churchill decided to undertake operations to capture it.

However, the sea approach to Constantinople was shielded by the easily defensible strait of the Dardanelles, where fortifications, minefields and a fierce current all combined to make its passage by a hostile fleet hazardous in the extreme. Yet in the state of unpreparedness of the Turks at the outbreak of war, it is probable that the straits could have been forced by a squadron of battleships if the attempt had been made at once and without warning, though not without some loss. The sacrifice of a few of the great number of old pre-dreadnoughts in commission would not have been a serious one. Whether a naval force alone could have captured and held Constantinople is at least open to doubt; on the other hand a combined operation, if launched at once in sufficient strength and prepared in secret, would certainly have taken the Turks by surprise and met with little opposition.

Such an operation was far beyond the capabilities of the Allied military organisation. At Churchill's urging, the British War Cabinet, therefore decided on a purely naval operation. The decision was forced through in opposition to the opinions of Lord Fisher, the First Sea Lord, and of almost every knowledgeable senior naval officer of the day. Sir Percy Scott described it as "crazy", Admiral Sturdee as impracticable; Admiral Sir Henry Jackson, later First Sea Lord, thought that it "would be a mad thing to try to do".

Unfortunately, the one condition which might have made success possible—surprise—had been sacrificed by a bombardment of the forts at the entrance to the Dardanelles on 3rd November by a force under Rear-Admiral Carden, comprising the battle-cruisers *Indefatigable* and *Indomitable* and the old French battleships *Verité* and *Suffren*. Seventy-six rounds of 12-inch caused considerable damage to the forts of Sedd-el-Bahr and Kum Kaleh, blew up the main magazine of Sedd-el-Bahr with heavy loss of life, and put both forts temporarily out of action, but the result of the bombardment was to put the Turks on the alert. With the aid of German experts, they set to work to repair and strengthen the defences along the whole length of the straits.

Thus when a large naval squadron under Admiral Carden arrived to begin the operation of forcing the straits on 19th February 1915, they found the defences altogether beyond the power of ships' guns to neutralise. Besides a series of permanent forts and earthworks in which were mounted guns of 14-inch, 11-inch, 10·2-inch, 9·4-inch, 8·2-inch and 6-inch calibre, there were ten lines of moored mines stretched at intervals across the channel, covered by searchlights and batteries of quick-firing guns.

It is a well-established principle of naval warfare that ships are not capable of defeating well-built land fortifications. Only for a brief period between the introduction of armour for warships and of explosive shell for guns has this principle been wrong. Its truth was now to be proved once again.

Carden's force consisted of the battle-cruiser *Inflexible*, the British pre-dreadnoughts *Agamemnon*, *Triumph*, *Vengeance*, *Albion* and *Cornwallis*, and the French pre-dreadnoughts *Suffren*, *Gaulois* and *Bouvet*. In addition the latest British battleship *Queen Elizabeth*, mounting eight 15-inch guns, was on her way to join him.

The attack opened on the morning of 19th February, with a bombardment of the forts on either side of the entrance to the straits at Kum Kaleh, Sedd-el-Bahr and Orkanieh.

Able to stand off at long range, the ships were able to silence the Turkish guns by deliberate, carefully spotted fire, and then close in and overwhelm them. As thick clouds of dust and smoke enveloped the silent forts it seemed that they must be reduced to ruins. Yet at 5 p.m. three batteries were able to open a brisk fire on the *Vengeance*, and another half-hour's bombardment was necessary to silence them.

Though the forts and earthworks were considerably damaged, only two guns, an 11-inch in Kum Kaleh and a 9·4-inch in Orkanieh, were in fact permanently disabled. However, had it been possible to resume the attack on the following day, the outer forts might have been kept out of action while the main bombardment moved on to the fortifications inside the straits.

Unfortunately the weather, always the chief factor in naval operations and insufficiently considered when the operation was planned, began to take a hand. Day after day high winds raised a heavy sea and brought poor visibility, conditions making accurate fire by ships of that day impossible.

While the ships were held idle, Turkish engineers repaired the damaged forts and gunners re-mounted the guns, so that when the weather moderated on the 25th all the work of silencing them had to be done again. Even though the 15-inch guns of the *Queen Elizabeth* were now added to the 12-inch of the older ships, it was not until 3 p.m. that it was accomplished. Furthermore, though these outer forts could be brought under fire from the open sea where the ships were free to manœuvre, the Turkish gunners were improving in performance, *Agamemnon* and *Gaulois* being repeatedly hit and suffering a number of casualties.

On the following day *Triumph*, *Albion* and *Majestic* entered the straits and engaged the next series of defences, while trawlers were set to sweeping for mines. Something of the real difficulties of the operation now became apparent as the battleships came under very heavy fire from 6-inch and 8·2-inch howitzers firing from concealed positions on railways, and which the naval guns were quite unable to silence. At 4 o'clock, after the *Majestic* had received a dangerous hit below the water-line, the force was recalled. The following day the weather again brought the bombardment to a halt for two days.

Perhaps the most ominous news to reach the commanding admiral at this time came from the landing party put ashore to complete the demolition of the fort at Sedd-el-Bahr. For all the weight of explosive that had been poured on it, they found that four out of the six heavy guns were intact.

By now it had become apparent to the War Cabinet that a military landing was necessary. Machinery for mounting the long and bloody operation which was to be known to history as Gallipoli was grinding slowly and haltingly into motion, but it would be two months before the troops and their equipment could be gathered and brought to the spot. Meanwhile the Navy was committed to the forcing of the straits on its own resources, and was being urged on to further efforts by Churchill to the dismay of Lord Fisher, who never ceased to rail against the folly of it all.

During the first week of March the attack was gradually shifted to the inner defences of the straits, though this was done more by ignoring the still-active shore batteries than by silencing them. The *Queen Elizabeth* bombarded the forts at the Chanak narrows from across the Gallipoli peninsula at a range of more than 14,000 yards. The thunder of the great guns and the flash and roar of the bursting shells were impressive to beholders, but all they achieved was a lucky hit which blew up a Turkish barracks.

While the battleships bombarded by day, the minesweepers were sent in by night. Held in the searchlight beams and subjected to a withering fire from quick-firing guns ashore, the trawler captains began to have serious doubts about the wisdom of the task given to them, for in the fierce swirling currents of the straits they could achieve little or nothing to justify the risk and casualties. After a particularly harsh experience on the night of 11th March they refused to continue. Volunteers from the fleet then took over, and made an attempt on the night of the 14th. The only result was four trawlers put out of action, while the light cruiser *Amethyst*, escorting them, was disabled and nearly lost when her steering gear was put out of action. Lying helpless for twenty minutes she was heavily hit, suffering 27 men killed and 45 wounded before she was brought under control again.

Thirty powerful trawlers were now ordered out from England, but could not be expected to arrive for a long time. Meanwhile Admiral Carden was under peremptory orders to press on with the attack regardless of casualties and loss. On the 16th his health broke down, and the command devolved upon Vice-Admiral J. M. de Robeck.

The new commander was by no means convinced of the wisdom or the value of a purely naval penetration of the Dardanelles, but he prepared to act with vigour on the orders which had come to him. Indeed it would have been difficult for him to refuse to make the attempt until experience had showed that it was not possible,

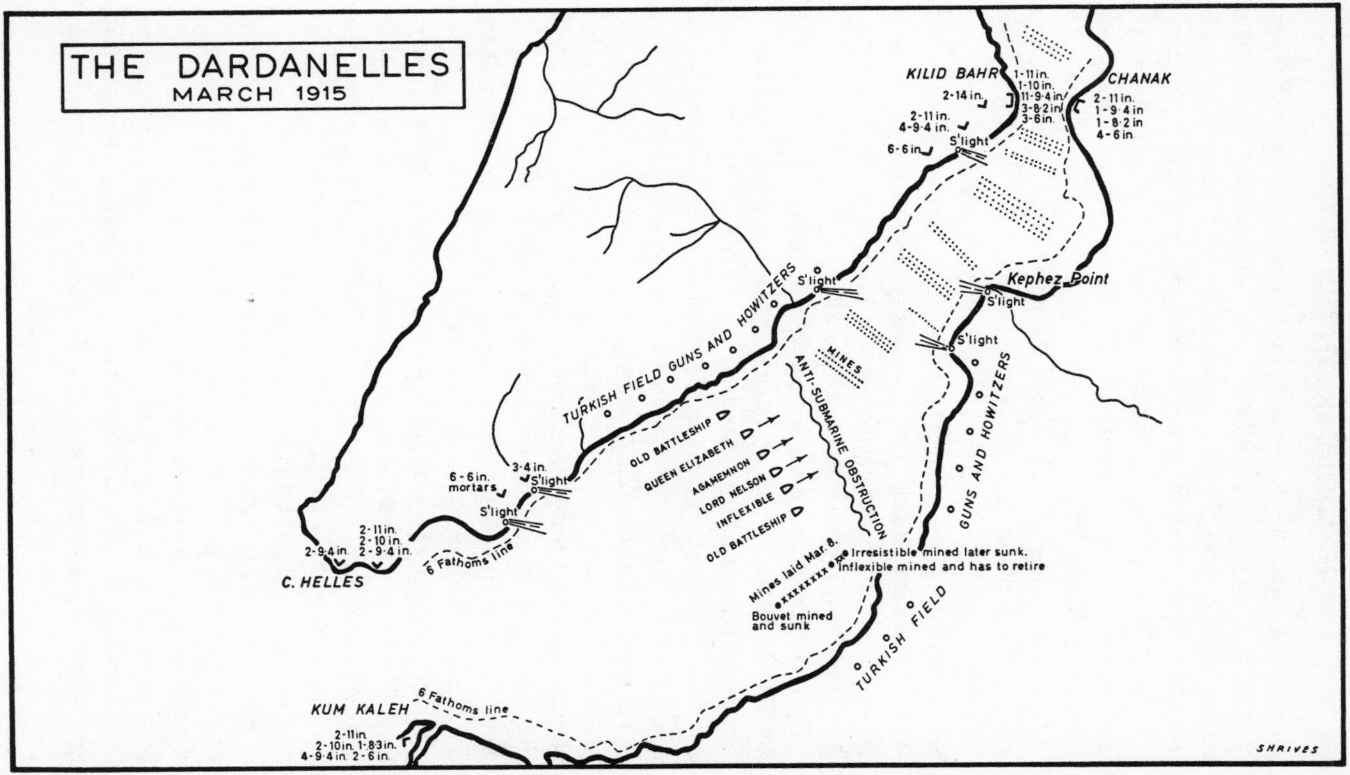
THE DARDANELLES
MARCH 1915
KILID BAHR
1-11in.
1-10in.
11-9·4in.
3-8·2in.
3-6in.
2-14in.
2-11in.
4-9·4in.
6-6in.
CHANAK
2-11in.
1-9·4in
1-8·2in
4-6in
S'light
Kephez Point
TURKISH FIELD GUNS AND HOWITZERS
GUNS AND HOWITZERS
MINES
ANTI-SUBMARINE OBSTRUCTION
OLD BATTLESHIP
QUEEN ELIZABETH
AGAMEMNON
LORD NELSON
INFLEXIBLE
OLD BATTLESHIP
Mines laid Mar. 8.
Irresistible mined later sunk.
Inflexible mined and has to retire
Bouvet mined and sunk
TURKISH FIELD
3·4in.
6-6in. mortars
2-11in.
2-10in.
2-9·4in.
2-9·4in.
C. HELLES
6 Fathoms line
KUM KALEH
6 Fathoms line
2-11in.
2-10in. 1-8·3in.
4-9·4in. 2-6in.
SHRIVES

for the force under his command was not inconsiderable. Besides the *Queen Elizabeth* and *Inflexible*, it comprised no less than sixteen French and British pre-dreadnought battleships each mounting four 12-inch guns, as well as powerful secondary batteries. These latter ships were considered to some extent "expendable", to use a phrase which was to become familiar in the Second World War.

On the morning of 18th March the great attack was therefore launched in brilliant weather. It was opened by the four most powerful ships, *Queen Elizabeth*, *Inflexible*, *Agamemnon* and *Lord Nelson* advancing into the straits in a line abreast with an old battleship on either flank. The plan was for these ships to smother the fire of the forts sufficiently for the older ships to move in to close range and silence them once for all.

By 11.30 action had been joined. Whatever may have been the damage inflicted on the permanent forts, the battleships found themselves quite unable to master the fire of the Turkish howitzers and smaller guns spread along the shore-line. The damage these could do was largely superficial, but the casualties they inflicted were numerous and galling. However, soon after noon the fire from the forts began to slacken, largely on account of the quantities of earth and sand thrown up around them by the bursting shells and choking the gun-barrels. Until they could be cleared the guns were forced, temporarily, to cease fire. It seemed the moment for the older battleships to go into action.

As they did so, the Turkish fire broke out again with renewed fury. The French ships *Gaulois* and *Bouvet*, and also the *Irresistible*, were repeatedly and heavily hit. The *Gaulois*, badly damaged, was the first to withdraw from the action, with a heavy list. Then the *Bouvet* was damaged by two 14-inch shells.

But the Turks had prepared another and more shocking surprise for their attackers. On the 8th March they had been able secretly to lay a minefield of twenty mines in water which had been reported cleared by Allied minesweepers, and had thereafter been regularly used by the bombarding battleships. It claimed its first victim at about 2 p.m., when the *Bouvet* disintegrated as she struck one of the mines which exploded a magazine. Of her crew of 800, 739 were killed.

The brunt of the enemy fire now turned on to the *Irresistible*. For an hour she was hit again and again. Both her turrets had been put out of action and she would soon have been forced to retire when at 4.15 she, too, struck a mine. Her crew were rescued, apart from twenty dead or missing, and she was left drifting in a sinking condition, to be finally sunk by Turkish gunfire.

While the *Irresistible* was being battered, the near-by *Inflexible* had also been suffering heavily, and at 4 o'clock she suddenly lurched as another of the same field of mines blew in her side forward, killing 29 men and admitting 2,000 tons of flood-water. With her bows almost awash and with a cruiser and destroyers standing by her expecting her to sink at any moment she was got painfully away, subsequently reaching Malta with great difficulty.

The attack was now called off, but the tale of Allied loss was not yet complete. The battleship *Ocean*, already severely damaged by gunfire, struck yet another mine and lay helpless, the target of a host of Turkish guns. She too had to be abandoned, to suffer the same fate as the *Irresistible*.

18th March had indeed been a disastrous day for the Allied cause. Besides the ships lost, the *Inflexible*, *Gaulois* and *Suffren* were making a perilous journey to Malta, barely able to keep afloat. The French *Charlemagne* had been badly holed; *Agamemnon* and *Albion* had turrets out of action. Furthermore the main minefields guarding the straits had not yet been tackled. Five days later the naval attack was finally abandoned. Misdirection of sea power was to give way to a combined operation in which extremes of heroism by the rank and file were to be wasted in pursuit of ill-conceived objectives, and any chance of success prejudiced from the start by bad planning and lack of foresight.

Naval support for the armies landed on the Gallipoli peninsula continued throughout the nine months during which the futile and tragic campaign continued, but the attempt to force the straits was never renewed. Even so, the employment of capital ships in what was virtually a close blockade was an unjustifiable risk. A Turkish destroyer commanded by a German, Lieutenant-Commander Firle, made a skilful night passage of the straits on 13th May to arrive undetected to within a hundred yards of the old battleship *Goliath*, into which she fired three torpedoes, sinking her with grievous loss of life.

Lord Fisher, who had unceasingly objected to the exposure of the precious *Queen Elizabeth* to such risks for an object so contrary to his wishes, at once demanded and obtained her recall. How justified he was became apparent when twelve days later the *Triumph*, in spite of torpedo-nets and a destroyer escort, was torpedoed and sunk by *U21*. On 27th May the *Majestic* suffered the same fate.

By December the futility of the Dardanelles campaign had become clear to all, and on the 20th a masterly withdrawal without the loss of a man brought the only laurels to be earned by the high command in the whole course of it. Indirectly it was to have an important effect on the higher direction of the naval war. It had first broken the partnership and for a long while the friendship of Churchill and Fisher, the latter resigning when his passionate opposition to the whole plan was ignored. When the campaign ended in failure, the reputation of its chief architect was so damaged, irreparably as it seemed at the time, that Churchill also was forced to resign. It is fascinating to speculate what changes might have been made in the command and strategy of the Grand Fleet in the months still to run before its great test in battle, if the Fisher-Churchill combination had still reigned at the Admiralty.

The stalemate in the North Sea was about to come to an end. In January 1916, the Commander-in-Chief of the High Seas Fleet, the inert von Pohl, was stricken with a mortal illness and forced to resign. In his place there came the brilliant and vigorous seaman Admiral Reinhard Scheer, lately in command of the Third Squadron of the High Seas Fleet, made up of seven of Germany's latest and most powerful dreadnoughts.

Scheer had no more desire than his predecessors to court a meeting with the Grand Fleet in all its strength. The odds were too unreasonable. But he believed, and was able to persuade the Kaiser, that by clever use of U-boats, scouting Zeppelins and the fleet in combination he had a good chance of catching a portion of the Grand Fleet in circumstances which would enable him to inflict serious loss on it before it could be reinforced. He was therefore given the free hand which his predecessors had sought in vain.

As a preliminary he decided to renew the tip-and-run raids on the English coast, well knowing that pressure would be brought to bear on Jellicoe to base a portion of the fleet farther south where it could counter them. Such sorties would also give the High Seas Fleet the activity and the sea experience of which it was so badly in need to raise its flagging morale.

Within a month of assuming the command, Scheer had ordered the first of such operations, sending his light forces to raid British minesweeping flotillas off the Dogger Bank on the night of 9th February. They succeeded in sinking only one minesweeper before scuttling back to harbour, but the whole Grand Fleet was sent pelting seaward, only to arrive too late from its northern bases. Though the German battle-cruisers were not employed on this raid, they could well have been. Once again came the old argument which Jellicoe had so far resisted, that the fleet should be based in the Forth and the Humber.

Jellicoe realised that this was just what the Germans wanted, and he continued to insist on the Grand Fleet's battleship squadron being kept concentrated at Scapa. With some justification he cited the lack of adequate submarine defences anywhere but at Scapa as a good reason for his insistence. The Battle-Cruiser Fleet, as Sir David Beatty's command was now designated, was already based in the Forth, and this was as far south as Jellicoe would permit. With the steady increase in the Grand Fleet's superiority in dreadnoughts over the High Seas Fleet, this caution was looked on by the Admiralty as excessive. For the moment they gave in to the Commander-in-Chief's wishes, but they insisted that new arrangements must be made as soon as anti-submarine defences were ready; such defences would be hastened towards completion.

This was the situation when on 24th April the Admiralty's radio monitoring stations reported unusual activity in the German fleet. At once warning signals went out to Scapa, to Rosyth and to Harwich, where a force of light craft under Rear-Admiral Tyrwhitt was based. The routine movements for such an occasion were cut and dried. The battle squadrons from Scapa would sail for their regular interception area in the middle of the North Sea "eastward of the Long Forties". The battle-cruiser fleet from Rosyth would take a more southerly route, but would in due course meet the remainder of the Grand Fleet at an agreed rendezvous from which position the whole force could cut off the German ships from their line of retreat.

But now came a complication which the Admiralty had always feared. A raging southerly gale in the Orkney area forced Jellicoe to report that his destroyers would be unable to sail with the fleet, and even the light cruisers would be unable to make more than 10 knots. To make matters worse it was soon known that the whole High Seas Fleet was coming out and was taking a southerly route close along the Dutch coast. The Channel and the Thames Estuary were wide open to attack, with only the pre-dreadnought squadrons and the light forces and submarines from Harwich available to meet it.

Though by the evening of the 24th the weather had moderated sufficiently for the battle squadrons to sail, and Jellicoe had sent the squadron of fast *Queen Elizabeths* to support Beatty's battle-cruisers, a situation had arisen whereby the enemy would be able to strike his blow and get away again unhindered. This, in fact, was exactly what happened, though fortunately only a tip-and-run raid by the battle-cruisers to bombard Lowestoft was aimed by Scheer on this occasion. Fortunately also, the Germans could not realise to what extent the British had been caught off balance; so that when Tyrwhitt's light cruisers and destroyers came in contact with the bombarding force of three battle-cruisers at dawn on the 25th, the Germans at once turned for home, uncertain what overwhelming force might be coming up behind Tyrwhitt's screen.

Tyrwhitt courageously followed the enemy ships, reporting their position and movements, but Jellicoe and Beatty were much too late to intercept. Once again the long-sought decision with the High Seas Fleet was postponed; and once again Jellicoe's insistence on concentration of the fleet so far north was blamed. A fresh approach was made to him by the Admiralty to get him to agree to a redistribution. It was decided that as soon as the Grand Fleet's dreadnought strength reached twenty-four, as was shortly expected, such a redistribution was to begin. In the meantime, as the Third Battle-Cruiser Squadron—*Invincible*, *Inflexible* and *Indomitable*—was due to come to Scapa for gunnery practice, the Fifth Battle Squadron, made up of the four *Queen Elizabeth* class ships, was to be sent to reinforce the Battle-Cruiser Fleet at Rosyth.

Such was the situation in the Spring of 1916 as, unknown to either side, the greatest encounter of the battleship age was drawing near. Exasperation with the endless game of hide-and-seek which the two fleets were playing was felt by British and Germans alike. The British, confident in the efficiency and overwhelming strength the Grand Fleet had now reached, were ready for a fight on any terms. The Germans, equally confident in the quality of their ships and their skill but unable to match the enemy in numbers, sought a meeting on their own conditions—in their own waters, close to their base, and with only a detached portion of the Grand Fleet.

As the unpredictable, difficult weather of the North Sea winter gave way with the approach of summer, staffs in each of the Fleet Flagships, Jellicoe's *Iron Duke* and Scheer's *Friedrich der Grosse* cudgelled their brains as to how to bring about the situation they desired. By May each had evolved a plan which, by pure coincidence was very similar to the other's and projected for roughly the same date. In the event neither was to be wholly carried out. Nevertheless, the final result was the meeting which each side professed to want.

12

Battle Fleets Engage

THE plans which emerged from the deliberations of the opposing Staffs were basically similar, each being designed to lure the enemy to sea and into the trap of an encounter with a superior force. The British scheme was quite simple. On 2nd June 1916, two squadrons of light cruisers would penetrate far into the straits between Denmark and Sweden, supported by a single squadron of battleships in the Skagerrak. This was the bait. Hovering out of sight to seaward would be the remainder of the Grand Fleet, the jaws of the trap.

Whether such a transparent scheme would have succeeded no one can say, for Scheer's own plan antedated it. Owing to his continued ignorance of the Admiralty's ability to read and partly decipher his signals, Scheer's action was to bring about the very situation which the Grand Fleet so badly wanted.

Scheer's intended stratagem was basically a repetition of the old familiar raid on an east coast port, though more intricate in detail. Beatty's strong force based at Rosyth was his primary target. By an attack on Sunderland he felt sure he could bring Beatty pelting out to sea into the arms of the waiting High Seas Fleet. Unfortunately for Scheer, long before he could reach Sunderland, the Admiralty would know from their wireless interception stations that he was under way. From Scapa and Rosyth both sections of the Grand Fleet would have come forth to rendezvous, as they had hopefully done a score of times before, "eastwards of the Long Forties".

The second part of the German plan was a prearranged ambush by U-boats stationed off Scapa, Cromarty and the Forth which would attack the battle squadrons as they swept past seaward on receiving news of the Sunderland raid. As early as 17th May sixteen U-boats had been sailed to their allotted stations. From that time onward, the limit of their endurance, which would take them to 30th May, was also the limit of the period during which the operation could be set in motion.

Any time between 22nd and 30th May that the weather was suitable for reconnaissance by Scheer's Zeppelins, the High Seas Fleet would be given orders to sail. The essence of Scheer's plan was that Zeppelins should be aloft and able to locate and warn against the approach of the battle fleet from Scapa which he had no intention of facing. This was the weakest link in Scheer's chain. The lumbering, unhandy airships could be grounded by high winds or rain or fog. Even with the summer weather approaching, as often as not the North Sea was covered by a misty haze in which visibility from the air was even less than from the bridge of a ship.

In case such conditions should persist throughout the vital period, an alternative plan was devised to be put into force on 30th May. To lure Beatty out to sea, Hipper's battle-cruisers would steam along the Norwegian coast where they were sure to be reported, while the High Seas Fleet waited out of sight ready to spring the trap at the right moment. It is a measure of the misunderstanding of Jellicoe's cautious strategy that Scheer should have thought that such a ruse could succeed.

While the last week of May slipped by, Scheer's U-boats kept their patient watch and wondered what the delay could be. In fact the period available for the start of the operation had been cut down by the need to wait for completion of repairs to the battle-cruiser *Seydlitz* which had been damaged by a mine during the fleet's previous sortie. She would not be ready until the 28th; so Scheer's Sunderland plan now depended upon good flying weather on the 29th and 30th. The fleet was ordered to be ready to sail by the morning of the 29th.

All through the 28th and 29th reports kept coming in of weather unsuitable for air reconnaissance. The 30th was the last possible day before the U-boats must be recalled; but again that morning the Zeppelins were unable to play their part, so the decision was made to revert to the alternative plan. By radio to all ships and authorities went out the cryptic message "31 Gg 2490", which meant simply "Carry out Top Secret Instruction 2490 on 31st May."

Though the British cryptographers had no way of knowing the meaning of this brief intercepted signal, it was obvious from the way it was handled and its wide distribution that it referred to some important operation by the High Seas Fleet. At once the familiar routine for concentrating the Grand Fleet at sea was begun. From Scapa, Invergordon and Rosyth the long lines of battleships battle-cruisers, cruisers and destroyers streamed seaward on the evening of 30th May, and vanished into the deepening dusk, while the High Seas Fleet still lay raising steam and preparing to sail at midnight.

Had Scheer's carefully placed submarine patrols achieved their object in sighting and reporting the various sections of the Grand Fleet as they hurried seaward, he would no doubt have changed his plans, and the great battle which was about to take place might have been indefinitely postponed. In fact, however, only small isolated squadrons were sighted. The U-boats' reports failed to show that the whole Grand Fleet was at sea, and so Scheer's plans went ahead unaltered.

The British fleet which was moving towards its assigned rendezvous for the following afternoon was the greatest concentration of naval power the world had ever seen. (Appendix A.) In the Battle Fleet which sailed from Scapa and Invergordon were twenty-four dreadnought battleships, three battle-cruisers, eight armoured cruisers, twelve light cruisers and fifty-one destroyers. From Rosyth, forming Sir David Beatty's Battle-Cruiser Fleet, went out six battle-cruisers, four dreadnought battleships, thirteen light cruisers, twenty-eight destroyers and a seaplane carrier. When formed in single line, the battleships of the Battle Fleet alone would cover some ten miles, the last ship of the line being on the horizon from the leading ship.

Such a force obviously had to have some compact form of

order in which to cruise, and in fact the battle squadrons normally steamed in six columns of four ships each, the columns disposed abreast of each other. Battle formation, on the other hand, could be nothing else but single line. There must therefore be a quick and simple method (or methods) whereby the cruising formation could be changed to fighting order, the "deployment" as it was commonly called. It was the cruising formation that the two sections of the Battle Fleet, from Scapa and from Invergordon, took up when they met at daylight on the 31st. They then continued on a south-easterly course to the afternoon rendezvous fixed with the Battle-Cruiser Fleet, converging on their course from farther south.

Meanwhile at 1 o'clock on the morning of 31st May, the ships of Hipper's Scouting Groups had weighed anchor and started up the swept channels out of the Schillig Roads, in blissful ignorance that the British Fleet was at sea. Following them came the main body of the High Seas Fleet. Normally every move they made would have been known to the Admiralty from the reports of the direction-finding radio stations. But, inexplicably, the operators were on this occasion misled by a simple device, not even intended to be a ruse, which transferred the German Commander-in-Chief's call sign from the Fleet Flagship, *Friedrich der Grosse*, to the shore wireless station, so that he would not be distracted by administrative signals while at sea. Until long after she had actually sailed, they therefore reported that the flagship was still in the Schillig Roads.

Jellicoe, so informed, continued to make his unhurried way towards the rendezvous with Beatty. On account of numerous delays while ships and fishing-boats encountered were examined, he was more than an hour behind schedule at 2 p.m., the time set for his rendezvous with Beatty. The battle-cruiser commander, similarly ignorant that the enemy was at sea, had sighted nothing by that time, and at 2.15 had turned northward to meet his Commander-in-Chief, another fruitless sweep apparently completed.

Beyond the horizon to the eastward of him on a slightly

converging course, Hipper's force of five battle-cruisers *Lützow* (flagship), *Derfflinger*, *Seydlitz*, *Moltke* and *Von der Tann*, and the Second Scouting Group of Light-Cruisers under Rear-Admiral Boedicker, *Frankfurt* (flagship), *Wiesbaden*, *Pillau* and *Elbing* with three flotillas of destroyers led by Commodore Heinrich in the light cruiser *Regensburg*, were also moving northward. If nothing happened to deflect them they would soon fall into the waiting, albeit unexpectant, arms of Jellicoe's Battle Fleet.

But something did. A small and peaceful Danish steamer, the *N. J. Fjord*, became the innocent cause of contact between the two battle-cruiser forces. Her smoke, rising high into the calm clear summer air, was sighted simultaneously by the light cruiser *Galatea*, flagship of Commodore Alexander-Sinclair, commanding the 1st Light Cruiser Squadron of Beatty's force, and by the left-wing ship of Hipper's scouting line, the light cruiser *Elbing*. Both turned to investigate. Each saw coming over the distant horizon, the unmistakable masts and funnels of a warship. A brief scrutiny and the signal "Enemy in Sight" was going out on the radio. At 2.28 p.m. the first shots flashed out as *Galatea* opened fire on the *Elbing*. They were the first of a long day's fighting packed with tragedy, drama and heroism which was to be called the Battle of Jutland by the Allies, and the Battle of Skagerrak by the Germans.

As the warning signal reached the two battle-cruiser force commanders, both turned inwards at high speed to support their light forces. Neither yet realised that enemy capital ships were present. It was a surprise for each, therefore, when at 3.20 black smoke which had been staining the horizon resolved itself into the unmistakable masts and funnels of battle-cruisers. The old enemies, Beatty and Hipper, were facing each other again, and this time both sides were ready to stay and fight it out.

Each thought the other was acting unsupported, and each acted so as to try to deliver the other in the hands of his own battle fleet—Beatty by steering to cut Hipper off from his line of retreat and to hold him until Jellicoe, just over the horizon to the north as he believed, could arrive on the scene; Hipper by turning back towards Scheer, still out of sight to the south, trying to lure Beatty into the arms of the German battle squadrons.

By turning southward Hipper foiled Beatty's plan, and the British admiral was forced to accept action on that course which was taking him away from the Grand Fleet. The impetuosity which was a marked characteristic of David Beatty had led him to lead off with his battle-cruisers at headlong speed without waiting for the 5th Battle Squadron of four *Queen Elizabeths* under Rear-Admiral Evan-Thomas which had been expressly given him to provide him with an overwhelming force for just such an occasion. Thus when action was joined, Beatty, with the *Lion* (flagship), *Princess Royal*, *Queen Mary*, *Tiger*, *New Zealand* and *Indefatigable* found himself with a superiority of one ship only over Hipper's battle-cruisers, while Evan-Thomas and his splendid ships *Barham* (flagship), *Valiant*, *Warspite* and *Malaya*, each mounting eight 15-inch guns, were pounding along 10 miles behind at their utmost speed of 25 knots, trying in vain to join the fight.

Had Beatty's ships been equal in material and training to the enemy's, this might have been sufficient to give him victory; but first of all the British battle-cruisers' gunnery and then their ability to take punishment proved inferior, with adverse results.

As the opposing squadrons turned southward on to parallel courses at 25 knots, and at 3.48 opened fire at a range of 16,500 yards, the British shells were falling as much as a mile beyond the enemy, the range having been grossly over-estimated. The Germans, on the other hand, quickly found the range, and three minutes after opening fire *Lion*, *Princess Royal* and *Tiger* had all been heavily hit. Not until 3.55, when the range was down to 12,900 yards, was a German ship hit. Then it was the *Queen Mary*, champion gunnery ship of the fleet, which sent two shells crashing home on the *Seydlitz*. For the second time in her career one of her barbettes was pierced, and a cordite fire started which burnt the handing room crew to death. The safety arrangements installed after Dogger Bank localised the fire, but the magazines had to be flooded and the turret was put out of action.

Meanwhile Beatty's ships had been repeatedly hit, *Princess*

Royal having her foremost turret put out of action and *Tiger*'s fire control system being destroyed. Except for the *Queen Mary*, which, having shifted her fire to the *Derfflinger*, second ship of Hipper's line, scored a hit at 3.58, the British fire had continued to be remarkably ineffective. About 4 o'clock both flagships were hit almost simultaneously. The *Lützow* escaped vital damage, but the *Lion* was hit on her midship turret, the shell plunging through the armoured wall and bursting in the gun house killing or wounding every man of the turret crew.

In the control officer's cabinet at the rear of the turret, Major F. J. W. Harvey of the Royal Marine Light Infantry, with both legs shattered and dying of his wounds, saw fire raging amongst the cordite, which must soon reach the magazines and blow the ship asunder. Somehow he got the order through to flood the magazines, and so saved the ship from certain destruction, an act which earned his memory the award of the Victoria Cross.

Damage to the *Lion* was heavy and mounting, fires raging and compartments flooded. To gain a respite Beatty led outwards a few degrees to increase the range; but at this moment tragedy struck the rear of his line, where *Indefatigable* had been exchanging fire with Hipper's rear ship, the *Von der Tann*. The British ship was hit by three heavy shells which plunged downwards through her armour into her vitals. Enveloped in smoke and flame, she struggled out of the line, sinking by the stern. Then as another salvo struck her, there was a violent explosion and the huge ship capsized and sank, carrying with her all but two of her company of 1,017 officers and men.

By now Beatty's situation was serious. All his ships were considerably damaged, while Hipper's were comparatively unharmed: and all the while the battle was rushing at headlong speed towards the approaching German battle fleet, still just out of sight over the horizon. But now at last relief began to come to the hard-pressed British ships as the 5th Battle Squadron, running through the pall of smoke left by the speeding battle-cruisers, came into sight and range of the enemy. The great 15-inch guns thundered into action. Unlike the battle-cruisers, the battleships found the

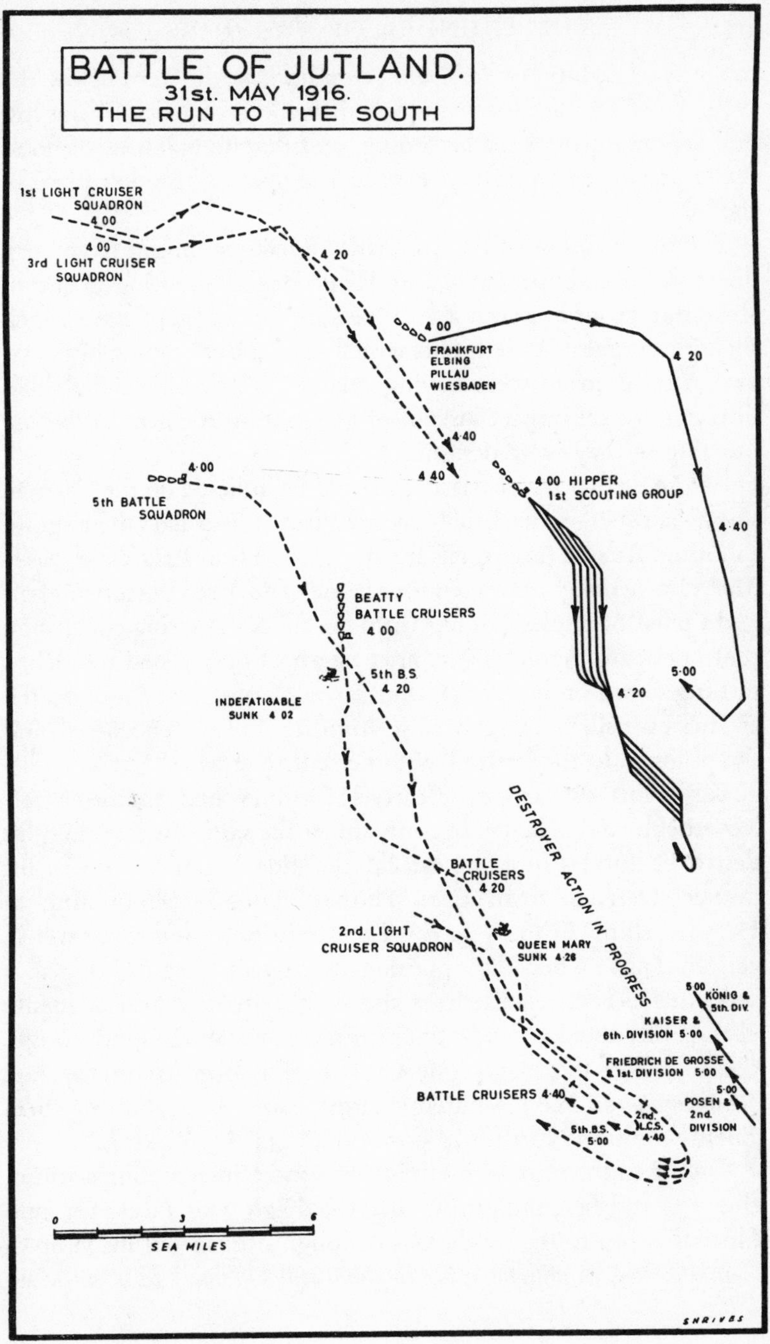
BATTLE OF JUTLAND.
31st. MAY 1916.
THE RUN TO THE SOUTH
1st LIGHT CRUISER SQUADRON
4 00
4 00
3rd LIGHT CRUISER SQUADRON
4 20
4 00
FRANKFURT
ELBING
PILLAU
WIESBADEN
4 20
4·40
4 40
4·00
5th BATTLE SQUADRON
4 00 HIPPER
1st SCOUTING GROUP
4·40
BEATTY
BATTLE CRUISERS
4 00
5th B.S.
4 20
INDEFATIGABLE
SUNK 4 02
4·20
5·00
DESTROYER ACTION IN PROGRESS
BATTLE CRUISERS
4 20
2nd. LIGHT CRUISER SQUADRON
QUEEN MARY
SUNK 4·26
5·00
KÖNIG &
5th. DIV.
KAISER &
6th. DIVISION 5·00
FRIEDRICH DE GROSSE
& 1st. DIVISION 5·00
5·00
POSEN &
2nd.
DIVISION
BATTLE CRUISERS 4·40
2nd.
L.C.S.
4·40
5th.B.S.
5·00
0
3
6
SEA MILES
SHRIVES

range at once, the *Von der Tann* being hit near the stern below the water-line. Though she was nearly driven out of action by this hit, emergency repairs kept her going, and despite 600 tons of flood water aboard and a distinct list she was able to keep her place in the line.

The intervention of the 5th Battle Squadron might have been disastrous for Hipper, as the excellent British shooting began to score numerous hits. But a weakness in the design of the 15-inch shells now revealed itself. Hits which should have caused heavy or even vital damage were having relatively little effect, the shells breaking up on impact instead of penetrating the armour before bursting as they were designed to do.

Before further serious damage could be inflicted on the German ships, another remarkable success had rewarded their good shooting. At 4.26 three shells from a salvo of four struck the *Queen Mary*. Immediately a tremendous flame of dark red burst from her, and a pillar of smoke shot high into the air. A shattering concussion rent her apart. As the *Tiger*, next astern of her, passed by, débris rattling down on her decks, the *Queen Mary*'s stern rose into the air, her propellers still revolving. Another explosion occurred, and she plunged to the bottom with her entire crew of 1,266.

With this catastrophe Beatty's fortunes had reached their lowest ebb, and as he held grimly on, at the same time sending his destroyer flotillas into the attack, the tide began to turn in his favour. Damage from Evan-Thomas' guns was mounting in Hipper's ships. In the *Von der Tann* only two guns were still in action. Then, while the opposing destroyers were fighting in a wild mêlée between the lines the whole situation was suddenly changed by the dramatic signal from Commodore Goodenough, commanding the 2nd Light Cruiser Squadron in his flagship, *Southampton*: "Have sighted enemy battle fleet, bearing S.E. Enemy's course North. My position 56° 34′ N, 6° 20′ E."

Owing to the mistake by the British radio interception stations, this was the first indication that the High Seas Fleet was out. Since the turn to the south, Goodenough's squadron, made up of *Southampton*, *Birmingham*, *Nottingham* and *Dublin*, had been doing its utmost to get ahead of the battle-cruisers to scout ahead, as was its duty. By 4.33 Goodenough had only succeeded in getting 2 miles ahead, and at that moment the topmasts of battleships hove into sight over the southern horizon.

Pressing on to get fuller information he had got within 13,000 yards without being fired at, since the enemy ships were unable to identify him as he approached them head-on: and now he could see that it was indeed the High Seas Fleet ahead of him, the tall ships stretching away in an interminable line to the far horizon. He had seen enough—and indeed more than was safe, for as he swung away to get out of range his four funnels were seen in silhouette. The great guns of the leading squadron of dreadnoughts opened fire, and as the four cruisers sped away, zig-zagging and weaving, the sea all around them spurted white columns of water. Fortunately they were able to get away unscathed.

It was time for Beatty, too, to retire. Recalling his destroyers, he led round 180 degrees on to a north-westerly course to fall back on the Grand Fleet, still far to the north but hurrying forward at 19 knots. The destroyers had fought a fierce drawn fight with their opposite numbers as the flotillas on each side leapt forward to deliver torpedo attacks on the big ships. Two boats on either side had been sunk but no torpedoes had found their mark until, as the British boats turned to obey the recall, the *Petard* sent her last two streaking for the enemy line, one of them hitting and severely damaging the *Seydlitz*. But so stout was the construction of the German ship that she was not put out of action, and continued in her place in the line.

While Beatty's battle-cruisers were turning northward in succession, a dangerous manœuvre when in gun range of a powerful enemy, Evan-Thomas continued southwards, engaging Hipper's ships and covering his chief's retirement. As the two British squadrons swept by on opposite courses, Beatty signalled for the 5th Battle Squadron to follow his example and turn back in succession. As soon as he had passed clear, Evan-Thomas complied. It was a serious tactical mistake on Beatty's part. If detailed manœuvring orders had to be given to a subordinate squadron at all, the wise signal would have been to order a turn about together, which would put all the ships on to their retirement course in a quarter the time taken by a turn in succession. During the precious minutes wasted the van of the German battle squadrons had time to draw abreast of the 5th Battle Squadron and concentrate their gunfire on the turning-point.

As each ship swung ponderously round in the wake of the next ahead, it plunged into a veritable forest of shell splashes. The *Barham* and *Valiant* were both hit and suffered casualties, but serious damage was somehow avoided. As the *Malaya*, the rear ship of the squadron, reached the turning-point, salvoes fell around her at ten-second intervals. A 12-inch shell burst in her starboard 6-inch battery, setting the ready-use ammunition ablaze and causing more than a hundred casualties. Another hit the roof of one of her after turrets, but the stout armour kept it out and it did no serious damage. When her seemingly interminable ordeal was over and she steadied her course in the wake of the squadron, *Malaya* miraculously emerged with her main armament undamaged and speed unimpaired.

Now the 5th Battle Squadron was able to get a measure of revenge. As it steamed northwards *Barham* and *Valiant* engaged, Hipper's battle-cruisers, scoring hits on *Lützow* and *Derfflinger* and heavily damaging the *Seydlitz*. Hipper's men, who had been somewhat contemptuous of the British battle-cruisers' gunnery, paid a grim tribute to that of Evan-Thomas' ships. *Warspite* and *Malaya* meanwhile engaged the leading German battleships and, in spite of the increasingly difficult light, got hits home on to the *Grosser Kurfürst* and *Markgraf*.

With their superior speed, however, the British ships gradually drew away from and out of range of Scheer's battle squadrons, though they were still able to obtain occasional glimpses of Hipper's ships—during which they did further damage to them, particularly to *Lützow* and *Seydlitz*, which were by now suffering heavily. In the *Von der Tann* the last remaining turret now went out of action for a time, due to a mechanical breakdown. Only the *Moltke* remained comparatively undamaged.

Scheer knew nothing of the parlous condition of Hipper's battle-cruisers. All he could see was a detached British squadron apparently fleeing before him, the situation he had dreamed of. To the yard-arm of the *Friedrich der Grosse* sped the signal for "General Chase", the rigid formation of the line gradually dissolving as each ship pressed forward at her utmost speed. As the great concourse of ships steamed northwards, Beatty's ships, by now out of range of any of the enemy, had respite to repair damage and in the *Lion* it was possible to deal with the numerous fires which until then had never been mastered. The battle-cruisers must be ready to play their part when the Grand Fleet hove in sight. As they drew away, they altered course gradually more easterly across the path of the German battle-cruisers so as to be able not only to cross their "T" and bring concentrated fire on their van, but also to press them away to prevent them from sighting and reporting the Grand Fleet, so prematurely springing the gigantic trap that was awaiting the High Seas Fleet.

* * *

Only one actor remained to complete the cast of this gigantic drama—Jellicoe, with his huge phalanx of battleships, still in cruising order and coming south-eastwards at his best speed. But though he was in the wings, he was an actor lacking a script. Except for Goodenough's report, not a word had reached him of the progress of the battle-cruiser action since it had developed on a southerly course. At 4.17, anxious for news, he had signalled to Evan-Thomas: "Are you in company with S.O. Battle-cruiser Fleet?" He received the wholly inadequate reply "Yes. I am engaging the enemy."

A little earlier the Admiralty had at last realised its mistake with regard to the enemy's wireless callsigns, and at 4.9 Jellicoe had been given the accurate position, course and speed of the High Seas Fleet. Even so this did not give him what he most wanted to know, the relative position of the two fleets, because after a night and a day of zig-zag steaming his own position was some four miles farther on than he thought. Until he knew with certainty the bearing on which the enemy would be met, he could not make the vital decision as to how to deploy into battle line. Nor, until he knew how far ahead of him they were could he know when to begin the complicated manœuvre.

If ordered on the wrong wing of his cruising formation, the deployment could expose him to having his "T" crossed and his van subjected to the concentrated fire of the whole enemy line. If ordered too late, the enemy might come on him in the middle of the lengthy manœuvre, many of his ships masked and unable to fire. Either could spell disaster.

As the afternoon had worn on, the clear air of midday had steadily thickened with the misty haze so common in the North Sea. Visibility had fallen until at times it was only five or six miles. In the area of the battle-cruiser action, drifting banks of smoke from funnels, guns and burning ships were making it even less. The enemy would, therefore, be already within gun range when sighted. It was vital to have completed the deployment before that happened.

Unfortunately the subordinate commanders in the British fleet had little idea of the over-riding importance of keeping the Commander-in-Chief informed of the situation—except for Commodore Goodenough, and even he threw doubt on the accuracy of his scouting reports when at 5.50 p.m. he reported the German battle-cruisers to be south-west of their battle squadrons, a palpable impossibility. He had in fact given the reciprocal of the proper bearing, Hipper being to the north-eastwards of Scheer at that time.

With his flagship severely knocked about and his wireless equipment destroyed, Beatty might have delegated the responsibility of making enemy reports to either Rear-Admiral Brock in the *Princess Royal* or Rear-Admiral Pakenham in the *New Zealand*. Either of them or Evan-Thomas might have used their initiative in the matter. Furthermore Beatty had with him two other light-cruiser squadrons besides Goodenough's, but neither of them deemed it their duty to keep touch with and report the movements of the High Seas Fleet.

So Jellicoe came on into the ever-gathering murk, starved of the information so critically needed. Eight miles ahead of his formation of battleships was a scouting line of eight armoured cruisers, two squadrons commanded by Rear-Admiral Arbuthnot in the *Defence* and Rear-Admiral Heath in the *Minotaur*. They might be able to give the information needed in time, but it would be a close thing. Some 20 miles ahead was the 3rd Squadron of battle-cruisers under Rear-Admiral Hood, *Invincible* (flagship), *Indomitable* and *Inflexible*. But having been sent off to the eastwards at the first alarm to interpose themselves between the enemy and an escape route through the Skagerrak, and then, when the fight had turned south, sent on at their best speed to support Beatty, they were actually too far to the eastward to be between Jellicoe and Scheer.

* * *

As Beatty had drawn ahead he had gradually edged round on to a north-north-easterly course across Hipper's line of advance. The respite had enabled the British ships to make hasty repairs and again prepare for battle, and Beatty now signalled "Prepare to renew the action."

Hipper for his part was by no means anxious to renew action with Beatty, though he had dutifully taken up his battle station ahead of Scheer's battle squadrons. His ships had suffered heavily from the 15-inch guns of the 5th Battle Squadron. He had certainly done his share by defeating the superior strength of the British battle-cruisers earlier on. There was a limit as to what could be expected of him. Furthermore the deteriorating visibility was worst in a north-westerly direction which Beatty now bore from him. But Scheer's order for "General Chase" left Hipper no alternative, and he altered course for the enemy.

Thus at 5.40, from the south-east, Hipper's ships came once again into view of Beatty's battle-cruisers at a range of 14,000 yards, and at somewhat longer range of the leading ships of the 5th Battle Squadron. Unable to see anything of their enemy except the orange flash of their guns, the German battle-cruisers came under a punishing fire. The *Derfflinger* was hit forward and began to sink by the head. Only by closing all watertight doors and openings and abandoning the fore part of the ship was she kept afloat. The *Seydlitz*, too, which had already suffered heavily from shell hits as well as the *Petard*'s torpedo, was further damaged and set on fire.

Unable to withstand such a hammering, Hipper bore away eastward, and Beatty turned to a parallel course to keep with him. The Grand Fleet was getting near now, and Beatty's new course was taking him right across its front. The boom and thud of the guns could be heard from the battleships. Excitement grew intense; but still Jellicoe lacked the information on which to base his deployment. At last at 5.50, the *Marlborough*, flagship of Vice-Admiral Sir Cecil Burney, commanding the 1st Battle Squadron and leading the starboard wing column, signalled gun flashes in sight ahead.

Jellicoe in the *Iron Duke*, leading the left hand of the two centre columns, could see nothing. Frantic for information, he signalled to Burney "What can you see?" to get the startling news that Beatty's ships were in sight ahead, steering across the front. By reckoning, they should still have been 11 miles farther to the south-eastwards. If it were they who had been heard firing, it meant that there was not a moment to be lost in starting the deployment. Yet he still had no information as to the position of the enemy's battle fleet. Grimly he held on until he could find out.

At 5.56 the *Lion* at last came in sight from the fleet flagship, and a message was at once flashed: "Where is the enemy's battle fleet?" Unfortunately Beatty did not know. In his race northward it had soon faded out of sight. All he could reply was "Enemy's battle-cruisers bearing south-west." Again from the *Iron Duke* came the urgent call "Where is the enemy's battle fleet?"

Outwardly impassive but inwardly seething, the little Admiral, on whose shoulders the responsibility for the great decision lay, waited and prayed for enlightenment. And at this moment the *Lion*'s searchlight began again to wink: "Have sighted enemy battle fleet bearing south-west."

At last Jellicoe could make the vital decision. A string of flags ran up to the *Iron Duke*'s yard-arm. Deployment was to be on the port-wing column on a course of south-east by south. The port-wing column led off on the course ordered, while the leading ships of the other columns swung together 90 degrees to port and were followed round by the ships of their respective columns until the whole great fleet was in single line forming a huge inverted "L" as it followed the port-wing column round on to the course ordered.

After all the puzzlement, anxiety and frustration, Jellicoe had shown himself a master of manœuvre by bringing off a perfect deployment in the nick of time, for into the two arms of the great "L" Scheer was pressing on in chase of Beatty, all unaware of the trap awaiting him. As the last of Jellicoe's ships were turning into line, the van of the High Seas Fleet loomed in sight of Jellicoe's rear division. It was a terrible moment for Scheer. With no warning whatever he suddenly found himself faced by an endless line of dreadnoughts vanishing into the mists, his own ships, somewhat disorganised after their long chase, steaming ponderously forward to destruction. Only a miracle, aided by superb tactics and perfect fighting discipline, could save the High Seas Fleet now,

* * *

While this tremendous drama was being played out, one last section of the great battle scene was being assembled at the other end of the stage. Here Hood's 3rd Battle-Cruiser Squadron, similarly ignorant of the position of the enemy and pressing on southwards to join Beatty, was so far to the eastward that it would have swept on without contact but for an encounter by Hood's attached light-cruiser *Chester*, which had been stationed 5 miles on his starboard beam as a scout.

At about 5.30, Captain Lawson of the *Chester* came within

sound of the guns of Hipper's battle-cruisers. He at once turned to investigate, only to run foul of Rear-Admiral Boedicker's 2nd Scouting Group, *Frankfurt*, *Wiesbaden*, *Pillau* and *Elbing*, which emerged from the haze at a range of little more than 6,000 yards. The *Chester* turned to escape but was caught in the greatly superior fire of the four German ships, and was badly damaged, with many casualties, before she could get out of range.

Hearing the gunfire, Hood swung his ships round to a north-westerly course and soon saw the *Chester* crossing ahead, surrounded by shell splashes. Then at 8,000 yards the German cruisers came into sight, and Hood's 12-inch guns came into action. Though Boedicker at once turned away under a smoke-screen, the *Wiesbaden* was reduced to a smoking wreck and the *Pillau*, with a 12-inch shell in her boiler-room, had four of her boilers out of action, a fire raging in her stokeholds and her speed reduced to 24 knots.

The unexpected thunder of big guns from a direction in which no British ships were thought to be, led Boedicker to think that it was the battle fleet which he had encountered. Commodore Heinrich, leading the destroyers of the scouting group thought likewise, and sent his boats into the attack. Met by the four destroyers of Hood's screen, they were however prevented from doing any damage, and the few torpedoes which they fired were ineffective. Hood meanwhile turned back and placed himself in his battle station ahead of Jellicoe's battle squadrons.

The two fleets were at last thus poised in their entirety for the great encounter. As they clashed, the Germans were to achieve their last major successes before the advantage finally passed to the immeasurably more powerful British fleet.

At the deployment, the cruisers of Arbuthnot's squadron, *Defence*, *Warrior* and *Black Prince*, which had been ahead, were left between the two fleets. Here they came upon the disabled *Wiesbaden*, and had just opened fire on her when out of the mist and smoke to the southward loomed Hipper's battle-cruisers. With no other target in sight at the time, they were able to concentrate their guns on the British cruisers with fearful effect.

All three were at once heavily damaged and turned to escape. But in the *Defence*, the old defect of exposed ammunition led to outbreaks of uncontrollable fires. Suddenly she blew up, leaving only a cloud of black smoke on the surface to mark her passing. The *Warrior*, also burning, and the *Black Prince* struggled away in different directions, the former shrouded in smoke, heading towards the 5th Battle Squadron which was about to take station in the rear of the battle line.

In order to do so, the *Barham* had led the squadron, still in action with the German battleships of the van, round to port—away from the enemy's line. As the *Warspite* reached the turning-point, her wheel, put to starboard to check her swing, suddenly jammed. Full in sight of the enemy fleet she swerved out of the line towards the enemy. Her commanding officer, Captain Philpotts, tried to bring her back into the line by use of her engines against the pull of the jammed rudder, but all that was achieved was to send her driving straight for the enemy—who promptly concentrated their fire on this easy and important target.

Unable to bring his ship back to port, Captain Philpotts had no alternative but to let her circle until his engineers had managed to restore some degree of steering control. As she did so she was hit over and over again, so that when at last she managed to settle on an escape course her damage was so extensive that she was ordered back to harbour. *Warspite*'s misfortune, however, was *Warrior*'s saving, as the cannonade which had followed her as she steamed away and which bid fair to destroy her had been transferred to the more valuable target. She was able to get away, though her accumulated damage was such that she had to be abandoned the following day.

By now the ships of the British battle line were coming into action, and both Hipper's battle-cruisers and Scheer's leading battleships were being hit. As out of the haze the orange flash of big guns was seen for mile on mile ahead of him, Scheer began to realise the desperate situation he was in, and he prepared to do his best to extricate himself.

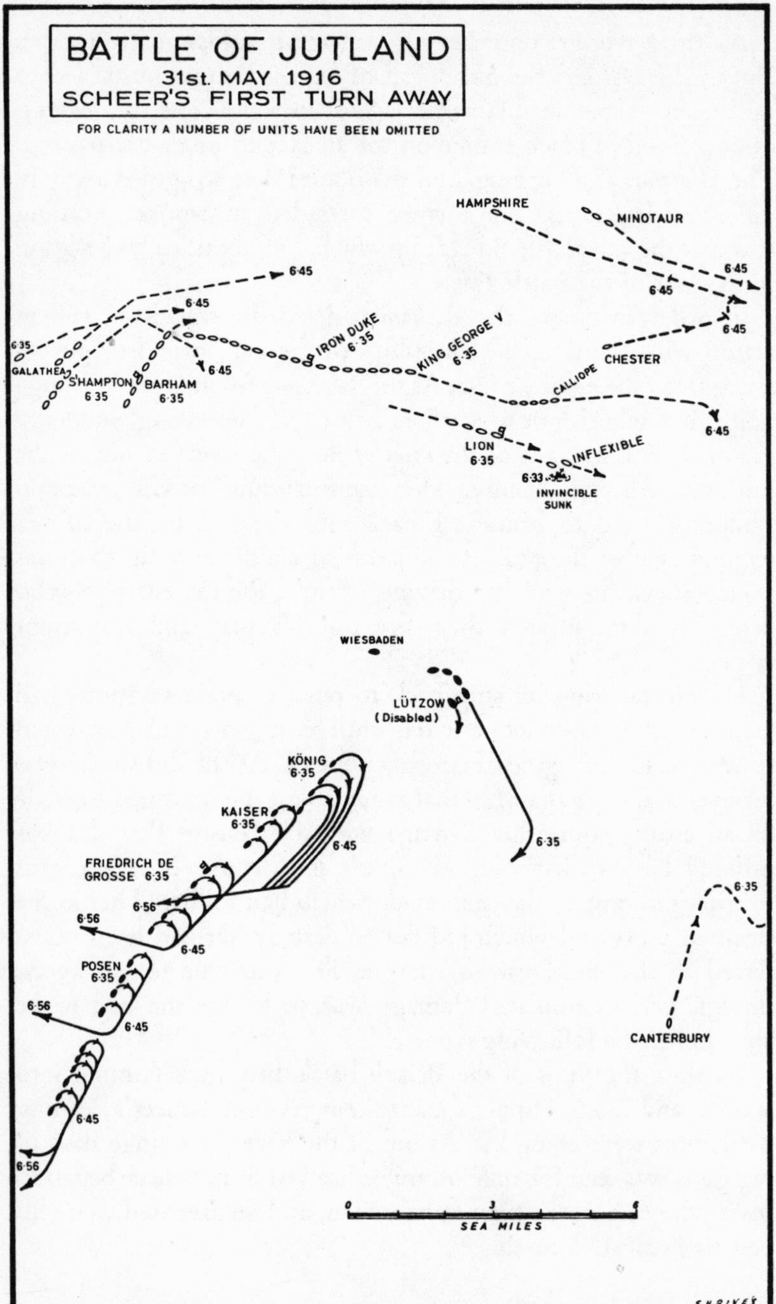
BATTLE OF JUTLAND
31st. MAY 1916
SCHEER'S FIRST TURN AWAY
FOR CLARITY A NUMBER OF UNITS HAVE BEEN OMITTED
HAMPSHIRE
MINOTAUR
6·45
6·45
6·45
6·45
6·45
6·35
GALATHEA
S'HAMPTON
6·35
BARHAM
6·35
6·45
IRON DUKE
6·35
KING GEORGE V
6·35
CALLIOPE
CHESTER
6·45
LION
6·35
INFLEXIBLE
6·33
INVINCIBLE
SUNK
WIESBADEN
LÜTZOW
(Disabled)
KÖNIG
6·35
KAISER
6·35
6·45
6·35
FRIEDRICH DE
GROSSE 6·35
6·56
6·56
6·45
POSEN
6·35
6·56
6·45
6·45
6·56
6·35
CANTERBURY
0
3
6
SEA MILES
SHRIVES

Before this was to come about yet another catastrophe was to occur to a British battle-cruiser, demonstrating once again the superiority of the German ship-design, at least so far as taking punishment was concerned. Hood's three ships at the head of the British line had crossed the "T" of Hipper's battle-cruisers at the comparatively short range of 10,000 yards, and were pouring an accurate and destructive fire into them. Hipper was forced to turn away on a parallel course and turn his guns on Hood's squadron. A fierce duel developed between the two squadrons, with *Lützow* and *Derfflinger* concentrating on Hood's flagship *Invincible*.

Standing out on the open bridge, Hood was delightedly watching the excellent shooting his gunnery officer was making as the 12-inch guns crashed out in rapid salvoes. "Keep at it as quickly as you can", he called up the voice-pipe to the spotting top. "Every shot is telling."

Hardly had he spoken when a salvo fell full on the *Invincible*, and a violent explosion tore her in half. By the time her two consorts swept by, only her bow and stern standing up out of the water remained. The gunnery officer and three ratings were all who survived.

Despite this instant destruction of a splendid vessel, a feat beyond all Hipper's reasonable expectations in view of the battered condition of the German ships, it was not sufficient to relieve Scheer's desperate situation. The pressure on his van was steadily bending back his line in a great bow. It would dissolve into chaos soon unless he did something about it. And now the incessant tactical exercises which Scheer had inflicted on his fleet since taking the command were to prove their worth.

The signal was hoisted for the Battle Turn Away, a simultaneous turn of 180 degrees by every ship of the long battle line.

13

Escape of the High Seas Fleet

As the signal fluttered down from the yard-arm of the *Friedrich der Grosse* and the German battleships began their simultaneous turn away, destroyers streaked across between them and the Grand Fleet laying a screen of black oily smoke, still further increasing the fog of battle. The British battleships, which had just settled down to make steady and accurate shooting, found that their targets had faded out of sight. The noise of guns died away.

From the *Iron Duke* the enemy's turn away could not be seen. All that Jellicoe knew was that the Germans had vanished to the westward in the increasing murk and thickness. Had he now turned his fleet by divisions in pursuit the battle would no doubt have developed into a pell-mell chase. But in Jellicoe's mind was an over-riding consideration—the danger of the torpedo.

Twelve years before, in the Russo-Japanese War, the torpedo had come into prominence but had had a surprising lack of success. Since then the weapon had increased greatly in range and explosive power. Every warship was equipped with torpedoes, fired either from tubes on deck which could be trained over the side, or, in capital ships, from fixed tubes in a torpedo compartment below the water-line. These latter were looked on as particularly sinister and menacing weapons, for unlike the upper-deck torpedoes of destroyers and cruisers, there was no way of knowing when they had been launched.

To use them, the firing ship had to be in a position of torpedo advantage, that is to say before the beam of its target, otherwise the torpedo would be given a stern chase and would reach the end of its run before overtaking the target. Thus it was a fleet being chased that would be able to resort to the torpedo. Jellicoe had always believed that the German fleet, inferior in strength, would manœuvre so as to gain such a position, deliberately turning away to do so. Furthermore he thought they might also carry mines, and would lay them in the path of the Grand Fleet.

In the absence of any information from his scouting forces—and except for Commodore Goodenough, he was badly served in this respect throughout the battle—Jellicoe had no idea that Scheer's turn-away had been so drastic. At first, therefore, he himself made only a moderate alteration of course, to south. When this brought no renewal of contact he ordered a further turn of 34 degrees, and steered to probe into the murk for the enemy.

Meanwhile Scheer, though greatly relieved at the success of his turn away, had come to realise that he had been badly out-manœuvred. The Grand Fleet lay in overwhelming numbers between him and his base, a situation which he had wished to avoid at all costs. Somehow he had to get to the eastward of the enemy and gain a clear route to the Horn's Reef Light, the entrance to his own protected waters. His only hope was to get away across the Grand Fleet's rear. He therefore ordered a second 180 degree turn by his whole line, and headed north-eastward again.

In his memoirs, Scheer later described this as a deliberate attack on the enemy's centre, "regardless of consequences", but it is hard to believe that he would have willingly taken so suicidal a step. It is more reasonable to believe that he had not yet fully realised the extent of the great arc extended by the Grand Fleet, effectually cutting off his retreat.

Warned by Goodenough, who had made another of his skilful reconnaissances, Jellicoe altered course back to south and waited for the Germans to appear. A few minutes after 7 p.m. they were in sight, and once again the whole British line opened up with their guns, pouring in a destructive fire. Hipper's battle-cruisers, still in the van, took the brunt of it, the leading German battleships, *König* and *Grosser Kürfurst*, also suffering.

Hipper himself had by now been forced to abandon his flagship *Lützow*, which was withdrawing from action in a desperate condition, screened by destroyers. Embarking in a destroyer, he was waiting for a lull in the action to transfer his flag to another of his ships. Meanwhile command of the battle-cruisers had devolved upon Captain Hartog of the *Derfflinger*.

The awe-inspiring sight of the eastern horizon lined with the rippling flash of battleships' guns concentrating on the head of his line was enough to show to Scheer that he had run into a deadly trap. Instant, emergency action was necessary to extricate himself. Though his line was in much confusion, ships bunching up on each other and some having to stop or go astern to avoid collision with the next ahead, he had no alternative but to order yet again the *Gefechtskehrtwendung* or Battle Turn Away.

This was not enough to hold off the enemy while he escaped. The battle-cruisers which had fought so splendidly must now, if necessary, be sacrificed. "Battle-cruisers at the Enemy. Charge!" went out his order. Without a moment's hesitation Captain Hartog turned his four remaining ships together, low in the water, battered and weary, on what was subsequently to be known as their "Death Ride".

That it would have meant their destruction can hardly be doubted, had it not been that at the same time the German destroyers were sent into attack with torpedoes. Two groups of destroyers, one of four boats and one of nine, came leaping out of the smoke pall to be greeted by the massed fire of a hundred or more guns from the secondary armament of the British battleships. Several were hit and two sunk. So thick were the shell splashes around them all that they had difficulty in selecting targets; nevertheless twenty-eight torpedoes in all were launched.

Here at last was the massed torpedo attack, means to counter which had been studied long and earnestly by the British Staff. Investigations on the tactical board had made it clear that there were only two possible ways of neutralising such an attack—by turning directly towards the destroyers at the moment of firing so as to "comb the tracks", or to turn away sufficiently so as to run beyond the range of the torpedoes.

The turn towards had the disadvantage that out of a line of

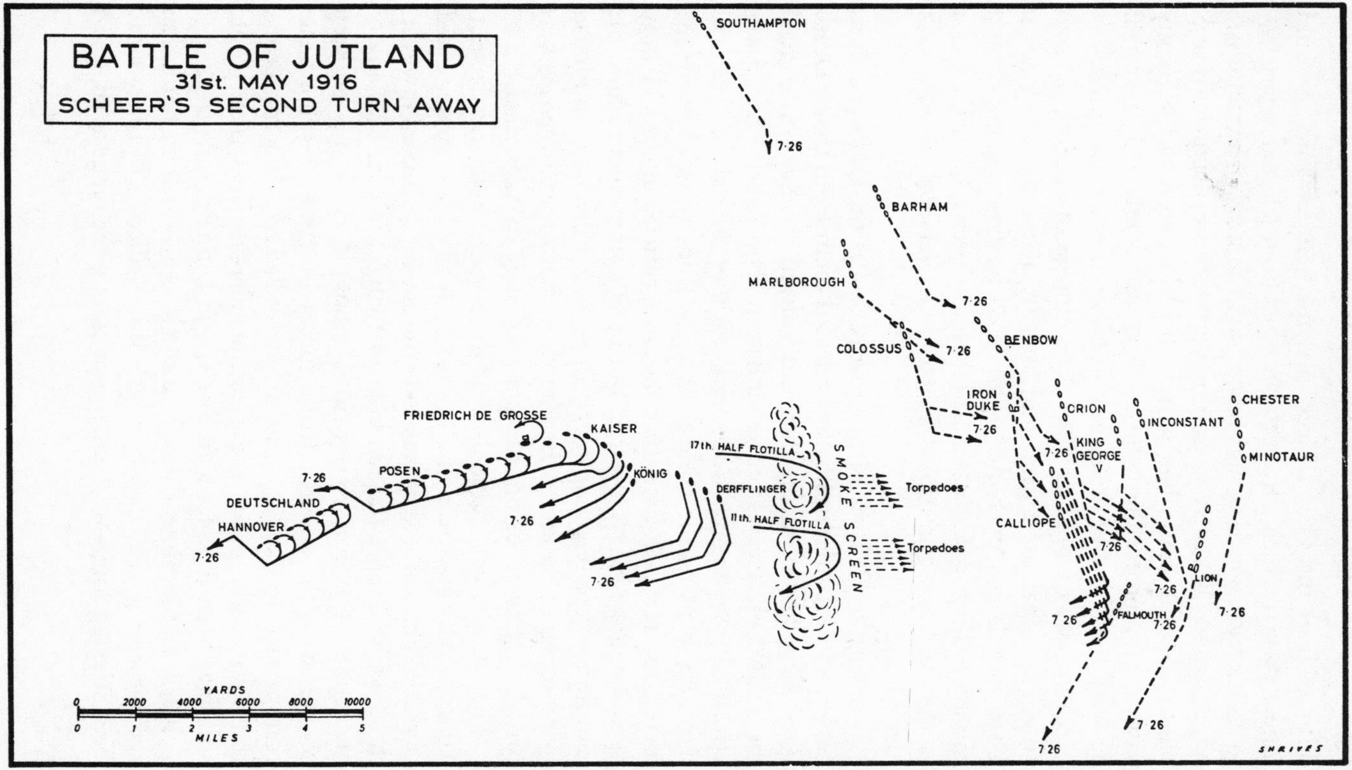
BATTLE OF JUTLAND
31st. MAY 1916
SCHEER'S SECOND TURN AWAY
SOUTHAMPTON
BARHAM
MARLBOROUGH
COLOSSUS
BENBOW
IRON DUKE
CRION
KING GEORGE V
INCONSTANT
CHESTER
MINOTAUR
CALLIOPE
LION
FALMOUTH
FRIEDRICH DE GROSSE
KAISER
KÖNIG
POSEN
DEUTSCHLAND
HANNOVER
17th. HALF FLOTILLA
DERFFLINGER
11th. HALF FLOTILLA
SMOKE SCREEN
Torpedoes
Torpedoes
7·26
YARDS
0 2000 4000 6000 8000 10000
0 1 2 3 4 5
MILES
SHRIVES

ships such as the Grand Fleet, perhaps 8 miles long, it could not be known which part of the line had been selected as target—so that a turn which would make, say, the head of the line safe might expose the centre squadrons. Furthermore, the turn towards might take the battle line within torpedo range of the enemy battleships, a proceeding which Jellicoe had firmly laid down that he would avoid until the enemy had been defeated by gunfire.

A turn away would have the disadvantage of opening the gun range, but only for a time, and only by a few thousand yards. Then, the danger over, the range could be closed again. Such a counter to the torpedo attack had therefore been standardised; and as the twenty-eight torpedoes raced for Jellicoe's line, it was carried out.

It saved the German battle-cruisers, for as the shells ceased to fall round his battleships Scheer released them from their "Death Ride", though not before they had suffered cruelly. It also saved the High Seas Fleet from annihilation. For Jellicoe had never visualised the enemy battle line turning directly about and steaming away at the same time as his ships were avoiding the torpedoes. He calculated that his own turn away would only open the range by 1,750 yards. But in fact, unknown to him, the two fleets were steaming away from each other at a combined speed of some 20 knots. By the time the torpedo menace was passed, they were far out of sight and range of each other.

The sun was now riding low on the horizon to the north-west. Time in which to reap the reward of his brilliant strategy and tactics earlier in the day was running out for Jellicoe. However, there was still more than an hour of twilight to run. Had any of his cruiser squadron commanders whose duty it was to keep contact with the enemy's battle force—or even his subordinate commanders in the line, some of whom had seen Scheer's second turn away—seen fit to tell the Commander-in-Chief, there would still have been time for a further assault before darkness.

It was not until nearly eight o'clock, nearly half an hour after the torpedo attack, during which time Jellicoe's squadrons had been steering south-west and so not closing the range at all, that a signal from Beatty—who had had the enemy in sight until 7.45—gave the vital news that the German battle squadrons had been at that time steering south by west. Jellicoe at once altered course, by divisions, to west, a course which he calculated should enable him to renew the action in twenty-five minutes.

* * *

Following his second encounter with the Grand Fleet, Scheer had had a respite in which he could take stock of his position. He was relieved to find that serious damage to his battleships had been confined to three ships, the dreadnoughts *Markgraf*, *Grosser Kürfurst* and *König*, and that even they had all their armament fit for action. Though the *König* and *Grosser Kürfurst* were extensively flooded, they could still keep up the fleet speed of 16 knots.

But the fact remained that the enemy was squarely across the line of retreat to the only safe area he could reach by early morning, Horn's Reef, and so avoid a renewal of the action on the morrow. There was no alternative therefore to setting a course for home and bludgeoning his way through during the night, which would soon be falling. For the time being he contented himself with a course of south to which he altered at 7.45, soon after Beatty, far ahead of the Grand Fleet's battle squadrons, had lost touch in the increasing gloom and had pushed his 3rd Light Cruiser Squadron out to reconnoitre.

The German line was gradually re-forming in reverse order, with the 2nd Squadron of pre-dreadnoughts under Rear-Admiral Mauve leading. Away to the north and limping away to the westward was the *Lützow*, her crew struggling manfully to keep her afloat. Abreast the battle line and to the eastward of it were the remaining battle-cruisers, overhauling the battleships in spite of the damage they had suffered, and making for their station in the van.

While the long summer twilight deepened the two fleets were again converging. Soon after 8, gunfire flared up once more as Rear-Admiral Napier's 3rd Light Cruiser Squadron, in the van, encountered the five light cruisers of the 4th Scouting Group and exchanged a brief cannonade with them, in which the *München* was damaged before the Germans turned away into the gloom. Then Beatty's battle-cruisers sighted their old antagonists and, having the advantage of the light, were able to pound the *Derfflinger* and *Seydlitz* unmercifully as they stood out against the afterglow of the sunset, before they too turned away to the westward.

To their rescue came Admiral Mauve's pre-dreadnoughts. Only present by reason of their commander's impassioned plea to Scheer not to be left behind, they had so far seen nothing of the fight. Now they were determined to make their mark, and stood boldly on to engage Beatty's ships, but they could not for long withstand even the reduced fire of which the battle-cruisers were capable after their long day of destructive battle. When the *Schleswig-Holstein*, *Pommern* and *Schlesien* had all been hit, Mauve also was forced to turn away to the west, and was soon lost to sight.

Meanwhile the British light cruisers *Calliope*, *Comus* and *Constance*, stationed abreast the leading division of the Grand Fleet, had also sighted Scheer's dreadnought divisions in the rear, and had been engaged and driven off. The Commodore's flagship *Calliope* had her wireless gear wrecked, and once again subordinate commanders failed to appreciate the vital importance of getting an enemy report through to the Commander-in-Chief. Before Jellicoe could gain any useful information, Scheer had sensed his danger and had reluctantly ordered the *Westfalen*, leading the two dreadnought squadrons, to alter away to the westward.

Yet there was to be one more chance given to the British battle squadrons to strike a blow before nightfall. As soon as possible the *Westfalen* had altered southward again, so that once more the two fleets were converging. A little before 9 o'clock, with the last of the light, the German dreadnoughts were again sighted by the leading British division, four ships of the 2nd Battle Squadron under Vice-Admiral Sir Martin Jerram. Though two of his light cruisers identified the German battleships and attacked with torpedoes, being met with a blast of fire from *Westfalen* and *Nassau*, Jerram did not feel sufficiently confident that they were indeed enemy to open fire. The Germans turned away to avoid the light cruisers' torpedoes; and soon afterwards, on receipt of a signal for a general alteration of course to the south, Jerram also led his squadron away.

It was a crowning example of lack of initiative amongst subordinate commanders in the British fleet to which can largely be ascribed the failure to reap the reward of Jellicoe's initial tactical masterpiece. After that triumphant moment, everything had gone steadily wrong. Scheer, caught in a perfect trap, had been allowed to escape the consequences again and again.

It is easy to apportion blame for the failure: but perhaps the key to it all is that fleets, and particularly the Grand Fleet, had grown too large and cumbersome to be handled as a single body with the primitive means of wireless communication then available. Radio channels were few, and wireless equipment the first to suffer from shell hits.

* * *

With darkness, Jellicoe had abandoned his probing towards the enemy, for he was firmly determined not to engage in a night action with his battleships. He had good reasons for this. A night action was always to the advantage of the smaller, more compact fleet in which there were fewer problems of identifying friend and foe. Furthermore he knew that the Germans were the better equipped with searchlights, and were better prepared generally for fighting at night. The destroyer flotillas, many of whom had not yet been in action, were to be left free to attack, night being the favoured time for their operations. Jellicoe therefore drew off his fleet, formed them into a compact night disposition and settled down to a southerly course which would place him in a position at daylight to renew the action should Scheer make for his own waters by way of the gap through the minefields to the south. In case the Germans decided to cut across the Grand Fleet's wake to reach the Horn's Reef Channel, the destroyers were stationed in the rear where their great strength—there were nearly fifty of them—was to be relied upon to make such an attempt a costly one.

Except for Jellicoe's determination not to become involved in the chance-ruled confusion of night action, the Grand Fleet was indeed still in control of the situation when darkness fell. Scheer was in no doubt of it. Again and again his efforts to win through to shelter had recoiled from the barrier of dreadnoughts. As the Grand Fleet settled down on its southerly course for the night, slowly taking up its cruising disposition in four columns, all that Jellicoe needed to know to bring the High Seas Fleet to action at daylight was which of the two escape routes Scheer had selected—Horn's Reef, or the southerly gap through the minefields.

At 9.10 p.m. Scheer had made his decision. The High Seas Fleet must steer undeviatingly for Horn's Reef. By radio the order went out: "Battle fleet's course SSE 1/4 E. This course is to be maintained. Speed sixteen knots." At the same time the battered battle-cruisers and the pre-dreadnought squadron were ordered to the rear.

In the Admiralty's radio-interception stations this message was taken in and deciphered. By 11.05 it was in Jellicoe's hands. An approximate knowledge of Scheer's position would now have given him the certain information he needed. Yet though none of his widespread force which had encountered the German battle line in the last hour of twilight had reported the fact in sufficient detail to give him this knowledge, the enemy's course could have been set for no other destination but Horn's Reef. Somehow the implication was missed by Jellicoe and his Staff.

In the Admiralty an even more conclusive piece of evidence was held. A message from Scheer asking for airship reconnaissance of the Horn's Reef area at dawn had been intercepted, but this vital news was not passed to the *Iron Duke*.

So as the dark hours slowly passed, the two great fleets headed southwards on converging courses. The British fleet, moving a knot faster than the German, was slowly drawing ahead so that the head of Scheer's line would cut close across the wake of Jellicoe's more compact formation. Astern of the British battle squadrons was the great mass of destroyers which must inevitably come in contact eventually with the German battleships.

Before this could come about light cruisers of both sides,

manœuvring in the area between the opposing battle squadrons, clashed in brief, explosive encounters at point-blank range before each side turned away, unable to withstand the shattering effect of rapid fire at a range at which every shot hit.

The cruiser encounters told neither Commander-in-Chief what he needed to know—the position of the opposing battle-squadrons. Both fleets held on. By 11 o'clock the head of the German line and the most westerly of the British destroyer flotillas were not far apart, each ignorant of the other's position. In the British destroyers, few of whom had as yet seen anything of the far-flung smoke and mist-obscured battle, there was an almost total absence of any knowledge of the whereabouts of the enemy fleet or of the outlying portions of their own.

As dark shapes loomed up to starboard of the 4th Flotilla of twelve boats led by Captain Wintour in the *Tipperary*, there was no certainty of their being hostile. Wintour ordered the challenge to be flashed. The reply came with the sudden blaze of searchlight beams and a storm of fire from every gun which could be brought to bear from the dreadnoughts leading the German line.

The *Tipperary* was quickly reduced to a burning shambles. Another destroyer, *Spitfire*, came into violent collision with the dreadnought *Nassau* and pulled away out of action. It was a scene of wildest confusion. Though all the ten torpedoes fired by the destroyers were avoided by the German ships as they sheered away, the light cruiser *Elbing*, trying to get through the German line, was rammed amidships by the battleship *Posen*, and so damaged that she had later to be abandoned and sunk.

Similar clashes took place at intervals throughout the night. The survivors of the 4th Flotilla made a second attack, as a result of which the light cruiser *Rostock* was torpedoed and sunk at a cost of one destroyer sunk and two others damaged and put out of action by collision. Yet a third time the remainder of this flotilla came up against the German line, but though they succeeded in inflicting much superficial damage with their small guns, no torpedoes found a target on this occasion. One destroyer was sunk, another driven out of action, and the flotilla finally dispersed.

On each occasion the German battleships swerved away from the torpedo threat only to be sternly ordered back on to the course for Horn's Reef as soon as the firing died away. The searchlights and gunflashes had been clearly in sight from the British battle squadrons, and from the rear ships the silhouette of a German dreadnought had been seen. Still no report was made to the fleet flagship, and the two fleets still drove steadily on.

By 1.0 a.m. on 1st June the head of the German line had crossed the Grand Fleet's wake. Except for more destroyer flotillas the way was clear to Horn's Reef. And now a line of twelve boats led by Commander Goldsmith in the *Lydiard* was passing across the bows of the *Westfalen*, the leading German dreadnought. The first ten had got across, unsuspecting and unseen, when the two rear boats found themselves on a collision course with the enemy battleship. By going ahead at full speed the eleventh boat, *Petard*, succeeded in scraping across her bows, but was badly shot about before escaping into the darkness. The *Turbulent*, in the rear, had no such fortune. As the searchlights came on once again, she was blown to pieces by the guns of the *Westfalen*.

Had the position of the head of the German line been given to Jellicoe as a result of this encounter, he might still have been able to bring Scheer to action again at dawn. But all was quiet in the British fleet as it ploughed onwards.

Daylight was not far off when the next British flotilla sighted the rear squadron of the enemy battle fleet. Captain Stirling in the *Faulknor* led his 12th Flotilla in to the attack at 2.15 a.m., torpedoes from his boats hitting the pre-dreadnought battleship *Pommern* and detonating her magazines—sinking her with all hands. This was the only result of an attack well pressed home in ideal conditions by the arm from which such great things had been expected in a night battle.

Before attacking, Stirling, alone amongst the flotilla leaders had tried to get an enemy report through to the Commander-in-Chief, but had received no acknowledgement. In fact, the message was not taken in by the *Iron Duke*.

With the completion of the 12th Flotilla's attack, the Battle of

Jutland was virtually over. Two hours steaming would bring the High Seas Fleet to the shelter of its own protected waters. Thirty miles away to the south-west and drawing ever farther away, the Grand Fleet was still steering south, about to turn back to the northward.

Jellicoe, ignorant of the events of the night as the enemy passed across astern of him, was in full expectation of renewing the action at daylight. Scheer, a few hours previously caught in an apparently fatal trap from which there seemed no way out without accepting battle against impossible odds, incredulously learnt that his way home was clear. For the loss of one battle-cruiser and one pre-dreadnought battleship from amongst his capital ships he had faced the whole might of the Grand Fleet, inflicting far heavier losses on it. The loss of the *Lützow* and the damage and casualties in the *Seydlitz* and *Derfflinger* were as nothing compared with the sight of British battle-cruisers disintegrating in magazine explosions.

One more German capital ship was to suffer before the day was over, as the dreadnought *Ostfriesland* struck a mine. But as the High Seas Fleet filed into the Schillig Roads, Scheer was already composing his dispatch announcing the victory of Skagerrak.

For Jellicoe, 1st June was a grim day. As the realisation of the escape of the German fleet grew, news began to reach him of the British losses. Only now did he learn of the destruction of the *Queen Mary* and *Indefatigable*. That of *Defence* and *Inflexible* he already knew. *Warrior* was struggling homewards and soon to be abandoned. *Warspite* was heavily damaged.

The great moment towards which all Jellicoe's careful strategy had been directed had come and gone. Brilliant opening tactics had delivered the enemy into his hands. Then a number of tactical errors and a lack of initiative on the part of subordinates combined with his own unwillingness to take any chances with his precious battleships had deprived him of a decisive victory.

Controversy after the battle was inevitable, as both sides claimed the victory. That the Germans had inflicted greater losses than they had themselves suffered was certainly true. That they had had only one desire, to escape to the security of their base, from the moment they found that they were facing the whole Grand Fleet was not surprising. But a fortunate escape from total destruction to which they had been exposed by the enemy's superior strategy can hardly justify a claim to victory. From the German point of view the risks of massed battle were too great, and never again would a serious attempt be made to bring on a fleet action.

From 1st June 1916 the Grand Fleet reigned supreme and unchallenged, while the Germans turned to their submarine arm to redress the balance. That the Grand Fleet failed to win a victory at Jutland is true; but it is equally true that they convinced their enemy that under no circumstances could the High Seas Fleet hope to wrest command of the sea from Britain, or to break the stranglehold of the blockade which was slowly but surely squeezing life and power out of Germany.

14

The Birth of Naval Air Power

THE age of the battleship saw its greatest day at the Battle of Jutland. Never again would long lines of the steel-clad Leviathans move ponderously into action and prepare to fight it out in an exchange of shell fire.

There were several reasons for this, the first being the mutual agreement by the leading naval powers to restrict the number and size of their capital ships, which was the outcome of the Washington Conference.

The agreement, which was embodied in the Washington Treaty of 1922, provided for a reduction in size of the battle fleets of Great Britain, the United States, France, Italy and Japan, which on completion would leave their relative strengths in capital ships in the ration of 5; 5; 3; 3; 3. The classification of a capital ships was any ship of more than 10,000 tons displacement.

So far as the British were concerned, utterly dependent on sea power for the defence of their wide-spread dominions as they were, this represented a crippling sacrifice and a final abandonment of the Two-Power Standard which successive generations had long insisted upon as necessary for security. The wave of revulsion against war which followed the appalling slaughter of 1914–18, and the steeply rising cost of armaments—battleships in particular—combined however to secure Britain's agreement.

Apart from this voluntary limitation of battleship strength, developments had already long been under way which would eventually depose the battleship from its position as monarch of the seas.

The first of these, in point of time, was the submarine. Fisher's "submarine boats" of the early 1900's had progressed until they had become ocean-going submersible craft of great endurance and high manœuvrability capable of spewing forth salvoes of high-speed, long-range torpedoes of great destructive power.

The slow and clumsy battleship could no longer venture to sea without an escort of destroyers to screen her; the screen required became ever larger and more complex as the manœuvring and diving capabilities of the submarine improved. Even with this protection it was necessary to seek further security by progressing in a nervous, irregular zig-zag course which could not be predicted by the submarine captain working his way into an attack position. Apart from making the submarine's torpedo-firing problem more difficult, this forced him to make more frequent use of his periscope, exposing him to visual detection, the only reliable form until the invention of the asdic or sonar device towards the end of the First World War. But the already moderate speed of advance of a battle squadron was thus further reduced.

The other development which was in the long run to drive the battleship from the surface of the seas was that of aircraft. Both airships and heavier-than-air craft on float undercarriages worked with the opposing fleets in the 1914–18 War. Both were too much at the mercy of the weather greatly to affect the fleet operations, though Zeppelins did save the High Seas Fleet from a second encounter with the Grand Fleet two months after Jutland.

By 1918, aircraft on wheels were being carried on platforms on top of battleships' turrets. On completion of any mission they had either to make for airfields ashore or to alight on the water, where they would be lost. Obviously the next development was to construct platforms on ships, and so the aircraft carrier was born.

For some time ship-borne aircraft were looked on as ancillaries to the battleship, to be used only for reconnaissance or artillery observation. It was not until they became capable of carrying an effective weapon, in the shape of a bomb or a torpedo, that they began to revolutionise naval warfare.

Controversy soon arose between the airmen and the more conservative amongst the sailors, each so exaggerating their claims that a reasonable compromise in the design and armaments of ships of war was never reached. The airmen contended that they could make it impossible for warships to operate within range of aircraft. The predominantly gun-dominated school of thought in the navies of the post-war years was confident that anti-aircraft fire could give the neccessary protection.

Each argued from false premisses. The airmen visualised only warships without fighter protection, the provision of which would, in fact, be one of the primary functions of the aircraft carrier. The sailors placed unrealistic faith in the capability of the gun alone to defeat air attack.

The Washington Treaty had also limited the size and number of aircraft carriers that each navy might have, in a similar ratio to that for capital ships. Though this did not cause so much dismay as the limitation of battleships, there were already forward-thinking minds who saw in it the real emasculation of British naval power. The veteran Sir Percy Scott, first to bring naval gunnery to its position of pre-eminence as a battle winner, was now amongst the first to realise that it had had its day. In 1922 he said: "Naval strength is no longer measured by the number of battleships a country has, but by the number of aeroplane-carriers and aeroplanes."

Had the majority of the naval hierarchy of any of the great powers had the same foresight, the naval side of the Second World War would have taken a very different course. When the Washington Treaty finally lapsed in 1936, much of the effort and financial resource of the naval powers was expended on new, monster battleships which would have been better diverted to the construction of aircraft carriers. France and Italy, indeed, built no carriers. The United States and Japan appreciated the shape of naval warfare of the future more clearly than any, and built up a powerful naval air service. Hamstrung by the disastrous decision of 1918 to entrust naval air development to a separate Air Force, Britain lagged seriously behind in this field.

At the outbreak of the Second World War, therefore, the battleship was still regarded as the hard core of any naval force, though aircraft carriers had already reached an advanced state of development in the British, American and Japanese fleets. Anti-aircraft guns had been added to the armament of cruisers and above, but they were in insufficient numbers to give any real degree of defence, particularly against dive and torpedo-bombers. Destroyers were still armed with low-angle guns suitable only for surface action.

The extreme schools of thought on either side were proved to be wrong when the test of war was applied. When the German and British surface fleets first clashed at the opening of the Norwegian campaign, the German land-trained airmen found it remarkably difficult to hit warships with their bombs, let alone sink them, even though they were presented with targets of greatly restricted mobility in the narrow fiords of Norway. On the other hand gunnery experts were dismayed and disillusioned at the low capability of their guns to bring aircraft down.

Thus while warships found that they could only operate within range of enemy dive-bombers at considerable risk of being immobilised by a lucky hit, the opposing air forces were considerably disappointed at the degree to which they were able to dominate even the sea areas close to their own coasts.

It quickly became apparent that to be free to manœuvre in restricted waters, a fleet must be capable of providing its own fighter defence; to be able to bring an unwilling enemy to action it must have its own force of "strike" aircraft always available. Both requirements called for aircraft carriers in greater numbers than had been visualised.

The British fleet, plunged into war with only one up-to-date carrier completed, was never to catch up with its requirements until nearly the end of hostilities. With two years of peace still to run, the American and Japanese fleets profited from the lessons learnt to launch a heavy programme of carrier construction. In the United States Fleet the destruction or heavy damage of a great portion of their battleship strength at the treacherous attack on Pearl Harbour in December 1941, and the fortunate absence at sea on that occasion of their existing aircraft carriers, helped to force on the Americans the development of a largely carrier Navy.

With it they were to hasten the end of the battleship as a fleet unit.

In the first two years of the war, however, while British naval air strength remained inadequate, battleships still played an irreplaceable rôle in the struggle for command of the sea. Even then it was only in combination with aircraft carriers that they were able to achieve any success. Prior to the entry of Japan into the war, Britain's sea power was threatened at two principal points. In the wide spaces of the Atlantic a long-drawn running fight was waged against her merchant convoys by German U-boats. In this battleships played no part. On the other hand Germany possessed a powerful surface fleet of battle-cruisers, pocket-battleships and heavy cruisers, any of which might attempt to break out into the Atlantic and fall on the convoys, virtually defenceless against such an attack.

Against this threat the British Home Fleet was based at Scapa Flow charged with barring the exit from the North Sea or, if that should fail, of hunting down any enemy ships which broke out.

The other threatened area was the Mediterranean. With the collapse of France, the British fleet found itself faced with commitments which stretched its resources to the limit. In that vital sea area an Italian fleet of splendidly designed, fast and powerful ships of which the hard core consisted of the two huge battleships *Littorio* and *Vittorio Veneto* about to come into service, opposed a British fleet of elderly though still serviceable *Queen Elizabeth* and *Royal Sovereign* class battleships, powerful in armament but some 6 knots slower than the Italians. For air support the Italians could count on the whole of their air force working from airfields in Southern Italy, Sardinia, Libya and the Dodecanese Islands in the Aegean; the British had only the few obsolescent aircraft in the solitary carrier which was all that was usually available.

East and west along the one thousand mile stretch from Gibraltar to Alexandria ran the supply route for Britain's armies defending Egypt. North and south across the central basin ran Italy's supply route to her armies in Libya. But whereas the former was flanked for much of its length by enemy airfields on both sides, the latter was but a brief passage which could be traversed in the dark hours of a single night. Malta, from which the Italian route might have been attacked, was almost devoid of fighter defence, and air attacks soon made it unusable by all but submarines and destroyers.

Naval operations were consequently linked to a great extent to the British efforts to run supply convoys to Malta and to Egypt and Italian efforts to prevent them. To cover such convoys the Mediterranean Fleet would move from Alexandria into the Central Mediterranean basin. Escorting the east-bound convoys would come the force of varying strength known as Force "H", usually including one or two battleships and an aircraft carrier. The convoy and fleet located by the Italian reconnaissance aircraft, they might be subjected to attack by bomber aircraft only, or the Italian battle fleet might put to sea to dispute their passage.

The Italian Air Force relied on high bombers and torpedo aircraft. Though the former were highly skilful and bombed with great accuracy, it was soon demonstrated that this form of attack enjoyed a low degree of probability of hitting ships. Salvoes of bombs would again and again fall all round their target which would vanish from sight in a forest of tall splashes and a cloud of smoke, but hits were extremely rare. The torpedo-bombers at first confined their efforts to attacks in twilight or by the light of the moon, and they achieved some success; but it was not until the German Air Force later moved into the Mediterranean, bringing their dive-bombers with them, that the central basin became unusable by British ships so long as the North African airfields were in enemy hands.

For the first year after Italy's entry into the war, therefore, the Italians could dispute the British control of the Mediterranean only by bringing their battle fleet into action. It was with something less than enthusiasm that they did so!

Before we examine the encounters which took place we should study the relative strength of the ships engaged.

With the defection of the French from the Allied cause, the British fleet in the Mediterranean consisted of five battleships,

Warspite, *Valiant*, *Malaya*, *Royal Sovereign* and *Ramillies*, the modern 6-inch gun cruisers *Orion*, *Neptune*, *Sydney*, *Liverpool* and *Gloucester*, and the old veterans *Capetown*, *Caledon*, *Calypso* and *Delhi*. At first the only aircraft carrier was the *Eagle*, a converted battleship carrying a handful of Swordfish aircraft which could double the rôles of reconnaissance and torpedo-attack. Later the *Illustrious*, an up-to-date and faster ship, was added.

Each of the battleships had a powerful battery of eight 15-inch guns; but three of them, *Malaya*, *Royal Sovereign* and *Ramillies* were old and unmodernised, their machinery and boilers coming to the end of their useful life, their guns on mountings which limited their range considerably.

The Italian fleet had four battleships, *Andrea Doria*, *Caio Duilio*, *Conte di Cavour* and *Giulio Cesare*, a little older than the *Warspite* and her consorts but all of them quite recently modernised, re-equipped and re-engined to give them a speed of 28 knots, which was 3 knots faster than the best of the British ships. Their main armament of ten 12·6-inch guns could throw a weight of broadside not far short of their opponents' and to a greater range than any but *Warspite* and *Valiant*—an important factor in the clear visibility of the average Mediterranean day.

Almost ready for service were the two splendid new battleships *Littorio* and *Vittorio Veneto* which had been laid down as soon as the Washington Treaty lapsed. Of 35,000 tons displacement, armed with nine 15-inch guns each and capable of a speed of more than 30 knots, they were, on paper, more than a match for anything the British could put against them.

In cruisers, the Italians were far superior in numbers, and in the *Zara* class of 10,000 ton ships mounting eight 8-inch guns they possessed a cruiser force which out-gunned, out-ranged and out-ran any British cruiser in the Mediterranean. Moreover, they were armoured to resist their 6-inch shells.

On paper, therefore, the Italian fleet had little to fear from an encounter with the British Mediterranean Fleet. To back their gun-power, they could call up a huge force of land-based bombing planes.

Though the Italian fleet was smaller than the British fleet as a whole, it enjoyed a local superiority in the Mediterranean. There was therefore no reason for it to adopt the strategy of maintenance of a "fleet in being", avoiding close action. For some reason nevertheless, this was what the Italians did. The incalculable influence of prestige, the one advantage the British could count on, was perhaps responsible. The first meeting between the two forces served to heighten the effect of this factor.

On 8th July 1940, the British Commander-in-Chief, Sir Andrew Cunningham, his flag in the *Warspite* and accompanied by the battleships *Royal Sovereign* and *Malaya*, the aircraft carrier *Eagle* and five 6-inch cruisers, at sea to the eastward of Malta to cover two convoys due to sail from that island to Alexandria, learnt from air reconnaissance that an Italian fleet of two battleships and a number of cruisers and destroyers was about 100 miles north of Benghazi, steering southwards. Cunningham at once steered towards Taranto to place himself between the enemy and his base.

During the night the Italians turned back to the northward, so that when next located by air reconnaissance at daylight on the following day they were some 145 miles to the westward of the British fleet, their way home clear. With their great superiority of speed they could be brought to action only if the torpedo-aircraft from the *Eagle* could damage one of their battleships, or if they themselves stood to fight.

In the event it was the latter which occurred, the *Eagle*'s small striking force failing to reduce the enemy's speed. The Italian Commander-in-Chief, Admiral Riccardi, could well turn with confidence to face Admiral Cunningham's fleet. Besides the two battleships *Giulio Cesare* and *Conte di Cavour*, able to out-range all the British ships present except the modernised *Warspite*, he had with him sixteen cruisers, more than half of them carrying 8-inch guns.

By noon the two fleets were 90 miles apart, the British cruisers pressing on ahead to gain contact with the enemy. Cunningham, impatient at the slow speed imposed on him in keeping company with the *Royal Sovereign*, soon abandoned her and the *Malaya*, and hurried on to support his cruisers, who were likely to be heavily outnumbered and out-gunned.

In the clear blue of a perfect Mediterranean day the British fleet, in three separate groups, thrust onward at its utmost speed, the Italians steering across ahead of them and awaiting their arrival. By 3 o'clock the Italian cruisers and destroyers were in sight from the British cruiser squadron made up of *Orion*, *Neptune*, *Liverpool* and *Sydney* under Vice-Admiral John Tovey. At 3.8 the *Neptune* reported the enemy battle fleet in sight.

For the first time since Jutland, twenty-four years before, a fleet action seemed imminent. Already the cruisers were hotly engaged, and soon the *Warspite* joined in to support her out-numbered cruisers while she waited for the enemy battleships to come within range.

Then at 3.30 the Italians suddenly turned away under a smoke-screen and were lost to sight. It seemed that after all they were not going to stand and fight. *Warspite* circled to allow her consorts to catch up before heading north-westwards again in pursuit. Hopes of bringing the Italian battleships to action had fallen low when out of the distant smoke-cloud their silhouettes were seen against the western horizon. At 3.52 the *Warspite*'s first broadside thundered out at a range of 26,000 yards. The Italian battleships replied at once. Both sides quickly demonstrated the advances made in gunnery since battleships had last been in action against each other; salvoes straddled the target again and again even at this huge distance of 13 miles.

Eight minutes after opening fire came the first hit as an orange flash blossomed at the base of the Italian flagship's funnels and a cloud of black smoke shot upwards. It was the first and only hit, for the Italian fleet at once turned away behind smoke. Piling on speed, the Italian heavy ships fled for the safety of their own waters, leaving their destroyers to make a few half-hearted and ineffective torpedo attacks before they too vanished in the smoke pall to the westward.

The Italian Air Force now came to rescue their discomfited

fleet, and after first attacking their own ships by mistake, dropped salvo after salvo from several hundred aircraft round the British battleships and the *Eagle*. As usual, the bombing was extremely accurate—and yet the British ships suffered no damage.

* * *

The fire of the Italian battleships had been quite as accurate as that of the *Warspite*, while neither *Royal Sovereign* nor *Malaya*, with their limited gun range, had been able to reach their target. It was therefore an outstanding piece of fortune for the British that so early in the initial encounter between the two fleets so spectacular a hit had been obtained. The confidence of the Italians in their ability to face British gunfire was badly and permanently shaken. This was to have a decisive influence on the naval campaign in the Mediterranean.

Nine days later two Italian 6-inch cruisers were brought to action by the Australian cruiser H.M.A.S. *Sydney*, which sank one of them and damaged the other. This further damped the morale of the Italians, and for the next few months the Mediterranean Fleet roamed unopposed except for air attacks—so much so that Admiral Cunningham felt able to attack the enemy in his own waters. On the night of 11th November, twenty-four torpedo-carrying Swordfish aircraft and two carrying flares and bombs left the deck of the aircraft carrier *Illustrious* and brought off a brilliant and successful attack, sinking three battleships at their moorings in the harbour of Taranto, and damaging a cruiser and two destroyers.

Until these battleships could be refloated and repaired, the threat from the Italian fleet was greatly reduced. Admiral Cunningham was even able to dispense with two of his unmodernised ships, *Malaya* and *Ramillies*. The situation in the Mediterranean in the winter of 1940 was one to give much quiet satisfaction to the fleet. On land the enemy were being rapidly pushed westwards out of Cyrenaica, and one by one the enemy airfields were falling into British hands.

But then the whole position was changed as German armies

poured into Greece to aid their Italian allies, who were finding they had made a serious miscalculation when they had attacked that country. Not only did this bring the German Air Force with its dive-bombers on to the scene, but the decision to send a British army to the help of the Greeks enormously increased the commitments of the Mediterranean Fleet.

The dive-bombing technique which, though it had been experienced by the British fleet in the Norway campaign and during the evacuation from Dunkirk, was new to the Mediterranean fleet, came as an unpleasant surprise. Since the early days when the German pilots had not been greatly successful, squadrons of JU87 dive-bombers, the famous Stukas, had been given special training in attacking ships. On 10th January 1941 a concentration of these highly skilled airmen swooped on the carrier *Illustrious*. The still inadequate anti-aircraft armament of British ships proved quite incapable of warding off the attack. Six bombs scored direct hits, and near misses by others caused further damage. The carrier was so badly hurt that she was forced out of action and out of the Mediterranean for repairs. On the following day the Stukas fell on the cruisers *Gloucester* and *Southampton*, damaging the former and sinking the *Southampton*.

Moreover, the tide of battle on land also turned. Once again the North African airfields, in enemy hands, outflanked the sea-route through the Mediterranean. The combination of all these factors, the heavy losses in cruisers and destroyers in the evacuation of Greece and Crete which resulted, were to rob the British fleet of its command of the sea for a complete year. But before Admiral Cunningham's battleships were to be virtually immobilised by the lack of destroyers to screen them, they were to take part in one more important fleet action.

By March 1941 the morale of the Italian fleet had somewhat recovered, perhaps being bolstered by the addition of the splendid new battleship *Vittorio Veneto*, a huge vessel armed with nine 15-inch guns and capable of a speed of 31 knots. Even so it was only the urging of the German Naval Staff, exasperated at the unopposed passage of British troop convoys between Alexandria and the Piraeus, that eventually roused their allies from their inertia. They were also encouraged by a false claim by the German Air Force to have put two of Admiral Cunningham's battleships out of action. During the 26th and 27th March, therefore, under Admiral Iachino in the *Vittorio Veneto*, a force composed of that ship, six cruisers and a number of destroyers had been making an abortive sweep of the empty Aegean Sea.

Early intelligence of an impending sortie by the Italian fleet had reached the British Commander-in-Chief, who had at once suspended the troop convoys. Sallying forth with his three battleships, *Warspite* (flagship), *Barham* and *Valiant* and the aircraft carrier *Formidable*, and screened by nine destroyers, he made rendezvous with his squadron of 6-inch cruisers, commanded by Vice-Admiral Pridham-Wippell in the *Orion*, leading the *Ajax*, *Perth* and *Gloucester*. The time of the rendezvous was dawn on 28th March south-west of Crete.

The cruisers stretched away ahead, to the westward, to look for the enemy. At the same time reconnaissance aircraft rose from the *Formidable*'s deck and sped away on a more extended search. It was one of these latter which first made contact, reporting a squadron of three Italian heavy cruisers to the northward of Pridham-Wippell's ships.

Meanwhile the scouting aircraft carried in the *Vittorio Veneto* had been sent up, and had sighted and reported the British cruisers. Iachino's whole force turned to fall on this apparently isolated force. For although his own reconnaissance aircraft from shore bases had reported the British battle squadron to him, position errors had convinced the Italian admiral that in fact it was his own fleet which the airmen had sighted. Even when it later became clear to him that Admiral Cunningham's battleships were in the vicinity, they were plotted on his charts more than 40 miles too far to the eastward, so that they were always that much closer than he suspected. The error was to have important consequences in the action which followed.

Barely had the report of enemy cruisers in his vicinity reached Pridham-Wippell when over the northern horizon came three

Italian 8-inch cruisers, closing him rapidly. The British cruisers, outclassed by the powerfully armed and armoured enemy, fell back to gain the support of their own battle squadron, and for an hour the Italians followed, shooting with considerable accuracy but without actually scoring any hits at their extreme range of 13 miles. At this distance the 6-inch guns of the British cruisers could not reach the enemy; but at 9 a.m. the Italians suddenly gave up the chase and turned away to the westward. Pridham-Wippell promptly turned after them to hold contact.

During the next two hours, as his battleships pounded westwards after the cruisers at their best speed of 24 knots, Admiral Cunningham was trying to get a clear picture from the none too reliable air reconnaissance reports which had been identifying battleships amongst the three separate groups of enemy ships sighted. All doubt was ended when at 11 o'clock, from the foretop of the *Orion*, a battleship was sighted on the northern sky-line.

It was the *Vittorio Veneto*, still bent on bringing the British cruisers to action. At the great range of 16 miles she opened a remarkably accurate fire, and the British cruisers were lucky not to be hit, being damaged by splinters from near misses before they turned away under smoke.

Confident that the 31 knots at his command would serve to preserve him from the undesired encounter with the British battleships, Iachino turned in chase as did his three cruisers, but already in the air coming towards him, was a squadron of torpedo-aircraft from the *Formidable*. Slow and clumsy, old-fashioned and highly vulnerable aircraft as they were, and available only in inadequate numbers, their first attack failed to achieve any hits; but they represented the shape of things to come in which battleships were to yield pride of place to aircraft carriers in ocean warfare. Even now, the threat they presented was enough to turn the Italians in flight.

With the *Vittorio Veneto*'s speed unimpaired, this was not at all what Admiral Cunningham wanted. At 3.15 the *Formidable*'s Albacore and Swordfish aircraft were again sent in to the attack. This time their leader, Lieutenant-Commander J. Dalyell-Stead, pressing valiantly into point-blank range, sent his torpedo streaking true for the enemy flagship, hitting her on her port quarter and fracturing her port outer propeller shaft. The pilot and his crew paid for their success with their lives; but now the battleship was crippled, her speed reduced temporarily as low as 16 knots.

Believing it to be even less, British hopes of catching her before dark rose high, but in fact the Italian flagship was soon able to increase to 19 knots. Further attacks during the afternoon by Royal Air Force bombers from Crete failed to achieve anything except to increase the Italians' determination to get away to the shelter of their own waters. Finally at dusk yet again a force from the *Formidable* struck, swooping through a vicious barrage to get their torpedoes away. One found a target. In the near darkness it could not be made out which ship had been hit, and though it was hoped that it might be the *Vittorio Veneto* it was in fact the cruiser *Pola*, steaming abreast the flagship. The *Pola* was brought to a standstill, but this was not known to the British.

Now it was time for the British Commander-in-Chief to decide on his plan for the night. The hazards of a night action between battleships in which so much turned on blind chance had always given pause to sea commanders up to this time. In this case the possibilities were more than usually unpleasant, for a disabled ship would be discovered at dawn within easy striking distance of the whole Italian Air Force and its German dive-bomber contingent.

On the other hand, radar, the device which was soon to revolutionise naval warfare, was installed in a few of the British ships, though not as yet in Cunningham's flagship. As far as was known, the Italian ships did not have it. The advantage thus conferred on the British ships inevitably encouraged a decision to press on in the hope of grasping the splendid prize so nearly in their hands.

The decision made, Cunningham unleashed his destroyers and sent them off into the dark to find and attack the enemy battle squadron. His own battleships pounded on at their best speed, but overtaking the enemy all too slowly. Cunningham was not to enjoy in full the triumph for which he had so successfully manœuvred, for his light forces never succeeded in locating the enemy's main force. Nevertheless a disastrous night for the Italians was to ensue.

The *Pola*, immobilised by her torpedo hit, had been left behind by the remainder of the Italian fleet full in the path of the oncoming British ships. Her crew, demoralised by their perilous situation, dissolved into an undisciplined mob; they broke into the wine stores, and soon many of them were drunk and incapable. Using radar, the British cruisers pelting on to gain contact with the main enemy force detected the solitary ship lying 5 miles to port of their track. Reporting it to the Commander-in-Chief, Pridham-Wippell swept onwards on his primary mission of reconnaissance.

Cunningham at once altered his ships together 40 degrees to port to close the reported contact. An hour later the *Valiant*'s radar picked up the target at 6 miles range. Excitement was intense as *Valiant* reported that the contact was a large ship and could be the *Vittorio Veneto*.

Meanwhile, ignorant of how closely he was being followed, Admiral Iachino had detached the heavy cruisers *Zara* and *Fiume* and sent them back with some destroyers to aid the crippled *Pola*. Now these ships were suddenly sighted on the starboard bow of the *Warspite*, crossing ahead. At once the battleships were swung together to starboard, to bring them into line ahead with all their guns bearing on the new target. The *Formidable* hauled out of the line to leave them to their gun play.

The ships turned ponderously to their new course, and the great turrets swivelled silently round, steadying on to the new target. The range was less than 3,000 yards. "Director layer sees the target" came a tense voice. Then came the order "Open Fire", the 15-inch guns erupted in orange flame and shattering blast.

In the glare of the searchlight-beams the huge one-ton shells could plainly be seen as they flew on their brief course before plunging into the hull of the leading Italian cruiser, *Fiume*. Then as *Valiant* and *Barham* joined their salvoes to those of the *Warspite*, the flagship shifted to the ship astern, the *Zara*. Watchers in the British ships saw whole turrets leaping in the air and falling into the sea as the two Italian cruisers were reduced in a few moments to blazing wrecks, as was the destroyer *Alfieri* which had been screening them.

Other Italian destroyers now came in to attack the British line, which turned 90 degrees to starboard to avoid their torpedoes. British and Italian destroyers mixed in a wild mêlée, appearing and disappearing as they passed through searchlight-beams, and for a time there was great danger of the battleships shooting up their own craft. At one moment, indeed, the destroyer *Havock* was squarely straddled by British gunfire and was fortunate to escape destruction.

Cunningham therefore withdrew his heavy ships from the scene, leaving the destroyers to deliver the coup-de-grâce to the *Zarà* and the destroyers *Alfieri* and *Carducci*. The *Fiume* had already blown up and sunk. As for the *Pola*, neither firing nor fired at, she took no part in the action. Her demoralised crew anxiously awaited whatever fate had in store for them. The senior officer of the British destroyer forces, Captain Philip Mack, took his ship, the *Jervis*, alongside and embarked the panic-stricken sailors while others of his flotilla picked up those who had leapt overboard. Torpedoes then sent the *Pola* to the bottom.

As the sun rose on another clear blue Mediterranean day, bringing promise of heavy air attack if he lingered in the vicinity, Admiral Cunningham could view the night's activities with much satisfaction as he turned back eastward. The main prize, the *Vittorio Veneto*, had escaped his grasp; yet for the loss of one Swordfish aircraft, that of the gallant Dalyell-Stead, his fleet had accounted for three of Italy's most powerful cruisers and two destroyers, while the *Vittorio Veneto* herself would be out of action for some time to come.

The Battle of Matapan, as it came to be called, was the swan-song of the battle squadron of the Mediterranean Fleet. With the loss of Greece and Crete to the enemy and the enemy's continued possession of the North African airfields, the eastern and central

Mediterranean passed under the domination of the German and Italian air forces until the Battle of Alamein drove the Afrika Korps from Libya. By that time the *Barham* had been sunk by a skilful torpedo attack by a German U-boat, and the *Queen Elizabeth* and *Valiant* had been heavily damaged in the harbour of Alexandria by Italian frogmen.

It is to the Atlantic that we must now turn to find battleships in action.

15

A Lion Brought to Bay

THE surface fleet with which Germany entered the war comprised a number of fast, powerful and well-designed ships. Forbidden by the terms of the Peace Treaty to have any large warships at all until 1928, she was even then restricted to ships below the capital-ship class, that is to say of no more than 10,000 tons displacement.

From the start she evaded the terms of her agreements by building the famous "pocket-battleships". Of highly ingenious design, these ships mounted six 11-inch guns, eight 5·9-inch and six 4·1-inch anti-aircraft guns and carried two seaplanes on catapults. It was brazenly claimed that these ships were of no more than 10,000 tons, though in fact they displaced more than 14,000. Three had been built before the war, *Graf Spee*, *Admiral Scheer* and *Deutschland* (later renamed *Lützow*).

These ships were very successful and were to stand the test of war well. When the Hitler régime cast off all restraints on rearmament, however, the Germans reverted to more orthodox types—heavy cruisers of 10,000 tons, mounting 8-inch guns, and fast battleships or battle-cruisers of 31,000 tons with nine 11-inch and twelve 5·9-inch guns, as well as a number of smaller cruisers with 6-inch guns.

Of the battle-cruisers, Germany had two in commission at the beginning of the war, *Scharnhorst* and *Gneisenau*, each capable of 30 knots. One heavy cruiser, the *Admiral Hipper*, was in service. Four more, *Prinz Eugen*, *Blücher*, *Seydlitz* and *Lützow* were building. The last-named was transferred to Russia in 1940 during the brief alliance between Hitler and Stalin.

Still on the stocks at the outbreak of the war were two enormous battleships, *Bismarck* and *Tirpitz*, each with a main battery of eight 15-inch guns and armour of great strength and thickness and capable of nearly 30 knots. Of 42,500 tons displacement, they were designed to be almost unsinkable by gunfire. Others were projected, but Hitler plunged Germany into war earlier than had been catered for by the naval building plan, and none of them was ever completed.

The naval strategy of Grand-Admiral Raeder, the Chief of the German Naval Staff, was based on an intention to use both U-boats and surface ships to attack Britain's merchant ships. This was perfectly sound. Raeder appreciated the lessons of the 1914–18 War, in which the High Seas Fleet was kept concentrated, waiting for a favourable moment to engage a portion of the Grand Fleet—a moment which never occurred. For the weaker fleet, a "guerre de course" was the most profitable employment.

Before war was declared, therefore, two pocket-battleships, the *Deutschland* and the *Graf Spee*, had slipped secretly away. Circling far to the north, they had reached their war stations in the North and South Atlantic oceans respectively. There, in unfrequented areas, they waited the order to begin operations which reached them on 26th September 1939.

The *Deutschland*'s efforts were remarkably unproductive, chiefly owing to the immediate institution by the British of a convoy system in that area. After roaming the North Atlantic for nearly two months during which she sank only two ships, the *Deutschland* slipped through the British northern patrols and returned to Germany. The *Graf Spee*, on the other hand, was able to reap a rich harvest in the South Atlantic before being brought to action on 13th December off the River Plate by a British squadron. Taking shelter in the neutral harbour of Montevideo, her captain scuttled her rather than face a renewal of the action.

The preoccupations of the Norwegian campaign, during which many of the German ships were damaged and the new heavy cruiser *Blücher* sunk, brought commerce-raiding operations to a standstill until the autumn of 1940. By then the fitness of the

German surface fleet had been restored. The first to be ready was the pocket-battleship *Scheer*, which got away round the north of Iceland into the Atlantic in the early days of November.

Apparently her luck was in, for almost at once she fell in with a convoy of thirty-seven ships homeward bound from Halifax. U-boats had not yet spread their operations so far westward, and the only escort with the convoy was the armed merchant cruiser *Jervis Bay*—a passenger liner armed with a few antiquated 6-inch guns. It seemed a soft, ripe plum ready for the picking by the powerful German ship.

But the difficulties under which a commerce-raider works, with no convenient repair base at hand, were quickly apparent. Accepting the hopeless odds, Captain Fegen of the *Jervis Bay* ordered his convoy to scatter and steered boldly into action. Until the *Jervis Bay* had been effectively silenced, the *Scheer* could not ignore the threat of her 6-inch guns and set about the destruction of the merchant ships. By the time this had been accomplished, the merchantmen were scattered far and wide. When darkness fell only five of the thirty-seven had been accounted for, the remainder reaching their destination in safety.

In the following month the heavy cruiser *Hipper* also broke out into the Atlantic, but her first encounter being with a strongly defended troop convoy she was driven off, damaged and forced to seek refuge in the French port of Brest, now in German hands.

The possession of this naval base on the Atlantic coast next emboldened the Germans to send out their two splendid battle-cruisers *Scharnhorst* and *Gneisenau*. Evading the Home Fleet, sent out to intercept them near Iceland, they arrived on the convoy route on 8th February. By now the convoys had each a battleship with them as escort. Though the German ships were more than a match for the solitary, out-of-date *Queen Elizabeth* or *Royal Sovereign* class ship which was all that could be spared to accompany each convoy, each time they fell in with them the Germans sheered off and refused action. But on 22nd of February 1941, coming across a number of merchantmen from convoys recently dispersed, they were able to sink five before shifting to a new area. On 15th and 16th March they repeated their success, sinking no less than sixteen ships before returning to Brest.

Grand-Admiral Raeder was greatly elated by these successes, and was determined to improve on them. Nearing completion were the new heavy cruiser *Prinz Eugen* and the monstrous great battleship *Bismarck*. In April they were to break out into the Atlantic together. There they would be joined by the *Scharnhorst* and *Gneisenau* from Brest. If brought to action the combined squadron would be a match for the whole Home Fleet, and until it was disposed of would be capable of bringing British shipping in the Atlantic to a standstill.

The British Admiralty was not blind to the possibilities. Such a combination would be disastrous. The War Cabinet was therefore persuaded to divert a massive portion of the Royal Air Force's bombing effort to the port of Brest. Though the results of repeated heavy attacks during the ensuing months fell far short of expectations and failed to disable *Scharnhorst* or *Gneisenau* for any great length of time, they were sufficient to disrupt Raeder's ambitious plan.

The *Scharnhorst*, refitting at Brest, was found to need more extensive repairs than had been expected, and could not be got ready in time. The *Gneisenau* was damaged by a torpedo fired by a Royal Air Force aircraft, and had to be dry-docked for repairs.

Impatient for his beautiful great ship to prove her worth and perhaps blind, as were many seamen of his generation, to the changing nature of naval strategy with the advance of air power, Raeder determined to press on with the operation, using only *Bismarck* and *Prinz Eugen*. After a delay until the third week of May occasioned by an engine-room defect in the *Prinz Eugen*, the two ships sailed in secrecy from Gdynia in the Baltic.

Raeder's hope of his ships getting away undetected was not fulfilled; they were sighted as they steamed through the Kattegat, and air reconnaissance located them on the morning of 21st May 1941 at anchor in Kors Fiord near Bergen. In thick weather with clouds hanging low on the Norwegian hillsides, defeating the Royal Air Force reconnaissance aircraft entrusted with the task of watching them, they slipped away to sea; but a naval aircraft braving fog and intense anti-aircraft fire penetrated to the Bergen fiords to gain the certain information that the *Bismarck* was out.

This was enough to set into motion the plans of Admiral Tovey, Commander-in-Chief, Home Fleet. His task was to intercept the enemy ships and prevent them reaching the Atlantic or, if that failed, to hunt them down in the wide ocean wastes. Already cruisers were patrolling the two most likely passages into the Atlantic—the Denmark Strait between Iceland and Greenland, and the strait between Iceland and the Faroes. The battle-cruiser *Hood*, flagship of Vice-Admiral L. E. Holland, and the new battleship *Prince of Wales* were on their way to Iceland. Now the Commander-in-Chief himself sailed in his flagship *King George V* with the aircraft carrier *Victorious*. From the Clyde the battle-cruiser *Repulse* would come to join him on passage to the north-west.

The *Hood* was more than twenty years old and was lightly armoured after the fashion of battle-cruisers of her generation; the *Prince of Wales* was only recently out of the builder's yard, her machinery still being cleared of "teething troubles" and her ship's company inexperienced. The aircrews of the *Victorious* were so untrained that many of them had not yet landed on a carrier's deck. Nevertheless the forces immediately available to Admiral Tovey could be looked on as adequate if the *Bismarck* could be intercepted before breaking clear into the open ocean.

However, any one of a number of unpredictable chances might enable the enemy to evade the British forces in the smoky northern seas, foggy, snow-laden and storm-tossed even in May. In that event, only a great preponderance of force could ensure the necessary concentration being brought to bear to engage the *Bismarck* successfully, even though air reconnaissance might succeed in locating her. Had foresight given the British Navy aircraft carriers in sufficient numbers first to ensure the location of an enemy vessel and then to deliver overwhelming massed air attacks, as demonstrated soon after by the Japanese, the problem would have not been difficult to solve. But as it was, the only two carriers available between Gibraltar and Iceland were the *Victorious* and the *Ark Royal*, the latter in Force "H" based on Gibraltar. Each carried only a handful of slow-flying, obsolescent Swordfish aircraft which combined the rôle of reconnaissance and torpedo attack aircraft. Yet it was to be the aircraft from the *Ark Royal* which were to bring eventual success.

During the night of 22nd May, as *King George V*, *Repulse* and *Victorious* punched their way north-westward into a moderate sea, there was no certainty with regard to the *Bismarck*'s intended movements. The Commander-in-Chief had deduced that a break-out into the Atlantic was the enemy's most probable intention, and he was making his plans to intercept with the forces immediately available. The 23rd dawned grey and wet, with low cloud covering the sky. Air patrols between Iceland and the Faroes were just possible, and were relied upon for that area; but in the Denmark Strait, the most likely route for the enemy, two cruisers, *Suffolk* and *Norfolk*, shared the task of interception in that fog-smothered channel between the ice-barrier to the north-west and the inhospitable coast of Iceland.

Two factors were to operate in favour of the British. The *Suffolk* was fitted with a modern surface-warning radar set, a device still in its primitive stage of development but still good enough to enable detection and shadowing of a large target in fog or snowstorms. Secondly, the German Admiral Lütjens, in the *Bismarck*, had chosen to pass through the Denmark Strait close in to the ice-barrier; and whereas on that side of the strait the weather was clear, towards Iceland dense fog covered the sea.

So on the evening of the 23rd the two German ships were sighted first by the *Suffolk* and soon afterwards by the *Norfolk*, and were then successfully shadowed through a night studded with snowstorms and fog patches. The reports coming regularly in from the cruisers brought the *Hood* and the *Prince of Wales* accurately on to the scene at dawn; and when at 3.35 as the distant shapes of two large enemy ships came into sight against the north-western horizon, Admiral Holland knew that he had made a perfect interception.

Holland's original intention had been to concentrate the four British ships, so that the fire of his two capital ships could be combined against the *Bismarck* while his cruisers engaged the *Prinz Eugen*. On sighting the enemy, however, he decided not to wait for *Norfolk* and *Suffolk* to come up, but immediately turned *Hood* and *Prince of Wales* 40 degrees together and steered to close the range. To all appearances he could well afford to do so. Against the *Bismarck*'s eight 15-inch guns, Holland could bring to bear the same number from the *Hood* and ten 14-inch from the *Prince of Wales*.

Unfortunately there were several adverse factors. The enemy ships were steaming with the cruiser leading the battleship. The similarity of their silhouettes led to the *Prinz Eugen* being taken for the *Bismarck* by the gun controllers in the *Hood*. A signal to concentrate the fire of both British ships on the leading enemy was made; and though it was corrected just before the first salvoes from the *Hood* crashed out, and in the *Prince of Wales* the mistake had been realised and the order ignored, it seems certain from German reports of the action that the *Hood* did in fact engage the *Prinz Eugen*.

Secondly, Holland's turn towards the enemy allowed only the forward turrets to bear, reducing the number of guns in action to four 15-inch and six 14-inch. This would not have been so serious had the British ships steered directly for the enemy while closing the range, thus presenting difficult end-on targets; but the course selected was only a partially converging one, so that neither was the target reduced nor the full fire-power brought to bear.

Finally, the "teething troubles" in the *Prince of Wales*'s turret machinery were to make themselves evident at her very first salvo. One gun was known to have a defect which would prevent it being reloaded after the first round. Of the remainder, first one and then another would miss a salvo; and though the contractor's workmen, still on board, strove manfully to keep the guns in action, it was only rarely that a full salvo was fired.

The action opened at 3.52 a.m. when the *Hood* fired her first salvo at a range of 25,000 yards, the *Prince of Wales* joining in thirty seconds later. Two minutes later the *Bismarck* replied. The German battleship's shooting was of remarkable accuracy, as well it might be, fresh as she was from intensive practice in the sheltered waters of the Baltic. The *Hood* was at once racing through the tall leaping columns of 15-inch shell splashes. A shell from one of the first salvoes scored a hit at the foot of her mainmast, and started a serious fire. Eight minutes after the action started another plunged down through her armour and penetrated to one of her after magazines, which blew up. The great ship was torn asunder by a violent explosion, broke in half, and in less than three minutes had vanished, leaving only a pall of smoke and three survivors.

Meanwhile the *Prince of Wales* had been left undisturbed to engage the *Bismark*—a fortunate circumstance, as in her untrained state it had taken six salvoes to find the range and straddle the target. Now the full fury of the enemy's fire descended on her. The range being down to 14,500 yards, the 8-inch guns of the *Prinz Eugen* joined those of the *Bismarck* to bring a continuous hail of fire accurately to bear. Shell after shell crashed home, and spray from near misses fell from masthead height as the water columns dissolved.

Then a 15-inch shell plunged full on to the bridge, smashing through it and exploding as it emerged. Everyone there except the captain and his Chief Yeoman of Signals was either killed or wounded. With his guns firing more and more spasmodically as breakdowns occurred, it was time for Captain Leach to withdraw and await the support he knew must be hurrying to the scene. Under shelter of a smoke-screen he turned his ship away.

Indeed, had Captain Leach realised it, he was fortunate to have escaped so lightly. One of the four 15-inch shells which had hit his ship had pierced her side well below the water-line, and had come to rest deep in her bowels without exploding. The damage had not all been one-sided, however. Three times the *Bismarck* too had been struck by the *Prince of Wales*'s 14-inch shells. One of these hits was to be of crucial significance. Plunging right through the ship it had holed two oil tanks and flooded a compartment in which were situated the suction valves for further oil tanks forward of it. At one blow Admiral Lütjens had been deprived of more than a thousand tons of precious, irreplaceable oil fuel.

At once all hope of carrying on with his commerce-raiding operation had vanished. Furthermore Lütjens had to make up his mind immediately whether to turn back for the North Sea and make for his home waters, or to head for a French Biscay port. He chose the latter, and his fate was sealed. For unknown to him, from the moment he was sighted by the *Norfolk* the British Admiralty had begun to gather forces from all over the Atlantic, out of which a net was to be woven in which the enemy must become entangled whichever way he shaped his course. Force "H" under Vice-Admiral Sir James Somerville, with his flag in the battle-cruiser *Renown*, and comprising in addition the aircraft carrier *Ark Royal*, the cruiser *Sheffield* and six destroyers, left Gibraltar and hurried north. The battleships *Rodney* and *Ramillies* were ordered to leave the convoy they were escorting, and to converge on the area south of Iceland. The *Revenge* sailed from Halifax to meet the *Bismarck* should she break westward. The cruisers *London* and *Edinburgh* were drawn in to make further strands of the net.

The Commander-in-Chief himself, in possession only of the news from the shadowing force that the *Hood* had been sunk and that the *Bismarck* was steering southward at undiminished speed into the Atlantic, was pushing ahead at his best speed to intercept.

However, he could not hope to come up with the enemy before the next morning. During the night the cruisers might lose touch in the steadily deteriorating weather. A rising gale from the north-west with rain and low cloud was making ideal conditions for evasion.

Admiral Tovey had one chance of damaging the enemy before dark: a torpedo attack by the *Victorious*'s aircraft. He accordingly detached the carrier to steer directly for the *Bismarck* and so gain a position within the range of her Swordfish aircraft, which it was estimated she could do by 7.0 p.m.

Meanwhile, the *Prince of Wales*, *Norfolk* and *Suffolk* had been shadowing the *Bismarck*, the *Suffolk*'s radar enabling contact to be maintained in spite of the increasingly foggy conditions. At about 4.30 p.m. Admiral Lütjens took advantage of a fog patch to turn briefly on the *Suffolk* to create a diversion during which the *Prinz Eugen* was detached to make her own way to safety, which she eventually succeeded in doing. The *Bismarck* then turned away westward.

This seriously upset the plans for the *Victorious*'s air "strike". At 8 p.m. the carrier was still 120 miles from the target, and closing it only slowly. Though darkness was not due for more than three hours, the increasing wind and sea, accompanied by ever more frequent rain squalls, persuaded Captain Bovell to delay no longer. The meagre handful of torpedo aircraft, nine Swordfish in three sub-flights of three each, lumbered heavily into the air from the heaving deck and droned away into the grey smother.

For all their old-fashioned appearance, the Swordfish had one important up-to-date piece of equipment in the shape of an early type of radar set. An hour later, using this radar, they detected a ship beneath them which was presumed to be the *Bismarck*. Breaking from their cloud cover, their pilots were dismayed to find that it was the *Norfolk* which they had located. The cruiser, however, was able to set them on their right course, and once more the aircraft flew off on their search.

Again their radar picked up a target. Again as they broke cloud they found that it was not the *Bismarck* beneath them, but an American coast-guard cutter on weather-reporting duties. The *Bismarck* too was indeed in sight some way farther on, but the premature descent from their cloud cover robbed the British aircraft of all possibility of achieving surprise. It was into a storm of anti-aircraft fire that they flew to deliver their torpedoes. In spite of it they pressed their attacks well home, so that for all her turning and twisting the *Bismarck* took one torpedo in her side.

That only one torpedo from this small number of aircraft should have hit, and that it happened to find a well-protected part of the battleship's hull and therefore achieved no more than a severe shaking, was not at all to the discredit of the airmen. Advocates of the air-borne torpedo for attack on surface ships had always visualised co-ordinated attacks by more than one squadron of aircraft. Now, as at Matapan, shortage of aircraft carriers in the British fleet had forced the use of the slow vulnerable Swordfish aircraft, a few at a time. That only one torpedo found a billet was far less surprising than that none of the aircraft was shot down.

As the nine Swordfish landed again on the *Victorious*'s deck in darkness and rain, bringing with them news of one certain torpedo hit, hopes rose high of the *Bismarck* being brought to action at daylight. They were to be sharply disappointed. Reliance had been concentrated on the *Suffolk*'s radar to hold contact during the night. As she zig-zagged to and fro, contact had inevitably been intermittently lost on her outward "legs" and regained when she turned and closed the range again. At 1.15 a.m. the usual restoration of contact failed to materialise at the expected moment. As minute after minute slipped by with no report from the radar operator, the *Suffolk*'s captain realised that the *Bismarck* had given him the slip.

Reporting this unwelcome news to his admiral, he had to make a quick decision as to how best to set about regaining touch. There were two alternatives. Lütjens had either piled on speed and made off to the westward, or else he had circled round through north, crossed astern of the shadowers and gone east or south-east. Captain Ellis of the *Suffolk* unluckily plumped quickly for the former, and at full speed shaped course to the south-west. He was followed by the *Norfolk*, and at daylight the *Victorious*'s aircraft flew in search to the north-west. All drew a blank. At this vital moment the *Bismarck* had been lost.

The problem now facing the Commander-in-Chief and the Admiralty was an extremely complex one. Apparently the enemy had the choice of a number of different courses—assuming that the *Bismarck* had not been seriously damaged.

Lütjens might be making for the west coast of Greenland where he might meet an oiler in some desolate inlet and then head out into the western Atlantic to attack merchant convoys; or he might have planned a rendezvous with an oiler in mid-ocean far to the south. He might have decided to return to Germany through the Denmark Strait or between Iceland and the Faroes; or he could be making for a French Biscay port.

Though the probability that *Bismarck* had suffered at least some damage made the last two alternatives the most likely, her most menacing course was a westerly one. Once there she would be able to wreak havoc amongst the Atlantic shipping, which had of course been her main object in coming to sea. In the absence of any other indications, Admiral Tovey felt bound to guard against this possibility, and for the next few hours his forces continued westerly on their various searches.

Thus they were actually opening the distance between themselves and the *Bismarck*. For Lütjens was in fact steering for Brest. Except for Admiral Somerville's Force "H" coming up from Gibraltar, and the battleship *Rodney*, where Captain Dalrymple-Hamilton had decided on his own initiative to remain to bar the way to a French port, Lütjens's escape route was clear. But then the German admiral cast away the advantage which his adroit manœuvre had given him. He transmitted a long wireless message to German naval headquarters.

At once the operators in the chain of radio direction-finding stations in the British Isles tuned in and took bearings of the transmission. By 8.30 on the morning of the 25th the Admiralty had enough information to appreciate that the *Bismarck* had gone south-eastward since last seen. Unfortunately, the bearings when received in the *King George V* and plotted on an ordinary navigational chart which introduced errors, gave a different picture. To the Commander-in-Chief it appeared that the enemy was going north-eastward—back towards the North Sea. The search by his forces was adjusted accordingly, and he himself turned north-eastward in chase.

Force "H" had not as yet been placed under the Commander-in-Chief's orders. Admiral Somerville therefore had the benefit of the Admiralty's own opinion, and was instructed to act on the assumption that the *Bismarck* was making for a French port. But throughout the forenoon the *King George V* was steering north-eastward, and no word came from the Admiralty to suggest that this was wrong. Admiral Tovey was therefore highly puzzled when at 1.30 in the afternoon he received from Whitehall a message giving the latest estimated position of the *Bismarck* which clearly indicated a course for the Bay of Biscay.

Unable to reconcile this latest information with the Admiralty's previous silence, it was not until 2.30, after fresh calculations had thrown doubts on his previously plotted position of the enemy, that Tovey signalled for the Admiralty's conclusions. Still no reply came, and at 4.10 he waited no longer, but turned back on what was in fact the right course to take. An hour later, to his infinite relief, a signal reached him which showed the Admiralty appreciation to be the same as his.

Even so, the long search in the wrong direction had reduced the force under Tovey's command to one ship, the *King George V*, and her stock of fuel remaining was now so low that economy was forcing a reduction of speed to 25 knots. The *Repulse* had already reached the end of her fuel endurance, and had been detached that morning to Newfoundland. To the north all but one of the cruisers and the *Prince of Wales* were similarly running short of oil, and now had to make for Iceland, taking the *Victorious* with them. The exception was the *Norfolk*, where at the risk of running down to a standstill, Rear-Admiral Wake-Walker decided to turn to join in the hunt to the south-eastward.

The night of 25/26th May was one of grim anxiety for Admiral Tovey as his flagship pressed on in pursuit, her stern lifting to the steadily growing following seas. A falling glass gave the promise of continued dirty weather on the morrow, weather to make air reconnaissance difficult. Unless the *Bismarck*'s rapid progress could be checked, there was little hope of bringing her to action before she came under the protection of shore-based aircraft. Only Force "H" lay between the enemy and safety. Somerville's flagship *Renown*, a battle-cruiser more than twenty years old and lightly armoured, was no match for the *Bismarck*. All British hopes now rested on the *Ark Royal* and her handful of Swordfish aircraft. Only if they could find the enemy and get a torpedo home to a vital spot could failure be turned into success.

But the enemy had first to be accurately located. Searches during the night by Catalina flying-boats of Coastal Command proved fruitless. By dawn the sands of Tovey's luck seemed to be running out fast. Yet in fact the agents which were to lead to the *Bismarck*'s destruction were already in motion. Soon after midnight, a Catalina aircraft had taken off from its British base for yet another long search. Through the night it had droned its way south, and dawn had revealed a blank, angry sea beneath low ragged rain clouds in and out of which the aircraft flew. At 8.30 a.m., 26th May, breaking out of one such cloud which had hung like a curtain almost to water-level, the pilot heard the American passenger sitting beside him suddenly say "What the devil's that?" Peering in the direction to which the American was pointing, the pilot saw the black bulk of the *Bismarck*. As the signal was going out, giving vital news which the Admiralty and the Commander-in-Chief had been nearly despairing of receiving, anti-aircraft fire from the battleship forced the pilot to sheer away and lose touch, which he could not thereafter regain.

But fortune had at last settled firmly on the British side. Even as the wireless operator in the Catalina was tapping out his message, reconnaissance Swordfish from the wildly heaving deck of the *Ark Royal* some 100 miles to the east-south-east were rumbling away to search, all ignorant of the Catalina's sighting. Half an hour after the flying-boat lost touch, one of the Swordfish sighted the *Bismarck*. From then onwards she was never to be let out of sight again.

Somerville sent the *Sheffield* on to gain surface contact, and meanwhile in the *Ark Royal* torpedoes were being got ready to arm the Swordfish as soon as they were back from their search. Not until nearly 1 p.m. could the fifteen aircraft be refuelled, armed and sent off, but at last they were on their way. After roughly the correct time of flight a contact appeared on their radar sets. They dived down out of the clouds, saw a large warship ahead and went at once into the attack.

The first flights to attack got their torpedoes away, only to see many of them explode as they hit the water. But before the later flights had reached their attacking position the pilots suddenly realised that their target was not the *Bismarck* but the *Sheffield*, of whose presence in the area they had been unaware. Calamitous as the mistake was, it was retrieved from disaster by the successful manœuvres of the *Sheffield* to avoid the few torpedoes which ran true. But the high hopes which had been placed on the air attack had collapsed in ruins.

The news was almost enough to cause Tovey to despair. With the *Rodney* now in company, he was still 130 miles behind the *Bismarck* and catching up only very slowly. *King George V*'s fuel was down to 30 per cent remaining, and Tovey was soon to be forced to tell Admiral Somerville that unless the enemy's speed could be reduced by midnight he would have to give up the chase. The only real hope was a second and more successful attack by the aircraft.

At this stage in the action Tovey's forces were joined by the 4th Destroyer Flotilla, commanded by Captain Vian in the *Cossack*. With the other ships of his flotilla, *Maori*, *Zulu*, *Sikh* and the Polish *Piorun*, Vian had been engaged on the more prosaic duty of escorting a troop convoy heading southward in the Atlantic when at midnight on the 25th he had been ordered to steer north to join the Commander-in-Chief. Tovey's own destroyers had been forced by shortage of fuel to drop out of the chase. The 4th Flotilla was to take their place.

As he came north, Vian had picked up the signal from the Catalina aircraft. In spite of his orders to join his Commander-in-Chief and give him the anti-submarine screen without which a battleship felt perilously naked, Vian felt sure during the coming night Tovey would wish him to be near the German ship. There he would be able perhaps to use his torpedoes to reduce the *Bismarck*'s speed, and with his shadowing reports to deliver her to the guns of the *King George V* at daybreak. Vian at once swung his ships on to a course to intercept, spreading them out to ensure a meeting.

As Vian ploughed on into the gale at the best speed which his destroyers could manage in the towering seas, the returning

Swordfish were hastily refuelled and rearmed for yet another sortie. The first abortive attack had not been valueless; for the premature torpedo explosions had exposed a defect in the magnetic pistols with which they had been armed. The well-tried and reliable contact pistols would be fitted this time. The crestfallen pilots, fully aware of the bitter disappointment their failure had caused, were filled with renewed resolution to succeed at their second attempt; and in this spirit they took off once more, soon after 5 p.m.

This time they were ordered to make contact with the *Sheffield* first. Soon after 6 p.m. they did so and, directed towards the enemy 12 miles farther on, they melted back into the cloud blanket. The low cloud and poor visibility made a co-ordinated attack impossible. Over a period of some thirty minutes from 6.55 onwards the Swordfish swooped down separately. How each aircrew succeeded no one could say, but at some time during the attack two torpedoes found a target, one of them hitting the *Bismarck* right aft, damaging her propellers, jamming her two rudders and putting the steering gear out of action.

It was the crucial blow of the long-drawn contest. For, reduced to 8 knots and unable to steer, the *Bismarck* was caught in the grip of the north-westerly gale and swung helplessly round into it. Soon she was lying wallowing, her bows to the north.

But it was not for some time that this startling change of fortune was known to the British forces. Not until the returning airmen were interrogated on board the *Ark Royal* was a conservative estimate of one torpedo hit arrived at; even this was believed to be amidships, in which case it might not have caused serious damage. The *Sheffield* had indeed reported that the enemy had swerved round on to a northerly course, but at the same moment she had been driven off by a sudden burst of accurate fire from the *Bismarck*'s 15-inch guns, which put the *Sheffield*'s radar out of action. The alteration of course might well have been simply part of the enemy's manœuvres to avoid torpedoes.

Then reports came in one after the other from the *Ark Royal*'s shadowing aircraft. Each gave the enemy's course as north. At last Admiral Tovey could allow himself to believe that the *Bismarck* had been brought to bay. When at a few minutes after 9 p.m. a first sighting report from the *Zulu* of Vian's flotilla assured him that contact would be held during the night, all doubt was dispersed, and he disposed his forces so as to bring them into action at daylight.

The rest of the story is the always pitiable tale of the agonising end of a splendid ship, be she friend or foe. In the darkness, wild wind and heavy seas, Vian's destroyers stationed themselves round the doomed giant to watch and report her every movement. As the night wore on, in spite of an accurate fire brought to bear on them whenever they closed, the destroyers crept in to launch torpedoes. *Maori*, *Cossack* and *Sikh* each scored hits, further ensuring the *Bismarck*'s complete disablement. At daybreak Vian's task was completed as the guns of the *King George V* and *Rodney* flashed out. Almost at once the 16-inch shells of the *Rodney* were hitting, and a minute later the 15-inch of the flagship also. For a few minutes the *Bismarck*'s return fire was fairly accurate, but as damage mounted it became ragged, and soon her big guns were knocked out of action one by one.

But the Germans had once again shown that they could build ships almost indestructible by gun-fire. Anxious to make an end, Tovey signalled for any ships still with torpedoes unexpended to close and sink the *Bismarck*. The task fell to a ship which up to then had taken no direct part in the great hunt and, indeed, had no real right to be there at all unless it be by reason of the unwritten privilege of any warship's captain to steer "for the sound of the guns" unless expressly forbidden to do so.

The cruiser *Dorsetshire* had been escorting a homeward-bound convoy from Freetown when she took in the Catalina's sighting report. Leaving the convoy to the care of an armed merchant cruiser, Captain Martin had headed immediately for the position, 600 miles to the northward. Driving her way through the heavy seas at her best speed, she arrived on the scene in time to add the fire of her 8-inch guns to that of the battleships. On receipt of Admiral Tovey's order she was in position to go straight on to put a torpedo into each side of the *Bismarck*. This was the coup-de-grâce. At 8.40 a.m. on 27th May 1941, the huge ship slowly capsized, and the fires blazing aboard her were extinguished as she plunged to the bottom. From the cold, rough seas 110 survivors were picked up by *Dorsetshire* and *Maori*. With barely enough fuel remaining to reach port, Tovey steered thankfully for home.

16

Twilight of the Battleship

THE hunting down and destruction of the *Bismarck*, an affair largely of battleships and cruisers groping for each other over the vast spaces of the ocean to bring their guns into action, was as outmoded as the blind "hit or miss" sweeps of the Grand Fleet during the First World War. A squadron of aircraft carriers would have brought the *Bismarck*'s brief excursion to an end more speedily and more certainly than the scattered force of ships, which after steaming great distances in search were only able to bring their weapons into play when the enemy had been immobilised by aircraft.

However, this was not yet fully appreciated, largely because the British Navy simply did not have aircraft carriers in sufficient numbers to employ them in delivering the massed air attacks which could swamp the gun-fire of ships and defeat all their efforts to elude bombs or torpedoes. Indeed, this deficiency was not remedied until nearly the end of the war.

The first massed attack by naval aircraft had indeed been executed with startling success by dive-bombers of the Royal Navy as long ago as the spring of 1940, when two squadrons of Skuas had swooped on the German light cruiser *Königsberg* in the harbour of Bergen and sent her to the bottom in one brief, hurtling attack. But so few were the carriers available at that time that it was from a naval air station ashore, in the Orkneys, that the aircraft had taken off, crossing the North Sea to reach their target, and finally landing back at their base with only a few gallons of petrol in their tanks.

Convincing as this demonstration was, the dive-bomber never found lasting favour with the Royal Navy; and when the Skua soon became obsolete on account of its poor flying performance, a replacement was never produced. Indeed, the dive-bomber had a limited value against heavily armoured ships. High-level precision bombing proved even less effective. It was underwater attack which was most lethal against such ships, so that the torpedo-carrying aircraft became first favourite. With the meagre air strength of which the Royal Navy could dispose in the early years of the war, the torpedo-carrier became the only form of "strike" aircraft.

Like the dive-bomber, it called for the massed, co-ordinated attack to achieve sure success. It was not surprising, therefore, that the small formations which were sent against enemy heavy ships from time to time from individual carriers, or by Coastal Command of the Royal Air Force from shore bases, often failed to produce the results expected of them.

On the other hand the Japanese Navy had built up a powerful naval air arm, carrier-borne and shore-based; and their high command showed at once that they understood how to wield it. The shore-based Japanese torpedo planes and bombers swarmed to the attack on the battleship *Prince of Wales* and the battle-cruiser *Repulse* off the Malayan coast. Swamping the anti-aircraft fire of these two powerful ships by a co-ordinated attack by twenty-seven bombers and sixty-one torpedo planes, they put torpedo after torpedo into them and sent them to the bottom.

Far to the north, aircraft from a squadron of six aircraft carriers, dive-bombers and torpedo-planes, had swooped in a devastating, treacherous attack on the unsuspecting Pacific Fleet of the United States Navy in Pearl Harbour. When the smoke cleared and the last aircraft droned away, two battleships had been destroyed and three others so damaged that they were out of action for a year. From Pearl Harbour the carrier force of Admiral Nagumo swept like a whirlwind through the East Indies, leaving a trail of ravaged naval bases. Then they pushed on into the Indian Ocean, where the British cruisers *Cornwall* and *Dorsetshire* and the small aircraft carrier *Hermes* fell victims to massed attacks.

It was a brilliant demonstration of the new look in naval warfare, but two principal factors were to halt the flow of Japanese successes. They had not been achieved without heavy loss of aircraft and pilots. The whole of Japan's first-line strength had been employed, and there were few reserves. The fine edge of the weapon had been blunted.

Besides this, there was the crucial fact that when Pearl Harbour was attacked the aircraft carriers of the United States Pacific Fleet had been absent. The weapon which the Japanese had wielded so skilfully was, in American hands, to bring them in their turn to defeat.

It was with the dual object of securing an outer defensive perimeter in mid-Pacific and of bringing the still inferior American fleet to action that the Japanese Commander-in-Chief, Admiral Yamamoto, took his fleet to sea on 26th May 1942. The aircraft of Admiral Nagumo's force of four aircraft carriers were to attack Midway, America's most westerly outpost. An invasion force under Admiral Kondo was then to occupy it. A subsidiary force would attack and occupy the western Aleutian Islands. In support, ready to engage the American fleet should it attempt to intervene, would be the battle fleet under the Commander-in-Chief himself, with his flag in the colossal battleship *Yamato*, mounting nine 18-inch guns. With him also were the two huge sister-ships *Nagato* and *Mutsu*, each mounting eight 16-inch guns, and a division of four other battleships in which the main battery consisted of twelve 14-inch guns.

It was a force irresistible by any fleet the Americans could assemble should they allow themselves to be brought to action. In the event, for all their massive gun-power, Yamamoto's battleships might just as well have remained in harbour. Where aircraft carriers were available to operate in numbers, the day of the battleship was over.

The American Pacific Command had received timely warning of the impending attack. Midway had been reinforced and provided with radar, and the fleet had put to sea. Lacking any battleships, the Commander-in-Chief, Admiral Nimitz, had to rely upon his three aircraft carriers, *Yorktown*, *Enterprise* and *Hornet*, for his main strength. Thus he was to inaugurate the new era in naval warfare.

Reconnaissance aircraft from Midway discovered the approaching Japanese landing force early on the morning of 3rd June, when the enemy ships were still 600 miles to the westward. That evening Flying Fortresses attacked the transports from a great height, but unsuccessfully. They were followed by a few torpedo-planes, which succeeded only in damaging a tanker. They were not carrier-borne types of aircraft, and gave no indication that American carriers were in the vicinity. Neither had the Japanese carriers been located.

At dawn on 4th June 1942, therefore, Nagumo's aircraft took off according to plan for their flight of 240 miles to Midway. At the same time four scouting aircraft were launched to search to the eastward, and more torpedo-aircraft were ranged on the decks of the four Japanese carriers ready to set off to attack any enemy ships located. But perhaps lulled into over-confidence by their past unbroken run of successes, the Japanese arrangements for reconnaissance lacked their usual efficiency. The catapult in the cruiser *Tone*, from which one of the scouts was to be launched, proved to be defective, delaying the aircraft for twenty minutes. As luck would have it this was the aircraft in whose sector of search the American fleet lay. Though the pilot failed to discover that in the American fleet there were three aircraft carriers, this twenty minutes delay in the detection of the enemy was to be of crucial importance. Furthermore the aircraft in the next sector, from which the three carriers were actually sighted, had a radio failure. Not until the pilot landed back on the deck of his carrier at 9.15 a.m. was the composition of the American fleet known.

Daybreak in the American carrier force commanded by Rear-Admiral Fletcher in the carrier *Yorktown*, with Rear-Admiral Spruance's task force comprising the carriers *Enterprise* and *Hornet* under him, disclosed a similar aerial activity. Reconnaissance aircraft were launched from the *Yorktown* in an attempt to locate the Japanese carriers, which from intelligence reports Fletcher knew must be approaching Midway from the north-west. While they were still searching, a report came in from a Catalina flying-boat from Midway. Nagumo's carriers had been found.

At once Fletcher ordered Spruance to take his force on to a position from which he could launch his attack planes, promising to follow as soon as he had recovered his scouting aircraft.

Meanwhile Nagumo, advised by the leader of the bombing planes over Midway that a further attack was necessary and still, at 7.15, ignorant of the presence of the American fleet within striking distance, had ordered his torpedo-planes to be struck down into the hangars and their torpedoes changed to bombs. Then at 7.45 came the first report from the *Tone*'s aircraft. At once Nagumo reversed his order. Torpedoes were to be put back again.

Thus when American torpedo-planes and dive-bombers from Midway roared into the attack, the Japanese hangar decks were littered with torpedoes and bombs. With the attack force due back from Midway, the flight decks had to be kept clear for them to land. No force could be sent to attack the American carriers.

However, the first waves of torpedo-aircraft to attack Nagumo's squadron found Japanese fighters waiting for them. Of sixteen Marine dive-bombers which attacked at 7.55, only eight, badly damaged, got back to base, and no hits were achieved. At 8.10, fifteen Flying Fortresses attacked from 20,000 feet quite ineffectively, after the fashion of high bombers. Then more dive-bombers screamed in to the attack, but were unsupported, and achieved nothing. Nagumo was not unjustifiably pleased with the successful defence offered. Confidently he steamed on, and soon after 8.30 started to recover the aircraft surviving from the attack on Midway.

But now his reconnaissance aircraft reported carrier aircraft approaching from eastward. As soon as the last bomber had been re-embarked and refuelling and rearming begun, he altered to east-north-east to take his force to locate and attack the American carriers. Winging towards him was a formidable force of no less than sixty-seven dive-bombers and twenty-nine torpedo-aircraft from *Enterprise* and *Hornet*. A further force of seventeen dive-bombers and twelve torpedo-aircraft from the *Yorktown* was also not far behind.

However, Nagumo's alteration of course greatly reduced the threat. The thirty-five dive-bombers from the *Hornet*, with the entire fighter escort, failed to find him; and after milling around searching for him, ran short of fuel and played no further part in the battle. This left the *Hornet*'s torpedo-aircraft unescorted. Attacking at 9.30, without waiting for *Enterprise*'s aircraft to co-ordinate their attack, they were shot down to a man, and made no hits. Coming in soon afterwards, the *Enterprise*'s torpedo-planes fared nearly as badly, losing ten out of their total of fourteen and again failing to achieve any hits.

But the gallant effort of the torpedo pilots was not entirely fruitless. Coming in low, they had drawn on to themselves the swarm of Japanese fighters protecting Nagumo's squadron. The upper air was left free for the dive-bombers from *Enterprise* and *Yorktown* to attack undisturbed. The Japanese carriers were by now somewhat scattered, owing to their manœuvres to avoid the American torpedoes. The *Hiryu* was far ahead; it was therefore on the *Akagi* and *Kaga* that the *Enterprise*'s aircraft swooped, while *Yorktown*'s dive-bombers chose the *Soryu* at the same moment.

In the next few minutes the Battle of Midway was lost and won.

Two bombs landed on Nagumo's flagship *Akagi*. One, plunging through the flight deck, burst in the hangar where the loaded torpedo-bombers were waiting. Fire at once broke out, and torpedoes and bombs exploded. The other bomb, landing squarely amidst the aircraft returned from Midway which were being refuelled on the flight deck, started further fierce fires. Above and below the *Akagi* was burning. All efforts of her crew to control them failed, and the carrier drifted away to be finally abandoned in the evening. Nagumo himself had meanwhile transferred his flag to a cruiser of his force.

The same fate was suffered by two others of the Japanese carrier force, the *Kaga* and the *Soryu*. Bombs set petrol, explosives and aircraft alight, and soon the ships were lapped in flame and smoke from bow to stern. The Emperor's portrait was ceremoniously transferred to destroyers which came alongside to embark all hands surplus to fire-fighting requirements. The efforts of the remainder were doomed to failure. As devastating internal explosions finally tore their ships apart, many hundreds of their ships' companies went down with them.

While this was going on, the fast battleships of Nagumo's squadron, *Haruna* and *Kirishima*, had been unable to protect the carriers despite their powerful gun armament. Clearly appreciating that it was the aircraft carriers which formed the main striking strength of a modern fleet, the American flyers had concentrated on them, ignoring the battleships—which were no longer the trumps in a fleet commander's hand.

That they were very right was soon to be demonstrated. Alone of Nagumo's squadron of carriers, the *Hiryu* had at first escaped destruction. By 11.10 a.m. a squadron of eighteen dive-bombers had been got ready, and set off to attack the *Yorktown*. With suicidal valour, encouraged by the desire to wipe out the stain of the Imperial Japanese Navy's first defeat, they plummeted down. Two bombs started dangerous fires; a third, exploding in the funnel, put several boilers out of action, reducing the *Yorktown*'s speed to 6 knots.

But the fires were quickly mastered, and the boilers repaired. At 20 knots again, the *Yorktown* had been able to land all her fighters for refuelling when a second wave of attackers, torpedo-planes this time, arrived from the *Hiryu*. Two torpedoes found their mark. The *Yorktown* was fatally damaged, soon to be abandoned as she heeled further and further over.

The *Hiryu* was not to survive long to enjoy her triumph. At 5.0 p.m. fresh waves of bombers from *Enterprise* and *Hornet* turned her into a blazing wreck. With the dawn, her crew were transferred to destroyers, and the *Hiryu* was sent to the bottom by torpedoes.

The Battle of Midway was over. The spear-head of the force with which the Japanese Navy had ruled the Eastern seas for six months was shattered. In this new form of naval battle, battleships had found themselves powerless to intervene. It may be thought that had Admiral Yamamoto added his powerful force of capital ships to the two fast battleships escorting Nagumo's carriers instead of holding them in support hundreds of miles in the rear, their tremendous volume of anti-aircraft fire might have saved the day. But the very possession of such splendid ships as the giant *Yamato* and the almost equally powerful *Nagato* and *Mutsu*, equipped to batter their armoured equals in thunderous gun duels, made it difficult for an admiral to appreciate that such ships had come to occupy a subsidiary position as anti-aircraft gun batteries defending the fleet's heart in the carriers. Its task completed, Admiral Spruance's force had turned away eastward. No target was left for the giant 18-inch and 16-inch guns of Yamamoto's ships. Their magazines full and their guns cold, they turned for home.

The Battle of Midway marked the end of Japanese expansion to the eastward. Far to the south, their probing towards Australia was halted by the American landing on the island of Guadalcanal in August 1942. For its possession and in particular for the air base of Henderson Field, the struggle was to be maintained with varying fortunes for months. Each side was bent on reinforcing their troops ashore on Guadalcanal and preventing the enemy from doing the same. In this the Americans were the most successful, but in the process they suffered sharp defeats when cruiser forces met in night battles.

In this form of warfare the Americans, in spite of the advantage of possessing radar sooner than the Japanese, proved to be less well-trained than their enemies. At the night Battle of Savo, which developed as the Japanese tried to get at the American transports which had just landed their expeditionary force, a mixed force of American and Australian ships lost four heavy cruisers without inflicting any serious damage on the enemy. Nevertheless, the Japanese were unable to carry on with their original plans.

Radar redressed the balance somewhat in October, when in another night cruiser action the Japanese, taken by surprise, lost the cruiser *Furutaka* and had two others badly damaged. As the battle ashore raged round Henderson Field, the Japanese brought their heavy ships, including battleships, into play to bombard the American air base. The Americans in their turn brought carrier task forces to the attack, supported by the two splendid new battleships *Washington* and *South Dakota*, each mounting nine 16-inch guns.

In a wide-spread carrier battle at the end of October, the Americans lost the *Hornet*. The *Wasp* had already been sunk by submarine attack, and for a time the Americans were reduced to a single carrier. Fortunately the continued possession of Henderson Field more than evened the odds.

By mid-November the fighting on Guadalcanal had reached a deadlock, but unless the Japanese could obtain substantial reinforcements they must soon give up the struggle for the island. In his flagship at Truk, Admiral Yamamoto was organising a full-scale expedition for this purpose. To cover a force of transports, he sent forward his fleet in two groups. A raiding group under Admiral Abe, consisting of the battleships *Hiei* and *Kirishima*, a light cruiser and fourteen destroyers, was to approach the northern shores of Guadalcanal, passing south of Savo Island about midnight on 12th November 1942 and bombard Henderson Field. In support would be Admiral Kondo with the battleships *Kongo* and *Haruna*, a heavy cruiser and destroyers.

Admiral Halsey, commanding the American fleet in the South Pacific from his headquarters at Noumea, had early news of the Japanese intentions, and ordered forward the powerful Task Force 16 under Admiral Kincaid, comprising the carrier *Enterprise*, two cruisers and destroyers and the battleships *Washington* and *South Dakota*. They could not hope to reach the area in time to intervene during the night of the 12th. Therefore the only force barring the way against Admiral Abe was made up of three heavy cruisers, *San Francisco*, *Portland* and *Helena*; two light cruisers, *Atlanta* and *Juneau*; and eight destroyers; the whole under Admiral Callaghan in the *San Francisco*.

At 1.30 on the morning of the 13th November the two forces

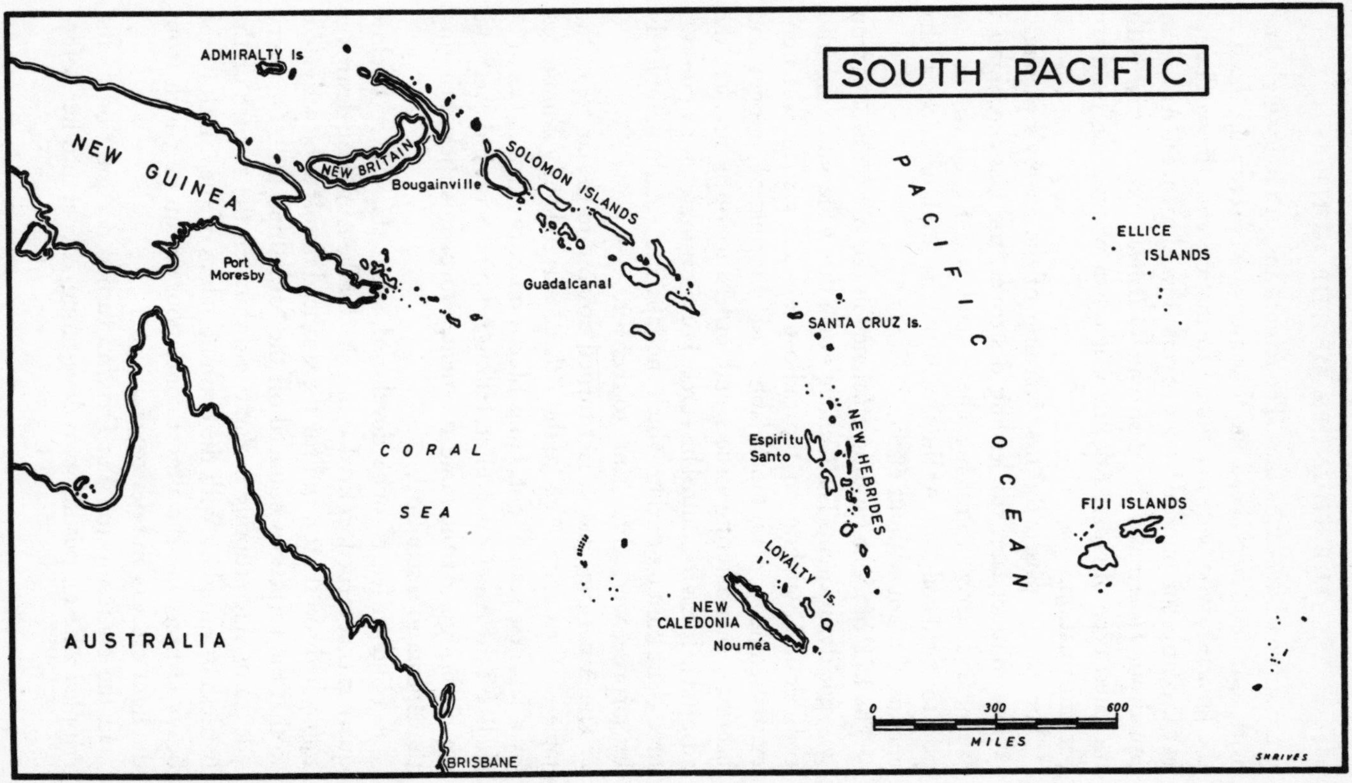
SOUTH PACIFIC
ADMIRALTY Is
NEW GUINEA
NEW BRITAIN
Bougainville
SOLOMON ISLANDS
Port
Moresby
Guadalcanal
PACIFIC OCEAN
ELLICE
ISLANDS
SANTA CRUZ Is.
Espiritu
Santo
NEW HEBRIDES
CORAL
SEA
FIJI ISLANDS
LOYALTY Is.
NEW
CALEDONIA
Nouméa
AUSTRALIA
0
300
600
MILES
BRISBANE
SHRIVES

were approaching each other. The Americans, in a long single line with four destroyers ahead and four astern, were crossing ahead of the Japanese, who were in a square formation with the battleships in the centre, surrounded by destroyers. Two ships of the American squadron, *Helena* and the destroyer *O'Bannon*, were fitted with the latest type of radar. Admiral Callaghan was relying on them for information.

The *Helena* passed the first warning of the enemy's presence. A few minutes later the leading destroyer, the *Cushing*, sighted Japanese destroyers crossing ahead, and was forced to turn to port to avoid collision. At the same time she fired torpedoes at the enemy, though without effect.

The lack of night-fighting efficiency in the American squadron was quickly apparent. The *Cushing*'s turn threw the whole line into confusion. Discipline on the radio-telephone system was non-existent, and a continuous jabber of information, ranges and bearings, manœuvring orders and orders to open fire left the admiral helpless to control his force. For six minutes not a gun was fired—six minutes during which the Japanese, caught completely by surprise, were given time to recover.

The Americans had in fact turned down into the centre of the Japanese formation. At 1.50 the *Atlanta* was suddenly illuminated by a Japanese searchlight. Guns blazed on both sides. A storm of shells hit the American cruiser, killing Admiral Scott and everyone on his bridge. At the same moment a torpedo struck, bringing the *Atlanta* to a standstill.

A blind mêlée at once developed, with ships at such close quarters that torpedoes fired at the *Hiei* by the American destroyer *Laffey* had too short a run for the warhead pistols to be activated, so that the torpedoes bounced off the battleship's hull. On every side guns were erupting in flame and thunder, the 14-inch of the battleships mingling with the crashing salvos of the 8-inch of the heavy cruisers and the almost continuous stream of 5-inch from the light cruisers and destroyers.

In the confusion the *San Francisco* turned her guns on to the crippled *Atlanta*, putting two devastating salvoes into her before

Admiral Callaghan, horror-struck at the mistake, sent out the agonised command over the radio "Cease fire—Own Ships." While other ships engaging the enemy were still questioning this incomprehensible order, the *San Francisco* came under the fire of the *Kirishima*'s big guns. As Callaghan, the captain of the *San Francisco*, and all on the bridge fell mortally wounded, steering and engine control were temporarily lost, leaving the ship unmanageable.

While the American ships were still trying to gain confirmation of the cease-fire order, torpedoes exploded against the *Portland* and *Juneau*, the latter almost at once in a sinking condition. The *Portland*, her steering gear damaged, turned a complete circle. As she completed it, the battleship *Hiei* loomed up in her sights. At the short range of 4,000 yards, the *Portland* turned her 8-inch guns on to the Japanese ship, and was joined by every undamaged American. At such a range even the strongly armoured battleship began to suffer severely. By the time Admiral Abe had ordered a retirement to the west, the *Hiei* was barely manœuvrable, and her speed had been reduced to a crawl.

Gradually the two entangled forces drew clear of each other. Of the American squadron two destroyers had been lost and a third disabled; the *Portland* was crippled and had to be towed to safety; the *Atlanta* was so damaged that she had to be scuttled the next day, while the *Juneau* was torpedoed and sunk by a Japanese submarine. Only the *Helena* and *San Francisco* survived from amongst the cruisers, and even they had been heavily damaged.

On the Japanese side, though two destroyers had been sunk, the parlous condition of the battleship *Hiei* was the most disastrous outcome of the engagement. Reduced to a crawl, she was delivered into the hands of the *Enterprise*'s aircraft the next morning. Repeatedly attacked and hit by four torpedoes as well as bombs, she survived until 6 p.m., but was then abandoned by her crew in a sinking condition.

In spite of this setback, the Japanese pressed on with their plans. In place of Admiral Abe's bombardment force, four heavy cruisers were sent in the following night, and succeeded in bombarding Henderson Field. In the meantime the Japanese convoy of troop transports sailed steadily on. But by now *Enterprise*'s aircraft were dominating the whole area. As the Japanese cruisers retired after their bombardment, they were set upon by dive-bombers; one was sunk and the remainder heavily damaged. Then it was the turn of the transports. Of the eleven merchantmen, seven were sunk or set ablaze. The remaining four pressed on with desperate courage, and during the night of 15th November succeeded in reaching the roadstead of Tassafaronga, where they ran themselves ashore and set about landing their troops and supplies.

In support of this desperate effort, Admiral Kondo, who had added the *Kirishima* and the survivors of the night action to his force, was planning to renew the bombardment of Henderson Field during the night. By now the *Enterprise*'s group had been withdrawn to refuel. Left to bar Kondo's way was Task Force 64, made up of the battleships *Washington* (flagship of Rear-Admiral Lee) and *South Dakota*, together with destroyers. By the evening of the 15th, Lee had rounded the western tip of Guadalcanal and was shaping course to pass in a wide sweep round Savo Island during the night.

By the light of a quarter-moon the Americans had circled Savo, and at 10.52 had turned west to pass south of Savo. They were about to meet the Japanese force, which was coming through the channel in three groups. Leading it was a group composed of a light cruiser and three destroyers; then came a screen of destroyers and the cruiser *Nagara*, and finally the actual bombardment group, composed of the *Kirishima* and two heavy cruisers.

The American force had been hastily got together, and the ships were unused to working together. The battleships were new and largely untried. In spite of the American advantage of radar, the Japanese again displayed the superiority of their night-fighting technique in the first clash. As the destroyer screens tangled, the Japanese at once got away well-aimed salvoes of torpedoes. In a few minutes two American destroyers had been sunk and another crippled.

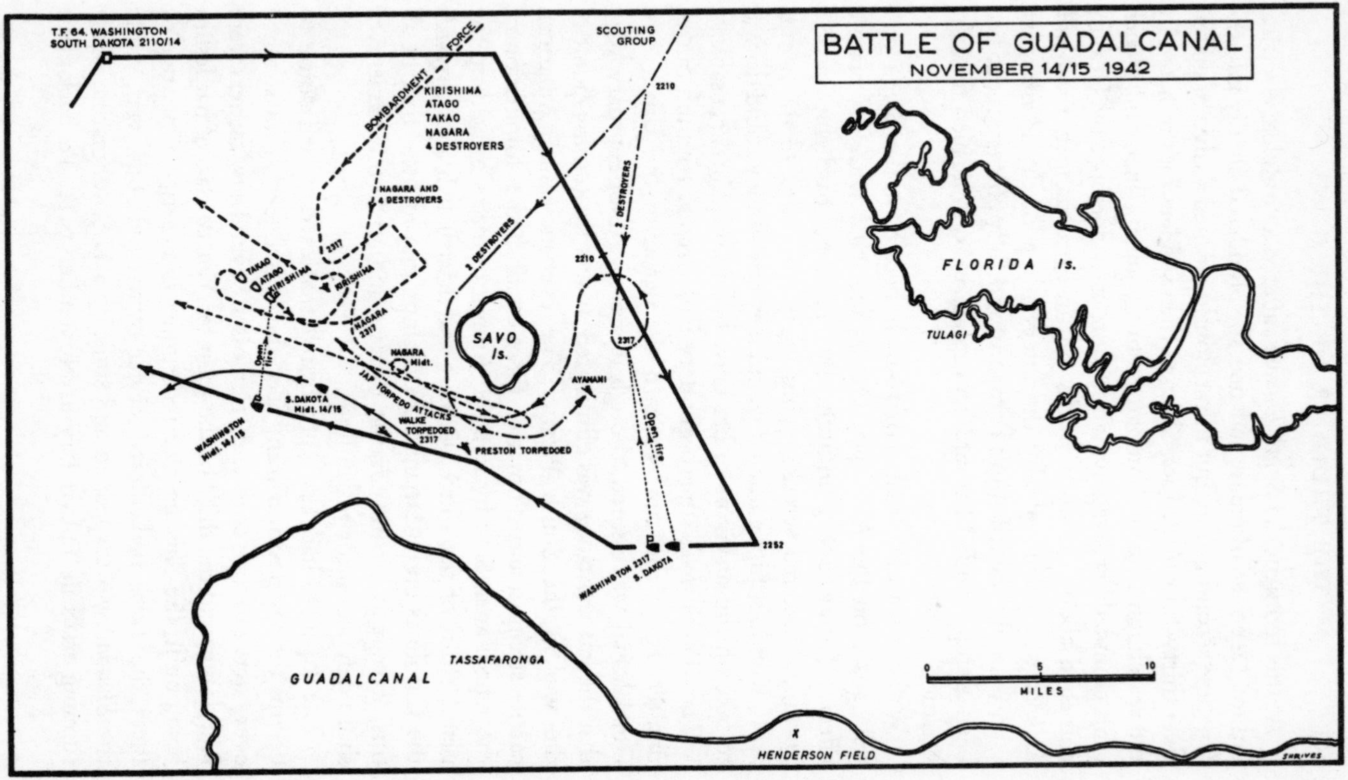
BATTLE OF GUADALCANAL
NOVEMBER 14/15 1942
T.F. 64. WASHINGTON
SOUTH DAKOTA 2110/14
SCOUTING GROUP
BOMBARDMENT FORCE
KIRISHIMA
ATAGO
TAKAO
NAGARA
4 DESTROYERS
NAGARA AND
4 DESTROYERS
2 DESTROYERS
2 DESTROYERS
2210
2210
2317
2317
TAKAO
ATAGO
KIRISHIMA
KIRISHIMA
NAGARA
2317
NAGARA
Midt.
SAVO
Is.
AYANAMI
Open fire
Open fire
JAP TORPEDO ATTACKS
S. DAKOTA
Midt. 14/15
WASHINGTON
Midt. 14/15
WALKE
TORPEDOED
2317
PRESTON TORPEDOED
WASHINGTON 2317
S. DAKOTA
2252
FLORIDA Is.
TULAGI
GUADALCANAL
TASSAFARONGA
HENDERSON FIELD
0
5
10
MILES
SHRIVES

At this moment the *South Dakota* suffered a complete electrical failure. Deprived of radar guidance, she blundered blindly into the Japanese second group, but miraculously escaped a salvo of no less than thirty-four torpedoes. She was then suddenly illuminated by the searchlights of the bombardment group. 14-inch and 8-inch guns pounded her savagely, while more torpedoes sped by. Heavily damaged about the upperworks and in great danger, the *South Dakota* was saved only by the intervention of the *Washington*, whose highly trained ship's company and fully efficient radar had been giving Admiral Lee and her captain an accurate picture of the situation.

Without warning a salvo of 16-inch shells from the *Washington* fell square on the *Kirishima*. Others followed with devastating effect. Within seven minutes the Japanese battleship was a burning, shattered wreck, trying vainly to escape to the north-west. Kondo's ships gathered round her, but all they could do was to take off the survivors of her crew before the *Kirishima* sank.

The *Washington*'s superb gunnery had wrested triumph out of disaster. From this time onward the defeat of the Japanese in Guadalcanal was assured, though it was not until February 1943 that the last resistance was eliminated. It was the turning-point of the war in the South Pacific. The ever-increasing American carrier strength and submarine force established a domination of the whole area. Step by step the American forces moved up the island chain of the Ellice, Gilbert and Marshall Islands towards the Carolines and Marianas. Battleships played little part in all this, except as escorts for the carriers and in bombardment of shore defences prior to landings.

The Japanese had also appreciated that carriers had come to occupy the key position in any fleet, and consequently they strained every nerve to replace their carrier losses. Several new carriers were laid down, and the third of the monster *Yamato* class of battleship being built, the *Shinano*, was redesigned as a carrier. Only one of these, the *Taiho*, had entered service by the end of the war, while the *Shinano* was torpedoed and sunk by a U.S. submarine while running trials in Tokyo Bay in November 1944. To back their three remaining large carriers, *Shokaku*, *Zuikaku* and *Taiho*, the Japanese had therefore to rely upon a number of small auxiliary carriers converted from cruisers and tankers.

By the middle of June 1944 the Americans were ready to assault the Marianas. Three strong task forces set out, comprising in all nine carriers and seven battleships. On the 15th, Vice-Admiral Ozawa, commanding the main Japanese fleet which, including six aircraft carriers and a battle squadron of five battleships, was exercising amongst the Philippines, received the startling news that American troops were landing on Saipan in the Marianas. It was an attack on the main defence barrier of the Japanese homeland, and could not be left unopposed. Ozawa's whole force sailed at once to the attack.

At daybreak on the 19th the reconnaissance aircraft of each side reported the enemy advancing. With a distance of more than 150 miles separating the two fleets, the battle began as torpedo-planes and dive-bombers roared off from the Japanese carriers' decks at 7.30 to attack the central American force. The Americans were in their element in this sort of battle. Long before the attackers had come within sight of the fleet, swarms of Grumman Wildcat fighters came tearing down out of the skies, throwing the Japanese formations into confusion and shooting down many aircraft. About half got through this first line of defence, only to meet an impenetrable wall of fire from the guns of the battleships and cruisers surrounding the American carriers.

The pilots, mostly inexperienced, and inheriting only courage from amongst the qualities of Nagumo's first-line aviators of the early months of war, came on with reckless gallantry but a lack of co-ordination, and were shot down one by one. A handful survived and made for the airfield on Guam, still in Japanese hands, only to find American fighter-planes waiting for them. Except for a few bomb hits on the battleships, which hurt the armoured monsters little, the attack had achieved nothing; neither did later attack waves, each of which broke against the solid American defence.

Meanwhile, all unknown to them, the Japanese carriers were

running into a submarine ambush. First the *Taiho*, Ozawa's flagship, was torpedoed, and the blow ruptured the piping for aviation spirit. As liquid poured into the hangar, explosive gases filled the ship, and at 11.00 a.m., soon after the Admiral had transferred to a cruiser, the carrier blew up in one tremendous explosion. Hardly had she vanished when four torpedoes struck the carrier *Shokaku*. In less than three hours, she, too, had gone to the bottom.

With only one large carrier left to him and barely a hundred aircraft out of the huge force with which he had started the day, Ozawa turned to escape. Now it was the turn of the Americans to attack. The Japanese force was somewhat scattered, and so the fighter defence and gun barrage was powerless to hold off the dive-bombers and torpedo-planes. The auxiliary carrier *Hiyo* was torpedoed and sunk; the *Junyo* was heavily damaged by bombs, and other ships were damaged by near misses.

The defeated remnants of the Japanese fleet fled to Okinawa, where they arrived on 22nd June, the carriers sailing on from there for repairs in the dockyards of Japan. Not until they were fit for battle again could the Japanese fleet offer any serious resistance. Island after island fell into American hands, driving the Japanese back on to their homeland. Desperately short of oil fuel and of tankers in which to transport it, the Japanese battle squadron under Admiral Kurita was forced to skulk in the Singapore area where some supplies were still available. Without aircraft carriers they were for the time being unable to intervene in the war.

By October the pattern of American air attacks showed that they were preparing to assault either the Philippine Islands or Formosa. By that time, too, the Japanese carriers had completed their repairs. Though ultimate defeat was now certain, and was realised by Japan's politicians, her military leaders were determined to fight on. Above all the loss of the Philippines and Formosa must be prevented; otherwise the oil regions of the south would be cut off from Japan, and the whole military machine would grind slowly to a halt.

A vast plan was therefore evolved to bring the American fleet to action as soon as landings were launched. Of great complexity, and relying for success on accurately timed arrivals of a number of different forces from as far apart as Singapore and Japan, it was to be the last defiant act of the Imperial Japanese Navy. There could be no question of an indecisive battle; it was to be victory or "hara-kiri".

Such was the position at 8 o'clock on the morning of 17th October 1944, when the Japanese Commander-in-Chief received the news that the Americans were landing on the islets at the entrance to the Gulf of Leyte. The order went out "Alert Plan Sho 1". The ride which was to end in the death of a navy had begun.

17

The Battle of Leyte—Overture

THE plan known as "Sho" devised by Imperial Japanese Naval Headquarters, was calculated to destroy any American landing force assaulting the Philippine Islands or Formosa. It consisted essentially in a strong force of Japan's last remaining aircraft carriers, coming south from Japan, luring the American Third Fleet—the main American carrier task force—away from the vicinity of the landings and engaging it in an all-out air battle, while from Singapore the Japanese battle fleet, including the giant battleships *Yamato* and *Musashi* and five others, would converge to annihilate the landing force and its defenders.

By October 1944 Japanese naval leaders no longer held any hope that the war could be won. The Japanese war machine was running down to a stop owing principally to the virtual elimination of her merchant fleet and in particular of her tankers. Dependent upon import of materials of all sorts, Japan could neither replace her losses in ships, especially aircraft carriers, nor in trained aviators, for whom there was insufficient aviation petrol for them to be given the necessary instruction and practice. Unable yet to contemplate surrender, the Japanese could only try to put off the inevitable end. This end would be brought immeasurably closer by the loss of the Philippines or Formosa, from either of which the supply route from the oil-fields of the south would be cut off.

At any cost, therefore, the loss of these places had to be postponed—even if it meant the destruction of the major portion of the Japanese fleet. There could be no doubt that the execution of the "Sho" plan would entail such a destruction. But in the process, a shattering blow might be struck at the American fleet also.

The "Sho" plan involved the simultaneous arrival in the threatened area of four separate forces, two from Singapore, with an advanced base at Brunei in Borneo, and two from Japan. At the given moment, the Second Fleet would sail from Brunei, organised in three sections A, B and C. Sections A and B would move as one force under Vice-Admiral Kurita; it consisted of the five most modern battleships, *Yamato*, *Musashi*, *Nagato*, *Kongo* and *Haruna*, ten heavy cruisers, two light cruisers and fifteen destroyers. Section C, under Vice-Admiral Nishimura, grouped round the older, slower battleships *Yamashiro* and *Fuso*, would take a shorter route. Timing its arrival with that of Kurita's force, it would form the other half of pincers between which the American landing fleet would be caught. To back Nishimura's force, a further squadron from the Fifth Fleet under Vice-Admiral Shima, made up of two heavy cruisers, one light cruiser and seven destroyers, would join him from Japan while on passage.

So much for the intended trap. For the lure which was to draw off the main American fleet, the Japanese Commander-in-Chief, Admiral Toyoda, planned to use the whole of the available Japanese carrier force, the last remaining large carrier *Zuikaku*; three light carriers *Zuiho*, *Chitose* and *Chiyoda*; two battleships *Hyuga* and *Ise*, which doubled the rôle of carrier, having a flight deck in place of their after turrets; three light cruisers, and ten destroyers. The whole of this force, under Vice-Admiral Ozawa, was based in Japan at the beginning of October, husbanding its precious fuel. Moreover the pilots of the two Carrier Divisions, 3 and 4, were still under training, and few of them were as yet fit to operate at sea. Only when the point of attack was known would this force, the Third Fleet, sail. The limited forces by now available to Toyoda, particularly of carrier-trained aviators, and the limited fuel that could be spared for the fleet, made it essential that exactly the right moment should be selected for committing his strength to battle. If the fleet were sent to sea too early it might run short of fuel, and would have to return just when the American attack was about to be launched. The heavy losses in large tankers made it no

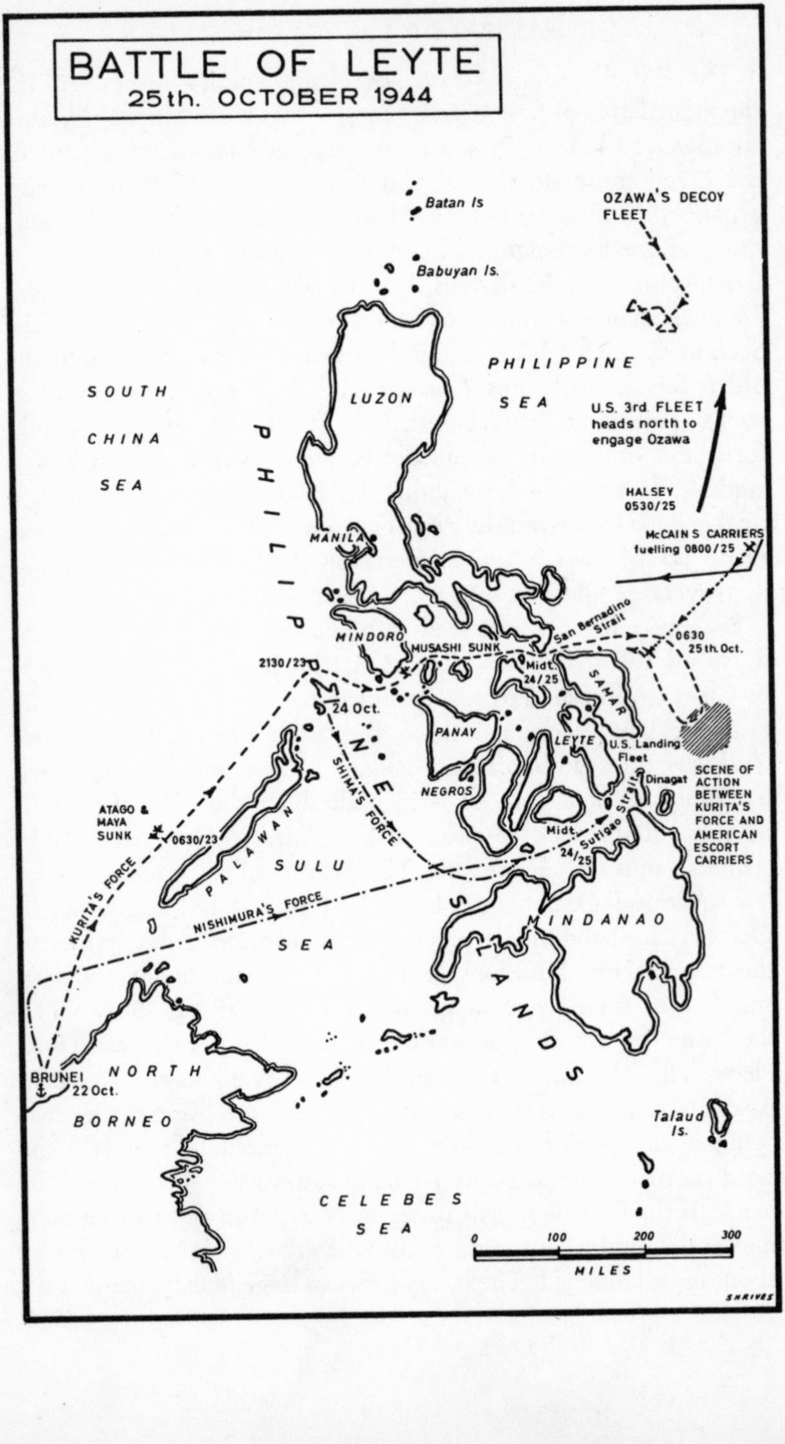

BATTLE OF LEYTE
25th. OCTOBER 1944
Batan Is
Babuyan Is.
OZAWA'S DECOY FLEET
PHILIPPINE SEA
SOUTH CHINA SEA
LUZON
U.S. 3rd. FLEET heads north to engage Ozawa
HALSEY 0530/25
McCAIN S CARRIERS fuelling 0800/25
MANILA
PHILIPPINE ISLANDS
San Bernadino Strait
MINDORO
MUSASHI SUNK
0630 25th Oct.
2130/23
Midt. 24/25
SAMAR
24 Oct.
PANAY
LEYTE
U.S. Landing Fleet
SHIMA'S FORCE
Dinagat
SCENE OF ACTION BETWEEN KURITA'S FORCE AND AMERICAN ESCORT CARRIERS
NEGROS
ATAGO & MAYA SUNK
0630/23
Surigao Strait
Midt. 24/25
PALAWAN
SULU SEA
KURITA'S FORCE
NISHIMURA'S FORCE
MINDANAO
BRUNEI 22 Oct.
NORTH BORNEO
Talaud Is.
CELEBES SEA
0 100 200 300
MILES
SHRIVES

longer possible to refuel at sea, whereas the American task forces, accompanied by their Fleet Train, could and did remain at sea for weeks on end.

So at the beginning of October, the stage was set. Somewhere to the eastward in the wide Pacific lay the U.S. Third Fleet under Admiral Halsey, with his flag in the fast and powerful new battleship *New Jersey*, the greatest naval force to be gathered in the war. Eight fleet carriers and eight light carriers were backed by six fast battleships, six heavy cruisers, nine light cruisers and fifty-eight destroyers, the whole force being designated Task Force 38 with Vice-Admiral M. A. Mitscher as Task Force Commander in the carrier *Lexington*. It was divided into four task groups, each centred on carriers.[1]

A separate organisation, coming under General MacArthur's South-west Pacific Command, was the U.S. Seventh Fleet, charged with carrying out the landings. Under the overall command of Vice-Admiral Kinkaid, a great force of transports was to have as close support a task force under Rear-Admiral Oldendorf, comprising six modernised older battleships, three heavy cruisers, five light cruisers and a number of destroyers. Air support was to come from a force under Rear-Admiral T. L. Sprague, made up of eighteen escort carriers—slow, lightly armed ships converted from merchantmen, carrying a comparatively small number of aircraft each.

It was primarily at the destruction of this Seventh Fleet and the repulse of its landing effort that the "Sho" plan was aimed. If Ozawa's force of carriers could succeed in reducing Halsey's Third Fleet, it would be in the nature of a bonus.

Meanwhile Toyoda, in his headquarters outside Tokyo, could only wait and see which point would be selected by the Americans for attack. Early in October every indication was that it would be Formosa. Halsey's carriers launched their air armada against the air-fields and installations there, and also in Luzon, the northern island of the Philippines. For six days, in tremendous strength, the American carrier planes swept in to attack after attack. Against

[1] See Appendix II for composition of the opposing fleets.

the carriers the Japanese launched their shore-based naval and military air forces from the Philippines and Formosa. Early reports of successes by these aircraft led Toyoda to believe that an opportunity had come to cripple Halsey's fleet really seriously. It seemed that the shore-based air force, which was suffering heavy losses, only needed strong reinforcement to achieve this object. But the only reinforcements available were the aircraft of Carrier Divisions 3 and 4, still incompletely trained and scheduled to embark in Ozawa's carriers as soon as the executive order for "Sho" was given.

Toyoda was called upon to make an agonising decision, similar to that of a general in a land battle whose last reserves, if committed and successful, would bring victory, but if thrown back might lead to a disastrous rout. Deceived by the exaggerated claims of the airmen, Toyoda made his gamble. The whole of the aircraft force of Carrier Divisions 3 and 4 was sent forward to join the battle raging to the eastward of Formosa.

The result appeared to justify Toyoda's action. Jubilant reports reached him of American carriers sinking and burning, as many as thirteen being reported destroyed. So complete seemed the havoc caused amongst the Americans that the cruisers of Admiral Shima's Fifth Fleet were sailed from the Inland Sea to mop up the few remaining units. Unfortunately for Toyoda, not one American ship had been actually sunk, the total serious damage being to two cruisers which had been torpedoed. As Admiral Halsey with grim humour signalled when he heard of these claims, his sunken ships had been salvaged and "were retiring at high speed towards the Japanese fleet".

On the other hand the air fleets of the Japanese Carrier Divisions 3 and 4 had been massacred by the fighters and guns of the American fleet. A vital component of the "Sho" plan had been virtually eliminated. Toyoda was still absorbing this disastrous news, which was coupled with reports of very large American carrier forces still at sea, exposing the falsity of his airmen's claims, when, on 18th October he heard that landings had been successfully made on the islands of Suluan and Dinagat in the mouth of the Gulf of Leyte. At dawn on the 20th the great guns of Rear-Admiral Oldendorf's battleships opened on the beaches to the north of the Gulf, and dive-bombers from Sprague's escort carriers screamed down on to the defences. Exactly on schedule, at 10 o'clock, the first waves of landing-craft beached. The target area was known at last. The executive order was given for the launching of "Sho".

Already Admiral Kurita's Second Fleet had been ordered forward to its advanced base, and at noon on the 20th it entered Brunei Bay to begin refuelling. Meanwhile Shima's Fifth Fleet, which had been awaiting orders at Amami-O-Shima, north of Okinawa, had reached the Pescadores, and was similarly fuelling ready for the great attack. The 25th had been decided upon as X-day, the day on which the Japanese forces would fall upon the American landing fleet.

Far to the north, Ozawa had been disconsolately discussing with Naval Headquarters what was to be the rôle of his force now that more than half of the air fleet for his carriers had been destroyed. Of the remainder, the pilots were so untrained that the aircraft would have to be hoisted aboard and not flown. Thus all hope had gone of fulfilling that part of his task which had been expected to cripple the U.S. Third Fleet carriers. Ozawa's own carriers could now take on simply the rôle of decoys—decoys which to be successful would inevitably be sacrificed to the overwhelming air power of Halsey's fleet. So it was decided and in the afternoon of the 20th October 1944, Ozawa's fleet passed out of the Inland Sea, heading south on its suicide mission.

* * *

The battle which was soon to unfold was probably the most tremendous sea-fight of all time, although since it occurred in the new air age and was spread over a thousand miles of sea, the various surface forces which actually clashed in gun battles were not so large as in the heyday of the battleship. Indeed, this battle gave the final proof that the day of the battleship was over. In the course of it the biggest battleship in the world was to go down under air attack alone, its giant 18-inch guns never having fired a shot in earnest during the whole course of its career. Other battleships were to steam fruitlessly and frantically from one battle area to another trying to bring their guns into action, while overhead the real striking power of modern fleets ranged to and fro delivering the blows which the guns were unable to do.

* * *

During 22nd October, Kurita's Second Fleet sailed from Brunei on its mission. On the previous evening the Admiral had given his orders. The First and Second Sections, comprising *Yamato*, *Musashi*, *Nagato*, *Kongo* and *Haruna*, all fast and powerful battleships, ten heavy cruisers, two light cruisers and fifteen destroyers, weighed anchor at 8 a.m. and set course to pass north of Palawan, south of Mindoro on the 24th and thence through the San Bernadino Strait during that night so as to arrive off the mouth of the Gulf of Leyte at 4 a.m. on the 25th. Kurita's flag flew in the heavy cruiser *Atago*.

The Third Section—the older battleships *Yamashiro* (flying Admiral Nishimura's flag) and *Fuso*, a heavy cruiser and four destroyers—sailed during the afternoon to take the shorter route to Leyte, through the Mindanao Sea and the Surigao Strait.

From Coron Bay in the Calamian Islands, Shima's three cruisers and four destroyers would sail early on the 24th to make the same final approach to Leyte as Nishimura, though neither admiral knew the other's movements in any detail.

Kurita's force duly steered north-eastward from Brunei. For the first day of its passage it was beyond the reach of reconnaissance aircraft from the American fleet, and had no fear of air attacks. By this time, however, American submarines, had established a very real ascendancy in the minds of the Japanese. Submarines were known to patrol the waters through which Kurita was passing, and throughout the 22nd look-outs were nervously alert, several false sighting reports being made. But when darkness fell all was still quiet, and during the night the fleet steamed peacefully up the coast of Palawan at 16 knots. But all unknown to the Japanese the dreaded submarines had indeed located them around midnight. Sending off sighting reports, the two American submarines *Darter* and *Dace* stationed themselves one on each bow of the advancing columns and waited for daybreak to attack. Just as daylight was beginning to grow, Kurita's peaceful progress was shattered as four torpedoes hit his flagship *Atago*. As smoke and flame burst from the whole length of the cruiser, two more torpedoes found the cruiser next astern, the *Takao*, bringing her to a standstill.

There was just time for Kurita and his staff to transfer to a destroyer before the *Atago* sank. Almost at once more torpedoes struck the other column of ships, where the cruiser *Maya* was blown to pieces, disappearing in four minutes. It was a disastrous opening to the day; and though no further attacks developed before dark, Japanese confidence was so shaken that alarm followed alarm, keeping the force manœuvring this way and that so continuously that it was not until late in the afternoon that Kurita was able to board the *Yamato* and resume active control of his force. Meanwhile, the Japanese ships had continued to follow their scheduled course past the Calamian Islands. By midnight they were in the Mindoro Strait. Daylight found them heading eastward to the south of Mindoro Island. A circular formation was taken up, with the battleships and cruisers ringed by destroyers, and the crews braced themselves for the air attacks which must surely come.

For the next two hours no attack developed, although radar, with which Japanese ships had at last been fitted, repeatedly made contact with aircraft formations. Tension had reached an unbearable degree when at 10.25 a.m. aircraft were seen sweeping into the attack. Kurita had asked for fighter protection, but all naval fighters were very fully occupied elsewhere. It is a measure of the absence of co-operation between the Japanese Naval and Army air forces that he neither asked for nor expected army fighters to be sent to his aid. Thus although the Japanese ships put up a gun barrage, using everything from 16-inch down to 20-millimetre, they were entirely unable to defend themselves from the twelve dive-bombers and thirteen torpedo-planes from the carriers *Intrepid* and *Cabot* of Halsey's fleet. One torpedo struck the *Musashi* on her starboard side. Another hit the cruiser *Myoko*. The *Myoko*, her speed reduced to 15 knots, rapidly dropped astern and was ordered back to Brunei. It took more than one torpedo seriously to damage such a monster as the *Musashi*, however; she steamed on, her speed and fighting power unaffected. By noon the force had debouched into the Sibuyan Sea.

Now came the second attack by *Intrepid*'s aircraft, as twelve dive-bombers and nine torpedo-planes streaked down from 15,000 feet in a co-ordinated effort which swamped the anti-aircraft defences. Concentrated on the *Musashi*, it resulted in two bomb and two torpedo hits. Now the great ship began to suffer from the accumulating damage. Her speed reduced to 22 knots, she began to drop astern of the formation. Further attacks followed throughout the afternoon, planes from the carriers *Lexington* and *Essex* joining those from *Intrepid*'s group. *Yamato* and *Nagato* were both hit by bombs, but these could cause only minor damage to such armoured giants, and they were able to evade all torpedoes. The *Musashi*, however, less manœuvrable after her previous damage, took three more torpedo hits. Her position was getting serious. With her forecastle almost awash, she dared not do more than 12 knots for fear of plunging by the bow. At 3 p.m. Kurita ordered her to make for Coron Bay, but the command came too late. A few minutes after she had turned back a further attack was concentrated on her, and ten bombs and four more torpedoes made her end certain. Though she was kept afloat for another four hours, she was abandoned at 7.20 p.m. Fifteen minutes later the most powerful battleship in the world rolled slowly over to port and sank. More than a thousand men perished with her.

Meanwhile the American carriers from which these attacks had been coming had been fighting off heavy raids by shore-based aircraft. Tremendous dog-fights had whirled furiously over their heads, particularly over the most northern of the four Task Groups into which the Third Fleet was divided, comprising the two large carriers *Lexington* and *Essex*, the light carriers *Princeton* and *Langley*, and several battleships and cruisers.

The American fighters completely dominated the Japanese aircraft everywhere, and no organised attacks got through. It was a single Japanese dive-bomber arriving over the *Princeton* unobserved which gave the Japanese their only success. Its bomb, plunging through the flight deck into the hangar before exploding, started uncontrollable fires amongst torpedo-aircraft waiting there, their torpedoes already slung beneath them. Heroic fire-fighting and damage control work assisted by cruisers and destroyers which secured alongside, at great risk, to play their hoses on the fires, had seemingly almost achieved final success in saving the ship by 3 p.m. The remaining fire still burning was around a torpedo stowage on the main deck in which, for want of space in the magazines, a number of bombs had been stowed.

It was thought that any explosion which was threatened would have occurred long ago, and so the cruiser *Birmingham* was brought alongside to complete the extinguishing of this last fire. As she lay close on the quarter of the burning carrier a violent explosion lifted a great section of the *Princeton*'s flight-deck into the air. Then on the blast came a whirlwind of steel débris ranging from small splinters to large sections of deck plating, which swept the crowded decks of the two ships. The upper deck of the cruiser was on the instant populated almost entirely by dead or wounded men. In the *Princeton*, scarcely a man escaped some injury.

It was a heavy price to pay (though who will be so rash as to say too heavy?) to support the U.S. Navy tradition never to give up the ship. But for all the sacrifice, though the *Princeton* was still in no danger of sinking, continued efforts to save her were interfering with the progress of operations. At 4.45 p.m., on orders from the Task Group commander, two torpedoes were put into the carrier to send her to the bottom.

★ ★ ★

By 4 o'clock the unceasing succession of air attacks had begun to dismay Kurita. For six hours of this day which had started with the shattering shock of torpedoes in his flagship, he had had to endure constant attacks with never a sight of a friendly aircraft. Everyone of his major units had suffered to some degree, and the speed of his squadron had been reduced to 22 knots. No word had reached him of the progress of attacks by the shore-based air fleets on the American heavy carriers, attacks which might bring him some relief before he left the open waters of the Sibuyan Sea for the narrow channels between the islands. For an hour, therefore, he reversed course and headed westwards; but by 5.20 p.m. he was once again on his heading for the San Bernadino Strait.

Indeed, Kurita had enjoyed an inexplicable respite from attack during his westward run—inexplicable to the Japanese, that is to say. The actual fact was that at about 4.40 the long-awaited news of the location of the Japanese carriers had reached Halsey. All day Ozawa had been pushing southwards, disappointed and puzzled that no enemy search planes had discovered him; for until he was discovered he could hardly play his assigned rôle of decoy. All day, too, Halsey had been wondering where the enemy carriers could be. Not realising that they were almost empty of aircraft, they seemed to form the main danger and therefore the main target, particularly as the sighting aircraft included several battleships in their reports. Kurita's force, so Halsey was assured by his airmen, had been thoroughly routed, and had been last seen retreating westwards. They were no longer a force seriously to be reckoned with. The two squadrons under Nishimura and Shima which had been sighted making for the Surigao Strait were adequately opposed by Vice-Admiral Kinkaid's Seventh Fleet with its six battleships. Only Ozawa's northern force, its strength greatly exaggerated by the air sighting reports, remained to be taken care of.

Halsey was no man to sit and wait for the enemy to come to him. Of the three alternatives open to him as dusk fell over the Pacific on the evening of 24th October, one, that of maintaining his station to eastward of San Bernadino Strait and so opposing the approach of both Kurita and Ozawa, meant a period of passive waiting. A second, that of leaving his battleships to guard the San

Bernadino Strait while the carrier force went north to engage Ozawa, would leave his battleships exposed to air attack by land-based air forces without fighter defence, a course which every lesson of the war to date condemned as unsound.

The third alternative, to go north with his whole force and engage Ozawa, leaving San Bernadino unguarded, commended itself strongly to Halsey's fighting spirit. On the strength of the information in his possession, the plan could not be faulted. At about 8.20 p.m. the decision was made. The various groups of Task Force 38 were directed to rendezvous and proceed northwards. Unfortunately, as has been seen, the two main pieces of intelligence upon which the decision was based were seriously inaccurate. Kurita's force had still four powerful battleships, including the *Yamato*; their fighting capacity had hardly been affected, and the Japanese were steaming hard at 20 knots for the San Bernadino Strait. Instead of comprising twenty-four ships including four battleships and carrying a formidable air fleet in its carriers, Ozawa's force was made up of only nineteen ships, of which the only two battleships had a third of their main armament removed and the carriers were empty shells with a mere handful of aircraft in their hangars.

But the die was cast, and now occurred a misunderstanding which was to have serious consequences. Informing Kinkaid of his decision, Halsey told him he was going north with *three* groups, presumably because his fourth group, which had been previously detached for replenishment, was given separate instructions and would not join the remainder of the Force until the following day. At the same time Kinkaid intercepted a message from Halsey to his Task Group Commanders in which reference was made to formation of a Task Force 34, composed of the battleships of the Third Fleet. The Seventh Fleet Commander assumed that this was Halsey's *fourth* group, and was being left to guard the San Bernadino Strait.

So while Halsey's great force was thus gathering and hurrying northwards through the night, and Nishimura's Third Section of the Second Fleet, with Shima's force some 40 miles astern of him, was approaching the Surigao Strait under a quarter-moon which would set soon after midnight, Kinkaid prepared to defend only that entrance to the Leyte Gulf area. Rear-Admiral Oldendorf's force of six battleships—elderly but modernised—three heavy cruisers, five light cruisers and twenty-six destroyers was overwhelmingly strong enough to take care of Nishimura and Shima. Kinkaid faced the night with an easy mind. The sixteen escort carriers of the landing force and their screens were to stay well clear in their usual flying stations to the eastward of Leyte Gulf.

Though contact with the Japanese Southern Force—Nishimura and Shima—had been lost during the 24th and had not been regained before dark, it was confidently and correctly assumed that the Japanese force was making for the Surigao Strait. Oldendorf therefore disposed his battleships in a single line, to patrol east and west across the mouth of the Strait and wait for the Japanese to emerge. Cruisers and destroyers would be on either flank, and the latter would be released to carry out torpedo attacks as the Japanese were threading their way through the Straits. The greatly improved radar fitted in most of the American ships, and lessons of the past from which the danger of using searchlights had been learnt, gave Oldendorf a marked ascendancy over the Japanese in night fighting. Altogether night operations were faced with great confidence. Only the battleships operated under some handicap, as half of them had not yet received the latest gunnery radar sets; furthermore, their task up to date having been bombardment support fire, on which they had already been engaged for the last five days, they were not only very short of ammunition but little of what they had was of the armour-piercing type needed for a ship action. Oldendorf therefore planned for a short, decisive gun battle, withholding fire until the enemy was within killing range, between 17,000 and 20,000 yards. Meanwhile the destroyers would have a free hand.

Oldendorf's force waited thus at the northern exit from the Surigao Strait. Out in the Mindanao Sea, motor-torpedo boats patrolled, with instructions to report any enemy contacts and then go in to the attack. At 10.15 p.m. the first radar contacts were made by a section of these P.T. boats, and they closed to sight the enemy. Over-anxious to get in their attacks, they found themselves in action and under fire before they had got a report away. By the time they had fired their torpedoes and disengaged, their radios had been put out of action. It was thus not until half an hour after midnight that a report reached Admiral Oldendorf in his flagship, the heavy cruiser *Louisville*. As Nishimura's force continued northward for the Strait, section after section of P.T. boats pressed their attacks in with great gallantry and dash, but under the concentrated fire of the Japanese ships they failed to secure any hits. Taking in their reports, Oldendorf was able to plot the enemy's progress, confirming that they were heading for the Strait; and at 2.15 in the morning his radar operators saw them appear on their screens at a range of 25 miles.

The contacts were watched coming steadily up the middle of the Strait, and at last Oldendorf sent his destroyers into the attack. For more than an hour, from 3 o'clock, running close in to the shore on either flank of the approaching enemy column and so baffling the Japanese radar, division after division closed to point-blank range and loosed their torpedoes. As one of the destroyer squadron commanders later observed, "The waters through which the enemy passed were so full of torpedoes it is difficult to see how any enemy ship could have failed to sustain damage."

Indeed, few did. Of the four destroyers leading the line, two were hit and sunk, a third was heavily damaged and drew away out of action. It was then the turn of the battleships. In the first attack the flagship *Yamashiro* received one hit, after which Nishimura's voice came over the radio telephone ordering his ships in to the attack. It was the last heard of him. More torpedoes found the *Yamashiro*, one reaching a magazine. A blinding flash and a deep, rumbling explosion, and the battleship broke in two and plunged to the bottom.

The *Fuso* also had been hit, but had not been put out of action.

Doggedly she pressed on up the Strait, the cruiser *Mogami* following. The ranges being passed by the radar operators in Oldendorf's heavy ships were coming down. At 3.37 a.m.

Squadron 56, the last of the destroyer squadrons, had started on its run in to the attack. In the American battleships the thrilling prospect of a gun battle from the classic point of advantage across the head of an approaching enemy line was inducing an almost unbearable tension. The opportunity was one which the crews of the elderly battleships had never hoped to enjoy. In the fast-moving air-dominated battles of the era, only the fast, powerful modern ships of the *Washington* class could normally hope to bring their guns to bear on an enemy ship; now, as they waited, the battleship crews half-feared that the target might be eliminated by the destroyers' torpedoes before they themselves could get into action. There was also a well-founded anxiety that their own destroyers might be brought under fire by mistake.

With the range down to 15,600 yards from the *Louisville* and 21,000 yards from the *Mississippi*, flagship of the battle line, Oldendorf at last gave the order to open fire, at 3.51. The 8-inch and 6-inch guns of the cruisers were the first to flame into action. Then the heavy guns of the battleships opened up, sending their shells tearing and rumbling over the mastheads of the smaller ships. The night was lit by the flashes of the guns and the stream of tracers arching away towards the target over 10 miles of sea. The modern radar of the cruisers and the battleships *West Virginia* and *Tennessee* directed a storm of shells which plunged into the *Fuso* and *Mogami*. The *Mogami* turned away south and, blazing brightly, tried to escape. The *Fuso*, heavily hit and burning, turned beam-on and stopped. As she lay thus, further salvoes crashed home. Great explosions shook the battleship.

At this moment Destroyer Squadron 56 reached its attacking position. Lit up and silhouetted by the gun flashes, the destroyers plunged through a storm of splashes from shells from both sides. One section retired up the Strait towards the American cruisers. Tragedy struck as the rear ship *Grant* was taken for an enemy and shattered by a continuous rain of shells; not until she had been brought to a standstill in a near-sinking condition did Admiral Oldendorf learn what was happening and order a general "Cease fire."

In the strange hush that followed, the flames flickering in the *Fuso* were suddenly extinguished as the last battleship of the Southern Force foundered. The time was 4.18 a.m. Of Nishimura's ships, there only survived the *Mogami*, heavily damaged and on fire, retreating southward, and the destroyer *Shigure*. After searching vainly for others of the force, the latter too had turned to escape, but a breakdown of her steering gear brought her to a standstill. As she lay, ships loomed out of the darkness to the south and were recognised as Shima's force advancing in their turn towards the Leyte Gulf.

Incredibly, after exchanging brief recognition signals, the captain of the *Shigure* allowed Shima's flagship *Nachi* to pass by without giving any news of what had happened to Nishimura. Except for a brief order to his force to reverse course to avoid torpedoes, intercepted at about 3 o'clock, Shima had heard nothing of Nishimura's fate. Twenty minutes later Shima had lost the light cruiser *Abukuma*, badly damaged by a P.T. boat's torpedo. At 3.45 the smoke and flame of burning ships, the dense cloud from smoke-screens and beyond, the flash of guns and the glitter of tracers showed him where the fight was still going on. At 28 knots he led forward to bring support.

Not until 4.20, however, could any enemy be made out, and then the two leading cruisers *Nachi* and *Ashigara* turned to starboard and fired torpedoes. At the same moment through the murk a large burning ship was sighted close ahead of the *Nachi*. Concentrating on the delivery of the torpedo attack, the bridge personnel of the flagship assumed it was stopped and would be passed clear. In fact it was the *Mogami*, still moving slowly, retiring towards the south, though barely under control. By the time the torpedo attack had been completed and attention could be given to her, collision was unavoidable. Though the *Nachi* put her wheel hard over and stopped both engines, the two ships came together with a grinding crash, a hole being torn from the *Nachi*'s side. As water poured in, Shima was quickly forced to conclude that the flagship could not continue in action. Followed by the *Ashigara*, he led the way southward in retreat.

With daylight the Japanese cripples were set upon by planes from the escort carriers and army bombers. The *Mogami* was given her final death-blow by a torpedo, the *Abukuma* by bombs, completing the rout of the southern section of the attack on Leyte. Of two battleships and four cruisers which had entered the Surigao Strait, only the *Nachi*, badly damaged, and the *Ashigara* survived. The Seventh Fleet was jubilant. From Kinkaid to Oldendorf went a signal "Well done."

Barely had this set the seal on the night's work, when shocked dismay took the place of elation. Shells from Japanese battleships and cruisers were falling round the defenceless escort carriers far to the eastward. Only Oldendorf's old battleships and his cruisers, their ammunition and fuel nearly exhausted and more than three hours' fast steaming from the scene, were available to intervene.

18

The End of a Navy

IN Halsey's force, there was complete confidence and excited anticipation as it sped northwards through the night. The Japanese carrier fleet had been delivered into the hands of the Third Fleet, and at daylight the Japanese would be wide open to attack. Furthermore, Halsey's splendid new fast battleships were at last to come into their own; indeed he planned to form them into a separate force thrown forward of the carriers. Then, as bombers and torpedo-planes swooped down on the Japanese ships, the 16-inch guns would join to bring simultaneous, overwhelming attack to bear, polishing off crippled ships and engaging the battleships reported to be with Ozawa's force. This was Task Force 34, reference to which had deceived Kinkaid into thinking that a force was to be left on guard at the San Bernadino Strait.

Shortly before 3 a.m. the reorganisation was ordered. Under Vice-Admiral Willis A. Lee, his flag still in the *Washington*, and comprising six battleships including the *New Jersey* (Halsey's flagship), two heavy cruisers, five light cruisers and eighteen destroyers, Task Force 34 pressed on ahead of the fleet, expecting to join action before daylight. Unfortunately the aircraft shadowing the Japanese was forced to return with engine trouble, and contact was not regained during the night. However, it was confidently expected that with daylight Ozawa's force would be rediscovered.

Day broke over a calm sea under a clear sky with a breeze from the north-east—perfect flying conditions. With the first streaks of dawn shortly before 6 o'clock, the carrier groups turned into wind; aircraft began to roar off their decks in endless succession, forming into strike groups and rumbling away northwards where it was expected the search planes would soon locate the enemy. But in fact it was not until after 7.30 that they were discovered, away to the north-east and 140 miles distant, so that bombers and torpedo-planes could be directed to their target.

In Ozawa's flagship, *Zuikaku*, the spirit of high resolve had given way to a feeling of frustration. In spite of long radio messages betraying his position to any listening direction-finding station, in spite of launching an air attack on the previous day on the northernmost of the Third Fleet carrier groups with the small number of strike planes available, planes which never returned, the Americans had obstinately refused to take any notice of him.

Indeed his aircraft had not been identified as coming from carriers, but had been presumed to come from shore bases—as had so many others. Half had been shot down; the other half, only partly trained and lacking confidence either to find or to land on their parent ships, had made for airfields in Luzon. It seemed that all Ozawa's efforts to decoy American forces north had been in vain. It was a bitter satisfaction, therefore, when at 7.40 that morning radar contacts of large formations of aircraft were reported to him. The lure had at least succeeded in drawing some of the American forces away from Kurita's hard-pressed squadron.

Now it was time to die. In two circular anti-aircraft formations Ozawa swung his force northward and awaited the onslaught. One group, centred on the hybrid battleship aircraft carrier *Hyuga*, in which flew Rear-Admiral Matsuda's flag, included the light carriers *Chiyoda* and *Chitose* and the light cruisers *Isuzu* and *Tama*, as well as two destroyers. In Ozawa's group there were, besides *Hyuga*'s sister-ship *Ise*, the light-carrier *Zuiho*, the light cruiser *Oyodo* and four destroyers. From the deck of the *Chiyoda* a small force of fighters manned by inexperienced, untrained pilots took the air. They were all that were available. For the rest, the Japanese ships had to rely upon gunfire for protection.

At 8.30 the American dive-bombers and torpedo-planes, some 120 aircraft in all, brushed aside this feeble fighter opposition and swept in to a well co-ordinated attack. The anti-aircraft fire was intense and accurate, but could achieve little against such a swarm of attackers. As the last plane sped away and the gunfire faltered and died, the *Chitose* lay stopped and listing heavily after a direct bomb hit forward and a number of damaging near misses. An hour later she foundered. The *Tama*, hit by a torpedo, had dropped astern as her crew struggled to repair the damage and get their ship under way again. The *Zuiho* had been hit, but was not yet seriously damaged. The *Zuikaku* had taken a torpedo aft, limiting her speed to 18 knots and leaving her barely manœuvrable, as she was steered manually. A destroyer had blown up, and her blazing wreck was soon to sink.

Japan's last carrier force was in its death-throes, but even as its agony began the aim of its sacrifice was being made clear to Halsey as an urgent signal from Kinkaid reached him announcing Japanese battleships and cruisers attacking the defenceless mass of escort carriers to the eastward of Leyte. Eight minutes later came a desperate appeal from Kinkaid asking for help from Task Force 34, which he still thought must be somewhere near San Bernadino Strait. At brief intervals further appeals poured in. With a fleeing enemy ahead and rapidly being overhauled, Halsey was far from anxious to turn back to the aid of the Seventh Fleet 350 miles, more than 14 hours steaming away. His fourth Task Group—three large carriers and two light carriers—under Rear-Admiral McCain, which had not yet rejoined him and was still refuelling away to the south-eastward, was closer to Leyte. McCain was ordered to make south-west at utmost speed, and launch air attacks as soon as possible against the enemy force attacking the landing force and its escort carriers.

By this time Halsey had no doubt realised the error into which he had been led by the over-sanguine reports of his airmen attacking Kurita's force on the previous day. If he turned his battleships back now, they could not be brought to the scene of action until the following morning, too late to save the Seventh Fleet. Ahead was at the very least a compensating, spectacular victory. Grimly the Admiral ordered Task Force 34 onwards to "Close the enemy at 25 knots."

Then at 10 o'clock, as the second air attack from his carriers was moving overhead towards the enemy, the Commander-in-Chief of the Pacific Fleet, Admiral Nimitz, Halsey's superior, signalled to Halsey, asking with some asperity what had happened to the fast battleships of the Third Fleet. For another hour Halsey held on northwards, the futility of a turn to the south at that late hour—and perhaps a great admiral's instinct that his enemy's day was over—steeling him against succumbing to the frantic appeals for aid.

But the signals from Kinkaid grew steadily more urgent. A picture was built up of unprecedented disaster and the annihilation of the Seventh Fleet, if Kurita was left free to corner the escort carriers in the Leyte Gulf amidst the transports and the almost ammunition-less old battleships of Oldendorf's force. By 11.15 a.m. Halsey could resist no further. On the bridges of the six battleships where the prospect of at last striking a blow from the gleaming, questing barrels of their 16-inch guns had seemed to be at long last at hand, the order to reverse course was received with incredulous dismay.

Yet in fact by the time Halsey's decision was made, the threat to the Seventh Fleet had been eliminated for more than two hours. Before we go south to share the Seventh Fleet's fortunes, however, the fate of Ozawa's force must be followed to the end.

The second air attack was a much smaller affair than the first; by now there was no fighter opposition, and the scattering of Ozawa's ships reduced the gun barrage. A direct bomb-hit and a number of near misses on the light carrier *Chiyoda* set her ablaze and brought her to a stop. For the next three hours her crew desperately fought the flames, while the *Hyuga* and a destroyer stood by, but renewal of air attacks then brought to an end efforts to take the carrier in tow. She was abandoned by her companions with her crew left aboard to fight to the end.

By this time the damage to the *Zuikaku*, and in particular the destruction of her wireless apparatus, had forced Ozawa to shift his flag to the cruiser *Oyodo*. With the fast-shrinking and battered remnants of his force he continued northwards at 18 knots, the speed to which the crippled *Zuikaku* limited him. The third air attack began at 1 o'clock in the afternoon, and went on sporadically for the next two hours. Selecting the two remaining apparently undamaged carriers for their target, the American airmen put bomb after bomb into the thin-shelled hulls of *Zuikaku* and *Zuiho*. The former, the last survivor of the attack on Pearl Harbour and a veteran of every major action of the war, rolled over and sank at 2.14 p.m., her crew having first defiantly hoisted a huge battle flag to the masthead. The *Zuiho*, which up to now had borne a charmed life through the war, and whose aircraft had been responsible for the sinking of the *Hornet* at the Battle of Santa Cruz, went down an hour later.

Of the Japanese carriers only the *Chiyoda* still floated, defiantly firing at any aircraft which approached her. Discovered by an American cruiser squadron ranging ahead of the carrier force, she was smothered by 8-inch and 6-inch shell fire, and within twenty minutes had been sent to the bottom.

Until dark the air attacks continued on the last two large ships of Ozawa's force, the *Hyuga* and *Ise*. But though battleships had by now small value in a naval action, they were still capable of putting up a sturdy fight in their own defence. The American aviators, too, after a long day of flying and combat, had lost some of their zest and skill. Except for a single bomb hit on the *Ise*, which caused heavy casualties but no serious damage, and a great many near misses which shook them and perforated their "blisters", the two battleships sailed on unharmed. Only one further loss was suffered by Ozawa's force, when the cruiser *Tama*, limping solitarily away seeking her base, was caught and sunk by American submarines. The Battle off Cape Engaño, as it came to be called, was over.

* * *

We must now examine the situation in the area more than 350 miles to the southward, eastward of the Island of Samar and the Gulf of Leyte, where the desperate plight of the escort carrier groups under Rear-Admiral Thomas L. Sprague had been the cause of Kinkaid's frantic appeals to Halsey for aid.

The night of the 24th had passed quietly, with only the prospect of operations in support of the ground troops ashore and perhaps an air raid or two to beat off on the morrow. Sprague's force was in three groups. The Northern Group, under another Sprague—Rear-Admiral C. A. F. Sprague—comprised the escort carriers *Fanshaw Bay* (his flagship), *Saint Lo*, *White Plains*, *Kalinin Bay*, *Kitkun Bay* and *Gambier Bay*, three destroyers, and four small destroyer escorts. At dawn they were in a position about half-way up the coast of Samar and 50 miles to seaward. Here they had launched the normal defensive combat air patrol and an anti-submarine patrol, and by 6.30 had turned out of wind on to a northerly course to await any calls for air support which might come in.

It was known that a powerful Japanese force had been intercepted on the previous day making for San Bernadino Strait, but it was believed to have been routed with severe losses. In any case the Third Fleet battleships were thought to be on guard. As a further precaution, Kinkaid had ordered a dawn air search of the area to be made. Unfortunately, however, this aircraft was not launched until half an hour after sunrise. Before it could be of any use, the placid morning flying routine of the carriers had been shattered.

Over the radio telephone crackled excited messages from patrolling aircraft, and finally a clear report from an aircraft of the *Saint Lo* announcing enemy battleships, cruisers and destroyers 20 miles to the north-west of Sprague's group. As the massive, pagoda-like top hamper of Kurita's battleships rose over the horizon, surprise was complete.

At once the Northern Group was turned at full speed on to an easterly course. This was not full into the wind, but at least aircraft could be launched. Very soon, armed with anything they had aboard them at the moment, they were roaring off the decks. They were still being sent away when the first 18-inch shells from the *Yamato*, fired at a range of 17½ miles, raised towering splashes in the midst of the carrier formation. By the third salvo the carrier *White Plains*, nearest to the enemy, was straddled and savagely shaken as the huge shells exploded under water near her. It was superb shooting by the Japanese gunners, who had waited through nearly three years of war for this opportunity.

As others of the Japanese ships joined the cannonade, the *White Plains* was surrounded by splashes, dyed in different colours to identify the ship firing them. Damage mounted from the near misses on the thin-shelled, converted merchantman. Black smoke to screen her began to pour from her funnel; and as it gathered in a cloud astern, relief came as the Japanese shifted their fire, believing that the *White Plains* had been sunk. The *Saint Lo* now became the target, and she too was so closely straddled that water from the splashes fell aboard her.

But now smoke from the carriers and from their escorting destroyers, who had been ordered to lay a screen, brought some respite. At the same time, aircraft swept in to attack the Japanese ships with a gallant abandon, machine-gunning them—the *Kongo*'s main range-finder was put out of action by this means—hurling the unsuitable ground-support bombs and a few launching torpedoes. Since the Japanese were forced to take avoiding action, the pursuit was repeatedly interrupted.

Then the Northern Group plunged gratefully into the shelter of a heavy rain squall and under its cover altered course southward, directly away from the enemy—who with their superior speed had been circling round to the northward. The Japanese gunnery radar was not good enough for accurate blind firing. For a while the shell splashes fell wide and died away, but not for long. When the carriers emerged from the rain squall the enemy's main force had closed to 25,000 yards, while heavy cruisers had been sent ahead hemming them in from the eastward and destroyers were on their other flank. Well might Admiral Sprague later write, "At this point it did not appear that any of our ships could survive another five minutes of the heavy-calibre fire being received, and some counter action was urgently and immediately required."

The time had in fact come for a sacrificial rearguard action of the kind which forms many of the heroic episodes of the history of war. To Commander Thomas in the destroyer *Hoel*, commanding the seven small ships of the screen, went the signal "Attack with torpedoes."

Dividing his force into two groups, Thomas ordered the three destroyers to make the first attack, to be followed by the four destroyer escorts. At once the little ships swung round to concentrate before plunging into the smoke and rain squalls, which would give them some cover and would afford them their only hope of surviving. The destroyer *Johnston* had indeed anticipated the order, and alone and unsupported had streaked away towards the heavy cruiser *Kumano*, which had been sighted through a gap in the smoke at a range of 18,000 yards. For the 4 miles of her desperate race towards the enemy the *Johnston* moved through a concentration of shell splashes, her own forward 5-inch guns blazing and scoring many hits, her curling bow wave tumbling away on either side as she raced forward at 40 knots. Still unscathed, the destroyer swung round as the range fell to 10,000 yards, and launched ten torpedoes before retiring again into the smoke-screens.

A hit aft on the *Kumano*, which put her out of action, rewarded this gallant effort. Furthermore as another cruiser, the *Suzuya*, also fell out of the chase to take aboard the squadron admiral from the *Kumano*, the *Johnston* had succeeded in removing two ships from the chase. But now she had to pay the penalty; as she emerged from the smoke she was heavily hit by 8-inch and 6-inch shells. Reduced to a crawl and barely manœuvrable, the tide of battle swept over her. For two hours she continued to engage every enemy who came in sight, from battleships to destroyers. She suffered heavy casualties, and at last her captain, Commander Evans, himself severely wounded, gave the order to abandon ship. Shortly afterwards the *Johnston* sank.

Meanwhile the two other destroyers *Hoel* and *Heermann* had been attacking no less gallantly in the face of tremendous fire which, concentrated at first on the *Hoel*, reduced her to a sinking wreck—but not before torpedoes had been launched at the battleship *Kongo* and others at cruisers. The *Heermann* also got her torpedoes away at the same targets. Avoiding serious damage, though several times hit, she brought her 5-inch guns to bear with good effect on cruisers which had been firing at the carriers.

Through the smoke and rain squalls the four destroyer escorts similarly closed to torpedo range before being seriously damaged. Salvoes of shells found their mark on two of them. One managed to escape into a smoke-screen, but the other, the *Roberts*, was quickly overwhelmed by more than forty direct hits. Yet even after 14-inch shells had brought her to a standstill and reduced the after part of the ship to a twisted mass of smoking metal, a solitary gun kept up a slow fire at any target that appeared, until the order came to abandon ship.

It was as heroic an episode as any of the war. Though it cannot be discovered how many of these ships' torpedoes hit or what damage they succeeded in doing with their guns, it is certain that the effect of the attacks was far in excess of any concrete successes. Forced to manœuvre to avoid the real or suspected torpedoes from the little ships sighted from time to time as they weaved in and out of smoke and rain, the Japanese battleships and cruisers lost ground in their pursuit of the carriers.

Even so, between 8 and 8.30 a.m. it seemed impossible that the carriers of the Northern Group could escape annihilation. Armed with one 5-inch gun apiece, they were under fire from the *Kongo* and *Haruna*, who had a clear view of them, and from *Yamato* and *Nagato* by radar. Four heavy cruisers, *Haguro*, *Tone*, *Chikuma* and *Chokai* had pressed far on in advance of the battleships. Their 8-inch guns were within killing range of the three carriers in the rear, *Gambier Bay*, *Kalinin Bay* and *Saint Lo*. All three began to take heavy punishment, and were probably only saved from immediate destruction by their thin skins, many of the Japanese armour-piercing shells passing through their hulls without exploding. Unhappily the *Gambier Bay*, in the windward station of the formation, was steaming clear of all smoke, and was exposed to direct fire from the Japanese cruisers. An almost continuous hail of 8-inch shells fell on her, and at 8.20 a hole was blown in her side; water poured into her machinery spaces, and at 8.50 she was abandoned shortly before capsizing and sinking.

But relief was coming to the hard-pressed carriers. Aircraft from all three groups of the escort carrier force had been recalled from the missions on which they had been flying when the alarm was first raised, and had now been rearmed, so that they could begin to harry the enemy's heavy ships. Catching the heavy cruiser squadron by surprise as the Japanese gunners were concentrating on sinking the *Gambier Bay*, they hit *Chokai* and *Chikuma*, putting them both out of action.

Turning next on to the battleships, they descended like a swarm of hornets, keeping the big ships continuously dodging their torpedoes and quite unable to keep up effective fire of the fleeing carriers at the same time. The fog of war covering the whole battle area had by now hidden the carriers from the bridge of the *Yamato*, and Kurita had lost all touch with or control of the battle. Believing from the start that the ships he had been engaging had been fast, large fleet carriers, his calculations appeared to show that they were outrunning him and escaping, and that a long stern chase at least would be needed to come up with them. Out of touch with the tactical situation, he had no idea that his two remaining cruisers had closed to within 10,500 yards of the carriers of the Northern Group and were poised for the kill. All he knew was that two of them had been put out of action, and that his ships had become widely scattered by their independent hot pursuit. Heavy air attacks were soon to be expected. With no fighter cover, only the concentrated fire of a close formation could give reasonable defence. The vision of the great *Musashi* beaten to a crippled wreck by air attack was far from reassuring and clearly it was time for Kurita to reform and concentrate his force. Then perhaps he could take it into Leyte Gulf to slaughter the mass of shipping there and isolate the beach-head on Samar.

At eleven minutes past nine Kurita signalled all ships to turn to the north and reassemble. From the carriers of the Northern Group, which had been preparing to suffer the same fate as the *Gambier Bay*, the *Tone* and *Haguro* were seen suddenly to swing round to a northerly course and rapidly disappear. The Americans could hardly believe their eyes, but they lost no time in repairing their damage and getting ready to launch their aircraft for further attacks.

It was an astonishing escape at the eleventh hour. For in addition to the seemingly certain destruction by Kurita's overwhelming force—and all unknown to him—the escort carriers had been experiencing the first of a new type of attack. The commanders of the two Japanese naval air fleets based ashore in Luzon, unable to train their pilots sufficiently to achieve any real success against ships had "decided that if the surface units were taking such desperate measures, we too must take similar desperate measures", and had started the first operation of the so-called Special Attack Force.

The Special Attack Force was the organisation which sent forth the famous "Kamikaze"—pilots dedicated to crashing their bomb-loaded planes on to enemy ships to ensure a hit. The first targets to be selected by the Kamikaze were the escort carriers of the Southern Group. Arriving over the force at 7.40 that morning, four Japanese fighters, each of them carrying a 300-lb. bomb, suddenly plummeted down through a thin layer of cloud. Two were shot down by gunfire and crashed harmlessly in the sea; but one hit the *Santee*, its explosion causing many casualties and blowing a huge hole in the flight deck; while the other took the carrier *Suwanee* for its target. Plunging through the flight deck, the bomb exploded between it and the hangar.

However, neither ship was fatally damaged, and even the *Santee*, which also suffered a torpedo hit from a submarine, was got back into operation after emergency repairs.

The next wave of Kamikaze attacked the already damaged carriers of the Northern Group, six fighters arriving over them at 10.49 when aircraft were busy landing-on. Out of a sky filled with waiting American aircraft, they streaked down without warning. The *White Plains*, *Kalinin Bay* and *Saint Lo* were each hit. The first two were heavily damaged and set on fire, but were saved by their repair parties. In the *Saint Lo*, however, the explosion of the aircraft's two bombs was followed by more and heavier ones which wreaked fearful damage and burst open the hull; within ten minutes she had to be abandoned, and at 11.25 she sank.

In spite of these calamities to American ships, Kurita was given little respite to gather in his force. Attack followed attack. Three of his heavy cruisers, *Kumano*, *Chokai* and *Chikuma* were crippled. The *Kumano* was withdrawing at slow speed, but the two others were unmanœuvrable, and soon destroyers took off their crews and sent them to the bottom. While this was taking place a fresh air attack added the *Suzuya* to the list of casualties, and she too was later abandoned and sunk. Kurita's force of four battleships, six heavy cruisers, two light cruisers and eleven destroyers had dwindled. He still had his four battleships and two heavy cruisers; but though the former had shown they could beat off attacks, the fate of the *Musashi* could not but remind him that a lucky torpedo hit in a tender spot could still destroy even the most powerful of battleships.

Until noon Kurita steered slowly south-west towards Leyte, pondering these things and assessing the situation. The question in his mind to which he sought an answer was whether it was of any value to press on into the restricted waters of Leyte Gulf, where he would have less freedom to manœuvre under air attack, in order to attack the now-empty American transports. Two long days of incessant air attack during which he had lost half the number of his ships, and another day of submarine alarms in which he had had his flagship sunk under him, were not conducive to unbiased consideration. When at about noon a fresh American task force was reported to the north-eastward of Samar, Kurita seized the opportunity to head northwards instead. In fact, the task force was never there. By 5.30 that evening, after another afternoon of fierce air attack in which aircraft from the Third Fleet's carrier task group under Rear-Admiral McCain were at last able to take part, Kurita knew it. With night approaching he was completely without information as to the enemy's whereabouts. Fuel was running short in his destroyers, and it was time to get back to base, so he turned westward for the San Bernadino Strait. The Battle off Samar was over.

In spite of the sacrificial efforts of Ozawa, which had successfully lured away the main striking fleet of the Americans, Kurita had failed to achieve the object for which the whole gigantic operation had been set on foot—the destruction of the American assault forces at Leyte. On the next day he could expect retribution from the hornet's nest he had stirred up but not destroyed, for he would still be within range at daylight of the carriers of McCain's group which were being joined by another Third Fleet group.

No doubt the exhausted Japanese gunners gained some uneasy rest as Kurita's fleet sped westward during the night through the San Bernadino Strait and the Sibuyan Sea. As day broke to show the coast of the island of Panay to port, they roused themselves to prepare for what might be the heaviest attack of all. And indeed between 8.30 and 9 o'clock they fought for their lives as more than a hundred planes from American carriers and others of the U.S. Army Air Force sought revenge. Though the light cruiser *Noshiro* was torpedoed, bombed and sunk, the already damaged *Kumano* again heavily hit and two destroyers sunk, Kurita's battleships could not be stopped. The *Yamato* took two bomb hits on her forward turrets, but torpedoes were needed to halt the great armoured vessel, and none reached her. On the 28th the survivors of the Japanese battle fleet anchored again in Brunei Bay. The Battle of Leyte also was over.

The comparison between losses in the two fleets is more than enough to rate the battle as a great American victory. Its results go further and deeper to make it one of the decisive battles of history. Against a loss to the Americans of one light carrier, two escort carriers, two destroyers and one destroyer escort can be set the Japanese loss of three battleships, one large carrier, three light carriers, six heavy cruisers, four light cruisers and nine destroyers. In addition, the last of Japan's trained naval airmen had gone.

It was the virtual end of the Imperial Japanese Navy. From now onward the U.S. Fleet roamed at will, striking ever closer to the heart of Japan, opposed only by a dwindling shore-based force of ill-trained airmen of whom the hard core were the Kamikaze.

19

Ichabod—The Glory has Departed

The Battle of Leyte was the final convincing demonstration that the battleship had outlived its name and usefulness in a sea-fight. Admiral Halsey's ships racing northwards in unavailing effort to bring their 16-inch guns into action, and their equally fruitless rush to engage Kurita's battleships, made this abundantly clear. Even Oldendorf's squadron in old-fashioned battle array, found itself all but robbed of its target by the torpedoes of the destroyers, though it did indeed come within hitting distance of the enemy.

After Leyte, Halsey's splendid new ships as well as their older sisters found themselves relegated to the ancillary rôle of escort for the carriers or bombardment in support of landing forces. For the Japanese, too, the end of the *Musashi* and the failure of the *Yamato* and her companions to annihilate the carrier force delivered into their hands, revealed the fallibility of the gigantic ships of which they had been so proud.

Even if the loss of the Philippines had not cut Japan's oil supply route, leaving insufficient fuel to send them to sea, they could not have faced the teeming carrier air fleets of the U.S. Pacific Fleet soon to be reinforced by those of the Royal Navy. Only when defeat was certain did the *Yamato*, with fuel enough to take her only to a warrior's end, steam out to meet her fate. On 7th April 1945, off Okinawa, she was set upon, bombed and torpedoed to a battered wreck, and sunk.

On the other side of the world, battleships' guns had thundered out against each other for the last time in December 1943 when Germany's last serviceable capital ship the *Scharnhorst*, sent out into the Arctic night to attack the convoys to Russia, fell a victim to the guns of the *Duke of York* and the torpedoes of cruisers and destroyers. In those wild winter waters, the long hours of darkness, the ceaseless succession of savage gales and the blinding swirling snowstorms delayed the era of air supremacy. Ship still sought ship in personal combat. To make contact they relied upon radar, in which British scientists had outstripped German. Thus the *Scharnhorst*, fumbling comparatively blindly through the dark, was trapped by ships in which her every move could be watched and plotted. Finally it was radar which enabled the first salvo of 14-inch shells from the *Duke of York* to strike the *Scharnhorst* and put her finally out of action.

But though this was the last sea-fight in which British battleships were to take part, for another year they were to be forced to keep guard in the north on account of a ship which in fact almost never went to sea. Since January 1942 the *Bismarck*'s sister-ship, *Tirpitz*, had lain in Norwegian waters. On guard against any sortie, it had been necessary to keep concentrated a much larger force under the Commander-in-Chief, Home Fleet. To give warning of her putting to sea, air reconnaissance had had to be maintained unceasingly. Within a few days of her arrival in Norway the first of a long series of raids by aircraft of the Royal Air Force was staged, but without success.

The deadly peril in which the break-out of the *Bismarck* had put the far-flung sea-traffic of the Allies, on which their whole war strategy depended, and the huge naval effort which had been required to deal with it, made a repetition by the *Tirpitz* a possibility to be prevented at all costs. In addition, convoys of merchantmen carrying vital war material to the hard-pressed Russians passed within twelve hours' steaming of the Norwegian coast twice every month.

Never was the principle of the "fleet in being" better illustrated than by the story of the *Tirpitz*. Fleets steamed thousands of miles or lay tied down when they were urgently needed elsewhere. Desperate, hazardous operations were set afoot. Crack bomber squadrons were diverted. A convoy to Russia was scattered and delivered piecemeal into the hands of U-boats—all on account of the brooding menace of one powerful battleship which did not need to go to sea to produce its effect.

The *Tirpitz* did indeed start her career by a sortie in March 1942 to attack the two Arctic convoys, one westbound, one eastbound, which were meeting and passing each other to the westward of the North Cape. Accompanied by four destroyers, and well-informed by U-boats of the convoys' positions, she put to sea on 4th March. A British submarine on patrol gave warning that she was out. The Home Fleet comprising two battleships, a battle-cruiser and the aircraft carrier *Victorious* went hurrying eastward. In the mists and snowstorms the carrier's aircraft could not be sent out to search, and in the blind-man's buff which followed the two forces passed unknown to each other some ninety miles apart. The same conditions gained the homeward-bound convoy an almost miraculous escape. Sweeping northward, the *Tirpitz* passed a few miles ahead of it, hidden in the murk. Her destroyers, spread to search, passed so close astern of it that they fell in with a straggler and sank it, but never detected the convoy itself which steamed slowly on unaware of its peril, escorted by only two minesweepers and two tiny corvettes.

The *Tirpitz* then veered northwards to find the outward convoy, but failed by a mere eighty miles. Admiral Tovey with the Home Fleet, waiting hundreds of miles to the southward to intercept the German on her return, would have been powerless to intervene had contact with the convoy been made. But luck was against the *Tirpitz*—luck and the German failure to develop an efficient radar. She turned back for Trondheim. Detected by *Victorious*' aircraft, she was attacked by the small force of torpedo-aircraft which the carrier could send forth. The attack was a failure, but it was sufficient to divert the *Tirpitz* into the shelter of Narvik.

Meagre as was the Royal Navy's carrier force, rarely more than one carrier being available in each theatre of operations, it was sufficient to make the German High Command forbid the commitment of their heavy ships from this time onward, and this applied to the *Tirpitz* in particular unless and until the carrier of the Home

Fleet had been located and neutralised by the Luftwaffe—a requirement hard to meet in Arctic winter weather.

For the next four months, therefore, she lay idle at Narvik, her great guns silent and useless while convoys to and from Russia passed by her doorstep with a few elderly destroyers and corvettes for escort. Yet her very presence, able at any moment to dash out for a surprise attack, was a constant menace—a menace which made every convoy to Russia an operation fraught with dire possibilities and also posed the ugly threat of a breakout into the Atlantic.

Therefore there began the long series of operations designed to neutralise this threat. To make an Atlantic sortie less attractive, a daring raid by Commandos and ships of the Royal Navy was launched on the port of St. Nazaire on 28th March to put the great dry dock there out of action. It was brilliantly successful, and from that moment the absence of any docking facilities for the great ship made an Atlantic adventure too hazardous to be undertaken. Efforts were now concentrated on attempts to immobilise the ship itself. At the end of March the Royal Air Force returned to the attack with another bombing raid. But, as the U.S. Army Air Force was similarly to discover, precision bombing from high altitude, even against a stationary ship, was rarely successful and required a force of picked, specially trained airmen to achieve any results. The *Tirpitz* emerged undamaged from this raid.

On 28th and 29th April two further raids were equally unsuccessful, and a high proportion of the aircraft involved were lost.

Thus when, on Russia's insistence and America's urging, convoys to Russia were continued into the summer when there was no darkness to shroud them and no snowstorms in which to hide, the mere fact of a move by the *Tirpitz* from Trondheim to Altenfiord in the extreme north of Norway was enough to induce the Admiralty to order the threatened convoy to scatter, the accepted tactics in face of surface attack. Split into single units or small unescorted groups, the ships of the convoy fell victims to the U-boats and bombers which had till then been unable to make much impression. Out of thirty-seven ships in the convoy, only eleven reached port. When finally the *Tirpitz* did go to sea, her work had been already done for her, and she returned to harbour after a brief uneventful cruise into the Barents Sea.

The one further Arctic convoy run before winter darkness came down was so heavily escorted that it did not tempt the *Tirpitz* out. But such large escort forces could not be spared permanently, and the need to cripple the *Tirpitz* was never far from the thoughts of the Admiralty. In October 1942 an enterprise was launched which might have been thought to emanate from the imagination of an adventure-story writer, but which happened to be true.

A fifty-five foot Norwegian fishing-boat, *Arthur*, commanded by Leif Larsen, the famous leader of Norwegian resistance, set off across the North Sea with two "human torpedoes" or "chariots" in her hold. On arrival in Norwegian waters the chariots were hoisted out and lashed under the hull; the four men of their crews were concealed behind a false bulkhead. Thus prepared, the *Arthur* chugged on into Trondheim fiord to face examination by the Germans. Bluff, good seamanship and an ice-cold nerve got Larsen through. Only 5 miles remained between the *Arthur* and the *Tirpitz* when disaster occurred. A squall swept down the fiord raising a steep short sea in which the *Arthur* rose and fell in jerky motion. The nose rings by which the chariots were secured snapped. Both broke away and sank. Another attempt to remove the menace of the *Tirpitz* had failed.

Through that winter the *Tirpitz* remained inactive, partly owing to an increasing shortage of fuel oil available for the fleet but chiefly to Hitler's refusal to allow any risks to be taken with his surface ships. Firmly believing that the Allies planned an invasion of Norway, every ship was to be reserved to repel it. Even when the cruiser *Hipper* and the pocket-battleship *Lützow* were loosed on to a passing convoy to Russia on New Year's Eve, they went out so hedged by cautionary restrictions that a bold fighting defence by the five old destroyers of the escort held off the two German heavy ships and six destroyers accompanying them until the intervention of two British light cruisers put the Germans to ignominious flight.

With the summer of 1943 the Arctic convoys were discontinued, all available escorts being required to augment those on the Atlantic convoy run where the decisive battle with the U-boats was being fought. *Tirpitz* and her smaller colleagues lay idle, morale seeping away from their crews. In September, no doubt to restore their self-respect, *Tirpitz* and *Scharnhorst* were sent on a raid to Spitsbergen to destroy the Norwegian weather reporting station there. To destroy a few huts and to overawe an almost defenceless handful of men was all the employment which could be found for the 15-inch and 11-inch guns

This was the last occasion when the *Tirpitz* put to sea in fighting trim. Even as she was expending her fury on the bleak landscape of Spitzbergen, a little force was assembling which was to put her out of action for the first time. It comprised the six midget submarines X5, 6, 7, 8, 9 and 10. They were to be towed across the North Sea by six conventional submarines, and released off the Norwegian coast to make their way some fifty miles up the fiords to where the *Tirpitz* and, it was thought, *Scharnhorst* and *Lützow* lay in Kaafiord, the steep narrow landward end of Altenfiord. Their weapons were two-ton charges of high explosive, one on each side, with delay-action fuses; these charges were intended to be released under the hull of the target ship.

In the event *Scharnhorst* and *Lützow* were found to have left. The *Tirpitz* was alone. Of the X-craft, two broke adrift on passage and were lost. A third developed a series of defects and, though she penetrated to within a few miles of the *Tirpitz*, was forced to give up the attempt when both compass and periscope retraction failed. After eight days of adventurous wandering she was recovered.

The three remaining boats pressed on to complete what Admiral Sir Max Horton, Britain's most renowned submariner, called "this magnificent feat of arms". With the handicap of an only partially effective periscope, X6, under the command of Lieutenant Donald Cameron, made its perilous way up Kaafiord in the half-light of early morning. Narrowly avoiding collisions, even passing between a destroyer and its mooring buoy on one occasion, she passed through the boat entrance of the net defences behind a picket-boat, and saw the gate hauled shut behind.

Now X6's luck showed signs of running out. Grounding on the north shore of the netted enclosure she was forced to break surface for a brief moment, during which she was sighted from the *Tirpitz*. But she was not confidently identified, and it was not until she struck a submerged rock 80 yards from the battleship and was thrust fully to the surface that the alarm was given. By this time she was so close that none of the battleship's guns could depress enough to fire at her. Putting his little craft down again, Cameron went on, only to be caught again in an obstruction. On surfacing he found that he was close under the port bows of the *Tirpitz*. Amidst a hail of small-arms fire and hand-grenades he dropped X6 astern until she was abreast the rearmost of the battleship's two forward turrets. There he released his two charges, set his craft to sink and gave the order to "Bail Out."

X6's crew were picked up by a German picket-boat and taken on board the *Tirpitz*. Meanwhile X7, commanded by Lieutenant Place, had tried to dive under the defensive nets, but had been entangled in them at a depth of 75 feet. For the next twenty minutes Place was in and out of nets, frantically manœuvring but getting ever closer to his object till at 7.30 a.m., a quarter of an hour after X6, X7 ran against the *Tirpitz*'s side. Dropping one charge roughly where Cameron had laid his, he then dropped back, placed his other under the after turrets and turned to escape.

Eight tons of explosive were now laid, waiting for the timing device to run out before detonating. Cameron and his crew, given coffee and schnapps and blankets to warm them, knew only of the four tons for which they were responsible. Taken for interrogation, they were unable to resist furtive looks at their watches; but there was little the Germans could do in spite of the warning this inevitably gave them. By working cable the Captain was able to slew the ship a few yards so that it was no longer directly over the spot where X6 had sunk, but even so when at 8.12 two heavy, almost simultaneous explosions took place, the great ship leapt bodily, tossing men into the air; all lights went out and her twisted hull settled back with a list to port with fuel pouring from her amidships.

Panic spread amongst the German crew, guns being fired wildly in every direction as well as at X7 which had been blown to the surface by the explosion and clear of the net in which she had been entangled. In the confusion the German gunners opened fire on their own tankers and picket-boats. One machine-gun firing at random wiped out a gun's crew on board their own ship. Besides one killed and forty injured by the explosion, some sixty more were killed or wounded by this undisciplined stampede.

In the brief view he had before taking his boat down and out of the fire being directed at him, Place was disappointed to see that the *Tirpitz* was still afloat. But in fact she had received heavy damage from which she never fully recovered, and which kept her completely immobilised for seven months.

Meanwhile X7, her compasses and depth-gauges damaged by the explosion, kept surfacing as Place struggled to extricate her from the maze of defensive netting. On each occasion she was smothered by gun-fire and suffered hull damage. The time came to abandon ship. Fortunately she came to the surface alongside a target raft, on to which Place was able to step out. Before the other three members of his crew could extricate themselves from the narrow, constricted spaces they occupied, the craft sank again. Two and a half hours later Sub-Lieutenant Aitken came to the surface with the aid of his escape apparatus, but the two other members of the crew had died when the oxygen gave out after the boat had filled with fumes.

X5, the third boat to get within sight of the *Tirpitz*, arrived later than the other two and after the explosion. When she broke surface at the outer net defence, she found a fully alerted defence. A blast of fire put her down, and depth-charges finished her destruction and that of her gallant crew.

* * *

In spite of this brilliant feat, the fact remained that the *Tirpitz* still remained afloat. By April 1944 there were signs that her repairs were nearly complete and, once again it became necessary to plan her destruction. By this time the Royal Navy's air arm had at last developed to such an extent that a squadron of carriers could be got together to form a striking force. True that out of the six carriers assembled, four were small escort carriers, adapted from merchant ships and carrying only a handful of aircraft; another was the veteran *Furious*, twenty-six years old and completely out of date. Only one, the *Victorious*, was a modern fleet carrier.

From these six ships two waves each comprising twenty-one dive-bombers and escorted by eighty fighters swept down over the mountain tops on to the *Tirpitz* at dawn on 3rd April, the very morning on which, her long repairs over, she was about to sail for trials. Complete surprise was achieved by the first wave. Before the smoke pots established round Kaafiord could come into operation, the bombs had been released with deadly accuracy to score hit after hit.

This sort of attack could never sink a battleship, for bombs of the size carried by dive-bombers could not penetrate the armoured deck; but more than three hundred of the *Tirpitz*'s crew had been killed, and she had been set on fire and damaged sufficiently to put her once more out of action. The repair crews wearily set about their task again in the dreary northern fiord, and for a while the *Tirpitz* could be wiped out of the Admiralty's calculations.

By August it was time to undo the repair crews' work yet again. Another force of carriers manœuvred for a week off Altenfiord, sending in striking forces of bombers. But by then the increased defences set up, the impossibility of achieving surprise and the speed with which the *Tirpitz*'s berth could be covered by a smoke-screen all combined to defeat their efforts. Other means had to be sought.

Though the task of destroying the *Tirpitz* was beyond the capacity of the normal heavy bomber squadron of the Royal Air

Force, there was one force which might do it—the famous "Dam Busters" of 617 Squadron. Their Lancaster bombers were fitted to carry six-ton armour piercing bombs. Their crews and those of No. 9 Squadron, which was now joined with them, were hand-picked, and were trained in attacking from the great heights necessary to give their bombs the necessary penetration.

On their first attack, delivered from a base in Russia, they succeeded in putting a bomb through the *Tirpitz*'s forecastle.

It was the end of the *Tirpitz* as a sea-going ship of war. She was so strained and damaged that even the indefatigable German ship-repairers at last threw in their hand. The battleship was to be moved to Tromsö and installed as a stationary defensive battery. Her parlous condition was a well-kept secret, however. Her destruction was still sought by the Admiralty, and the "Dam Busters" were sent out against her again.

An attack at the end of October was defeated by a last minute change of weather which obscured the target by clouds. But then, in November, fortune smiled on the bomber squadrons. Coming in from landward in clear blue weather they achieved a measure of surprise. The few smoke generators yet installed at Tromsö failed to screen the ship. From 14,000 feet the huge "Tall-Boys", six-ton bombs with hardened steel noses, plunged unerringly for the target. Three direct hits, one of which detonated a magazine, put an end to the three-year career of the ship which, though only three times putting to sea for brief and ineffectual forays, had tied down an embarrassing proportion of Britain's available naval force.

By herself the *Tirpitz* had comprised a "fleet in being". But in fact long before she rolled over and settled on the mud in Tromsö's harbour, she had become an example of a form of naval warfare that was really past. Had the Royal Navy been able to muster a single carrier task force such as those being deployed in the Pacific, the menace of the *Tirpitz* would have been eliminated long ago. She could only have come to sea to face destruction as did her much larger fellows of the Japanese Navy

At the beginning of 1945, the splendid floating citadels which had ruled the seas for a hundred years were yielding pride of place to the aircraft carrier in every part of the world. Today the carrier still represents the capital ship of all first-class navies except that of Russia. How long it will remain so is doubtful. Certainly it is unlikely to enjoy the long reign of the battleship. The development of atomic power has enabled ship-designers to produce the true submarine, a vessel which can remain indefinitely entirely submerged and requires no contact with the outside air to do so.

Such a submarine holds an immense advantage over any surface warship. It can maintain a high speed even in rough weather which reduces a surface ship to a crawl or forces it to heave-to. Its ability to move in three dimensions compels the use of complicated, three-dimensional weapons to attack it, weapons which must have capabilities of searching for and homing on to their invisible target in the depths.

The true submarine bids fair to make all purely surface warships obsolete. Such a development is likely to be a slow process in time of peace; but should war break out and the use of nuclear bombs not bring an end to the civilisation of the machine age, the submarine will surely become the principal if not the only type of warship.

The aircraft carrier has never achieved the air of majestic dignity or the symmetrical beauty of some of the battleships, particularly those of the last decade of the era. Similarly submarines, by their very nature, are unlikely ever to attain the individuality and the grace of surface warships of the battleship epoch. Sinister power and an air of mystery will be their characteristics; but not the beauty which has inspired artists to paint portraits of the famous battleships.

When the last battleship passes sadly to the breaker's yard, the seamen of yesterday will no doubt sigh: "Ichabod. The glory has departed." But so, no doubt, did the men of the epoch of galleys, when sails replaced the flashing oars and ugly cannon superseded swords and bows. So indeed did the salty sailormen who saw masts and yards and the noble spread of white sails disappear from the seas in favour of funnels and tripods, the long broadsides of cannon replaced by a few monster guns.

So it had always been. The old order changes, giving place to new. Giving welcome to the latter, we can spare a sigh for the former, and record its great days as we have tried to do in this volume. *Ave atque vale.*

APPENDIX A

THE OPPOSING FLEETS AT JUTLAND

Organization of the Grand Fleet as it sailed on 30th May 1916

BATTLE FLEET

FLEET FLAGSHIP: *Iron Duke*

2ND BATTLE SQUADRON

1ST DIVISION:

King George V—Vice-Admiral Sir Martyn Jerram

Ajax *Centurion* *Erin*

2ND DIVISION:

Orion—Rear-Admiral A. C. Leveson

Monarch *Conqueror* *Thunderer*

4TH BATTLE SQUADRON

3RD DIVISION:

Iron Duke—Admiral Sir John Jellicoe

Royal Oak *Superb* *Canada*

4TH DIVISION:

Benbow—Vice-Admiral Sir Doveton Sturdee

Bellerophon *Temeraire* *Vanguard*

1ST BATTLE SQUADRON

6TH DIVISION:

Marlborough—Vice-Admiral Sir Cecil Burney

Revenge *Hercules* *Agincourt*

5TH DIVISION:

Colossus—Rear-Admiral E. F. A. Gaunt

Collingwood *Neptune* *St. Vincent*

ATTACHED BATTLE CRUISERS

3RD BATTLE CRUISER SQUADRON

Invincible—Rear-Admiral The Hon. H. L. A. Hood

Inflexible *Indomitable*

CRUISERS

1ST CRUISER SQUADRON:

Defence—Rear-Admiral Sir Robert Arbuthnot

Warrior *Duke of Edinburgh* *Black Prince*

2ND CRUISER SQUADRON:

Minotaur—Rear-Admiral H. L. Heath

Hampshire *Cochrane* *Shannon*

LIGHT CRUISERS

4TH LIGHT CRUISER SQUADRON:	*Attached*
Calliope	*Boadicea*
(Commodore C. E. Le Mesurier)	*Blanche*
Caroline	*Bellona*
Royalist	*Active*
Comus	*Canterbury*
	Chester

Castor (Light Cruiser) and 49 Destroyers

ATTACHED TO BATTLE FLEET

Oak *Abdiel* (Minelayer)

BATTLE CRUISER FLEET

FLEET FLAGSHIP: *Lion*—Vice-Admiral Sir David Beatty

1ST BATTLE CRUISER SQUADRON

Princess Royal—Rear-Admiral O. de B. Brock

Queen Mary *Tiger*

2ND BATTLE CRUISER SQUADRON

New Zealand—Rear-Admiral W. C. Pakenham

Indefatigable

5TH BATTLE SQUADRON

Barham—Rear-Admiral H. Evan-Thomas

Valiant *Warspite* *Malaya*

LIGHT CRUISERS

1ST LIGHT CRUISER SQUADRON

Galatea
(Commodore E. S. Alexander-Sinclair)
Phaeton
Inconstant
Cordelia

2ND LIGHT CRUISER SQUADRON

Southampton
(Commodore W. E. E. Goodenough)
Birmingham
Nottingham
Dublin

3RD LIGHT CRUISER SQUADRON

Falmouth—Rear-Admiral T. A. W. Napier
Yarmouth
Birkenhead
Gloucester

Fearless, *Champion* (Light Cruisers) and 27 Destroyers

SEAPLANE CARRIER

Engadine

Organization of the High Seas Fleet as it sailed on 31st May 1916

BATTLE FLEET

FLEET FLAGSHIP: *Friedrich der Grosse*

3RD SQUADRON

König—Rear-Admiral Behncke
Grosser Kurfürst
Kronprinz
Markgraf
Kaiser—Rear-Admiral Nordmann
Kaiserin
Prinzregent Leopold

1ST SQUADRON

Friedrich der Grosse—Vice-Admiral Reinhard Scheer
Ostfriesland—Vice-Admiral E. Schmidt
Thuringen
Helgoland
Oldenburg
Posen—Rear-Admiral Engelhardt
Rheinland
Nassau
Westfalen

2ND SQUADRON

Deutschland—Rear-Admiral Mauve
Hessen
Pommern
Hannover—Rear-Admiral Freiherr von Dulwigk zu Lichtenfels
Schlesien
Schleswig Holstein

LIGHT CRUISERS

FOURTH SCOUTING GROUP

Stettin—Commodore von Reuter
München *Hamburg* *Frauenlob* *Stuttgart*

TORPEDO-BOAT FLOTILLAS

Rostock (Light Cruiser)—Commodore Michelsen
1st Flotilla (1st Half)—Lieutenant-Commander C. Albrecht
3rd Flotilla—Commander Hollmann
5th Flotilla—Commander Heinecke
7th Flotilla—Commander von Koch

BATTLE CRUISER FORCE

BATTLE CRUISERS

FIRST SCOUTING GROUP

Lützow—Vice-Admiral Hipper
Derfflinger
Seydlitz
Moltke
Von der Tann

LIGHT CRUISERS

SECOND SCOUTING GROUP

Frankfurt—Rear-Admiral Boedicker
Wiesbaden
Pillau
Elbing

TORPEDO-BOAT FLOTILLAS

Regensburg (Light Cruiser)—Commodore Heinrich
2nd Flotilla—Captain Schuur
6th Flotilla—Commander M. Schultz
9th Flotilla—Commander Goehle

APPENDIX B

The Opposing Fleets in the Battle of Leyte

JAPANESE

(*a*) *Vice-Admiral Kurita's Second Fleet*

BATTLESHIPS	HEAVY CRUISERS	LIGHT CRUISERS
Yamato	*Atago* (Fleet Flagship)	*Noshiro*
Musashi	*Maya*	*Yahagi*
Nagato	*Takao*	
Kongo	*Chokai*	
Haruna	*Myoko*	
	Haguro	
	Kumano	
	Suzuya	
	Tone	
	Chikuma	

15 DESTROYERS

(*b*) *Vice-Admiral Nishimura's Squadron*

BATTLESHIPS	HEAVY CRUISERS
Fuso	*Mogami*
Yamashiro (Flagship)	

4 DESTROYERS

(*c*) *Vice-Admiral Shima's Squadron*

HEAVY CRUISERS	LIGHT CRUISER
Nachi (Flagship)	*Abukuma*
Ashigara	

4 DESTROYERS

(*d*) *Admiral Ozawa's Fleet*

BATTLESHIP–CARRIERS

Ise
Hyuga

FLEET CARRIER

Zuikaku (Flagship)

LIGHT CARRIERS

Chitose
Chiyoda
Zuiho

LIGHT CRUISERS

Oyodo
Tama
Isuzu

10 DESTROYERS

AMERICAN

(*a*) *Seventh Fleet Bombardment and Support Group* (Rear-Admiral Jesse B. Oldendorf)

BATTLESHIPS

West Virginia
Maryland
Mississippi
Tennessee
California
Pennsylvania

CRUISERS

Louisville (Flagship)
Portland
Minneapolis
Denver
Columbia
Phoenix
Boise
H.M.A.S. *Shropshire*

21 DESTROYERS

(*b*) *Seventh Fleet Escort Carrier Force* (Rear-Admiral Thomas L. Sprague)

NORTHERN GROUP

CARRIERS

Fanshaw Bay
Saint Lo
White Plains
Kalinin Bay
Kitkun Bay
Gambier Bay

3 DESTROYERS
4 DESTROYER ESCORTS

MIDDLE GROUP

CARRIERS

Natoma Bay
Manila Bay
Marcus Island
Kadashan Bay
Savo Island
Ommaney Bay

3 DESTROYERS
4 DESTROYER ESCORTS

SOUTHERN GROUP

CARRIERS

Sangamon
Suwannee
Santee
Petrof Bay

3 DESTROYERS
3 DESTROYER ESCORTS

(*c*) *U.S. Third Fleet*

(Admiral William F. Halsey)

Task Force 38 (Vice-Admiral Marc A. Mitscher)

Task Group 38.1

(Vice-Admiral S. McCain)

CARRIERS	CRUISERS
Wasp	*Chester*
Hornet	*Pensacola*
Hancock	*Salt Lake City*
Monterey	*Boston*
Cowpens	*San Diego*
	Oakland

14 DESTROYERS

Task Group 38.2

(Rear-Admiral Gerald F. Bogan)

CARRIERS	BATTLESHIPS
Intrepid	*Iowa*
Cabot	*New Jersey* (Fleet Flagship)
Independence	

CRUISERS

Biloxi *Vincennes* *Miami*

16 DESTROYERS

Task Group 38.3

(Rear-Admiral Frederick C. Sherman)

CARRIERS	BATTLESHIPS	CRUISERS
Lexington	*Massachusetts*	*Santa Fe*
Essex	*South Dakota*	*Birmingham*
Princeton		*Mobile*
Langley		*Reno*

13 DESTROYERS

Task Group 38.4

(Rear-Admiral Ralph E. Davison)

CARRIERS	BATTLESHIPS	CRUISERS
Enterprise	*Washington*	*Wichita*
Franklin	*Alabama*	*New Orleans*
San Jacinto		
Belleau Wood		

15 DESTROYERS

INDEX

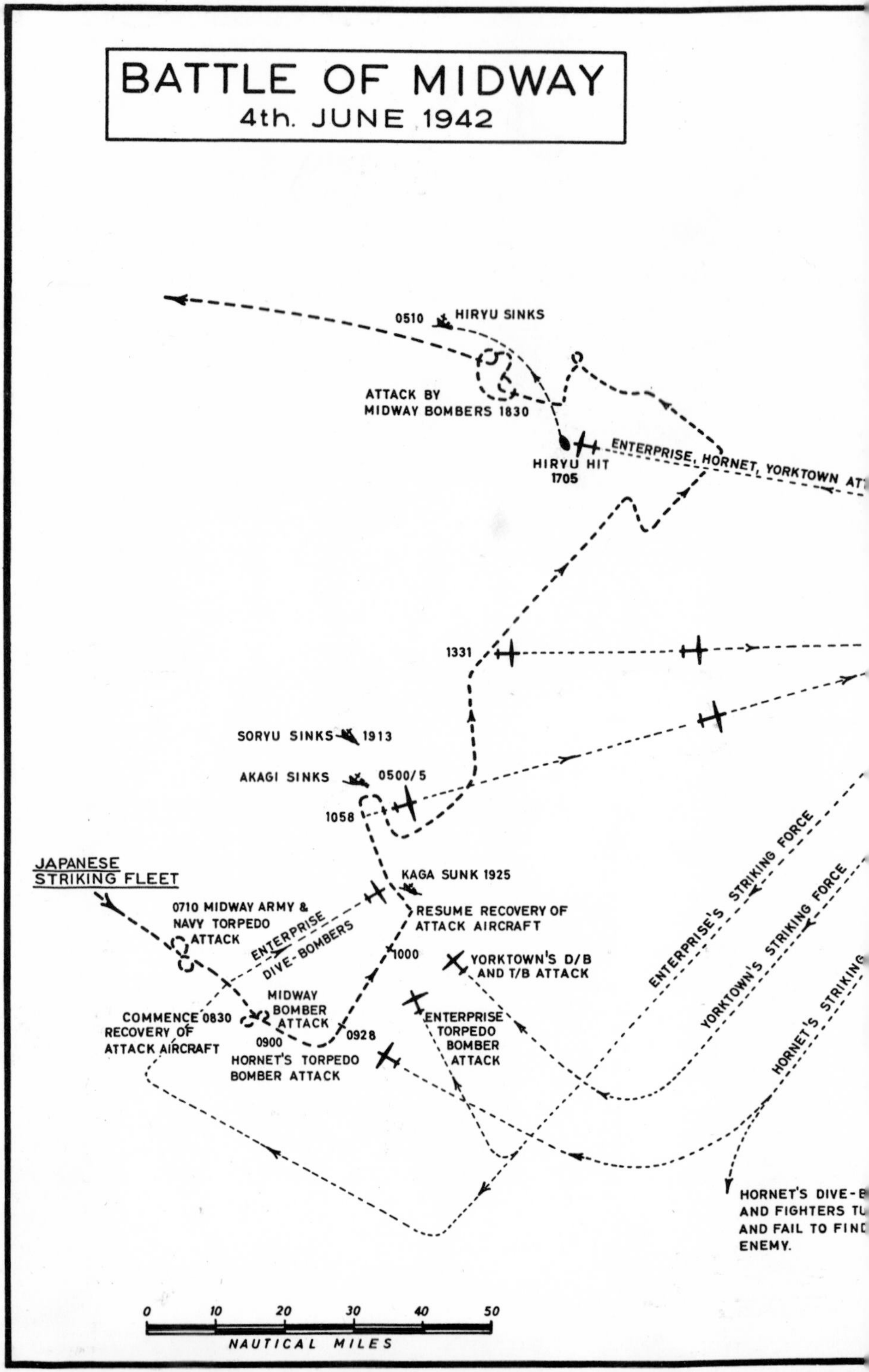
BATTLE OF MIDWAY
4th. JUNE 1942
0510
HIRYU SINKS
ATTACK BY
MIDWAY BOMBERS 1830
HIRYU HIT
1705
ENTERPRISE, HORNET, YORKTOWN AT
1331
SORYU SINKS 1913
AKAGI SINKS 0500/5
1058
JAPANESE
STRIKING FLEET
KAGA SUNK 1925
0710 MIDWAY ARMY &
NAVY TORPEDO
ATTACK
RESUME RECOVERY OF
ATTACK AIRCRAFT
ENTERPRISE
DIVE-BOMBERS
1000
YORKTOWN'S D/B
AND T/B ATTACK
MIDWAY
BOMBER
ATTACK
COMMENCE 0830
RECOVERY OF
ATTACK AIRCRAFT
0900
0928
ENTERPRISE
TORPEDO
BOMBER
ATTACK
HORNET'S TORPEDO
BOMBER ATTACK
ENTERPRISE'S STRIKING FORCE
YORKTOWN'S STRIKING FORCE
HORNET'S STRIKING
HORNET'S DIVE-B
AND FIGHTERS TU
AND FAIL TO FIND
ENEMY.
0
10
20
30
40
50
NAUTICAL MILES